W9-BDQ-314

SUSPENSE •
MANNERS AND MORALS •
REALISM • MODERNISM

From tradition to innovation and back again, the strength of the British short story is evidenced by the thirty-four outstanding stories chosen for this volume. There are mystery tales blended with social observation, such as Dickens's "Hunted Down" . . . adventure stories like Joseph Conrad's "Youth" that mark a trend toward individual concerns . . . the influence of Continental modernism, felt in Virginia Woolf's brilliant interior monologue, "The Mark on the Wall" . . . and the post-World War II return to traditional form to describe nontraditional subjects, as in Edna O'Brien's "How to Grow a Wisteria," a sharply witty portrait of a woman's disillusionment with sexual liberation.

These selections, along with many others by favorite authors or distinguished contemporary writers, demonstrate not only the diversity of the British short story, but their own enduring value as entertainment.

FREDERICK R. KARL, a noted critic and professor of English at New York University, is the author of *Joseph Conrad: The Three Lives; American Fictions: 1940–1980;* and *Modern and Modernism.*

THE
SIGNET CLASSIC
BOOK OF BRITISH
SHORT STORIES

EDITED AND WITH AN
INTRODUCTION BY
Frederick R. Karl

A SIGNET CLASSIC

NEW AMERICAN LIBRARY

NEW YORK
PUBLISHED IN CANADA BY
PENGUIN BOOKS CANADA LIMITED, MARKHAM, ONTARIO

Copyright © 1985 by Frederick R. Karl

Grateful acknowledgment is made for permission
to reprint the following:

"The Open Window," from THE COMPLETE SHORT STORIES OF
    SAKI by H. H. Munro. Copyright 1930, renewed © 1958 by The
    Viking Press, Inc. Reprinted by permission of Viking Penguin, Inc.

"Mr. Know-All," from COMPLETE SHORT STORIES by W. Somer-
    set Maugham. Copyright 1924 by W. Somerset Maugham. Reprinted
    by permission of Doubleday & Company, Inc.

"The Story of a Panic" by E. M. Forster. Reprinted by permission from
    Sidgwick & Jackson, Ltd.

(The following pages constitute an extension of this copyright page.)

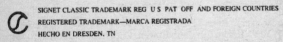

SIGNET CLASSIC TRADEMARK REG U S PAT OFF AND FOREIGN COUNTRIES
REGISTERED TRADEMARK—MARCA REGISTRADA
HECHO EN DRESDEN, TN

SIGNET, SIGNET CLASSIC, MENTOR, ONYX, PLUME, MERIDIAN and NAL BOOKS are published *in the United States* by NAL PENGUIN INC., 1633 Broadway, New York, New York 10019, *in Canada* by Penguin Books Canada Limited, 2801 John Street, Markham, Ontario L3R 1B4

First Printing, October, 1985

3   4   5   6   7   8   9   10   11

PRINTED IN CANADA

Contents

THE
SIGNET CLASSIC
BOOK OF BRITISH
SHORT STORIES

INTRODUCTION

This anthology has several functions. It is, first, an attempt to show the historical development of the British short story, from its (more or less) beginnings in the mid-nineteenth century to the present time. These developments are not only in subject matter but in techniques, innovations, and experimentations with form and language. Such innovative structures accompany themes of isolation, alienation, and ambiguity—the received matter of the twentieth century.

The second guiding principle of organization has been to mix the familiar with the unfamiliar. Some of these stories have been much anthologized, others very little, and some not at all. The reasons for this type of mix are apparent: to present to the reader those stories that have achieved a "classic" status and, at the same time, to introduce into the short fictional canon those stories that may, in time, themselves become classics.

A third principle of selection aims at crowding in as many well-known figures as possible, while also introducing some lesser anthologized writers. While the nineteenth century in England is a period mainly of the novel, we can nevertheless discover important short fiction among the major novelists. Mixed in with the great figures of the English tradition such as Dickens, Eliot, and Meredith are others who need to be recalled, Wilkie Collins among them. In the late nineteenth and in the twentieth century, the same principle of selection has remained: to include the obvious authors—Hardy, Conrad, Wells, Kipling, Joyce, Woolf, Forster—as well as those usually not seen in an anthology: Sansom, Hughes, and others.

The final function of the collection—and what has governed it throughout—has been to demonstrate the multiplicity of experience that English short fiction is capable of reflecting. The range is huge, displaying an intense awareness of the inner world as well as the more expected analysis of social and class structures. The near constant in English short fiction is a class system that permeates virtually every aspect of experience, but one that has not hobbled the English writer from making profound inner explorations as well. This collection, in fact, stands or falls on this very point: its ability to provide the reader with variety, intensity, and social analysis, all within innovative fictional structures that meet the material on its own terms.

The British short story as the product of that "tight little island" nevertheless shows as much versatility and diversity as the short fiction of any nation. It encompasses the full range of the form, from its stress on mystery and suspense in the nineteenth century to its emphasis, directly or indirectly, on political and social issues in the twentieth. Furthermore, in both centuries, it demonstrates a sharp awareness of innovation in narrative strategies, presentation of character, point of view, and other matters we associate with Modernism. The arrangement of this collection has been made so as to exhibit the British short story as it moves through several phases. This will be a demonstration of historical development of the form, but also a presentation of stories that exist for their own value, regardless of their historical placement. Every story is of consequence.

While the British novel has received deservedly lavish attention from scholars, critics, and general readers, the shorter forms of fiction have been neglected. Part of the reason is that several of the major novelists either were not interested in writing short fiction or else were not themselves significant short story writers. Those who neglected or ignored the form included Jane Austen, Sir Walter Scott, the Brontës, Thackeray (except for satirical sketches), and several others of like stature. Yet Dickens worked in the shorter forms, as did George Eliot, George Meredith, Wilkie Collins, Bulwer-Lytton, and Sheridan Le Fanu. What they created, however, is not quite what we mean now by the short story, for most of them wrote, in the main, a longer version, a form somewhat between story and novella, or short novel. Sometimes, as with Eliot and Meredith, their short stories were closer to novellas. The novella is not simply a lengthened story; but in its development it has many of the ingredients of the novel, although it is briefer. Since the short story is defined, in one respect, by its brevity and succinctness, we see few exact examples of it in the major nineteenth-century novelists, for whom swiftness and succinctness were not recognizable values.

Later in the century, the short story form flourished. The form as we know it did not develop from English sources, but chiefly could be found in Poe, Gogol, or Pushkin, or in folktales, fairy tales, allegories, fables, and other short forms that come to us from early literary history. Before there was a "story," there was a "tale," and tale-making goes back almost as far as speech. Tales are less consciously artful—usually they are connected to oral forms and, therefore, are less susceptible to the devices of narration we associate with a reading audience. Also, tales, like fables, fairy tales, legends, and so on, have a spontaneity, in that they are fitted to listeners who are responding at the moment.

The short story that we find in the English tradition goes through three major stages. These stages, incidentally, do not occur at any precise time—they enter, overlap, and alter themselves often imperceptibly. Only with hindsight do we see that the English short story has undergone enormous transformations in less than one hundred years; from, generally, the mid-nineteenth century to the years following World War I.

The earlier forms such as fables, legends, and myths were concerned with explaining reality, with giving some shape to chaotic or supernatural events. The short story, however, is engaged in shaping and reshaping that reality, tilted more to change and development than to stability. By the mid-nineteenth century, in England at least, the stress on development, socially, politically, and economically, was so strong that it carried the country through the disasters of World War I. Fiction, both longer and shorter forms, reflected the desire for change, social mobility, and new advances in democratic institutions. The society was itself on the move, shifting from a village and agricultural economy to an urban and industrialized one. By midcentury, that shift had occurred, creating in effect a dualistic England that still connected ideologically to country, even as it was passing, and that linked pragmatically to city, even as urban life stifled and shackled the individual. As Raymond Williams, in *The Country and the City*, wrote: "An unequal interaction between country and city was now far advanced and pervasive. There was the recourse to law, to the capital market and to the marriage market, in the consolidation and extension of the landlords. . . . It was a case of a capital city drawing the character of an economy and a society into its extraordinary centre: order and chaos both."

Much short fiction—that of Dickens, Eliot, and Meredith, at least—was socially based, as were their novels. Not surprisingly, their shorter work reads like novels cut down to briefer length, rather than as a distinct form of fictional achievement, which the short story would become. Other factors, however, were involved—the influence of Poe, as well as his French imitators, would shortly begin to filter in; and this would result in stories that intermixed social observation with elements of mystery and the supernatural, class conflicts with emotions of horror and terror.

This type of mixture characterized short fiction by Wilkie Collins, a friend and collaborator of Dickens, as well as that of Bulwer-Lytton, another member of the Dickens circle. But the influence of mystery and the supernatural extended well into the next phase of the short story, as we can see in Wells, Stevenson, and some authors not included here, Sheridan Le Fanu or Arthur Conan Doyle and his Sherlock Holmes stories. It is fair to state that the mystery and social aspects of the short story—as of the novel—were staples from midcentury.

The reasons for this development are several. Even without Poe and his imitators, we must recognize the persistence of the Gothic tradition in English fiction, reaching back to Walpole's *The Castle of Otranto* and Matthew Lewis's *The Monk*, continuing through Mary Shelley's *Frankenstein* and Charles Maturin's *Melmoth the Wanderer*, and on into the second half of the nineteenth century. Further, even as "social reality" prevailed in the society, development and progress came under attack from those—like Dickens—who found in it qualities of dehumanization, loss of spiritual centers, elements of antilife itself. The reaction was almost as forceful as the original impulse. Fiction based on realistic social forms, no matter how intense and how tragicomic, began to give way to fiction that introduced other dimensions: the potentiality of mysterious, supernatural events and the suspense attendant upon the unwinding of great crimes. In a way, the energies once connected to myth and legend began to creep back into fiction, but now divested of religious content. The purpose was still to entertain, but entertainment now suggested an extension of the reader into new, hitherto inaccessible worlds. The culmination of this phase of fiction would come in H. G. Wells's science fictions at the turn of the century, or Stevenson's psychological thriller "The Strange Case of Dr. Jekyll and Mr. Hyde," or the Sherlock Holmes stories of Conan Doyle.

As the social aspects of the English short story began to be displaced—but by no means exorcised—other elements began to prevail. Exotic places became the setting for stories—in Conrad, Kipling, and a little later in Maugham, Forster, Lawrence, and others. The story as a genre moved into individual decisions and destinies, as distinct from stressing background influences. The language of the short story itself began to shift, from realistic, denotative, analytic prose toward elusiveness, uncertainty, connotation. This aspect of language was perhaps less apparent in the English writers than in those on the continent, but in Lawrence, Woolf, and, of course, Joyce, the language of the nineteenth century would be permanently transformed. Language was internalized by several of these writers, so that what we call voice—that element expressing attitude, intention, tone—comes from within, or someplace within. The omniscient author or third-person narrator still remains, but he or she is being questioned and, in some instances, displaced.

Along with the new internalized voice, we find many other elements shifting as we move from our second to our third phase of the short story. Although we have seen that the English were slower than their continental counterparts to embrace the full thrust of Modernism, its special qualities become apparent. Most of the traditional elements of shorter fiction begin to drop away, though not all at the same time or at the same speed. Plot, character, theme, and even setting gave way to more ambiguous elements such as tone, atmosphere, and symbolism of an abstruse kind. Even a "realist" such as D. H. Lawrence in a story like "Things" uses the remoteness of external objects to say something powerful about sexuality; while the method here is not difficult to comprehend, it is indirect. Everything in the story is subservient to the power of the objects, not to character or setting as such. Theme grows not from anything we learn from the author's mouth, but from externalities, and the distinctions they create between two people.

All this is fairly standard in the beginning of this third phase of the English short story in and around World War I. In its later developments, the third phase becomes more innovative, moving closer to what a Modernistic story has come to be. We find such avant-garde elements in Elizabeth Bowen's "The Demon Lover," Samuel Beckett's "Yellow," Ted

Hughes's "Snow," and others. Yet even as this move into experimentation in theme, voice, and language becomes clear, the English story retains more of its traditional matter than either American or continental shorter fiction. The English brand rarely achieves the experimental quality we associate with—to mention only Americans—Donald Barthelme, William Gass, or other minimalists who have purged the story of nearly everything but words.

Possibly because of their strong mooring in social classes and in historical antecedents, the English have never settled for words, but have insisted on some realistic shape. Even Joyce, in the stories called *Dubliners*, anchored his subjects securely in a time and a place. Several stories in this collection retain that naturalistic-realistic orientation: we can cite those by O'Connor, Maugham, O'Flaherty, Greene, Lessing, Gordimer, and Moore. These stories fit into the category known as "well-made," which means they more or less have a beginning, middle, and end. Even when they depart somewhat into areas of modern uncertainty, or when they mask part of the beginning, middle, or end, as in the Greene, they are in a line of traditional English fiction. With their empirical, utilitarian, pragmatic philosophical traditions, the English have found it difficult to retreat from a substantial, tactile world; whereas their continental counterparts—Kafka is exemplary here—were not restricted by pragmatics, having grown and developed in a very difficult philosophical atmosphere of Kant, Hegel, Marx, and Nietzsche. As for the American writers, once the influence of Poe, Hawthorne, Melville, and James was assimilated, the story moved into a Hemingway, Fitzgerald, and Faulkner phase, which later gave way to a full penetration by European Modernism. The American story was spatial, the English story more temporal; the American moving out, the latter caught up by the past.

Conrad's "Youth" is a good example of a short piece that looks both backward and forward. As a sharp view of youthful behavior and experience, it falls into the genre known as the *Bildungsroman*, the novel of learning, building, and formation—what we have generally called apprenticeship fiction. Yet by turning all physical detail to spiritual or experiential data, "Youth" upsets that pattern: the external exists, finally, only to be internalized. Conrad works in the great tradition of English fiction, but deflects it toward another area of experience. In the very details of the story, space is denied, in favor of temporal matters—tradition, growth, sudden development of a young man into awareness. That grasping for consciousness that is so central to "Youth" is part of the second phase of the English short story. One may grasp, but one may or may not reach.

Virginia Woolf's "The Mark on the Wall" indicates a further stage of that development from external to internal. It comes two decades after the Conrad story and suggests how the English writer is getting further away from naturalism-realism, but still without forsaking some dimensions of it. The question we may ask at first is whether or not it is even a "short story." Or does its existence throw into confusion any effort to define that genre as it moved into its Modernist phase? "The Mark on the Wall" has no discernible or describable characters; it lacks story and plot; its setting is barely alluded to; and it has internalized all experience so that nothing measurable happens.

It turns a mark on the wall into the focus of all kinds of free association by the "voice" who controls the words. These free associations range into history, philosophy (questioning the very nature of being), Shakespeare, feminist issues, matters of identity, questions of reality (about the mark itself, about whether or not one can even determine what it is), the experience of Sundays, the standards in *Whitaker's Almanak* of British aristocracy and notables, and so on. The "matter" of the associations is infinite in its potentiality; the story, such as it is, can end at any point. The control is not the theme, plot, or story line, but the extent of consciousness exerted by the voice.

The Woolf piece, nevertheless, is a short story—or, more aptly called, a short fiction—according to the standards of what short fiction was becoming in the Modern era. In terms of the first and even second phase of the English short story, however, it would be classified as an essay of sorts, a kind of ruminative, associative rambling, such as we associate with Coleridge and Hazlitt. But in postwar England and continental Europe, the roaming essay took on fictional trappings, and whatever emanated from the single consciousness was considered a fictional voice. Such fictions, both shorter and longer, would come to dominate.

We need only compare Woolf's brief piece with Ted Hughes's equally brief "Snow" more than forty years later. While Woolf's short work fits into certain fictional expectations, even while probing the "mark," Hughes's was entering a seemingly surreal landscape. As a symbol, the snow is vaguely equivalent to the mark, but it derives from some mysterious source, and the life of the survivor is sustained in ways we cannot fathom. After five months, he is without food, and only his control keeps him going—going where? from where to where? Setting means only snow. The chair somehow is his salvation because he can doze off in it without being smothered. While the vagueness of the setting is familiar—recalling the experience of Hans Castorp in the "Snow" section of Thomas Mann's *The Magic Mountain*—the sequence of events is far removed from familiar objects. The influence of Samuel Beckett appears strong, especially those novels that make up the trilogy, and their questing, yearning, never-arriving protagonists: what keeps them going is will and little else. Or else the landscape and effort are what we find in *Waiting for Godot*, a lunar landscape in its forbidding solitude. Whatever values we assign to the story, Hughes has stretched the "mark" of Woolf's story to something far more uncertain and ambiguous.

Some writers resisted these developments, and several of them are included here to demonstrate that short fiction can be of several varieties, even when a movement creates tremendous pressure to capitulate to the new. Somerset Maugham, for one, Aldous Huxley for another, Graham Greene for a third, and Nadine Gordimer for a fourth continued within the short story tradition of theme, plot, character, setting—qualities that throw us back to the beginnings of the genre. Yet even within these traditional terms, Modernism still meant something to them, in terms of leanness and a certain elliptical way of approaching their material. If nothing else, they accepted minimalism—an economy of word and pacing—forsaking that earlier slowness of development that often made short fiction seem like cut-down novels.

What, then, happened to realism in the short story? Has it gone the way of realism in the arts in general, toward some form of abstraction, such as we find in painting for the last fifty years? Or has realism in short fiction come to mean something else? First of all, we must return to our earliest practitioners of the short story. When the form was developed by Pushkin and Gogol in Russia or by Poe and Hawthorne in America, it was hardly realistic. Poe, for example, stressed extremes of behavior, and he used numerous devices—horrible crimes, terror of the victims, bizarre events—to move the reader from everyday routine. Hawthorne, likewise, devised several strategies for undermining realism: light and dark imagery, use of the American past, portrayal of acts of desperation, and often extreme behavior that marked the individual as a modern-day Cain. From the beginning of the short story genre, realism may have been the main mode of portrayal, but it was consistently subverted by other strategies—so that it was rarely unadorned, rarely purely "realistic."

When we turn to the English contemporaries of Poe and Hawthorne, we find—in Eliot, Dickens, Meredith, Trollope, Elizabeth Gaskell—a greater adherence to realism: especially to what Lionel Trilling called the mainstay of the English novel, its reliance on manners and morals. Even such an adventurous and adversarial writer like Wilkie Collins was solidly embedded in social realism—not the least when his main concern was creating or solving a mystery. In "Mr. Marmaduke and the Minister," the working out of the plot (itself an adjunct of realistic fiction) depends on our sharp awareness of English class structuring. A minister in a Scottish kirk, his daughter, the stranger who is really an actor—all of the interplay among them depends on attitudes deeply linked to "manners and morals," class gradations that dictate behavior, language, and attitude.

Yet even here, in the very heartland of realism in the English nineteenth century, we find dimensions and strategies that run counter to realism and that qualify its presence. Dickens's emphasis on Gothic terror or horror is one; the element of mystery or the prevalence of the mystery tale in Dickens and Eliot is another; the sense of impending or potential doom in Meredith is a third. These elements do not destroy realism, but they prepare us for the slow shift away from it that occurs in the second phase of the short story. Hardy's "The Three Strangers" is a good example: a story deeply rooted in realistic detail of a house, a place, a way of life that has continued for centuries. Yet the three strangers immediately conjure up the three magi—after all, the event being celebrated is a christening, and the parents are humble people. Yet these three strangers are clearly not bearing gifts. They introduce the world of death into the celebration, and they create distinct rumbles of another kind of world, quite alien to the celebration of a christening. What appears to be a most realistic story in the opening pages becomes something else as the plot unravels: the theme of the story, in fact, depends on the "mysterious" element overtaking the realistic. The Hardy piece is dated 1883, and it appeared in a volume of *Wessex Tales*, in 1888. This is a good date to locate what was clearly becoming a major shift in the English short story.

Stevenson's "The Strange Case of Dr. Jekyll and Mr. Hyde," in 1886, its writing overlapping with the Hardy, plays with a dualism: the realistic surface of the story reflected by Dr. Jekyll and the antirealistic, mysterious, bizarre world represented by Mr. Hyde. Here, unlike his predecessors, Stevens has structured the antirealism directly into the major character. He has closed up the gaps, as it were, so that the conflicting elements no longer exist only in the telling or in the plot elements, but in the vehicle carrying those elements, his protagonist. This is a major development in short fiction, since an author not only recognizes an irrational component in man's personality—and this well before Freud's digging into the unconscious—but perceives, further, that this irrational dimension cannot be covered by a veneer of logic and rationality, that it must surface and take over. Such a recognition of irrationality strikes a twofold blow, first at late Victorian order and then at our sense of how that order can be contained in fiction. Here short fiction is the avant-garde, well ahead of its longer cousin.

However dissimilar to each other the short fictions in this second phase may appear—bringing together Hardy and Stevenson with Conrad, Wells, and Kipling—their qualities overlap. They all differ, obviously, in their stress on various elements. Kipling insists on strong plotting, Hardy on setting, attitudes, and customs, Stevenson and Conrad on psychological schisms, Wells on mystery and the supernatural—but they overlap in their insistence on economy of expression, use of irrational impulses as the driving motivation, and, perhaps most of all, stress on extreme areas for their subject matter.

In the third phase, which stretches, as we have seen, from the time just before World War I until well after World War II, the retreat from realism becomes intense, even when the writers are themselves sympathetic to realistic portrayal. A case in point is E. M. Forster, in "The Story of a Panic." Here Pan and Panic dominate, irrational elements that are not an integral part of the world represented by the narrator, a proper Englishman. As much as Stevenson in Jekyll and Hyde, Forster has separated man's experience into dual functions; so that while the tourists reflect an ordered, proper world, the young boy, Eustace (whose name, ironically, means "steadfast"), and his Italian friend, Gennaro, represent the "other world." That "other" is, apparently, nature, the primitive, the natural and normative, as against the ordered, limited, death-oriented existence of the tourists. But Forster has gone beyond merely suggesting a world that is antirealistic; he has shown it in action, and yet, at the same time, denied its validity through his narrator.

Further, in this third phase of the short story, we have narrators with whom we do not agree, or whose presence is opposed by the author who created them. This is a considerable shift from earlier realistic fiction, in which the narrator represented universal values, certainly the social and class values of the reader. He was the surrogate reader, as it were, or the reader if he could enter the fiction. But as the genre developed in complexity, the narrator takes on qualities of the enemy—enemy to ordered life, to what is natural, even to what is normal. All of this is part of the redeployment of the narrator in fiction, from being merely an acceptable voice to being part of the complexity of the tale, or providing some of its tension. Similarly, it is a new stage in the use of voice or attitude. In order to read correctly, we must adapt to the voice, which may be antipathetic to our own views. If we agree with the narrator of "The Story of a Panic"—that is, if we identify not with his snobbishness but with his need for order, stability, and civility of behavior—then we cannot come to terms with Forster's themes. His theme is nothing less than that we must rethink who and what we are, if we wish to survive whole.

Questions of narrator, narrative voice or attitude, and tone become increasingly significant in this third phase, as we have already seen. Stories such as Jean Rhys's "Mannequin," Samuel Beckett's "Yellow," or Dylan Thomas's "One Warm Saturday" involve complicated or montagelike narrating techniques, even when the story line appears relatively uncluttered. In "Mannequin," for example, the narrator is outside the protagonist, Anna, and yet the experience reflected seems to derive from within her. The way in which the reader experiences the story involves at least a dual response: to the details that come from outside and, at the same time, to the experience that suggests the internal workings of Anna. This intimacy in narrative is achieved because Rhys has moved the third-person authorial voice close to interior monologue; and this tactic we find also in the Beckett and Thomas stories. Such a strategy, which maintains the realism of the narrative while questioning its order and stability by delving within, is one of the major distinctions between first- and third-phase short (or long) fiction.

In both the Thomas and Beckett stories, style dominates, to the exclusion of more traditional elements of plot, theme, story line, or even character. By the dominance of style, we mean that language has itself preempted other considerations. The writer has called attention to his words instead of allowing words to be subservient to other elements in the story; and because of this stress on language we must pay particular attention to tones, movements, rhythms, pacing, and other less tactile qualities. In "One Warm Saturday," the substance—whatever it is—exists within a cloud or haze of language. Whenever we see anything, it is fleeting and distorted, what we associate with dreams. Everything is indeterminate, condensed, uncertain. Another way of looking at the story is to see it as part of a fairy-tale world, so distant from the "real" that it has its own rules of communication.

While Beckett's "Yellow" is somewhat firmer, it, too, explores a similar sensibility. Common to such stories—and to several others in this third phase—is a movement to extremes for subject matter: in "Yellow," the patient awaits an operation. Such reliance on extremes not only allows an opening up of experience heretofore neglected in short fiction, but permits the author to move toward unconscious and sub- or preconscious experience. Part of the difficulty we find with such fiction comes in locating "where we are," cutting through ambiguities of place and idea and linking the isolated character to something we are familiar with. Yet we cannot ignore the fact that artistic movements toward abstraction and nonrepresentation after World War I inevitably influenced every aspect of fiction; and the response of short fiction in the area I have called style is typical.

Nevertheless, as has already been suggested, several authors of considerable craft and accomplishment have continued to write in older forms, and frequently with great power and cogency. Even though in this third phase we have come to expect innovation and experimentation, we should not judge fiction solely by its technical daring, especially when we are dealing with English fiction. Resistance to innovation has characterized the form from its beginnings, and when we do think of innovators, except for Virginia Woolf, they tend to derive from outside England: Joyce from Ireland; Conrad from Poland via France; Ford Madox Ford was half-German. The strength of English short fiction from its earliest phases to the present has been based on several constants: its sensitivity to subtle shifts in class structure, its responsiveness to language, and its adherence to a darkly comic rather than a tragic view of life.

Within this frame of reference, we find many "well-made" stories: fictions that have the snap and zip of a good tale, presented with great craft. Certainly Somerset Maugham's "Mr. Know-All" fits into that group, as do Frank O'Connor's "The Face of Evil," Liam O'Flaherty's "The Touch," Sylvia Townsend Warner's "The Phoenix," Saki's "The Open Window," even Arthur C. Clarke's "The Star." We could add several others. This does not mean that such fictions lack meaning, but that they are, foremost, tales that entertain. Somewhat between, still in this third phase, are more or less conventionally narrated stories that have considerable symbolic significance, such as Edna O'Brien's "How to Grow a Wisteria," Graham Greene's "Brother," William Sansom's "How Claeys Died," and Katherine Mansfield's "Marriage à la Mode."

In a related category is James Joyce's "Araby," from his collection *Dubliners*. The stories here are not innovative in technical terms, nor are they intended to be experimental in the way Joyce was later. They are a young man's work, not yet the mature fiction of *Ulysses* and *Finnegans Wake*. And yet even here, a story like "Araby," written while Joyce was still working on *A Portrait of the Artist as a Young Man*, depends on the reader's sensitivity to detail, nuance, and matters of tone and attitude. It is not descriptive, it has no plot to unroll, it states no theme, it barely sketches in character, and yet it has tremendous density from the accrual of small things. It is fleeting in its registry of points that count, and we know it is part of the later phase of short fiction because it makes traditional elements secondary to tones, atmosphere, and rhythms. It has less matter than manner, which is not to say it lacks matter.

Joyce would, of course, go much further as an innovator, as would Woolf, Rhys, Beckett, and Thomas. Nevertheless, the textures of the English short story lie not in incessant experimentation, but in persistent reassessment of psychological, moral, and social possibilities for the genre. With writers such as O'Brien, Moore, Gordimer, Lessing, and Greene, to name only a sampling, we see aspects of the short story returning to its origins. This is not a self-conscious return to tradition, but it is a recognition that while continental fiction is rooted in change, often in radical change, English short fiction will depend on continuity, stability, and balance.

The interlude of Modernism that so strongly affected English short and long fiction was, somehow, a phase, an interruption or a disruption. The genre regained its own native momentum and returned to what it had been, although on a different scale and with no loss of craft.

—FREDERICK R. KARL

The
Nineteenth
Century

Charles Dickens
(1812–1870)

Charles Dickens's early years, lived in poverty and solitude, proved to be a very valuable resource for him when he became a novelist. Born in Portsmouth, Dickens suffered a traumatic experience when at age twelve he found himself abandoned by his parents (who were in debtors' prison) and forced to work in a blacking warehouse. He recovered, however, and at seventeen became a court stenographer and then a parliamentary reporter. His novelistic skills were already becoming evident in the sketches he began to publish when barely out of his teens. These were collected as Sketches by Boz (1836). When Victoria ascended to the throne of England in 1837, her renown was soon to be matched by that of this former street urchin, whose the Posthumous Papers of the Pickwick Club (1836–37) made him as famous as the young queen. Dickens had married in 1836, but the union with Catherine Hogarth, who bore him ten children, soon began to tire him. He threw himself into several activities: traveling, editing, acting in club theatricals, and, of course, novel writing. Beginning with Oliver Twist in 1837–38, Dickens's fiction made him the most-read writer in England, and he kept his audience happy with a novel virtually every other year: Nicholas Nickleby (1838–39); The Old Curiosity Shop (1840–41), Barnaby Rudge (1841), Martin Chuzzlewit (1843–44), Christmas Books (1843–48), Dombey and Son (1847–48), David Copperfield (1849–50), Bleak House (1852–53), Hard Times (1854), Little Dorrit (1857–58), A Tale of Two Cities (1859), Great Expectations (1860–61), Our Mutual Friend (1864), and the unfinished The Mystery of Edwin Drood (1870). Dickens's themes became familiar: praise for the virtues of the heart; incessant attacks on those who could offer only logic and rationality; sympathy for the downtrodden and isolated; emphasis on violence, crime, and criminal behavior; evocation of city sounds and smells and bizarre people; attacks upon institutions that neglected human values; and yet support, curiously, of the status quo. The Dickens prose style also became distinctive, with its mixture of comic play, detail of observation, and sentimentality. Along with his friend Wilkie Collins, Dickens helped to introduce detective fiction, what we see in a story like "Hunted Down." In his later years, he became obsessed with giving read-

*ings from his work—especially from passages of extreme vio-
lence—and his health broke, so that he died two years short of his
sixtieth birthday.*

Hunted Down

I

Most of us see some romances in life. In my capacity as Chief
Manager of a Life Assurance Office, I think I have within the
last thirty years seen more romances than the generality of
men, however unpromising the opportunity may, at first sight,
seem.

As I have retired, and live at my ease, I possess the means
that I used to want, of considering what I have seen, at leisure.
My experiences have a more remarkable aspect, so reviewed,
than they had when they were in progress. I have come home
from the Play now, and can recall the scenes of the Drama
upon which the curtain has fallen, free from the glare, bewilderment, and bustle of the Theatre.

Let me recall one of these Romances of the real world.

There is nothing truer than physiognomy, taken in connection with manner. The art of reading that book of which
Eternal Wisdom obliges every human creature to present his
or her own page with the individual character written on it,
is a difficult one, perhaps, and is little studied. It may require
some natural aptitude, and it must require (for everything
does) some patience and some pains. That there are not usually given to it,—that numbers of people accept a few stock
commonplace expressions of face as the whole list of char-
acteristics, and neither seek nor know the refinements that
are truest,—that You, for instance, give a great deal of time
and attention to the reading of music, Greek, Latin, French,
Italian, Hebrew if you please, and do not qualify yourself to
read the face of the master or mistress looking over your
should teaching to you,—I assume to be five hundred times
more probable than improbable. Perhaps a little self-suffi-
ciency may be at the bottom of this; facial expression requires

no study from you, you think; it comes by nature to you to know enough about it, and you are not to be taken in.

I confess, for my part, that I *have* been taken in, over and over again. I have been taken in by acquaintances, and I have been taken in (of course) by friends; far oftener by friends than by any other class of persons. How came I to be so deceived? Had I quite misread their faces?

No. Believe me, my first impression of those people, founded on face and manner alone, was invariably true. My mistake was in suffering them to come nearer to me and explain themselves away.

II

The partition which separated my own office from our general outer office in the City was of thick plate-glass. I could see through it what passed in the outer office, without hearing a word. I had it put up, in place of a wall that had been there for years,—ever since the house was built. It was no matter whether I did or did not make the change in order that I might derive my first impression of strangers, who came to us on business, from their faces alone, without being influenced by anything they said. Enough to mention that I turned my glass partition to that account, and that a Life Assurance Office is at all times exposed to be practised upon by the most crafty and cruel of the human race.

It was through my glass partition that I first saw the gentleman whose story I am going to tell.

He had come in without my observing it, and had put his hat and umbrella on the broad counter, and was bending over it to take some papers from one of the clerks. He was about forty or so, exceedingly well dressed in black,—being in mourning,—and the hand he extended with a polite air had a particularly well-fitting black kid glove upon it. His hair, which was elaborately brushed and oiled, was parted straight up the middle; and he presented this parting to the clerk, exactly (to my thinking) as if he had said, in so many words: "You must take me, if you please, my friend, just as I show myself. Come straight up here; follow the gravel path; keep off the grass; I allow no trespassing."

I conceived a very great aversion to that man the moment I thus saw him.

He had asked for some of our printed forms, and the clerk was giving them to him and explaining them. An obliged and agreeable smile was on his face, and his eyes met those of the clerk with a sprightly look. (I have known a vast quantity of nonsense talked about bad men not looking you in the face. Don't trust that conventional idea. Dishonesty will stare honesty out of countenance, any day in the week, if there is anything to be got by it.)

I saw, in the corner of his eyelash, that he became aware of my looking at him. Immediately he turned the parting in his hair toward the glass partition, as if he said to me with a sweet smile. "Straight up here, if you please. Off the grass!"

In a few moments he had put on his hat and taken up his umbrella, and was gone.

I beckoned the clerk into my room, and asked, "Who was that?"

He had the gentleman's card in his hand. "Mr. Julius Slinkton, Middle Temple."

"A barrister, Mr. Adams?"

"I think not, sir."

"I should have thought him a clergyman, but for his having no Reverend here," said I.

"Probably, from his appearance," Mr. Adams replied, "he is reading for orders."

I should mention that he wore a dainty white cravat, and dainty linen altogether.

"What did he want, Mr. Adams?"

"Merely a form of proposal, sir, and form of reference."

"Recommended here? Did he say?"

"Yes, he said he was recommended here by a friend of yours. He noticed you, but said that as he had not the pleasure of your personal acquaintance he would not trouble you."

"Did he know my name?"

"O yes, sir! He said, 'There *is* Mr. Sampson, I see!' "

"A well-spoken gentleman, apparently?"

"Remarkably so, sir."

"Insinuating manners, apparently?"

"Very much so, indeed, sir."

"Hah!" said I. "I want nothing at present, Mr. Adams."

Within a fortnight of that day I went to dine with a friend of mine, a merchant, a man of taste who buys pictures and books; and the first man I saw among the company was Mr. Julius Slinkton. There he was, standing before the fire, with good large eyes and an open expression of face; but still (I thought) requiring everybody to come at him by the prepared way he offered, and by no other.

I noticed him ask my friend to introduce him to Mr. Sampson, and my friend did so. Mr. Slinkton was very happy to see me. Not too happy; there was no over-doing of the matter; happy in a thoroughly well-bred, perfectly unmeaning way.

"I thought you had met," our host observed.

"No," said Mr. Slinkton. "I did look in at Mr. Sampson's office, on your recommendation; but I really did not feel justified in troubling Mr. Sampson himself, on a point in the everyday routine of an ordinary clerk."

I said I should have been glad to show him any attention on our friend's introduction.

"I am sure of that," said he, "and am much obliged. At another time, perhaps, I may be less delicate. Only, however, if I have real business; for I know, Mr. Sampson, how precious business time is, and what a vast number of impertinent people there are in the world."

I acknowledged his consideration with a slight bow. "You were thinking," said I, "of effecting a policy on your life."

"O dear, no! I am afraid I am not so prudent as you pay me the compliment of supposing me to be, Mr. Sampson. I merely inquired for a friend. But you know what friends are in such matters. Nothing may ever come of it. I have the greatest reluctance to trouble men of business with inquiries for friends, knowing the probabilities to be a thousand to one that the friends will never follow them up. People are so fickle, so selfish, so inconsiderate. Don't you, in your business, find them so every day, Mr. Sampson?"

I was going to give a qualified answer; but he turned his smooth, white parting on me with its "Straight up here, if you please!" and I answered, "Yes."

"I hear, Mr. Sampson," he resumed, presently, for our friend had a new cook, and dinner was not so punctual as usual, "that your profession has recently suffered a great loss."

"In money!" said I.

He laughed at my ready association of loss with money, and replied, "No, in talent and vigour."

Not at once following out his allusion, I considered for a moment. "*Has* it sustained a loss of that kind?" said I. "I was not aware of it."

"Understand me, Mr. Sampson. I don't imagine that you have retired. It is not so bad as that. But Mr. Meltham—"

"O, to be sure!" said I. "Yes! Mr. Meltham, the young actuary of the 'Inestimable.' "

"Just so," he returned, in a consoling way.

"He is a great loss. He was at once, the most profound, the most original, and the most energetic man I have ever known connected with Life Assurance."

I spoke strongly; for I had a high esteem and admiration for Meltham, and my gentleman had indefinitely conveyed to me some suspicion that he wanted to sneer at him. He recalled me to my guard by presenting that trim pathway up his head, with its infernal "Not on the grass, if you please,— the gravel."

"You knew him, Mr. Slinkton."

"Only by reputation. To have known him as an acquaintance, or as a friend, is an honour I should have sought if he had remained in society, though I might never have had the good fortune to attain it, being a man of far inferior mark. He was scarcely above thirty, I suppose?"

"About thirty."

"Ah!" He sighed in his former consoling way. "What creatures we are! To break up, Mr. Sampson, and become incapable of business, at that time of life!—Any reason assigned for the melancholy fact?"

("Humph!" thought I, as I looked at him. "But I WON'T go up the track, and I WILL go on the grass.")

"What reason have you heard assigned, Mr. Slinkton?" I asked point blank.

"Most likely a false one. You know what Rumour is, Mr. Sampson. I never repeat what I hear; it is the only way of paring the nails and shaving the head of Rumour. But, when *you* ask me what reason I have heard assigned for Mr. Meltham's passing away from among men, it is another thing. I am not gratifying idle gossip then. I was told, Mr. Sampson, that Mr. Meltham had relinquished all his avocations and all prospects, because he was, in fact, broken-hearted. A disappointed attachment I heard,—though it hardly seems probable, in the case of a man so distinguished and so attractive."

"Attractions and distinctions are no armour against death," said I.

"Oh! she died? Pray pardon me. I did not hear that. That, indeed, makes it very sad. Poor Mr. Meltham! She died? Ah, dear me! Lamentable, lamentable!"

I still thought his pity was not quite genuine, and I still suspected an unaccountable sneer under all this, until he said as we were parted, like the other knots of talkers, by the announcement of dinner,

"Mr. Sampson, you are surprised to see me so moved on

behalf of a man whom I have never known. I am not so disinterested as you may suppose. I have suffered, and recently too, from death myself. I have lost one of two charming nieces, who were my constant companions. She died young,— barely three-and-twenty,—and even her remaining sister is far from strong. The world is a grave!"

He said this with deep feeling, and I felt reproached for the coldness of my manner. Coldness and distrust had been engendered in me, I knew, by my bad experiences; they were not natural to me; and I often thought how much I had lost in life, losing trustfulness, and how little I had gained, gaining hard caution. This state of mind being habitual to me, I troubled myself more about this conversation than I might have troubled myself about a greater matter. I listened to his talk at dinner, and observed how readily other men responded to it, and with what a graceful instinct he adapted his subjects to the knowledge and habits of those he talked with. As, in talking with me, he had easily started the subject I might be supposed to understand best, and to be the most interested in, so, in talking with others, he guided himself by the same rule. The company was of varied character; but he was not at fault, that I could discover, with any member of it. He knew just as much of each man's pursuit as made him agreeable to that man in reference to it, and just as little as made it natural in him to seek modestly for information when the theme was broached.

As he talked and talked,—but really not too much, for the rest of us seemed to force it upon him,—I became quite angry with myself. I took his face to pieces in my mind, like a watch, and examined it in detail. I could not say much against any of his features separately; I could say even less against them when they were put together. "Then is it not monstrous," I asked myself, "that because a man happens to part his hair straight up the middle of his head, I should permit myself to suspect, and even to detest him?"

(I may stop to remark that this was no proof of my sense. An observer of men who finds himself steadily repelled by some apparently trifling thing in a stranger is right to give it great weight. It may be the clue to the whole mystery. A hair or two will show where a lion is hidden. A very little key will open a very heavy door.)

I took my part in the conversation with him after a time, and we got on remarkably well. In the drawing-room I asked the host how long he had known Mr. Slinkton? He answered,

not many months; he had met him at the house of a celebrated
painter then present, who had known him well when he was
travelling with his nieces in Italy for their health. His plans
in life being broken by the death of one of them, he was
reading with the intention of going back to college as a matter
of form, taking his degree, and going into orders. I could not
but argue with myself that here was the true explanation of
his interest in poor Meltham, and that I had been almost
brutal in my distrust on that simple head.

III

On the very next day but one, I was sitting behind my glass
partition, as before, when he came into the outer office as
before. The moment I saw him again without hearing him, I
hated him worse than ever.

It was only for a moment that I had this opportunity; for
he waved his tight-fitting black glove the instant I looked at
him, and came straight in.

"Mr. Sampson, good day! I presume, you see, upon your
kind permission to intrude upon you. I don't keep my word
in being justified by business, for my business here—if I may
so abuse the word—is of the slightest nature."

I asked, was it anything I could assist him in?

"I thank you, no. I merely called to inquire outside, whether
my dilatory friend had been so false to himself as to be practical and sensible. But, of course, he has done nothing. I gave
him your papers with my own hand, and he was hot upon
the intention, but of course he has done nothing. Apart from
the general human disinclination to do anything that ought
to be done I dare say there is a specialty about assuring one's
life? You find it like will-making? People are so superstitious,
and take it for granted they will die soon afterwards?"

"Up here, if you please. Straight up here, Mr. Sampson.
Neither to the right nor to the left!" I almost fancied I could
hear him breathe the words, as he sat smiling at me, with
that intolerable parting exactly opposite the bridge of my
nose.

"There is such a feeling sometimes, no doubt," I replied;
"but I don't think it obtains to any great extent."

"Well," said he, with a shrug and a smile, "I wish some
good angel would influence my friend in the right direction.
I rashly promised his mother and sister in Norfolk, to see it

done, and he promised them that he would do it. But I suppose he never will.''

He spoke for a minute or two on indifferent topics and went away.

I had scarcely unlocked the drawers of my writing-table next morning when he reappeared. I noticed that he came straight to the door in the glass partition, and did not pause a single moment outside.

"Can you spare me two minutes, my dear Mr. Sampson?''

"By all means.''

"Much obliged," laying his hat and umbrella on the table, "I came early, not to interrupt you. The fact is, I am taken by surprise, in reference to this proposal my friend has made.''

"Has he made one?" said I.

"Ye-es," he answered, deliberately looking at me; and then a bright idea seemed to strike him;—"or he only tells me he has. Perhaps that may be a new way of evading the matter. By Jupiter, I never thought of that!''

Mr. Adams was opening the morning's letters in the outer office. "What is the name, Mr. Slinkton?" I asked.

"Beckwith.''

I looked out at the door and requested Mr. Adams, if there were a proposal in that name, to bring it in. He had already laid it out of his hand on the counter. It was easily selected from the rest, and he gave it me. Alfred Beckwith. Proposal to effect a policy with us for two thousand pounds. Dated yesterday.

"From the Middle Temple, I see, Mr. Slinkton.''

"Yes. He lives on the same staircase with me; his door is opposite. I never thought he would make me his reference though.''

"It seems natural enough that he should.''

"Quite so, Mr. Sampson; but I never thought of it. Let me see." He took the printed paper from his pocket. "How am I to answer all these questions!''

"According to the truth, of course," said I.

"O, of course!" he answered, looking up from the paper with a smile; "I meant they were so many. But, you do right to be particular. Will you allow me to use your pen and ink?''

"Certainly.''

"And your desk?''

"Certainly.''

He had been hovering about between his hat and his umbrella, for a place to write on. He now sat down in my chair, at my blotting paper and inkstand, with the long walk up his head in accurate perspective before me, as I stood with my back to the fire.

Before answering each question he ran over it aloud, and discussed it. How long had he known Mr. Alfred Beckwith? That he had to calculate by years upon his fingers. What were his habits? No difficulty about them; temperate in the last degree, and took a little too much exercise, if anything. All the answers were satisfactory. When he had written them all, he looked them over, and finally signed them in a very pretty hand. He supposed he had now done with the business? I told him he was not likely to be troubled any further. Should he leave the papers there? If he pleased. Much obliged. Good morning!

I had had one other visitor before him; not at the office, but at my own house. The visitor had come to my bedside when it was not yet daylight, and had been seen by no one else but my faithful confidential servant.

A second reference paper (for we required always two) was sent down into Norfolk, and was duly received back by post. This, likewise, was satisfactorily answered in every respect. Our forms were all complied with, we accepted the proposal, and the premium for one year was paid.

IV

For six or seven months, I saw no more of Mr. Slinkton. He called once at my house, but I was not at home; and he once asked me to dine with him in the Temple, but I was engaged. His friend's Assurance was effected in March. Late in September or early in October, I was down in Scarborough for a breath of sea air, where I met him on the beach. It was a hot evening; he came toward me with his hat in his hand; and there was the walk I had felt so strongly disinclined to take, in perfect order again, exactly in front of the bridge of my nose.

He was not alone, but had a young lady on his arm.

She was dressed in mourning, and I looked at her with great interest. She had the appearance of being extremely delicate, and her face was remarkably pale and melancholy; but she was very pretty. He introduced her as his niece, Miss Niner.

"Are you strolling, Mr. Sampson? Is it possible you can be idle?"

It *was* possible, and I *was* strolling.

"Shall we stroll together?"

"With pleasure."

The young lady walked between us, and we walked on the cool sea sand, in the direction of Filey.

"There have been wheels here," said Mr. Slinkton. "And now I look again, the wheels of a hand-carriage! Margaret, my love, our shadow, without doubt!"

"Miss Niner's shadow?" I repeated, looking down at it on the sand.

"Not that one," Mr. Slinkton returned, laughing. "Margaret, my dear, tell Mr. Sampson."

"Indeed," said the young lady, turning to me, "there is nothing to tell,—except that I constantly see the same invalid old gentleman, at all times, wherever I go. I have mentioned it to my uncle, and he calls the gentleman my shadow."

"Does he live in Scarborough?" I asked.

"He is staying here."

"Do you live in Scarborough?"

"No, I am staying here. My uncle has placed me with a family here, for my health."

"And your shadow?" said I, smiling.

"My shadow," she answered, smiling too, "is—like myself—not very robust, I fear; for I lose my shadow sometimes, as my shadow loses me at other times. We both seem liable to confinement to the house. I have not seen my shadow for days and days; but it does oddly happen, occasionally, that wherever I go, for many days together, this gentleman goes. We have come together in the most unfrequent nooks on this shore."

"Is this he?" said I, pointing before us.

The wheels had swept down to the water's edge, and described a great loop on the sand in turning. Bringing the loop back towards us, and spinning it out as it came, was a hand-carriage drawn by a man.

"Yes," said Miss Niner, "this really is my shadow, uncle!"

As the carriage approached us and we approached the carriage, I saw within it an old man, whose head was sunk on his breast, and who was enveloped in a variety of wrappers. He was drawn by a very quiet but very keen-looking man, with iron-grey hair, who was slightly lame. They had passed us, when the carriage stopped, and the old gentleman within, putting out his arm, called to me by my name. I went back, and was absent from Mr. Slinkton and his niece for about five minutes.

When I rejoined them, Mr. Slinkton was the first to speak. Indeed, he said to me in a raised voice before I came up with him: "It is well you have not been longer, or my niece might have died of curiosity to know who her shadow is, Mr. Sampson."

"An old East India Director," said I. "An intimate friend of our friend's at whose house I first had the pleasure of meeting you. A certain Major Banks. You have heard of him?"

"Never."

"Very rich, Miss Niner; but very old, and very crippled. An amiable man, sensible,—much interested in you. He has just been expatiating on the affection that he has observed to exist between you and your uncle."

Mr. Slinkton was holding his hat again, and he passed his hand up the straight walk, as if he himself went up it serenely, after me.

"Mr. Sampson," he said, tenderly pressing his niece's arm in his, "our affection was always a strong one, for we have had but few near ties. We have still fewer now. We have associations to bring us together, that are not of this world, Margaret."

"Dear uncle!" murmured the young lady, and turned her face aside to hide her tears.

"My niece and I have such remembrances and regrets in common, Mr. Sampson," he feelingly pursued, "that it would be strange indeed if the relations between us were cold or indifferent. If I remember a conversation we once had together, you will understand the reference I make. Cheer up, dear Margaret. Don't droop, don't droop. My Margaret! I cannot bear to see you droop!"

The poor young lady was very much affected, but controlled herself. His feelings, too, were very acute. In a word, he found himself under such great need of a restorative, that he presently went away, to take a bath of sea-water, leaving the young lady and me sitting by a point of rock, and probably presuming—but that you will say was a pardonable indulgence in a luxury—that she would praise him with all her heart.

She did, poor thing! With all her confiding heart, she praised him to me, for his care of her dead sister, and for his untiring devotion in her last illness. The sister had wasted away very slowly, and wild and terrible fantasies had come over her toward the end, but he had never been impatient with her, or at a loss; had always been gentle, watchful, and self-possessed. The sister had known him, as she had known him, to be the best of men, the kindest of men, and yet a man of such admirable strength of character, as to be a very tower for the support of their weak natures while their poor lives endured.

"I shall leave him, Mr. Sampson, very soon," said the young lady; "I know my life is drawing to an end; and when I am gone, I hope he will marry and be happy. I am sure he has lived single so long, only for my sake, and for my poor sister's."

The little hand-carriage had made another great loop on the damp sand, and was coming back again, gradually spinning out a slim figure of eight, half a mile long.

"Young lady," said I, looking around, laying my hand upon her arm, and speaking in a low voice, "time presses. You hear the gentle murmur of that sea?"

She looked at me with the utmost wonder and alarm, saying,

"Yes!"

"And you know what a voice is in it when the storm comes?"

"Yes!"

"You see how quiet and peaceful it lies before us, and you know what an awful sight of power without pity it might be, this very night!"

"Yes!"

"But if you had never heard or seen it, or heard of it in its cruelty, could you believe that it beats every inanimate thing in its way to pieces, without mercy, and destroys life without remorse?"

"You terrify me, sir, by these questions!"

"To save you, young lady, to save you! For God's sake, collect your strength and collect your firmness! If you were here alone, and hemmed in by the rising tide on the flow to fifty feet above your head, you could not be in greater danger than the danger you are now to be saved from."

The figure on the sand was spun out, and straggled off into a crooked little jerk that ended at the cliff very near us.

"As I am, before Heaven and the Judge of all mankind, your friend, and your dead sister's friend, I solemnly entreat you, Miss Niner, without one moment's loss of time, to come to this gentleman with me!"

If the little carriage had been less near us, I doubt if I could

have got her away; but it was so near that we were there
before she had recovered the hurry of being urged from the
rock. I did not remain there with her two minutes. Certainly
within five, I have the inexpressible satisfaction of seeing
her—from the point we had sat on, and to which I had returned—half supported and half carried up some rude steps
notched in the cliff, by the figure of an active man. With that
figure beside her, I knew she was safe anywhere.

I sat alone on the rock, awaiting Mr. Slinkton's return. The
twilight was deepening and the shadows were heavy, when
he came round the point, with his hat hanging at his button-
hole, smoothing his wet hair with one of his hands, and picking out the old path with the other and a pocket-comb.

"My niece not here, Mr. Sampson?" he said, looking about.

"Miss Niner seemed to feel a chill in the air after the sun
was down, and has gone home."

He looked surprised, as though she were not accustomed
to do anything without him; even to originate so slight a
proceeding. "I persuaded Miss Niner," I explained.

"Ah!" said he. "She is easily persuaded—for her good.
Thank you, Mr. Sampson; she is better within doors. The
bathing-place was farther than I thought, to say the truth."

"Miss Niner is very delicate," I observed.

He shook his head and drew a deep sigh. "Very, very,
very. You may recollect my saying so. The time that has since
intervened has not strengthened her. The gloomy shadow that
fell upon her sister so early in life seems, in my anxious eyes,
to gather over her, ever darker, ever darker. Dear Margaret,
dear Margaret! But we must hope."

The hand-carriage was spinning away before us at a most
indecorous pace for an invalid vehicle, and was making most
irregular curves upon the sand. Mr. Slinkton, noticing it after
he had put his handkerchief to his eyes, said,

"If I may judge from appearances, your friend will be upset
Mr. Sampson."

"It looks probable, certainly," said I.

"The servant must be drunk."

"The servants of old gentlemen will get drunk stometimes,"
said I.

"The major draws very light, Mr. Sampson."

"The major does draw light," said I.

By this time the carriage, much to my relief, was lost in
the darkness. We walked on for a little, side by side over the
sand, in silence. After a short while he said, in a voice still

affected by the emotion that his niece's state of health had awakened in him,

"Do you stay here long, Mr. Sampson?"

"Why, no. I am going away to-night."

"So soon? But business always holds you in request. Men like Mr. Sampson are too important to others, to be spared to their own need of relaxation and enjoyment."

"I don't know about that," said I. "However, I am going back."

"To London?"

"To London."

"I shall be there too, soon after you."

I knew that as well as he did. But I did not tell him so. Any more than I told him what defensive weapon my right hand rested on in my pocket, as I walked by his side. Any more than I told him why I did not walk on the sea side of him with the night closing in.

We left the beach, and our ways diverged. We exchanged good night, and had parted indeed, when he said, returning,

"Mr. Sampson, *may* I ask? Poor Meltham, whom we spoke of,—dead yet?"

"Not when I last heard of him; but too broken a man to live long, and hopelessly lost to his old calling."

"Dear, dear, dear!" said he, with great feeling. "Sad, sad, sad! The world is a grave!" And so went his way.

It was not his fault if the world were not a grave; but I did not call that observation after him, any more than I had mentioned those other things just now enumerated. He went his way, and I went mine with all expedition. This happened, as I have said, either at the end of September or beginning of October. The next time I saw him, and the last time, was late in November.

V

I had a very particular engagement to breakfast in the Temple. It was a bitter northeasterly morning, and the sleet and slush lay inches deep in the streets. I could get no conveyance, and was soon wet to the knees; but I should have been true to that appointment though I had had to wade to it up to my neck in the same impediments.

The appointment took me to some chambers in the Temple. They were at the top of a lonely corner house overlooking the river. The name, MR. ALFRED BECKWITH, was painted on the outer door. On the opposite side, on the same landing, Mr. Julius Slinkton. The doors of both sets of chambers stood open, so that anything said aloud in one could be heard in the other.

I had never been in those chambers before. They were dismal, close, unwholesome, and oppressive; the furniture, originally good, and not yet old, was faded and dirty,—the rooms were in great disorder; there was a strong pervading smell of opium, brandy, and tobacco; the grate and fire-irons were splashed all over with unsightly blotches of rust; and on a sofa by the fire, in the room where breakfast had been prepared, lay the host, Mr. Beckwith, a man with all the appearances of the worst kind of drunkard, very far advanced upon his shameful way to death.

"Slinkton is not come yet," said this creature, staggering up when I went in; "I'll call him. Halloa! Julius Cæsar! Come and drink!" As he hoarsely roared this out, he beat the poker and tongs together in a mad way, as if that were his usual manner of summoning his associate.

The voice of Mr. Slinkton was heard through the clatter from the opposite side of the staircase, and he came in. He had not expected the pleasure of meeting me. I have seen several artful men brought to a stand, but I never saw a man so aghast as when his eyes rested on mine.

"Julius Cæsar," cried Beckwith, staggering between us, "Mist' Sampson! Mist' Sampson, Julius Cæsar! Julius, Mist' Sampson, is the friend of my soul. Julius keeps me plied with liquor, morning, noon, and night. Julius is a real benefactor. Julius threw the tea and coffee out of the window when I used to have any. Julius empties all the water jugs of their contents, and fills 'em with spirits. Julius winds me up and keeps me going.—Boil the brandy, Julius!"

There was a rusty and furred saucepan in the ashes,—the ashes looked like the accumulation of weeks,—and Beckwith, rolling and staggering between us as if he were going to plunge headlong into the fire, got the saucepan out, and tried to force it into Slinkton's hand.

"Boil the brandy, Julius Cæsar! Come! Do your usual office.—Boil the brandy!"

He became so fierce in his gesticulations with the saucepan, that I expected to see him lay open Slinkton's head with it. I therefore put out my hand to check him. He reeled back to the sofa, and sat there, panting, shaking and red-eyed, in his rags of dressing-gown, looking at us both. I noticed then that there was nothing to drink on the table but brandy, and nothing to eat but salted herrings, and a hot, sickly, highly peppered stew.

"At all events, Mr. Sampson," said Slinkton, offering me the smooth gravel path for the last time, "I thank you for interfering between me and this unfortunate man's violence. However you came here, Mr. Sampson, or with whatever motive you came here, at least I thank you for that."

"Boil the brandy," muttered Beckwith.

Without gratifying his desire to know how I came there, I said, quietly, "How is your niece, Mr. Slinkton?"

He looked hard at me, and I looked hard at him.

"I am sorry to say, Mr. Sampson, that my niece has proved treacherous and ungrateful to her best friend. She left me without a word of notice or explanation. She was misled, no doubt, by some designing rascal. Perhaps you may have heard of it?"

"I did hear that she was misled by a designing rascal. In fact, I have proof of it."

"Are you sure of that?" said he.

"Quite."

"Boil the brandy," muttered Beckwith. "Company to breakfast, Julius Cæsar! Do your usual office—provide the usual breakfast, dinner, tea, and supper.—Boil the brandy!"

The eyes of Slinkton looked from him to me, and he said, after a moment's consideration,

"Mr. Sampson, you are a man of the world, and so am I. I will be plain with you."

"O no, you won't," said I, shaking my head.

"I tell you sir, I will be plain wth you."

"And I tell you, you will not," said I. "I know all about you. *You* plain with any one? Nonsense, nonsense!"

"I tell you, Mr. Sampson," he went on, with a manner almost composed, "that I understand your object. You want to save your funds, and escape from your liabilities; these are old tricks of trade with you Office gentlemen. But you will not do it, sir; you will not succeed. You have not an easy adversary to play against, when you play against me. We shall have to inquire, in due time, when and how Mr. Beckwith fell into his present habits. With that remark, sir, I put this poor creature and his incoherent wanderings of speech, aside, and wish you a good morning and a better case next time."

While he was saying this, Beckwith had filled a half-pint glass with brandy. At this moment, he threw the brandy at his face, and threw the glass after it. Slinkton put his hands up, half blinded with the spirit, and cut with the glass across the forehead. At the sound of the breakage, a fourth person came into the room, closed the door, and stood at it; he was a very quiet but very keen looking man, with iron-gray hair, and slightly lame.

Slinkton pulled out his handkerchief, assuaged the pain in his smarting eyes, and dabbled the blood on his forehead. He was a long time about it, and I saw that, in the doing of it, a tremendous change came over him, occasioned by the change in Beckwith,—who ceased to pant and tremble, sat upright, and never took his eyes off him. I never in my life saw a face in which abhorrence and determination were so forcibly painted, as in Beckwith's then.

"Look at me, you villain," said Beckwith, "and see me as I really am. I took these rooms, to make them a trap for you. I came into them as a drunkard, to bait the trap for you. You fell into the trap, and you will never leave it alive. On the morning when you last went to Mr. Sampson's office, I had seen him first. Your plot has been known to both of us, all along, and you have been counterplotted all along. What? Having been cajoled into putting that prize of two thousand pounds in your power, I was to be done to death with brandy, and, brandy not proving quick enough, with something quicker? Have I never seen you, when you thought my senses gone, pouring from your little bottle into my glass? Why, you Murderer and Forger, alone here with you in the dead of night, as I have so often been, I have had my hand upon the trigger of a pistol, twenty times, to blow your brains out!"

This sudden starting up of the thing that he had supposed to be his imbecile victim into a determined man, wtih a settled resolution to hunt him down and be the death of him, mercilessly expressed from head to foot, was in the first shock too much for him. Without any figure of speech, he staggered under it. But there is no greater mistake than to suppose that a man who is a calculating criminal is, in any phase of his guilt, otherwise than true to himself and perfectly consistent with his whole character. Such a man commits murder, and murder is the natural culmination of his course; such a man has to outface murder, and will do it with hardihood and effrontery. It is a sort of fashion to express surprise that any notorious criminal, having such crime upon his conscience, can so brave it out. Do you think that if he had it on his conscience at all, or had a conscience to have it upon, he would ever have committed the crime?

Perfectly consistent with himself, as I believe all such monsters to be, this Slinkton recovered himself, and showed a defiance that was sufficiently cold and quiet. He was white, he was haggard, he was changed; but only as a sharper who had played for a great stake and had been outwitted and had lost the game.

"Listen to me, you villain," said Beckwith, "and let every word you hear me say be a stab in your wicked heart. When I took these rooms, to throw myself in your way and lead you on to the scheme that I knew my appearance and supposed character and habits would suggest to such a devil, how did I know that? Because you were no stranger to me. I knew you well. And I knew you to be the cruel wretch who, for so much money, had killed one innocent girl while she trusted him implicitly, and who was by inches killing another."

Slinkton took out a snuff-box, took a pinch of snuff, and laughed.

"But see here," said Beckwith, never looking away, never raising his voice, never relaxing his face, never unclenching his hand. "See what a dull wolf you have been, after all! The infatuated drunkard who never drank a fiftieth part of the liquor you plied him with, but poured it away, here, there, everywhere,—almost before your eyes; who bought over the fellow you set to watch him and to ply him, by outbidding you in his bribe, before he had been at his work three days,— with whom you have observed no caution, yet who was so bent on ridding the earth of you as a wild beast, that he would have defeated you if you had been ever so prudent,—that drunkard whom you have, many a time, left on the floor of this room, and who has even let you go out of it, alive and undeceived, when you have turned him over with your foot,— has, almost as often, on the same night, within an hour, within a few minutes, watched you awake, had his hand at your pillow when you were asleep, turned over your papers, taken samples from your bottles and packets of powder, changed their contents, rifled every secret of your life!"

He had had another pinch of snuff in his hand, but had gradually let it drop from between his fingers to the floor; where he now smoothed out with his foot, looking down at it the while.

"That drunkard," said Beckwith, "who had free access to your rooms at all times, that he might drink the strong drinks that you left in his way and be the sooner ended, holding no more terms with you than he would hold with a tiger, has had his master-key for all your locks, his test for all your poisons, his clew to your cipher-writing. He can tell you, as well as you can tell him, how long it took to complete that deed, what doses there were, what intervals, what signs of gradual decay upon mind and body; what distempered fancies were produced, what observable changes, what physical pain. He can tell you as well as I can tell him, that all this was recorded day by day, as a lesson of experience for future service. He can tell you, better than you can tell him, where that journal is at this moment."

Slinkton stopped the action of his foot, and looked at Beckwith.

"No," said the latter, as if answering a question from him. "Not in the drawer of the writing-desk that opens with the spring; it is not there, and it never will be there again."

"Then you are a thief!" said Slinkton.

Without any change whatever in the inflexible purpose, which it was terrific even to me to contemplate, and from the power of which I had always felt convinced it was impossible for this wretch to escape, Beckwith returned,

"And I am your niece's shadow, too."

With an imprecation, Slinkton put his hand to his head, tore out some hair, and flung it to the ground. It was the end of the smooth walk; he destroyed it in the action, and it will soon be seen that his use for it was past.

Beckwith went on: "Whenever you left here, I left here. Although I understood that you found it necessary to pause in the completion of that purpose, to avert suspicion, still I watched you close, with the poor, confiding girl. When I had the diary, and could read it word by word,—it was only about the night before your last visit to Scarborough,—you remember the night? you slept with a small flat vial tied to your wrist,—I sent to Mr. Sampson, who was kept out of view. This is Mr. Sampson's trusty servant standing by the door. We three saved your niece among us."

Slinkton looked at us all, took an uncertain step or two from the place where he had stood, returned to it, and glanced about him in a very curious way,—as one of the meaner reptiles might, looking for a hole to hide in. I noticed at the same time, that a singular change took place in the figure of the man,—as if it collapsed within his clothes, and they consequently became ill-shaped and ill-fitting.

"You shall know," said Beckwith, "for I hope the knowledge will be bitter and terrible to you, why you have been pursued by one man, and why, when the whole interest that Mr. Sampson represents would have expended any money in hunting you down, you have been tracked to death at a single individual's charge. I hear you have had the name of Meltham on your lips sometimes?"

I saw, in addition to those other changes, a sudden stoppage come upon his breathing.

"When you sent the sweet girl whom you murdered (you know with what artfully made-out surroundings and probabilities you sent her) to Meltham's office, before taking her abroad to originate the transaction that doomed her to the grave, it fell to Meltham's lot to see her and to speak with her. It did not fall to his lot to save her, though I know he would freely give his own life to have done it. He admired her;—I would say, he loved her deeply, if I thought it possible that you could understand the word. When she was sacrificed, he was thoroughly assured of your guilt. Having lost her, he had but one object left in life, and that was to avenge her and destroy you."

I saw the villain's nostrils rise and fall, convulsively; but I saw no moving at his mouth.

"That man, Meltham," Beckwith steadily pursued, "was as absolutely certain that you could never elude him in this world, if he devoted himself to your destruction with his utmost fidelity and earnestness, and if he divided the sacred duty with no other duty in life, as he was certain that in achieving it he would be a poor instrument in the hands of Providence, and would do well before Heaven in striking you out from among living men. I am that man, and I thank God that I have done my work!"

If Slinkton had been running for his life from swift-footed savages, a dozen miles, he could not have shown more emphatic signs of being oppressed at heart and labouring for breath, than he showed now, when he looked at the pursuer who had so relentlessly hunted him down.

"You never saw me under my right name before; you see me under my right name now. You shall see me once again in the body, when you are tried for your life. You shall see me once again in the spirit, when the cord is round your neck, and the crowd are crying against you!"

When Meltham had spoken these last words, the miscreant suddenly turned away his face, and seemed to strike his mouth with his open hand. At the same instant, the room was filled with a new and powerful odour, and, almost at the same instant, he broke into a crooked run, leap, start,—I have no name for the spasm,—and fell, with a dull weight that shook the heavy old doors and windows in their frames.

That was the fitting end of him.

When we saw that he was dead, we drew away from the room, and Meltham, giving me his hand, said with a weary air,—

"I have no more work on earth, my friend. But I shall see her again elsewhere."

It was in vain that I tried to rally him. He might have saved her, he said; he had not saved her, and he reproached himself; he had lost her, and he was broken-hearted.

"The purpose that sustained me is over, Sampson, and there is nothing now to hold me to life. I am not fit for life; I am weak and spiritless; I have no hope and no object; my day is done."

In truth, I could hardly have believed that the broken man who then spoke to me was the man who had so strongly and so differently impressed me when his purpose was before him. I used such entreaties with him as I could; but he still said, and always said, in a patient, undemonstrative way,—nothing could avail him,—he was broken-hearted.

He died early in the next spring. He was buried by the side of the poor young lady for whom he had cherished those tender and unhappy regrets; and he left all that he had to her sister. She lived to be a happy wife and mother: she married my sister's son, who succeeded poor Meltham; she is living now, and her children ride about the garden on my walking stick when I go to see her.

George Eliot
(1819–1880)

George Eliot and Charles Dickens are generally considered the greatest English novelists of the nineteenth century. Born Mary Ann or Marian Evans in Warwickshire, George Eliot took on the male pseudonym when she first started to write fiction, the sketches that became known as Scenes of Clerical Life *(1857–58). Before that, she did translations from the German (Strauss's Life of Jesus) and served as subeditor on the* Westminster Review, *to which she also contributed articles and reviews. In 1854, she formed a life-long relationship with George Henry Lewes, a versatile writer who encouraged Eliot to write fiction and who remained a strong influence on her and her work until his death in 1878. After* Scenes, *she wrote the novels that strengthened and spread her reputation:* Adam Bede *(1859),* The Mill on the Floss *(1860),* Silas Marner *(1861),* Romola *(1863),* Felix Holt the Radical *(1866),* Middlemarch *(1871–72), and* Daniel Deronda *(1876). Having given up formal religion and having endured the social osctracism of living unmarried with Lewes (whose wife was still alive), Eliot turned to themes of individual morality and personal responsibility. Her most mature statement of how individual lives can be interwoven with social values comes in* Middlemarch, *but elements of that great nineteenth-century theme may already be glimpsed in "The Lifted Veil," one of those early "scenes" of clerical life.*

The Lifted Veil

Give me no light, great Heaven, but such as turns
To energy of human fellowship;
No powers beyond the growing heritage
That makes completer manhood.

CHAPTER I

The time of my end approaches. I have lately been subject
to attacks of *angina pectoris*; and in the ordinary course of
things, my physician tells me, I may fairly hope that my life
will not be protracted many months. Unless, then, I am cursed
with an exceptional physical constitution, as I am cursed with
an exceptional mental character, I shall not much longer groan
under the wearisome burthen of this earthly existence. If it
were to be otherwise—if I were to live on to the age most
men desire and provide for—I should for once have known
whether the miseries of elusive expectation can outweigh the
miseries of true prevision. For I foresee when I shall die, and
everything that will happen in my last moments.

Just a month from this day, on September 20, 1850, I shall
be sitting in this chair, in this study, at ten o'clock at night,
longing to die, weary of incessant insight and foresight, without delusions and without hope. Just as I am watching a
tongue of blue flame rising in the fire, and my lamp is burning
low, the horrible contraction will begin at my chest. I shall
only have time to reach the bell, and pull it violently, before
the sense of suffocation will come. No one will answer my
bell. I know why. My two servants are lovers, and will have
quarrelled. My housekeeper will have rushed out of the house
in a fury, two hours before, hoping that Perry will believe
she has gone to drown herself. Perry is alarmed at last, and
is gone out after her. The little scullery-maid is asleep on a
bench: she never answers the bell; it does not wake her. The
sense of suffocation increases: my lamp goes out with a horrible stench: I make a great effort, and snatch at the bell
again. I long for life, and there is no help. I thirsted for the
unknown: the thirst is gone. O God, let me stay with the
known, and be weary of it: I am content. Agony of pain and

suffocation—and all the while the earth, the fields, the pebbly brook at the bottom of the rookery, the fresh scent after the rain, the light of the morning through my chamber-window, the warmth of the hearth after the frosty air—will darkness close over them for ever?

Darkness—darkness—no pain—nothing but darkness: but I am passing on and on through the darkness: my thought stays in the darkness, but always with a sense of moving onward. . . .

Before that time comes, I wish to use my last hours of ease and strength in telling the strange story of my experience. I have never fully unbosomed myself to any human being; I have never been encouraged to trust much in the sympathy of my fellow-men. But we have all a chance of meeting with some pity, some tenderness, some charity, when we are dead: it is the living only who cannot be forgiven—the living only from whom men's indulgence and reverence are held off, like the rain by the hard east wind. While the heart beats, bruise it—it is your only opportunity; while the eye can still turn towards you with moist, timid entreaty, freeze it with an icy unanswering gaze; while the ear, that delicate messenger to the inmost sanctuary of the soul, can still take in the tones of kindness, put it off with hard civility, or sneering compliment, or envious affectation of indifference; while the creative brain can still throb with the sense of injustice, with the yearning for brotherly recognition—make haste—oppress it with your ill-considered judgements, your trivial comparisons, your careless misrepresentations. The heart will by and by be still— "ubi saeva indignatio ulterius cor lacerare nequit[1]"; the eye will cease to entreat; the ear will be deaf; the brain will have ceased from all wants as well as from all work. Then your charitable speeches may find vent; then you may remember and pity the toil and the struggle and the failure; then you may give due honour to the work achieved; then you may find extenuation for errors, and may consent to bury them.

That is a trivial schoolboy text; why do I dwell on it? It has little reference to me, for I shall leave no works behind me for men to honour. I have no near relatives who will make up, by weeping over my grave, for the wounds they inflicted on me when I was among them. It is only the story of my life that will perhaps win a little more sympathy from strangers

---

[1] Inscription on Swift's tombstone.

when I am dead, than I ever believed it would obtain from my friends while I was living.

My childhood perhaps seems happier to me than it really was, by contrast with all the after-years. For then the curtain of the future was as impenetrable to me as to other children: I had all their delight in the present hour, their sweet indefinite hopes for the morrow; and I had a tender mother: even now, after the dreary lapse of long years, a slight trace of sensation accompanies the remembrance of her caress as she held me on her knee—her arms round my little body, her cheek pressed on mine. I had a complaint of the eyes that made me blind for a little while, and she kept me on her knee from morning till night. That unequalled love soon vanished out of my life, and even to my childish consciousness it was as if that life had become more chill. I rode my little white pony with the groom by my side as before, but there were no loving eyes looking at me as I mounted, no glad arms opened to me when I came back. Perhaps I missed my mother's love more than most children of seven or eight would have done, to whom the other pleasures of life remained as before; for I was certainly a very sensitive child. I remember still the mingled trepidation and delicious excitement with which I was affected by the tramping of the horses on the pavement in the echoing stables, by the loud resonance of the groom's voices, by the booming bark of the dogs as my father's carriage thundered under the archway of the courtyard, by the din of the gong as it gave notice of luncheon and dinner. The measured tramp of soldiery which I sometimes heard—for my father's house lay near a county town where there were large barracks—made me sob and tremble; and yet when they were gone past, I longed for them to come back again.

I fancy my father thought me an odd child, and had little fondness for me; though he was very careful in fulfilling what he regarded as a parent's duties. But he was already past the middle of life, and I was not his only son. My mother had been his second wife, and he was five-and-forty when he married her. He was a firm, unbending, intensely orderly man, in root and stem a banker, but with a flourishing graft of the active landholder, aspiring to county influence: one of those people who are always like themselves from day to day, who are uninfluenced by the weather, and neither know melancholy nor high spirits. I held him in great awe, and appeared more timid and sensitive in his presence than at other times;

a circumstance which, perhaps, helped to confirm him in the intention to educate me on a different plan from the prescriptive one with which he had complied in the case of my elder brother, already a tall youth at Eton. My brother was to be his representative and successor; he must go to Eton and Oxford, for the sake of making connexions, of course: my father was not a man to underrate the bearing of Latin satirists or Greek dramatists on the attainment of an aristocratic position. But, intrinsically, he had slight esteem for "those dead but sceptred spirits"; having qualified himself for forming an independent opinion by reading Potter's *Æschylus*, and dipping into Francis's *Horace*. To this negative view he added a positive one, derived from a recent connexion with mining speculations; namely, that a scientific education was the really useful training for a younger son. Moreover, it was clear that a shy, sensitive boy like me was not fit to encounter the rough experience of a public school. Mr. Letherall had said so very decidedly. Mr. Letherall was a large man in spectacles, who one day took my small head between his large hands, and pressed it here and there in an exploratory, suspicious manner—then placed each of his great thumbs on my temples, and pushed me a little way from him, and stared at me with glittering spectacles. The contemplation appeared to displease him, for he frowned sternly, and said to my father, drawing his thumbs across my eyebrows—

"The deficiency is there, sir—there; and here," he added, touching the upper sides of my head, "here is the excess. That must be brought out, sir, and this must be laid to sleep."

I was in a state of tremor, partly at the vague idea that I was the object of reprobation, partly in the agitation of my first hatred—hatred of this big, spectacled man, who pulled my head about as if he wanted to buy and cheapen it.

I am not aware how much Mr. Letherall had to do with the system afterwards adopted towards me, but it was presently clear that private tutors, natural history, science, and the modern languages, were the appliances by which the defects of my organization were to be remedied. I was very stupid about machines, so I was to be greatly occupied with them; I had no memory for classification, so it was particularly necessary that I should study systematic zoology and botany; I was hungry for human deeds and humane motions, so I was to be plentifully crammed with the mechanical powers, the elementary bodies, and the phenomena of electricity and magnetism. A better-constituted boy would certainly have profited under my intelligent tutors, with their scientific apparatus; and would, doubtless, have found the phenomena of electricity and magnetism as fascinating as I was, every Thursday, assured they were. As it was, I could have paired off, for ignorance of whatever was taught me, with the worst Latin scholar that was ever turned out of a classical academy. I read Plutarch, and Shakespeare, and Don Quixote by the sly, and supplied myself in that way with wandering thoughts, while my tutor was assuring me that "an improved man, as distinguished from an ignorant one, was a man who knew the reason why water ran downhill." I had no desire to be this improved man; I was glad of the running water; I could watch it and listen to it gurgling among the pebbles, and bathing the bright green water-plants, by the hour together. I did not want to know *why* it ran; I had perfect confidence that there were good reasons for what was so very beautiful.

There is no need to dwell on this part of my life. I have said enough to indicate that my nature was of the sensitive, unpractical order, and that it grew up in an uncongenial medium, which could never foster it into happy, healthy development. When I was sixteen I was sent to Geneva to complete my course of education; and the change was a very happy one to me, for the first sight of the Alps, with the setting sun on them, as we descended the Jura, seemed to me like an entrance into heaven; and the three years of my life there were spent in a perpetual sense of exaltation, as if from a draught of delicious wine, at the presence of Nature in all her awful loveliness. You will think, perhaps, that I must have been a poet, from this early sensibility to Nature. But my lot was not so happy as that. A poet pours forth his song and *believes* in the listening ear and answering soul, to which his song will be floated sooner or later. But the poet's sensibility without his voice—the poet's sensibility that finds no vent but in silent tears on the sunny bank, when the noonday light sparkles on the water, or in an inward shudder at the sound of harsh human tones, the sight of a cold human eye—this dumb passion brings with it a fatal solitude of soul in the society of one's fellow-men. My least solitary moments were those in which I pushed off in my boat, at evening, towards the centre of the lake; it seemed to me that the sky, and the glowing mountain-tops, and the wide blue water, surrounded me with a cherishing love such as no human face had shed on me since my mother's love had vanished out of my life. I used to do as Jean Jacques did—lie down in my boat and let it glide where it would, while I looked up at the departing glow leaving one mountain-top after the other, as if the prophet's chariot of fire were passing over them on its way to the home of light. Then, when the white summits were all sad and corpse-like, I had to push homeward, for I was under careful surveillance, and was allowed no late wanderings. This disposition of mine was not favourable to the formation of intimate friendships among the numerous youths of my own age who are always to be found studying at Geneva. Yet I made *one* such friendship; and, singularly enough, it was with a youth whose intellectual tendencies were the very reverse of my own. I shall call him Charles Meunier; his real surname—an English one, for he was of English extraction—having since become celebrated. He was an orphan, who lived on a miserable pittance while he pursued the medical studies for which he had a special genius. Strange! that with my vague mind, susceptible and unobservant, hating inquiry and given up to contemplation, I should have been drawn towards a youth whose strongest passion was science. But the bond was not an intellectual one; it came from a source that can happily bend the stupid with the brilliant, the dreamy with the practical: it came from community of feeling. Charles was poor and ugly, derided by Genevese *gamins*, and not acceptable in drawing-rooms. I saw that he was isolated, as I was, though from a different cause, and, stimulated by a sympathetic resentment, I made timid advances towards him. It is enough to say that there sprang up as much comradeship between us as our different habits would allow; and in Charles's rare holidays we went up the Salève together, or took the boat to Vevay, while I listened dreamily to the monologues in which he unfolded his bold conceptions of future experiment and discovery. I mingled them confusedly in my thought with glimpses of blue water and delicate floating cloud, with the notes of birds and the distant glitter of the glacier. He knew quite well that my mind was half absent, yet he liked to talk to me in this way; for don't we talk of our hopes and our projects even to dogs and birds, when they love us? I have mentioned this one friendship because of its connexion with a strange and terrible scene which I shall have to narrate in my subsequent life.

This happier life at Geneva was put an end to by a severe illness, which is partly a blank to me, partly a time of dimly-remembered suffering, with the presence of my father by my bed from time to time. Then came the languid monotony of convalescence, the days gradually breaking into variety and distinctness as my strength enabled me to take longer and longer drives. On one of these more vividly remembered days, my father said to me, as he sat beside my sofa—

"When you are quite well enough to travel, Latimer, I shall take you home with me. The journey will amuse you and do you good, for I shall go through the Tyrol and Austria, and you will see many new places. Our neighbours, the Filmores, are come; Alfred will join us at Basle, and we shall all go together to Vienna, and back by Prague" . . .

My father was called away before he had finished his sentence, and he left my mind resting on the word *Prague*, with a strange sense that a new and wondrous scene was breaking upon me: a city under the broad sunshine, that seemed to me as if it were the summer sunshine of a long-past century arrested in its course—unrefreshed for ages by dews of night, or the rushing rain-cloud; scorching the dusty, weary, time-eaten grandeur of a people doomed to live on in the stale repetition of memories, like deposed and superannuated kings in their regal gold-inwoven tatters. The city looked so thirsty that the broad river seemed to me a sheet of metal; and the blackened statues, as I passed under their blank gaze, along the unending bridge, with their ancient garments and their saintly crowns, seemed to me the real inhabitants and owners of this place, while the busy, trivial men and women, hurrying to and fro, were a swarm of ephemeral visitants infesting it for a day. It is such grim, stony beings as these, I thought, who are the fathers of ancient faded children, in those tanned time-fretted dwellings that crowd the steep before me; who pay their court in the worn and crumbling pomp of the palace which stretches its monotonous length on the height; who worship wearily in the stifling air of the churches, urged by no fear or hope, but compelled by their doom to be ever old and undying, to live on in the rigidity of habit, as they live on in perpetual midday, without the repose of night or the new birth of morning.

A stunning clang of metal suddenly thrilled through me, and I became conscious of the objects in my room again: one of the fire-irons had fallen as Pierre opened the door to bring me my draught. My heart was palpitating violently, and I begged Pierre to leave my draught beside me; I would take it presently.

As soon as I was alone again, I began to ask myself whether I had been sleeping. Was this a dream—this wonderfully distinct vision—minute in its distinctness down to a patch of rainbow light on the pavement, transmitted through a coloured lamp in the shape of a star—of a strange city, quite unfamiliar to my imagination? I had seen no picture of Prague: it lay in my mind as a mere name, with vaguely-remembered historical associations—ill-defined memories of imperial grandeur and religious wars.

Nothing of this sort had ever occurred in my dreaming experience before, for I had often been humiliated because my dreams were only saved from being utterly disjointed and commonplace by the frequent terrors of nightmare. But I could not believe that I had been asleep, for I remembered distinctly the gradual breaking-in of the vision upon me, like the new images in a dissolving view, or the growing distinctness of the landscape as the sun lifts up the veil of the morning mist. And while I was conscious of this incipient vision, I was also conscious that Pierre came to tell my father Mr. Filmore was waiting for him, and that my father hurried out of the room. No, it was not a dream; was it—the thought was full of tremulous exultation—was it the poet's nature in me, hitherto only a troubled yearning sensibility, now manifesting itself suddenly as spontaneous creation? Surely it was in this way that Homer saw the plain of Troy, that Dante saw the abodes of the departed, that Milton saw the earthward flight of the Tempter. Was it that my illness had wrought some happy change in my organization—given a firmer tension to my nerves—carried off some dull obstruction? I had often read of such effects—in works of fiction at least. Nay; in genuine biographies I had read of the subtilizing or exalting influence of some diseases on the mental powers. Did not Novalis feel his inspiration intensified under the progress of consumption?

When my mind had dwelt for some time on this blissful idea, it seemed to me that I might perhaps test it by an exertion of my will. The vision had begun when my father was speaking of our going to Prague. I did not for a moment believe it was really a representation of that city; I believed—I hoped it was a picture that my newly liberated genius had painted in fiery haste, with the colours snatched from lazy memory. Suppose I were to fix my mind on some other place—Venice, for example, which was far more familiar to my imagination than Prague: perhaps the same sort of result would follow. I concentrated my thoughts on Venice; I stimulated my imagination with poetic memories, and strove to feel myself present in Venice, as I had felt myself present in Prague. But in vain. I was only colouring the Canaletto engravings that hung in my old bedroom at home; the picture was a shifting one, my mind wandering uncertainly in search of more vivid images; I could see no accident of form or shadow without conscious labour after the necessary conditions. It was all prosaic effort, not rapt passivity, such as I had experienced half an hour before. I was discouraged; but I remembered that inspiration was fitful.

For several days I was in a state of excited expectation, watching for a recurrence of my new gift. I sent my thoughts ranging over my world of knowledge, in the hope that they would find some object which would send a reawakening vibration through my slumbering genius. But no; my world remained as dim as ever, and that flash of strange light refused to come again, though I watched for it with palpitating eagerness.

My father accompanied me every day in a drive, and a gradually lengthening walk as my powers of walking increased; and one evening he had agreed to come and fetch me at twelve the next day, that we might go together to select a musical box, and other purchases rigorously demanded of a rich Englishman visiting Geneva. He was one of the most punctual of men and bankers, and I was always nervously anxious to be quite ready for him at the appointed time. But, to my surprise, at a quarter past twelve he had not appeared. I felt all the impatience of a convalescent who has nothing particular to do, and who has just taken a tonic in the prospect of immediate exercise that would carry off the stimulus.

Unable to sit still and reserve my strength, I walked up and down the room, looking out on the current of the Rhone, just where it leaves the dark-blue lake; but thinking all the while of the possible causes that could detain my father.

Suddenly I was conscious that my father was in the room, but not alone: there were two persons with him. Strange! I had heard no footstep, I had not seen the door open; but I saw my father, and at his right hand our neighbour Mrs. Filmore, whom I remembered very well, though I had not seen her for five years. She was a commonplace middle-aged woman, in silk and cashmere; but the lady on the left of my father was not more than twenty, a tall, slim, willowy figure, with luxuriant blond hair, arranged in cunning braids and folds that looked almost too massive for the slight figure and the small-featured, thin-lipped face they crowned. But the face had not a girlish expression: the features were sharp, the pale grey eyes at once acute, restless, and sarcastic. They were fixed on me in half-smiling curiosity, and I felt a painful sensation as if a sharp wind were cutting me. The pale/green dress, and the green leaves that seemed to form a border about her pale blond hair, made me think of a Water-Nixie— for my mind was full of German lyrics, and this pale, fatal-eyed woman, with the green weeds, looked like a birth from some cold sedgy stream, the daughter of an aged river.

"Well, Latimer, you thought me long," my father said. . . .

But while the last word was in my ears, the whole group vanished, and there was nothing between me and the Chinese painted folding-screen that stood before the door. I was cold and trembling; I could only totter forward and throw myself on the sofa. This strange new power had manifested itself again. . . . But *was* it a power? Might it not rather be a disease—a sort of intermittent delirium, concentrating my energy of brain into moments of unhealthy activity, and leaving my saner hours all the more barren? I felt a dizzy sense of unreality in what my eye rested on; I grasped the bell convulsively, like one trying to free himself from nightmare, and rang it twice. Pierre came with a look of alarm in his face.

"Monsieur ne se trouve pas bien?" he said anxiously.

"I'm tired of waiting, Pierre," I said, as distinctly and emphatically as I could, like a man determined to be sober in spite of wine; "I'm afraid something has happened to my father—he's usually so punctual. Run to the Hôtel des Bergues and see if he is there."

Pierre left the room at once, with a soothing "Bien, Monsieur"; and I felt the better for this scene of simple, waking prose. Seeking to calm myself still further, I went into my bedroom, adjoining the *salon*, and opened a case of eau-de-Cologne; took out a bottle; went through the process of taking out the cork very neatly, and then rubbed the reviving spirit over my hands and forehead, and under my nostrils, drawing a new delight from the scent because I had procured it by slow details of labour, and by no strange sudden madness. Already I had begun to taste something of the horror that belongs to the lot of a human being whose nature is not adjusted to simple human conditions.

Still enjoying the scent, I returned to the *salon*, but it was not unoccupied, as it had been before I left it. In front of the Chinese folding-screen there was my father, with Mrs. Filmore on his right hand, and on his left—the slim, blond-

haired girl, with the keen face and the keen eyes fixed on me
in half-smiling curiosity.

"Well, Latimer, you thought me long," my father
said. . . .

I heard no more, felt no more, till I became conscious that
I was lying with my head low on the sofa, Pierre, and my
father by my side. As soon as I was thoroughly revived, my
father left the room, and presently returned, saying—

"I've been to tell the ladies how you are, Latimer. They
were waiting in the next room. We shall put off our shopping
expedition to-day."

Presently he said, "That young lady is Bertha Grant, Mrs.
Filmore's orphan niece. Filmore has adopted her, and she
lives with them, so you will have her for a neighbour when
we go home—perhaps for a near relation; for there is a tenderness between her and Alfred, I suspect, and I should be
gratified by the match, since Filmore means to provide for
her in every way as if she were his daughter. It had not
occurred to me that you knew nothing about her living with
the Filmores."

He made no further allusion to the fact of my having fainted
at the moment of seeing her, and I would not for the world
have told him the reason: I shrank from the idea of disclosing
to any one what might be regarded as a pitiable peculiarity,
most of all from betraying it to my father, who would have
suspected my sanity ever after.

I do not mean to dwell with particularity on the details of
my experience. I have described these two cases at length,
because they had definite, clearly traceable results in my af-
terlot.

Shortly after this last occurrence—I think the very next
day—I began to be aware of a phase in my abnormal sensibility, to which, from the languid and slight nature of my
intercourse with others since my illness, I had not been alive
before. This was the obtrusion on my mind of the mental
process going forward in first one person, and then another,
with whom I happened to be in contact: the vagrant, frivolous
ideas and emotions of some uninteresting acquintance—Mrs.
Filmore, for example—would force themselves on my consciousness like an importunate, ill-played musical instrument,
or the loud activity of an imprisoned insect. But this unplesant
sensibility was fitful, and left me moments of rest, when the
souls of my companions were once more shut out from me,
and I felt a relief such as silence brings to wearied nerves. I

might have believed this importunate insight to be merely a diseased activity of the imagination, but that my prevision of incalculable words and actions proved it to have a fixed relation to the mental process in other minds. But this super-added consciousness, wearying and annoying enough when it urged on me the trivial experience of indifferent people, became an intense pain and grief when it seemed to be opening to me the souls of those who were in a close relation to me—when the rational talk, the graceful attentions, the wittily-turned phrases, and the kindly deeds, which used to make the web of their characters, were seen as if thrust asunder by a microscopic vision, that showed all the intermediate frivolities, all the suppressed egoism, all the struggling chaos of puerilities, meanness, vague capricious memories, and indolent make-shift thoughts, from which human words and deeds emerge like leaflets covering a fermenting heap.

At Basle we were joined by my brother Alfred, now a handsome, self-confident man of six-and-twenty—a thorough contrast to my fragile, nervous, ineffectual self. I believe I was held to have a sort of half-womanish, half-ghostly beauty; for the portrait-painters, who are thick as weeds at Geneva, had often asked me to sit to them, and I had been the model of a dying minstrel in a fancy picture. But I thoroughly disliked my own physique and nothing but the belief that it was a condition of poetic genius would have reconciled me to it. That brief hope was quite fled, and I saw in my face now nothing but the stamp of a morbid organization, framed for passive suffering—too feeble for the sublime resistance of poetic production. Alfred, from whom I had been almost constantly separated, and who, in his present stage of character and appearance, came before me as a perfect stranger, was bent on being extremely friendly and brother-like to me. He had the superficial kindness of a good-humoured, self-satisfied nature, that fears no rivalry, and has encountered no contrarieties. I am not sure that my disposition was good enough for me to have been quite free from envy towards him, even if our desires had not clashed, and if I had been in the healthy human condition which admits of generous confidence and charitable construction. There must always have been an antipathy between our natures. As it was, he became in a few weeks an object of intense hatred to me; and when he entered the room, still more when he spoke, it was as if a sensation of grating metal had set my teeth on edge. My diseased consciousness was more intensely and continually occupied with his thoughts and emotions, than with those of any other person who came in my way. I was perpetually exasperated with the petty promptings of his conceit and his love of patronage, with his self-complacent belief in Bertha Grant's passion for him, with his half-pitying contempt for me—seen not in the ordinary indications of intonation and phrase and slight action, which an acute and suspicious mind is on the watch for, but in all their naked skinless complication.

For we were rivals, and our desires clashed, though he was not aware of it. I have said nothing yet of the effect Bertha Grant produced in me on a nearer acquaintance. That effect was chiefly determined by the fact that she made the only exception, among all the human beings about me, to my unhappy gift of insight. About Bertha I was always in a state of uncertainty: I could watch the expression of her face, and speculate on its meaning; I could ask for her opinion with the real interest of ignorance; I could listen for her words and watch for her smile with hope and fear: she had for me the fascination of an unravelled destiny. I say it was this fact that chiefly determined the strong effect she produced on me: for, in the abstract, no womanly character could seem to have less affinity for that of a shrinking, romantic, passionate youth than Bertha's. She was keen, sarcastic, unimaginative, prematurely cynical, remaining critical and unmoved in the most impressive scenes, inclined to dissect all my favourite poems, and especially contemptuous towards the German lyrics which were my pet literature at that time. To this moment I am unable to define my feeling towards her: it was not ordinary boyish admiration, for she was the very opposite, even to the colour of her hair, of the ideal woman who still remained to me the type of loveliness; and she was without that enthusiasm for the great and good, which, even at the moment of her strongest dominion over me, I should have declared to be the highest element of character. But there is no tyranny more complete than that which a self-centred negative nature exercises over a morbidly sensitive nature perpetually craving sympathy and support. The most independent people feel the effect of a man's silence in heightening their value for his opinion—feel an additional triumph in conquering the reverence of a critic habitually captious and satirical: no wonder, then, that an enthusiastic self-distrusting youth should watch and wait before the closed secret of a sarcastic woman's face, as if it were the shrine of the doubtfully benignant deity who

ruled his destiny. For a young enthusiast is unable to imagine
the total negation in another mind of the emotions which are
stirring his own: they may be feeble, latent, inactive, he thinks,
but they are there—they may be called forth; sometimes, in
moments of happy hallucination, he believes they may be
there in all the greater strength because he sees no outward
sign of them. And this effect, as I have intimated, was heightened to its utmost intensity in me, because Bertha was the
only being who remained for me in the mysterious seclusion
of soul that renders such youthful delusion possible. Doubtless there was another sort of fascination at work—that subtle
physical attraction which delights in cheating our psychological predictions, and in compelling the men who paint sylphs,
to fall in love with some *bonne et brave femme*, heavy-heeled
and freckled.

Bertha's behaviour towards me was such as to encourage
all my illusions, to heighten my boyish passion, and make me
more and more dependent on her smiles. Looking back with
my present wretched knowledge, I conclude that her vanity
and love of power were intensely gratified by the belief that
I had fainted on first seeing her purely from the strong impression her person had produced on me. The most prosaic woman
likes to believe herself the object of a violent, a poetic passion;
and without a grain of romance in her, Bertha had that spirit
of intrigue which gave piquancy to the idea that the brother
of the man she meant to marry was dying with love and
jealousy for her sake. That she meant to marry my brother,
was what at that time I did not believe; for though he was
assiduous in his attentions to her, and I knew well enough
that both he and my father had made up their minds to this
result, there was not yet an understood engagement—there
had been no explicit declaration; and Bertha habitually, while
she flirted with my brother, and accepted his homage in a
way that implied to him a thorough recognition of its intention, made me believe, by the subtlest looks and phrases—
feminine nothings which could never be quoted against her—
that he was really the object of her secret ridicule; that she
thought him, as I did, a coxcomb, whom she would have
pleasure in disappointing. Me she openly petted in my brother's presence, as if I were too young and sickly ever to be
thought of as a lover; and that was the view he took of me.
But I believe she must inwardly have delighted in the tremors
into which she threw me by the coaxing way in which she
patted my curls, while she laughed at my quotations. Such

caresses were always given in the presence of our friends; for when we were alone together, she affected a much greater distance towards me, and now and then took the opportunity, by words or slight actions, to stimulate my foolish timid hope that she really preferred me. And why should she not follow her inclination? I was not in so advantageous a position as my brother, but I had fortune, I was not a year younger than she was, and she was an heiress, who would soon be of age to decide for herself.

The fluctuations of hope and fear, confined to this one channel, made each day in her presence a delicious torment. There was one deliberate act of hers which especially helped to intoxicate me. When we were at Vienna her twentieth birthday occurred, and as she was very fond of ornaments, we all took the opportunity of the splendid jewellers' shops in that Teutonic Paris to purchase her a birthday present of jewellery. Mine, naturally, was the least expensive; it was an opal ring—the opal was my favourite stone, because it seems to blush and turn pale as if it had a soul. I told Bertha so when I gave it her, and said that it was an emblem of the poetic nature, changing with the changing light of heaven and of woman's eyes. In the evening she appeared elegantly dressed, and wearing conspicuously all the birthday presents except mine. I looked eagerly at her fingers, but saw no opal. I had no opportunity of noticing this to her during the evening; but the next day, when I found her seated near the window alone, after breakfast, I said, "You scorn to wear my poor opal. I should have remembered that you despised poetic natures, and should have given you coral, or turquoise, or some other opaque unresponsive stone." "Do I despise it?" she answered, taking hold of a delicate gold chain which she always wore round her neck and drawing out the end from her bosom with my ring hanging to it; "it hurts me a little, I can tell you," she said, with her usual dubious smile, "to wear it in that secret place; and since your poetical nature is so stupid as to prefer a more public position, I shall not endure the pain any longer."

She took off the ring from the chain and put it on her finger, smiling still, while the blood rushed to my cheeks, and I could not trust myself to say a word of entreaty that she would keep the ring where it was before.

I was completely fooled by this, and for two days shut myself up in my own room whenever Bertha was absent, that

I might intoxicate myself afresh with the thought of this scene and all it implied.

I should mention that during these two months—which seemed a long life to me from the novelty and intensity of the pleasures and pains I underwent—my diseased participation in other people's consciousness continued to torment me; now it was my father, and now my brother, now Mrs. Filmore or her husband, and now our German courier, whose stream of thought rushed upon me like a ringing in the ears not to be got rid of, though it allowed my own impulses and ideas to continue their uninterrupted course. It was like a preternaturally heightened sense of hearing, making audible to one a roar of sound where others find perfect stillness. The weariness and disgust of this involuntary intrusion into other souls was counteracted only by my ignorance of Bertha, and my growing passion for her; a passion enormously stimulated, if not produced, by that ignorance. She was my oasis of mystery in the dreary desert of knowledge. I had never allowed my diseased condition to betray itself, or to drive me into any unusual speech or action, except once, when, in a moment of peculiar bitterness against my brother, I had forestalled some words which I knew he was going to utter—a clever observation, which he had prepared beforehand. He had occasionally a slightly-affected hesitation in his speech, and when he paused an instant after the second word, my impatience and jealousy impelled me to continue the speech for him, as if it were something we had both learned by rote. He coloured and looked astonished, as well as annoyed; and the words had no sooner escaped my lips than I felt a shock of alarm lest such an anticipation of words—very far from being words of course, easy to divine—should have betrayed me as an exceptional being, a sort of quiet energumen, whom every one, Bertha above all, would shudder at and avoid. But I magnified, as usual, the impression any word or deed of mine could produce on others; for no one gave any sign of having noticed my interruption as more than a rudeness, to be forgiven me on the score of my feeble nervous condition.

While this superadded consciousness of the actual was almost constant with me, I had never had a recurrence of that distinct prevision which I have described in relation to my first interview with Bertha; and I was waiting with eager curiosity to know whether or not my vision of Prague would prove to have been an instance of the same kind. A few days after the incident of the opal ring, we were paying one of our

frequent visits to the Lichtenberg Palace. I could never look
at many pictures in succession; for pictures, when they are
at all powerful, affect me so strongly that one or two exhaust
all my capability of contemplation. This morning I had been
looking at Giorgione's picture of the cruel-eyed woman, said
to be a likeness of Lucrezia Borgia. I had stood long alone
before it, fascinated by the terrible reality of that cunning,
relentless face, till I felt a strange poisoned sensation, as if I
had long been inhaling a fatal odour, and was just beginning
to be conscious of its effects. Perhaps even then I should not
have moved away, if the rest of the party had not returned
to this room, and announced that they were going to the
Belvedere Gallery to settle a bet which had arisen between
my brother and Mr. Filmore about a portrait. I followed them
dreamily, and was hardly alive to what occurred till they had
all gone up to the gallery, leaving me below; for I refused to
come within sight of another picture that day. I made my way
to the Grand Terrace, since it was agreed that we should
saunter in the gardens when the dispute had been decided. I
had been sitting here a short space, vaguely conscious of trim
gardens, with a city and green hills in the distance, when,
wishing to avoid the proximity of the sentinel, I rose and
walked down the broad stone steps, intending to seat myself
farther on in the gardens. Just as I reached the gravel-walk,
I felt an arm slipped within mine, and a light hand gently
pressing my wrist. In the same instant a strange intoxicating
numbness passed over me, like the continuance or climax of
the sensation I was still feeling from the gaze of Lucrezia
Borgia. The gardens, the summer sky, the consciousness of
Bertha's arm being within mine, all vanished, and I seemed
to be suddenly in darkness, out of which there gradually broke
a dim firelight, and I felt myself sitting in my father's leather
chair in the library at home. I knew the fireplace—the dogs
for the wood-fire—the black marble chimneypiece with the
white marble medallion of the dying Cleopatra in the centre.
Intense and hopeless misery was pressing on my soul; the
light became stronger, for Bertha was entering with a candle
in her hand—Bertha, my wife—with cruel eyes, with green
jewels and green leaves on her white ball-dress; every hateful
thought within her present to me. . . . "Madman, idiot! why
don't you kill yourself, then?" It was a moment of hell. I saw
into her pitiless soul—saw its barren worldliness, its scorching
hate—and felt it clothe me round like an air I was obliged to
breathe. She came with her candle and stood over me with

a bitter smile of contempt; I saw the great emerald brooch on her bosom, a studded serpent with diamond eyes. I shuddered—I despised this woman with the barren soul and mean thoughts; but I felt helpless before her, as if she clutched my bleeding heart, and would clutch it till the last drop of life-blood ebbed away. She was my wife, and we hated each other. Gradually the hearth, the dim library, the candle-light disappeared—seemed to melt away into a background of light, the green serpent with the diamond eyes remaining a dark image on the retina. Then I had a sense of my eyelids quivering, and the living daylight broke in upon me; I saw gardens, and heard voices; I was seated on the steps of the Belvedere Terrace, and my friends were round me.

The tumult of mind into which I was thrown by this hideous vision made me ill for several days, and prolonged our stay at Vienna. I shuddered with horror as the scene recurred to me; and it recurred constantly, with all its minutiæ, as if they had been burnt into my memory; and yet, such is the madness of the human heart under the influence of its immediate desires, I felt a wild hell-braving joy that Bertha was to be mine; for the fulfilment of my former prevision concerning her first appearance before me, left me little hope that this last hideous glimpse of the future was the mere diseased play of my own mind, and had no relation to external realities. One thing alone I looked towards as a possible means of casting doubt on my terrible conviction—the discovery that my vision of Prague had been false—and Prague was the next city on our route.

Meanwhile, I was no sooner in Bertha's society again, than I was as completely under her sway as before. What if I saw into the heart of Bertha, the matured woman—Bertha, my wife? Bertha, the *girl*, was a fascinating secret to me still: I trembled under her touch; I felt the witchery of her presence; I yearned to be assured of her love. The fear of poison is feeble against the sense of thirst. Nay, I was just as jealous of my brother as before—just as much irritated by his small patronizing ways; for my pride, my diseased sensibility, were there as they had always been, and winced as inevitably under every offence as my eye winced from an intruding mote. The future, even when brought within the compass of feeling by a vision that made me shudder, had still no more than the force of an idea, compared with the force of present emotion—of my love for Bertha, of my dislike and jealousy towards my brother.

It is an old story, that men sell themselves to the tempter, and sign a bond with their blood, because it is only to take effect at a distant day; then rush on to snatch the cup their souls thirst after with an impulse not the less savage because there is a dark shadow beside them for evermore. There is no short cut, no patent tram-road, to wisdom: after all the centuries of invention, the soul's path lies through the thorny wilderness which must be still trodden in solitude, with bleeding feet, with sobs for help, as it was trodden by them of old time.

My mind speculated eagerly on the means by which I should become my brother's successful rival, for I was still too timid, in my ignorance of Bertha's actual feeling, to venture on any step that would urge from her an avowal of it. I thought I should gain confidence even for this, if my vision of Prague proved to have been veracious; and yet, the horror of that certitude! Behind the slim girl Bertha, whose words and looks I watched for, whose touch was bliss, there stood continually that Bertha with the fuller form, the harder eyes, the more rigid mouth—with the barren, selfish soul laid bare; no longer a fascinating secret, but a measured fact, urging itself perpetually on my unwilling sight. Are you unable to give me your sympathy—you who read this? Are you unable to imagine this double consciousness at work within me, flowing on like two parallel streams which never mingle their waters and blend into a common hue? Yet you must have known something of the presentiments that spring from an insight at war with passion; and my visions were only like presentiments intensified to horror. You have known the powerlessness of ideas before the might of impulse; and my visions, when once they had passed into memory, were mere ideas—pale shadows that beckoned in vain, while my hand was grasped by the living and the loved.

In after-days I thought with bitter regret that if I had foreseen something more or something different—if instead of that hideous vision which poisoned the passion it could not destroy, or if even along with it I could have had a foreshadowing of that moment when I looked on my brother's face for the last time, some softening influence would have been shed over my feeling towards him: pride and hatred would surely have been subdued into pity, and the record of those hidden sins would have been shortened. But this is one of the vain thoughts with which we men flatter ourselves. We try to believe that the egoism within us would have easily been melted, and that it was only the narrowness of our knowledge which hemmed in our generosity, our awe, our human piety, and hindered them from submerging our hard indifference to the sensations and emotions of our fellows. Our tenderness and self-renunciation seem strong when our egoism has had its day—when, after our mean striving for a triumph that is to be another's loss, the triumph comes suddenly, and we shudder at it, because it is held out by the chill hand of death.

Our arrival in Prague happened at night, and I was glad of this, for it seemed like a deferring of a terribly decisive moment, to be in the city for hours without seeing it. As we were not to remain long in Prague, but to go on speedily to Dresden, it was proposed that we should drive out the next morning and take a general view of the place, as well as visit some of its specially interesting spots, before the heat became oppressive—for we were in August, and the season was hot and dry. But it happened that the ladies were rather late at their morning toilet, and to my father's politely-repressed but perceptible annoyance, we were not in the carriage till the morning was far advanced. I thought with a sense of relief, as we entered the Jews' quarter, where we were to visit the old synagogue, that we should be kept in this flat, shut-up part of the city, until we should all be too tired and too warm to go farther, and so we should return without seeing more than the streets through which we had already passed. That would give me another day's suspense—suspense, the only form in which a fearful spirit knows the solace of hope. But, as I stood under the blackened, groined arches of that old synagogue, made dimly visible by the seven thin candles in the sacred lamp, while our Jewish cicerone reached down the Book of the Law, and read to us in its ancient tongue—I felt a shuddering impression that this strange building, with its shrunken lights, this surviving withered remnant of medieval Judaism, was of a piece with my vision. Those darkened dusty Christian saints, with their loftier arches and their larger candles, needed the consolatory scorn with which they might point to a more shrivelled death-in-life than their own.

As I expected, when we left the Jews' quarter the elders of our party wished to return to the hotel. But now, instead of rejoicing in this, as I had done beforehand, I felt a sudden overpowering impulse to go on at once to the bridge, and put an end to the suspense I had been wishing to protract. I declared, with unusual decision, that I would get out of the carriage and walk on alone; they might return without me. My father, thinking this merely a sample of my usual "poetic nonsense," objected that I should only do myself harm by walking in the heat; but when I persisted, he said angrily that I might follow my own absurd devices, but that Schmidt (our courier) must go with me. I assented to this, and set off with Schmidt towards the bridge. I had no sooner passed from under the archway of the grand old gate leading on to the bridge, than a trembling seized me, and I turned cold under the mid-day sun; yet I went on; I was in search of something— a small detail which I remembered with special intensity as part of my vision. There it was—the patch of rainbow light on the pavement transmitted through a lamp in the shape of a star.

CHAPTER II

Before the autumn was at an end, and while the brown leaves still stood thick on the beeches in our park, my brother and Bertha were engaged to each other, and it was understood that their marriage was to take place early in the next spring. In spite of the certainty I had felt from that moment on the bridge at Prague, that Bertha would one day be my wife, my constitutional timidity and distrust had continued to benumb me, and the words in which I had sometimes premeditated a confession of my love, had died away unuttered. The same conflict had gone on within me as before—the longing for an assurance of love from Bertha's lips, the dread lest a word of contempt and denial should fall upon me like a corrosive acid. What was the conviction of a distant necessity to me? I trembled under a present glance, I hungered after a present joy, I was clogged and chilled by a present fear. And so the days passed on: I witnessed Bertha's engagement and heard her marriage discussed as if I were under a conscious nightmare—knowing it was a dream that would vanish, but feeling stifled under the grasp of hard-clutching fingers.

When I was not in Bertha's presence—and I was with her very often, for she continued to treat me with a playful patronage that wakened no jealousy in my brother—I spent my time chiefly in wandering, in strolling, or taking long rides while the daylight lasted, and then shutting myself up with my unread books; for books had lost the power of chaining my attention. My self-consciousness was heightened to that pitch of intensity in which our own emotions take the form of a drama which urges itself imperatively on our contemplation, and we begin to weep, less under the sense of our suffering than at the thought of it. I felt a sort of pitying anguish over the pathos of my own lot: the lot of a being finely organized for pain, but with hardly any fibres that responded to pleasure—to whom the idea of future evil robbed the present of its joy, and for whom the idea of future good did not still the uneasiness of a present yearning or a present dread. I went dumbly through that stage of the poet's suffering, in which he feels the delicious pang of utterance, and makes an image of his sorrows.

I was left entirely without remonstrance concerning this dreamy wayward life: I knew my father's thought about me: "That lad will never be good for anything in life: he may waste his years in an insignificant way on the income that falls to him: I shall not trouble myself about a career for him."

One mild morning in the beginning of November, it happened that I was standing outside the portico patting lazy old Caesar, a Newfoundland almost blind with age, the only dog that ever took any notice of me—for the very dogs shunned me, and fawned on the happier people about me—when the groom brought up my brother's horse which was to carry him to the hunt, and my brother himself appeared at the door, florid, broad-chested, and self-complacent, feeling what a good-natured fellow he was not to behave insolently to us all on the strength of his great advantages.

"Latimer, old boy," he said to me in a tone of compassionate cordiality, "what a pity it is you don't have a run with the hounds now and then! The finest thing in the world for low spirits!"

"Low spirits!" I thought bitterly, as he rode away; "that is the sort of phrase with which coarse, narrow natures like yours think to describe experience of which you can know no more than your horse knows. It is to such as you that the good of this world falls: ready dulness, healthy selfishness, good-tempered conceit—these are the keys to happiness.

The quick thought came, that my selfishness was even stronger than his—it was only a suffering selfishness instead of an enjoying one. But then, again, my exasperating insight into Alfred's self-complacent soul, his freedom from all the doubts and fears, the unsatisfied yearnings, the exquisite tortures of sensitiveness, that had made the web of my life, seemed to absolve me from all bonds towards him. This man needed no pity, no love; those fine influences would have been as little felt by him as the delicate white mist is felt by the rock it caresses. There was no evil in store for *him*: if he was not to marry Bertha, it would be because he had found a lot pleasanter to himself.

Mr. Filmore's house lay not more than half a mile beyond our own gates, and whenever I knew my brother was gone in another direction, I went there for the chance of finding Bertha at home. Later on in the day I walked thither. By a rare accident she was alone, and we walked out in the grounds together, for she seldom went on foot beyond the trimly-swept gravel-walks. I remember what a beautiful sylph she looked to me as the low November sun shone on her blond hair, and she tripped along teasing me with her usual light banter, to which I listened half fondly, half moodily; it was all the sign Bertha's mysterious inner self ever made to me. To-day perhaps the moodiness predominated, for I had not yet shaken off the access of jealous hate which my brother had raised in me by his parting patronage. Suddenly I interrupted and startled her by saying, almost fiercely, "Bertha, how can you love Alfred?"

She looked at me with surprise for a moment, but soon her light smile came again, and she answered sarcastically, "Why do you suppose I love him?"

"How can you ask that, Bertha?"

"What! Your wisdom thinks I must love the man I'm going to marry? The most unpleasant thing in the world. I should quarrel with him; I should be jealous of him; our *ménage* would be conducted in a very ill-bred manner. A little quiet contempt contributes gently to the elegance of life."

"Bertha, that is not your real feeling. Why do you delight in trying to deceive me by inventing such cynical speeches?"

"I need never take the trouble of invention in order to deceive you, my small Tasso"—(that was the mocking name she usually gave me). "The easiest way to deceive a poet is to tell him the truth."

She was testing the validity of her epigram in a daring way, and for a moment the shadow of my vision—the Bertha whose soul was no secret to me—passed between me and the radiant girl, the playful sylph whose feelings were a fascinating mystery. I suppose I must have shuddered, or betrayed in some other way my momentary chill of horror.

"Tasso!" she said, seizing my wrist, and peeping round into my face, "are you really beginning to discern what a heartless girl I am? Why, you are not half the poet I thought you were;

you are actually capable of believing the truth about me."

The shadow passed from between us, and was no longer the object nearest to me. The girl whose light fingers grasped me, whose elfish charming face looked into mine—who, I thought, was betraying an interest in my feelings that she would not have directly avowed,—this warm breathing presence again possessed my senses and imagination like a returning siren melody which had been overpowered for an instant by the roar of threatening waves. It was a moment as delicious to me as the waking up to a consciousness of youth after a dream of middle age. I forgot everything but my passion and said with swimming eyes—

"Bertha, shall you love me when we are first married? I wouldn't mind if you really loved me only for a little while."

Her look of astonishment, as she loosed my hand and started away from me, recalled me to a sense of my strange, my criminal indiscretion.

"Forgive me," I said, hurriedly, as soon as I could speak again; "I did not know what I was saying."

"Ah, Tasso's mad fit has come on, I see," she answered quietly, for she had recovered herself sooner than I had. "Let him go home and keep his head cool. I must go in, for the sun is setting."

I left her—full of indignation against myself. I had let slip words which, if she reflected on them, might rouse in her a suspicion of my abnormal mental condition—a suspicion which of all things I dreaded. And besides that, I was ashamed of the apparent baseness I had committed in uttering them to my brother's betrothed wife. I wandered home slowly, entering our park through a private gate instead of by the lodges. As I approached the house, I saw a man dashing off at full speed from the stable-yard across the park. Had any accident happened at home? No; perhaps it was only one of my father's peremptory business errands that required this headlong haste.

Nevertheless I quickened my pace without any distinct motive, and was soon at the house. I will not dwell on the scene I found there. My brother was dead—had been pitched from his horse, and killed on the spot by a concussion of the brain.

I went up to the room where he lay, and where my father was seated beside him with a look of rigid despair. I had shunned my father more than any one since our return home, for the radical antipathy between our natures made my insight into his inner self a constant affliction to me. But now, as I went up to him, and stood beside him in sad silence, I felt the presence of a new element that blended us as we had never been blent before. My father had been one of the most successful men in the money-getting world: he had had no sentimental sufferings, no illness. The heaviest trouble that had befallen him was the death of his first wife. But he married my mother soon after; and I remember he seemed exactly the same, to my keen childish observation, the week after her death as before. But now, at last, a sorrow had come—the sorrow of old age, which suffers the more from the crushing of its pride and its hopes, in proportion as the pride and hope are narrow and prosaic. His son was to have been married soon—would probably have stood for the borough at the next election. That son's existence was the best motive that could be alleged for making new purchases of land every year to round off the estate. It is a dreary thing to live on doing the same things year after year, without knowing why we do them. Perhaps the tragedy of disappointed youth and passion is less piteous than the tragedy of disappointed age and worldliness.

As I saw into the desolation of my father's heart, I felt a movement of deep pity towards him, which was the beginning of a new affection—an affection that grew and strengthened in spite of the strange bitterness with which he regarded me in the first month or two after my brother's death. If it had not been for the softening influence of my compassion for him—the first deep compassion I had ever felt—I should have been stung by the perception that my father transferred the inheritance of an eldest son to me with a mortified sense that fate had compelled him to the unwelcome course of caring for me as an important being. It was only in spite of himself that he began to think of me with anxious regard. There is hardly any neglected child for whom death has made vacant a more favoured place, who will not understand what I mean.

Gradually, however, my new deference to his wishes, the effect of that patience which was born of my pity for him, won upon his affection, and he began to please himself with the endeavour to make me fill my brother's place as fully as my feebler personality would admit. I saw that the prospect which by and by presented itself of my becoming Bertha's husband was welcome to him, and he even contemplated in my case what he had not intended in my brother's—that his son and daughter-in-law should make one household with him. My softened feeling towards my father made this the happiest time I had known since childhood;—these last months in which I retained the delicious illusion of loving Bertha, of longing and doubting and hoping that she might love me. She behaved with a certain new consciousness and distance towards me after my brother's death; and I too was under a double constraint—that of delicacy towards my brother's memory, and of anxiety as to the impression my abrupt words had left on her mind. But the additional screen this mutual reserve erected between us only brought me more completely under her power: no matter how empty the adytum, so that the veil be thick enough. So absolute is our soul's need of something hidden and uncertain for the maintenance of that doubt and hope and effort which are the breath of its life, that if the whole future were laid bare to us beyond to-day, the interest of all mankind would be bent on the hours that lie between; we should pant after the uncertainties of our one morning and our one afternoon; we should rush fiercely to the Exchange for our last possibility of speculation, of success, of disappointment: we should have a glut of political prophets foretelling a crisis or a no-crisis within the only twenty-four hours left open to prophecy. Conceive the condition of the human mind if all propositions whatsoever were self-evident except one, which was to become self-evident at the close of a summer's day, but in the meantime might be the subject of question, of hypothesis, of debate. Art and philosophy, literature and science, would fasten like bees on that one proposition which had the honey of probability in it, and be the more eager because their enjoyment would end with sunset. Our impulses, our spiritual activities, no more adjust themselves to the idea of their future nullity, than the beating of our heart, or the irritability of our muscles.

Bertha, the slim, fair-haired girl, whose present thoughts and emotions were an enigma to me amidst the fatiguing obviousness of the other minds around me, was as absorbing to me as a single unknown to-day—as a single hypothetic proposition to remain problematic till sunset; and all the cramped, hemmed-in belief and disbelief, trust and distrust, of my nature, welled out in this one narrow channel.

And she made me believe that she loved me. Without ever quitting her tone of *badinage* and playful superiority, she intoxicated me with the sense that I was necessary to her, that she was never at ease unless I was near her, submitting to her playful tyranny. It costs a woman so little effort to besot us in this way! A half-repressed word, a moment's unexpected silence, even an easy fit of petulance on our account,

will serve us as *hashish* for a long while. Out of the subtlest
web of scarcely perceptible signs, she set me weaving the
fancy that she had always unconsciously loved me better than
Alfred, but that, with the ignorant fluttered sensibility of a
young girl, she had been imposed on by the charm that lay
for her in the distinction of being admired and chosen by a
man who made so brilliant a figure in the world as my brother.
She satirized herself in a very graceful way for her vanity and
ambition. What was it to me that I had the light of my wretched
provision on the fact that now it was I who possessed at least
all but the personal part of my brother's advantages? Our
sweet illusions are half of them conscious illusions, like effects
of colour that we know to be made up of tinsel, broken glass,
and rags.

We were married eighteen months after Alfred's death,
one cold, clear morning in April, when there came hail and
sunshine both together; and Bertha, in her white silk and
pale-green leaves, and the pale hues of her hair and face,
looked like the spirit of the morning. My father was happier
than he had thought of being again: my marriage, he felt sure,
would complete the desirable modification of my character,
and make me practical and worldly enough to take my place
in society among sane men. For he delighted in Bertha's tact
and acuteness, and felt sure she would be mistress of me, and
make me what she chose: I was only twenty-one, and madly
in love with her. Poor father! He kept that hope a little while
after our first year of marriage, and it was not quite extinct
when paralysis came and saved him from utter disappointment.

I shall hurry through the rest of my story, not dwelling so
much as I have hitherto done in my inward experience. When
people are well known to each other, they talk rather of what
befalls them externally, leaving their feelings and sentiments
to be inferred.

We lived in a round of visits for some time after our return
home, giving splendid dinner-parties, and making a sensation
in our neighbourhood by the new lustre of our equipage, for
my father had reserved this display of his increased wealth
for the period of his son's marriage; and we gave our acquaintances liberal opportunity for remarking that it was a
pity I made so poor a figure as an heir and a bridegroom.
The nervous fatigue of this existence, the insincerities and
platitudes which I had to live through twice over—through
my inner and outward sense—would have been maddening

to me, if I had not had that sort of intoxicated callousness which came from the delights of a first passion. A bride and bridegroom, surrounded by all the appliances of wealth, hurried through the day by the whirl of society, filling their solitary moments with hastily-snatched caresses, are prepared for their future life together as the novice is prepared for the cloister—by experiencing its utmost contrast.

Through all these crowded excited months, Bertha's inward self remained shrouded from me, and I still read her thoughts only through the language of her lips and demeanour: I had still the human interest of wondering whether what I did and said pleased her, of longing to hear a word of affection, of giving a delicious exaggeration of meaning to her smile. But I was conscious of a growing difference in her manner towards me; sometimes strong enough to be called haughty coldness, cutting and chilling me as the hail had done that came across the sunshine on our marriage morning; sometimes only perceptible in the dexterous avoidance of a *tête-à-tête* walk or dinner to which I had been looking forward. I had been deeply pained by this—had even felt a sort of crushing of the heart, from the sense that my brief day of happiness was near its setting; but still I remained dependent on Bertha, eager for the last rays of a bliss that would soon be gone for ever, hoping and watching for some after-glow more beautiful from the impending night.

I remember—how should I not remember?—the time when that dependance and hope utterly left me, when the sadness I had felt in Bertha's growing estrangement became a joy that I looked back upon with longing as a man might look back on the last pains in a paralysed limb. It was just after the close of my father's last illness, which had necessarily withdrawn us from society and thrown us more upon each other. It was the evening of my father's death. On that evening the veil which had shrouded Bertha's soul from me—had made me find in her alone among my fellow-beings the blessed possibility of mystery, and doubt, and expectation—was first withdrawn. Perhaps it was the first day since the beginning of my passion for her, in which that passion was completely neutralized by the presence of an absorbing feeling of another kind. I had been watching by my father's deathbed: I had been witnessing the last fitful yearning glance his soul had cast back on the spent inheritance of life—the last faint consciousness of love he had gathered from the pressure of my hand. What are all our personal loves when we have been sharing in that supreme agony? In the first moments when we come away from the presence of death, every other relation to the living is merged, to our feeling, in the great relation of a common nature and a common destiny.

In that state of mind I joined Bertha in her private sitting-room. She was seated in a leaning posture on a settee, with her back towards the door; the great rich coils of her pale blond hair surmounting her small neck, visible above the back of the settee. I remember, as I closed the door behind me, a cold tremulousness seizing me, and a vague sense of being hated and lonely—vague and strong, like a presentiment. I know how I looked at that moment, for I saw myself in Bertha's thought as she lifted her cutting grey eyes, and looked at me: a miserable ghost-seer, surrounded by phantoms in the noonday, trembling under a breeze when the leaves were still, without appetite for the common objects of human desires, but pining after the moon-beams. We were front to front with each other, and judged each other. The terrible moment of complete illumination had come to me, and I saw that the darkness had hidden no landscape from me, but only a blank prosaic wall: from that evening forth, through the sickening years which followed, I saw all round the narrow room of this woman's soul—saw petty artifice and mere negation where I had delighted to believe in coy sensibilities and in wit at war with latent feeling—saw the light floating vanities of the girl defining themselves into the systematic coquetry, the scheming selfishness, of the woman—saw repulsion and antipathy harden into cruel hatred, giving pain only for the sake of wreaking itself.

For Bertha too, after her kind, felt the bitterness of disillusion. She had believed that my wild poet's passion for her would make me her slave; and that, being her slave, I should execute her will in all things. With the essential shallowness of a negative, unimaginative nature, she was unable to conceive the fact that sensibilities were anything else than weaknesses. She had thought my weaknesses would put me in her power, and she found them unmanageable forces. Our positions were reversed. Before marriage she had completely mastered my imagination, for she was a secret to me; and I created the unknown thought before which I trembled as if it were hers. But now that her soul was laid open to me, now that I was compelled to share the privacy of her motives, to follow all the petty devices that preceded her words and acts, she found herself powerless with me, except to produce in me the chill shudder of repulsion—powerless, because I could be acted on by no lever within her reach. I was dead to worldly ambitions, to social vanities, to all the incentives within the compass of her narrow imagination, and I lived under influences utterly invisible to her.

She was really pitiable to have such a husband, and so all the world thought. A graceful, brilliant woman, like Bertha, who smiled on morning callers, made a figure in ball-rooms, and was capable of that light repartee which, from such a woman, is accepted as wit, was secure of carrying off all sympathy from a husband who was sickly, abstracted, and, as some suspected, crack-brained. Even the servants in our house gave her the balance of their regard and pity. For there were no audible quarrels between us; our alienation, our repulsion from each other, lay within the silence of our own hearts; and if the mistress went out a great deal, and seemed to dislike the master's society, was it not natural, poor thing? The master was odd. I was kind and just to my dependants, but I excited in them a shrinking, half-contemptuous pity; for this class of men and women are but slightly determined in their estimate of others by general considerations, or even experience, of character. They judge of persons as they judge of coins, and value those who pass current at a high rate.

After a time I interfered so little with Bertha's habits that it might seem wonderful how her hatred towards me could grow so intense and active as it did. But she had begun to suspect, by some involuntary betrayal of mine, that there was an abnormal power of penetration in me—that fitfully, at least, I was strangely cognizant of her thoughts and intentions, and she began to be haunted by a terror of me, which alternated every now and then with defiance. She meditated continually how the incubus could be shaken off her life—how she could be freed from this hateful bond to a being whom she at once despised as an imbecile, and dreaded as an inquisitor. For a long while she lived in the hope that my evident wretchedness would drive me to the commission of suicide; but suicide was not in my nature. I was too completely swayed by the sense that I was in the grasp of unknown forces, to believe in my power of self-release. Towards my own destiny I had become entirely passive; for my one ardent desire had spent itself, and impulse no longer predominated over knowledge. For this reason I never thought of taking any steps towards a complete separation, which would have made our alienation evident to the world. Why should I rush for help to a new course, when I was only suffering from the consequences of a deed which had been the act of my intensest will? That would have been the logic of one who had desires to gratify, and I had no desires. But Bertha and I lived more and more aloof from each other. The rich find it easy to live married and apart.

That course of our life which I have indicated in a few sentences filled the space of years. So much misery—so slow and hideous a growth of hatred and sin, may be compressed into a sentence! And men judge of each other's lives through this summary medium. They epitomize the experience of their fellow-mortal, and pronounce judgement on him in neat syntax, and feel themselves wise and virtuous—conquerors over the temptations they define in well-selected predicates. Seven years of wretchedness glide glibly over the lips of the man who has never counted them out in moments of chill disappointment, of head and heart throbbings, of dread and vain wrestling, of remorse and despair. We learn *words* by rote, but not their meaning; *that* must be paid for with our life-blood, and printed in the subtle fibres of our nerves.

But I will hasten to finish my story. Brevity is justified at once to those who readily understand, and to those who will never understand.

Some years after my father's death, I was sitting by the dim firelight in my library one January evening—sitting in the leather chair that used to be my father's—when Bertha appeared at the door, with a candle in her hand, and advanced towards me. I knew the ball-dress she had on—the white ball-dress, with the green jewels, shone upon by the light of the wax candle which lit up the medallion of the dying Cleopatra on the mantelpiece. Why did she come to me before going out? I had not seen her in the library, which was my habitual place for months. Why did she stand before me with the candle in her hand, with her cruel contemptuous eyes fixed on me, and the glittering serpent, like a familiar demon, on her breast? For a moment I thought this fulfilment of my vision at Vienna marked some dreadful crisis in my fate, but I saw nothing in Bertha's mind, as she stood before me, except scorn for the look of overwhelming misery with which I sat before her. . . . "Fool, idiot, why don't you kill yourself, then?"—that was her thought. But at length her thoughts reverted to her errand, and she spoke aloud. The apparently indifferent nature of the errand seemed to make a ridiculous anti-climax to my prevision and my agitation.

"I have had to hire a new maid. Fletcher is going to be married, and she wants me to ask you to let her husband have the public-house and farm at Molton. I wish him to have it. You must give the promise now, because Fletcher is going to-morrow morning—and quickly, because I'm in a hurry."

"Very well; you may promise her," I said, indifferently, and Bertha swept out of the library again.

I always shrank from the sight of a new person, and all the more when it was a person whose mental life was likely to weary my reluctant insight with worldly ignorant trivialities. But I shrank especially from the sight of this new maid, because her advent had been announced to me at a moment to which I could not cease to attach some fatality: I had a vague dread that I should find her mixed up with the dreary drama of my life—that some new sickening vision would reveal her to me as an evil genius. When at last I did unavoidably meet her, the vague dread was changed into definite disgust. She was a tall, wiry, dark-eyed woman, this Mrs. Archer, with a face handsome enough to give her coarse hard nature the odious finish of bold, self-confident coquetry. That was enough to make me avoid her, quite apart from the contemptuous feeling with which she contemplated me. I seldom saw her; but I perceived that she rapidly became a favourite with her mistress, and, after the lapse of eight or nine months, I began to be aware that there had arisen in Bertha's mind towards this woman a mingled feeling of fear and dependence, and that this feeling was associated with ill-defined images of candle-light scenes in her dressing-room, and the locking-up of something in Bertha's cabinet. My interviews with my wife had become so brief and so rarely solitary, that I had no opportunity of perceiving these images in her mind with more definiteness. The recollections of the past become contracted in the rapidity of thought till they sometimes bear hardly a more distinct resemblance to the external reality than the forms of an oriental alphabet to the objects that suggested them.

Besides, for the last year or more a modification had been going forward in my mental condition, and was growing more and more marked. My insight into the minds of those around me was becoming dimmer and more fitful, and the ideas that crowded my double consciousness became less and less dependent on any personal contact. All that was personal in me seemed to be suffering a gradual death, so that I was losing the organ through which the personal agitations and projects of others could affect me. But along with this relief from wearisome insight, there was a new development of what I concluded—as I have since found rightly—to be a prevision of external scenes. It was as if the relation between me and my fellow-men was more and more deadened, and my relation to what we call the inanimate was quickened into new life. The more I lived apart from society, and in proportion as my wretchedness subsided from the violent throb of agonized passion into the dulness of habitual pain, the more frequent and vivid became such visions as that I had had of Prague—of strange cities, of sandy plains, of gigantic ruins, of midnight skies with strange bright constellations, of mountain-passes, of grassy nooks flecked with the afternoon sunshine through the boughs: I was in the midst of such scenes, and in all of them one presence seemed to weigh on me in all these mighty shapes—the presence of something unknown and pitiless. For continual suffering had annihilated religious faith within me: to the utterly miserable—the unloving and the unloved—there is no religion possible, no worship but a worship of devils. And beyond all these, and continually recurring, was the vision of my death—the pangs, the suffocation, the last struggle, when life would be grasped at in vain.

Things were in this state near the end of the seventh year. I had become entirely free from insight, from my abnormal cognizance of any other consciousness than my own, and instead of intruding involuntarily into the world of other minds, was living continually in my own solitary future. Bertha was aware that I was greatly changed. To my surprise she had of late seemed to seek opportunities of remaining in my society, and had cultivated that kind of distant yet familiar talk which is customary between a husband and wife who live in polite and irrevocable alienation. I bore this with languid submission, and without feeling enough interest in her motives to be roused into keen observation; yet I could not help perceiving something triumphant and excited in her carriage and the expression of her face—something too subtle to express itself in words or tones, but giving one the idea that she lived in a state of expectation or hopeful suspense. My chief feeling was satisfaction that her inner self was once more shut out from me; and I almost revelled for the moment in the absent melancholy that made me answer her at cross purposes, and betray utter ignorance of what she had been saying. I remember well the look and the smile with which she one day said, after a mistake of this kind on my part: "I used to think you were a clairvoyant, and that was the reason why you were so bitter against other clairvoyants, wanting to keep your monopoly; but I see now you have become rather duller than the rest of the world."

I said nothing in reply. It occurred to me that her recent obtrusion of herself upon me might have been prompted by the wish to test my power of detecting some of her secrets; but I let the thought drop again at once: her motives and her deeds had no interest for me, and whatever pleasures she might be seeking, I had no wish to baulk her. There was still pity in my soul for every living thing, and Bertha was living— was surrounded with possibilities of misery.

Just at this time there occurred an event which roused me somewhat from my inertia, and gave me an interest in the passing moment that I had thought impossible for me. It was a visit from Charles Meunier, who had written me word that he was coming to England for relaxation from too strenuous labour, and would like to see me. Meunier had now a European reputation; but his letter to me expressed that keen remembrance of an early regard, an early debt of sympathy, which is inseparable from nobility of character: and I too felt as if his presence would be to me like a transient resurrection into a happier pre-existence.

He came, and as far as possible, I renewed our old pleasure of making *tête-à-tête* excursions, though, instead of mountains and glaciers and the wide blue lake, we had to content ourselves with mere slopes and ponds and artificial plantations. The years had changed us both, but with what different result! Meunier was now a brilliant figure in society, to whom elegant women pretended to listen, and whose acquaintance was boasted of by noblemen ambitious of brains. He repressed with the utmost delicacy all betrayal of the shock which I am sure he must have received from our meeting, or of a desire to penetrate into my condition and circumstances, and sought by the utmost exertion of his charming social powers to make our reunion agreeable. Bertha was much struck by the unexpected fascinations of a visitor whom she had expected to find presentable only on the score of his celebrity, and put forth all her coquetries and accomplishments. Apparently she succeeded in attracting his admiration, for his manner towards her was attentive and flattering. The effect of his presence on me was so benignant, especially in those renewals of our old *tête-à-tête* wanderings, when he poured forth to me wonderful narratives of his professional experience, that more than once, when his talk turned on the psychological relations of disease, the thought crossed my mind that, if his stay with me were long enough, I might possibly bring myself to tell this man the secrets of my lot. Might there not lie some remedy for *me*, too, in his science? Might there not at least lie some comprehension and sympathy ready for me in his large and susceptible mind? But the thought only flickered feebly now and then, and died out before it could become a wish. The horror I had of again breaking in on the privacy of another soul, made me, by an irrational instinct, draw the shroud of concealment more closely around my own, as we automatically perform the gesture we feel to be wanting in another.

When Meunier's visit was approaching its conclusion, there happened an event which caused some excitement in our household, owing to the surprisingly strong effect it appeared to produce on Bertha—on Bertha, the self-possessed, who usually seemed inaccessible to feminine agitations, and did even her hate in a self-restrained hygienic manner. This event was the sudden severe illness of her maid, Mrs. Archer. I have reserved to this moment the mention of a circumstance which had forced itself on my notice shortly before Meunier's arrival, namely, that there had been some quarrel between Bertha and this maid, apparently during a visit to a distant family, in which she had accompanied her mistress. I had overheard Archer speaking in a tone of bitter insolence, which I should have thought an adequate reason for immediate dismissal. No dismissal followed; on the contrary, Bertha seemed to be silently putting up with personal inconveniences from the exhibitions of this woman's temper. I was the more astonished to observe that her illness seemed a cause of strong solicitude to Bertha; that she was at the bedside night and day, and would allow no one else to officiate as head-nurse. It happened that our family doctor was out on a holiday, an accident which made Meunier's presence in the house doubly welcome, and he apparently entered into the case with an interest which seemed so much stronger than the ordinary professional feeling, that one day when he had fallen into a long fit of silence after visiting her, I said to him—

"Is this a very peculiar case of disease, Meunier?"

"No," he answered, "it is an attack of peritonitis, which will be fatal, but which does not differ physically from many other cases that have come under my observation. But I'll tell you what I have on my mind. I want to make an experiment on this woman, if you will give me permission. It can do her no harm—will give her no pain—for I shall not make it until life is extinct to all purposes of sensation. I want to try the effect of transfusing blood into her arteries after the heart has ceased to beat for some minutes. I have tried the experiment again and again with animals that have died of this disease, with astounding results, and I want to try it on a human subject. I have the small tubes necessary, in a case I have with me, and the rest of the apparatus could be prepared readily. I should use my own blood—take it from my own arm. This woman won't live through the night, I'm convinced, and I want you to promise me your assistance in making the experiment. I can't do without another hand, but it would perhaps not be well to call in a medical assistant from among your provincial doctors. A disagreeable foolish version of the thing might get abroad."

"Have you spoken to my wife on the subject?" I said, "because she appears to be peculiarly sensitive about this woman: she has been a favourite maid."

"To tell you the truth," said Meunier, "I don't want her to know about it. There are always insuperable difficulties with women in these matters, and the effect on the supposed dead body may be startling. You and I will sit up together, and be in readiness. When certain symptoms appear I shall take you in, and at the right moment we must manage to get every one else out of the room."

I need not give our farther conversation on the subject. He entered very fully into the details, and overcame my repulsion from them, by exciting in me a mingled awe and curiosity concerning the possible results of his experiment.

We prepared everything, and he instructed me in my part as assistant. He had not told Bertha of his absolute conviction that Archer would not survive through the night, and endeavoured to persuade her to leave the patient and take a night's rest. But she was obstinate, suspecting the fact that death was at hand, and supposing that he wished merely to save her nerves. She refused to leave the sick-room. Meunier and I sat up together in the library, he making frequent visits to the sick-room, and returning with the information that the case was taking precisely the course he expected. Once he said to me, "Can you imagine any cause of ill-feeling this woman has against her mistress, who is so devoted to her?"

"I think there was some misunderstanding between them before her illness. Why do you ask?"

"Because I have observed for the last five or six hours—

since, I fancy, she has lost all hope of recovery—there seems a strange prompting in her to say something which pain and failing strength forbid her to utter; and there is a look of hideous meaning in her eyes, which she turns continually towards her mistress. In this disease the mind often remains singularly clear to the last."

"I am not surprised at an indication of malevolent feeling in her," I said. "She is a woman who has always inspired me with distrust and dislike, but she managed to insinuate herself into her mistress's favour." He was silent after this, looking at the fire with an air of absorption, till he went upstairs again. He stayed away longer than usual, and on returning, said to me quietly, "Come now."

I followed him to the chamber where death was hovering. The dark hangings of the large bed made a background that gave a strong relief to Bertha's pale face as I entered. She started forward as she saw me enter, and then looked at Meunier with an expression of angry inquiry; but he lifted up his hand as if to impose silence, while he fixed his glance on the dying woman and felt her pulse. The face was pinched and ghastly, a cold perspiration was on the forehead, and the eyelids were lowered so as to conceal the large dark eyes. After a minute or two, Meunier walked round to the other side of the bed where Bertha stood, and with his usual air of gentle politeness towards her begged her to leave the patient under our care—everything should be done for her—she was no longer in a state to be conscious of an affectionate presence. Bertha was hesitating, apparently almost willing to believe his assurance and to comply. She looked round at the ghastly dying face, as if to read the confirmation of that assurance, when for a moment the lowered eyelids were raised again, and it seemed as if the eyes were looking towards Bertha, but blankly. A shudder passed through Bertha's frame, and she returned to her station near the pillow, tacitly implying that she would not leave the room.

The eyelids were lifted no more. Once I looked at Bertha as she watched the face of the dying one. She wore a rich *peignoir*, and her blond hair was half covered by a lace cap: in her attire she was, as always, an elegant woman, fit to figure in a picture of modern aristocratic life: but I asked myself how that face of hers could ever have seemed to me the face of a woman born of woman, with memories of childhood, capable of pain, needing to be fondled? The features at that moment seemed so preternaturally sharp, the eyes were so hard and eager—she looked like a cruel immortal, finding her spiritual feast in the agonies of a dying race. For across those hard features there came something like a flash when the last hour had been breathed out, and we all felt that the dark veil had completely fallen. What secret was there between Bertha and this woman? I turned my eyes from her with a horrible dread lest my insight should return, and I should be obliged to see what had been breeding about two unloving women's hearts. I felt that Bertha had been watching for the moment of death as the sealing of her secret: I thanked Heaven it could remain sealed for me.

Meunier said quietly, "She is gone." He then gave his arm to Bertha, and she submitted to be led out of the room.

I suppose it was at her order that two female attendants came into the room, and dismissed the younger one who had been present before. When they entered, Meunier had already opened the artery in the long thin neck that lay rigid on the pillow, and I dismissed them, ordering them to remain at a distance till we rang: the doctor, I said, had an operation to perform—he was not sure about the death. For the next twenty minutes I forgot everything but Meunier and the experiment in which he was so absorbed, that I think his senses would have been closed against all sounds or sights which had no relation to it. It was my task at first to keep up the artificial respiration in the body after the transfusion had been effected, but presently Meunier relieved me, and I could see the wondrous slow return of life; the breast began to heave, the inspirations became stronger, the eyelids quivered, and the soul seemed to have returned beneath them. The artificial respiration was withdrawn: still the breathing continued, and there was a movement of the lips.

Just then I heard the handle of the door moving: I suppose Bertha had heard from the women that they had been dismissed: probably a vague fear had arisen in her mind, for she entered with a look of alarm. She came to the foot of the bed and gave a stifled cry.

The dead woman's eyes were wide open, and met hers in full recognition—the recognition of hate. With a sudden strong effort, the hand that Bertha had thought for ever still was pointed towards her, and the haggard face moved. The gasping eager voice said—

"You mean to poison your husband . . . the poison is in the black cabinet . . . I got it for you . . . you laughed at me, and told lies about me behind my back, to make me disgusting

. . . because you were jealous . . . are you sorry . . . now?"

The lips continued to murmur, but the sounds were no longer distinct. Soon there was no sound—only a slight movement: the flame had leaped out, and was being extinguished the faster. The wretched woman's heart-strings had been set to hatred and vengeance; the spirit of life had swept the chords for an instant, and was gone again for ever. Great God! Is this what it is to live again . . . to wake up with our unstilled thirst upon us, with our unuttered curses rising to our lips, with our muscles ready to act out their half-committed sins?

Bertha stood pale at the foot of the bed, quivering and helpless, despairing of devices, like a cunning animal whose hiding-places are surrounded by swift-advancing flame. Even Meunier looked paralysed; life for that moment ceased to be a scientific problem to him. As for me, this scene seemed of one texture with the rest of my existence: horror was my familiar, and this new relation was only like an old pain recurring with new circumstances.

Since then Bertha and I have lived apart—she in her own neighbourhood, the mistress of half our wealth, I as a wanderer in foreign countries, until I came to this Devonshire nest to die. Bertha lives pitied and admired; for what had I against that charming woman, whom every one but myself could have been happy with? There had been no witness of the scene in the dying room except Meunier, and while Meunier lived his lips were sealed by a promise to me.

Once or twice, weary of wandering, I rested in a favourite spot, and my heart went out towards the men and women and children whose faces were becoming familiar to me; but I was driven away again in terror at the approach of my old insight—driven away to live continually with the one Unknown Presence revealed and yet hidden by the moving curtain of the earth and sky. Till at last disease took hold of me and forced me to rest here—forced me to live in dependence on my servants. And then the curse of insight—of my double consciousness, came again, and has never left me. I know all their narrow thoughts, their feeble regard, their half-wearied pity.

It is the 20th of September, 1850. I know these figures I have just written, as if they were a long familiar inscription. I have seen them on this page in my desk unnumbered times, when the scene of my dying struggle has opened upon me. . . .

Wilkie Collins
(1824–1889)

Wilkie Collins was born in London into a family of painters. After attendance at Maida Hall, an elite private school, he traveled for almost two years in Italy with his family. Italy apparently greatly influenced him, especially in the turn his fiction would take, toward elements of mystery, horror, and the Gothic. Upon his return from Italy, he returned to school and then followed a series of aborted career choices before he turned to writing. In 1851, he formed the most important association of his life, meeting Dickens and becoming his collaborator on theatricals and a traveling companion. From 1850 until his death Collins turned out a succession of novels and shorter fictions, but his reputation rests firmly on a few works: The Woman in White *in 1860, and* The Moonstone *in 1868. To these, we should add* Hide and Seek *(1861),* Basil *(1862),* No Name *(1862),* Armadale *(1866), and a collection of stories,* The Frozen Deep and Other Stories *(1874). Collins is generally considered to be the progenitor of the detective novel in English, and his work and presence deeply affected Dickens's fiction in this respect. Wilkie Collins's detective novel depended far more on melodramatic effects than did the kind developed and made famous by Conan Doyle in his Sherlock Holmes series. T. S. Eliot made this point when he asserted that the best English detective fiction, deriving from Collins, "has relied less on the beauty of the mathematical problem and much more on the intangible human element," which is melodramatic. In nearly all of his major work, Collins transcended what we call pure crime fiction in order to flesh out and give social weight to his tale.*

Mr. Marmaduke and the Minister

I

September 13*th.*—Winter seems to be upon us, on the Highland Border, already.

I looked out of window, as the evening closed in, before I barred the shutters and drew the curtains for the night. The clouds hid the hilltops on either side of our valley. Fantastic mists parted and met again on the lower slopes, as the varying breeze blew them. The blackening waters of the lake before our window seemed to anticipate the coming darkness. On the more distant hills the torrents were just visible, in the breaks of the mist, stealing their way over the brown ground like threads of silver. It was a dreary scene. The stillness of all things was only interrupted by the splashing of our little waterfall at the back of the house. I was not sorry to close the shutters, and confine the view to the four walls of our sitting-room.

The day happened to be my birthday. I sat by the peat-fire, waiting for the lamp and the tea-tray, and contemplating my past life from the vantage-ground, so to speak, of my fifty-fifth year.

There was wonderfully little to look back on. Nearly thirty years since, it pleased an all-wise Providence to cast my lot in this remote Scottish hamlet, and to make me Minister of Cauldkirk, on a stipend of seventy-four pounds sterling per annum. I and my surroundings have grown quietly older and older together. I have outlived my wife; I have buried one generation among my parishioners, and married another; I have borne the wear and tear of years better than the kirk in which I minister and the manse (or parsonage-house) in which I live—both sadly out of repair, and both still trusting for the means of reparation to the pious benefactions of persons richer than myself. Not that I complain, be it understood, of the humble position which I occupy. I possess many blessings; and I thank the Lord for them. I have my little bit of land and my cow. I have also my good daughter, Felicia;

named after her deceased mother, but inheriting her comely looks, it is thought, rather from myself.

Neither let me forget my elder sister, Judith; a friendless single person, sheltered under my roof, whose temperament I could wish somewhat less prone to look at persons and things on the gloomy side, but whose compensating virtues Heaven forbid that I should deny. No; I am grateful for what has been given me (from on high), and resigned to what has been taken away. With what fair prospects did I start in life! Springing from a good old Scottish stock, blest with every advantage of education that the institutions of Scotland and England in turn could offer; with a career at the Bar and in Parliament before me—and all cast to the winds, as it were, by the measureless prodigality of my unhappy father, God forgive him! I doubt if I had five pounds left in my purse, when the compassion of my relatives on the mother's side opened a refuge to me at Cauldkirk, and hid me from the notice of the world for the rest of my life.

September 14*th.*—Thus far I had posted up my Diary on the evening of the 13th, when an event occurred so completely unexpected by my household and myself, that the pen, I may say, dropped incontinently from my hand.

It was the time when we had finished our tea, or supper— I hardly know which to call it. In the silence, we could hear the rain pouring against the window, and the wind that had risen with the darkness howling round the house. My sister Judith, taking the gloomy view according to custom—copious draughts of good Bohea and two helpings of such a mutton ham as only Scotland can produce had no effect in raising her spirits—my sister, I say, remarked that there would be ships lost at sea and men drowned this night. My daughter Felicia, the brightest-tempered creature of the female sex that I have ever met with, tried to give a cheerful turn to her aunt's depressing prognostication. "If the ships must be lost," she said, "we may surely hope that the men will be saved." "God willing," I put in—thereby giving to my daughter's humane expression of feeling the fit religious tone that was all it wanted—and then went on with my written record of the events and reflections of the day. No more was said. Felicia took up a book. Judith took up her knitting.

On a sudden, the silence was broken by a blow on the house-door.

My two companions, as is the way of women, set up a

scream. I was startled myself, wondering who could be out in the rain and the darkness, and striking at the door of the house. A stranger it must be. Light or dark, any person in or near Cauldkirk, wanting admission, would know where to find the bell-handle at the side of the door. I waited awhile to hear what might happen next. The stroke was repeated, but more softly. It became me as a man and a minister to set an example. I went out into the passage, and I called through the door, "Who's there?"

A man's voice answered—so faintly that I could barely hear him—"A lost traveller."

Immediately upon this my cheerful sister expressed her view of the matter through the open parlour door. "Brother Noah, it's a robber. Don't let him in!"

What would the Good Samaritan have done in my place? Assuredly he would have run the risk and opened the door. I imitated the Good Samaritan.

A man, dripping wet, with a knapsack on his back and a thick stick in his hand, staggered in, and would I think have fallen in the passage if I had not caught him by the arm. Judith peeped out at the parlour door, and said, "He's drunk." Felicia was behind her, holding up a lighted candle the better to see what was going on. "Look at his face, aunt," says she. "Worn out with fatigue, poor man. Bring him in, father— bring him in."

Good Felicia! I was proud of my girl. "He'll spoil the carpet," says sister Judith. I said, "Silence, for shame!" and brought him in, and dropped him dripping into my own armchair. Would the Good Samaritan have thought of his carpet or his chair? I did think of them, but I overcame it. Ah, we are a decadent generation in these latter days!

"Be quick, father!" says Felicia; "he'll faint if you don't give him something!"

I took out one of our little drinking cups (called among us a "Quaigh"), while Felicia, instructed by me, ran to the kitchen for the cream-jug. Filling the cup with whisky and cream in equal proportions, I offered it to him. He drank it off as if it had been so much water. "Stimulant and nourishment, you'll observe, sir, in equal portions," I remarked to him. "How do you feel now?"

"Ready for another," says he.

Felicia burst out laughing. I gave him another. As I turned to hand it to him, sister Judith came behind me, and snatched away the cream-jug. Never a generous person, sister Judith, at the best of times—more especially in the matter of cream.

He handed me back the empty cup. "I believe, sir, you have saved my life," he said. "Under Providence," I put in—adding, "But I would remark, looking to the state of your clothes, that I have yet another service to offer you, before you tell us how you came into this pitiable state." With that reply, I led him upstairs, and set before him the poor resources of my wardrobe, and left him to do the best he could with them. He was rather a small man, and I am in stature nigh on six feet. When he came down to us in my clothes, we had the merriest evening that I can remember for years past. I thought Felicia would have had an hysteric fit; and even sister Judith laughed—he did look such a comical figure in the minister's garments.

As for the misfortune that had befallen him, it offered one more example of the preternatural rashness of the English traveller in countries unknown to him. He was on a walking tour through Scotland; and he had set forth to go twenty miles a-foot, from a town on one side of the Highland Border to a town on the other, without a guide. The only wonder is that he found his way to Cauldkirk, instead of perishing of exposure among the lonesome hills.

"Will you offer thanks for your preservation to the Throne of Grace, in your prayers to-night?" I asked him. And he answered, "Indeed I will!"

We have a spare room at the manse; but it had not been inhabited for more than a year past. Therefore we made his bed, for that night, on the sofa in the parlour; and so left him, with the fire on one side of his couch, and the whisky and the mutton ham on the other in case of need. He mentioned his name when we bade him good-night. Marmaduke Falmer of London, son of a minister of the English Church Establishment, now deceased. It was plain, I may add, before he spoke, that we had offered the hospitality of the manse to a man of gentle breeding.

September 15*th*.—I have to record a singularly pleasant day; due partly to a return of the fine weather, partly to the good social gifts of our guest.

Attired again in his own clothing, he was, albeit wanting in height, a finely proportioned man, with remarkably small hands and feet; having also a bright mobile face, and large dark eyes of an extraordinary diversity of expression. Also, he was of a sweet and cheerful humour; easily pleased with

little things, and amiably ready to make his gifts agreeable
to all of us. At the same time, a person of my experience and
penetration could not fail to perceive that he was most content
when in company with Felicia. I have already mentioned my
daughter's comely looks and good womanly qualities. It was
in the order of nature that a young man (to use his own
phrase) getting near to his thirty-first birthday should feel
drawn by sympathy towards a well-favoured young woman
in her four-and-twentieth year. In matters of this sort I have
always cultivated a liberal turn of mind, not forgetting my
own youth.

As the evening closed in, I was sorry to notice a certain
change in our guest for the worse. He showed signs of fatigue—falling asleep at intervals in his chair, and waking up
and shivering. The spare room was now well aired, having
had a roaring fire in it all day.

I begged him not to stand on ceremony, and to betake
himself at once to his bed. Felicia (having learned the accomplishment from her excellent mother) made him a warm
sleeping-draught of eggs, sugar, nutmeg, and spirits, delicious
alike to the senses of smell and taste. Sister Judith waited
until he had closed the door behind him, and then favoured
me with one of her dismal predictions. "You'll rue the day,
brother, when you let him into the house. He is going to fall
ill on our hands."

II

November 28th.—God be praised for all His mercies! This
day, our guest, Marmaduke Falmer, joined us downstairs in
the sitting-room for the first time since his illness.

He is sadly deteriorated, in a bodily sense, by the wasting
rheumatic fever that brought him nigh to death; but he is still
young, and the doctor (humanly speaking) has no doubt of
his speedy and complete recovery. My sister takes the opposite view. She remarked, in his hearing, that nobody ever
thoroughly got over a rheumatic fever. Oh, Judith! Judith!
it's well for humanity that you're a single person! If, haply,
there had been any man desperate enough to tackle such a
woman in the bonds of marriage, what a pessimist progeny
must have proceeded from you!

Looking back over my Diary for the last two months and
more, I see one monotonous record of the poor fellow's sufferings; cheered and varied, I am pleased to add, by the

devoted services of my daughter at the sick man's bedside.
With some help from her aunt (most readily given when he
was nearest to the point of death), and with needful services
performed in turn by two of our aged women in Cauldkirk,
Felicia could not have nursed him more assiduously if he had
been her own brother. Half the credit of bringing him through
it belonged (as the doctor himself confessed) to the discreet
young nurse, always ready through the worst of the illness,
and always cheerful through the long convalescence that followed. I must also record to the credit of Marmaduke that
he was indeed duly grateful. When I led him into the parlour,
and he saw Felicia waiting by the armchair, smiling and patting the pillows for him, he took her by the hand, and burst
out crying. Weakness, in part, no doubt—but sincere gratitude at the bottom of it, I am equally sure.

November 29th.—However, there are limits even to sincere
gratitude. Of this truth Mr. Marmaduke seems to be insuf-
ficiently aware. Entering the sitting-room soon after noon to-
day, I found our convalescent guest and his nurse alone. His
head was resting on her shoulder; his arm was around her
waist—and (the truth before everything) Felicia was kissing
him.

A man may be of a liberal turn of mind, and may yet
consistently object to freedom when it takes the form of un-
licensed embracing and kissing; the person being his own
daughter, and the place his own house. I signed to my girl
to leave us, and I advanced to Mr. Marmaduke, with my
opinion of his conduct just rising in words to my lips—when
he staggered me with amazement by asking for Felicia's hand
in marriage.

"You need feel no doubt of my being able to offer to your
daughter a position of comfort and respectability," he said.
"I have a settled income of eight hundred pounds a year."

His raptures over Felicia; his protestations that she was the
first woman he had ever really loved; his profane declaration
that he preferred to die, if I refused to let him be her husband—all these flourishes, as I may call them, passed in at
one of my ears and out at the other. But eight hundred pounds
sterling per annum, descending as it were in a golden avalanche on the mind of a Scottish minister (accustomed to
thirty years' annual contemplation of seventy-four pounds)—
eight hundred a year, in one young man's pocket, I say,
completely overpowered me. I just managed to answer, "Wait

till to-morrow"—and hurried out of doors to recover my self-respect, if the thing was to be anywise done. I took my way through the valley. The sun was shining, for a wonder. When I saw my shadow on the hillside, I saw the Golden Calf as an integral part of me, bearing this inscription in letters of flame—"Here's another of them!"

November 30*th*.—I have made amends for yesterday's backsliding; I have acted as becomes my parental dignity and my sacred calling.

The temptation to do otherwise has not been wanting. Here is sister Judith's advice: "Make sure that he has got the money first; and, for Heaven's sake, nail him!" Here is Mr. Marmaduke's proposal: "Make any conditions you please, so long as you give me your daughter." And, lastly, here is Felicia's confession: "Father, my heart is set on him. Oh, don't be unkind to me for the first time in your life!"

But I have stood firm. I have refused to hear any more words on the subject from any one of them, for the next six months to come.

"So serious a venture as the venture of marriage," I said, "is not to be undertaken on impulse. As soon as Mr. Marmaduke can travel, I request him to leave us, and not to return again for six months. If, after that interval, he is still of the same mind, and my daughter is still of the same mind, let him return to Cauldkirk, and (premising that I am in all other respects satisfied) let him ask me for his wife."

There were tears, there were protestations; I remained immovable. A week later, Mr. Marmaduke left us, on his way by easy stages to the south. I am not a hard man. I rewarded the lovers for their obedience by keeping sister Judith out of the way, and letting them say their farewell words (accompaniments included) in private.

III

May 28*th*.—A letter from Mr. Marmaduke, informing me that I may expect him at Cauldkirk, exactly at the expiration of the six months' interval—viz., on June the seventh.

Writing to this effect, he added a timely word on the subject of his family. Both his parents were dead; his only brother held a civil appointment in India, the place being named. His uncle (his father's brother) was a merchant resident in London; and to this near relative he referred me, if I wished to make inquiries about him. The names of his bankers, authorised to give me every information in respect to his pecuniary affairs, followed. Nothing could be more plain and straightforward. I wrote to his uncle, and I wrote to his bankers. In both cases the replies were perfectly satisfactory—nothing in the slightest degree doubtful, no prevarications, no mysteries. In a word, Mr. Marmaduke himself was thoroughly well vouched for, and Mr. Marmaduke's income was invested in securities beyond fear and beyond reproach. Even sister Judith, bent on picking a hole in the record somewhere, tried hard, and could make nothing of it.

The last sentence in Mr. Marmaduke's letter was the only part of it which I failed to read with pleasure.

He left it to me to fix the day for the marriage, and he entreated that I would make it as early a day as possible. I had a touch of the heartache when I thought of parting with Felicia, and being left at home with nobody but Judith. However, I got over it for that time; and, after consulting my daughter, we decided on naming a fortnight after Mr. Marmaduke's arrival—that is to say, the twenty-first of June. This gave Felicia time for her preparations, besides offering to me the opportunity of becoming better acquainted with my son-in-law's disposition. The happiest marriage does indubitably make its demands on human forbearance; and I was anxious, among other things, to assure myself of Mr. Marmaduke's good temper.

IV

June 22nd.—The happy change in my daughter's life (let me say nothing of the change in *my* life) has come: they were married yesterday. The manse is a desert; and sister Judith was never so uncongenial a companion to me as I feel her to be now. Her last words to the married pair, when they drove away, were: "Lord help you both; you have all your troubles before you!"

I had no heart to write yesterday's record, yesterday evening, as usual. The absence of Felicia at the supper-table completely overcame me. I, who have so often comforted others in their afflictions, could find no comfort for myself. Even now that the day has passed, the tears come into my eyes, only with writing about it. Sad, sad weakness! Let me close my Diary, and open the Bible—and be myself again.

June 23rd.—More resigned since yesterday; a more becoming and more pious frame of mind—obedient to God's holy will, and content in the belief that my dear daughter's married life will be a happy one.

They have gone abroad for their holiday—to Switzerland, by way of France. I was anything rather than pleased when I heard that my son-in-law proposed to take Felicia to that sink of iniquity, Paris. He knows already what I think of balls and playhouses, and similar devils' diversions, and how I have brought up my daughter to think of them—the subject having occurred in conversation among us more than a week since. That he could meditate taking a child of mine to the head-quarters of indecent jiggings and abominable stage-plays, of spouting rogues and painted Jezebels, was indeed a heavy blow.

However, Felicia reconciled me to it in the end. She declared that her only desire in going to Paris was to see the picture-galleries, the public buildings, and the fair outward aspect of the city generally. "Your opinions, father, are my opinions," she said; "and Marmaduke, I am sure, will so shape our arrangements as to prevent our passing a Sabbath in Paris." Marmaduke not only consented to this (with the perfect good temper of which I have observed more than one gratifying example in him), but likewise assured me that, speaking for himself personally, it would be a relief to him when they got to the mountains and the lakes. So that matter was happily settled. Go where they may, God bless and prosper them!

Speaking of relief, I must record that Judith has gone away to Aberdeen on a visit to some friends. "You'll be wretched enough here," she said at parting, "all by yourself." Pure vanity and self-complacence! It may be resignation to her absence, or it may be natural force of mind, I began to be more easy and composed the moment I was alone, and this blessed state of feeling has continued uninterruptedly ever since.

V

September 5th.—A sudden change in my life, which it absolutely startles me to record. I am going to London!

My purpose in taking this most serious step is of a twofold nature. I have a greater and a lesser object in view.

The greater object is to see my daughter, and to judge for myself whether certain doubts on the vital question of her happiness, which now torment me night and day, are unhappily founded on truth. She and her husband returned in August from their wedding-tour, and took up their abode in Marmaduke's new residence in London. Up to this time, Felicia's letters to me were, in very truth, the delight of my life—she was so entirely happy, so amazed and delighted with all the wonderful things she saw, so full of love and admiration for the best husband that ever lived. Since her return to London, I perceive a complete change.

She makes no positive complaint, but she writes in a tone of weariness and discontent; she says next to nothing of Marmaduke, and she dwells perpetually on the one idea of my going to London to see her. I hope with my whole heart that I am wrong; but the rare allusions to her husband, and the constantly repeated desire to see her father (while she has not been yet three months married), seem to me to be bad signs. In brief, my anxiety is too great to be endured. I have so arranged matters with one of my brethren as to be free to travel to London cheaply by steamer; and I begin the journey to-morrow.

My lesser object may be dismissed in two words. Having already decided on going to London, I propose to call on the wealthy nobleman who owns all the land hereabouts, and represent to him the discreditable, and indeed dangerous, condition of the parish kirk for want of means to institute the necessary repairs. If I find myself well received, I shall put in a word for the manse, which is almost in as deplorable a condition as the church. My lord is a wealthy man—may his heart and his purse be opened unto me!

Sister Judith is packing my portmanteau. According to custom, she forebodes the worst. "Never forget," she says, "that I warned you against Marmaduke, on the first night when he entered the house."

VI

September 10*th.*—After more delays than one, on land and sea, I was at last set ashore near the Tower, on the afternoon of yesterday. God help us, my worst anticipations have been realized! My beloved Felicia has urgent and serious need of me.

It is not to be denied that I made my entry into my son-in-law's house in a disturbed and irritated frame of mind. First, my temper was tried by the almost interminable journey, in the noisy and comfortless vehicle which they call cab, from the river-wharf to the west-end of London, where Marmaduke lives. In the second place, I was scandalised and alarmed by an incident which took place—still on the endless journey from east to west—in a street hard by the market of Covent Garden.

We had just approached a large building, most profusely illuminated with gas, and exhibiting prodigious coloured placards having inscribed on them nothing but the name of Barrymore. The cab came suddenly to a standstill; and looking out to see what the obstacle might be, I discovered a huge concourse of men and women drawn across the pavement and road alike, so that it seemed impossible to pass by them. I inquired of my driver what this assembling of the people meant. "Oh," says he, "Barrymore has made another hit." This answer being perfectly unintelligible to me, I requested some further explanation, and discovered that "Barrymore" was the name of a stage-player favoured by the populace; that the building was a theatre; and that all these creatures with immortal souls were waiting, before the doors opened, to get places at the show!

The emotions of sorrow and indignation caused by this discovery so absorbed me, that I failed to notice an attempt the driver made to pass through, where the crowd seemed to be thinner, until the offended people resented the proceeding. Some of them seized the horse's head; others were on the point of pulling the driver off his box, when providentially the police interfered. Under their protection, we drew back, and reached our destination in safety, by another way. I record this otherwise unimportant affair, because it grieved and revolted me (when I thought of the people's souls), and so indisposed my mind to take cheerful views of anything. Under these circumstances, I would fain hope that I have exaggerated the true state of the case, in respect to my daughter's married life.

My good girl almost smothered me with kisses. When I at last got a fair opportunity of observing her, I thought her looking pale and worn and anxious. Query: Should I have arrived at this conclusion if I had met with no example of the wicked dissipations of London, and if I had ridden at my ease in a comfortable vehicle?

They had a succulent meal ready for me, and, what I call, fair enough whisky out of Scotland. Here again I remarked that Felicia ate very little, and Marmaduke nothing at all. He drank wine too—and good heavens, champagne wine!—a needless waste of money surely when there was whisky on the table. My appetite being satisfied, my son-in-law went out of the room, and returned with his hat in his hand. "You and Felicia have many things to talk about on your first evening together. I'll leave you for a while—I shall only be in the way." So he spoke. It was in vain that his wife and I assured him he was not in the way at all. He kissed his hand, and smiled pleasantly, and left us.

"There, father!" says Felicia. "For the last ten days, he has gone out like that, and left me alone for the whole evening. When we first returned from Switzerland, he left me in the same mysterious way, only it was after breakfast then. Now he stays at home in the daytime, and goes out at night."

I inquired if she had not summoned him to give her some explanation.

"I don't know what to make of his explanation," says Felicia. "When he went away in the daytime, he told me he had business in the City. Since he took to going out at night, he says he goes to his club."

"Have you asked where his club is, my dear?"

"He ways it's in Pall Mall. There are dozens of clubs in that street—and he has never told me the name of *his* club. I am completely shut out of his confidence. Would you believe it, father? He has not introduced one of his friends to me since we came home. I doubt if they know where he lives, since he took this house."

What could I say?

I said nothing, and looked round the room. It was fitted up with perfectly palatial magnificence. I am an ignorant man in matters of this sort, and partly to satisfy my curiosity, partly to change the subject, I asked to see the house. Mercy preserve us, the same grandeur everywhere! I wondered if even such an income as eight hundred a year could suffice for it all. In a moment when I was considering this, a truly frightful suspicion crossed my mind. Did these mysterious absences, taken in connection with the unbridled luxury that surrounded us, mean that my son-in-law was a gamester? a shameless shuffler of cards, or a debauched bettor on horses? While I was still completely overcome by my own previsions of evil, my daughter put her arm in mine to take me to the top of the house.

For the first time I observed a bracelet of dazzling gems on her wrist. "Not diamonds?" I said. She answered, with as much composure as if she had been the wife of a nobleman, "Yes, diamonds—a present from Marmaduke." This was too much for me; my previsions, so to speak, forced their way into words. "Oh, my poor child!" I burst out, "I'm in mortal fear that your husband's a gamester!"

She showed none of the horror I had anticipated; she only shook her head and began to cry.

"Worse than that, I'm afraid," she said.

I was petrified; my tongue refused its office, when I would fain have asked her what she meant. Her besetting sin, poor soul, is a proud spirit. She dried her eyes on a sudden, and spoke out freely, in these words: "I am not going to cry about it. The other day, father, we were out walking in the park. A horrid, bold, yellow-haired woman passed us in an open carriage. She kissed her hand to Marmaduke, and called out to him, 'How are you, Marmy?' I was so indignant that I pushed him away from me, and told him to go and take a drive with his lady. He burst out laughing. 'Nonsense!' he said; 'she has known me for years—you don't understand our easy London manners.' We have made it up since then; but I have my own opinion of the creature in the open carriage."

Morally speaking, this was worse than all. But, logically viewed, it completely failed as a means of accounting for the diamond bracelet and the splendour of the furniture.

We went on to the uppermost story. It was cut off from the rest of the house by a stout partition of wood, and a door covered with green baize.

When I tried the door it was locked. "Ha!" says Felicia, "I wanted you to see it for yourself!" More suspicious proceedings on the part of my son-in-law! He kept the door constantly locked, and the key in his pocket. When his wife asked him what it meant, he answered: "My study is up there—and I like to keep it entirely to myself." After such a reply as that, the preservation of my daughter's dignity permitted but one answer: "Oh, keep it to yourself, by all means!"

My previsions, upon this, assumed another form.

I now asked myself—still in connection with my son-in-law's extravagant expenditure—whether the clue to the mystery might not haply be the forging of banknotes on the other side of the baize door. My mind was prepared for anything by this time. We descended again to the dining-room. Felicia saw how my spirits were dashed, and came and perched upon my knee. "Enough of my troubles for to-night, father," she said. "I am going to be your little girl again, and we will talk of nothing but Cauldkirk, until Marmaduke comes back." I am one of the firmest men living, but I could not keep the hot tears out of my eyes when she put her arm round my neck and said those words. By good fortune I was sitting with my back to the lamp; she didn't notice me.

A little after eleven o'clock, Marmaduke returned. He looked pale and weary. But more champagne, and this time something to eat with it, seemed to set him to rights again—no doubt by relieving him from the reproaches of a guilty conscience.

I had been warned by Felicia to keep what had passed between us a secret from her husband for the present; so we had (superficially speaking) a merry end to the evening. My son-in-law was nearly as good company as ever, and wonderfully fertile in suggestions and expedients when he saw they were wanted. Hearing from his wife, to whom I had mentioned it, that I purposed representing the decayed condition of the kirk and manse to the owner of Cauldkirk and the country round about, he strongly urged me to draw up a list of repairs that were most needful, before I waited on my lord. This advice, vicious and degraded as the man who offered it may be, is sound advice nevertheless. I shall assuredly take it.

So far I had written in my Diary, in the forenoon. Returning to my daily record, after lapse of some hours, I have a new mysery of iniquity to chronicle. My abominable son-in-law now appears (I blush to write it) to be nothing less than an associate of thieves!

After the meal they call luncheon, I thought it well, before recreating myself with the sights of London, to attend first to the crying necessities of the kirk and the manse. Furnished with my written list, I presented myself at his lordship's residence. I was immediately informed that he was otherwise engaged, and could not possibly receive me. If I wished to see my lord's secretary, Mr. Helmsley, I could do so. Consenting to this, rather than fail entirely in my errand, I was shown into the secretary's room.

Mr. Helmsley heard what I had to say civilly enough; expressing, however, grave doubts whether his lordship would do anything for me, the demands on his purse being insupportably numerous already. However, he undertook to place my list before his employer, and to let me know the result. "Where are you staying in London?" he asked. I answerd, "With my son-in-law, Mr. Marmaduke Falmer." Before I could add the address, the secretary started to his feet, and tossed my list back to me across the table in the most uncivil manner.

"Upon my word," says he, "your assurance exceeds anything I ever heard of. Your son-in-law is concerned in the robbery of her ladyship's diamond bracelet—the discovery was made not an hour ago. Leave the house, sir, and consider yourelf lucky that I have no instructions to give you in charge to the police." I protested against this unprovoked outrage, with a violence of language which I would rather not recall. As a minister I ought, under every provocation, to have preserved my self-control.

The one thing to do next was to drive back to my unhappy daughter.

Her guilty husband was with her. I was too angry to wait for a fit opportunity of speaking. The Christian humility which I have all my life cultivated as the first of virtues sank, as it were, from under me. In terms of burning indignation I told them what had happened. The result was too distressing to be described. It ended in Felicia giving her husband back the bracelet. The hardened reprobate laughed at us. "Wait till I have seen his lordship and Mr. Helmsley," he said, and left the house.

Does he mean to escape to foreign parts? Felicia, womanlike, believes in him still; she is quite convinced that there must be some mistake. I am myself in hourly expectation of the arrival of the police.

With gratitude to Providence, I note before going to bed the harmless termination of the affair of the bracelet—so far as Marmaduke is concerned. The agent who sold him the jewel has been forced to come forward and state the truth. His lordship's wife is the guilty person; the bracelet was hers—a present from her husband. Harassed by debts that she dare not acknowledge, she sold it; my lord discovered that it was gone; and in terror of his anger the wretched woman took refuge in a lie.

She declared that the bracelet had been stolen from her. Asked for the name of the thief, the reckless woman (having no other name in her mind at the moment) mentioned the man who had innocently bought the jewel of her agent, otherwise my unfortunate son-in-law. Oh, the profligacy of the modern Babylon! It was well I went to the secretary when I did, or we should really have had the police in the house. Marmaduke found them in consultation over the supposed robbery, asking for his address. There was a dreadful exhibition of violence and recrimination at his lordship's residence: in the end he repurchased the bracelet. My son-in-law's money has been returned to him; and Mr. Helmsley has sent me a written apology.

In a worldly sense, this would, I suppose, be called a satisfactory ending.

It is not so, to my mind. I freely admit that I too hastily distrusted Marmaduke; but am I, on that account, to give him back immediately the place which he once occupied in my esteem? Again this evening he mysteriously quitted the house, leaving me alone with Felicia, and giving no better excuse for his conduct than that he had an engagement. And this when I have a double claim on his consideration, as his father-in-law and his guest!

September 11th.—The day began well enough. At breakfast, Marmaduke spoke feelingly of the unhappy result of my visit to his lordship, and asked me to let him look at the list of repairs. "It's just useless to expect anything from my lord, after what has happened," I said. "Besides, Mr. Helmsley gave me no hope when I stated my case to him." Marmaduke still held out his hand for the list. "Let me try if I can get some subscribers," he replied. This was kindly meant, at any rate. I gave him the list; and I began to recover some of my old friendly feeling for him. Alas! the little gleam of tranquillity proved to be of short duration.

We made out our plans for the day pleasantly enough. The check came when Felicia spoke next of our plans for the evening. "My father has only four days more to pass with us," she said to her husband. "Surely you won't go out again to-night, and leave him?" Marmaduke's face clouded over directly; he looked embarrassed and annoyed. I sat perfectly silent, leaving them to settle it by themselves.

"You will stay with us this evening, won't you?" says Felicia. No: he was not free for that evening. "What! another engagement? Surely you can put it off?" No; impossible to put it off. "Is it a ball, or a party of some kind?" No answer;

he changed the subject—he offered Felicia the money repaid
to him for the bracelet. "Buy one for yourself, my dear, this
time." Felicia handed him back the money, rather too haughtily perhaps. "I don't want a bracelet," she said: "I want your
company in the evening."

He jumped up, good-tempered as he was, in something
very like a rage—then looked at me, and checked himself on
the point (as I believe) of using profane language. "This is
downright persecution!" he burst out, with an angry turn of
his head towards his wife. Felicia got up, in her turn. "Your
language is an insult to my father and to me!" He looked
thoroughly staggered at this: it was evidently their first serious
quarrel.

Felicia took no notice of him. "I will get ready directly,
father; and we will go out together." He stopped her as she
was leaving the room—recovering his good temper with a
readiness which it pleased me to see. "Come, come, Felicia!
We have not quarrelled yet, and we won't quarrel now. Let
me off this one time more, and I will devote the next three
evenings of your father's visit to him and to you. Give me a
kiss, and make it up." My daughter doesn't do things by
halves. She gave him a dozen kisses, I should think—and
there was a happy end to it.

"But what shall we do to-morrow evening?" says Marmaduke, sitting down by his wife, and patting her hand as it
lay in his.

"Take us somewhere," says she. Marmaduke laughed. "Your
father objects to public amusements. Where does he want to
go to?" Felicia took up the newspaper. "There is an oratorio
at Exeter Hall," she said; "my father likes music." He turned
to me. "You don't object to oratorios, sir?" I don't object
to music," I answered, "so long as I am not required to enter
a theatre." Felicia handed the newspaper to me. "Speaking
of theatres, father, have you read what they say about the
new play? What a pity it can't be given out of a theatre!" I
looked at her in speechless amazement. She tried to explain
herself. "The paper says that the new play is a service rendered to the cause of virtue; and that the great actor, Barrymore, has set an example in producing it which deserves
the encouragement of all truly religious people. Do read it,
father!" I held up my hands in dismay. My own daughter
perverted! pinning her faith on a newspaper! speaking, with
a perverse expression of interest, of a stage-play and an actor!
Even Marmaduke witnessed this lamentable exhibition of

backsliding with some appearance of alarm. "It's not her fault, sir," he said, interceding with me. "It's the fault of the newspaper. Don't blame her!" I held my peace; determining inwardly to pray for her. Shortly afterwards my daughter and I went out. Marmaduke accompanied us part of the way, and left us at a telegraph-office. "Who are you going to telegraph to?" Felicia asked. Another mysery! He answered, "Business of my own, my dear"—and went into the office.

September 12*th*.—Is my miserable son-in-law's house under a curse? The yellow-haired woman in the open carriage drove up to the door at half-past ten this morning, in a state of distraction. Felicia and I saw her from the drawing-room balcony—a tall woman in gorgeous garments. She knocked with her own hand at the door—she cried out distractedly, "Where is he? I must see him!" At the sound of her voice, Marmaduke (playing with his little dog in the drawing-room) rushed downstairs, and out into the street. "Hold your tongue!" we heard him say to her. "What are you here for?"

What she answered we failed to hear; she was certainly crying. Marmaduke stamped on the pavement like a man beside himself—took her roughly by the arm, and led her into the house.

Before I could utter a word, Felicia left me, and flew headlong down the stairs.

She was in time to hear the dining-room door locked. Following her, I prevented the poor jealous creature from making a disturbance at the door. God forgive me—not knowing how else to quiet her—I degraded myself by advising her to listen to what they said. She instantly opened the door of the back dining-room, and beckoned to me to follow. I naturally hesitated. "I shall go mad," she whispered, "if you leave me by myself!" What could I do? I degraded myself for the second time. For my own child—in pity for my own child!

We heard them, through the flimsy modern folding-doors, at those times when he was most angry, and she most distracted. That is to say, we heard them when they spoke in their loudest tones.

"How did you find out where I live?" says he. "Oh, you're ashamed of me?" says she. "Mr. Helmsley was with us yesterday evening. That's how I found out!" "What do you mean?" "I mean that Mr. Helmsley had your card and address in his pocket. Ah, you were obliged to give your address when you had to clear up that matter of the bracelet! You cruel, cruel man, what have I done to deserve such a note as you sent me this morning?" "Do what the note tells you!" "Do what the note tells me? Did anybody ever hear a man talk so, out of a lunatic asylum? Why, you haven't even the grace to carry out your own wicked deception—you haven't even gone to bed!" There the voices grew less angry, and we missed what followed. Soon the lady burst out again, piteously entreating him this time. "Oh, Marmy, don't ruin me! Has anybody offended you? Is there anything you wish to have altered? Do you want more money? It is too cruel to treat me in this way—it is indeed!" He made some answer, which we were not able to hear; we could only suppose that he had upset her temper again. She went on louder than ever. "I've begged and prayed of you—and you're as hard as iron. I've told you about the Prince—and *that* has had no effect on you. I have done now. We'll see what the doctor says." He got angry, in his turn; we heard him again. "I won't see the doctor!" "Oh, you refuse to see the doctor? I shall make your refusal known— and if there's law in England, you shall feel it!" Their voices dropped again; some new turn seemed to be taken by the conversation. We heard the lady once more, shrill and joyful this time. "There's a dear! You see it, don't you, in the right light? And you haven't forgotten the old times, have you? You're the same dear, honourable, kind-hearted fellow that you always were!"

I caught hold of Felicia, and put my hand over her mouth. There was a sound in the next room which might have been—I cannot be certain—the sound of a kiss. The next moment, we heard the door of the room unlocked. Then the door of the house was opened, and the noise of retreating carriage-wheels followed. We met him in the hall, as he entered the house again.

My daughter walked up to him, pale and determined.

"I insist on knowing who that woman is, and what she wants here." Those were her first words. He looked at her like a man in utter confusion. "Wait till this evening; I am in no state to speak to you now!" With that, he snatched his hat off the hall table, and rushed out of the house.

It is little more than three weeks since they returned to London from their happy wedding-tour—and it has come to this!

The clock has just struck seven; a letter has been left by a messenger, addressed to my daughter. I had persuaded her, poor soul, to lie down in her own room. God grant that the letter may bring her some tidings of her husband! I please myself in the hope of hearing good news.

My mind has not been kept long in suspense. Felicia's waiting-woman has brought me a morsel of writing-paper, with these lines pencilled on it in my daughter's handwriting: "Dearest father, make your mind easy. Everything is explained. I cannot trust myself to speak to you about it tonight—and *he* doesn't wish me to do so. Only wait till tomorrow, and you shall know all. He will be back about eleven o'clock. Please don't wait up for him—he will come straight to me."

September 13*th*.—The scales have fallen from my eyes; the light is set in on me at last. My bewilderment is not to be uttered in words—I am like a man in a dream.

Before I was out of my room in the morning, my mind was upset by the arrival of a telegram addressed to myself. It was the first thing of the kind I ever received; I trembled under the prevision of some new misfortune as I opened the envelope.

Of all the people in the world, the person sending the telegram was sister Judith! Never before did this distracting relative confound me as she confounded me now. Here is her message: "You can't come back. An architect from Edinburgh asserts his resolution to repair the kirk and the manse. The man only waits for his lawful authority to begin. The money is ready—but who has found it? Mr. Architect is forbidden to tell. We live in awful times. How is Felicia?"

Naturally concluding that Judith's mind must be deranged, I went downstairs to meet my son-in-law (for the first time since the events of yesterday) at the late breakfast which is customary in this house. He was waiting for me—but Felicia was not present. "She breakfasts in her room this morning," says Marmaduke; "and I am to give you the explanation which has already satisfied your daughter. Will you take it at great length, sir? or will you have it in one word?" There was something in his manner that I did not at all like—he seemed to be setting me at defiance. I said, stiffly, "Brevity is best; I will have it in one word."

"Here it is then," he answered. "I am Barrymore."

POSTSCRIPT ADDED BY FELICIA

If the last line extracted from my dear father's Diary does
not contain explanation enough in itself, I add some sentences
from Marmaduke's letter to me, sent from the theatre last
night. (N.B.—I leave out the expressions of endearment: they
are my own private property.)

* * * "Just remember how your father talked about theatres
and actors, when I was at Cauldkirk, and how you listened
in dutiful agreement with him. Would he have consented to
your marriage if he had known that I was one of the 'spouting
rogues,' associated with the 'painted Jezebels' of the play-
house? He would never have consented—and you yourself,
my darling, would have trembled at the bare idea of marrying
an actor.

"Have I been guilty of any serious deception? and have
my friends been guilty in helping to keep my secret? My birth,
my name, my surviving relatives, my fortune inherited from
my father—all these important particulars have been truly
stated. The name of Barrymore is nothing but the name that
I assumed when I went on the stage.

"As to what has happened, since our return from Switzerland, I own that I ought to have made my confession to
you. Forgive me if I weakly hesitated. I was so fond of you;
and I so distrusted the Puritanical convictions which your
education had rooted in your mind, that I put it off from day
to day. Oh, my angel * * * !

"Yes, I kept the address of my new house a secret from
all my friends, knowing they would betray me if they paid us
visits. As for my mysteriously-closed study, it was the place
in which I privately rehearsed my new part. When I left you
in the mornings, it was to go to the theatre-rehearsals. My
evening absences began of course with the first performance.

"Your father's arrival seriously embarrassed me. When you
(most properly) insisted on my giving up some of my evenings
to him, you necessarily made it impossible for me to appear
on the stage. The one excuse I could make to the theatre
was, that I was too ill to act. It did certainly occur to me to
cut the Gordian knot by owning the truth. But your father's
horror, when you spoke of the newspaper review of the play,
and the shame and fear you showed at your own boldness,
daunted me once more.

"The arrival at the theatre of my written excuse brought
the manageress down upon me, in a state of distraction. No-

body could supply my place; all the seats were taken; and the Prince was expected. There was, what we call, a scene between the poor lady and myself. I felt I was in the wrong; I saw that the position in which I had impulsively placed myself was unworthy of me—and it ended in my doing my duty to the theatre and the public. But for the affair of the bracelet, which obliged me as an honourable man to give my name and address, the manageress would not have discovered me. She, like everyone else, only knew of my address at my bachelor chambers. How could you be jealous of the old theatrical comrade of my first days on the stage? Don't you know yet that you are the one woman in the world * * * ?

"A last word relating to your father, and I have done.

"Do you remember my leaving you at the telegraph-office? It was to send a message to a friend of mine, an architect in Edinburgh, instructing him to go immediately to Cauldkirk, and provide for the repairs at my expense. The theatre, my dear, more than trebles my paternal income, and I can well afford it. Will your father refuse to accept a tribute of respect to a Scottish minister, because it is paid out of an actor's pocket? You shall ask him the question.

"And, I say, Felicia—will you come and see me act? I don't expect your father to enter a theatre; but, by way of further reconciling him to his son-in-law, suppose you ask him to hear me read the play?"

George Meredith
(1828–1909)

George Meredith, like Thomas Hardy, was that rare bird, both a major novelist and a poet. Meredith began his career, after schooling with the Moravian Brothers in Germany, as a journalist. At twenty-three, he published his first volume of poetry; two years earlier, in 1849, he had married Mary Ellen Nicoll, the daughter of the novelist Thomas Love Peacock, a marriage whose disasters Meredith would chart in his poetic sequence Modern Love (1862). Once the marriage broke up, in 1858, when Nicoll left him, Meredith seemed liberated to write fiction. The novels that established his reputation followed rapidly: The Ordeal of Richard Feverel (1859), Evan Harrington (1861), Emilia in England (1864), Rhoda Fleming (1865), Vittoria (1867), The Adventures of Harry Richmond (1871), Beauchamp's Career (1876), The Egoist (1877), Diana of the Crossways (1885), One of Our Conquerors (1891), and The Amazing Marriage (1895). Besides being a comic novelist, Meredith was a theorist, and his important essay, On the Idea of Comedy and the Uses of the Comic Spirit, was delivered in 1877 as a lecture. Although Meredith's career as a novelist ended by 1895, he continued to write poetry until his death. Well ahead of his time, Meredith was pro-feminist, critical of nineteenth-century logic, and a strong supporter of the emotional life; but the rhetorical swirls of his writing prevented his work from becoming popular. Since his death, his reputation has fluctuated; yet for those who can enter his world of language, he is considered one of the four or five major novelists of the previous century.

The Case of General Ople and Lady Camper

CHAPTER I

An excursion beyond the immediate suburbs of London, projected long before his pony-carriage was hired to conduct him, in fact ever since his retirement from active service, led General Ople across a famous common, with which he fell in love at once, to a lofty highway along the borders of a park, for which he promptly exchanged his heart, and so gradually within a stone's-throw or so of the river-side, where he determined not solely to bestow his affections but to settle for life. It may be seen that he was of an adventurous temperament, though he had thought fit to loosen his sword-belt. The pony-carriage, however, had been hired for the very special purpose of helping him to pass in review the lines of what he called country houses, cottages, or even sites for building, not too remote from sweet London: and as when Cœlebs goes forth intending to pursue and obtain, there is no doubt of his bringing home a wife, the circumstance that there stood a house to let, in an airy situation, at a certain distance in hail of the metropolis he worshipped, was enough to kindle the General's enthusiasm. He would have taken the first he saw, had it not been for his daughter, who accompanied him, and at the age of eighteen was about to undertake the management of his house. Fortune, under Elizabeth Ople's guiding restraint, directed him to an epitome of the comforts. The place he fell upon is only to be described in the tongue of auctioneers, and for the first week after taking it he modestly followed them by terming it bijou. In time, when his own imagination, instigated by a state of something more than mere contentment, had been at work on it, he chose the happy phrase, "a gentlemanly residence." For it was, he declared, a small estate. There was a lodge to it, resembling two sentry-boxes forced into union, where in one half an old couple sat bent, in the other half lay compressed; there was a back-drive to discoverable stables; there was a bit of grass that would have appeared a meadow if magnified; and there was a wall round the kitchen-garden and a strip of wood round the flower-garden. The prying of the outside world was impossible. Comfort, fortification, and gentlemanliness made the place, as the General said, an ideal English home.

The compass of the estate was half an acre, and perhaps a perch or two, just the size for the hugging love General Ople was happiest in giving. He wisely decided to retain the old couple at the lodge, whose members were used to restriction, and also not to purchase a cow, that would have wanted pasture. With the old man, while the old woman attended to the bell at the handsome front entrance with its gilt-spiked gates, he undertook to do the gardening; a business he delighted in, so long as he could perform it in a gentlemanly manner, that is to say, so long as he was not overlooked. He was perfectly concealed from the road. Only one house, and curiously indeed, only one window of the house, and further to show the protection extended to Douro Lodge, that window an attic, overlooked him. And the house was empty.

The house (for who can hope, and who should desire a commodious house, with conservatories, aviaries, pond and boat-shed, and other joys of wealth, to remain unoccupied) was taken two seasons later by a lady, of whom Fame, rolling like a dust-cloud from the place she had left, reported that she was eccentric. The word is uninstructive: it does not frighten. In a lady of a certain age, it is rather a characteristic of aristocracy in retirement. And at least it implies wealth.

General Ople was very anxious to see her. He had the sentiment of humble respectfulness toward aristocracy, and there was that in riches which aroused his admiration. London, for instance, he was not afraid to say he thought the wonder of the world. He remarked, in addition, that the sacking of London would suffice to make every common soldier of the foreign army of occupation an independent gentleman for the term of his natural days. But this is a nightmare! said he, startling himself with an abhorrent dream of envy of those enriched invading officers: for Booty is the one lovely thing which the military mind can contemplate in the abstract. His habit was to go off in an explosion of heavy sighs, when he had delivered himself so far, like a man at war with himself.

The lady arrived in time: she received the cards of the neighbourhood, and signalized her eccentricity by paying no attention to them, excepting the card of a Mrs. Baerens, who had audience of her at once. By express arrangement, the card of General Wilson Ople, as her nearest neighbour, followed the card of the rector, the social head of the district; and the rector was granted an interview, but Lady Camper was not at home to General Ople. She is of superior station to me, and may not wish to associate with me, the General modestly said. Nevertheless he was wounded: for in spite of himself, and without the slightest wish to obtrude his own person, as he explained the meaning that he had in him, his rank in the British army forced him to be the representative of it, in the absence of any one of a superior rank. So that he was professionally hurt, and his heart being in his profession, it may be honestly stated that he was wounded in his feelings, though he said no, and insisted on the distinction. Once a day his walk for constitutional exercise compelled him to pass before Lady Camper's windows, which were not bashfully withdrawn, as he said humorously of Douro Lodge, in the seclusion of half-pay, but bowed out imperiously, militarily, like a generalissimo on horseback, and had full command of the road and levels up to the swelling park-foliage. He went by at a smart stride, with a delicate depression of his upright bearing, as though hastening to greet a friend in view, whose hand was getting ready for the shake. This much would have been observed by a housemaid; and considering his fine figure and the peculiar shining silveriness of his hair, the acceleration of his gait was noticeable. When he drove by, the pony's right ear was flicked, to the extreme indignation of a mettlesome little animal. It ensued in consequence that the General was borne flying under the eyes of Lady Camper, and such pace displeasing him, he reduced it invariably at a step or two beyond the corner of her grounds.

But neither he nor his daughter Elizabeth attached importance to so trivial a circumstance. The General punctiliously avoided glancing at the windows during the passage past them, whether in his wild career or on foot. Elizabeth took a side-shot, as one looks at a wayside tree. Their speech concerning Lady Camper was an exchange of commonplaces over her loneliness: and this condition of hers was the more perplexing to General Ople on his hearing from his daughter that the lady was very fine-looking, and not so very old, as he had fancied eccentric ladies must be. The rector's account of her, too, excited the mind. She had informed him bluntly, that she now and then went to church to save appearances, but was not a church-goer, finding it impossible to support the length of the service; might, however, be reckoned in subscriptions for all the charities, and left her pew open to poor people, and none but the poor. She had travelled over Europe, and knew the East. Sketches in water-colours of the scenes she had visited adorned her walls, and a pair of pistols, that she had found useful, she affirmed, lay on the writing-desk in her drawing-room. General Ople gathered from the rector that she had a great contempt for men: yet it was curiously varied with lamentations over the weakness of women. "Really she cannot possibly be an example of that," said the General, thinking of the pistols.

Now, we learn from those who have studied women on the chess-board, and know what ebony or ivory will do along particular lines, or hopping, that men much talked about will take possession of their thoughts; and certainly the fact may be accepted for one of their moves. But the whole fabric of our knowledge of them, which we are taught to build on this originally acute perception, is shattered when we hear, that it is exactly the same, in the same degree, in proportion to the amount of work they have to do, exactly the same with men and their thoughts in the case of women much talked about. So it was with General Ople, and nothing is left for me to say except, that there is broader ground than the chess-board. I am earnest in protesting the similarity of the singular couples on common earth, because otherwise the General is in peril of the accusation that he is a feminine character; and not simply was he a gallant officer, and a veteran in gunpowder strife, he was also (and it is an extraordinary thing that a genuine humility did not prevent it, and did survive it) a lord and conqueror of the sex. He had done his pretty bit of mischief, all in the way of honour, of course, but hearts had knocked. And now, with his bright white hair, his close-brushed white whiskers on a face burnt brown, his clear-cut features, and a winning droop of his eyelids, there was powder in him still, if not shot.

There was a lamentable susceptibility to ladies' charms. On the other hand, for the protection of the sex, a remainder of shyness kept him from active enterprise and in the state of suffering, so long as indications of encouragement were wanting. He had killed the soft ones, who came to him, attracted by the softness in him, to be killed: but clever women alarmed and paralyzed him. Their aptness to question and require immediate sparkling answers; their demand for fresh wit, of a kind that is not furnished by publications which strike it into heads with a hammer, and supply it wholesale; their various reading; their power of ridicule too; made them awful in his contemplation.

Supposing (for the inflammable officer was now thinking, and deeply thinking, of a clever woman), supposing that Lady Camper's pistols were needed in her defence one night: at the first report proclaiming her extremity, valour might gain an introduction to her upon easy terms, and would not be expected to be witty. She would, perhaps, after the excitement, admit his masculine superiority, in the beautiful old fashion, by fainting in his arms. Such was the reverie he passingly indulged, and only so could he venture to hope for an acquaintance with the formidable lady who was his next neighbour. But the proud society of the burglarious denied him opportunity.

Meanwhile, he learnt that Lady Camper had a nephew, and the young gentleman was in a cavalry regiment. General Ople met him outside his gates, received and returned a polite salute, liked his appearance and manners, and talked of him to Elizabeth, asking her if by chance she had seen him. She replied that she believed she had, and praised his horsemanship. The General discovered that he was an excellent sculler. His daughter was rowing him up the river when the young gentleman shot by, with a splendid stroke, in an outrigger, backed, and floating alongside presumed to enter into conversation, during which he managed to express regrets at his aunt's turn for solitariness. As they belonged to sister branches of the same Service, the General and Mr. Reginald Rolles had a theme in common, and a passion. Elizabeth told her father that nothing afforded her so much pleasure as to hear him talk with Mr. Rolles on military matters. General Ople assured her that it pleased him likewise. He began to spy about for Mr. Rolles, and it sometimes occurred that they conversed across the wall; it could hardly be avoided. A hint or two, an undefinable flying allusion, gave the General to understand that Lady Camper had not been happy in her marriage. He was pained to think of her misfortune; but as she was not over forty, the disaster was, perhaps, not irremediable; that is to say, if she could be taught to extend her forgiveness to men, and abandon her solitude. "If," he said to his daughter, "Lady Camper should by any chance be induced to contract a second alliance, she would, one might expect, be humanized, and we should have highly agreeable neighbours." Elizabeth artlessly hoped for such an event to take place.

She rarely differed with her father, up to whom, taking example from the world around him, she looked as the pattern of a man of wise conduct.

And he was one; and though modest, he was in good humour with himself, approved himself, and could say, that without boasting of success, he was a satisfied man, until he met his touchstone in Lady Camper.

CHAPTER II

This is the pathetic matter of my story, and it requires pointing out, because he never could explain what it was that seemed to him so cruel in it, for he was no brilliant son of fortune, he was no great pretender, none of those who are logically displaced from the heights they have been raised to, manifestly created to show the moral in Providence. He was modest, retiring, humbly contented; a gentlemanly residence appeased his ambition. Popular, he could own that he was, but not meteorically; rather by reason of his willingness to receive light than his desire to shed it. Why, then, was the terrible test brought to bear upon him, of all men? He was one of us; no worse, and not strikingly or perilously better; and he could not but feel, in the bitterness of his reflections upon an inexplicable destiny, that the punishment befalling him, unmerited as it was, looked like absence of Design in the scheme of things Above. It looked as if the blow had been dealt him by reckless chance. And to believe that, was for the mind of General Ople the having to return to his alphabet and recommence the ascent of the laborious mountain of understanding.

To proceed, the General's introduction to Lady Camper was owing to a message she sent him by her gardener, with a request that he would cut down a branch of a wych-elm, obscuring her view across his grounds toward the river. The General consulted with his daughter, and came to the conclusion, that as he could hardly despatch a written reply to a verbal message, yet greatly wished to subscribe to the wishes of Lady Camper, the best thing for him to do was to apply for an interview. He sent word that he would wait on Lady Camper immediately, and betook himself forthwith to his toilette. She was the niece of an earl.

Elizabeth commended his appearance, "passed him," as he would have said; and well she might, for his hat, surtout, trousers and boots, were worthy of an introduction to Royalty.

A touch of scarlet silk round the neck gave him bloom, and
better than that, the blooming consciousness of it.

"You are not to be nervous, papa," Elizabeth said.

"Not at all," replied the General. "I say, not at all, my
dear," he repeated, and so betrayed that he had fallen into
the nervous mood. "I was saying, I have known worse mornings than this." He turned to her and smiled brightly, nodded,
and set his face to meet the future.

He was absent an hour and a half.

He came back with his radiance a little subdued, by no
means eclipsed; as, when experience has afforded us matter
for thought, we cease to shine dazzlingly, yet are not clouded;
the rays have merely grown serener. The sum of his impres-
sions was conveyed in the reflective utterance—"It only shows,
my dear, how different the reality is from our anticipation of
it!"

Lady Camper had been charming; full of condescension,
neighbourly, friendly, willing to be satisfied with the sacrifice
of the smallest branch of the wych-elm, and only requiring
that much for complimentary reasons.

Elizabeth wished to hear what they were, and she thought
the request rather singular; but the General begged her to
bear in mind, that they were dealing with a very extraordinary
woman; "highly accomplished, really exceedingly handsome," he said to himself, aloud.

The reasons were, her liking for air and view, and desire
to see into her neighbour's grounds without having to mount
to the attic.

Elizabeth gave a slight exclamation, and blushed.

"So, my dear, we are objects of interest to her ladyship,"
said the General.

He assured her that Lady Camper's manners were delightful. Strange to tell, she knew a great deal of his antecedent
history, things he had not supposed were known: "little matters," he remarked, by which his daughter faintly conceived
a reference to the conquests of his dashing days. Lady Camper
had deigned to impart some of her own, incidentally; that
she was of Welsh blood, and born among the mountains.
"She has a romantic look," was the General's comment; and
that her husband had been an insatiable traveller before he
became an invalid, and had never cared for Art. "Quite an
extraordinary circumstance, with such a wife!" the General
said.

He fell upon the wych-elm with his own hands, under cover

of the leafage, and the next day he paid his respects to Lady
Camper, to inquire if her ladyship saw any further obstruction
to the view.

"None," she replied. "And now we shall see what the two
birds will do."

Apparently, then, she entertained an animosity to a pair
of birds in the tree.

"Yes, yes; I say they chirp early in the morning," said
General Ople.

"At all hours."

"The song of birds? . . ." he pleaded softly for nature.

"If the nest is provided for them; but I don't like vagabond
chirping."

The General perfectly acquiesced. This, in an engagement
with a clever woman, is what you should do, or else you are
likely to find yourself planted unawares in a high wind, your
hat blown off, and your coat-tails anywhere; in other words,
you will stand ridiculous in your bewilderment; and General
Ople ever footed with the utmost caution to avoid that quag-
mire of the ridiculous. The extremer quags he had hitherto
escaped; the smaller, into which he fell in his agile evasions
of the big, he had hitherto been blest in finding none to notice.

He requested her ladyship's permission to present his
daughter. Lady Camper sent in her card.

Elizabeth Ople beheld a tall, handsomely-mannered lady,
with good features and penetrating dark eyes, an easy carriage
of her person and an agreeable voice, but (the vision of her
age flashed out under the compelling eyes of youth) fifty if a
day. The rich colouring confessed to it. But she was very
pleasing, and Elizabeth's perception dwelt on it only because
her father's manly chivalry had defended the lady against one
year more than forty.

The richness of the colouring, Elizabeth feared, was artificial, and it caused her ingenuous young blood a shudder.
For we are so devoted to nature when the dame is flattering
us with her gifts, that we loathe the substitute, omitting to
think how much less it is an imposition than a form of practical
adoration of the genuine.

Our young detective, however, concealed her emotion of
childish horror.

Lady Camper remarked of her, "She seems honest, and
that is the most we can hope of girls."

"She is a jewel for an honest man," the General sighed,
"some day!"

"Let us hope it will be a distant day."

"Yet," said the General, "girls expect to marry."

Lady Camper fixed her black eyes on him, but did not speak.

He told Elizabeth that her ladyship's eyes were exceedingly searching: "Only," said he, "as I have nothing to hide, I am able to submit to inspection;" and he laughed slightly up to an arresting cough, and made the mantelpiece ornaments pass muster.

General Ople was the hero to champion a lady whose airs of haughtiness caused her to be somewhat backbitten. He assured everybody, that Lady Camper was much misunderstood; she was a most remarkable woman; she was a most affable and highly intelligent lady. Building up her attributes on a splendid climax, he declared she was pious, charitable, witty, and really an extraordinary artist. He laid particular stress on her artistic qualities, describing her power with the brush, her water-colour sketches, and also some immensely clever caricatures. As he talked of no one else, his friends heard enough of Lady Camper, who was anything but a favourite. The Pollingtons, the Wilders, the Wardens, the Baerens, the Goslings, and others of his acquaintance, talked of Lady Camper and General Ople rather maliciously. They were all City people, and they admired the General, but mourned that he should so abjectly have fallen at the feet of a lady as red with rouge as a railway bill. His not seeing it showed that state he was in. The sister of Mrs. Pollington, an amiable widow, relict of a large City warehouse, named Barcop, was chilled by a falling off in his attentions. His apology for not appearing at garden parties was, that he was engaged to wait on Lady Camper.

And at one time, her not condescending to exchange visits with the obsequious General was a topic fertile in irony. But she did condescend.

Lady Camper came to his gate unexpectedly, rang the bell, and was let in like an ordinary visitor. It happened that the General was gardening—not the pretty occupation of pruning, he was digging—and of necessity his coat was off, and he was hot, dusty, unpresentable. From adoring earth as the mother of roses, you may pass into a lady's presence without purification; you cannot (or so the General thought) when you are caught in the act of adoring the mother of cabbages. And though he himself loved the cabbage equally with the rose, in his heart respected the vegetable yet more than he esteemed the flower, for he gloried in his kitchen-garden, this was not a secret for the world to know, and he almost heeled over on his beam ends when word was brought of the extreme honour Lady Camper had done him. He worked his arms hurriedly into his fatigue jacket, trusting to get away to the house and spend a couple of minutes on his adornment; and with any other visitor it might have been accomplished, but Lady Camper disliked sitting alone in a room. She was on the square of lawn as the General stole along the walk. Had she kept her back to him, he might have rounded her like the shadow of a dial, undetected. She was frightfully acute of hearing. She turned while he was in the agony of hesitation, in a queer attitude, one leg on the march, projected by a frenzied tiptoe of the hinder leg, the very fatallest moment she could possibly have selected for unveiling him.

Of course there was no choice but to surrender on the spot.

He began to squander his dizzy wits in profuse apologies. Lady Camper simply spoke of the nice little nest of a garden, smelt the flowers, accepted a Niel rose and a Rohan, a Céline, a Falcot, and La France.

"A beautiful rose indeed," she said of the latter, "only it smells of macassar oil."

"Really, it never struck me, I say it never struck me before," rejoined the General, smelling it as at a pinch of snuff. "I was saying, I always . . ." And he tacitly, with the absurdest of smiles, begged permission to leave unterminated a sentence not in itself particularly difficult.

"I have a nose," observed Lady Camper.

Like the nobly-bred person she was, according to General Ople's version of the interview on his estate, when he stood before her in his gardening costume, she put him at his ease, or she exerted herself to do so; and if he underwent considerable anguish, it was the fault of his excessive scrupulousness regarding dress, propriety, appearance.

He conducted her at her request to the kitchen-garden and the handful of paddock, the stables and coach-house, then back to the lawn.

"It is the home for a young couple," she said.

"I am no longer young," the General bowed, with the sigh peculiar to this confession. "I say, I am no longer young, but I call the place a gentlemanly residence. I was saying, I . . ."

"Yes, yes!" Lady Camper tossed her head, half closing her eyes, with a contraction of the brows, as if in pain.

He perceived a similar expression whenever he spoke of his residence.

Perhaps it recalled happier days to enter such a nest. Perhaps it had been such a home for a young couple that she had entered on her marriage with Sir Scrope Camper, before he inherited his title and estates.

The General was at a loss to conceive what it was.

It recurred at another mention of his idea of the nature of the residence. It was almost a paroxysm. He determined not to vex her reminiscences again; and as this resolution directed his mind to his residence, thinking it pre-eminently gentlemanly, his tongue committed the error of repeating it, with "gentlemanlike" for a variation.

Elizabeth was out—he knew not where. The housemaid informed him, that Miss Elizabeth was out rowing on the water.

"Is she alone?" Lady Camper inquired of him.

"I fancy so," the General replied.

"The poor child has no mother."

"It has been a sad loss to us both, Lady Camper."

"No doubt. She is too pretty to go out alone."

"I can trust her."

"Girls!"

"She has the spirit of a man."

"That is well. She has a spirit; it will be tried."

The General modestly furnished an instance or two of her spiritedness.

Lady Camper seemed to like this theme; she looked graciously interested.

"Still, you should not suffer her to go out alone," she said.

"I place implicit confidence in her," said the General; and Lady Camper gave it up.

She proposed to walk down the lanes to the river-side, to meet Elizabeth returning.

The General manifested alacrity checked by reluctance. Lady Camper had told him she objected to sit in a strange room by herself; after that, he could hardly leave her to dash upstairs to change his clothes; yet how, attired as he was, in a fatigue jacket, that warned him not to imagine his back view, and held him constantly a little to the rear of Lady Camper, lest she should be troubled by it;—and he knew the habit of the second rank to criticise the front—how consent to face the outer world in such style side by side with the lady he admired?

"Come," said she; and he shot forward a step, looking as if he had missed fire.

"Are you not coming, General?"

He advanced mechanically.

Not a soul met them down the lanes, except a little one, to whom Lady Camper gave a small silver-piece, because she was a picture.

The act of charity sank into the General's heart, as any pretty performance will do upon a warm waxen bed.

Lady Camper surprised him by answering his thoughts.

"No; it's for my own pleasure."

Presently she said, "Here they are."

General Ople beheld his daughter by the river-side at the end of the lane, under escort of Mr. Reginald Rolles.

It was another picture, and a pleasing one. The young lady and the young gentleman wore boating hats, and were both dressed in white, and standing by or just turning from the outrigger and light skiff they were about to leave in charge of a waterman. Elizabeth stretched a finger at arm's-length, issuing directions, which Mr. Rolles took up and worded further to the man, for the sake of emphasis; and he, rather than Elizabeth, was guilty of the half-start at sight of the persons who were approaching.

"My nephew, you should know, is intended for a working soldier," said Lady Camper; "I like that sort of soldier best."

General Ople drooped his shoulders at the personal compliment.

She resumed. "His pay is a matter of importance to him. You are aware of the smallness of a subaltern's pay."

"I," said the General, "I say I feel my poor half-pay, having always been a working soldier myself, very important, I was saying, very important to me."

"Why did you retire?"

Her interest in him seemed promising. He replied conscientiously, "Beyond the duties of General of Brigade, I could not, I say I could not, dare to aspire; I can accept and execute orders; I shrink from responsibility."

"It is a pity," said she, "that you were not, like my nephew Reginald, entirely dependent on your profession."

She laid such stress on her remark, that the General, who had just expressed a very modest estimate of his abilities, was unable to reject the flattery of her assuming him to be a man of some fortune. He coughed, and said, "Very little." The thought came to him that he might have to make a statement to her in time, and he emphasized, "Very little indeed. Sufficient," he assured her, "for a gentlemanly appearance."

"I have given you your warning," was her inscrutable rejoinder, uttered within earshot of the young people, to whom, especially to Elizabeth, she was gracious. The damsel's boating uniform was praised, and her sunny flush of exercise and exposure.

Lady Camper regretted that she could not abandon her parasol: "I freckle so easily."

The General, puzzling over her strange words about a warning, gazed at the red rose of art on her cheek with an air of profound abstraction.

"I freckle so easily," she repeated, dropping her parasol to defend her face from the calculating scrutiny.

"I burn brown," said Elizabeth.

Lady Camper laid the bud of a Falcot rose against the young girl's cheek, but fetched streams of colour, that overwhelmed the momentary comparison of the sun-swarthed skin with the rich dusky yellow of the rose in its deepening inward to soft brown.

Reginald stretched his hand for the prvileged flower, and she let him take it; then she looked at the General; but the General was looking, with his usual air of satisfaction, nowhere.

CHAPTER III

"Lady Camper is no common enigma," General Ople observed to his daughter.

Elizabeth inclined to be pleased with her, for at her suggestion the General had bought a couple of horses, that she might ride in the park, accompanied by her father or the little groom. Still, the great lady was hard to read. She tested the resources of his income by all sorts of instigation to expenditure, which his gallantry could not withstand; she encouraged him to talk of his deeds in arms; she was friendly, almost affectionate, and most bountiful in the presents of fruit, peaches, nectarines, grapes, and hot-house wonders that she showered on his table; but she was an enigma in her evident dissatisfaction with him for something he seemed to have left unsaid. And what could that be?

At their last interview she had asked him, "Are you sure, General, you have nothing more to tell me?"

And as he remarked, when relating it to Elizabeth, "One

might really be tempted to misapprehend her ladyship's . . . I say one might commit oneself beyond recovery. Now, my dear, what do you think she intended?"

Elizabeth was "burning brown," or darkly blushing, as her manner was.

She answered, "I am certain you know of nothing that would interest her; nothing, unless . . ."

"Well?" the General urged her.

"How can I speak it, papa?"

"You really can't mean . . ."

"Papa, what could I mean?"

"If I were fool enough!" he murmured. "No, no, I am an old man. I was saying, I am past the age of folly."

One day Elizabeth came home from her ride in a thoughtful mood. She had not, further than has been mentioned, incited her father to think of the age of folly; but voluntarily or not, Lady Camper had, by an excess of graciousness amounting to downright invitation; as thus, "Will you persist in withholding your confidence from me, General?" She added, "I am not so difficult a person." These prompting speeches occurred on the morning of the day when Elizabeth sat at his table, after a long ride into the country, profoundly meditative.

A note was handed to General Ople, with the request that he would step in to speak with Lady Camper in the course of the evening, or next morning. Elizabeth waited till his hat was on, then said, "Papa, on my ride to-day, I met Mr. Rolles."

"I am glad you had an agreeable escort, my dear."

"I could not refuse his company."

"Certainly not. And where did you ride?"

"To a beautiful valley; and there we met . . ."

"Her ladyship?"

"Yes."

"She always admires you on horseback."

"So you know it, papa, if she should speak of it."

"And I am bound to tell you, my child," said the General, "that this morning Lady Camper's manner to me was . . . if I were a fool . . . I say, this morning I beat a retreat, but apparently she . . . I see no way out of it, supposing she . . ."

"I am sure she esteems you, dear papa," said Elizabeth.

"You take to her, my dear?" the General inquired anxiously; "a little?—a little afraid of her?"

"A little," Elizabeth replied, "only a little."

"Don't be agitated about me."

"No, papa; you are sure to do right."

"But you are trembling."

"Oh! no. I wish you success."

General Ople was overjoyed to be reinforced by his daughter's good wishes. He kissed her to thank her. He turned back to her to kiss her again. She had greatly lightened the difficulty at least of a delicate position.

It was just like the imperious nature of Lady Camper to summon him in the evening to terminate the conversation of the morning, from the visible pitfall of which he had beaten a rather precipitate retreat. But if his daughter cordially wished him success, and Lady Camper offered him the crown of it, why then he had only to pluck up spirit, like a good commander who has to pass a fordable river in the enemy's presence; a dash, a splash, a rattling volley or two, and you are over, established on the opposite bank. But you must be positive of victory, otherwise, with the river behind you, your new position is likely to be ticklish. So the General entered Lady Camper's drawing-room warily, watching the fair enemy. He knew he was captivating, his old conquests whispered in his ears, and her reception of him all but pointed to a footstool at her feet. He might have fallen there at once, had he not remembered a hint that Mr. Reginald Rolles had dropped concerning Lady Camper's amazing variability.

Lady Camper began.

"General, you ran away from me this morning. Let me speak. And, by the way, I must reproach you; you should not have left it to me. Things have now gone so far that I cannot pretend to be blind. I know your feelings as a father. Your daughter's happiness . . ."

"My lady," the General interposed, "I have her distinct assurance that it is, I say it is wrapt up in mine."

"Let me speak. Young people will say anything. Well, they have a certain excuse for selfishness; we have not. I am in some degree bound to my nephew; he is my sister's son."

"Assuredly, my lady. I would not stand in his light, be quite assured. If I am, I was saying if I am not mistaken, I . . . and he is, or has the making of an excellent soldier in him, and is likely to be a distinguished cavalry officer."

"He has to carve his own way in the world, General."

"All good soldiers have, my lady. And if my position is not, after a considerable term of service, I say if . . ."

"To continue," said Lady Camper: "I never have liked early marriages. I was married in my teens before I knew men. Now I do know them, and now . . ."

The General plunged forward: "The honour you do us now:—a mature experience is worth:—my dear Lady Camper, I have admired you:—and your objection to early marriages cannot apply to . . . indeed, madam, vigour, they say . . . though youth, of course . . . yet young people, as you observe . . . and I have, though perhaps my reputation is against it, I was saying I have a natural timidity with your sex, and I am grey-headed, white-headed, but happily without a single malady."

Lady Camper's brows showed a trifling bewilderment. "I am speaking of these young people, General Ople."

"I consent to everything beforehand, my dear lady. He should be, I say Mr. Rolles should be provided for."

"So should she, General, so should Elizabeth."

"She shall be, she will, dear madam. What I have, with your permission, if—good heaven! Lady Camper, I scarcely know where I am. She would . . . I shall not like to lose her: you would not wish it. In time she will . . . she has every quality of a good wife."

"There, stay there, and be intelligible," said Lady Camper. "She has every quality. Money should be one of them. Has she money?"

"Oh! my lady," the General exclaimed, "we shall not come upon your purse when her time comes."

"Has she ten thousand pounds?"

"Elizabeth? She will have, at her father's death . . . but as for my income, it is moderate, and only sufficient to maintain a gentlemanly appearance in proper self-respect. I make no show. I say I make no show. A wealthy marriage is the last thing on earth I should have aimed at. I prefer quiet and retirement. Personally, I mean. That is my personal taste. But if the lady: I say if it should happen that the lady . . . and indeed I am not one to press a suit: but if she who distinguishes and honours me should chance to be wealthy, all I can do is to leave her wealth at her disposal, and that I do: I do that unreservedly. I feel I am very confused, alarmingly confused. Your ladyship merits a superior . . . I trust I have not . . . I am entirely at your ladyship's mercy."

"Are you prepared, if your daughter is asked in marriage, to settle ten thousand pounds on her, General Ople?"

The General collected himself. In his heart he thoroughly

appreciated the moral beauty of Lady Camper's extreme solicitude on behalf of his daughter's provision; but he would
have desired a postponement of that and other material questions belonging to a distant future until his own fate was
decided.

So he said: "Your ladyship's generosity is very marked. I
say it is very marked."

"How, my good General Ople! how is it marked in any
degree?" cried Lady Camper. "I am not generous. I don't
pretend to be; and certainly I don't want the young people
to think me so. I want to be just. I have assumed that you
intend to be the same. Then will you do me the favour to
reply to me?"

The General smiled winningly and intently, to show her
that he prized her, and would not let her escape his eulogies.

"Marked, in this way, dear madam, that you think of my
daughter's future more than I. I say, more than her father
himself does. I know I ought to speak more warmly, I feel
warmly. I was never an eloquent man, and if you take me as
a soldier, I am, as I have ever been in the service, I was saying
I am Wilson Ople, of the grade of General, to be relied on
for executing orders; and, madam, you are Lady Camper,
and you command me. I cannot be more precise. In fact, it
is the feeling of the necessity for keeping close to the business
that destroys what I would say. I am in fact lamentably in-
competent to conduct my own case."

Lady Camper left her chair.

"Dear me, this is very strange, unless I am singularly in
error," she said.

The General now faintly guessed that he might be in error,
for his part.

But he had burned his ships, blown up his bridges; retreat
could not be thought of.

He stood, his head bent and appealing to her side-face,
like one pleadingly in pursuit, and very deferentially, with a
courteous vehemence, he entreated first her ladyship's pardon
for his presumption, and then the gift of her ladyship's hand.

As for his language, it was the tongue of General Ople.
But his bearing was fine. If his clipped white silken hair spoke
of age, his figure breathed manliness. He was a picture, and
she loved pictures.

For his own sake, she begged him to cease. She dreaded
to hear of something "gentlemanly."

"This is a new idea to me, my dear General," she said.

"You must give me time. People at our age have to think of fitness. Of course, in a sense, we are both free to do as we like. Perhaps I may be of some aid to you. My preference is for absolute independence. And I wished to talk of a different affair. Come to me to-morrow. Do not be hurt if I decide that we had better remain as we are."

The General bowed. His efforts, and the wavering of the fair enemy's flag, had inspired him with a positive reawakening of masculine passion to gain this fortress. He said well: "I have, then, the happiness, madam, of being allowed to hope until to-morrow?"

She replied, "I would not deprive you of a moment of happiness. Bring good sense with you when you do come."

The General asked eagerly, "I have your ladyship's permission to come early?"

"Consult your happiness," she answered; and if to his mind she seemed returning to the state of enigma, it was on the whole deliciously. She restored him his youth. He told Elizabeth that night, he really must begin to think of marrying her to some worthy young fellow. "Though," said he, with an air of frank intoxication, "my opinion is, the young ones are not so lively as the old in these days, or I should have been besieged before now."

The exact substance of the interview he forbore to relate to his inquisitive daughter, with a very honourable discretion.

CHAPTER IV

Elizabeth came riding home to breakfast from a gallop round the park, and passing Lady Camper's gates, received the salutation of her parasol. Lady Camper talked with her through the bars. There was not a sign to tell of a change or twist in her neighbourly affability. She remarked simply enough, that it was her nephew's habit to take early gallops, and possibly Elizabeth might have seen him, for his quarters were proximate; but she did not demand an answer. She had passed a rather restless night, she said. "How is the General?"

"Papa must have slept soundly, for he usually calls to me through his door when he hears I am up," said Elizabeth.

Lady Camper nodded kindly and walked on.

Early in the morning General Ople was ready for battle. His forces were, the anticipation of victory, a carefully arranged toilette, and an unaccustomed spirit of enterprise in the realms of speech; for he was no longer in such awe of Lady Camper.

"You have slept well?" she inquired.

"Excellently, my lady."

"Yes, your daughter tells me she heard you, as she went by your door in the morning for a ride to meet my nephew. You are, I shall assume, prepared for business."

"Elizabeth? . . . to meet? . . ." General Ople's impression of anything extraneous to his emotion was feeble and passed instantly. "Prepared! Oh, certainly;" and he struck in a compliment on her ladyship's fresh morning bloom.

"It can hardly be visible," she responded; "I have not painted yet."

"Does your ladyship proceed to your painting in the very early morning?"

"Rouge. I rouge."

"Dear me! I should not have supposed it."

"You have speculated on it very openly, General. I remember your trying to see a freckle through the rouge; but the truth is, I am of a supernatural paleness if I do not rouge, so I do. You understand, therefore, I have a false complexion. Now to business."

"If your ladyship insists in calling it business. I have little to offer—myself!"

"You have a gentlemanly residence."

"It is, my lady, it is. It is a bijou."

"Ah!" Lady Camper sighed dejectedly.

"It is a perfect bijou!"

"Oblige me, General, by not pronouncing the French word as if you were swearing by something in English, like a trooper."

General Ople started, admitted that the word was French, and apologized for his pronunciation. Her variability was now visible over a corner of the battlefield like a thundercloud.

"The business we have to discuss concerns the young people, General."

"Yes," brightened by this, he assented: "Yes, dear Lady Camper; it is a part of the business; it is a secondary part; it has to be discussed; I say I subscribe beforehand. I may say, that honouring, esteeming you as I do, and hoping ardently for your consent . . ."

"They must have a home and an income, General."

"I presume, dearest lady, that Elizabeth will be welcome in your home. I certainly shall never chase Reginald out of mine."

Lady Camper threw back her head. "Then you are not yet awake, or you practice the art of sleeping with open eyes! Now listen to me. I rouge, I have told you. I like colour, and I do not like to see wrinkles or have them seen. Therefore I rouge. I do not expect to deceive the world so flagrantly as to my age, and you I would not deceive for a moment. I am seventy."

The effect of this noble frankness on the General was to raise him from his chair in a sitting posture as if he had been blown up.

Her countenance was inexorably imperturbable under his alternate blinking and gazing that drew her close and shot her distant, like a mysterious toy.

"But," said she, "I am an artist; I dislike the look of extreme age, so I conceal it as well as I can. You are very kind to fall in with the deception; an innocent and, I think, a proper one, before the world, though not to the gentleman who does me the honour to propose to me for my hand. You desire to settle our business first. You esteem me; I suppose you mean as much as young people mean when they say they love. Do you? Let us come to an understanding."

"I can," the melancholy General gasped, "I say I can—I cannot—I cannot credit your ladyship's . . ."

"You are at liberty to call me Angela."

"Ange . . ." he tried it, and in shame relapsed. "Madam, yes. Thanks."

"Ah," cried Lady Camper, "do not use these vulgar contractions of decent speech in my presence. I abhor the word 'thanks.' It is fit for fribbles."

"Dear me, I have used it all my life," groaned the General.

"Then, for the remainder, be it understood that you renounce it. To continue, my age is . . ."

"Oh, impossible, impossible," the General almost wailed; there was really a crack in his voice.

"Advancing to seventy. But, like you, I am happy to say I have not a malady. I bring no invalid frame to an union that necessitates the leaving of the front door open day and night to the doctor. My belief is, I could follow my husband still on a campaign, if he were a warrior instead of a pensioner."

General Ople winced.

He was about to say humbly, "As General of Brigade . . ."

"Yes, yes, you want a commanding officer, and that I have

seen, and that has caused me to meditate on your proposal," she interrupted him; while he, studying her countenance hard, with the painful aspect of a youth who lashes a donkey memory in an examination by word of mouth, attempted to marshal her signs of younger years against her awful confession of the extremely ancient, the witheringly ancient. But for the manifest rouge, manifest in spite of her declaration that she had not yet that morning proceeded to her paint-brush, he would have thrown down his glove to challenge her on the subject of her age. She had actually charms. Her mouth had a charm; her eyes were lively; her figure, mature if you like, was at least full and good; she stood upright, she had a queenly seat. His mental ejaculation was, "What a wonderful constitution!"

By a lapse of politeness, he repeated it to himself half aloud; he was shockingly nervous.

"Yes, I have finer health than many a younger woman," she said. "An ordinary calculation would give me twenty good years to come. I am a widow, as you know. And, by the way, you have a leaning for widows. Have you not? I thought I had heard of a widow Barcop in this parish. Do not protest. I assure you I am a stranger to jealousy. My income . . ."

The General raised his hands.

"Well, then," said the cool and self-contained lady, "before I go farther, I may ask you, knowing what you have forced me to confess, are you still of the same mind as to marriage? And one moment, General. I promise you most sincerely that your withdrawing a step shall not, as far as it touches me, affect my neighbourly and friendly sentiments; not in any degree. Shall we be as we were?"

Lady Camper extended her delicate hand to him.

He took it respectfully, inspected the aristocratic and unshrunken fingers, and kissing them, said, "I never withdraw from a position, unless I am beaten back. Lady Camper, I . . ."

"My name is Angela."

The General tried again: he could not utter the name.

To call a lady of seventy Angela is difficult in itself. It is, it seems, thrice difficult in the way of courtship.

"Angela!" said she.

"Yes. I say, there is not a more beautiful female name, dear Lady Camper."

"Spare me that word 'female' as long as you live. Address me by that name, if you please."

The General smiled. The smile was meant for propitiation and sweetness. It became a brazen smile.

"Unless you wish to step back," said she.

"Indeed, no. I am happy, Lady Camper. My life is yours. I say, my life is devoted to you, dear madam."

"Angela!"

General Ople was blushingly delivered of the name.

"That will do," said she. "And as I think it possible one may be admired too much as an artist, I must request you to keep my number of years a secret."

"To the death, madam," said the General.

"And now we will take a turn in the garden, Wilson Ople. And beware of one thing, for a commencement, for you are full of weeds, and I mean to pluck out a few: never call any place a gentlemanly residence in my hearing, nor let it come to my ears that you have been using the phrase elsewhere. Don't express astonishment. At present it is enough that I dislike it. But this only," Lady Camper added, "this only if it is not your intention to withdraw from your position."

"Madam, my lady, I was saying—hem!—Angela, I *could* not wish to withdraw."

Lady Camper leaned with some pressure on his arm, observing, "You have a curious attachment to antiquities."

"My dear lady, it is your mind; I say, it is your mind: I was saying, I am in love with your mind," the General endeavoured to assure her, and himself too.

"Or is it my powers as an artist?"

"Your mind, your extraordinary powers of mind."

"Well," said Lady Camper, "a veteran General of Brigade is as good a crutch as a childless old grannam can have."

And, as a crutch, General Ople, parading her grounds with the aged woman, found himself used and treated.

The accuracy of his perceptions might be questioned. He was like a man stunned by some great tropical fruit, which responds to the longing of his eyes by falling on his head; but it appeared to him, that she increased in bitterness at every step they took, as if determined to make him realize her wrinkles.

He was even so inconsequent, or so little recognized his position, as to object in his heart to hear himself called Wilson.

It is true that she uttered Wilsonople as if the names formed one word. And on a second occasion (when he inclined to feel hurt) she remarked, "I fear me, Wilsonople, if we are to speak plainly, thou art but a fool." He, perhaps, naturally objected to that. He was, however, giddy, and barely knew.

Yet once more the magical woman changed. All semblance of harshness, and harridan-like spike-tonguedness, vanished when she said adieu.

The astronomer, looking at the crusty jag and scoria of the magnified moon through his telescope, and again with naked eyes at the soft-beaming moon, when the crater-ridges are faint as eyebrow-pencillings, has a similar sharp alternation of prospect to that which mystified General Ople.

But between watching an orb that is only variable at our caprice, and contemplating a woman who shifts and quivers ever with her own, how vast the difference!

And consider that this woman is about to be one's wife!

He could have believed (if he had not known full surely that such things are not) he was in the hands of a witch.

Lady Camper's "adieu" was perfectly beautiful—a kind, cordial, intimate, above all, to satisfy his present craving, it was a lady-like adieu—the adieu of a delicate and elegant woman, who had hardly left her anchorage by forty to sail into the fifties.

Alas! he had her word for it, that she was not less than seventy. And, worse, she had betrayed most melancholy signs of sourness and agedness as soon as he had sworn himself to her fast and fixed.

"The road is open to you to retreat," were her last words.

"My road," he answered gallantly, "is forward."

He was drawing backward as he said it, and something provoked her to smile.

CHAPTER V

It is a noble thing to say that your road is forward, and it befits a man of battles. General Ople was too loyal a gentleman to think of any other road. Still, albeit not gifted with imagination, he could not avoid the feeling that he had set his face to Winter. He found himself suddenly walking straight into the heart of Winter, and a nipping Winter. For her ladyship had proved acutely nipping. His little customary phrases, to which Lady Camper objected, he could see no harm in whatever. Conversing with her in the privacy of domestic life would never be the flowing business that it is for other men.

It would demand perpetual vigilance, hop, skip, jump, flounderings, and apologies.

This was not a pleasing prospect.

On the other hand, she was the niece of an earl. She was wealthy. She might be an excellent friend to Elizabeth; and she could be, when she liked, both commandingly and bewitchingly ladylike.

Good! But he was a General Officer of not more than fifty-five, in his full vigour, and she a woman of seventy!

The prospect was bleak. It resembled an outlook on the steppes. In point of the discipline he was to expect, he might be compared to a raw recruit, and in his own home!

However, she was a woman of mind. One would be proud of her.

But did he know the worst of her? A dreadful presentiment, that he did not know the worst of her, rolled an ocean of gloom upon General Ople, striking out one solitary thought in the obscurity, namely, that he was about to receive punishment for retiring from active service to a life of ease at a comparatively early age, when still in marching trim. And the shadow of the thought was, that he deserved the punishment!

He was in his garden with the dawn. Hard exercise is the best of opiates for dismal reflections. The General discomposed his daughter by offering to accompany her on her morning ride before breakfast. She considered that it would fatigue him. "I am not a man of eighty!" he cried. He could have wished he had been.

He led the way to the park, where they soon had sight of young Rolles, who checked his horse and spied them like a vedette, but, perceiving that he had been seen, came cantering, and hailing the General with hearty wonderment.

"And what's this the world says, General?" said he. "But we all applaud your taste. My aunt Angela was the handsomest woman of her time."

The General murmured in confusion, "Dear me!" and looked at the young man, thinking that he could not have known the time.

"Is all arranged, my dear General?"

"Nothing is arranged, and I beg—I say I beg . . . I came out for fresh air and pace."

The General rode frantically.

In spite of the fresh air, he was unable to eat at breakfast. He was bound, of course, to present himself to Lady Camper, in common civility, immediately after it.

And first, what were the phrases he had to avoid uttering in her presence? He could remember only the "gentlemanly residence." And it was a gentlemanly residence, he thought as he took leave of it. It was one, neatly named to fit the place. Lady Camper is indeed a most eccentric person! he decided from his experience of her.

He was rather astonished that young Rolles should have spoken so coolly of his aunt's leaning to matrimony; but perhaps her exact age was unknown to the younger members of her family.

This idea refreshed him by suggesting the extremely honourable nature of Lady Camper's uncomfortable confession.

He himself had an uncomfortable confession to make. He would have to speak of his income. He was living up to the edges of it.

She is an upright woman, and I must be the same! he said, fortunately not in her hearing.

The subject was disagreeable to a man sensitive on the topic of money, and feeling that his prudence had recently been misled to keep up appearances.

Lady Camper was in her garden, reclining under her parasol. A chair was beside her, to which, acknowledging the salutation of her suitor, she waved him.

"You have met my nephew Reginald this morning, General?"

"Curiously, in the park, this morning, before breakfast, I did, yes. Hem! I, I say I did meet him. Has your ladyship seen him?"

"No. The park is very pretty in the early morning."

"Sweetly pretty."

Lady Camper raised her head, and with the mildness of assured dictatorship, pronounced: "Never say that before me."

"I submit, my lady," said the poor scourged man.

"Why, naturally you do. Vulgar phrases have to be endured, except when our intimates are guilty, and then we are not merely offended, we are compromised by them. You are still of the mind in which you left me yesterday? You are one day older. But I warn you, so am I."

"Yes, my lady, we cannot, I say we cannot check time. Decidedly of the same mind. Quite so."

"Oblige me by never saying 'Quite so.' My lawyer says it. It reeks of the City of London. And do not look so miserable."

"I, madam? my dear lady!" the General flashed out in a radiance that dulled instantly.

"Well," said she, cheerfully, "and you're for the old woman?"

"For Lady Camper."

"You are seductive in your flatteries, General. Well, then, we have to speak of business."

"My affairs—" General Ople was beginning, with perturbed forehead; but Lady Camper held up her finger.

"We will touch on your affairs incidentally. Now listen to me, and do not exclaim until I have finished. You know that these two young ones have been whispering over the wall for some months. They have been meeting on the river and in the park habitually, apparently with your consent."

"My lady!"

"I did not say with your connivance."

"You mean my daughter Elizabeth?"

"And my nephew Reginald. We have named them, if that advances us. Now, the end of such meetings is marriage, and the sooner the better, if they are to continue. I would rather they should not; I do not hold it good for young soldiers to marry. But if they do, it is very certain that their pay will not support a family; and in a marriage of two healthy young people, we have to assume the existence of the family. You have allowed matters to go so far that the boy is hot in love; I suppose the girl is, too. She is a nice girl. I do not object to her personally. But I insist that a settlement be made on her before I give my nephew one penny. Hear me out, for I am not fond of business, and shall be glad to have done with these explanations. Reginald has nothing of his own. He is my sister's son, and I loved her, and rather like the boy. He has at present four hundred a-year from me. I will double it, on the condition that you at once make over ten thousand— not less; and let it be yes or no!—to be settled on your daughter and go to her children, independent of the husband—*cela va sans dire*. Now you may speak, General."

The General spoke, with breath fetched from the deeps:

"Ten thousand pounds! Hem! Ten! Hem, frankly—ten, my lady! One's income—I am quite taken by surprise. I say Elizabeth's conduct—though, poor child! it is natural to her to seek a mate, I mean, to accept a mate and an establishment, and Reginald is a very hopeful fellow—I was saying, they jump on me out of an ambush, and I wish them every happiness. And she is an ardent soldier, and a soldier she must marry. But ten thousand!"

"It is to secure the happiness of your daughter, General."

"Pounds! my lady. It would rather cripple me."

"You would have my house, General; you would have the moiety, as the lawyers say, of my purse; you would have horses, carriages, servants; I do not divine what more you would wish to have."

"But, madam—a pensioner on the Government! I can look back on past services, I say old services, and I accept my position. But, madam, a pensioner on my wife, bringing next to nothing to the common estate! I fear my self-respect would, I say would . . ."

"Well, and what would it do, General Ople?"

"I was saying, my self-respect as my wife's pensioner, my lady. I could not come to her empty-handed."

"Do you expect that I should be the person to settle money on your daughter, to save her from mischances? A rakish husband, for example; for Reginald is young, and no one can guess what will be made of him."

"Undoubtedly your ladyship is correct. We might try absence for the poor girl. I have no female relation, but I could send her to the sea-side to a lady-friend."

"General Ople, I forbid you, as you value my esteem, ever—and I repeat, I forbid you ever—to afflict my ears with that phrase, 'lady-friend!' "

The General blinked in a state of insurgent humility.

These incessant whippings could not but sting the humblest of men; and "lady-friend," he was sure, was a very common term, used, he was sure, in the very best society. He had never heard Her Majesty speak at levées of a lady-friend, but he was quite sure that she had one; and if so, what could be the objection to her subjects mentioning it as a term to suit their own circumstances?

He was harassed and perplexed by old Lady Camper's treatment of him, and he resolved not to call her Angela even upon supplication—not that day, at least.

She said, "You will not need to bring property of any kind to the common estate; I neither look for nor desire it. The generous thing for you to do would be to give your daughter all you have, and come to me."

"But, Lady Camper, if I denude myself or curtail my income—a man at his wife's discretion, I was saying a man at his wife's mercy! . . ."

General Ople was really forced, by his manly dignity, to make this protest on its behalf. He did not see how he could have escaped doing so; he was more an agent than a principal. "My wife's mercy," he said again, but simply as a herald proclaiming superior orders.

Lady Camper's brows were wrathful. A deep blood-crimson overcame the rouge, and gave her a terrible stormy look.

"The congress now ceases to sit, and the treaty is not concluded," was all she said.

She rose, bowed to him, "Good morning, General," and turned her back.

He sighed. He was a free man. But this could not be denied—whatever the lady's age, she was a grand woman in her carriage, and when looking angry, she had a queen-like aspect that raised her out of the reckoning of time.

So now he knew there was a worse behind what he had previously known. He was precipitate in calling it the worst. "Now," said he to himself, "I know the worst!"

No man should ever say it. Least of all, one who has entered into relations with an eccentric lady.

CHAPTER VI

Politeness required that General Ople should not appear to rejoice in his dismissal as a suitor, and should at least make some show of holding himself at the beck of a reconsidering mind. He was guilty of running up to London early next day, and remaining absent until nightfall; and he did the same on the two following days. When he presented himself at Lady Camper's lodge-gates, the astonishing intelligence, that her ladyship had departed for the Continent and Egypt, gave him qualms of remorse, which assumed a more definite shape in something like awe of her triumphant constitution. He forbore to mention her age, for he was the most honourable of men, but a habit of tea-table talkativeness impelled him to say and repeat an idea that had visited him, to the effect, that Lady Camper was one of those wonderful women who are comparable to brilliant generals, and defend themselves from the siege of Time by various aggressive movements. Fearful of not being understood, owing to the rarity of the occasions when the squat plain squad of honest Saxon regulars at his command were called upon to explain an idea, he re-cast the sentence. But, as it happened that the regulars of his vocabulary were not numerous, and not accustomed to work upon thoughts and images, his repetitions rather succeeded in exposing the piece of knowledge he had recently acquired than in making his meaning plainer. So we need not marvel that his acquaintances should suppose him to be secretly aware of an extreme degree in which Lady Camper was a veteran.

General Ople entered into the gaieties of the neighbourhood once more, and passed through the Winter cheerfully. In justice to him, however, it should be said that to the intent dwelling of his mind upon Lady Camper, and not to the festive life he led, was due his entire ignorance of his daughter's unhappiness. She lived with him, and yet it was in other houses he learnt that she was unhappy. After his last interview with Lady Camper, he had informed Elizabeth of the ruinous and preposterous amount of money demanded of him for a settlement upon her: and Elizabeth, like the girl of good sense that she was, had replied immediately, "It could not be thought of, papa." He had spoken to Reginald likewise. The young man fell into a dramatic tearing-of-hair and long-stride fury, not ill becoming an enamoured dragoon. But he maintained that his aunt, though an eccentric, was a cordially kind woman. He seemed to feel, if he did not partly hint, that the General might have accepted Lady Camper's terms. The young officer could no longer be welcome at Douro Lodge, so the General paid him a morning call at his quarters, and was distressed to find him breakfasting very late, tapping eggs that he forgot to open—one of the surest signs of a young man downright and deep in love, as the General knew from experience— and surrounded by uncut sporting journals of past weeks, which dated from the day when his blow had struck him, as accurately as the watch of the drowned man marks his minute. Lady Camper had gone to Italy, and was in communication with her nephew: Reginald was not further explicit. His legs were very prominent in his despair, and his fingers frequently performed the part of blunt combs; consequently the General was impressed by his passion for Elizabeth. The girl who, if she as often meditative, always met his eyes with a smile, and quietly said "Yes, papa," and "No, papa," gave him little concern as to the state of her feelings. Yet everybody said now that she was unhappy. Mrs. Barcop, the widow, raised her voice above the rest. So attentive was she to Elizabeth that the General had it kindly suggested to him, that someone was courting him through his daughter. He gazed at the widow. Now she was not much past thirty; and it was really singular— he could have laughed—thinking of Mrs. Barcop set him persistently thinking of Lady Camper. That is to say, his mad fancy reverted from the lady of perhaps thirty-five to the lady of seventy! Such, thought he, is genius in a woman! Of his neighbours generally, Mrs. Baerens, the wife of a German merchant, an exquisite player on the pianoforte, was the most inclined to lead him to speak of Lady Camper. She was a kind prattling woman, and was known to have been a governess before her charms withdrew the gastronomic Gottfried Baerens from his devotion to the well-served City Club, where, as he exclaimed (ever turning fondly to his wife as he vocalized the compliment), he had found every necessity, every luxury, in life, "as you cannot have dem out of London—all save de female!" Mrs. Baerens, a lady of Teutonic extraction, was distinguishable as of that sex; at least, she was not masculine. She spoke with great respect of Lady Camper and her family, and seemed to agree in the General's eulogies of Lady Camper's constitution. Still he thought she eyed him strangely.

One April morning the General received a letter with the Italian postmark. Opening it with his usual calm and happy curiosity, he perceived that it was composed of pen-and-ink drawings. And suddenly his heart sank like a scuttled ship. He saw himself the victim of a caricature.

The first sketch had merely seemed picturesque, and he supposed it a clever play of fancy by some travelling friend, or perhaps an actual scene slightly exaggerated. Even on reading, "A distant view of the city of Wilsonople," he was only slightly enlightened. His heart beat still with befitting regularity. But the second and the third sketches betrayed the terrible hand. The distant view of the city of Wilsonople was fair with glittering domes, which, in the succeeding near view, proved to have been soap-bubbles, for place of extreme flatness, begirt with crazy old-fashioned fortifications, was shown; and in the third view, representing the interior, stood for sole place of habitation, a sentry-box.

Most minutely drawn, and, alas! with fearful accuracy, a military gentleman in undress occupied the box. Not a doubt could exist as to the person it was meant to be.

The General tried hard to remain incredulous. He remembered too well who had called him Wilsonople.

But here as the extraordinary thing that sent him over the neighbourhood canvassing for exclamations: on the fourth page was the outline of a lovely feminine hand, holding a pen, as in the act of shading, and under it these words: *"What I say is, I say I think it exceedingly unladylike."*

Now consider the General's feelings when, turning to this fourth page, having these very words in his mouth, as the

accurate expression of his thoughts, he discovered them written!

An enemy who anticipates the actions of our mind has a
quality of the malignant divine that may well inspire terror.
The senses of General Ople were struck by the aspect of a
lurid Goddess, who penetrated him, read him through, and
had both power and will to expose and make him ridiculous
for ever.

The loveliness of the hand, too, in a perplexing manner
contested his denunciation of her conduct. It was ladylike
eminently, and it involved him in a confused mixture of the
moral and material, as great as young people are known to
feel when they make the attempt to separate them, in one of
their frenzies.

With a petty bitter laugh he folded the letter, put it in his
breast-pocket, and sallied forth for a walk, chiefly to talk to
himself about it. But as it absorbed him entirely, he showed
it to the rector, whom he met, and what the rector said is of
no consequence, for General Ople listened to no remarks,
calling in succession on the Pollingtons, the Goslings, the
Baerens', and others, early though it was, and the lords of
those houses absent amassing hoards; and to the ladies everywhere he displayed the sketches he had received, observing,
that Wilsonople meant himself; and there he was, he said,
pointing at the capped fellow in the sentry-box, done unmistakably. The likeness indeed was remarkable. "She is a woman
of genius," he ejaculated, with utter melancholy. Mrs. Baerens, by the aid of a magnifying glass, assisted him to read a
line under the sentry-box, that he had taken for a mere trembling dash; it ran, *A gentlemanly residence.*

"What eyes she has!" the General exclaimed; "I say it is
miraculous what eyes she has at her time of . . . I was saying,
I should never have known it was writing."

He sighed heavily. His shuddering sensitiveness to caricature was increased by a certain evident dread of the hand which
struck; the knowing that he was absolutely bare to this woman,
defenceless, open to exposure in his little whims, foibles,
tricks, incompetencies, in what lay in his heart, and the words
that would come to his tongue. He felt like a man haunted.

So deeply did he feel the blow, that people asked how it
was that he could be so foolish as to dance about assisting
Lady Camper in her efforts to make him ridiculous; he acted
the parts of publisher and agent for the fearful caricaturist.
In truth, there was a strangely double reason for his conduct;

he danced about for sympathy, he had the intensest craving for sympathy, but more than this, or quite as much, he desired to have the powers of his enemy widely appreciated; in the first place, that he might be excused to himself for wincing under them, and secondly, because an awful admiration of her, that should be deepened by a corresponding sentiment around him, helped him to enjoy luxurious recollections of an hour when he was near making her his own—his own, in the holy abstract contemplation of marriage, without realizing their probable relative conditions after the ceremony.

"I say, that is the very image of her ladyship's hand," he was especially fond of remarking, "I say it is a beautiful hand."

He carried the letter in his pocket-book; and beginning to fancy that she had done her worst, for he could not imagine an inventive malignity capable of pursuing the theme, he spoke of her treatment of him with compassionate regret, not badly assumed from being partly sincere.

Two letters dated in France, the one Dijon, the other Fontainebleau, arrived together; and as the General knew Lady Camper to be returning to England, he expected that she was anxious to excuse herself to him. His fingers were not so confident, for he tore one of the letters to open it.

The City of Wilsonople was recognizable immediately. So likewise was the sole inhabitant.

General Ople's petty bitter laugh recurred, like a weak-chested patient's cough in the shifting of our winds eastward.

A faceless woman's shadow kneels on the ground near the sentry-box, weeping. A faceless shadow of a young man on horseback is beheld galloping toward a gulf. The sole inhabitant contemplates his largely substantial full fleshed face and figure in a glass.

Next, we see the standard of Great Britain furled; next, unfurled and borne by a troop of shadows to the sentry-box. The officer within says, "I say I should be very happy to carry it, but I cannot quit this gentlemanly residence."

Next, the standard is shown assailed by popguns. Several of the shadows are prostrate. "I was saying, I assure you that nothing but this gentlemanly residence prevents me from heading you," says the gallant officer.

General Ople trembled with protestant indignation when he saw himself reclining in a magnified sentry-box, while detachments of shadows hurry to him to show him the standard of his country trailing in the dust; and he is maliciously made to say, "I dislike responsibility. I say I am a fervent patriot, and very fond of my comforts, but I shun responsibility."

The second letter contained scenes between Wilsonople and the Moon.

He addresses her as his neighbour, and tells her of his triumphs over the sex.

He requests her to inform him whether she is a "female," that she may be triumphed over.

He hastens past her window on foot, with his head bent, just as the General had been in the habit of walking.

He drives a mouse-pony furiously by.

He cuts down a tree, that she may peep through.

Then, from the Moon's point of view, Wilsonople, a Silenus, is discerned in an arm-chair winking at a couple too plainly pouting their lips for a doubt of their intentions to be entertained.

A fourth letter arrived, bearing date of Paris. This one illustrated Wilsonople's courtship of the Moon, and ended with his "saying," in his peculiar manner, *In spite of her paint I could not have conceived her age to be so enormous.*

How break off his engagement with the Lady Moon? Consent to none of her terms!

Little used as he was to read behind a veil, acuteness of suffering sharpened the General's intelligence to a degree that sustained him in animated dialogue with each succeeding sketch, or poisoned arrow whirring at him from the moment his eyes rested on it; and here are a few samples:—

"Wilsonople informs the Moon that she is 'sweetly pretty.'

He thanks her with 'thanks' for a handsome piece of lunar green cheese.

He points to her, apparently telling some one, 'my lady-friend.'

He sneezes 'Bijou! bijou! bijou!' "

They were trifles, but they attacked his habits of speech; and he began to grow more and more alarmingly absurd in each fresh caricature of his person.

He looked at himself as the malicious woman's hand had shaped him. It was unjust; it was no resemblance—and yet it was! There was a corner of likeness left that leavened the lump; henceforth he must walk abroad with this distressing image of himself before his eyes, instead of the satisfactory reflex of the man who had, and was happy in thinking that he had, done mischief in his time. Such an end for a conquering man was too pathetic.

The General surprised himself talking to himself in something louder than a hum at neighbours' dinner-tables. He looked about and noticed that people were silently watching him.

CHAPTER VII

Lady Camper's return was the subject of speculation in the neighbourhood, for most people thought she would cease to persecute the General with her preposterous and unwarrantable pen-and-ink sketches when living so closely proximate; and how he would behave was the question. Those who made a hero of him were sure he would treat her with disdain. Others were uncertain. He had been so severely hit that it seemed possible he would not show much spirit.

He, for his part, had come to entertain such dread of the post, that Lady Camper's return relieved him of his morning apprehensions; and he would have forgiven her, though he feared to see her, if only she had promised to leave him in peace for the future. He feared to see her, because of the too probable furnishing of fresh matter for her ladyship's hand. Of course he could not avoid being seen by her, and that was a particular misery. A gentlemanly humility, or demureness of aspect, when seen, would, he hoped, disarm his enemy. It should, he thought. He had borne unheard-of things. No one of his friends and acquaintances knew, they could not know, what he had endured. It had caused him fits of stammering. It had destroyed the composure of his gait. Elizabeth had informed him that he talked to himself incessantly, and aloud. She, poor child, looked pale too. She was evidently anxious about him.

Young Rolles, whom he had met now and then, persisted in praising his aunt's good heart. So, perhaps, having satiated her revenge, she might now be inclined for peace, on the terms of distant civility.

"Yes! poor Elizabeth!" sighed the General, in pity of the poor girl's disappointment; "poor Elizabeth! she little guesses what her father has gone through. Poor child! I say, she hasn't an idea of my sufferings."

General Ople delivered his card at Lady Camper's lodge gates, and escaped to his residence in a state of prickly heat that required the brushing of his hair with hard brushes for several minutes to comfort and re-establish him.

He had fallen to working in his garden, when Lady Camper's card was brought to him an hour after the delivery of his own; a pleasing promptitude, showing signs of repentance, and suggesting to the General instantly some sharp sarcasms upon women, which he had come upon in quotations in the papers and the pulpit, his two main sources of information.

Instead of handing back the card to the maid, he stuck it in his hat and went on digging.

The first of a series of letters containing shameless realistic caricatures was handed to him the afternoon following. They came fast and thick. Not a day's interval of grace was allowed. Niobe under the shafts of Diana was hardly less violently and mortally assailed. The deadliness of the attack lay in the ridicule of the daily habits of one of the most sensitive of men, as to his personal appearance, and the opinion of the world. He might have concealed the sketches, but he could not have concealed the bruises, and people were perpetually asking the unhappy General what he was saying, for he spoke to himself as if he were repeating something to them for the tenth time.

"I say," said he, "I say that for a lady, really an educated lady, to sit, as she must—I was saying, she must have sat in an attic to have the right view of me. And there you see— this is what she has done. This is the last, this is the afternoon's delivery. Her ladyship has me correctly as to costume, but I could not exhibit such a sketch to ladies."

A back view of the General was displayed in his act of digging.

"I say I could not allow ladies to see it," he informed the gentlemen, who were suffered to inspect it freely.

"But you see, I have no means of escape; I am at her mercy from morning to night," the General said, with a quivering tongue, "unless I stay at home inside the house; and that is death to me, or unless I abandon the place, and my lease; and I shall—I say, I shall find nowhere in England for anything like the money or conveniences such a gent—a residence you would call fit for a gentleman. I call it a bi . . . it is, in short, a gem. But I shall have to go."

Young Rolles offered to expostulate with his aunt Angela.

The General said, "Tha . . . I thank you very much. I would not have her ladyship suppose I am so susceptible. I hardly know," he confessed pitiably, "what it is right to say, and what not—what not. I—I—I never know when I am not looking a fool. I hurry from tree to tree to shun the light. I am seriously affected in my appetite. I say, I shall have to go."

Reginald gave him to understand that if he flew, the shafts would follow him, for Lady Camper would never forgive his running away, and was quite equal to publishing a book of the adventures of Wilsonople.

Sunday afternoon, walking in the park with his daughter on his arm, General Ople met Mr. Rolles. He saw that the young man and Elizabeth were mortally pale, and as the very idea of wretchedness directed his attention to himself, he addressed them conjointly on the subject of his persecution, giving neither of them a chance of speaking until they were constrained to part.

A sketch was the consequence, in which a withered Cupid and a fading Psyche were seen divided by Wilsonople, who keeps them forcibly asunder with policeman's fists, while courteously and elegantly entreating them to hear him. "Meet," he tells them, "as often as you like, in my company, so long as you listen to me;" and the pathos of his aspect makes hungry demand for a sympathetic audience.

Now, this, and not the series representing the martyrdom of the old couple at Douro Lodge Gates, whose rigid frames bore witness to the close packing of a gentlemanly residence, this was the sketch General Ople, in his madness from the pursuing bite of the gadfly, handed about at Mrs. Pollington's lawn-party. Some have said, that he should not have betrayed his daughter; but it is reasonable to suppose he had no idea of his daughter's being the Psyche. Or if he had, it was indistinct, owing to the violence of his personal emotion. Assuming this to have been the very sketch; he handed it to two or three ladies in turn, and was heard to deliver himself at intervals in the following snatches: "As you like, my lady, as you like; strike, I say strike; I bear it; I say I bear it. . . . If her ladyship is unforgiving, I say I am enduring. . . . I may go, I was saying I may go mad, but while I have my reason I walk upright, I walk upright."

Mr. Pollington and certain City gentlemen hearing the poor General's renewed soliloquies, were seized with disgust of Lady Camper's conduct, and stoutly advised an application to the Law Courts.

He gave ear to them abstractedly, but after pulling out the whole chapter of the caricatures (which it seemed that he kept in a case of morocco leather in his breast-pocket), showing them, with comments on them; and observing, "There will be more, there must be more, I say I am sure there are things I do that her ladyship will discover and expose," he declined to seek redress or simple protection; and the miserable spectacle was exhibited soon after of this courtly man listening to Mrs. Barcop on the weather, and replying in acquiescence: "It is hot.—If your ladyship will only abstain from colours. Very hot as you say, madam,—I do not complain of pen and ink, but I would rather escape colours. And I dare say you find it hot too?"

Mrs. Barcop shut her eyes and sighed over the wreck of a handsome military officer.

She asked him: "What is your objection to colours?"

His hand was at his breast-pocket immediately, as he said: "Have you not seen?"—though but a few minutes back he had shown her the contents of the packet, including a hurried glance of the famous digging scene.

By this time the entire district was in fervid sympathy with General Ople. The ladies did not, as their lords did, proclaim astonishment that a man should suffer a woman to goad him to a state of semi-lunacy; but one or two confessed to their husbands, that it required a great admiration of General Ople not to despise him, both for his susceptibility and his patience. As for the men, they knew him to have faced the balls in bellowing battle-strife; they knew him to have endured privation, not only cold but downright want of food and drink—an almost unimaginable horror to these brave daily feasters; so they could not quite look on him in contempt; but his want of sense was offensive, and still more so his submission to a scourging by a woman. Not one of them would have deigned to feel it. Would they have allowed her to see that she could sting them? They would have laughed at her. Or they would have dragged her before a magistrate.

It was a Sunday in early Summer when General Ople walked to morning service, unaccompanied by Elizabeth, who was unwell. The church was of the considerate old-fashioned order, with deaf square pews, permitting the mind to abstract itself from the sermon, or wrestle at leisure with the difficulties presented by the preacher, as General Ople often did, feeling not a little in love with his sincere attentiveness for grappling with the knotty point and partially allowing the struggle to be seen.

The Church was, besides, a sanctuary for him. Hither his enemy did not come. He had this one place of refuge, and he almost looked a happy man again.

He had passed into his hat and out of it, which he habitually did standing, when who should walk up to within a couple of yards of him but Lady Camper. Her pew was full of poor people, who made signs of retiring. She signified to them that they were to sit, then quietly took her seat among them, fronting the General across the aisle.

During the sermon a low voice, sharp in contradistinction to the monotone of the preacher's, was heard to repeat these words: "I say I am not sure I shall survive it." Considerable muttering in the same quarter was heard besides.

After the customary ceremonious game, when all were free to move, of nobody liking to move first, Lady Camper and a charity boy were the persons who took the lead. But Lady Camper could not quit her pew, owing to the sticking of the door. She smiled as with her pretty hand she twice or thrice essayed to shake it open. General Ople strode to her aid. He pulled the door, gave the shadow of a respectful bow, and no doubt he would have withdrawn, had not Lady Camper, while acknowledging the civility, placed her Prayer-book in his hands to carry at her heels. There was no choice for him. He made a sort of slipping dance back for his hat, and followed her lady-ship. All present being eager to witness the spectacle, the passage of Lady Camper dragging the victim General behind her was observed without a stir of the well-dressed members of the congregation, until a desire overcame them to see how Lady Camper would behave to her fish when she had him outside the sacred edifice.

None could have imagined such a scene. Lady Camper was in her carriage; General Ople was holding her Prayer-book, hat in hand at the carriage step, and he looked as if he were toasting before the bars of a furnace; for while he stood there, Lady Camper was rapidly pencilling outlines in a small pocket sketch-book. There are dogs whose shyness is put to it to endure human observation and a direct address to them, even on the part of their masters; and these dear simple dogs wag tail and turn their heads aside waveringly, as though to entreat you not to eye them and talk to them so. General Ople, in the presence of the sketch-book, was much like the nervous animal. He would fain have run away. He glanced at it, and round about, and again at it, and at the heavens. Her lady-ship's cruelty, and his inexplicable submission to it, were witnessed of the multitude.

The General's friends walked very slowly. Lady Camper's carriage whirled by, and the General came up with them, accosting them and himself alternately. They asked him where

Elizabeth was, and he replied, "Poor child, yes! I am told she is pale, but I cannot believe I am so perfectly, I say so perfectly ridiculous when I join the responses." He drew forth half a dozen sheets, and showed them sketches that Lady Camper had taken in church, caricaturing him in the sitting down and the standing up. She had torn them out of the book, and presented them to him when driving off. "I was saying, worship in the ordinary sense will be interdicted to me if her lady-ship . . . ," said the General, woefully shuffling the sketchpaper sheets in which he figured.

He made the following odd confession to Mr. and Mrs. Gosling on the road:—that he had gone to his chest, and taken out his sword-belt to measure his girth, and found himself thinner than when he left the service, which had not been the case before his attendance at the last levée of the foregoing season. So the deduction was obvious, that Lady Camper had reduced him. She had reduced him as effectually as a harassing siege.

"But why do you pay atention to her? Why! . . ," exclaimed Mr. Gosling, a gentleman of the City, whose roundness would have turned a rifle-shot.

"To allow her to wound you so seriously!" exclaimed Mrs. Gosling.

"Madam, if she were my wife," the General explained, "I should feel it. I say it is the fact of it; I feel it, if I appear so extremely ridiculous to a human eye, to any one eye."

"To Lady Camper's eye!"

He admitted it might be that. He had not thought of ascribing the acuteness of his pain to the miserable image he presented in this particular lady's eye. No; it really was true, curiously true: another lady's eye might have transformed him to a pumpkin shape, exaggerated all his foibles fifty-fold, and he, though not liking it, of course not, would yet have preserved a certain manly equanimity. How was it Lady Camper had such power over him?—a lady concealing seventy years with a rouge-box or paint-pot! It was witchcraft in its worst character. He had for six months at her bidding been actually living the life of a beast, degraded in his own esteem; scorched by every laugh he heard; running, pursued, overtaken, and as it were scored or branded, and then let go for the process to be repeated.

CHAPTER VIII

Our young barbarians have it all their own way with us when
they fall into love-liking; they lead us whither they please,
and interest us in their wishings, their weepings, and that fine
performance, their kissings. But when we see our veterans
tottering to their fall, we scarcely consent to their having a
wish; as for a kiss, we halloo at them if we discover them on
a byway to the sacred grove where such things are supposed
to be done by the venerable. And this piece of rank injustice,
not to say impoliteness, is entirely because of an unsound
opinion that Nature is not in it, as though it were our esteem
for Nature which caused us to disrespect them. They, in truth,
show her to us discreet, civilized, in a decent moral aspect:
vistas of real life, views of the mind's eye, are opened by
their touching little emotions; whereas those bully youngsters
who come bellowing at us and catch us by the senses plainly
prove either that we are no better than they, or that we give
our attention to Nature only when she makes us afraid of
her. If we cared for her, we should be up and after her rev-
erentially in her sedater steps, deeply studying her in her
slower paces. She teaches them nothing when they are whirl-
ing. Our closest instructors, the true philosophers—the story-
tellers, in short—will learn in time that Nature is not of necessity always roaring, and as soon as they do, the world may
be said to be enlightened. Meantime, in the contemplation
of a pair of white whiskers fluttering round a pair of manifestly
painted cheeks, be assured that Nature is in it: not that hec-
toring wanton—but let the young have their fun. Let the
superior interest of the passions of the aged be conceded,
and not a word shall be said against the young.

If, then, Nature is in it, how has she been made active?
The reason of her launch upon this last adventure is, that she
has perceived the person who can supply the virtue known
to her by experience to be wanting. Thus, in the broader
instance, many who have journeyed far down the road, turn
back to the worship of youth, which they have lost. Some are
for the graceful worldliness of wit, of which they have just
share enough to admire it. Some are captivated by hands that
can wield the rod, which in earlier days they escaped to their
cost. In the case of General Ople, it was partly her whippings
of him, partly her penetration; her ability, that sat so finely
on a wealthy woman, her indifference to conventional manners, that so well beseemed a nobly-born one, and more than

all, her correction of his little weaknesses and incompetencies, in spite of his dislike of it, won him. He began to feel a sort of nibbling pleasure in her grotesque sketches of his person; a tendency to recur to the old ones while dreading the arrival of new. You hear old gentlemen speak fondly of the swish; and they are not attached to pain, but the instrument revives their feeling of youth; and General Ople half enjoyed, while shrinking, Lady Camper's foregone outlines of him. For in the distance, the whip's-end may look like a clinging caress instead of a stinging flick. But this craven melting in his heart was rebuked by a very worthy pride, that flew for support to the injury she had done to his devotions, and the offence to the sacred edifice. After thinking over it, he decided that he must quit his residence; and as it appeared to him in the light of duty, he, with an unspoken anguish, commissioned the house-agent of his town to sell his lease or let the house furnished, without further parley.

From the house-agent's shop he turned into the chemist's, for a tonic—a foolish proceeding, for he had received bracing enough in the blow he had just dealt himself, but he had been cogitating on tonics recently, imagining certain valiant effects of them, with visions of a former careless happiness that they were likely to restore. So he requested to have the tonic strong, and he took one glass of it over the counter.

Fifteen minutes after the draught, he came in sight of his house, and beholding it, he could have called it a gentlemanly residence aloud under Lady Camper's windows, his insurgency was of such violence. He talked of it incessantly, but forbore to tell Elizabeth, as she was looking pale, the reason why its modest merits touched him so. He longed for the hour of his next dose, and for a caricature to follow, that he might drink and defy it. A caricature was really due to him, he thought; otherwise why had he abandoned his bijou dwelling? Lady Camper, however, sent none. He had to wait a fortnight before one came, and that was rather a likeness, and a handsome likeness, except as regarded a certain disorderliness in his dress, which he knew to be very unlike him. Still it despatched him to the looking-glass, to bring that verifier of facts in evidence against the sketch. While sitting there he heard the housemaid's knock at the door, and the strange intelligence that his daughter was with Lady Camper, and had left word that she hoped he would not forget his engagement to go to Mrs. Baerens' lawn-party.

The General jumped away from the glass, shouting at the

absent Elizabeth in a fit of wrath so foreign to him, that he returned hurriedly to have another look at himself, and exclaimed at the pitch of his voice, "I say I attribute it to an indigestion of that tonic. Do you hear?" The housemaid faintly answered outside the door that she did, alarming him, for there seemed to be confusion somewhere. His hope was that no one would mention Lady Camper's name, for the mere thought of her caused a rush to his head. "I believe I am in for a touch of apoplexy," he said to the rector, who greeted him, in advance of the ladies, on Mr. Baerens' lawn. He said it smilingly, but wanting some show of sympathy, instead of the whisper and meaningless hand at his clerical band, with which the rector responded, he cried, "Apoplexy," and his friend seemed then to understand, and disappeared among the ladies.

Several of them surrounded the General, and one inquired whether the series was being continued. He drew forth his pocket-book, handed her the latest, and remarked on the gross injustice of it; for, as he requested them to take note, her ladyship now sketched him as a person inattentive to his dress, and she begged them to observe that she had drawn him with his necktie hanging loose. "And that, I say that has never been known of me since I first entered society."

The ladies exchanged looks of profound concern; for the fact was, the General had come without any necktie and any collar, and he appeared to be unaware of the circumstance. The rector had told them, that in answer to a hint he had dropped on the subject of neckties, General Ople expressed a slight apprehension of apoplexy; but his careless or merely partial observance of the laws of buttonment could have nothing to do with such fears. They signified rather a disorder of the intelligence. Elizabeth was condemned for leaving him to go about alone. The situation was really most painful, for a word to so sensitive a man would drive him away in shame and for good; and still, to let him parade the ground in the state, compared with his natural self, of scarecrow, and with the dreadful habit of talking to himself quite raging, was a horrible alternative. Mrs. Baerens at last directed her husband upon the General, trembling as though she watched for the operations of a fish torpedo; and other ladies shared her excessive anxiousness, for Mr. Baerens had the manner and the look of artillery, and on this occasion carried a surcharge of powder.

The General bent his ear to Mr. Baerens, whose German-

English and repeated remark, "I am to do it wid delicassy," did not assist his comprehension; and when he might have been enlightened, he was petrified by seeing Lady Camper walk on the lawn with Elizabeth. The great lady stood a moment beside Mrs. Baerens; she came straight over to him, contemplating him in silence.

Then she said, "Your arm, General Ople," and she made one circuit of the lawn with him, barely speaking.

At her request, he conducted her to her carriage. He took a seat beside her, obediently. He felt that he was being sketched, and comported himself like a child's flat man, that jumps at the pulling of a string.

"Where have you left your girl, General?"

Before he could rally his wits to answer the question, he was asked:

"And what have you done with your necktie and collar?"

He touched his throat.

"I am rather nervous to-day, I forgot Elizabeth," he said, sending his fingers in a dotting run of wonderment round his neck.

Lady Camper smiled with a triumphing humour on her close-drawn lips.

The verified absence of necktie and collar seemed to be choking him.

"Never mind, you have been abroad without them," said Lady Camper, "and that is a victory for me. And you thought of Elizabeth first when I drew your attention to it, and that is a victory for you. It is a very great victory. Pray, do not be dismayed, General. You have a handsome campaigning air. And no apologies, if you please; I like you well enough as you are. There is my hand."

General Ople understood her last remark. He pressed the lady's hand in silence, very nervously.

"But do not shrug your head into your shoulders as if there were any possibility of concealing the thunderingly evident," said Lady Camper, electrifying him, what with her cordial squeeze, her kind eyes, and her singular language. "You have omitted the collar. Well? The collar is the fatal finishing touch in men's dress; it would make Apollo look bourgeois."

Her hand was in his: and watching the play of her features, a spark entered General Ople's brain, causing him, in forgetfulness of collar and caricatures, to ejaculate, "Seventy? Did your ladyship say seventy? Utterly impossible! You trifled with me."

"We will talk when we are free of this accompaniment of carriage-wheels, General," said Lady Camper.

"I will beg permission to go and fetch Elizabeth, madam."

"Rightly thought of. Fetch her in my carriage. And, by the way, Mrs. Baerens was my old music-mistress, and is, I think, one year older than I. She can tell you on which side of seventy I am."

"I shall not require to ask, my lady," he said, sighing.

"Then we will send the carriage for Elizabeth, and have it out together at once. I am impatient; yes, General, impatient: for what?—forgiveness."

"Of me, my lady?" The General breathed profoundly.

"Of whom else? Do you know what it is?—I don't think you do. You English have the smallest experience of humanity. I mean this: to strike so hard that, in the end, you soften your heart to the victim. Well, that is my weakness. And we of our blood put no restraint on the blows we strike when we think them wanted, so we are always overdoing it."

General Ople assisted Lady Camper to alight from the carriage, which was forthwith despatched for Elizabeth.

He prepared to listen to her with a disconnected smile of acute attentiveness.

She had changed. She spoke of money. Ten thousand pounds must be settled on his daughter. "And now," said she, "you will remember that you are wanting a collar."

He acquiesced. He craved permission to retire for ten minutes.

"Simplest of men! what will cover you?" she exclaimed, and peremptorily bidding him sit down in the drawing-room, she took one of the famous pair of pistols in her hand, and said, "If I put myself in a similar position, and make myself *décolletée* too, will that satisfy you? You see these murderous weapons. Well, I am a coward. I dread fire-arms. They are laid there to impose on the world, and I believe they do. They have imposed on you. Now, you would never think of pretending to a moral quality you do not possess. But, silly, simple man that you are! You can give yourself the airs of wealth, buy horses to conceal your nakedness, and when you are taken upon the standard of your apparent income, you would rather seem to be beating a miserly retreat than behave frankly and honestly. I have a little overstated it, but I am near the mark."

"Your ladyship wanting courage!" cried the General.

"Refresh yourself by meditating on it," said she. "And to

prove it to you, I was glad to take this house when I knew I was to have a gallant gentleman for a neighbour. No visitors will be admitted, General Ople, so you are bare-throated only to me: sit quietly. One day you speculated on the paint in my cheeks for the space of a minute and a half:—I had said that I freckled easily. Your look signified that you really could not detect a single freckle for the paint. I forgave you, or I did not. But when I found you, on closer acquaintance, as indifferent to your daughter's happiness as you had been to her reputation . . ."

"My daughter! her reputation! her happiness!" General Ople raised his eyes under a wave, half uttering the outcries.

"So indifferent to her reputation, that you allowed a young man to talk with her over the wall, and meet her by appointment: so reckless of the girl's happiness, that when I tried to bring you to a treaty, on her behalf, you could not be dragged from thinking of yourself and your own affair. When I found that, perhaps I was predisposed to give you some of what my sisters used to call my spice. You would not honestly state the proportions of your income, and you affected to be faithful to the woman of seventy. Most preposterous! Could any caricature of mine exceed in grotesqueness your sketch of yourself? You are a brave and a generous man all the same: and I suspect it is more hoodwinking than egotism—or extreme egotism—that blinds you. A certain amount you must have to be a man. You did not like my paint, still less did you like my sincerity; you were annoyed by my corrections of your habits of speech; you were horrified by the age of seventy, and you were credulous—General Ople, listen to me, and remember that you have no collar on!—you were credulous of my statement of my great age, or you chose to be so, or chose to seem so, because I had brushed your cat's coat against the fur. And then, full of yourself, not thinking of Elizabeth, but to withdraw in the chivalrous attitude of the man true to his word to the old woman, only stickling to bring a certain independence to the common stock, because—I quote you! and you have no collar on, mind—'you could not be at your wife's mercy,' you broke from your proposal on the money question. Where was your consideration for Elizabeth then?

"Well, General, you were fond of thinking yourself, and I thought I would assist you. I gave you plenty of subject matter. I will not say I meant to work a homœopathic cure. But if I drive you to forget your collar, is it or is it not a triumph?

"No," added Lady Camper, "it is no triumph for me, but

it is one for you, if you like to make the most of it. Your fault has been to quit active service, General, and love your ease too well. It is the fault of your countrymen. You must get a militia regiment, or inspectorship of militia. You are ten times the man in exercise. Why, do you mean to tell me that you would have cared for those drawings of mine when marching?"

"I think so, I say I think so," remarked the General seriously.

"I doubt it," said she. "But to the point; here comes Elizabeth. If you have not much money to spare for her, according to your prudent calculation, reflect how this money has enfeebled you and reduced you to the level of the people round about us here—who are, what? Inhabitants of gentlemanly residences, yes! But what kind of creature? They have no mental standard, no moral aim, no native chivalry. You were rapidly becoming one of them, only, fortunately for you, you were sensitive to ridicule."

"Elizabeth shall have half my money settled on her," said the General; "though I fear it is not much. And if I can find occupation, my lady . . ."

"Something worthier than *that*," said Lady Camper, pencilling outlines rapidly on the margin of a book, and he saw himself lashing a pony; "or *that*," and he was plucking at a cabbage; "or *that*," and he was bowing to three petticoated posts.

"The likeness is exact," General Ople groaned.

"So you may suppose I have studied you," said she. "But there is no real likeness. Slight exaggerations did more harm to truth than reckless violations of it. You would not have cared one bit for a caricature, if you had not nursed the absurd idea of being one of our conquerors. It is the very tragedy of modesty for a man like you to have such notions, my poor dear good friend. The modest are the most easily intoxicated when they sip at vanity. And reflect whether you have not been intoxicated, for these young people have been wretched, and you have not observed it, though one of them was living with you, and is the child you love. There, I have done. Pray show a good face to Elizabeth."

The General obeyed as well as he could. He felt very like a sheep that has come from a shearing, and when released he wished to run away. But hardly had he escaped before he had a desire for the renewal of the operation. "She sees me through, she sees me through," he was heard saying to himself, and in the end he taught himself to say it with a secret exultation, for as it was on her part an extraordinary piece of insight to see him through, it struck him that in acknowledging the truth of it, he made a discovery of new powers in human nature.

General Ople studied Lady Camper diligently for fresh proofs of her penetration of the mysteries in his bosom; by which means, as it happened that she was diligently observing the two betrothed young ones, he began to watch them likewise, and took a pleasure in the sight. Their meetings, their partings, their rides out and home furnished him themes of converse. He soon had enough to talk of, and previously, as he remembered, he had never sustained a conversation of any length with composure and the beneficent sense of fulness. Five thousand pounds, to which sum Lady Camper reduced her stipulation for Elizabeth's dowry, he signed over to his dear girl gladly, and came out with the confession to her ladyship that a well-invested twelve thousand comprised his fortune. She shrugged: she had left off pulling him this way and that, so his chains were enjoyable, and he said to himself: "If ever she should in the dead of night want a man to defend her!" He mentioned it to Reginald, who had been the repository of Elizabeth's lamentations about her father being left alone, forsaken, and the young man conceived a scheme for causing his aunt's great bell to be rung at midnight, which would certainly have led to a dramatic issue and the happy re-establishment of our masculine ascendancy at the close of this history. But he forgot it in his bridegroom's delight, until he was making his miserable official speech at the wedding-breakfast, and set Elizabeth winking over a tear. As she stood in the hall ready to depart, a great van was observed in the road at the gates of Douro Lodge; and this, the men in custody declared to contain the goods and knick-knacks of the people who had taken the house furnished for a year, and were coming in that very afternoon.

"I remember, I say now I remember, I had a notice," the General said cheerily to his troubled daughter.

"But where are you to go, papa?" the poor girl cried, close on sobbing.

"I shall get employment of some sort," said he. "I was saying I want it, I need it, I require it!"

"You are saying three times what once would have sufficed for," said Lady Camper, and she asked him a few questions, frowned with a smile, and offered him a lodgement in his neighbour's house.

"Really, dearest Aunt Angela?" said Elizabeth.

"What else can I do, child? I have, it seems, driven him out of a gentlemanly residence, and I must give him a ladylike one. True, I would rather have had him at call, but as I have always wished for a policeman in the house, I may as well be satisfied with a soldier."

"But if you lose your character, my lady?" said Reginald.

"Then I must look to the General to restore it."

General Ople immediately bowed his head over Lady Camper's fingers.

"An odd thing to happen to a woman of forty-one!" she said to her great people, and they submitted with the best grace in the world, while the General's ears tingled till he felt younger than Reginald. This, his reflections ran, or it would be more correct to say waltzed, this is the result of painting!—that you can believe a woman to be any age when her cheeks are tinted.

As for Lady Camper, she had been floated accidentally over the ridicule of the bruit of a marriage at a time of life as terrible to her as her fiction of seventy had been to General Ople; she resigned herself to let things go with the tide. She had not been blissful in her first marriage, she had abandoned the chase of an ideal man, and she had found one who was tuneable so as not to offend her ears, likely ever to be a fund of amusement for her humour, good, impressible, and above all, very picturesque. There is the secret of her, and of how it came to pass that a simple man and a complex woman fell to union after the strangest division.

Between Centuries

Thomas Hardy
(1840–1928)

Thomas Hardy was one of the great literary figures of the nine-teenth and early twentieth centuries. As a poet, he was the equal of Tennyson, Browning, and Arnold; as a novelist, he was in the rank of Dickens, Eliot, Thackeray, Trollope, and Meredith. Trained as an architect, Hardy did not begin to publish fiction until he was over thirty. Deeply influenced by Darwin, Hardy's work often demonstrates man as an alien figure in an indifferent universe; he would work out his philosophy most fully in his epic drama, The Dynasts, *written in 1903–8. His early fiction,* Desperate Remedies *(1871) and* A Pair of Blue Eyes *(1873), gained him little attention, but his fourth novel,* Far from the Madding Crowd, *in 1874, enabled him to leave architecture and devote himself to writing. In the same year, he married Emma Lavinia Gifford. With* The Return of the Native *in 1878, Hardy came into his characteristic fictional voice: a deep sense of place, the fictional Wessex; the use of folktales and folk traditions as a constant pressure on present behavior and activity; a loving regard for the land, even when it proves harsh and ungiving; an awareness of the disparity between man's wants and what the universe permits or provides in the way of gratification; the recognition of women as victims, especially when they attempt to expand their roles. While also writing poetry, Hardy published in the next fifteen years the novels on which his reputation rests:* The Mayor of Casterbridge *(1886),* The Wood-landers *(1887),* Tess of the D'Urbervilles *(1891), and* Jude the Obscure *(1896). When the latter novel was attacked for its sup-posed immorality and sexual explicitness, Hardy wrote no more long fiction and devoted himself to poetry. In 1912, when his wife died, he married Florence Emily Dugdale, a much younger woman and herself a writer of children's books. Volumes of poetry suc-ceeded each other in rapid sequence until his death:* Poems *(1898),* Poems of the Past and Present *(1902),* Time's Laughing-Stocks *(1909),* Satires of Circumstance *(1914),* Moments of Vision *(1917), and* Winter Words *(1928).*

The Three Strangers

Among the few features of agricultural England which retain an appearance but little modified by the lapse of centuries, may be reckoned the long, grassy and furzy downs, coombs, or ewe-leases, as they are called according to their kind, that fill a large area of certain counties in the south and south-west. If any mark of human occupation is met with hereon, it usually takes the form of the solitary cottage of some shepherd.

Fifty years ago such a lonely cottage stood on such a down, and may possibly be standing there now. In spite of its loneliness, however, the spot, by actual measurement, was not three miles from a county-town. Yet that affected it little. Three miles of irregular upland, during the long inimical seasons, with their sleets, snows, rains, and mists, afford withdrawing space enough to isolate a Timon or a Nebuchadnezzar; much less, in fair weather, to please that less repellent tribe, the poets, philosophers, artists, and others who "conceive and meditate of pleasant things."

Some old earthen camp or barrow, some clump of trees, at least some starved fragment of ancient hedge is usually taken advantage of in the erection of these forlorn dwellings. But, in the present case, such a kind of shelter had been disregarded. Higher Crowstairs, as the house was called, stood quite detached and undefended. The only reason for its precise situation seemed to be the crossing of two footpaths at right angles hard by, which may have crossed there and thus for a good five hundred years. Hence the house was exposed to the elements on all sides. But, though the wind up here blew unmistakably when it did blow, and the rain hit hard whenever it fell, the various weathers of the winter season were not quite so formidable on the down as they were imagined to be by dwellers on low ground. The raw rimes were not so pernicious as in the hollows, and the frosts were scarcely so severe. When the shepherd and his family who tenanted the house were pitied for their sufferings from the exposure, they said that upon the whole they were less inconvenienced by "wuzzes and flames" (hoarses and phlegms) than when they had lived by the stream of a snug neighbouring valley.

The night of March 28, 182–, was precisely one of the nights that were wont to call forth these expressions of commiseration. The level rainstorm smote walls, slope, and hedges like the clothyard shafts of Senlac and Crecy. Such sheep and outdoor animals as had no shelter stood with their buttocks to the winds; while the tails of little birds trying to roost on some scraggy thorn were blown inside-out like umbrellas. The gable-end of the cottage was stained with wet, and the eaves-droppings flapped against the wall. Yet never was commiseration for the shepherd more misplaced. For that cheerful rustic was entertaining a large party in glorification of the christening of his second girl.

The guests had arrived before the rain began to fall, and they were all now assembled in the chief or living room of the dwelling. A glance into the apartment at eight o'clock on this eventful evening would have resulted in the opinion that it was as cosy and comfortable a nook as could be wished for in boisterous weather. The calling of its inhabitant was proclaimed by a number of highly-polished sheep-crooks without stems that were hung ornamentally over the fireplace, the curl of each shining crook varying from the antiquated type engraved in the patriarchal pictures of old family Bibles to the most approved fashion of the last local sheep-fair. The room was lighted by half-a-dozen candles, having wicks only a trifle smaller than the grease which enveloped them, in candlesticks that were never used but at high-days, holy-days, and family feasts. The lights were scattered about the room, two of them standing on the chimney-piece. This position of candles was in itself significant. Candles on the chimney-piece always meant a party.

On the hearth, in front of a back-brand to give substance, blazed a fire of thorns, that crackled "like the laughter of the fool."

Nineteen persons were gathered here. Of these, five women, wearing gowns of various bright hues, sat in chairs along the wall; girls shy and not shy filled the window-bench; four men, including Charley Jake the hedge-carpenter, Elijah New the parish-clerk, and John Pitcher, a neighbouring dairyman, the shepherd's father-in-law, lolled in the settle; a young man and maid, who were blushing over tentative *pourparlers* on a life-companionship, sat beneath the corner-cupboard; and an elderly engaged man of fifty or upward moved restlessly about from spots where his betrothed was not to the spot where she was. Enjoyment was pretty general, and so much the more prevailed in being unhampered by conventional restrictions. Absolute confidence in each other's good opinion begat perfect ease, while the finishing stroke of manner, amounting to a truly princely serenity, was lent to the majority by the absence of any expression or trait denoting that they wished to get on in the world, enlarge their minds, or do any eclipsing thing whatever—which nowadays so generally nips the bloom and *bonhomie* of all except the two extremes of the social scale.

Shepherd Fennel had married well, his wife being a dairyman's daughter from a vale at a distance, who brought fifty guineas in her pocket—and kept them there, till they should be required for ministering to the needs of a coming family. This frugal woman had been somewhat exercised as to the character that should be given to the gathering. A sit-still party had its advantages; but an undistrubed position of ease in chairs and settles was apt to lead on the men to such an unconscionable deal of toping that they would sometimes fairly drink the house dry. A dancing-party was the alternative; but this, while avoiding the foregoing objection on the score of good drink, had a counter-balancing disadvantage in the matter of good victuals, the ravenous appetites engendered by the exercise causing immense havoc in the buttery. Shepherdess Fennel fell back upon the intermediate plan of mingling short dances with short periods of talk and singing, so as to hinder any ungovernable rage in either. But this scheme was entirely confined to her own gentle mind: the shepherd himself was in the mood to exhibit the most reckless phases of hospitality.

The fiddler was a boy of those parts, about twelve years of age, who had a wonderful dexterity in jigs and reels, though his fingers were so small and short as to necessitate a constant shifting for the high notes, from which he scrambled back to the first position with sounds not of unmixed purity of tone. At seven the shrill tweedle-dee of this youngster had begun, accompanied by a booming ground-bass from Elijah New, the parish-clerk, who had thoughtfully brought with him his favourite musical instrument, the serpent. Dancing was instantaneous, Mrs. Fennel privately enjoining the players on no account to let the dance exceed the length of a quarter of an hour.

But Elijah and the boy in the excitement of their position quite forgot the injunction. Moreover, Oliver Giles, a man of seventeen, one of the dancers, who was enamoured of his

partner, a fair girl of thirty-three rolling years, had recklessly
handed a new crown-piece to the musicians, as a bribe to
keep going as long as they had muscle and wind. Mrs. Fennel,
seeing the steam begin to generate on the countenances of
her guests, crossed over and touched the fiddler's elbow and
put her hand on the serpent's mouth. But they took no notice,
and fearing she might lose her character of genial hostess if
she were to interfere too markedly, she retired and sat down
helpless. And so the dance whizzed on with cumulative fury,
the performers moving in their planet-like courses, direct and
retrograde, from apogee to perigee, till the hand of the well-
kicked clock at the bottom of the room had travelled over
the circumference of an hour.

While these cheerful events were in course of enactment
within Fennel's pastoral dwelling, an incident having considerable bearing on the party had occurred in the gloomy night
without. Mrs. Fennel's concern about the growing fierceness
of the dance corresponded in point of time with the ascent
of a human figure to the solitary hill of Higher Crowstairs
from the direction of the distant town. This personage strode
on through the rain without a pause, following the little-worn
path which, further on in its course, skirted the shepherd's
cottage.

It was nearly the time of full moon, and on this account,
though the sky was lined with a uniform sheet of dripping
cloud, ordinary objects out of doors were readily visible. The
said wan light revealed the lonely pedestrian to be a man of
supple frame; his gait suggested that he had somewhat passed
the period of perfect and instinctive agility, though not so far
as to be otherwise than rapid of motion when occasion required. At a rough guess, he might have been about forty
years of age. He appeared tall, but a recruiting sergeant, or
other person accustomed to the judging of men's heights by
the eye, would have discerned that this was chiefly owing to
his gauntness, and that he was not more than five-feet-eight
or nine.

Notwithstanding the regularity of his tread there was caution in it, as in that of one who mentally feels his way; and
despite the fact that there was something about him which
suggested that he naturally belonged to the black-coated tribes
of men. His clothes were of fustian, and his boots hobnailed,
yet in his progress he showed not the mud-accustomed bearing of hobnailed and fustianed peasantry.

By the time that he had arrived abreast of the shepherd's

premises the rain came down, or rather came along, with yet
more determined violence. The outskirts of the little settlement partially broke the force of wind and rain, and this
induced him to stand still. The most salient of the shepherd's
domestic erections was an empty sty at the forward corner of
his hedgeless garden, for in these latitudes the principle of
masking the homelier features of your establishment by a
conventional frontage was unknown. The traveller's eye was
attracted to this small building by the pallid shine of the wet
slates that covered it. He turned aside, and, finding it empty,
stood under the pent-roof for shelter.

While he stood the boom of the serpent within the adjacent
house, and the lesser strains of the fiddler, reached the spot
as an accompaniment to the surging hiss of the flying rain on
the sod, its louder beating on the cabbage-leaves of the garden, on the straw hackles of eight or ten beehives just discernible by the path, and its dripping from the eaves into a
row of buckets and pans that had been placed under the walls
of the cottage. For at Higher Crowstairs, as at all such ele-
vated domiciles, the grand difficulty of housekeeping was an
insufficiency of water; and a casual rainfall was utilized by
turning out, as catchers, every utensil that the house contained. Some queer stories might be told of the contrivances
for economy in suds and dishwaters that are absolutely ne-
cessitated in upland habitations during the droughts of summer. But at this season there were no such exigencies; a mere
acceptance of what the skies bestowed was sufficient for an
abundant store.

At last the notes of the serpent ceased and the house was
silent. This cessation of activity aroused the solitary pedestrian from the reverie into which he had lapsed, and, emerging
from the shed, with an apparently new intention, he walked
up the path to the house-door. Arrived here, his first act was
to kneel down on a large stone beside the row of vessels, and
to drink a copious draught from one of them. Having quenched
his thirst he rose and lifted his hand to knock, but paused
with his eye upon the panel. Since the dark surface of the
wood revealed absolutely nothing, it was evident that he must
be mentally looking through the door, as if he wished to
measure thereby all the possibilities that a house of this sort
might include, and how they might bear upon the question
of his entry.

In his indecision he turned and surveyed the scene around.
Not a soul was anywhere visible. The garden-path stretched

downward from his feet, gleaming like the rack of a snail; the roof of the little well (mostly dry), the well-cover, the top rail of the garden-gate, were varnished with the same dull liquid glaze; while, far away in the vale, a faint whiteness of more than usual extent showed that the rivers were high in the meads. Beyond all this winked a few bleared lamplights through the beating drops—lights that denoted the situation of the county-town from which he had appeared to come. The absence of all notes of life in that direction seemed to clinch his intentions, and he knocked at the door.

Within, a desultory chat had taken the place of movement and musical sound. The hedge-carpenter was suggesting a song to the company, which nobody just then was inclined to undertake, so that the knock afforded a not unwelcome diversion.

"Walk in!" said the shepherd promptly.

The latch clicked upward, and out of the night our pedestrian appeared upon the door-mat. The shepherd arose, snuffed two of the nearest candles, and turned to look at him.

Their light disclosed that the stranger was dark in complexion and not unprepossessing as to feature. His hat, which for a moment he did not remove, hung low over his eyes, without concealing that they were large, open, and determined, moving with a flash rather than a glance round the room. He seemed pleased with his survey, and, baring his shaggy head, said, in a rich deep voice, "The rain is so heavy, friends, that I ask leave to come in and rest awhile."

"To be sure, stranger," said the shepherd. "And faith, you've been lucky in choosing your time, for we are having a bit of a fling for a glad cause—though, to be sure, a man could hardly wish that glad cause to happen more than once a year."

"Nor less," spoke up a woman. "For 'tis best to get your family over and done with, as soon as you can, so as to be all the earlier out of the fag o't."

"And what may be this glad cause?" asked the stranger.

"A birth and christening," said the shepherd.

The stranger hoped his host might not be made unhappy either by too many or too few of such episodes, and being invited by a gesture to a pull at the mug, he readily acquiesced. His manner, which, before entering, had been so dubious, was now altogether that of a careless and candid man.

"Late to be traipsing athwart this coomb—hey?" said the engaged man of fifty.

"Late it is, master, as you say.—I'll take a seat in the chimney-corner, if you have nothing to urge against it, ma'am; for I am a little moist on the side that was next the rain."

Mrs. Shepherd Fennel assented, and made room for the self-invited comer, who, having got completely inside the chimney-corner, stretched out his legs and his arms with the expansiveness of a person quite at home.

"Yes, I am rather cracked in the vamp," he said freely, seeing that the eyes of the shepherd's wife fell upon his boots, "and I am not well fitted either. I have had some rough times lately, and have been forced to pick up what I can get in the way of wearing, but I must find a suit better fit for working-days when I reach home."

"One of hereabouts?" she inquired.

"Not quite that—further up the country."

"I thought so. And so be I; and by your tongue you come from my neighbourhood."

"But you would hardly have heard of me," he said quickly. "My time would be long before yours, ma'am, you see."

This testimony to the youthfulness of his hostess had the effect of stopping her cross-examination.

"There is only one thing more wanted to make me happy," continued the new-comer. "And that is a little baccy, which I am sorry to say I am out of."

"I'll fill your pipe," said the shepherd.

"I must ask you to lend me a pipe likewise."

"A smoker, and no pipe about 'ee?"

"I have dropped it somewhere on the road."

The shepherd filled and handed him a new clay pipe, saying, as he did so, "Hand me your baccy-box—I'll fill that too, now I am about it."

The man went through the movement of searching his pockets.

"Lost that too?" said his entertainer, with some surprise.

"I am afraid so," said the man with some confusion. "Give it to me in a screw of paper." Lighting his pipe at the candle with a suction that drew the whole flame into the bowl, he resettled himself in the corner and bent his looks upon the faint steam from his damp legs, as if he wished to say no more.

Meanwhile, the general body of guests had been taking little notice of this visitor by reason of an absorbing discussion in which they were engaged with the band about a tune for the next dance. The matter being settled, they were about to stand up when an interruption came in the shape of another knock at the door.

At sound of the same the man in the chimney-corner took up the poker and began stirring the brands as if doing it thoroughly were the one aim of his existence; and a second time the shepherd said, "Walk in!" In a moment another man stood upon the straw-woven door-mat. He too was a stranger.

This individual was one of a type radically different from the first. There was more of the commonplace in his manner, and a certain jovial cosmopolitanism sat upon his features. He was several years older than the first arrival, his hair being slightly frosted, his eyebrows bristly, and his whiskers cut back from his cheeks. His face was rather full and flabby, and yet it was not altogether a face without power. A few grog-blossoms marked the neighbourhood of his nose. He flung back his long drab greatcoat, revealing that beneath it he wore a suit of cinder-grey shade throughout, large heavy seals, of some metal or other that would take a polish, dangling from his fob as his only personal ornament. Shaking the water-drops from his low-crowned glazed hat, he said, "I must ask for a few minutes' shelter, comrades, or I shall be wetted to my skin before I get to Casterbridge."

"Make yourself at home, master," said the shepherd, perhaps a trifle less heartily than on the first occasion. Not that Fennel had the least tinge of niggardliness in his composition; but the room was far from large, spare chairs were not numerous, and damp companions were not altogether desirable at close quarters for the women and girls in their bright-coloured gowns.

However, the second comer, after taking off his greatcoat, and hanging his hat on a nail in one of the ceiling-beams as if he had been specially invited to put it there, advanced and sat down at the table. This had been pushed so closely into the chimney-corner, to give all available room to the dancers, that its inner edge grazed the elbow of the man who had ensconced himself by the fire; and thus the two strangers were brought into close companionship. They nodded to each other by way of breaking the ice of unacquaintance, and the first stranger handed his neighbour the family mug—a huge vessel of brown ware, having its upper edge worn away like a threshold by the rub of whole generations of thirsty lips that had gone the way of all flesh, and bearing the following inscription burnt upon its rotund side in yellow letters:—

THERE IS NO FUN
UNTILL I CUM.

The other man, nothing loth, raised the mug to his lips, and drank on, and on, and on—till a curious blueness overspread the countenance of the shepherd's wife, who had regarded with no little surprise the first stranger's free offer to the second of what did not belong to him to dispense.

"I knew it!" said the toper to the shepherd with much satisfaction. "When I walked up your garden before coming in, and saw the hives all of a row, I said to myself, 'Where there's bees there's honey, and where there's honey there's mead.' But mead of such a truly comfortable sort as this I really didn't expect to meet in my older days." He took yet another pull at the mug, till it assumed an ominous elevation.

"Glad you enjoy it!" said the shepherd warmly.

"It is goodish mead," assented Mrs. Fennel, with an absence of enthusiasm which seemed to say that it was possible to buy praise for one's cellar at too heavy a price. "It is trouble enough to make—and really I hardly think we shall make any more. For honey sells well, and we ourselves can make shift with a drop o' small mead and metheglin for common use from the comb-washings."

"O, but you'll never have the heart!" reproachfully cried the stranger in cinder-grey, after taking up the mug a third time and setting it down empty. "I love mead, when 'tis old like this, as I love to go to church o' Sundays, or to relieve the needy any day of the week."

"Ha, ha, ha!" said the man in the chimney-corner, who, in spite of the taciturnity induced by the pipe of tobacco, could not or would not refrain from this slight testimony to his comrade's humour.

Now the old mead of those days, brewed of the purest first-year or maiden honey, four pounds to the gallon—with its due complement of white of eggs, cinnamon, ginger, cloves, mace, rosemary, yeast, and processes of working, bottling, and cellaring—tasted remarkably strong; but it did not taste so strong as it actually was. Hence, presently, the stranger in cinder-grey at the table, moved by its creeping influence, unbuttoned his waistcoat, threw himself back in his chair, spread his legs, and made his presence felt in various ways.

"Well, well, as I say," he resumed, "I am going to Casterbridge, and to Casterbridge I must go. I should have been almost there by this time; but the rain drove me into your dwelling, and I'm not sorry for it."

"You don't live in Casterbridge?" said the shepherd.

"Not as yet; though I shortly mean to move there."

"Going to set up in trade, perhaps?"

"No, no," said the shepherd's wife. "It is easy to see that the gentleman is rich, and don't want to work at anything."

The cinder-grey stranger paused, as if to consider whether he would accept that definition of himself. He presently rejected it by answering, "Rich is not quite the word for me, dame. I do work, and I must work. And even if I only get to Casterbridge by midnight I must begin work there at eight to-morrow morning. Yes, het or wet, blow or snow, famine or sword, my day's work to-morrow must be done."

"Poor man! Then, in spite o' seeming, you be worse off than we?" replied the shepherd's wife.

" 'Tis the nature of my trade, men and maidens. 'Tis the nature of my trade more than my poverty. . . . But really and truly I must up and off, or I shan't get a lodging in the town." However, the speaker did not move, and directly added, "There's time for one more draught of friendship before I go; and I'd perform it at once if the mug were not dry."

"Here's a mug o' small," said Mrs. Fennel. "Small, we call it, though to be sure 'tis only the first wash o' the combs."

"No," said the stranger disdainfully. "I won't spoil your first kindness by partaking o' your second."

"Certainly not," broke in Fennel. "We don't increase and multiply every day, and I'll fill the mug again." He went away to the dark place under the stairs where the barrel stood. The shepherdess followed him.

"Why should you do this?" she said reproachfully, as soon as they were alone. "He's emptied it once, though it held enough for ten people; and now he's not contented wi' the small, but must needs call for more o' the strong! And a stranger unbeknown to any of us. For my part, I don't like the look o' the man at all."

"But he's in the house, my honey; and 'tis a wet night, and a christening. Daze it, what's a cup of mead more or less? There'll be plenty more next bee-burning."

"Very well—this time, then," she answered, looking wistfully at the barrel. "But what is the man's calling, and where is he one of, that he should come in and join us like this?"

"I don't know. I'll ask him again."

The catastrophe of having the mug drained dry at one pull

by the stranger in cinder-grey was effectually guarded against this time by Mrs. Fennel. She poured out his allowance in a small cup, keeping the large one at a discreet distance from him. When he had tossed off his portion the shepherd renewed his inquiry about the stranger's occupation.

The latter did not immediately reply, and the man in the chimney-corner, with sudden demonstrativeness, said, "Anybody may know my trade—I'm a wheelwright."

"A very good trade for these parts," said the shepherd.

"And anybody may know mine—if they've the sense to find it out," said the stranger in cinder-grey.

"You may generally tell what a man is by his claws," observed the hedge-carpenter, looking at his own hands. "My fingers be as full of thorns as an old pin-cushion is of pins."

The hands of the man in the chimney-corner instinctively sought the shade, and he gazed into the fire as he resumed his pipe. The man at the table took up the hedge-carpenter's remark, and added smartly, "True; but the oddity of my trade is that, instead of setting a mark upon me, it sets a mark upon my customers."

No observation being offered by anybody in elucidation of this enigma, the shepherd's wife once more called for a song. The same obstacles presented themselves as at the former time—one had no voice, another had forgotten the first verse. The stranger at the table, whose soul had now risen to a good working temperature, relieved the difficulty by exclaiming that, to start the company, he would sing himself. Thrusting one thumb into the arm-hole of his waistcoat, he waved the other hand in the air, and, with an extemporizing gaze at the shining sheep-crooks above the mantelpiece, began:—

> "O my trade it is the rarest one,
> Simple shepherds all—
> My trade is a sight to see;
> For my customers I tie, and take them up on high,
> And waft 'em to a far countree!"

The room was silent when he had finished the verse—with one exception, that of the man in the chimney-corner, who, at the singer's word, "Chorus!" joined him in a deep bass voice of musical relish—

> "And waft 'em to a far countree!"

Oliver Giles, John Pitcher the dairyman, the parish-clerk, the engaged man of fifty, the row of young women against the wall, seemed lost in thought not of the gayest kind. The shepherd looked meditatively on the ground, the shepherdess gazed keenly at the singer, and with some suspicion; she was doubting whether this stranger were merely singing an old song from recollection, or was composing one there and then for the occasion. All were as perplexed at the obscure revelation as the guests at Belshazzar's Feast, except the man in the chimney-corner, who quietly said, "Second verse, stranger," and smoked on.

The singer thoroughly moistened himself from his lips inwards, and went on with the next stanza as requested:—

> "My tools are but common ones,
> Simple shepherds all—
> My tools are no sight to see:
> A little hempen string, and a post whereon to swing,
> Are implements enough for me!"

Shepherd Fennel glanced round. There was no longer any doubt that the stranger was answering his question rhythmically. The guests one and all started back with suppressed exclamations. The young woman engaged to the man of fifty fainted half-way, and would have proceeded, but finding him wanting in alacrity for catching her she sat down trembling.

"O, he's the——!" whispered the people in the background, mentioning the name of an ominous public officer. "He's come to do it! 'Tis to be at Casterbridge jail to-morrow—the man for sheep-stealing—the poor clock-maker we heard of, who used to live away at Shottsford and had no work to do. Timothy Summers, whose family were a-starving, and so he went out of Shottsford by the highroad, and took a sheep in open daylight, defying the farmer and the farmer's wife and the farmer's lad, and every man jack among 'em. He" (and they nodded towards the stranger of the deadly trade) "is come from up the country to do it because there's not enough to do in his own county-town, and he's got the place here now our own county man's dead; he's going to live in the same cottage under the prison wall."

The stranger in cinder-grey took no notice of this whispered string of observations, but again wetted his lips. Seeing that his friend in the chimney-corner was the only one who reciprocated his joviality in any way, he held out his cup towards that appreciative comrade, who also held out his own. They clinked together, the eyes of the rest of the room hanging upon the singer's actions. He parted his lips for the third verse; but at that moment another knock was audible upon the door. This time the knock was faint and hesitating.

The company seemed scared; the shepherd looked with consternation towards the entrance, and it was with some effort that he resisted his alarmed wife's deprecatory glance, and uttered for the third time the welcoming words, "Walk in!"

The door was gently opened, and another man stood upon the mat. He, like those who had preceded him, was a stranger. This time it was a short, small personage, of fair complexion, and dressed in a decent suit of dark clothes.

"Can you tell me the way to——?" he began: when, gazing round the room to observe the nature of the company amongst whom he had fallen, his eyes lighted on the stranger in cindergrey. It was just at the instant when the latter, who had thrown his mind into his song with such a will that he scarcely heeded the interruption, silenced all whispers and inquiries by bursting into his third verse:

> "To-morrow is my working day,
>
> > Simple shepherds all—
> > To-morrow is a working day for me:
> For the farmer's sheep is slain, and the lad who did it ta'en,
> And on his soul may God ha' merc-y!"

The stranger in the chimney-corner, waving cups with the singer so heartily that his mead splashed over on the hearth, repeated in his bass voice as before:

> "And on his soul may God ha' merc-y!"

All this time the third stranger had been standing in the doorway. Finding now that he did not come forward or go on speaking, the guests particularly regarded him. They noticed to their surprise that he stood before them the picture of abject terror—his knees trembling, his hand shaking so violently that the door-latch by which he supported himself rattled audibly: his white lips were parted, and his eyes fixed on the merry officer of justice in the middle of the room. A moment more and he had turned, closed the door, and fled.

"What a man can it be?" said the shepherd.

The rest, between the awfulness of their late discovery and the odd conduct of this third visitor, looked as if they knew not what to think, and said nothing. Instinctively they withdrew further and further from the grim gentleman in their midst, whom some of them seemed to take for the Prince of

Darkness himself, till they formed a remote circle, an empty space of floor being left between them and him—

". . . circulus, cujus centrum diabolus."

The room was so silent—though there were more than twenty people in it—that nothing could be heard but the patter of the rain against the window-shutters, accompanied by the occasional hiss of a stray drop that fell down the chimney into the fire, and the steady pulling of the man in the corner, who had now resumed his pipe of long clay.

The stillness was unexpectedly broken. The distant sound of a gun reverberated through the air apparently from the direction of the county-town.

"Be jiggered!" cried the stranger who had sung the song, jumping up.

"What does that mean?" asked several.

"A prisoner escaped from the jail—that's what it means."

All listened. The sound was repeated, and none of them spoke but the man in the chimney-corner, who said quietly, "I've often been told that in this county they fire a gun at such times; but I never heard it till now."

"I wonder if it is *my* man?" murmured the personage in cinder-grey.

"Surely it is!" said the shepherd involuntarily. "And surely we've zeed him! That little man who looked in at the door by now, and quivered like a leaf when he zeed ye and heard your song!"

"His teeth chattered, and the breath went out of his body," said the diaryman.

"And his heart seemed to sink within him like stone," said Oliver Giles.

"And he bolted as if he'd been shot at," said the hedge-carpenter.

"True—his teeth chattered, and his heart seemed to sink; and he bolted as if he'd been shot at," slowly summed up the man in the chimney-corner.

"I didn't notice it," remarked the hangman.

"We were all a-wondering what made him run off in such a fright," faltered one of the women against the wall, "and now 'tis explained!"

The firing of the alarm-gun went on at intervals, low and sullenly, and their suspicions became a certainty. The sinister gentleman in cinder-grey roused himself. "Is there a constable here?" he asked, in thick tones. "If so, let him step forward."

The engaged man of fifty stepped quavering out from the wall, his betrothed beginning to sob on the back of the chair.

"You are a sworn constable?"

"I be, sir."

"Then pursue the criminal at once, with assistance, and bring him back here. He can't have gone far."

"I will, sir, I will—when I've got my staff. I'll go home and get it, and come sharp here, and start in a body."

"Staff!—never mind your staff; the man'll be gone!"

"But I can't do nothing without my staff—can I, William, and John, and Charles Jake? No; for there's the king's royal crown a painted on en in yaller and gold, and the lion and the unicorn, so as when I raise en up and hit my prisoner, 'tis made a lawful blow thereby. I wouldn't 'tempt to take up a man without my staff—no, not I. If I hadn't the law to gie me courage, why, instead o' my taking up him he might take up me!"

"Now, I'm a king's man myself, and can give you authority enough for this," said the formidable officer in grey. "Now then, all of ye, be ready. Have ye any lanterns?"

"Yes—have ye any lanterns?—I demand it!" said the constable.

"And the rest of you able-bodied—"

"Able-bodied men—yes—the rest of ye!" said the constable.

"Have you some good stout staves and pitchforks—"

"Staves and pitchforks—in the name o' the law! And take 'em in yer hands and go in quest, and do as we in authority tell ye!"

Thus aroused, the men prepared to give chase. The evidence was, indeed, though circumstantial, so convincing, that but little argument was needed to show the shepherd's guests that after what they had seen it would look very much like connivance if they did not instantly pursue the unhappy third stranger, who could not as yet have gone more than a few hundred yards over such uneven country.

A shepherd is always well provided with lanterns; and, lighting these hastily, and with hurdle-staves in their hands, they poured out of the door, taking a direction along the crest of the hill, away from the town, the rain having fortunately a little abated.

Disturbed by the noise, or possibly by unpleasant dreams of her baptism, the child who had been christened began to cry heart-brokenly in the room overhead. These notes of grief came down through the chinks of the floor to the ears of the women below, who jumped up one by one, and seemed glad of the excuse to ascend and comfort the baby, for the incidents of the last half-hour greatly oppressed them. Thus in the space of two or three minutes the room on the ground-floor was deserted quite.

But it was not for long. Hardly had the sound of footsteps died away when a man returned round the corner of the house from the direction the pursuers had taken. Peeping in at the door, and seeing nobody there, he entered leisurely. It was the stranger of the chimney-corner, who had gone out with the rest. The motive of his return was shown by his helping himself to a cut piece of skimmer-cake that lay on a ledge beside where he had sat, and which he had apparently forgotten to take with him. He also poured out half a cup more mead from the quantity that remained, ravenously eating and drinking these as he stood. He had not finished when another figure came in just as quietly—his friend in cinder-grey.

"O—you here?" said the latter, smiling. "I thought you had gone to help in the capture." And this speaker also revealed the object of his return by looking solicitously round for the fascinating mug of old mead.

"And I thought you had gone," said the other, continuing his skimmer-cake with some effort.

"Well, on second thoughts, I felt there were enough without me," said the first confidentially, "and such a night as it is, too. Besides, 'tis the business o' the Government to take care of its criminals—not mine."

"True; so it is. And I felt as you did, that there were enough without me."

"I don't want to break my limbs running over the humps and hollows of this wild country."

"Nor I neither, between you and me."

"These shepherd-people are used to it—simple-minded souls, you know, stirred up to anything in a moment. They'll have him ready for me before the morning, and no trouble to me at all."

"They'll have him, and we shall have saved ourselves all labour in the matter."

"True, true. Well, my way is to Casterbridge; and 'tis as much as my legs will do to take me that far. Going the same way?"

"No, I am sorry to say! I have to get home over there" (he nodded indefinitely to the right), "and I feel as you do, that it is quite enough for my legs to do before bedtime."

The other had by this time finished the mead in the mug,

after which, shaking hands heartily at the door, and wishing each other well, they went their several ways.

In the meantime the company of pursuers had reached the end of the hog's-back elevation which dominated this part of the down. They had decided on no particular plan of action; and, finding that the man of the baleful trade was no longer in their company, they seemed quite unable to form any such plan now. They descended in all directions down the hill, and straightway several of the party fell into the snare set by Nature for all misguided midnight ramblers over this part of the cretaceous formation. The "lanchets," or flint slopes, which belted the escarpment at intervals of a dozen yards, took the less cautious ones unawares, and losing their footing on the rubbly steep they slid sharply downwards, the lanterns rolling from their hands to the bottom, and there lying on their sides till the horn was scorched through.

When they had again gathered themselves together the shepherd, as the man who knew the country best, took the lead, and guided them round these treacherous inclines. The lanterns, which seemed rather to dazzle their eyes and warn the fugitive than to assist them in the exploration, were extinguished, due silence was observed; and in this more rational order they plunged into the vale. It was a grassy, briery, moist defile, affording some shelter to any person who had sought it; but the party perambulated it in vain, and ascended on the other side. Here they wandered apart, and after an interval closed together again to report progress. At the second time of closing in they found themselves near a lonely ash, the single tree on this part of the coomb, probably sown there by a passing bird some fifty years before. And here, standing a little to one side of the trunk, as motionless as the trunk itself, appeared the man they were in quest of, his outline being well defined agianst the sky beyond. The band noiselessly drew up and faced him.

"Your money or your life!" said the constable sternly to the still figure.

"No, no," whispered John Pitcher. " 'Tisn't our side ought to say that. That's the doctrine of vagabonds like him, and we be on the side of the law."

"Well, well," replied the constable impatiently; "I must say something, mustn't I? and if you had all the weight o' this undertaking upon your mind, perhaps you'd say the wrong thing too!—Prisoner at the bar, surrender, in the name of the Father—the Crown, I mane!"

The man under the tree seemed now to notice them for the first time, and giving them no opportunity whatever for exhibiting their courage, he strolled slowly towards them. He was, indeed, the little man, the third stranger; but his trepidation had in a great measure gone.

"Well, travellers," he said, "did I hear ye speak to me?"

"You did: you've got to come and be our prisoner at once!" said the constable. "We arrest 'ee on the charge of not biding in Casterbridge jail in a decent proper manner to be hung to-morrow morning. Neighbours, do your duty and seize the culpet!"

On hearing the charge the man seemed enlightened, and, saying not another word, resigned himself with preternatural civility to the search-party, who, with their staves in their hands, surrounded him on all sides, and marched him back towards the shepherd's cottage.

It was eleven o'clock by the time they arrived. The light shining from the open door, a sound of men's voices within, proclaimed to them as they approached the house that some new events had arisen in their absence. On entering they discovered the shepherd's living room to be invaded by two officers from Casterbridge jail, and a well-known magistrate who lived at the nearest country-seat, intelligence of the escape having become generally circulated.

"Gentlemen," said the constable, "I have brought back your man—not without risk and danger; but every one must do his duty! He is inside this circle of able-bodied persons, who have lent me useful aid, considering their ignorance of Crown work. Men, bring forward your prisoner!" And the third stranger was led to the light.

"Who is this?" said one of the officials.

"The man," said the constable.

"Certainly not," said the turnkey; and the first corroborated his statement.

"But how can it be otherwise?" asked the constable. "Or why was he so terrified at sight o' the singing instrument of the law who sat there?" Here he related the strange behaviour of the third stranger on entering the house during the hangman's song.

"Can't understand it," said the officer coolly. "All I know is that it is not the condemned man. He's quite a different character from this one; a gauntish fellow, with dark hair and eyes, rather good-looking, and with a musical bass voice that if you heard it once you'd never mistake as long as you lived."

"Why, souls—'twas the man in the chimney-corner!"

"Hey—what?" said the magistrate, coming forward after inquiring particulars from the shepherd in the background. "Haven't you got the man after all?"

"Well, sir," said the constable, "he's the man we were in search of, that's true; and yet he's not the man we were in search of. For the man we were in search of was not the man we wanted, sir, if you understand my every-day way; for 'twas the man in the chimney-corner!"

"A pretty kettle of fish altogether!" said the magistrate. "You had better start for the other man at once."

The prisoner now spoke for the first time. The mention of the man in the chimney-corner seemed to have moved him as nothing else could do. "Sir," he said, stepping forward to the magistrate, "take no more trouble about me. The time is come when I may as well speak. I have done nothing; my crime is that the condemned man is my brother. Early this afternoon I left home at Shottsford to tramp it all the way to Casterbridge jail to bid him farewell. I was benighted, and called here to rest and ask the way. When I opened the door I saw before me the very man, my brother, that I thought to see in the condemned cell at Casterbridge. He was in this chimney-corner; and jammed close to him, so that he could not have got out if he had tried, was the executioner who'd come to take his life, singing a song about it and not knowing that it was his victim who was close by, joining in to save appearances. My brother threw a glance of agony at me, and I knew he meant, 'Don't reveal what you see; my life depends on it.' I was so terror-struck that I could hardly stand, and, not knowing what I did, I turned and hurried away."

The narrator's manner and tone had the stamp of truth, and his story made a great impression on all around. "And do you know where your brother is at the present time?" asked the magistrate.

"I do not. I have never seen him since I closed this door."

"I can testify to that, for we've been between ye ever since," said the constable.

"Where does he think to fly to?—what is his occupation?"

"He's a watch-and-clock-maker, sir."

" 'A said 'a was a wheelwright—a wicked rogue," said the constable.

"The wheels of clocks and watches he meant, no doubt," said Shepherd Fennel. "I thought his hands were palish for's trade."

"Well, it appears to me that nothing can be gained by

retaining this poor man in custody," said the magistrate; "your business lies with the other, unquestionably."

And so the little man was released off-hand; but he looked nothing the less sad on that account, it being beyond the power of magistrate or constable to raze out the written troubles in his brain, for they concerned another whom he regarded with more solicitude than himself. When this was done, and the man had gone his way, the night was found to be so far advanced that it was deemed useless to renew the search before the next morning.

Next day, accordingly, the quest for the clever sheep-stealer became general and keen, to all appearance at least. But the intended punishment was cruelly disproportioned to the transgression, and the sympathy of a great many country-folk in that district was strongly on the side of the fugitive. Moreover, his marvellous coolness and daring in hob-and-nobbing with the hangman, under the unprecedented circumstances of the shepherd's party, won their admiration. So that it may be questioned if all those who ostensibly make themselves so busy in exploring woods and fields and lanes were quite so thorough when it came to the private examination of their own lofts and out-houses. Stories were afloat of a mysterious figure being occasionally seen in some old overgrown trackway or other, remote from turnpike roads; but when a search was instituted in any of these suspected quarters nobody was found. Thus the days and weeks passed without tidings.

In brief, the bass-voiced man of the chimney-corner was never recaptured. Some said that he went across the sea, others that he did not, but buried himself in the depths of a populous city. At any rate, the gentleman in cinder-grey never did this morning's work at Casterbridge, nor met anywhere at all, for business purposes, the genial comrade with whom he had passed an hour of relaxation in the lonely house on the slope of the coomb.

The grass has long been green on the graves of Shepherd Fennel and his frugal wife; the guests who made up the christening party have mainly followed their entertainers to the tomb; the baby in whose honour they all had met is a matron in the sere and yellow leaf. But the arrival of the three strangers at the shepherd's that night, and the details connected therewith, is a story as well known as ever in the country about Higher Crowstairs.

Robert Louis Stevenson
(1850–1894)

*Although he died young, Robert Louis Stevenson, like D.H.
Lawrence, packed many kinds of writing into his forty-four years.
Born in Edinburgh, Stevenson started out as a lawyer, but his
poor health—he suffered from tuberculosis—made a writing career
more congenial. He began with essays, later published as* Virgin-
ibus Puerisque *(1881) and* Familiar Studies of Men and Books
(1882), and then turned to stories, collected as New Arabian Nights
(1882). However, with Treasure Island *in 1883, he came into his
own. This was followed in quick succession by* A Child's Garden
of Verses *(1885),* Kidnapped *(1886), and "The Strange Case of
Dr. Jekyll and Mr. Hyde" (1886). The latter demonstrates his
sensitivity to many of the developments occurring in the study of
the unconscious in the years preceding Freud. Because of continuing illness, Stevenson would settle in Samoa, in the South Pacific,
for the rest of his years, but before setting out for the South Seas
he wrote* The Master of Ballantrae *(1889). He lived on Samoa
for the final five years of his life and wrote both poetry and several
more novels, including* The Ebb Tide *(1894) and the incomplete*
Weir of Hermiston *(1896). He was buried on Samoa.*

The Strange Case
of Dr. Jekyll
and Mr. Hyde

STORY OF THE DOOR

Mr. Utterson the lawyer was a man of a rugged countenance
that was never lighted by a smile; cold, scanty and embarrassed in discourse; backward in sentiment; lean, long, dusty,

dreary and yet somehow lovable. At friendly meetings, and when the wine was to his taste, something eminently human beaconed from his eye; something indeed which never found its way into his talk, but which spoke not only in these silent symbols of the after-dinner face, but more often and loudly in the acts of his life. He was austere with himself; drank gin when he was alone, to mortify a taste for vintages; and though he enjoyed the theatre, had not crossed the doors of one for twenty years. But he had an approved tolerance for others; sometimes wondering, almost with envy, at the high pressure of spirits involved in their misdeeds; and in any extremity inclined to help rather than to reprove. "I incline to Cain's heresy," he used to say quaintly: "I let my brother go to the devil in his own way." In this character, it was frequently his fortune to be the last reputable acquaintance and the last good influence in the lives of downgoing men. And to such as these, so long as they came about his chambers, he never marked a shade of change in his demeanour.

No doubt the feat was easy to Mr. Utterson; for he was undemonstrative at the best, and even his friendship seemed to be founded in a similar catholicity of good-nature. It is the mark of a modest man to accept his friendly circle ready-made from the hands of opportunity; and that was the law-yer's way. His friends were those of his own blood or those whom he had known the longest; his affections, like ivy, were the growth of time, they implied no aptness in the object. Hence, no doubt, the bond that united him to Mr. Richard Enfield, his distant kinsman, the well-known man about town. It was a nut to crack for many, what these two could see in each other, or what subject they could find in common. It was reported by those who encountered them in their Sunday walks, that they said nothing, looked singularly dull, and would hail with obvious relief the appearance of a friend. For all that, the two men put the greatest store by these excursions, counted them the chief jewel of each week, and not only set aside occasions of pleasure, but even resisted the calls of business, that they might enjoy them uninterrupted.

It chanced on one of these rambles that their way led them down a by-street in a busy quarter of London. The street was small and what is called quiet, but it drove a thriving trade on the week-days. The inhabitants were all doing well, it seemed, and all emulously hoping to do better still, and laying out the surplus of their gains in coquetry; so that the shop fronts stood along that thoroughfare with an air of invitation,

like rows of smiling saleswomen. Even on Sunday, when it
veiled its more florid charms and lay comparatively empty of
passage, the street shone out in contrast to its dingy neighbourhood, like a fire in a forest; and with its freshly
painted shutters, well-polished brasses, and general cleanliness and
gaiety of note, instantly caught and pleased the eye of the
passenger.

Two doors from one corner, on the left hand going east,
the line was broken by the entry of a court; and just at that
point, a certain sinister block of building thrust forward its
gable on the street. It was two storeys high; showed no window, nothing but a door on the lower storey and a blind
forehead of discoloured wall on the upper; and bore in every
feature, the marks of prolonged and sordid negligence. The
door, which was equipped with neither bell nor knocker, was
blistered and distained. Tramps slouched into the recess and
struck matches on the panels; children kept shop upon the
steps; the schoolboy had tried his knife on the mouldings;
and for close on a generation, no one had appeared to drive
away these random visitors or to repair their ravages.

Mr. Enfield and the lawyer were on the other side of the
by-street; but when they came abreast of the entry, the former
lifted up his cane and pointed.

"Did you ever remark that door?" he asked; and when his
companion had replied in the affirmative, "It is connected in
my mind," added he, "with a very odd story."

"Indeed?" said Mr. Utterson, with a slight change of voice,
"and what was that?"

"Well, it was this way," returned Mr. Enfield: "I was coming home from some place at the end of the world, about
three o'clock of a black winter morning, and my way lay
through a part of town where there was literally nothing to
be seen but lamps. Street after street, and all the folks asleep—
street after street, all lighted up as if for a procession and all
as empty as a church—till at last I got into that state of mind
when a man listens and listens and begins to long for the sight
of a policeman. All at once, I saw two figures: one a little
man who was stumping along eastward at a good walk, and
the other a girl of maybe eight or ten who was running as
hard as she was able down a cross street. Well, sir, the two
ran into one another naturally enough at the corner; and then
came the horrible part of the thing; for the man trampled
calmly over the child's body and left her screaming on the
ground. It sounds nothing to hear, but it was hellish to see.

It wasn't like a man; it was like some damned Juggernaut. I gave a view halloa, took to my heels, collared my gentleman, and brought him back to where there was already quite a group about the screaming child. He was perfectly cool and made no resistance, but gave me one look, so ugly that it brought out the sweat on me like running. The people who had turned out were the girl's own family; and pretty soon, the doctor, for whom she had been sent, put in his appearance. Well, the child was not much the worse, more frightened, according to the Sawbones; and there you might have supposed would be an end to it. But there was one curious circumstance. I had taken a loathing to my gentleman at first sight. So had the child's family, which was only natural. But the doctor's case was what struck me. He was the usual cut and dry apothecary, of no particular age and colour, with a strong Edinburgh accent, and about as emotional as a bagpipe. Well, sir, he was like the rest of us; every time he looked at my prisoner, I saw that Sawbones turn sick and white with the desire to kill him. I knew what was in his mind, just as he knew what was in mine; and killing being out of the question, we did the next best. We told the man we could and would make such a scandal out of this, as should make his name stink from one end of London to the other. If he had any friends or any credit, we undertook that he should lose them. And all the time, as we were pitching it in red hot, we were keeping the women off him as best we could, for they were as wild as harpies. I never saw a circle of such hateful faces; and there was the man in the middle, with a kind of black, sneering coolness—frightened too, I could see that— but carrying it off, sir, really like Satan. 'If you choose to make capital out of this accident,' said he, 'I am naturally helpless. No gentleman but wishes to avoid a scene,' says he. 'Name your figure.' Well, we screwed him up to a hundred pounds for the child's family; he would have clearly liked to stick out; but there was something about the lot of us that meant mischief, and at last he struck. The next thing was to get the money; and where do you think he carried us but to that place with the door?—whipped out a key, went in, and presently came back with the matter of ten pounds in gold and a cheque for the balance on Coutts's, drawn payable to bearer and signed with a name that I can't mention, though it's one of the points of my story, but it was a name at least very well known and often printed. The figure was stiff; but the signature was good for more than that, if it was only genuine. I took the liberty of pointing out to my gentleman that the whole business looked apocryphal, and that a man does not, in real life, walk into a cellar door at four in the morning and come out of it with another man's cheque for close upon a hundred pounds. But he was quite easy and sneering. 'Set your mind at rest,' says he, 'I will stay with you till the banks open and cash the cheque myself.' So we all set off, the doctor, and the child's father, and our friend and myself, and passed the rest of the night in my chambers; and next day, when we had breakfasted, went in a body to the bank. I gave in the cheque myself, and said I had every reason to believe it was a forgery. Not a bit of it. The cheque was genuine."

"Tut-tut," said Mr. Utterson.

"I see you feel as I do," said Mr. Enfield. "Yes, it's a bad story. For my man was a fellow that nobody could have to do with, a really damnable man; and the person that drew the cheque is the very pink of the proprieties, celebrated too, and (what makes it worse) one of your fellows who do what they call good. Black mail, I suppose; an honest man paying through the nose for some of the capers of his youth. Black Mail House is what I call that place with the door, in consequence. Though even that, you know, is far from explaining all," he added, and with the words fell into a vein of musing.

From this he was recalled by Mr. Utterson asking rather suddenly: "And you don't know if the drawer of the cheque lives there?"

"A likely place, isn't it?" returned Mr. Enfield. "But I happen to have noticed his address; he lives in some square or other."

"And you never asked about the—place with the door?" said Mr. Utterson.

"No, sir: I had a delicacy," was the reply. "I feel very strongly about putting questions; it partakes too much of the style of the day of judgment. You start a question, and it's like starting a stone. You sit quietly on the top of a hill; and away the stone goes, starting others; and presently some bland old bird (the last you would have thought of) is knocked on the head in his own back garden and the family have to change their name. No, sir, I make it a rule of mine: the more it looks like Queer Street, the less I ask."

"A very good rule, too," said the lawyer.

"But I have studied the place for myself," continued Mr. Enfield. "It seems scarcely a house. There is no other door, and nobody goes in or out of that one but, once in a great while, the gentleman of my adventure. There are three windows looking on the court on the first floor; none below; the windows are always shut but they're clean. And then there is a chimney which is generally smoking; so somebody must live there. And yet it's not so sure; for the buildings are so packed together about that court, that it's hard to say where one ends and another begins.''

The pair walked on again for a while in silence; and then "Enfield," said Mr. Utterson, "that's a good rule of yours."

"Yes, I think it is," returned Enfield.

"But for all that," continued the lawyer, "there's one point I want to ask: I want to ask the name of that man who walked over the child."

"Well," said Mr. Enfield, "I can't see what harm it would do. It was a man of the name of Hyde."

"Hm," said Mr. Utterson. "What sort of a man is he to see?"

"He is not easy to describe. There is something wrong with his appearance; something displeasing, something downright detestable. I never saw a man I so disliked, and yet I scarce know why. He must be deformed somewhere; he gives a strong feeling of deformity, although I couldn't specify the point. He's an extraordinary looking man, and yet I really can name nothing out of the way. No, sir; I can make no hand of it; I can't describe him. And it's not want of memory; for I declare I can see him this moment."

Mr. Utterson again walked some way in silence and obviously under a weight of consideration. "You are sure he used a key?" he inquired at last.

"My dear sir . . .'' began Enfield, surprised out of himself.

"Yes, I know," said Utterson; "I know it must seem strange. The fact is, if I do not ask you the name of the other party, it is because I know it already. You see, Richard, your tale has gone home. If you have been inexact in any point, you had better correct it."

"I think you might have warned me," returned the other with a touch of sullenness. "But I have been pedantically exact, as you call it. The fellow had a key; and what's more, he has it still. I saw him use it, not a week ago."

Mr. Utterson sighed deeply but said never a word; and the young man presently resumed. "Here is another lesson to say nothing," said he. "I am ashamed of my long tongue. Let us make a bargain never to refer to this again."

"With all my heart," said the lawyer. "I shake hands on that, Richard."

SEARCH FOR MR. HYDE

That evening Mr. Utterson came home to his bachelor house in sombre spirits and sat down to dinner without relish. It was his custom of a Sunday, when this meal was over, to sit close by the fire, a volume of some dry divinity on his reading desk, until the clock of the neighbouring church rang out the hour of twelve, when he would go soberly and gratefully to bed. On this night, however, as soon as the cloth was taken away, he took up a candle and went into his business room. There he opened his safe, took from the most private part of it a document endorsed on the envelope as Dr. Jekyll's Will, and sat down with a clouded brow to study its contents. The will was holograph, for Mr. Utterson, though he took charge of it now that it was made, had refused to lend the least assistance in the making of it; it provided not only that, in case of the decease of Henry Jekyll, M.D., D.C.L., L.L.D., F.R.S., etc., all his possessions were to pass into the hands of his "friend and benefactor Edward Hyde," but that in case of Dr. Jekyll's "disappearance or unexplained absence for any period exceeding three calendar months," the said Edward Hyde should step into the said Henry Jekyll's shoes without further delay and free from any burthen or obligation, beyond the payment of a few small sums to the members of the doctor's household. This document had long been the lawyer's eyesore. It offended him both as a lawyer and as a lover of the sane and customary sides of life, to whom the fanciful was the immodest. And hitherto it was his ignorance of Mr. Hyde that had swelled his indignation; now, by a sudden turn, it was his knowledge. It was already bad enough when the name was but a name of which he could learn no more. It was worse when it began to be clothed upon with detestable attributes; and out of the shifting, insubstantial mists that had so long baffled his eye, there leaped up the sudden, definite presentment of a fiend.

"I thought it was madness," he said, as he replaced the obnoxious paper in the safe, "and now I begin to fear it is disgrace."

With that he blew out his candle, put on a greatcoat, and set forth in the direction of Cavendish Square, that citadel of medicine, where his friend, the great Dr. Lanyon, had his house and received his crowding patients. "If anyone knows, it will be Lanyon," he had thought.

The solemn butler knew and welcomed him; he was subjected to no stage of delay, but ushered direct from the door to the dining-room where Dr. Lanyon sat alone over his wine. This was a hearty, healthy, dapper, red-faced gentleman, with a shock of hair prematurely white, and a boisterous and decided manner. At sight of Mr. Utterson, he sprang up from his chair and welcomed him with both hands. The geniality, as was the way of the man, was somewhat theatrical to the eye; but it reposed on genuine feeling. For those two were old friends, old mates both at school and college, both thorough respecters of themselves and of each other, and, what does not always follow, men who thoroughly enjoyed each other's company.

After a little rambling talk, the lawyer led up to the subject which so disagreeably preoccupied his mind.

"I suppose, Lanyon," said he, "you and I must be the two oldest friends that Henry Jekyll has?"

"I wish the friends were younger," chuckled Dr. Lanyon. "But I suppose we are. And what of that? I see little of him now."

"Indeed?" said Utterson. "I thought you had a bond of common interest."

"We had," was the reply. "But it is more than ten years since Henry Jekyll became too fanciful for me. He began to go wrong, wrong in mind; and though of course I continue to take an interest in him for old sake's sake, as they say, I see and I have seen devilish little of the man. Such unscientific balderdash," added the doctor, flushing suddenly purple, "would have estranged Damon and Pythias."

This little spirit of temper was somewhat of a relief to Mr. Utterson. "They have only differed on some point of science," he thought; and being a man of no scientific passions (except in the matter of conveyancing), he even added: "It is nothing worse than that!" He gave his friend a few seconds to recover his composure, and then approached the question he had come to put. "Did you ever come across a protégé of his—one Hyde?" he asked.

"Hyde?" repeated Lanyon. "No. Never heard of him. Since my time."

That was the amount of information that the lawyer carried back with him to the great, dark bed on which he tossed to and fro, until the small hours of the morning began to grow large. It was a night of little ease to his toiling mind, toiling in mere darkness and besieged by questions.

Six o'clock struck on the bells of the church that was so conveniently near to Mr. Utterson's dwelling, and still he was digging at the problem. Hitherto it had touched him on the intellectual side alone; but now his imagination also was engaged, or rather enslaved; and as he lay and tossed in the gross darkness of the night and the curtained room, Mr. Enfield's tale went by before his mind in a scroll of lighted pictures. He would be aware of the great field of lamps of a nocturnal city; then of the figure of a man walking swiftly; then of a child running from the doctor's; and then these met, and that human Juggernaut trod the child down and passed on regardless of her screams. Or else he would see a room in a rich house, where his friend lay asleep, dreaming and smiling at his dreams; and then the door of that room would be opened, the curtains of the bed plucked apart, the sleeper recalled, and lo! there would stand by his side a figure to whom power was given, and even at that dead hour, he must rise and do its bidding. The figure in these two phases haunted the lawyer all night; and if at any time he dozed over, it was but to see it glide more stealthily through sleeping houses, or move the more swiftly and still the more swiftly, even to dizziness, through wider labyrinths of lamplighted city, and at every street corner crush a child and leave her screaming. And still the figure had no face by which he might know it; even in his dreams, it had no face, or one that baffled him and melted before his eyes; and thus it was that there sprang up and grew apace in the lawyer's mind a singularly strong, almost an inordinate, curiosity to behold the features of the real Mr. Hyde. If he could but once set eyes on him, he thought the mystery would lighten and perhaps roll altogether away, as was the habit of mysterious things when well examined. He might see a reason for his friend's strange preference or bondage (call it which you please) and even for the startling clause of the will. At least it would be a face worth seeing: the face of a man who was without bowels of mercy: a face which had but to show itself to raise up, in the mind of the unimpressionable Enfield, a spirit of enduring hatred.

From that time forward, Mr. Utterson began to haunt the door in the by-street of shops. In the morning before office hours, at noon when business was plenty, and time scarce, at night under the face of the fogged city moon, by all lights and at all hours of solitude or concourse, the lawyer was to be found on his chosen post.

"If he be Mr. Hyde," he had thought, "I shall be Mr. Seek."

And at last his patience was rewarded. It was a fine dry night; frost in the air; the streets as clean as a ballroom floor; the lamps, unshaken by any wind, drawing a regular pattern of light and shadow. By ten o'clock, when the shops were closed, the by-street was very solitary and, in spite of the low growl of London from all round, very silent. Small sounds carried far; domestic sounds out of the houses were clearly audible on either side of the roadway; and the rumour of the approach of any passenger preceded him by a long time. Mr. Utterson had been some minutes at his post, when he was aware of an odd, light footstep drawing near. In the course of his nightly patrols, he had long grown accustomed to the quaint effect with which the footfalls of a single person, while he is still a great way off, suddenly spring out distinct from the vast hum and clatter of the city. Yet his attention had never before been so sharply and decisively arrested; and it was with a strong, superstitious prevision of success that he withdrew into the entry of the court.

The steps drew swiftly nearer, and swelled out suddenly louder as they turned the end of the street. The lawyer, looking forth from the entry, could soon see what manner of man he had to deal with. He was small and very plainly dressed, and the look of him, even at that distance, went somehow strongly against the watcher's inclination. But he made straight for the door, crossing the roadway to save time; and as he came, he drew a key from his pocket like one approaching home.

Mr. Utterson stepped out and touched him on the shoulder as he passed. "Mr. Hyde, I think?"

Mr. Hyde shrank back with a hissing intake of the breath. But his fear was only momentary; and though he did not look the lawyer in the face, he answered coolly enough: "That is my name. What do you want?"

"I see you are going in," returned the lawyer. "I am an old friend of Dr. Jekyll's—Mr. Utterson of Gaunt Street— you must have heard of my name; and meeting you so conveniently, I thought you might admit me."

"You will not find Dr. Jekyll; he is from home," replied Mr. Hyde, blowing in the key. And then suddenly, but still without looking up, "How did you know me?" he asked.

"On your side," said Mr. Utterson, "will you do me a favour?"

"With pleasure," replied the other. "What shall it be?"

"Will you let me see your face?" asked the lawyer.

Mr. Hyde appeared to hesitate, and then, as if upon some sudden reflection, fronted about with an air of defiance; and the pair stared at each other pretty fixedly for a few seconds. "Now I shall know you again," said Mr. Utterson. "It may be useful."

"Yes," returned Mr. Hyde, "it is as well we have met; and *à propos*, you should have my address." And he gave a number of a street in Soho.

"Good God!" thought Mr. Utterson, "can he, too, have been thinking of the will?" But he kept his feelings to himself and only grunted in acknowledgment of the address.

"And now," said the other, "how did you know me?"

"By description," was the reply.

"Whose description?"

"We have common friends," said Mr. Utterson.

"Common friends?" echoed Mr. Hyde, a little hoarsely. "Who are they?"

"Jekyll, for instance," said the lawyer.

"He never told you," cried Mr. Hyde, with a flush of anger. "I did not think you would have lied."

"Come," said Mr. Utterson, "that is not fitting language."

The other snarled aloud into a savage laugh; and the next moment, with extraordinary quickness, he had unlocked the door and disappeared into the house.

The lawyer stood awhile when Mr. Hyde had left him, the picture of disquietude. Then he began slowly to mount the street, pausing every step or two and putting his hand to his brow like a man in mental perplexity. The problem he was thus debating as he walked, was one of a class that is rarely solved. Mr. Hyde was pale and dwarfish, he gave an impression of deformity without any nameable malformation, he had a displeasing smile, he had borne himself to the lawyer with a sort of murderous mixture of timidity and boldness, and he spoke with a husky, whispering and somewhat broken voice; all these were points against him, but not all of these together could explain the hitherto unknown disgust, loathing and fear with which Mr. Utterson regarded him. "There must be something else," said the perplexed gentleman. "There *is* something more, if I could find a name for it. God bless me, the man seems hardly human! Something troglodytic, shall we say? or can it be the old story of Dr. Fell? or is it the mere radiance of a foul soul that thus transpires through, and transfigures, its clay continent? The last, I think; for, O my poor old Harry Jekyll, if ever I read Satan's signature upon a face, it is on that of your new friend."

Round the corner from the by-street, there was a square of ancient, handsome houses, now for the most part decayed from their high estate and let in flats and chambers to all sorts and conditions of men; map-engravers, architects, shady lawyers and the agents of obscure enterprises. One house, however, second from the corner, was still occupied entire; and at the door of this, which wore a great air of wealth and comfort, though it was now plunged in darkness except for the fan-light, Mr. Utterson stopped and knocked. A well-dressed, elderly servant opened the door.

"Is Dr. Jekyll at home, Poole?" asked the lawyer.

"I will see, Mr. Utterson," said Poole, admitting the visitor, as he spoke, into a large, low-roofed, comfortable hall, paved with flags, warmed (after the fashion of a country house) by a bright, open fire, and furnished with costly cabinets of oak. "Will you wait here by the fire, sir? or shall I give you a light in the dining-room?"

"Here, thank you," said the lawyer, and he drew near and leaned on the tall fender. This hall, in which he was now left alone, was a pet fancy of his friend the doctor's; and Utterson himself was wont to speak of it as the pleasantest room in London. But tonight there was a shudder in his blood; the face of Hyde sat heavy on his memory; he felt (what was rare with him) a nausea and distaste of life; and in the gloom of his spirits, he seemed to read a menace in the flickering of the firelight on the polished cabinets and the uneasy starting of the shadow on the roof. He was ashamed of his relief, when Poole presently returned to announce that Dr. Jekyll was gone out.

"I saw Mr. Hyde go in by the old dissecting-room door, Poole," he said.

"Is that right, when Dr. Jekyll is from home?"

"Quite right, Mr. Utterson, sir," replied the servant. "Mr. Hyde has a key."

"Your master seems to repose a great deal of trust in that young man, Poole," resumed the other musingly.

"Yes, sir, he do indeed," said Poole. "We have all orders to obey him."

"I do not think I ever met Mr. Hyde?" asked Utterson.

"O, dear no, sir. He never *dines* here," replied the butler. "Indeed we see very little of him on this side of the house; he mostly comes and goes by the laboratory."

"Well, good-night, Poole."

"Good-night, Mr. Utterson."

And the lawyer set out homeward with a very heavy heart. "Poor Harry Jekyll," he thought, "my mind misgives me he is in deep waters! He was wild when he was young; a long while ago to be sure; but in the law of God, there is no statute of limitations. Ay, it must be that; the ghost of some old sin, the cancer of some concealed disgrace: punishment coming, *pede claudo*, years after memory has forgotten and self-love condoned the fault." And the lawyer, scared by the thought, brooded awhile on his own past, groping in all the corners of memory, lest by chance some Jack-in-the-Box of an old in-iquity should leap to light there. His past was fairly blameless; few men could read the rolls of their life with less apprehen-sion; yet he was humbled to the dust by the many ill things he had done, and raised up again into a sober and fearful gratitude by the many he had come so near to doing, yet avoided. And then by a return on his former subject, he conceived a spark of hope. "This Master Hyde, if he were studied," thought he, "must have secrets of his own; black secrets, by the look of him; secrets compared to which poor Jekyll's worst would be like sunshine. Things cannot continue as they are. It turns me cold to think of this creature stealing like a thief to Harry's bedside; poor Harry, what a wakening! And the danger of it; for if this Hyde suspects the existence of the will, he may grow impatient to inherit. Ay, I must put my shoulder to the wheel—if Jekyll will but let me," he added, "if Jekyll will only let me." For once more he saw before his mind's eye, as clear as transparency, the strange clauses of the will.

DR. JEKYLL WAS QUITE AT EASE

A fortnight later, by excellent good fortune, the doctor gave one of his pleasant dinners to some five or six old cronies, all intelligent, reputable men and all judges of good wine; and Mr. Utterson so contrived that he remained behind after the others had departed. This was no new arrangement, but a thing that had befallen many scores of times. Where Ut-terson was liked, he was liked well. Hosts loved to detain the dry lawyer, when the light-hearted and loose-tongued had already their foot on the threshold; they liked to sit awhile in his unobtrusive company, practising for solitude, sobering their minds in the man's rich silence after the expense and strain of gaiety. To this rule, Dr. Jekyll was no exception; and as he now sat on the opposite side of the fire—a large, well-made, smooth-faced man of fifty, with something of a slyish cast perhaps, but every mark of capacity and kindness— you could see by his looks that he cherished for Mr. Utterson a sincere and warm affection.

"I have been waiting to speak to you, Jekyll," began the latter. "You know that will of yours?"

A close observer might have gathered that the topic was distasteful; but the doctor carried it off gaily. "My poor Utterson," said he, "you are unfortunate in such a client. I never saw a man so distressed as you were by my will; unless it were that hide-bound pedant, Lanyon, at what he called my scientific heresies. O, I know he's a good fellow—you needn't frown—an excellent fellow, and I always mean to see more of him; but a hide-bound pedant for all that; an ignorant, blatant pedant. I was never more disappointed in any man than Lanyon."

"You know I never approved of it," pursued Utterson, ruthlessly disregarding the fresh topic.

"My will? Yes, certainly, I know that," said the doctor, a trifle sharply. "You have told me so."

"Well, I tell you so again," continued the lawyer. "I have been learning something of young Hyde."

The large handsome face of Dr. Jekyll grew pale to the very lips, and there came a blackness about his eyes. "I do not care to hear more," said he. "This is a matter I thought we had agreed to drop."

"What I heard was abominable," said Utterson.

"It can make no change. You do not understand my position," returned the doctor, with a certain incoherency of manner. "I am painfully situated, Utterson; my position is a very strange—a very strange one. It is one of those affairs that cannot be mended by talking."

"Jekyll," said Utterson, "you know me: I am a man to be trusted. Make a clean breast of this in confidence; and I make no doubt I can get you out of it."

"My good Utterson," said the doctor, "this is very good of you, this is downright good of you, and I cannot find words to thank you in. I believe you fully; I would trust you before any man alive, ay, before myself, if I could make the choice;

but indeed it isn't what you fancy; it is not as bad as that; and just to put your good heart at rest, I will tell you one thing: the moment I choose, I can be rid of Mr. Hyde. I give you my hand upon that; and I thank you again and again; and I will just add one little word, Utterson, that I'm sure you'll take in good part: this is a private matter, and I beg of you to let it sleep."

Utterson reflected a little, looking in the fire.

"I have no doubt you are perfectly right," he said at last, getting to his feet.

"Well, but since we have touched upon this business, and for the last time I hope," continued the doctor, "there is one point I should like you to understand. I have really a very great interest in poor Hyde. I know you have seen him; he told me so; and I fear he was rude. But I do sincerely take a great, a very great interest in that young man; and if I am taken away, Utterson, I wish you to promise me that you will bear with him and get his rights for him. I think you would, if you knew all; and it would be a weight off my mind if you would promise."

"I can't pretend that I shall ever like him," said the lawyer.

"I don't ask that," pleaded Jekyll, laying his hand upon the other's arm; "I only ask for justice; I only ask you to help him for my sake, when I am no longer here."

Utterson heaved an irrepressible sigh. "Well," said he, "I promise."

THE CAREW MURDER CASE

Nearly a year later, in the month of October, 18—, London was startled by a crime of singular ferocity and rendered all the more notable by the high position of the victim. The details were few and startling. A maid servant living alone in a house not far from the river, had gone upstairs to bed about eleven. Although a fog rolled over the city in the small hours, the early part of the night was cloudless, and the lane, which the maid's window overlooked, was brilliantly lit by the full moon. It seems she was romantically given, for she sat down upon her box, which stood immediately under the window, and fell into a dream of musing. Never (she used to say, with streaming tears, when she narrated that experience), never had she felt more at peace with all men or thought more kindly of the world. And as she so sat she became aware of an aged beautiful gentleman with white hair, drawing near along the lane; and advancing to meet him, another and very small gentleman, to whom at first she paid less attention. When they had come within speech (which was just under the maid's eyes) the older man bowed and accosted the other with a very pretty manner of politeness. It did not seem as if the subject of his address were of great importance; indeed, from his pointing, it sometimes appeared as if he were only inquiring his way; but the moon shone on his face as he spoke, and the girl was pleased to watch it, it seemed to breathe such an innocent and old-world kindness of disposition, yet with something high too, as of a well-founded self-content. Presently her eye wandered to the other, and she was surprised to recognise in him a certain Mr. Hyde, who had once visited her master and for whom she had conceived a dislike. He had in his hand a heavy cane, with which he was trifling; but he answered never a word, and seemed to listen with an ill-contained impatience. And then all of a sudden he broke out in a great flame of anger, stamping with his foot, brandishing the cane, and carrying on (as the maid described it) like a madman. The old gentleman took a step back, with the air of one very much surprised and a trifle hurt; and at that Mr. Hyde broke out of all bounds and clubbed him to the earth. And next moment, with ape-like fury, he was trampling his victim under foot and hailing down a storm of blows, under which the bones were audibly shattered and the body jumped upon the roadway. At the horror of these sights and sounds, the maid fainted.

It was two o'clock when she came to herself and called for the police. The murderer was gone long ago; but there lay his victim in the middle of the lane, incredibly mangled. The stick with which the deed had been done, although it was of some rare and very tough and heavy wood, had broken in the middle under the stress of this insensate cruelty; and one splintered half had rolled in the neighbouring gutter—the other, without doubt, had been carried away by the murderer. A purse and gold watch were found upon the victim; but no cards or papers, except a sealed and stamped envelope, which he had been probably carrying to the post, and which bore the name and address of Mr. Utterson.

This was brought to the lawyer the next morning, before he was out of bed; and he had no sooner seen it, and been told the circumstances, than he shot out a solemn lip. "I shall say nothing till I have seen the body," said he; "this may be very serious. Have the kindness to wait while I dress." And with the same grave countenance he hurried through his breakfast and drove to the police station, whither the body had been carried. As soon as he came into the cell, he nodded.

"Yes," said he, "I recognise him. I am sorry to say that this is Sir Danver Carew."

"Good God, sir," exclaimed the officer, "is it possible?" And the next moment his eye lighted up with professional ambition. "This will make a deal of noise," he said. "And perhaps you can help us to the man." And he briefly narrated what the maid had seen, and showed the broken stick.

Mr. Utterson had already quailed at the name of Hyde; but when the stick was laid before him, he could doubt no longer; broken and battered as it was, he recognised it for one that he had himself presented many years before to Henry Jekyll.

"Is this Mr. Hyde a person of small stature?" he inquired.

"Particularly small and particularly wicked-looking, is what the maid calls him," said the officer.

Mr. Utterson reflected; and then, raising his head, "If you will come with me in my cab," he said, "I think I can take you to his house."

It was by this time about nine in the morning, and the first fog of the season. A great chocolate-coloured pall lowered over heaven, but the wind was continually charging and routing these embattled vapours; so that as the cab crawled from street to street, Mr. Utterson beheld a marvelous number of degrees and hues of twilight; for here it would be dark like the back-end of evening; and there would be a glow of a rich, lurid brown, like the light of some strange conflagration; and here, for a moment, the fog would be quite broken up, and a haggard shaft of daylight would glance in between the swirling wreaths. The dismal quarter of Soho seen under these changing glimpses, with its muddy ways, and slatternly passengers, and its lamps, which had never been extinguished or had been kindled afresh to combat this mournful reinvasion of darkness, seemed, in the lawyer's eyes, like a district of some city in a nightmare. The thoughts of his mind, besides, were of the gloomiest dye; and when he glanced at the companion of his drive, he was conscious of some touch of that terror of the law and the law's officers, which may at times assail the most honest.

As the cab drew up before the address indicated, the fog lifted a little and showed him a dingy street, a gin palace, a low French eating house, a shop for the retail of penny numbers and twopenny salads, many ragged children huddled in the doorways, and many women of many different nationalities passing out, key in hand, to have a morning glass; and the next moment the fog settled down again upon that part, as brown as umber, and cut him off from his blackguardly surroundings. This was the home of Henry Jekyll's favourite; of a man who was heir to a quarter of a million sterling.

An ivory-faced and silvery-haired old woman opened the door. She had an evil face, smoothed by hypocrisy: but her manners were excellent. Yes, she said, this was Mr. Hyde's, but he was not at home; he had been in that night very late, but he had gone away again in less than an hour; there was nothing strange in that; his habits were very irregular, and he was often absent; for instance, it was nearly two months since she had seen him till yesterday.

"Very well, then, we wish to see his rooms," said the lawyer; and when the woman begin to declare it was impossible, "I had better tell you who this person is," he added. "This is Inspector Newcomen of Scotland Yard."

A flash of odious joy appeared upon the woman's face. "Ah!" said she, "he is in trouble! What has he done?"

Mr. Utterson and the inspector exchanged glances. "He don't seem a very popular character," observed the latter. "And now, my good woman, just let me and this gentleman have a look about us."

In the whole extent of the house, which but for the old woman remained otherwise empty, Mr. Hyde had only used a couple of rooms; but these were furnished with luxury and good taste. A closet was filled with wine; the plate was of silver, the napery elegant; a good picture hung upon the walls, a gift (as Utterson supposed) from Henry Jekyll, who was much of a connoisseur; and the carpets were of many plies and agreeable in colour. At this moment, however, the rooms bore every mark of having been recently and hurriedly ransacked; clothes lay about the floor, with their pockets inside out; lock-fast drawers stood open; and on the hearth there lay a pile of grey ashes, as though many papers had been burned. From these embers the inspector disinterred the butt end of a green cheque book, which had resisted the action of the fire; the other half of the stick was found behind the door; and as this clinched his suspicions, the officer declared himself delighted. A visit to the bank, where several thousand pounds were found to be lying to the murderer's credit, completed his gratification.

"You may depend upon it, sir," he told Mr. Utterson: "I have him in my hand. He must have lost his head, or he never would have left the stick or, above all, burned the cheque book. Why, money's life to the man. We have nothing to do but wait for him at the bank, and get out the handbills."

This last, however, was not so easy of accomplishment; for Mr. Hyde had numbered few familiars—even the master of the servant maid had only seen him twice; his family could nowhere be traced; he had never been photographed; and the few who could describe him differed widely, as common observers will. Only on one point were they agreed; and that was the haunting sense of unexpressed deformity with which the fugitive impressed his beholders.

INCIDENT OF THE LETTER

It was late in the afternoon, when Mr. Utterson found his way to Dr. Jekyll's door, where he was at once admitted by Poole, and carried down by the kitchen offices and across a yard which had once been a garden, to the building which was indifferently known as the laboratory or dissecting rooms. The doctor had bought the house from the heirs of a celebrated surgeon; and his own tastes being rather chemical than anatomical, had changed the destination of the block at the bottom of the garden. It was the first time that the lawyer had been received in that part of his friend's quarters; and he eyed the dingy, windowless structure with curiosity, and gazed round with a distasteful sense of strangeness as he crossed the theatre, once crowded with eager students and now lying gaunt and silent, the tables laden with chemical apparatus, the floor strewn with crates and littered with packing straw, and the light falling dimly through the foggy cupola. At the further end, a flight of stairs mounted to a door covered with red baize; and through this, Mr. Utterson was at last received into the doctor's cabinet. It was a large room fitted round with glass presses, furnished, among other things, with a cheval-glass and a business table, and looking out upon the court by three dusty windows barred with iron. The fire burned in the grate; a lamp was set lighted on the chimney shelf, for even in the houses the fog began to lie thickly; and there, close up to the warmth, sat Dr. Jekyll, looking deadly sick. He did not rise to meet his visitor, but held out a cold hand and bade him welcome in a changed voice.

"And now," said Mr. Utterson, as soon as Poole had left them, "you have heard the news?"

The doctor shuddered. "They were crying it in the square," he said. "I heard them in my dining-room."

"One word," said the lawyer. "Carew was my client, but so are you, and I want to know what I am doing. You have not been mad enough to hide this fellow?"

"Utterson, I swear to God," cried the doctor, "I swear to God I will never set eyes on him again. I bind my honour to you that I am done with him in this world. It is all at an end. And indeed he does not want my help; you do not know him as I do; he is safe, he is quite safe; mark my words, he will never more be heard of."

The lawyer listened gloomily; he did not like his friend's feverish manner. "You seem pretty sure of him," said he; "and for your sake, I hope you may be right. If it came to a trial, your name might appear."

"I am quite sure of him," replied Jekyll; "I have grounds for certainty that I cannot share with anyone. But there is one thing on which you may advise me. I have—I have received a letter; and I am at a loss whether I should show it to the police. I should like to leave it in your hands, Utterson; you would judge wisely, I am sure; I have so great a trust in you."

"You fear, I suppose, that it might lead to his detection?" asked the lawyer.

"No," said the other. "I cannot say that I care what becomes of Hyde; I am quite done with him. I was thinking of my own character, which this hateful business has rather exposed."

Utterson ruminated awhile; he was surprised at his friend's selfishness, and yet relieved by it. "Well," said he, at last, "let me see the letter."

The letter was written in an odd, upright hand and signed "Edward Hyde": and it signified, briefly enough, that the writer's benefactor, Dr. Jekyll, whom he had long so unworthily repaid for a thousand generosities, need labour under no alarm for his safety, as he had means of escape on which he placed a sure dependence. The lawyer liked this letter well enough; it put a better colour on the intimacy than he had looked for; and he blamed himself for some of his past suspicions.

"Have you the envelope?" he asked.

"I burned it," replied Jekyll, "before I thought what I was

about. But it bore no postmark. The note was handed in."

"Shall I keep this and sleep upon it?" asked Utterson.

"I wish you to judge for me entirely," was the reply. "I have lost confidence in myself."

"Well, I shall consider," returned the lawyer. "And now one word more: it was Hyde who dictated the terms in your will about that disappearance?"

The doctor seemed seized with a qualm of faintness; he shut his mouth tight and nodded.

"I knew it," said Utterson. "He meant to murder you. You had a fine escape."

"I have had what is far more to the purpose," returned the doctor solemnly: "I have had a lesson—O God, Utterson, what a lesson I have had!" And he covered his face for a moment with his hands.

On his way out, the lawyer stopped and had a word or two with Poole. "By the bye," said he, "there was a letter handed in to-day: what was the messenger like?" But Poole was positive. nothing had come except by post; "and only circulars by that," he added.

This news sent off the visitor with his fears renewed. Plainly the letter had come by the laboratory door; possibly, indeed, it had been written in the cabinet; and if that were so, it must be differently judged, and handled with the more caution. The newsboys, as he went, were crying themselves hoarse along the footways: "Special edition. Shocking murder of an M.P." That was the funeral oration of one friend and client; and he could not help a certain apprehension lest the good name of another should be sucked down in the eddy of the scandal. It was, at least, a ticklish decision that he had to make; and self-reliant as he was by habit, he began to cherish a longing for advice. It was not to be had directly; but perhaps, he thought, it might be fished for.

Presently after, he sat on one side of his own hearth, with Mr. Guest, his head clerk, upon the other, and midway between, at a nicely calculated distance from the fire, a bottle of a particular old wine that had long dwelt unsunned in the foundations of his house. The fog still slept on the wing above the drowned city, where the lamps glimmered like carbuncles; and through the muffle and smother of these fallen clouds, the procession of the town's life was still rolling in through the great arteries with a sound as of a mighty wind. But the room was gay with firelight. In the bottle the acids were long ago resolved; the imperial dye had softened with time, as the colour grows richer in stained windows; and the glow of hot autumn afternoons on hillside vineyards, was ready to be set free and to disperse the fogs of London. Insensibly the lawyer melted. There was no man from whom he kept fewer secrets than Mr. Guest; and he was not always sure that he kept as many as he meant. Guest had often been on business to the doctor's; he knew Poole; he could scarce have failed to hear of Mr. Hyde's familiarity about the house; he might draw conclusions: was it not as well, then, that he should see a letter which put that mystery to rights? and above all since Guest, being a great student and critic of handwriting, would consider the step natural and obliging? The clerk, besides, was a man of counsel; he could scarce read so strange a document without dropping a remark; and by that remark Mr. Utterson might shape his future course.

"This is a sad business about Sir Danvers," he said.

"Yes, sir, indeed. It has elicited a great deal of public feeling," returned Guest. "The man, of course, was mad."

"I should like to hear your views on that," replied Utterson. "I have a document here in his handwriting; it is between ourselves, for I scarce know what to do about it; it is an ugly business at the best. But there it is; quite in your way: a murderer's autograph."

Guest's eyes brightened, and he sat down at once and studied it with passion. "No sir," he said: "not mad; but it is an odd hand."

"And by all accounts a very odd writer," added the lawyer.

Just then the servant entered with a note.

"Is that from Dr. Jekyll, sir?" inquired the clerk. "I thought I knew the writing. Anything private, Mr. Utterson?"

"Only an invitation to dinner. Why? Do you want to see it?"

"One moment. I thank you, sir;" and the clerk laid the two sheets of paper alongside and sedulously compared their contents. "Thank you, sir," he said at last, returning both; "it's a very interesting autograph."

There was a pause, during which Mr. Utterson struggled with himself. "Why did you compare them, Guest?" he inquired suddenly.

"Well, sir," returned the clerk, "there's a rather singular resemblance; the two hands are in many points identical: only differently sloped."

"Rather quaint," said Utterson.

"It is, as you say, rather quaint," returned Guest.

"I wouldn't speak of this note, you know," said the master.

"No, sir," said the clerk. "I understand."

But no sooner was Mr. Utterson alone that night, than he locked the note into his safe, where it reposed from that time forward. "What!" he thought. "Henry Jekyll forge for a murderer!" And his blood ran cold in his veins.

REMARKABLE INCIDENT OF DR. LANYON

Time ran on; thousands of pounds were offered in reward, for the death of Sir Danvers was resented as a public injury; but Mr. Hyde had disappeared out of the ken of the police as though he had never existed. Much of his past was unearthed, indeed, and all disreputable: tales came out of the man's cruelty, at once so callous and violent; of his vile life, of his strange associates, of the hatred that seemed to have surrounded his career; but of his present whereabouts, not a whisper. From the time he had left the house in Soho on the morning of the murder, he was simply blotted out; and gradually, as time drew on, Mr. Utterson began to recover from the hotness of his alarm, and to grow more at quiet with himself. The death of Sir Danvers was, to his way of thinking, more than paid for by the disappearance of Mr. Hyde. Now that that evil influence had been withdrawn, a new life began for Dr. Jekyll. He came out of his seclusion, renewed relations with his friends, became once more their familiar guest and entertainer; and whilst he had always been known for charities, he was now no less distinguished for religion. He was busy, he was much in the open air, he did good; his face seemed to open and brighten, as if with an inward consciousness of service; and for more than two months, the doctor was at peace.

On the 8th of January Utterson had dined at the doctor's with a small party; Lanyon had been there; and the face of the host had looked from one to the other as in the old days when the trio were inseparable friends. On the 12th, and again on the 14th, the door was shut against the lawyer. "The doctor was confined to the house," Poole said, "and saw no one." On the 15th, he tried again, and was again refused; and having now been used for the last two months to see his friend almost daily, he found this return of solitude to weigh upon his spirits. The fifth night he had in Guest to dine with him; and the sixth he betook himself to Dr. Lanyon's.

There at least he was not denied admittance; but when he

came in he was shocked at the change which had taken place in the doctor's appearance. He had his death-warrant written legibly upon his face. The rosy man had grown pale; his flesh had fallen away; he was visibly balder and older; and yet it was not so much these tokens of a swift physical decay that arrested the lawyer's notice, as a look in the eye and quality of manner that seemed to testify to some deep-seated terror of the mind. It was unlikely that the doctor should fear death; and yet that was what Utterson was tempted to suspect. "Yes," he thought; "he is a doctor, he must know his own state and that his days are counted; and the knowledge is more than he can bear." And yet when Utterson remarked on his ill-looks, it was with an air of great firmness that Lanyon declared himself a doomed man.

"I have had a shock," he said, "and I shall never recover. It is a question of weeks. Well, life has been pleasant; I liked it; yes, sir, I used to like it. I sometimes think if we knew all, we should be more glad to get away."

"Jekyll is ill, too," observed Utterson. "Have you seen him?"

But Lanyon's face changed, and he held up a trembling hand. "I wish to see or hear no more of Dr. Jekyll," he said in a loud, unsteady voice. "I am quite done with that person; and I beg that you will spare me any allusion to one whom I regard as dead."

"Tut-tut," said Mr. Utterson; and then after a considerable pause, "Can't I do anything?" he inquired. "We are three very old friends, Lanyon; we shall not live to make others."

"Nothing can be done," returned Lanyon; "ask himself."

"He will not see me," said the lawyer.

"I am not surprised at that," was the reply. "Some day, Utterson, after I am dead, you may perhaps come to learn the right and wrong of this. I cannot tell you. And in the meantime, if you can sit and talk with me of other things, for God's sake, stay and do so; but if you cannot keep clear of this accursed topic, then in God's name, go, for I cannot bear it."

As soon as he got home, Utterson sat down and wrote to Jekyll, complaining of his exclusion from the house, and asking the cause of this unhappy break with Lanyon; and the next day brought him a long answer, often very pathetically worded, and sometimes darkly mysterious in drift. The quarrel with Lanyon was incurable. "I do no blame our old friend," Jekyll wrote, "but I share his view that we must never meet.

I mean from henceforth to lead a life of extreme seclusion; you must not be surprised, nor must you doubt my friendship, if my door is often shut even to you. You must suffer me to go my own dark way. I have brought on myself a punishment and a danger that I cannot name. If I am the chief of sinners, I am the chief of sufferers also. I could not think that this earth contained a place for sufferings and terrors so unmanning; and you can do but one thing, Utterson, to lighten this destiny, and that is to respect my silence." Utterson was amazed; the dark influence of Hyde had been withdrawn, the doctor had returned to his old tasks and amities; a week ago, the prospect had smiled with every promise of a cheerful and an honoured age; and now in a moment, friendship, and peace of mind, and the whole tenor of his life were wrecked. So great and unprepared a change pointed to madness; but in view of Lanyon's manner and words, there must lie for it some deeper ground.

A week afterwards Dr. Lanyon took to his bed, and in something less than a fortnight he was dead. The night after the funeral, at which he had been sadly affected, Utterson locked the door of his business room, and sitting there by the light of a melancholy candle, drew out and set before him an envelope addressed by the hand and sealed with the seal of his dead friend. "PRIVATE: for the hands of G. J. Utterson ALONE, and in case of his predecease *to be destroyed unread*," so it was emphatically superscribed; and the lawyer dreaded to behold the contents. "I have buried one friend to-day," he thought: "what if this should cost me another?" And then he condemned the fear as a disloyalty, and broke the seal. Within there was another enclosure, likewise sealed, and marked upon the cover as "not to be opened till the death or disappearance of Dr. Henry Jekyll." Utterson could not trust his eyes. Yes, it was disappearance; here again, as in the mad will which he had long ago restored to its author, here again were the idea of a disappearance and the name of Henry Jekyll bracketted. But in the will, that idea had sprung from the sinister suggestion of the man Hyde; it was set there with a purpose all too plain and horrible. Written by the hand of Lanyon, what should it mean? A great curiosity came on the trustee, to disregard the prohibition and dive at once to the bottom of these mysteries; but professional honour and faith to his dead friend were stringent obligations; and the packet slept in the inmost corner of his private safe.

It is one thing to mortify curiosity, another to conquer it;

and it may be doubted if, from that day forth, Utterson desired the society of his surviving friend with the same eagerness. He thought of him kindly; but his thoughts were dis-
quieted and fearful. He went to call indeed; but he was perhaps
relieved to be denied admittance; perhaps, in his heart, he
preferred to speak with Poole upon the doorstep and surrounded by the air and sounds of the open city, rather than
to be admitted into that house of voluntary bondage, and to
sit and speak with its inscrutable recluse. Poole had, indeed,
no very pleasant news to communicate. The doctor, it appeared, now more than ever confined himself to the cabinet
over the laboratory, where he would sometimes even sleep;
he was out of spirits, he had grown very silent, he did not
read; it seemed as if he had something on his mind. Utterson
became so used to the unvarying character of these reports,
that he fell off little by little in the frequency of his visits.

INCIDENT AT THE WINDOW

It chanced on Sunday, when Mr. Utterson was on his usual
walk with Mr. Enfield, that their way lay once again through
the by-street; and that when they came in front of the door,
both stopped to gaze on it.

"Well," said Enfield, "that story's at an end at least. We
shall never see more of Mr. Hyde."

"I hope not," said Utterson. "Did I ever tell you that I
once saw him, and shared your feeling of repulsion?"

"It was impossible to do the one without the other," returned Enfield. "And by the way, what an ass you must have
thought me, not to know that this was a back way to Dr.
Jekyll's! It was partly your own fault that I found it out, even
when I did."

"So you found it out, did you?" said Utterson. "But if that
be so, we may step into the court and take a look at the
windows. To tell you the truth, I am uneasy about poor Jekyll;
and even outside, I feel as if the presence of a friend might
do him good."

The court was very cool and a little damp, and full of
premature twilight, although the sky, high up overhead, was
still bright with sunset. The middle one of the three windows
was half-way open; and sitting close beside it, taking the air
with an infinite sadness of mien, like some disconsolate prisoner, Utterson saw Dr. Jekyll.

"What! Jekyll!" he cried. "I trust you are better."

"I am very low, Utterson," replied the doctor drearily, "very low. It will not last long, thank God."

"You stay too much indoors," said the lawyer. "You should be out, whipping up the circulation like Mr. Enfield and me. (This is my cousin—Mr. Enfield—Dr. Jekyll.) Come now; get your hat and take a quick turn with us."

"You are very good," sighed the other. "I should like to very much; but no, no, no, it is quite impossible; I dare not. But indeed, Utterson, I am very glad to see you; this is really a great pleasure; I would ask you and Mr. Enfield up, but the place is really not fit."

"Why then," said the lawyer, good-naturedly, "the best thing we can do is to stay down here and speak with you from where we are."

"That is just what I was about to venture to propose," returned the doctor with a smile. But the words were hardly uttered, before the smile was struck out of his face and succeeded by an expression of such abject terror and despair, as froze the very blood of the two gentlemen below. They saw it but for a glimpse for the window was instantly thrust down; but that glimpse had been sufficient, and they turned and left the court without a word. In silence, too, they traversed the by-street; and it was not until they had come into a neighbouring thoroughfare, where even upon a Sunday there were still some stirrings of life, that Mr. Utterson at last turned and looked at his companion. They were both pale; and there was an answering horror in their eyes.

"God forgive us, God forgive us," said Mr. Utterson.

But Mr. Enfield only nodded his head very seriously, and walked on once more in silence.

THE LAST NIGHT

Mr. Utterson was sitting by his fireside one evening after dinner, when he was surprised to receive a visit from Poole.

"Bless me, Poole, what brings you here?" he cried; and then taking a second look at him, "What ails you?" he added; "is the doctor ill?"

"Mr. Utterson," said the man, "there is something wrong."

"Take a seat, and here is a glass of wine for you," said the lawyer. "Now, take your time, and tell me plainly what you want."

"You know the doctor's ways, sir," replied Poole, "and how he shuts himself up. Well, he's shut up again in the cabinet; and I don't like it, sir—I wish I may die if I like it. Mr. Utterson, sir, I'm afraid."

"Now, my good man," said the lawyer, "be explicit. What are you afraid of?"

"I've been afraid for about a week," returned Poole, doggedly disregarding the question, "and I can bear it no more."

The man's appearance amply bore out his words; his manner was altered for the worse; and except for the moment when he had first announced his terror, he had not once looked the lawyer in the face. Even now, he sat with the glass of wine untasted on his knee, and his eyes directed to a corner of the floor. "I can bear it no more," he repeated.

"Come," said the lawyer, "I see you have some good reason, Poole; I see there is something seriously amiss. Try to tell me what it is."

"I think there's been foul play," said Poole, hoarsely.

"Foul play!" cried the lawyer, a good deal frightened and rather inclined to be irritated in consequence. "What foul play! What does the man mean?"

"I daren't say, sir," was the answer; "but will you come along with me and see for yourself?"

Mr. Utterson's only answer was to rise and get his hat and greatcoat; but he observed with wonder the greatness of the relief that appeared upon the butler's face, and perhaps with no less, that the wine was still untasted when he set it down to follow.

It was a wild, cold, seasonable night of March, with a pale moon, lying on her back as though the wind had tilted her, and a flying wrack of the most diaphanous and lawny texture. The wind made talking difficult, and flecked the blood into the face. It seemed to have swept the streets unusually bare of passengers, besides; for Mr. Utterson thought he had never seen that part of London so deserted. He could have wished it otherwise; never in his life had he been conscious of so sharp a wish to see and touch his fellow-creatures; for struggle as he might, there was borne in upon his mind a crushing anticipation of calamity. The square, when they got there, was full of wind and dust, and the thin trees in the garden were lashing themselves along the railing. Poole, who had kept all the way a pace or two ahead, now pulled up in the middle of the pavement, and in spite of the biting weather, took off his hat and mopped his brow with a red pocket-handkerchief. But for all the hurry of his coming, these were not the dews of exertion that he wiped away, but the moisture of some strangling anguish; for his face was white and his voice, when he spoke, harsh and broken.

"Well, sir," he said, "here we are, and God grant there be nothing wrong."

"Amen, Poole," said the lawyer.

Thereupon the servant knocked in a very guarded manner; the door was opened on the chain; and a voice from within, "Is that you, Poole?"

"It's all right," said Poole. "Open the door."

The hall, when they entered it, was brightly lighted up; the fire was built high; and about the hearth the whole of the servants, men and women, stood huddled together like a flock of sheep. At the sight of Mr. Utterson, the housemaid broke into hysterical whimpering; and the cook, crying out "Bless God! it's Mr. Utterson," ran forward as if to take him in her arms.

"What, what? Are you all here?" said the lawyer peevishly. "Very irregular, very unseemly; your master would be far from pleased."

"They're all afraid," said Poole.

Blank silence followed, no one protesting; only the maid lifted up her voice and now wept loudly.

"Hold your tongue!" Poole said to her, with a ferocity of accent that testified to his own jangled nerves; and indeed, when the girl had so suddenly raised the note of her lamentation, they had all started and turned towards the inner door with faces of dreadful expectation. "And now," continued the butler, addressing the knife-boy, "reach me a candle, and we'll get this through hands at once." And then he begged Mr. Utterson to follow him, and led the way to the back garden.

"Now, sir," said he, "you come as gently as you can. I want you to hear, and I don't want you to be heard. And see here, sir, if by any chance he was to ask you in, don't go."

Mr. Utterson's nerves, at this unlooked-for termination, gave a jerk that nearly threw him from his balance; but he recollected his courage and followed the butler into the laboratory building and through the surgical theatre, with its lumber of crates and bottles, to the foot of the stair. Here Poole motioned him to stand on one side and listen; while he himself, setting down the candle and making a great and obvious call on his resolution, mounted the steps and knocked with a somewhat uncertain hand on the red baize of the cabinet door.

"Mr. Utterson, sir, asking to see you," he called; and even as he did so, once more violently signed to the lawyer to give ear.

A voice answered from within: "Tell him I cannot see anyone," it said complainingly.

"Thank you, sir," said Poole, with a note of something like triumph in his voice; and taking up his candle, he led Mr. Utterson back across the yard and into the great kitchen, where the fire was out and the beetles were leaping on the floor.

"Sir," he said, looking Mr. Utterson in the eyes, "was that my master's voice?"

"It seems much changed," replied the lawyer, very pale, but giving look for look.

"Changed? Well, yes, I think so," said the butler. "Have I been twenty years in this man's house, to be deceived about his voice? No, sir; master's made away with; he was made away with eight days ago, when we heard him cry out upon the name of God; and *who's* in there instead of him, and *why* it stays there, is a thing that cries to Heaven, Mr. Utterson!"

"This is a very strange tale, Poole; this is rather a wild tale, my man," said Mr. Utterson, biting his finger. "Suppose it were as you suppose, supposing Dr. Jekyll to have been— well, murdered, what could induce the murderer to stay? That won't hold water; it doesn't commend itself to reason."

"Well, Mr. Utterson, you are a hard man to satisfy, but I'll do it yet," said Poole. "All this last week (you must know) him, or it, whatever it is that lives in that cabinet, has been crying night and day for some sort of medicine and cannot get it to his mind. It was sometimes his way—the master's, that is—to write his orders on a sheet of paper and throw it on the stair. We've had nothing else this week back; nothing but papers, and a closed door, and the very meals left there to be smuggled in when nobody was looking. Well, sir, every day, ay, and twice and thrice in the same day, there have been orders and complaints, and I have been sent flying to all the wholesale chemists in town. Every time I brought the stuff back, there would be another paper telling me to return it, because it was not pure, and another order to a different firm. This drug is wanted bitter bad, sir, whatever for."

"Have you any of these papers?" asked Mr. Utterson.

Poole felt in his pocket and handed out a crumpled note,

which the lawyer, bending nearer to the candle, carefully examined. Its contents ran thus: "Dr. Jekyll presents his compliments to Messrs. Maw. He assures them that their last sample is impure and quite useless for his present purpose. In the year 18—, Dr. J. purchased a somewhat large quantity from Messrs. M. He now begs them to search with most sedulous care, and should any of the same quality be left, to forward it to him at once. Expense is no consideration. The importance of this to Dr. J. can hardly be exaggerated." So far the letter had run composedly enough, but here with a sudden splutter of the pen, the writer's emotion had broken loose. "For God's sake," he added, "find me some of the old."

"This is a strange note," said Mr. Utterson; and then sharply, "How do you come to have it open?"

"The man at Maw's was main angry, sir, and he threw it back to me like so much dirt," returned Poole.

"This is unquestionably the doctor's hand, do you know?" resumed the lawyer.

"I thought it looked like it," said the servant rather sulkily; and then, with another voice, "But what matters hand of write?" he said. "I've seen him!"

"Seen him?" repeated Mr. Utterson. "Well?"

"That's it!" said Poole. "It was this way. I came suddenly into the theatre from the garden. It seems he had slipped out to look for this drug or whatever it is; for the cabinet door was open, and there he was at the far end of the room digging among the crates. He looked up when I came in, gave a kind of cry, and whipped upstairs into the cabinet. It was but one minute that I saw him, but the hair stood upon my head like quills. Sir, if that was my master, why had he a mask upon his face? If it was my master, why did he cry out like a rat, and run from me? I have served him long enough. And then . . ." The man paused and passed his hand over his face.

"These are all very strange circumstances," said Mr. Utterson, "but I think I begin to see daylight. Your master, Poole, is plainly seized with one of those maladies that both torture and deform the sufferer; hence, for aught I know, the alteration of his voice; hence the mask and the avoidance of his friends; hence his eagerness to find this drug, by means of which the poor soul retains some hope of ultimate recovery—God grant that he be not deceived! There is my explanation; it is sad enough, Poole, ay, and appalling to consider; but it is plain and natural, hangs well together, and delivers us from all exorbitant alarms."

"Sir," said the butler, turning to a sort of mottled pallor, "that thing was not my master, and there's the truth. My master"—here he looked round him and began to whisper—"is a tall, fine build of a man, and this was more of a dwarf." Utterson attempted to protest. "O, sir," cried Poole, "do you think I do not know my master after twenty years? Do you think I do not know where his head comes to in the cabinet door, where I saw him every morning of my life? No, sir, that thing in the mask was never Dr. Jekyll—God knows what it was, but it was never Dr. Jekyll; and it is the belief of my heart that there was murder done."

"Poole," replied the lawyer, "if you say that, it will become my duty to make certain. Much as I desire to spare your master's feelings, much as I am puzzled by this note which seems to prove him to be still alive, I shall consider it my duty to break in that door."

"Ah, Mr. Utterson, that's talking!" cried the butler.

"And now comes the second question," resumed Utterson: "Who is going to do it?"

"Why, you and me, sir," was the undaunted reply.

"That's very well said," returned the lawyer; "and whatever comes of it, I shall make it my business to see you are no loser."

"There is an axe in the theatre," continued Poole; "and you might take the kitchen poker for yourself."

The lawyer took that rude but weighty instrument into his hand, and balanced it. "Do you know, Poole," he said, looking up, "that you and I are about to place ourselves in a position of some peril?"

"You may say so, sir, indeed," returned the butler.

"It is well, then, that we should be frank," said the other. "We both think more than we have said; let us make a clean breast. This masked figure that you saw, did you recognise it?"

"Well, sir, it went so quick, and the creature was so doubled up, that I could hardly swear to that," was the answer. "But if you mean, was it Mr. Hyde?—why, yes, I think it was! You see, it was much of the same bigness; and it had the same quick, light way with it; and then who else could have got in by the laboratory door? You have not forgot, sir, that at the time of the murder he had still the key with him? But that's not all. I don't know, Mr. Utterson, if you ever met this Mr. Hyde?"

"Yes," said the lawyer, "I once spoke with him."

"Then you must know as well as the rest of us that there was something queer about that gentleman—something that gave a man a turn—I don't know rightly how to say it, sir, beyond this: that you felt in your marrow kind of cold and thin."

"I own I felt something of what you describe," said Mr. Utterson.

"Quite so, sir," returned Poole. "Well, when that masked thing like a monkey jumped from among the chemicals and whipped into the cabinet, it went down my spine like ice. O, I know it's not evidence, Mr. Utterson; I'm book-learned enough for that; but a man has his feelings, and I give you my bible-word it was Mr. Hyde!"

"Ay, ay," said the lawyer. "My fears incline to the same point. Evil, I fear, founded—evil was sure to come—of that connection. Ay truly, I believe you; I believe poor Harry is killed; and I believe his murderer (for what purpose, God alone can tell) is still lurking in his victim's room. Well, let our name be vengeance. Call Bradshaw."

The footman came at the summons, very white and nervous.

"Pull yourself together, Bradshaw," said the lawyer. "This suspense, I know, is telling upon all of you; but it is now our intention to make an end of it. Poole, here, and I are going to force our way into the cabinet. If all is well, my shoulders are broad enough to bear the blame. Meanwhile, lest anything should really be amiss, or any malefactor seek to escape by the back, you and the boy must go round the corner with a pair of good sticks and take your post at the laboratory door. We give you ten minutes, to get to your stations."

As Bradshaw left, the lawyer looked at his watch. "And now, Poole, let us get to ours," he said; and taking the poker under his arm, led the way into the yard. The scud had banked over the moon, and it was now quite dark. The wind, which only broke in puffs and draughts into that deep well of building, tossed the light of the candle to and fro about their steps, until they came into the shelter of the theatre, where they sat down silently to wait. London hummed solemnly all around; but nearer at hand, the stillness was only broken by the sounds of a footfall moving to and fro along the cabinet floor.

"So it will walk all day, sir," whispered Poole; "ay, and

the better part of the night. Only when a new sample comes from the chemist, there's a bit of a break. Ah, it's an ill conscience that's such an enemy to rest! Ah, sir, there's blood foully shed in every step of it! But hark again, a little closer— put your heart in your ears, Mr. Utterson, and tell me, is that the doctor's foot?"

The steps fell lightly and oddly, with a certain swing, for all they went so slowly; it was different indeed from the heavy creaking tread of Henry Jekyll. Utterson sighed. "Is there never anything else?" he asked.

Poole nodded. "Once," he said. "Once I heard it weeping!"

"Weeping? how that?" said the lawyer, conscious of a sudden chill of horror.

"Weeping like a woman or a lost soul," said the butler. "I came away with that upon my heart, that I could have wept too."

But now the ten minutes drew to an end. Poole disinterred the axe from under a stack of packing straw; the candle was set upon the nearest table to light them to the attack; and they drew near with bated breath to where that patient foot was still going up and down, up and down, in the quiet of the night. "Jekyll," cried Utterson, with a loud voice, "I demand to see you." He paused a moment, but there came no reply. "I give you fair warning, our suspicions are aroused, and I must and shall see you," he resumed; "if not by fair means, then by foul—if not of your consent, then by brute force!"

"Utterson," said the voice, "for God's sake, have mercy!"

"Ah, that's not, Jekyll's voice—it's Hyde's!" cried Utterson. "Down with the door, Poole!"

Poole swung the axe over his shoulder; the blow shook the building, and the red baize door leaped against the lock and hinges. A dismal screech, as of mere animal terror, rang from the cabinet. Up went the ax again, and again the panels crashed and the frame bounded; four times the blow fell; but the wood was tough and the fittings were of excellent workmanship; and it was not until the fifth, that the lock burst and the wreck of the door fell inwards on the carpet.

The besiegers, appalled by their own riot and the stillness that had succeeded, stood back a little and peered in. There lay the cabinet before their eyes in the quiet lamplight, a good fire glowing and chattering on the hearth, the kettle singing its thin strain, a drawer or two open, papers neatly set forth on the business table, and nearer the fire, the things laid out for tea; the quietest room, you would have said, and, but for the glazed presses full of chemicals, the most commonplace that night in London.

Right in the midst there lay the body of a man sorely contorted and still twitching. They drew near on tiptoe, turned it on its back and beheld the face of Edward Hyde. He was dressed in clothes far too large for him, clothes of the doctor's bigness; the cords of his face still moved with a semblance of life, but life was quite gone: and by the crushed phial in the hand and the strong smell of kernels that hung upon the air, Utterson knew that he was looking on the body of a self-destroyer.

"We have come too late," he said sternly, "whether to save or punish. Hyde is gone to his account; and it only remains for us to find the body of your master."

The far greater proportion of the building was occupied by the theatre, which filled almost the whole ground storey and was lighted from above, and by the cabinet, which formed an upper storey at one end and looked upon the court. A corridor joined the theatre to the door on the by-street; and with this the cabinet communicated separately by a second flight of stairs. There were besides a few dark closets and a spacious cellar. All these they now thoroughly examined. Each closet needed but a glance, for all were empty, and all, by the dust that fell from their doors, had stood long unopened. The cellar, indeed, was filled with crazy lumber, mostly dating from the times of the surgeon who was Jekyll's predecessor; but even as they opened the door they were advertised of the uselessness of further search, by the fall of a perfect mat of cobweb which had for years sealed up the entrance. Nowhere was there any trace of Henry Jekyll, dead or alive.

Poole stamped on the flags of the corridor. "He must be buried here," he said, hearkening to the sound.

"Or he may have fled," said Utterson, and he turned to examine the door in the by-street. It was locked; and lying near by on the flags, they found the key, already stained with rust.

"This does not look like use," observed the lawyer.

"Use!" echoed Poole. "Do you not see, sir, it is broken? much as if a man had stamped on it."

"Ay," continued Utterson, "and the fractures, too, are rusty." The two men looked at each other with a scare. "This is beyond me, Poole," said the lawyer. "Let us go back to the cabinet."

They mounted the stair in silence, and still with an occasional awestruck glance at the dead body, proceeded more thoroughly to examine the contents of the cabinet. At one table, there were traces of chemical work, various measured heaps of some white salt being laid on glass saucers, as though for an experiment in which the unhappy man had been prevented.

"That is the same drug that I was always bringing him," said Poole; and even as he spoke, the kettle with a startling noise boiled over.

This brought them to the fireside, where the easychair was drawn cosily up, and the tea things stood ready to the sitter's elbow, the very sugar in the cup. There were several books on a shelf; one lay beside the tea things open, and Utterson was amazed to find it a copy of a pious work, for which Jekyll had several times expressed a great esteem, annotated, in his own hand, with startling blasphemies.

Next, in the course of their review of the chamber, the searchers came to the cheval-glass, into whose depths they looked with an involuntary horror. But it was so turned as to show them nothing but the rosy glow playing on the roof, the fire sparkling in a hundred repetitions along the glazed front of the presses, and their own pale and fearful countenances stooping to look in.

"This glass has seen some strange things, sir," whispered Poole.

"And surely none stranger than itself," echoed the lawyer in the same tones. "For what did Jekyll"—he caught himself up at the word with a start, and then conquering the weakness—"what could Jekyll want with it?" he said.

"You may say that!" said Poole.

Next they turned to the business table. On the desk, among the neat array of papers, a large envelope was uppermost, and bore, in the doctor's hand, the name of Mr. Utterson. The lawyer unsealed it, and several enclosures fell to the floor. The first was a will, drawn in the same eccentric terms as the one which he had returned six months before, to serve as a testament in case of death and as a deed of gift in a case of disappearance; but in the place of the name of Edward Hyde, the lawyer, with indescribable amazement, read the name of Gabriel John Utterson. He looked at Poole, and then back at the paper, and last of all at the dead malefactor stretched upon the carpet.

"My head goes round," he said. "He has been all these

days in possession; he had no cause to like me; he must have raged to see himself displaced; and he has not destroyed this document."

He caught up the next paper; it was a brief note in the doctor's hand and dated at the top. "O Poole!" the lawyer cried, "he was alive and here this day. He cannot have been disposed of in so short a space; he must be still alive, he must have fled! And then, why fled? and how? and in that case, can we venture to declare this suicide? O, we must be careful. I foresee that we may yet involve your master in some dire catastrophe."

"Why don't you read it, sir?" asked Poole.

"Because I fear," replied the lawyer solemnly. "God grant I have no cause for it!" And with that he brought the paper to his eyes and read as follows:

> "MY DEAR UTTERSON,—When this shall fall into your hands, I shall have disappeared, under what circumstances I have not the penetration to foresee, but my instinct and all the circumstances of my nameless situation tell me that the end is sure and must be early. Go then, and first read the narrative which Lanyon warned me he was to place in your hands; and if you care to hear more, turn to the confession of
>
> "Your unworthy and unhappy friend,
>
> "HENRY JEKYLL."

"There was a third enclosure?" asked Utterson.

"Here, sir," said Poole, and gave into his hands a considerable packet sealed in several places.

The lawyer put it in his pocket. "I would say nothing of this paper. If your master has fled or is dead, we may at least save his credit. It is now ten; I must go home and read these documents in quiet; but I shall be back before midnight, when we shall send for the police."

They went out, locking the door of the theatre behind them; and Utterson, once more leaving the servants gathered about the fire in the hall, trudged back to his office to read the two narratives in which this mystery was now to be explained.

DR. LANYON'S NARRATIVE

On the ninth of January, now four days ago, I received by the evening delivery a registered envelope, addressed in the hand of my colleague and old school companion, Henry Jekyll. I was a good deal surprised by this; for we were by no means in the habit of correspondence; I had seen the man, dined with him, indeed, the night before; and I could imagine nothing in our intercourse that should justify formality of registration. The contents increased my wonder; for this is how the letter ran:

> "10th December, 18—.

"DEAR LANYON,—You are one of my oldest friends; and although we may have differed at times on scientific questions, I cannot remember, at least on my side, any break in our affection. There was never a day when, if you had said to me, 'Jekyll, my life, my honour, my reason, depend upon you,' I would not have sacrificed my left hand to help you. Lanyon, my life, my honour, my reason, are all at your mercy; if you fail me to-night, I am lost. You might suppose, after this preface, that I am going to ask you for something dishonourable to grant. Judge for yourself.

"I want you to postpone all other engagements for to-night—ay, even if you were summoned to the bedside of an emperor; to take a cab, unless your carriage should be actually at the door; and with this letter in your hand for consultation, to drive straight to my house. Poole, my butler, has his orders; you will find him waiting your arrival with a locksmith. The door of my cabinet is then to be forced: and you are to go in alone; to open the glazed press (letter E) on the left hand, breaking the lock if it be shut; and to draw out, *with all its contents as they stand*, the fourth drawer from the top or (which is the same thing) the third from the bottom. In my extreme distress of mind, I have a morbid fear of misdirecting you; but even if I am in error, you may know the right drawer by its contents: some powders, a phial and a paper book. This drawer I beg of you to carry back with you to Cavendish Square exactly as it stands.

"That is the first part of the service: now for the second. You should be back, if you set out at once on the receipt of this, long before midnight; but I will leave you that amount of margin, not only in the fear of one of those obstacles that can neither be prevented nor foreseen, but because an hour when your servants are in bed is to be preferred for what will then remain to do. At midnight, then, I have to ask you to be alone in your

consulting room, to admit with your own hand into the
house a man who will present himself in my name, and
to place in his hands the drawer that you will have brought
with you from my cabinet. Then you will have played
your part and earned my gratitude completely. Five minutes afterwards, if you insist upon an explanation, you
will have understood these arrangements are of capital
importance; and that by the neglect of one of them,
fantastic as they must appear, you might have charged
your conscience with my death or the shipwreck of my
reason.

"Confident as I am that you will not trifle with this
appeal, my heart sinks and my hand trembles at the bare
thought of such a possibility. Think of me at this hour,
in a strange place, labouring under a blackness of distress
that no fancy can exaggerate, and yet well aware that,
if you will but punctually serve me, my troubles will roll
away like a story that is told. Serve me, my dear Lanyon,
and save

"Your friend,
"H. J.

"P.S.—I had already sealed this up when a fresh terror
struck upon my soul. It is possible that the post-office
may fail me, and this letter not come into your hands
until to-morrow morning. In that case, dear Lanyon, do
my errand when it shall be most convenient for you in
the course of the day; and once more expect my messenger at midnight. It may then already be too late; and
if that night passes without event, you will know that
you have seen the last of Henry Jekyll."

Upon the reading of this letter, I made sure my colleague
was insane; but till that was proved beyond the possibility of
doubt, I felt bound to do as he requested. The less I understood of this farrago, the less I was in a position to judge of
its importance; and an appeal so worded could not be set
aside without a grave responsibility. I rose accordingly from
table, got into a hansom, and drove straight to Jekyll's house.
The butler was awaiting my arrival; he had received by the
same post as mine a registered letter of instruction, and had
sent at once for a locksmith and a carpenter. The tradesmen
came while we were yet speaking; and we moved in a body
to old Dr. Denman's surgical theatre, from which (as you are
doubtless aware) Jekyll's private cabinet is most conveniently

entered. The door was very strong, the lock excellent; the carpenter avowed he would have great trouble and have to do much damage, if force were to be used; and the locksmith was near despair. But this last was a handy fellow, and after two hours' work, the door stood open. The press marked E was unlocked; and I took out the drawer, had it filled up with straw and tied in a sheet, and returned with it to Cavendish Square.

Here I proceeded to examine its contents. The powders were neatly enough made up, but not with the nicety of the dispensing chemist; so that it was plain they were of Jekyll's private manufacture: and when I opened one of the wrappers I found what seemed to me a simple crystalline salt of a white colour. The phial, to which I next turned my attention, might have been about half full of a blood-red liquor, which was highly pungent to the sense of smell and seemed to me to contain phosphorus and some volatile ether. At the other ingredients I could make no guess. The book was an ordinary version book and contained little but a series of dates. These covered a period of many years, but I observed that the entries ceased nearly a year ago and quite abruptly. Here and there a brief remark was appended to a date, usually no more than a single word: "double" occurring perhaps six times in a total of several hundred entries; and once very early in the list and followed by several marks of exclamation, "total failure!!!" All this, though it whetted my curiosity, told me little that was definite. Here was a phial of some tincture, a paper of some salt, and the record of a series of experiments that had led (like too many of Jekyll's investigations) to no end of practical usefulness. How could the presence of these articles in my house affect either the honour, the sanity, or the life of my flighty colleague? If his messenger could go to one place, why could he not go to another? And even granting some impediment, why was this gentleman to be received by me in secret? The more I reflected the more convinced I grew that I was dealing with a case of cerebral disease; and though I dismissed my servants to bed, I loaded an old revolver, that I might be found in some posture of self-defence.

Twelve o'clock had scarce rung out over London, ere the knocker sounded very gently on the door. I went myself at the summons, and found a small man crouching against the pillars of the portico.

"Are you come from Dr. Jekyll?" I asked.

He told me "yes" by a constrained gesture; and when I

had bidden him enter, he did not obey me without a searching backward glance into the darkness of the square. There was a policeman not far off, advancing with his bull's eye open; and at the sight, I thought my visitor started and made greater haste.

These particulars struck me, I confess, disagreeably; and as I followed him into the bright light of the consulting room, I kept my hand ready on my weapon. Here, at last, I had a chance of clearly seeing him. I had never set eyes on him before, so much was certain. He was small, as I have said; I was struck besides with the shocking expression of his face, with his remarkable combination of great muscular activity and great apparent debility of constitution, and—last but not least—with the odd, subjective disturbance caused by his neighbourhood. This bore some resemblance to incipient rigour, and was accompanied by a marked sinking of the pulse. At the time, I set it down to some idiosyncratic, personal distaste, and merely wondered at the acuteness of the symptoms; but I have since had reason to believe the cause to lie much deeper in the nature of man, and to turn on some nobler hinge than the principle of hatred.

This person (who had thus, from the first moment of his entrance, struck in me what I can only describe as a disgustful curiosity) was dressed in a fashion that would have made an ordinary person laughable; his clothes, that is to say, although they were of rich and sober fabric, were enormously too large for him in every measurement—the trousers hanging on his legs and rolled up to keep them from the ground, the waist of the coat below his haunches, and the collar sprawling wide upon his shoulders. Strange to relate, this ludicrous accoutrement was far from moving me to laughter. Rather, as there was something abnormal and misbegotten in the very essence of the creature that now faced me—something seizing, surprising and revolting—this fresh disparity seemed but to fit in with and to reinforce it; so that to my interest in the man's nature and character, there was added a curiosity as to his origin, his life, his fortune and status in the world.

These observations, though they have taken so great a space to be set down in, were yet the work of a few seconds. My visitor was, indeed, on fire with sombre excitement.

"Have you got it?" he cried. "Have you got it?" And so lively was his impatience that he even laid his hand upon my arm and sought to shake me.

I put him back, conscious at his touch of a certain icy pang along my blood. "Come, sir," said I. "You forget that I have not yet the pleasure of your acquaintance. Be seated, if you please." And I showed him an example, and sat down myself in my customary seat and with as fair an imitation of my ordinary manner to a patient, as the lateness of the hour, the nature of my preoccupations, and the horror I had of my visitor, would suffer me to muster.

"I beg your pardon, Dr. Lanyon," he replied civilly enough. "What you say is very well founded; and my impatience has shown its heels to my politeness. I come here at the instance of your colleague, Dr. Henry Jekyll, on a piece of business of some moment; and I understood . . ." He paused and put his hand to his throat, and I could see, in spite of his collected manner, that he was wrestling against the approaches of the hysteria—"I understood, a drawer . . ."

But here I took pity on my visitor's suspense, and some perhaps on my own growing curiosity.

"There it is, sir," said I, pointing to the drawer, where it lay on the floor behind a table and still covered with the sheet.

He sprang to it, and then paused, and laid his hand upon his heart: I could hear his teeth grate with the convulsive action of his jaws; and his face was so ghastly to see that I grew alarmed both for his life and reason.

"Compose yourself," said I.

He turned a dreadful smile to me, and as if with the decision of despair, plucked away the sheet. At sight of the contents, he uttered one loud sob of such immense relief that I sat petrified. And the next moment, in a voice that was already fairly well under control, "Have you a graduated glass?" he asked.

I rose from my place with something of an effort and gave him what he asked.

He thanked me with a smiling nod, measured out a few minims of the red tincture and added one of the powders. The mixture, which was at first of a reddish hue, began, in proportion as the crystals melted, to brighten in colour, to effervesce audibly, and to throw off small fumes of vapour. Suddenly and at the same moment, the ebullition ceased and the compound changed to a dark purple, which faded again more slowly to a watery green. My visitor, who had watched these metamorphoses with a keen eye, smiled, set down the glass upon the table, and then turned and looked upon me with an air of scrutiny.

"And now," he said, "to settle what remains. Will you be

wise? will you be guided? will you suffer me to take this glass
in my hand and to go forth from your house without further
parley? or has the greed of curiosity too much command of
you? Think before you answer, for it shall be done as you
decide. As you decide, you shall be left as you were before,
and neither richer nor wiser, unless the sense of service rendered to a man in mortal distress may be counted as a kind
of riches of the soul. Or, if you shall so prefer to choose, a
new province of knowledge and new avenues to fame and
power shall be laid open to you, here, in this room, upon the
instant; and your sight shall be blasted by a prodigy to stagger
the unbelief of Satan."

"Sir," said I, affecting a coolness that I was far from truly
possessing, "you speak enigmas, and you will perhaps not
wonder that I hear you with no very strong impression of
belief. But I have gone too far in the way of inexplicable
services to pause before I see the end."

"It is well," replied my visitor. "Lanyon, you remember
your vows: what follows is under the seal of our profession.
And now, you who have so long been bound to the most
narrow and material views, you who have denied the virtue
of transcendental medicine, you who have derided your su-
periors—behold!"

He put the glass to his lips and drank at one gulp. A cry
followed; he reeled, staggered, clutched at the table and held
on, staring with injected eyes, gasping with open mouth; and
as I looked there came, I thought, a change—he seemed to
swell—his face became suddenly black and the features seemed
to melt and alter—and the next moment I had sprung to my
feet and leaped back against the wall, my arm raised to shield
me from that prodigy, my mind submerged in terror.

"O God!" I screamed, and "O God!" again and again; for
there before my eyes—pale and shaken, and half fainting,
and groping before him with his hands, like a man restored
from death—there stood Henry Jekyll!

What he told me in the next hour, I cannot bring my mind
to set on paper. I saw what I saw, I heard what I heard, and
my soul sickened at it; and yet now when that sight has faded
from my eyes, I ask myself if I believe it, and I cannot answer.
My life is shaken to its roots; sleep has left me; the deadliest
terror sits by me at all hours of the day and night; and I feel
that my days are numbered, and that I must die; and yet I
shall die incredulous. As for the moral turpitude that man
unveiled to me, even with tears of penitence, I cannot, even

in memory, dwell on it without a start of horror. I will say but one thing, Utterson, and that (if you can bring your mind to credit it) will be more than enough. The creature who crept into my house that night was, on Jekyll's own confession, known by the name of Hyde and hunted for in every corner of the land as the murderer of Carew.

HASTIE LANYON

HENRY JEKYLL'S FULL STATEMENT OF THE CASE

I was born in the year 18—to a large fortune, endowed besides with excellent parts, inclined by nature to industry, fond of the respect of the wise and good among my fellow-men, and thus, as might have been supposed, with every guarantee of an honourable and distinguished future. And indeed the worst of my faults was a certain impatient gaiety of disposition, such as has made the happiness of many, but such as I found it hard to reconcile with my imperious desire to carry my head high, and wear a more than commonly grave countenance before the public. Hence it came about that I concealed my pleasures; and that when I reached years of reflection, and began to look round me and take stock of my progress and position in the world, I stood already committed to a profound duplicity of life. Many a man would have even blazoned such irregularities as I was guilty of; but from the high views that I had set before me, I regarded and hid them with an almost morbid sense of shame. It was thus rather the exacting nature of my aspirations than any particular degradation in my faults, that made me what I was, and, with even a deeper trench than in the majority of men, severed in me those provinces of good and ill which divide and compound man's dual nature. In this case, I was driven to reflect deeply and inveterately on that hard law of life, which lies at the root of religion and is one of the most plentiful springs of distress. Though so profound a double-dealer, I was in no sense a hypocrite; both sides of me were in dead earnest; I was no more myself when I laid aside restraint and plunged in shame, than when I laboured, in the eye of day, at the furtherance of knowledge or the relief of sorrow and suffering. And it chanced that the direction of my scientific studies, which led wholly towards the mystic and the transcendental, reacted and shed a strong light on this consciousness of the perennial war among my members. With every day, and from both sides of my intelligence, the moral and the intellectual,

I thus drew steadily nearer to that truth, by whose partial discovery I have been doomed to such a dreadful shipwreck: that man is not truly one, but truly two. I say two, because the state of my own knowledge does not pass beyond that point. Others will follow, others will outstrip me on the same lines; and I hazard the guess that man will be ultimately known for a mere polity of multifarious, incongruous and independent denizens. I, for my part, from the nature of my life, advanced infallibly in one direction and in one direction only. It was on the moral side, and in my own person, that I learned to recognise the thorough and primitive duality of man; I saw that, of the two natures that contended in the field of my consciousness, even if I could rightly be said to be either, it was only because I was radically both; and from an early date, even before the course of my scientific discoveries had begun to suggest the most naked possibility of such a miracle, I had learned to dwell with pleasure, as a beloved daydream, on the thought of the separation of these elements. If each, I told myself, could be housed in separate identities, life would be relieved of all that was unbearable; the unjust might go his way, delivered from the aspirations and remorse of his more upright twin; and the just could walk steadfastly and securely on his upward path, doing the good things in which he found his pleasure, and no longer exposed to disgrace and penitence by the hands of this extraneous evil. It was the curse of mankind that these incongruous faggots were thus bound together—that in the agonised womb of consciousness, these polar twins should be continuously struggling. How, then, were they dissociated?

I was so far in my reflections when, as I have said, a side light began to shine upon the subject from the laboratory table. I began to perceive more deeply than it has ever yet been stated, the trembling immateriality, the mistlike transience, of this seemingly so solid body in which we walk attired. Certain agents I found to have the power to shake and pluck back that fleshy vestment, even as a wind might toss the curtains of a pavilion. For two good reasons, I will not enter deeply into this scientific branch of my confession. First, because I have been made to learn that the doom and burthen of our life is bound for ever on man's shoulders, and when the attempt is made to cast it off, it but returns upon us with more unfamiliar and more awful pressure. Second, because, as my narrative will make, alas! too evident, my discoveries were incomplete. Enough, then, that I not only recognised my natural body from the mere aura and effulgence of certain of the powers that made up my spirit, but managed to compound a drug by which these powers should be dethroned from their supremacy, and a second form and countenance substituted, none the less natural to me because they were the expression, and bore the stamp of lower elements in my soul.

I hesitated long before I put this theory to the test of practice. I knew well that I risked death; for any drug that so potently controlled and shook the very fortress of identity, might, by the least scruple of an overdose or at the least inopportunity in the moment of exhibition, utterly blot out that immaterial tabernacle which I looked to it to change. But the temptation of a discovery so singular and profound at last overcame the suggestions of alarm. I had long since prepared my tincture; I purchased at once, from a firm of wholesale chemists, a large quantity of a particular salt which I knew, from my experiments, to be the last ingredient rquired; and late one accursed night, I compounded the elements, watched them boil and smoke together in the glass, and when the ebullition had subsided, with a strong glow of courage, drank off the potion.

The most racking pangs succeeded: a grinding in the bones, deadly nausea, and a horror of the spirit that cannot be exceeded at the hour of birth or death. Then these agonies began swiftly to subside, and I came to myself as if out of a great sickness. There was something strange in my sensations, something indescribably new and, from its very novelty, incredibly sweet. I felt younger, lighter, happier in body; within I was conscious of a heady recklessness, a current of disordered sensual images running like a millrace in my fancy, a solution of the bonds of obligation, an unknown but not an innocent freedom of the soul. I knew myself, at the first breath of this new life, to be more wicked, tenfold more wicked, sold a slave to my original evil; and the thought, in that moment, braced and delighted me like wine. I stretched out my hands, exulting in the freshness of these sensations; and in the act, I was suddenly aware that I had lost in stature.

There was no mirror, at that date, in my room; that which stands beside me as I write, was brought there later on and for the very purpose of these transformations. The night, however, was far gone into the morning—the morning, black as it was, was nearly ripe for the conception of the day—the inmates of my house were locked in the most rigorous hours of slumber; and I determined, flushed as I was with hope and triumph, to venture in my new shape as far as to my bedroom. I crossed the yard, wherein the constellations looked down upon me, I could have thought, with wonder, the first creature of that sort that their unsleeping vigilance had yet disclosed to them; I stole through the corridors, a stranger in my own house; and coming to my room, I saw for the first time the appearance of Edward Hyde.

I must here speak by theory alone, saying not that which I know, but that which I suppose to be most probable. The evil side of my nature, to which I had now transferred the stamping efficacy, was less robust and less developed than the good which I had just deposed. Again, in the course of my life, which had been, after all, nine tenths a life of effort, virtue and control, it had been much less exercised and much less exhausted. And hence, as I think, it came about that Edward Hyde was so much smaller, slighter and younger than Henry Jekyll. Even as good shone upon the countenance of the one, evil was written broadly and plainly on the face of the other. Evil besides (which I must still believe to be the lethal side of man) had left on that body an imprint of deformity and decay. And yet when I looked upon that ugly idol in the glass, I was conscious of no repugnance, rather of a leap of welcome. This, too, was myself. It seemed natural and human. In my eyes it bore a livelier image of the spirit, it seemed more express and single, than the imperfect and divided countenance I had been hitherto accustomed to call mine. And in so far I was doubtless right. I have observed that when I wore the semblance of Edward Hyde, none could come near to me at first without a visible misgiving of the flesh. This, as I take it, was because all human beings, as we met them, are commingled out of good and evil: and Edward Hyde, alone in the ranks of mankind, was pure evil.

I lingered but a moment at the mirror: the second and conclusive experiment had yet to be attempted; it yet remained to be seen if I had lost my identity beyond redemption and must flee before daylight from a house that was no longer mine; and hurrying back to my cabinet, I once more prepared and drank the cup, once more suffered the pangs of dissolution, and came to myself once more with the character, the stature and the face of Henry Jekyll.

That night I had come to the fatal cross-roads. Had I approached my discovery in a more noble spirit, had I risked the experiment while under the empire of generous or pious aspirations, all must have been otherwise, and from these agonies of death and birth, I had come forth an angel instead of a fiend. The drug had no discriminating action; it was neither diabolical nor divine; it but shook the doors of the prisonhouse of my disposition; and like the captives of Philippi, that which stood within ran forth. At that time my virtue slumbered; my evil, kept awake by ambition, was alert and swift to seize the occasion; and the thing that was projected was Edward Hyde. Hence, although I had now two characters as well as two appearances, one was wholly evil, and the other was still the old Henry Jekyll, that incongruous compound of whose reformation and improvement I had already learned to despair. The movement was thus wholly toward the worse.

Even at that time, I had not conquered my aversions to the dryness of a life of study. I would still be merrily disposed at times; and as my pleasures were (to say the least) undignified, and I was not only well known and highly considered, but growing towards the elderly man, this incoherency of my life was daily growing more unwelcome. It was on this side that my new power tempted me until I fell in slavery. I had but to drink the cup, to doff at once the body of the noted professor, and to assume, like a thick cloak, that of Edward Hyde. I smiled at the notion; it seemed to me at the time to be humourous; and I made my preparations with the most studious care. I took and furnished that house in Soho, to which Hyde was tracked by the police; and engaged as a housekeeper a creature whom I knew too well to be silent and unscrupulous. On the other side, I announced to my servants that a Mr. Hyde (whom I described) was to have full liberty and power about my house in the square; and to parry mishaps, I even called and made myself a familiar object, in my second character. I next drew up that will to which you so much objected; so that if anything befell me in the person of Dr. Jekyll, I could enter on that of Edward Hyde without pecuniary loss. And thus fortified, as I supposed, on every side, I began to profit by the strange immunities of my position.

Men have before hired bravos to transact their crimes, while their own person and reputation sat under shelter. I was the first that ever did so for his pleasures. I was the first that could plod in the public eye with a load of genial respectability, and in a moment, like a school-boy, strip off these lendings and spring headlong into the sea of liberty. But for me, in my impenetrable mantle, the safety was com-

plete. Think of it—I did not even exist! Let me but escape
into my laboratory door, give me but a second or two to mix
and swallow the draught that I had always standing ready;
and whatever he had done, Edward Hyde would pass away
like the stain of breath upon a mirror; and there in his stead,
quietly at home, trimming the midnight lamp in his study, a
man who could afford to laugh at suspicion, would be Henry
Jekyll.

The pleasures which I made haste to seek in my disguise
were, as I have said, undignified; I would scarce use a harder
term. But in the hands of Edward Hyde, they soon began to
turn toward the monstrous. When I would come back from
these excursions, I was often plunged into a kind of wonder
at my vicarious depravity. This familiar that I called out of
my own soul, and sent forth alone to do his good pleasure,
was a being inherently malign and villainous; his every act
and thought centered on self; drinking pleasure with bestial
avidity from any degree of torture to another; relentless like
a man of stone. Henry Jekyll stood at times aghast before
the acts of Edward Hyde; but the situation was apart from
ordinary laws, and insidiously relaxed the grasp of conscience.
It was Hyde, after all, and Hyde alone, that was guilty. Jekyll
was no worse; he woke again to his good qualities seemingly
unimpaired; he would even make haste, where it was possible,
to undo the evil done by Hyde. And thus his conscience
slumbered.

Into the details of the infamy in which I thus connived (for
even now I can scarce grant that I committed it) I have no
design of entering; I mean but to point out the warnings and
the successive steps with which my chastisement approached.
I met with one accident which, as it brought on no consequence, I shall no more than mention. An act of cruelty to
a child aroused against me the anger of a passerby, whom I
recognised the other day in the person of your kinsman; the
doctor and the child's family joined him; there were moments
when I feared for my life; and at last, in order to pacify their
too just resentment, Edward Hyde had to bring them to the
door, and pay them in a cheque drawn in the name of Henry
Jekyll. But this danger was easily eliminated from the future,
by opening an account at another bank in the name of Edward
Hyde himself; and when, by sloping my own hand backward,
I had supplied my double with a signature, I thought I sat
beyond the reach of fate.

Some two months before the murder of Sir Danvers, I had

been out for one of my adventures, had returned at a late hour, and woke the next day in bed with somewhat odd sensations. It was in vain I looked about me; in vain I saw the decent furniture and tall proportions of my room in the square; in vain that I recognised the pattern of the bed curtains and the design of the mahogany frame; something still kept insisting that I was not where I was, that I had not wakened where I seemed to be, but in the little room in Soho where I was accustomed to sleep in the body of Edward Hyde. I smiled to myself, and, in my psychological way, began lazily to inquire into the elements of this illusion, occasionally, even as I did so, dropping back into a comfortable morning doze. I was still so engaged when, in one of my more wakeful moments, my eyes fell upon my hand. Now the hand of Henry Jekyll (as you have often remarked) was professional in shape and size: it was large, firm, white and comely. But the hand which I now saw, clearly enough, in the yellow light of a mid-London morning, lying half shut on the bedclothes, was lean, corded, knuckly, of a dusky pallor and thickly shaded with a swart growth of hair. It was the hand of Edward Hyde.

I must have stared upon it for near half a minute, sunk as I was in the mere stupidity of wonder, before terror woke up in my breast as sudden and startling as the crash of cymbals; and bounding from my bed, I rushed to the mirror. At the sight that met my eyes, my blood was changed into something exquisitely thin and icy. Yes, I had gone to bed Henry Jekyll, I had awakened Edward Hyde. How was this to be explained? I asked myself; and then, with another bound of terror—how was it to be remedied? It was well on in the morning; the servants were up; all my drugs were in the cabinet—a long journey down two pairs of stairs, through the back passage, across the open court and through the anatomical theatre, from where I was then standing horror-struck. It might indeed be possible to cover my face; but of what use was that, when I was unable to conceal the alteration in my stature? And then with an overpowering sweetness of relief, it came back upon my mind that the servants were already used to the coming and going of my second self. I had soon dressed, as well as I was able, in clothes of my own size: had soon passed through the house, where Bradshaw stared and drew back at seeing Mr. Hyde at such an hour and in such a strange array; and ten minutes later, Dr. Jekyll had returned to his own shape and was sitting down, with a darkened brow, to make a feint of breakfasting.

Small indeed was my appetite. This inexplicable incident, this reversal of my previous experience, seemed, like the Babylonian finger on the wall, to be spelling out the letters of my judgment; and I began to reflect more seriously than ever before on the issues and possibilities of my double existence. That part of me which I had the power of projecting, had lately been much exercised and nourished; it had seemed to me of late as though the body of Edward Hyde had grown in stature, as though (when I wore that form) I were conscious of a more generous tide of blood; and I began to spy a danger that, if this were much prolonged, the balance of my nature might be permanently overthrown, the power of voluntary change be forfeited, and the character of Edward Hyde become irrevocably mine. The power of the drug had not been always equally displayed. Once, very early in my career, it had totally failed me; since then I had been obliged on more than one occasion to double, and once, with infinite risk of death, to treble the amount; and these rare uncertainties had cast hitherto the sole shadow on my contentment. Now, however, and in the light of that morning's accident, I was led to remark that whereas, in the beginning, the difficulty had been to throw off the body of Jekyll, it had of late gradually but decidedly transferred itself to the other side. All things therefore seemed to point to this; that I was slowly losing hold of my original and better self, and becoming slowly incorporated with my second and worse.

Between these two, I now felt I had to choose. My two natures had memory in common, but all other faculties were most unequally shared between them. Jekyll (who was composite) now with the most sensitive apprehensions, now with a greedy gusto, projected and shared in the pleasures and adventures of Hyde; but Hyde was indifferent to Jekyll, or but remembered him as the mountain bandit remembers the cavern in which he conceals himself from pursuit. Jekyll had more than a father's interest; Hyde had more than a son's indifference. To cast in my lot with Jekyll, was to die to those appetites which I had long secretly indulged and had of late begun to pamper. To cast it in with Hyde, was to die to a thousand interests and aspirations, and to become, at a blow and forever, despised and friendless. The bargain might appear unequal; but there was still another consideration in the scales; for while Jekyll would suffer smartingly in the fires of abstinence, Hyde would be not even conscious of all that he had lost. Strange as my circumstances were, the terms of this debate are as old and commonplace as man; much the same inducements and alarms cast the die for any tempted and trembling sinner; and it fell out with me, as it falls with so vast a majority of my fellows, that I chose the better part and was found wanting in the strength to keep to it.

Yes, I preferred the elderly and discontented doctor, surrounded by friends and cherishing honest hopes; and bade a resolute farewell to the liberty, the comparative youth, the light step, leaping impulses and secret pleasures, that I had enjoyed in the disguise of Hyde. I made this choice perhaps with some unconscious reservation, for I neither gave up the house in Soho, nor destroyed the clothes of Edward Hyde, which still lay ready in my cabinet. For two months, however, I was true to my determination; for two months, I led a life of such severity as I had never before attained to, and enjoyed the compensations of an approving conscience. But time began at last to obliterate the freshness of my alarm; the praises of conscience began to grow into a thing of course; I began to be tortured with throes and longings, as of Hyde struggling after freedom; and at last, in an hour of moral weakness, I once again compounded and swallowed the transforming draught.

I do not suppose that, when a drunkard reasons with himself upon his vice, he is once out of five hundred times affected by the dangers that he runs through his brutish, physical insensibility; neither had I, long as I had considered my position, made enough allowance for the complete moral insensibility and insensate readiness to evil, which were the leading characters of Edward Hyde. Yet it was by these that I was punished. My devil had been long caged, he came out roaring. I was conscious, even when I took the draught, of a more unbridled, a more furious propensity to ill. It must have been this, I suppose, that stirred in my soul that tempest of impatience with which I listened to the civilities of my unhappy victim; I declare, at least, before God, no man morally sane could have been guilty of that crime upon so pitiful a provocation; and that I struck in no more reasonable spirit than that in which a sick child may break a play-thing. But I had voluntarily stripped myself of all those balancing instincts by which even the worst of us continues to walk with some degree of steadiness among temptations; and in my case, to be tempted, however slightly, was to fall.

Instantly the spirit of hell awoke in me and raged. With a transport of glee, I mauled the unresisting body, tasting delight from every blow; and it was not till weariness had begun to succeed, that I was suddenly, in the top fit of my delirium, struck through the heart by a cold thrill of terror. A mist dispersed; I saw my life to be forfeit; and fled from the scene of these excesses, at once glorying and trembling, my lust of evil gratified and stimulated, my love of life screwed to the topmost peg. I ran to the house in Soho, and (to make assurance doubly sure) destoyed my papers; thence I set out through the lamplit streets, in the same divided ecstasy of mind, gloating on my crime, light-headedly devising others in the future, and yet still hastening and still hearkening in my wake for the steps of the avenger. Hyde had a song upon his lips as he compounded the draught, and as he drank it, pledged the dead man. The pangs of transformation had not done tearing him, before Henry Jekyll, with streaming tears of gratitude and remorse, had fallen upon his knees and lifted his clasped hands to God. The veil of self-indulgence was rent from head to foot. I saw my life as a whole: I followed it up from the days of childhood, when I had walked with my father's hand, and through the self-denying toils of my professional life, to arrive again and again, with the same sense of unreality, at the damned horrors of the evening. I could have screamed aloud; I sought with tears and prayers to smother down the crowd of hideous images and sounds with which my memory swarmed against me; and still, between the petitions, the ugly face of my iniquity stared into my soul. As the acuteness of this remorse began to die away, it was succeeded by a sense of joy. The problem of my conduct was solved. Hyde was thenceforth impossible; whether I would or not, I as now confined to the better part of my existence; and O, how I rejoiced to think of it! with what willing humility I embraced anew the restrictions of natural life! with what sincere renunciation I locked the door by which I had so often gone and come, and ground the key under my heel!

The next day, came the news that the murder had been overlooked, that the guilt of Hyde was patent to the world, and that the victim was a man in public estimation. It was not only a crime, it had been a tragic folly. I think I was glad to know it; I think I was glad to have my better impulses thus buttressed and guarded by the terrors of the scaffold. Jekyll was now my city of refuge; let but Hyde peep out an instant, and the hands of all men would be raised to take and slay him.

I resolved in my future conduct to redeem the past; and I

can say with honesty that my resolve was fruitful of some good. You know yourself how earnestly, in the last months of the last year, I laboured to relieve suffering; you know that much was done for others, and that the days passed quietly, almost happily for myself. Nor can I truly say that I wearied of this beneficent and innocent life; I think instead that I daily enjoyed it more completely; but I was still cursed with my duality of purpose; and as the first edge of my penitence wore off, the lower side of me, so long indulged, so recently chained down, began to growl for licence. Not that I dreamed of resuscitating Hyde; the bare idea of that would startle me to frenzy: no, it was in my own person that I was once more tempted to trifle with my conscience; and it was as an ordinary secret sinner that I at last fell before the assaults of temptation.

There comes an end to all things; the most capacious measure is filled at last; and this brief condescension to my evil finally destroyed the balance of my soul. And yet I was not alarmed; the fall seemed natural, like a return to the old days before I had made my discovery. It was a fine, clear, January day, wet under foot where the frost had melted, but cloudless overhead; and the Regent's Park was full of winter chirrupings and sweet with spring odours. I sat in the sun on a bench; the animal within me licking the chops of memory; the spiritual side a little drowsed, promising subsequent penitence, but not yet moved to begin. After all, I reflected, I was like my neighbours; and then I smiled, comparing myself with other men, comparing my active good-will with the lazy cruelty of their neglect. And at the very moment of that vainglorious thought, a qualm came over me, a horrid nausea and the most deadly shuddering. These passed away, and left me faint; and then as in its turn faintness subsided, I began to be aware of a change in the temper of my thoughts, a greater boldness, a contempt of danger, a solution of the bonds of obligation. I looked down; my clothes hung formlessly on my shrunken limbs; the hand that lay on my knee was corded and hairy. I was once more Edward Hyde. A moment before I had been safe of all men's respect, wealthy, beloved—the cloth laying for me in the dining-room at home; and now I was the common quarry of mankind, hunted, houseless, a known murderer, thrall to the gallows.

My reason wavered, but it did not fail me utterly. I have more than once observed that, in my second character, my faculties seemed sharpened to a point and my spirits more tensely elastic; thus it came about that, where Jekyll perhaps might have succumbed, Hyde rose to the importance of the moment. My drugs were in one of the presses of my cabinet; how was I to reach them? That was the problem that (crushing my temples in my hands) I set myself to solve. The laboratory door I had closed. If I sought to enter by the house, my own servants would consign me to the gallows. I saw I must employ another hand, and thought of Lanyon. How was he to be reached? how persuaded? Supposing that I escaped capture in the streets, how was I to make my way into his presence? and how should I, an unknown and displeasing visitor, prevail on the famous physician to rifle the study of his colleague, Dr. Jekyll? Then I remembered that of my original character, one part remained to me: I could write my own hand; and once I had conceived that kindling spark, the way that I must follow became lighted up from end to end.

Thereupon, I arranged my clothes as best I could, and summoning a passing hansom, drove to an hotel in Portland Street, the name of which I chanced to remember. At my appearance (which was indeed comical enough, however tragic a fate these garments covered) the driver could not conceal his mirth. I gnashed my teeth upon him with a gust of devilish fury; and the smile withered from his face—happily for him— yet more happily for myself, for in another instant I had certainly dragged him from his perch. At the inn, as I entered, I looked about me with so black a countenance as made the attendants tremble; not a look did they exchange in my presence; but obsequiously took my orders, led me to a private room, and brought me wherewithal to write. Hyde in danger of his life was a creature new to me; shaken with inordinate anger, strung to the pitch of murder, lusting to inflict pain. Yet the creature was astute; mastered his fury with a great effort of the will; composed his two important letters, one to Lanyon and one to Poole; and that he might receive actual evidence of their being posted, sent them out with directions that they should be registered. Thenceforward, he sat all day over the fire in the private room, gnawing his nails; there he dined, sitting alone with his fears, the waiter visibly quailing before his eye; and thence, when the night was fully come, he set forth in the corner of a closed cab, and was driven to and fro about the streets of the city. He, I say—I cannot say, I. That child of Hell had nothing human; nothing lived in him but fear and hatred. And when at last, thinking the driver had begun to grow suspicious, he discharged the cab and ventured on foot, attired in his misfitting clothes, an object marked out for observation, into the midst of the nocturnal passengers, these two base passions raged within him like a tempest. He walked fast, hunted by his fears, chattering to himself, skulking through the less frequented thoroughfares, counting the minutes that still divided him from midnight. Once a woman spoke to him, offering, I think, a box of lights. He smote her in the face, and she fled.

When I came to myself at Lanyon's, the horror of my old friend perhaps affected me somewhat: I do not know; it was at least but a drop in the sea to the abhorrence with which I looked back upon these hours. A change had come over me. It was no longer the fear of the gallows, it was the horror of being Hyde that racked me. I received Lanyon's condemnation partly in a dream; it was partly in a dream that I came home to my own house and got into bed. I slept after the prostration of the day, with a stringent and profound slumber which not even the nightmares that wrung me could avail to break. I awoke in the morning shaken, weakened, but refreshed. I still hated and feared the thought of the brute that slept within me, and I had not of course forgotten the appalling dangers of the day before; but I was once more at home, in my own house and close to my drugs; and gratitude for my escape shone so strong in my soul that it almost rivalled the brightness of hope.

I was stepping leisurely across the court after breakfast, drinking the chill of the air with pleasure, when I was seized again with those indescribable sensations that heralded the change; and I had but the time to gain the shelter of my cabinet, before I was once again raging and freezing with the passions of Hyde. It took on this occasion a double dose to recall me to myself; and alas! six hours after, as I sat looking sadly in the fire, the pangs returned, and the drug had to be re-administered. In short, from that day forth it seemed only by a great effort as of gymnastics, and only under the immediate stimulation of the drug, that I was able to wear the countenance of Jekyll. At all hours of the day and night, I would be taken with the premonitory shudder; above all, if I slept, or even dozed for a moment in my chair, it was always as Hyde that I awakened. Under the strain of this continually impending doom and by the sleeplessness to which I now condemned myself, ay, even beyond what I had thought possible to man, I became, in my own person, a creature eaten up and emptied by fever, languidly weak both in body and

mind, and solely occupied by one thought: the horror of my
other self. But when I slept, or when the virtue of the medicine wore off, I would leap almost without transition (for the
pangs of transformation grew daily less marked) into the possession of a fancy brimming with images of terror, a soul
boiling with causeless hatreds, and a body that seemed not
strong enough to contain the raging energies of life. The
powers of Hyde seemed to have grown with the sickliness of
Jekyll. And certainly the hate that now divided them was
equal on each side. With Jekyll, it was a thing of vital instinct.
He had now seen the full deformity of that creature that
shared with him some of the phenomena of consciousness,
and was co-heir with him to death: and beyond these links
of community, which in themselves made the most poignant
part of his distress, he thought of Hyde, for all his energy of
life, as of something not only hellish but inorganic. This was
the shocking thing; that the slime of the pit seemed to utter
cries and voices; that the amorphous dust gesticulated and
sinned; that what was dead, and had no shape, should usurp
the offices of life. And this again, that that insurgent horror
was knit to him closer than a wife, closer than an eye; lay
caged in his flesh, where he heard it mutter and felt it struggle
to be born; and at every hour of weakness, and in the confidence of slumber, prevailed against him, and deposed him
out of life. The hatred of Hyde for Jekyll was of a different
order. His terror of the gallows drove him continually to
commit temporary suicide, and return to his subordinate station of a part instead of a person; but he loathed the necessity,
he loathed the despondency into which Jekyll was now fallen,
and he resented the dislike with which he was himself regarded. Hence the ape-like tricks that he would play me,
scrawling in my own hand blasphemies on the pages of my
books, burning the letters and destroying the portrait of my
father; and indeed, had it not been for his fear of death, he
would long ago have ruined himself in order to involve me
in the ruin. But his love of life is wonderful; I go further: I,
who sicken and freeze at the mere thought of him, when I
recall the abjection and passion of this attachment, and when
I know how he fears my power to cut him off by suicide, I
find it in my heart to pity him.

It is useless, and the time awfully fails me, to prolong this
description; no one has ever suffered such torments, let that
suffice; and yet even to these, habit brought—no, not alle-
viation—but a certain callousness of soul, a certain acquies-

cence of despair; and my punishment might have gone on for years, but for the last calamity which has now fallen, and which has finally severed me from my own face and nature. My provision of the salt, which had never been renewed since the date of the first experiment, began to run low. I sent out for a fresh supply and mixed the draught; the ebullition followed, and the first change of colour, not the second; I drank it and it was without efficiency. You will learn from Poole how I have had London ransacked; it was in vain; and I am now persuaded that my first supply was impure, and that it was that unknown impurity which lent efficacy to the draught.

About a week has passed, and I am now finishing this statement under the influence of the last of the old powders. This, then, is the last time, short of a miracle, that Henry Jekyll can think his own thoughts or see his own face (now how sadly altered!) in the glass. Nor must I delay too long to bring my writing to an end; for if my narrative has hitherto escaped destruction, it has been by a combination of great prudence and great good luck. Should the throes of change take me in the act of writing it, Hyde will tear it in pieces; but if some time shall have elapsed after I have laid it by, his wonderful selfishness and circumscription to the moment will probably save it once again from the action of his ape-like spite. And indeed the doom that is closing on us both has already changed and crushed him. Half an hour from now, when I shall again and forever reindue that hated personality, I know how I shall sit shuddering and weeping in my chair, or continue, with the most strained and fearstruck ecstasy of listening, to pace up and down this room (my last earthly refuge) and give ear to every sound of menace. Will Hyde die upon the scaffold? or will he find courage to release himself at the last moment? God knows; I am careless; this is my true hour of death, and what is to follow concerns another than myself. Here then, as I lay down the pen and proceed to seal up my confession, I bring the life of that unhappy Henry Jekyll to an end.

Joseph Conrad
(1857–1924)

Joseph Conrad (Józef Teodor Konrad Korzeniowski) was born in Berdichev, the Ukraine, the son of Polish parents. He Anglicized his name when he turned to writing, but well before that he became a British citizen, in 1886. Leaving Poland just short of his seventeenth birthday, Conrad pursued a sea career on French and English ships for almost twenty years, rising to captain in the British merchant service. After his first efforts at fiction, Almayer's Folly *(1895),* An Outcast of the Islands *(1896), and* The Nigger of the "Narcissus" *(1897), he devoted himself completely to writing. Although popular acclaim was slow in coming, he gained critical acclaim from his earliest days. In a ten-to-twelve-year period, he produced most of his greatest work:* Heart of Darkness *(1899), based on his 1890 journey into the Congo;* Lord Jim *(1900), which drew on his own voyages in and around the Dutch East Indies and Singapore;* Nostromo *(1904);* The Secret Agent *(1907); and* Under Western Eyes *(1911). The latter three were deeply political novels that derived from his view of Europe on the eve of World War I. His other notable fictions include* Chance *(1913),* Victory *(1915),* The Shadow-Line *(1917), and* The Rover *(1923).*

Youth

This could have occurred nowhere but in England, where men and sea interpenetrate, so to speak—the sea entering into the life of most men, and the men knowing something or everything about the sea, in the way of amusement, of travel, or of breadwinning.

We were sitting round a mahogany table that reflected the bottle, the claret glasses, and our faces as we leaned on our elbows. There was a director of companies, an accountant, a lawyer, Marlow, and myself. The director had been a *Conway* boy, the accountant had served four years at sea, the lawyer—a fine crusted Tory, High Churchman, the best of old fellows, the soul of honor—had been chief officer in the P. & O. service in the good old days when mailboats were square-rigged at least on two masts, and used to come down the China Sea before a fair monsoon with stun'sails set alow and aloft. We all began life in the merchant service. Between the five of us there was the strong bond of the sea, and also the fellowship of the craft, which no amount of enthusiasm for yachting, cruising, and so on can give, since one is only the amusement of life and the other is life itself.

Marlow (at least I think that is how he spelt his name) told the story, or rather the chronicle, of a voyage:

"Yes, I have seen a little of the Eastern seas; but what I remember best is my first voyage there. You fellows know there are those voyages that seem ordered for the illustration of life, that might stand for a symbol of existence. You fight, work, sweat, nearly kill yourself, sometimes do kill yourself, trying to accomplish something—and you can't. Not from any fault of yours. You simply can do nothing, neither great nor little—not a thing in the world—not even marry an old maid, or get a wretched 600-ton cargo of coal to its port of destination.

"It was altogether a memorable affair. It was my first voyage to the East, and my first voyage as second mate; it was also my skipper's first command. You'll admit it was time. He was sixty if a day; a little man, with a broad, not very straight back, with bowed shoulders and one leg more bandy than the other, he had that queer twisted-about appearance you see so often in men who work in the fields. He had a nutcracker face—chin and nose trying to come together over a sunken mouth—and it was framed in iron-gray fluffy hair, that looked like a chinstrap of cotton-wool sprinkled with coaldust. And he had blue eyes in that old face of his, which were amazingly like a boy's, with that candid expression some quite common men preserve to the end of their days by a rare internal gift of simplicity of heart and rectitude of soul. What induced him to accept me was a wonder. I had come out of a crack Australian clipper, where I had been third officer, and he seemed to have a prejudice against crack clippers as aristocratic and high-toned. He said to me, 'You know, in this ship you will have to work.' I said I had to work in

every ship I had ever been in. 'Ah, but this is different, and
you gentlemen out of them big ships; . . . but there! I dare
say you will do. Join tomorrow.'

"I joined tomorrow. It was twenty-two years ago; and I
was just twenty. How time passes! It was one of the happiest
days of my life. Fancy! Second mate for the first time—a
really responsible officer! I wouldn't have thrown up my new
billet for a fortune. The mate looked me over carefully. He
was also an old chap, but of another stamp. He had a Roman
nose, a snow-white, long beard, and his name was Mahon,
but he insisted that it should be pronounced Mann. He was
well connected; yet there was something wrong with his luck,
and he had never got on.

"As to the captain, he had been for years in coasters, then
in the Mediterranean, and last in the West Indian trade. He
had never been round the Capes. He could just write a kind
of sketchy hand, and didn't care for writing at all. Both were
thorough good seamen of course, and between those two old
chaps I felt like a small boy between two grandfathers.

"The ship also was old. Her name was the *Judea*. Queer
name, isn't it? She belonged to a man Wilmer, Wilcox—some
name like that; but he has been bankrupt and dead these
twenty years or more, and his name don't matter. She had
been laid up in Shadwell basin for ever so long. You may
imagine her state. She was all rust, dust, grime—soot aloft,
dirt on deck. To me it was like coming out of a palace into
a ruined cottage. She was about 400 tons, had a primitive
windlass, wooden latches to the doors, not a bit of brass about
her, and a big square stern. There was on it, below her name
in big letters, a lot of scrollwork, with the gilt off, and some
sort of a coat of arms, with the motto 'Do or Die' underneath.
I remember it took my fancy immensely. There was a touch
of romance in it, something that made me love the old thing—
something that appealed to my youth!

"We left London in ballast—sand ballast—to load a cargo
of coal in a northern port for Bankok. Bankok! I thrilled. I
had been six years at sea, but had only seen Melbourne and
Sydney, very good places, charming places in their way—but
Bankok!

"We worked out of the Thames under canvas, with a North
Sea pilot on board. His name was Jermyn, and he dodged all
day along about the galley drying his handkerchief before the
stove. Apparently he never slept. He was a dismal man, with
a perpetual tear sparkling at the end of his nose, who either

had been in trouble, or was in trouble, or expected to be in trouble—couldn't be happy unless something went wrong. He mistrusted my youth, my common sense, and my seamanship, and made a point of showing it in a hundred little ways. I dare say he was right. It seems to me I knew very little then, and I know not much more now; but I cherish a hate for that Jermyn to this day.

"We were a week working up as far as Yarmouth Roads, and then we got into a gale—the famous October gale of twenty-two years ago. It was wind, lightning, sleet, snow, and a terrific sea. We were flying light, and you may imagine how bad it was when I tell you we had smashed bulwarks and a flooded deck. On the second night she shifted her ballast into the lee bow, and by that time we had been blown off somewhere on the Dogger Bank. There was nothing for it but go below with shovels and try to right her, and there we were in that vast hold, gloomy like a cavern, the tallow dips stuck and flickering on the beams, the gale howling above, the ship tossing about like mad on her side; there we all were, Jermyn, the captain, everyone, hardly able to keep our feet, engaged on that gravedigger's work, and trying to toss shovelfuls of wet sand up to windward. At every tumble of the ship you could see vaguely in the dim light men falling down with a great flourish of shovels. One of the ship's boys (we had two), impressed by the weirdness of the scene, wept as if his heart would break. We could hear him blubbering somewhere in the shadows.

"On the third day the gale died out, and by and by a north-country tug picked us up. We took sixteen days in all to get from London to the Tyne! When we got into dock we had lost our turn for loading, and they hauled us off to a pier where we remained for a month. Mrs. Beard (the captain's name was Beard) came from Colchester to see the old man. She lived on board. The crew of runners had left, and there remained only the officers, one boy and the steward, a mulatto who answered to the name of Abraham. Mrs. Beard was an old woman, with a face all wrinkled and ruddy like a winter apple, and the figure of a young girl. She caught sight of me once, sewing on a button, and insisted on having my shirts to repair. This was something different from the captains' wives I had known on board crack clippers. When I brought her the shirts, she said: 'And the socks? They want mending, I am sure, and John's—Captain Beard's—things are all in order now. I would be glad of something to do.' Bless the

old woman. She overhauled my outfit for me, and meantime
I read for the first time *Sartor Resartus* and Burnaby's *Ride
to Khiva*. I didn't understand much of the first then: but I
remember I preferred the soldier to the philosopher at the
time; a preference which life has only confirmed. One was a
man, and the other was either more—or less. However, they
are both dead and Mrs. Beard is dead, and youth, strength,
genius, thoughts, achievements, simple hearts—all dies. . . .
No matter.

"They loaded us at last. We shipped a crew. Eight able
seamen and two boys. We hauled off one evening to the buoys
at the dock gates, ready to go out, and with a fair prospect
of beginning the voyage next day. Mrs. Beard was to start
for home by a late train. When the ship was fast we went to
tea. We sat rather silent through the meal—Mahon, the old
couple, and I. I finished first, and slipped away for a smoke,
my cabin being in a deckhouse just against the poop. It was
high water, blowing fresh with a drizzle; the double dock
gates were opened, and the steam colliers were going in and
out in the darkness with their lights burning bright, a great
plashing of propellers, rattling of winches, and a lot of hailing
on the pierheads. I watched the procession of headlights gliding high and of green lights gliding low in the night, when
suddenly a red gleam flashed at me, vanished, came into view
again, and remained. The fore end of a steamer loomed up
close. I shouted down the cabin, 'Come up, quick!' and then
heard a startled voice saying afar in the dark, 'Stop her, sir.'
A bell jingled. Another voice cried warningly, 'We are going
right into that bark, sir.' The answer to this was a gruff 'All
right,' and the next thing was a heavy crash as the steamer
struck a glancing blow with the bluff of her bow about our
forerigging. There was a moment of confusion, yelling, and
running about. Steam roared. Then somebody was heard saying, 'All clear, sir.' . . . 'Are you all right?' asked the gruff
voice. I had jumped forward to see the damage, and hailed
back. 'I think so.' 'Easy astern,' said the gruff voice. A bell
jingled. 'What steamer is that?' screamed Mahon. By that
time she was no more to us than a bulky shadow maneuvering
a little way off. They shouted at us some name—a woman's
name, Miranda or Melissa—or some such thing. 'This means
another month in this beastly hole,' said Mahon to me, as we
peered with lamps about the splintered bulwarks and broken
braces. 'But where's the captain?'

"We had not heard or seen anything of him all that time.

We went aft to look. A doleful voice arose hailing somewhere in the middle of the dock, '*Judea* ahoy!' . . . How the devil did he get there? . . . 'Hallo!' we shouted. 'I am adrift in our boat without oars,' he cried. A belated water-man offered his services, and Mahon struck a bargain with him for half-a-crown to tow our skipper alongside; but it was Mrs. Beard that came up the ladder first. They had been floating about the dock in that mizzly cold rain for nearly an hour. I was never so surprised in my life.

"It appears that when he heard my shout 'Come up' he understood at once what was the matter, caught up his wife, ran on deck, and across, and down into our boat, which was fast to the ladder. Not bad for a sixty-year-old. Just imagine that old fellow saving heroically in his arms that old woman—the woman of his life. He set her down on a thwart, and was ready to climb back on board when the painter came adrift somehow, and away they went together. Of course in the confusion we did not hear him shouting. He looked abashed. She said cheerfully, 'I suppose it does not matter my losing the train now?' 'No, Jenny—you go below and get warm,' he growled. Then to us: 'A sailor has no business with a wife—I say. There I was, out of the ship. Well, no harm done this time. Let's go and look at what that fool of a steamer smashed.'

"It wasn't much, but it delayed us three weeks. At the end of that time, the captain being engaged with his agents, I carried Mrs. Beard's bag to the railway station and put her all comfy into a third-class carriage. She lowered the window to say, 'You are a good young man. If you see John—Captain Beard—without his muffler at night, just remind him from me to keep his throat well wrapped up.' 'Certainly, Mrs. Beard,' I said. 'You are a good young man; I noticed how attentive you are to John—to Captain—' The train pulled out suddenly; I took my cap off to the old woman: I never saw her again. . . . Pass the bottle.

"We went to sea next day. When we made that start for Bankok we had been already three months out of London. We had expected to be a fortnight or so—at the outside.

"It was January, and the weather was beautiful—the beautiful sunny winter weather that has more charm than in the summertime, because it is unexpected, and crisp, and you know it won't, it can't, last long. It's like a windfall, like a godsend, like an unexpected piece of luck.

"It lasted all down the North Sea, all down Channel; and it lasted till we were three hundred miles or so to the westward of the Lizards; then the wind went round to the sou'west and began to pipe up. In two days it blew a gale. The *Judea*, hove to, wallowed on the Atlantic like an old candle-box. It blew day after day: it blew with spite, without interval, without mercy, without rest. The world was nothing but an immensity of great foaming waves rushing at us, under a sky low enough to touch with hand and dirty like a smoked ceiling. In the stormy space surrounding us there was as much flying spray as air. Day after day and night after night there was nothing round the ship but the howl of the wind, the tumult of the sea, the noise of water pouring over her deck. There was no rest for her and no rest for us. She tossed, she pitched, she stood on her head, she sat on her tail, she rolled, she groaned, and we had to hold on while on deck and cling to our bunks when below, in a constant effort of body and worry of mind.

"One night Mahon spoke through the small window of my berth. It opened right into my very bed, and I was lying there sleepless, in my boots, feeling as though I had not slept for years, and could not if I tried. He said excitedly:

" 'You got the sounding rod in here, Marlow? I can't get the pumps to suck. By God! It's no child's play!'

"I gave him the sounding rod and lay down again, trying to think of various things—but I thought only of the pumps. When I came on deck they were still at it, and my watch relieved at the pumps. By the light of the lantern brought on deck to examine the sounding rod I caught a glimpse of their weary, serious faces. We pumped all the four hours. We pumped all night, all day, all the week—watch and watch. She was working herself loose, and leaked badly—not enough to drown us at once, but enough to kill us with the work at the pumps. And while we pumped the ship was going from us piecemeal: the bulwarks went, the stanchions were torn out, the ventilators smashed, the cabin door burst in. There was not a dry spot in the ship. She was being gutted bit by bit. The longboat changed, as if by magic, into matchwood where she stood in her gripes. I had lashed her myself, and was rather proud of my handiwork, which had withstood so long the malice of the sea. And we pumped. And there was no break in the weather. The sea was white like a sheet of foam, like a caldron of boiling milk; there was not a break in the clouds, no—not the size of a man's hand—no, not for so much as ten seconds. There was for us no sky, there were for us no stars, no sun, no universe—nothing but angry clouds and an infuriated sea. We pumped watch and watch, for dear life; and it seemed to last for months, for years, for all eternity, as though we had been dead and gone to a hell for sailors. We forgot the day of the week, the name of the month, what year it was, and whether we had ever been ashore. The sails blew away, she lay broadside on under a weather cloth, the ocean poured over her, and we did not care. We turned those handles, and had the eyes of idiots. As soon as we had crawled on deck I used to take a round turn with a rope about the men, the pumps, and the mainmast, and we turned, we turned incessantly, with the water to our waists, to our necks, over our heads. It was all one. We had forgotten how it felt to be dry.

"And there was somewhere in me the thought: By Jove! This is the deuce of an adventure—something you read about; and it is my first voyage as second mate—and I am only twenty—and here I am lasting it out as well as any of these men, and keeping my chaps up to the mark. I was pleased. I would not have given up the experience for worlds. I had moments of exultation. Whenever the old dismantled craft pitched heavily with her counter high in the air, she seemed to me to throw up, like an appeal, like a defiance, like a cry to the clouds without mercy, the words written on her stern: '*Judea*, London. Do or Die.'

"O youth! The strength of it, the faith of it, the imagination of it! To me she was not an old rattletrap carting about the world a lot of coal for a freight—to me she was the endeavor, the test, the trial of life. I think of her with pleasure, with affection, with regret—as you would think of someone dead you have loved. I shall never forget her. . . . Pass the bottle.

"One night when tied to the mast, as I explained, we were pumping on, deafened with the wind, and without spirit enough in us to wish ourselves dead, a heavy sea crashed aboard and swept clean over us. As soon as I got my breath I shouted, as in duty bound, 'Keep on, boys!' when suddenly I felt something hard floating on deck strike the calf of my leg. I made a grab at it and missed. It was so dark we could not see each other's faces within a foot—you understand.

"After that thump the ship kept quiet for a while, and the thing, whatever it was, struck my leg again. This time I caught it—and it was a saucepan. At first, being stupid with fatigue and thinking of nothing but the pumps, I did not understand what I had in my hand. Suddenly it dawned upon me, and I shouted, 'Boys, the house on deck is gone. Leave this, and let's look for the cook.'

"There was a deckhouse forward, which contained the galley, the cook's berth, and the quarters of the crew. As we had expected for days to see it swept away, the hands had been ordered to sleep in the cabin—the only safe place in this ship. The steward, Abraham, however, persisted in clinging to his berth, stupidly, like a mule—from sheer fright I believe, like an animal that won't leave a stable falling in an earthquake. So we went to look for him. It was chancing death, since once out of our lashings we were as exposed as if on a raft. But we went. The house was shattered as if a shell had exploded inside. Most of it had gone overboard—stove, men's quarters, and their property, all was gone; but two posts, holding a portion of the bulkhead to which Abraham's bunk was attached, remained as if by a miracle. We groped in the ruins and came upon this, and there he was, sitting in his bunk, surrounded by foam and wreckage, jabbering cheerfully to himself. He was out of his mind; completely and forever mad, with this sudden shock coming upon the fag-end of his endurance. We snatched him up, lugged him aft, and pitched him headfirst down the cabin companion. You understand there was no time to carry him down with infinite precautions and wait to see how he got on. Those below would pick him up at the bottom of the stairs all right. We were in a hurry to go back to the pumps. That business could not wait. A bad leak is an inhuman thing.

"One would think that the sole purpose of that fiendish gale had been to make a lunatic of that poor devil of a mulatto. It eased before morning, and next day the sky cleared, and as the sea went down the leak took up. When it came to bending a fresh set of sails the crew demanded to put back—and really there was nothing else to do. Boats gone, decks swept clean, cabin gutted, men without a stitch but what they stood in, stores spoiled, ship strained. We put her head for home, and—would you believe it? The wind came east right in our teeth. It blew fresh, it blew continuously. We had to beat up every inch of the way, but she did not leak so badly, the water keeping comparatively smooth. Two hours' pumping in every four is no joke—but it kept her afloat as far as Falmouth.

"The good people there live on casualties of the sea, and no doubt were glad to see us. A hungry crowd of shipwrights sharpened their chisels at the sight of that carcass of a ship. And, by Jove! they had pretty pickings off us before they were done. I fancy the owner was already in a tight place.

There were delays. Then it was decided to take part of the cargo out and calk her topsides. This was done, the repairs finished, cargo reshipped; a new crew came on board, and we went out—for Bankok. At the end of a week we were back again. The crew said they weren't going to Bankok—a hundred and fifty days' passage—in a something hooker that wanted pumping eight hours out of the twenty-four; and the nautical papers inserted again the little paragraph: '*Judea*. Bark. Tyne to Bankok; coals; put back to Falmouth leaky and with crew refusing duty.'

"There were more delays—more tinkering. The owner came down for a day, and said she was as right as a little fiddle. Poor old Captain Beard looked like the ghost of a Geordie skipper—through the worry and humiliation of it. Remember he was sixty, and it was his first command. Mahon said it was a foolish business, and would end badly. I loved the ship more than ever, and wanted awfully to get to Bankok. To Bankok! Magic name, blessed name. Mesopotamia wasn't a patch on it. Remember I was twenty, and it was my first second-mate's billet, and the East was waiting for me.

"We went out and anchored in the outer roads with a fresh crew—the third. She leaked worse than ever. It was as if those confounded shipwrights had actually made a hole in her. This time we did not even go outside. The crew simply refused to man the windlass.

"They towed us back to the inner harbor, and we became a fixture, a feature, an institution of the place. People pointed us out to visitors as 'That 'ere bark that's going to Bankok—has been here six months—put back three times.' On holidays the small boys pulling about in boats would hail, '*Judea*, ahoy!' and if a head showed above the rail shouted, 'Where you bound to?—Bankok?' and jeered. We were only three on board. The poor old skipper mooned in the cabin. Mahon undertook the cooking, and unexpectedly developed all a Frenchman's genius for preparing nice little messes. I looked languidly after the rigging. We became citizens of Falmouth. Every shopkeeper knew us. At the barber's or tobacconist's they asked familiarly, 'Do you think you will ever get to Bankok?' Meantime the owner, the underwriters, and the charterers squabbled amongst themselves in London, and our pay went on. . . . Pass the bottle.

"It was horrid. Morally it was worse than pumping for life. It seemed as though we had been forgotten by the world, belonged to nobody, would get nowhere; it seemed that, as if bewitched, we would have to live for ever and ever in that inner harbor, a derision and a bywork to generations of longshore loafers and dishonest boatmen. I obtained three months' pay and a five days' leave, and made a rush for London. It took me a day to get there and pretty well another to come back—but three months' pay went all the same. I don't know what I did with it. I went to a music hall, I believe, lunched, dined, and supped in a swell place in Regent Street, and was back on time, with nothing but a complete set of Byron's works and a new railway rug to show for three months' work. The boatman who pulled me off to the ship said: 'Hallo! I thought you had left the old thing. *She* will never get to Bankok.' 'That's all *you* know about it,' I said, scornfully—but I didn't like that prophecy at all.

"Suddenly a man, some kind of agent to somebody, appeared with full powers. He had grog-blossoms all over his face, an indomitable energy, and was a jolly soul. We leaped into life again. A hulk came alongside, took our cargo, and then we went into dry dock to get our copper stripped. No wonder she leaked. The poor thing, strained beyond endurance by the gale, had, as if in disgust, spat out all the oakum of her lower seams. She was recalked, new-coppered, and made as tight as a bottle. We went back to the hulk and reshipped our cargo.

"Then, on a fine moonlight night, all the rats left the ship.

"We had been infested with them. They had destroyed our sails, consumed more stores than the crew, affably shared our beds and our dangers, and now, when the ship was made seaworthy, concluded to clear out. I called Mahon to enjoy the spectacle. Rat after rat appeared on our rail, took a last look over his shoulder, and leaped with a hollow thud into the empty hulk. We tried to count them, but soon lost the tale. Mahon said: 'Well, well! don't talk to me about the intelligence of rats. They ought to have left before, when we had that narrow squeak from foundering. There you have the proof how silly is the superstition about them. They leave a good ship for an old rotten hulk, where there is nothing to eat, too, the fools! . . . I don't believe they know what is safe or what is good for them, any more than you or I.'

"And after some more talk we agreed that the wisdom of rats had been grossly overrated, being in fact no greater than that of men.

"The story of the ship was known, by this, all up the Channel from Land's End to the Forelands, and we could get no crew on the south coast. They sent us one all complete from Liverpool and we left once more—for Bankok.

"We had fair breezes, smooth water right into the tropics, and the old *Judea* lumbered along in the sunshine. When she went eight knots everything cracked aloft, and we tied our caps to our heads; but mostly she strolled on at the rate of three miles an hour. What could you expect? She was tired—that old ship. Her youth was where mine is—where yours is—you fellows who listen to this yarn; and what friend would throw your years and your weariness in your face? We didn't grumble at her. To us aft, at least, it seemed as though we had been born in her, reared in her, had lived in her for ages, had never known any other ship. I would just as soon have abused the old village church at home for not being a cathedral.

"And for me there was also my youth to make me patient. There was all the East before me, and all life, and the thought that I had been tried in that ship and had come out pretty well. And I thought of men of old who, centuries ago, went that road in ships that sailed no better, to the land of palms, and spices, and yellow sands, and of brown nations ruled by kings more cruel than Nero the Roman, and more splendid than Solomon the Jew. The old bark lumbered on, heavy with her age and the burden of her cargo, while I lived the life of youth in ignorance and hope. She lumbered on through an interminable procession of days; and the fresh gilding flashed back at the setting sun, seemed to cry out over the darkening sea the words painted on her stern, '*Judea*, London. Do or Die.'

"Then we entered the Indian Ocean and steered northerly for Java Head. The winds were light. Weeks slipped by. She crawled on, do or die, and people at home began to think of posting us as overdue.

"One Saturday evening, I being off duty, the men asked me to give them an extra bucket of water or so—for washing clothes. As I did not wish to screw on the fresh-water pump so late, I went forward whistling, and with a key in my hand to unlock the forepeak scuttle, intending to serve the water out of a spare tank we kept there.

"The smell down below was as unexpected as it was frightful. One would have thought hundreds of paraffin lamps had been flaring and smoking in that hole for days. I was glad to get out. The man with me coughed and said, 'Funny smell, sir.' I answered negligently, 'It's good for the health, they say,' and walked aft.

"The first thing I did was to put my head down the square of the midship ventilator. As I lifted the lid a visible breath, something like a thin fog, a puff of faint haze, rose from the opening. The ascending air was hot, and had a heavy, sooty, paraffiny smell. I gave one sniff, and put down the lid gently. It was no use choking myself. The cargo was on fire.

"Next day she began to smoke in earnest. You see it was to be expected, for though the coal was of a safe kind, that cargo had been so handled, so broken up with handling, that it looked more like smithy coal than anything else. Then it had been wetted—more than once. It rained all the time we were taking it back from the hulk, and now with this long passage it got heated, and there was another case of spontaneous combustion.

"The captain called us into the cabin. He had a chart spread on the table, and looked unhappy. He said, 'The coast of West Australia is near, but I mean to proceed to our destination. It is the hurricane month, too; but we will just keep her head for Bankok, and fight the fire. No more putting back anywhere, if we all get roasted. We will try first to stifle this 'ere damned combustion by want of air.'

"We tried. We battened down everything, and still she smoked. The smoke kept coming out through imperceptible crevices; it forced itself through bulkheads and covers; it oozed here and there and everywhere in slender threads, in an invisible film, in an incomprehensible manner. It made its way into the cabin, into the forecastle; it poisoned the sheltered places on the deck; it could be sniffed as high as the mainyard. It was clear that if the smoke came out the air came in. This was disheartening. This combustion refused to be stifled.

"We resolved to try water, and took the hatches off. Enormous volumes of smoke, whitish, yellowish, thick, greasy, misty, choking, ascended as high as the trucks. All hands cleared out aft. Then the poisonous cloud blew away, and we went back to work in a smoke that was no thicker now than that of an ordinary factory chimney.

"We rigged the force pump, got the hose along, and by and by it burst. Well, it was as old as the ship—a prehistoric hose, and past repair. Then we pumped with the feeble head pump, drew water with buckets, and in this way managed in time to pour lots of Indian Ocean into the main hatch. The bright stream flashed in sunshine, fell into a layer of white crawling smoke, and vanished on the black surface of coal. Steam ascended mingling with the smoke. We poured salt water as into a barrel without a bottom. It was our fate to pump in that ship, to pump out of her, to pump into her; and after keeping water out of her to save ourselves from being drowned, we frantically poured water into her to save ourselves from being burnt.

"And she crawled on, do or die, in the serene weather. The sky was a miracle of purity, a miracle of azure. The sea was polished, was blue, was pellucid, was sparkling like a precious stone, extending on all sides, all round to the horizon—as if the whole terrestrial globe had been one jewel, one colossal sapphire, a single gem fashioned into a planet. And on the luster of the great calm waters the *Judea* glided imperceptibly, enveloped in languid and unclean vapors, in a lazy cloud that drifted to leeward, light and slow; a pestiferous cloud defiling the splendor of sea and sky.

"All this time of course we saw no fire. The cargo smoldered at the bottom somewhere. Once Mahon, as we were working side by side, said to me with a queer smile: 'Now, if she only would spring a tidy leak—like that time when we first left the Channel—it would put a stopper on this fire. Wouldn't it?' I remarked irrelevantly, 'Do you remember the rats?'

"We fought the fire and sailed the ship too as carefully as though nothing had been the matter. The steward cooked and attended on us. Of the other twelve men, eight worked while four rested. Everyone took his turn, captain included. There was equality, and if not exactly fraternity, then a deal of good feeling. Sometimes a man, as he dashed a bucketful of water down the hatchway, would yell out, 'Hurrah for Bankok!' and the rest laughed. But generally we were taciturn and serious—and thirsty. Oh! how thirsty! And we had to be careful with the water. Strict allowance. The ship smoked, the sun blazed. . . . Pass the bottle.

"We tried everything. We even made an attempt to dig down to the fire. No good, of course. No man could remain more than a minute below. Mahon, who went first, fainted there, and the man who went to fetch him out did likewise. We lugged them out on deck. Then I leaped down to show how easily it could be done. They had learned wisdom by that time, and contented themselves by fishing for me with a chainhook tied to a broom handle, I believe. I did not offer to go and fetch up my shovel, which was left down below.

"Things began to look bad. We put the longboat into the water. The second boat was ready to swing out. We had also another, a fourteen-foot thing, on davits aft, where it was quite safe.

"Then, behold, the smoke suddenly decreased. We redoubled our efforts to flood the bottom of the ship. In two days there was no smoke at all. Everybody was on the broad grin. This was on a Friday. On Saturday no work, but sailing the ship of course, was done. The men washed their clothes and their faces for the first time in a fortnight, and had a special dinner given them. They spoke of spontaneous combustion with contempt, and implied *they* were the boys to put out combustions. Somehow we all felt as though we each had inherited a large fortune. But a beastly smell of burning hung about the ship. Captain Beard had hollow eyes and sunken cheeks. I had never noticed so much before how twisted and bowed he was. He and Mahon prowled soberly about hatches and ventilators, sniffing. It struck me suddenly poor Mahon was a very, very old chap. As to me, I was pleased and proud as though I had helped to win a great naval battle. O youth!

"The night was fine. In the morning a homeward-bound ship passed us hull down—the first we had seen for months; but we were nearing the land at last, Java Head being about 190 miles off, and nearly due north.

"Next day it was my watch on deck from eight to twelve. At breakfast the captain observed, 'It's wonderful how that smell hangs about the cabin.' About ten, the mate being on the poop, I stepped down on the main deck for a moment. The carpenter's bench stood abaft the mainmast: I leaned against it sucking at my pipe, and the carpenter, a young chap, came to talk to me. He remarked, 'I think we have done very well, haven't we?' and then I perceived with annoyance the fool was trying to tilt the bench. I said curtly, 'Don't, Chips,' and immediately became aware of a queer sensation, of an absurd delusion—I seemed somehow to be in the air. I heard all round me like a pent-up breath released—as if a thousand giants simultaneously had said Phoo!—and felt a dull concussion which made my ribs ache suddenly. No doubt about it—I was in the air, and my body was describing a short parabola. But short as it was, I had the time to think several thoughts in, as far as I can remember, the following order: 'This can't be the carpenter—What is it?—Some accident—Submarine volcano?—Coals, gas!—By Jove!

We are being blown up—Everybody's dead—I am falling into the afterhatch—I see fire in it.'

"The coaldust suspended in the air of the hold had glowed dull-red at the moment of the explosion. In the twinkling of an eye, in an infinitesimal fraction of a second since the first tilt of the bench, I was sprawling full length on the cargo. I picked myself up and scrambled out. It was quick like a rebound. The deck was a wilderness of smashed timber, lying crosswise like trees in a wood after a hurricane; an immense curtain of soiled rags waved gently before me—it was the mainsail blown to strips. I thought: the masts will be toppling over directly; and to get out of the way bolted on all fours towards the poop ladder. The first person I saw was Mahon, with eyes like saucers, his mouth open, and the long white hair standing straight on end round his head like a silver halo. He was just about to go down when the sight of the main deck stirring, heaving up, and changing into splinters before his eyes, petrified him on the top step. I stared at him in unbelief, and he stared at me with a queer kind of shocked curiosity. I did not know that I had no hair, no eyebrows, no eyelashes, that my young mustache was burnt off, that my face was black, one cheek laid open, my nose cut, and my chin bleeding. I had lost my cap, one of my slippers, and my shirt was torn to rags. Of all this I was not aware. I was amazed to see the ship still afloat, the poop deck whole—and, most of all, to see anybody alive. Also the peace of the sky and the serenity of the sea were distinctly surprising. I suppose I expected to see them convulsed with horror. . . . Pass the bottle.

"There was a voice hailing the ship from somewhere—in the air, in the sky—I couldn't tell. Presently I saw the captain—and he was mad. He asked me eagerly, 'Where's the cabin table?' and to hear such a question was a frightful shock. I had just been blown up, you understand, and vibrated with that experience—I wasn't quite sure whether I was alive. Mahon began to stamp with both feet and yelled at him, 'Good God! don't you see the deck's blown out of her?' I found my voice, and stammered out as if conscious of some gross neglect of duty, 'I don't know where the cabin table is.' It was like an absurd dream.

"Do you know what he wanted next? Well, he wanted to trim the yards. Very placidly, and as if lost in thought, he insisted on having the foreyard squared. 'I don't know if there's anybody alive,' said Mahon, almost tearfully. 'Surely,' he said, gently, 'there will be enough left to square the fore-yard.'

"The old chap, it seems, was in his own berth winding up the chronometers, when the shock sent him spinning. Immediately it occurred to him—as he said afterwards—that the ship had struck something, and he ran out into the cabin. There, he saw, the cabin table had vanished somewhere. The deck being blown up, it had fallen down into the lazarette of course. Where we had our breakfast that morning he saw only a great hole in the floor. This appeared to him so awfully mysterious, and impressed him so immensely, that what he saw and heard after he got on deck were mere trifles in comparison. And mark, he noticed directly the wheel deserted and his bark off her course—and his only thought was to get that miserable, stripped, undecked, smoldering shell of a ship back again with her head pointing at her port of destination. Bankok! That's what he was after. I tell you this quiet, bowed, bandy-legged, almost deformed little man was immense in the singleness of his idea and in his placid ignorance of our agitation. He motioned us forward with a commanding gesture, and went to take the wheel himself.

"Yes; that was the first thing we did—trim the yards of that wreck! No one was killed, or even disabled, but everyone was more or less hurt. You should have seen them! Some were in rags, with black faces, like coal heavers, like sweeps, and had bullet heads that seemed closely cropped, but were in fact singed to the skin. Others, of the watch below, awakened by being shot out from their collapsing bunks, shivered incessantly, and kept on groaning even as we went about our work. But they all worked. That crew of Liverpool hard cases had in them the right stuff. It's my experience they always have. It is the sea that gives it—the vastness, the loneliness surrounding their dark stolid souls. Ah! Well! We stumbled, we crept, we fell, we barked our shins on the wreckage, we hauled. The masts stood, but we did not know how much they might be charred down below. It was nearly calm, but a long swell ran from the west and made her roll. They might go at any moment. We looked at them with apprehension. One could not foresee which way they would fall.

"Then we retreated aft and looked about us. The deck was a tangle of planks on edge, of planks on end, of splinters, of ruined woodwork. The masts rose from that chaos like big trees above a matted undergrowth. The interstices of that mass of wreckage were full of something whitish, sluggish, stirring—of something that was like a greasy fog. The smoke of the invisible fire was coming up again, was trailing, like a poisonous thick mist in some valley choked with dead wood. Already lazy wisps were beginning to curl upwards amongst the mass of splinters. Here and there a piece of timber, stuck upright, resembled a post. Half of a fife rail had been shot through the foresail, and the sky made a patch of glorious blue in the ignobly soiled canvas. A portion of several boards holding together had fallen across the rail, and one end protruded overboard, like a gangway leading upon nothing, like a gangway leading over the deep sea, leading to death—as if inviting us to walk the plank at once and be done with our ridiculous troubles. And still the air, the sky—a ghost, something invisible was hailing the ship.

"Someone had the sense to look over, and there was the helmsman, who had impulsively jumped overboard, anxious to come back. He yelled and swam lustily like a merman, keeping up with the ship. We threw him a rope, and presently he stood amongst us streaming with water and very crestfallen. The captain had surrendered the wheel, and apart, elbow on rail and chin in hand, gazed at the sea wistfully. We asked ourselves, What next? I thought, Now, this is something like. This is great. I wonder what will happen. O youth!

"Suddenly Mahon sighted a steamer far astern. Captain Beard said, 'We may do something with her yet.' We hoisted two flags, which said in the international language of the sea, 'On fire. Want immediate assistance.' The steamer grew bigger rapidly, and by and by spoke with two flags on her foremast, 'I am coming to your assistance.'

"In half an hour she was abreast, to windward, within hail, and rolling slightly, with her engines stopped. We lost our composure, and yelled all together with excitement, 'We've been blown up.' A man in a white helmet, on the bridge, cried, 'Yes! All right! all right!' and he nooded his head, and smiled, and made soothing motions with his hand as though at a lot of frightened children. One of the boats dropped in the water, and walked towards us upon the sea with her long oars. Four Calashes pulled a swinging stroke. This was my first sight of Malay seamen. I've known them since, but what struck me then was their unconcern: they came alongside, and even the bowman standing up and holding to our main chains with the boathook did not deign to lift his head for a glance. I thought people who had been blown up deserved more attention.

"A little man, dry like a chip and agile like a monkey, clambered up. It was the mate of the steamer. He gave one look, and cried, 'O boys—you had better quit!'

"We were silent. He talked apart with the captain for a time—seemed to argue with him. Then they went away together to the steamer.

"When our skipper came back we learned that the steamer was the *Sommerville*, Captain Nash, from West Austrailia to Singapore via Batavia with mails, and that the agreement was she should tow us to Anjer or Batavia, if possible, where we could extinguish the fire by scuttling, and then proceed on our voyage—to Bankok! The old man seemed excited. 'We will do it yet,' he said to Mahon, fiercely. He shook his fist at the sky. Nobody else said a word.

"At noon the steamer began to tow. She went ahead slim and high, and what was left of the *Judea* followed at the end of seventy fathom of towrope—followed her swiftly like a cloud of smoke with mastheads protruding above. We went aloft to furl the sails. We coughed on the yards, and were careful about the bunts. Do you see the lot of us there, putting a neat furl on the sails of that ship doomed to arrive nowhere? There was not a man who didn't think that at any moment the masts would topple over. From aloft we could not see the ship for smoke, and they worked carefully, passing the gaskets with even turns. 'Harbor furl'—aloft there!' cried Mahon from below.

"You understand this? I don't think one of those chaps expected to get down in the usual way. When we did I heard them saying to each other, 'Well, I thought we would come down overboard, in a limp—sticks and all—blame me if I didn't.' 'That's what I was thinking to myself,' would answer wearily another battered and bandaged scarecrow. And, mind, these were men without the drilled-in habit of obedience. To an onlooker they would be a lot of profane scallywags without a redeeming point. What made them do it—what made them obey me when I, thinking consciously how fine it was, made them drop the bunt of the foresail twice to try and do it better? What? They had no professional reputation—no examples, no praise. It wasn't a sense of duty; they all knew well enough how to shirk, and laze, and dodge—when they had a mind to it—and mostly they had. Was it the two pounds ten a month that sent them there? They didn't think their pay half good enough. No; it was something in them, something inborn and subtle and everlasting. I don't say positively that the crew of a French or German merchantman wouldn't have done it, but I doubt whether it would have been done in the same way. There was a completeness in it, something solid like a principle, and masterful like an instinct—a disclosure of something secret—of that hidden something, that gift of good or evil that makes racial difference, that shapes the fate of nations.

"It was that night, at ten that, for the first time since we had been fighting it, we saw the fire. The speed of the towing had fanned the smoldering destruction. A blue gleam appeared forward, shining below the wreck of the deck. It wavered in patches, it seemed to stir and creep like the light of a glowworm. I saw it first, and told Mahon. 'Then the game's up,' he said. 'We had better stop this towing, or she will burst out suddenly fore and aft before we can clear out.' We set up a yell; rang bells to attract their attention; they towed on. At last Mahon and I had to crawl forward and cut the rope with an axe. There was no time to cast off the lashings. Red tongues could be seen licking the wilderness of splinters under our feet as we made our way back to the poop.

"Of course they very soon found out in the steamer that the rope was gone. She gave a loud blast of her whistle, her lights were seen sweeping in a wide circle, she came up ranging close alongside, and stopped. We were all in a tight group on the poop looking at her. Every man had saved a little bundle or a bag. Suddenly a conical flame with a twisted top shot up forward and threw upon the black sea a circle of light, with the two vessels side by side and heaving gently in its center. Captain Beard had been sitting on the gratings still and mute for hours, but now he rose slowly and advanced in front of us, to the mizzen-shrouds. Captain Nash hailed: 'Come along! Look sharp. I have mailbags on board. I will take you and your boats to Singapore.'

" 'Thank you! No!' said our skipper. 'We must see the last of the ship.'

" 'I can't stand by any longer,' shouted the other. 'Mails— you know.'

" 'Ay! ay! We are all right.'

" 'Very well! I'll report you in Singapore. . . . Good-by!'

"He waved his hand. Our men dropped their bundles quietly. The steamer moved ahead, and passing out of the circle of light, vanished at once from our sight, dazzled by the fire which burned fiercely. And then I knew that I would see the East first as commander of a small boat. I thought it fine; and the fidelity to the old ship was fine. We should see the last of her. Oh, the glamor of youth! Oh, the fire of it, more dazzling than the flames of the burning ship, throwing a magic light on the wide earth, leaping audaciously to the sky, presently to be quenched by time, more cruel, more pitiless, more bitter than the sea—and like the flames of the burning ship surrounded by an impenetrable night.

"The old man warned us in his gentle and inflexible way that it was part of our duty to save for the underwriters as much as we could of the ship's gear. Accordingly we went to work aft, while she blazed forward to give us plenty of light. We lugged out a lot of rubbish. What didn't we save? An old barometer fixed with an absurd quantity of screws nearly cost me my life: a sudden rush of smoke came upon me, and I just got away in time. There were various stores, bolts of canvas, coils of rope; the poop looked like a marine bazaar, and the boats were lumbered to the gunwales. One would have thought the old man wanted to take as much as he could of his first command with him. He was very, very quiet, but off his balance evidently. Would you believe it? He wanted to take a length of old stream-cable and a kedge anchor with him in the longboat. We said, 'Ay, ay, sir,' deferentially, and on the quiet let the things slip overboard. The heavy medicine chest went that way, two bags of green coffee, tins of paint—fancy, paint!—a whole lot of things. Then I was ordered with two hands into the boats to make a stowage and get them ready against the time it would be proper for us to leave the ship.

"We put everything straight, stepped the longboat's mast for our skipper, who was to take charge of her, and I was not sorry to sit down for a moment. My face felt raw, every limb ached as if broken, I was aware of all my ribs, and would have sworn to a twist in the backbone. The boats, fast astern, lay in a deep shadow, and all around I could see the circle of the sea lighted by the fire. A gigantic flame arose forward straight and clear. It flared fierce, with noises like the whirr of wings, with rumbles as of thunder. There were cracks, detonations, and from the cone of flame the sparks flew upwards, as man is born to trouble, to leaky ships, and to ships that burn.

"What bothered me was that the ship, lying broadside to the swell and to such wind as there was—a mere breath—the boats would not keep astern where they were safe, but persisted, in a pigheaded way boats have, in getting under the counter and then swinging alongside. They were knocking about dangerously and coming near the flame, while the ship rolled on them, and, of course, there was always the danger of the masts going over the side at any moment. I and my two boatkeepers kept them off as best we could, with oars and boathooks; but to be constantly at it became exasperating, since there was no reason why we should not leave at once. We could not see those on board, nor could we imagine what caused the delay. The boatkeepers were swearing feebly, and I had not only my share of the work but also had to keep at it two men who showed a constant inclination to lay themselves down and let things slide.

"At last I hailed, 'On deck there,' and someone looked over. 'We're ready here,' I said. The head disappeared, and very soon popped up again. 'The captain says, All right, sir, and to keep the boats well clear of the ship.'

"Half an hour passed. Suddenly there was a frightful racket, rattle, clanking of chain, hiss of water, and millions of sparks flew up into the shivering column of smoke that stood leaning slightly above the ship. The catheads had burned away, and the two red-hot anchors had gone to the bottom, tearing out after them two hundred fathom of red-hot chain. The ship trembled, the mass of flame swayed as if ready to collapse, and the fore-topgallant mast fell. It darted down like an arrow of fire, shot under, and instantly leaping up within an oar's length of the boats, floated quietly, very black on the luminous sea. I hailed the deck again. After some time a man in an unexpectedly cheerful but also muffled tone, as though he had been trying to speak with his mouth shut, informed me, 'Coming directly, sir,' and vanished. For a long time I heard nothing but the whirr and roar of the fire. There were also whistling sounds. The boats jumped, tugged at the painters, ran at each other playfully, knocked their sides together, or, do what we would, swung in a bunch against the ship's side. I couldn't stand it any longer, and swarming up a rope, clambered aboard over the stern.

"It was as bright as day. Coming up like this, the sheet of fire facing me was a terrifying sight, and the heat seemed hardly bearable at first. On a settee cushion dragged out of the cabin Captain Beard, his legs drawn up and one arm under his head, slept with the light playing on him. Do you know what the rest were busy about? They were sitting on deck right aft, round an open case, eating bread and cheese and drinking bottled stout.

"On the background of flames twisting in fierce tongues above their heads they seemed at home like salamanders, and looked like a band of desperate pirates. The fire sparkled in the whites of their eyes, gleamed on patches of white skin seen through the torn shirts. Each had the marks as of a battle about him—bandaged heads, tied-up arms, a strip of dirty rag round a knee—and each man had a bottle between his legs and a chunk of cheese in his hand. Mahon got up. With his handsome and disreputable head, his hooked profile, his long white beard, and with an uncorked bottle in his hand, he resembled one of those reckless sea robbers of old making merry amidst violence and disaster. 'The last meal on board,' he explained solemnly. 'We had nothing to eat all day, and it was no use leaving all this.' He flourished the bottle and indicated the sleeping skipper. 'He said he couldn't swallow anything, so I got him to lie down,' he went on; and as I stared, 'I don't know whether you are aware, young fellow, the man had no sleep to speak of for days—and there will be dam' little sleep in the boats.' 'There will be no boats by and by if you fool about much longer,' I said, indignantly. I walked up to the skipper and shook him by the shoulder. At last he opened his eyes, but did not move. 'Time to leave her, sir,' I said quietly.

"He got up painfully, looked at the flames, at the sea sparkling round the ship, and black, black as ink farther away; he looked at the stars shining dim through a thin veil of smoke in a sky black, black as Erebus.

" 'Youngest first.' he said.

"And the ordinary seaman, wiping his mouth with the back of his hand, got up, clambered over the taffrail and vanished. Others followed. One, on the point of going over, stopped short to drain his bottle, and with a great swing of his arm flung it at the fire. 'Take this!' he cried.

"The skipper lingered disconsolately, and we left him to commune alone for a while with his first command. Then I went up again and brought him away at last. It was time. The ironwork on the poop was hot to the touch.

"Then the painter of the longboat was cut, and the three boats, tied together, drifted clear of the ship. It was just sixteen hours after the explosion when we abandoned her. Mahon had charge of the second boat, and I had the smallest—the fourteen-foot thing. The longboat would have taken the lot of us; but the skipper said we must save as much property as we could—for the underwriters—and so I got my first command. I had two men with me, a bag of biscuits, a few tins of meat, and a breaker of water. I was ordered to keep close to the longboat, that in case of bad weather we might be taken into her.

"And do you know what I thought? I thought I would part company as soon as I could. I wanted to have my first command all to myself. I wasn't going to sail in a squadron if there were a chance for independent cruising. I would make land by myself. I would beat the other boats. Youth! All youth! The silly, charming, beautiful youth.

"But we did not make a start at once. We must see the last of the ship. And so the boats drifted about that night, heaving and setting on the swell. The men dozed, waked, sighed, groaned. I looked at the burning ship.

"Between the darkness of earth and heaven she was burning fiercely upon a disc of purple sea shot by the blood-red play of gleams; upon a disc of water glittering and sinister. A high, clear flame, an immense and lonely flame, ascended from the ocean, and from its summit the black smoke poured continuously at the sky. She burned furiously; mournful and imposing like a funeral pile kindled in the night, surrounded by the sea, watched over by the stars. A magnificent death had come like a grace, like a gift, like a reward to that old ship at the end of her laborious days. The surrender of her weary ghost to the keeping of stars and sea was stirring like the sight of a glorious triumph. The masts fell just before daybreak, and for a moment there was a burst and turmoil of sparks that seemed to fill with flying fire the night patient and watchful, the vast night lying silent upon the sea. At daylight she was only a charred shell, floating still under a cloud of smoke and bearing a glowing mass of coal within.

"Then the oars were got out, and the boats forming in a line moved round her remains as if in procession—the longboat leading. As we pulled across her stern a slim dart of fire shot out viciously at us, and suddenly she went down, head first, in a great hiss of steam. The unconsumed stern was the last to sink; but the paint had gone, had cracked, had peeled off, and there were no letters, there was no word, no stubborn device that was like her soul, to flash at the rising sun her creed and her name.

"We made our way north. A breeze sprang up, and about noon all the boats came together for the last time. I had no mast or sail in mine, but I made a mast out of a spare oar and hoisted a boat-awning for a sail, with a boathook for a yard. She was certainly over-masted, but I had the satisfaction of knowing that with the wind aft I could beat the other two. I had to wait for them. Then we all had a look at the captain's chart, and, after a sociable meal of hard bread and water, got our last instructions. These were simple: steer north, and keep together as much as possible. 'Be careful with that jury-rig, Marlow,' said the captain; and Mahon, as I sailed proudly past his boat, wrinkled his curved nose and hailed, 'You will sail that ship of yours under water, if you don't look out, young fellow.' He was a malicious old man—and may the deep sea where he sleeps now rock him gently, rock him tenderly to the end of time!

"Before sunset a thick rain-squall passed over the two boats, which were far astern, and that was the last I saw of them for a time. Next day I sat steering my cockleshell—my first command—with nothing but water and sky round me. I did sight in the afternoon the upper sails of a ship far away, but said nothing, and my men did not notice her. You see I was afraid she might be homeward bound, and I had no mind to turn back from the portals of the East. I was steering for Java—another blessed name—like Bankok, you know. I steered many days.

"I need not tell you what it is to be knocking about in an open boat. I remember nights and days of calm, when we pulled, we pulled, and the boat seemed to stand still, as if bewitched within the circle of the sea horizon. I remember the heat, the deluge of rain-squalls that kept us baling for dear life (but filled our water cask), and I remember sixteen hours on end with a mouth dry as a cinder and a steering oar over the stern to keep my first command head on to a breaking sea. I did not know how good a man I was till then. I remember the drawn faces, the dejected figures of my two men, and I remember my youth and the feeling that will never come back any more—the feeling that I could last forever, outlast the sea, the earth, and all men; the deceitful feeling that lures us on to joys, to perils, to love, to vain effort—to death; the triumphant conviction of strength, the heat of life in the handful of dust, the glow in the heart that with every year grows dim, grows cold, grows small, and expires—and expires, too soon, too soon—before life itself.

"And this is how I see the East. I have seen its secret places and have looked into its very soul; but now I see it always

from a small boat, a high outline of mountains, blue and afar
in the morning; like faint mist at noon; a jagged wall of purple
at sunset. I have the feel of the oar in my hand, the vision
of a scorching blue sea in my eyes. And I see a bay, a wide
bay, smooth as glass and polished like ice, shimmering in the
dark. A red light burns far off upon the gloom of the land,
and the night is soft and warm. We drag at the oars with
aching arms, and suddenly a puff of wind, a puff faint and
tepid and laden with strange odors of blossoms, of aromatic
wood, comes out of the still night—the first sigh of the East
on my face. That I can never forget. It was impalpable and
enslaving, like a charm, like a whispered promise of mysterious delight.

"We had been pulling this finishing spell for eleven hours.
Two pulled, and he whose turn it was to rest sat at the tiller.
We had made out the red light in that bay and steered for it,
guessing it must mark some small coasting port. We passed
two vessels, outlandish and highsterned, sleeping at anchor,
and, approaching the light, now very dim, ran the boat's nose
against the end of a jutting wharf. We were blind with fatigue.
My men dropped the oars and fell off the thwarts as if dead.
I made fast to a pile. A current rippled softly. The scented
obscurity of the shore was grouped into vast masses, a density
of colossal clumps of vegetation, probably—mute and fantastic shapes. And at their foot the semicircle of a beach
gleamed faintly, like an illusion. There was not a light, not
a stir, not a sound. The mysterious East faced me, perfumed
like a flower, silent like death, dark like a grave.

"And I sat weary beyond expression, exulting like a conqueror, sleepless and entranced as if before a profound, a
fateful enigma.

"A splashing of oars, a measured dip reverberating on the
level of water, intensified by the silence of the shore into loud
claps, made me jump up. A boat, a European boat, was
coming in. I invoked the name of the dead; I hailed: '*Judea*
ahoy!' A thin shout answered.

"It was the captain. I had beaten the flagship by three
hours, and I was glad to hear the old man's voice again,
tremulous and tired. 'Is it you, Marlow?' 'Mind the end of
that jetty, sir,' I cried.

"He approached cautiously, and brought up with the deep-
sea lead line which we had saved—for the underwriters. I
eased my painter and fell alongside. He sat, a broken figure
at the stern, wet with dew, his hands clasped in his lap. His

men were asleep already. 'I had a terrible time of it,' he murmured. 'Mahon is behind—not very far.' We conversed in whispers, in low whispers, as if afraid to wake up the land. Guns, thunder, earthquakes would not have awakened the men just then.

"Looking round as we talked, I saw away at sea a bright light traveling in the night. 'There's a steamer passing the bay,' I said. She was not passing, she was entering, and she even came close and anchored. 'I wish,' said the old man, 'you would find out whether she is English. Perhaps they could give us a passage somewhere.' He seemed nervously anxious. So by dint of punching and kicking I started one of my men into a state of somnambulism, and giving him an oar, took another and pulled towards the lights of the steamer.

"There was a murmur of voices in her, metallic hollow clangs of the engine room, footsteps on the deck. Her ports shone, round like dilated eyes. Shapes moved about, and there was a shadowy man high up on the bridge. He heard my oars.

"And then, before I could open my lips, the East spoke to me, but it was in a Western voice. A torrent of words was poured into the enigmatical, the fateful silence; outlandish, angry words, mixed with words and even whole sentences of good English, less strange but even more surprising. The voice swore and cursed violently; it riddled the solemn peace of the bay by a volley of abuse. It began by calling me Pig, and from that went crescendo into unmentionable adjectives—in English. The man up there raged aloud in two languages, and with a sincerity in his fury that almost convinced me I had, in some way, sinned against the harmony of the universe. I could hardly see him, but began to think he would work himself into a fit.

"Suddenly he ceased, and I could hear him snorting and blowing like a porpoise. I said:

" 'What steamer is this, pray?'

" 'Eh? What's this? And who are you?'

" 'Castaway crew of an English bark burnt at sea. We came here tonight. I am the second mate. The captain is in the longboat, and wishes to know if you would give us a passage somewhere.'

" 'Oh, my goodness! I say. . . . This is the *Celestial* from Singapore on her return trip. I'll arrange with your captain in the morning, . . . and, . . . I say, . . . did you hear me just now?'

" 'I should think the whole bay heard you.'

" 'I thought you were a shoreboat. Now, look here—this infernal lazy scoundrel of a caretaker has gone to sleep again—curse him. The light is out, and I nearly ran foul of the end of this damned jetty. This is the third time he plays me this trick. Now, I ask you, can anybody stand this kind of thing? It's enough to drive a man out of his mind. I'll report him. . . . I'll get the Assistant Resident to give him the sack, by—! See—there's no light. It's out, isn't it? I take you to witness the light's out. There should be a light, you know. A red light on the—'

" 'There was a light,' I said, mildly.

" 'But it's out, man! What's the use of talking like this? You can see for yourself it's out—don't you? If you had to take a valuable steamer along this God-forsaken coast you would want a light, too. I'll kick him from end to end of his miserable wharf. You'll see if I don't. I will—'

" 'So I may tell my captain you'll take us?' I broke in.

" 'Yes, I'll take you. Good night,' he said, brusquely.

"I pulled back, made fast again to the jetty, and then went to sleep at last. I had faced the silence of the East. I had heard some of its language. But when I opened my eyes again the silence was as complete as though it had never been broken. I was lying in a flood of light, and the sky had never looked so far, so high, before. I opened my eyes and lay without moving.

"And then I saw the men of the East—they were looking at me. The whole length of the jetty was full of people. I saw brown, bronze, yellow faces, the black eyes, the glitter, the color of an Eastern crowd. And all these beings stared without a murmur, without a sigh, without a movement. They stared down at the boats, at the sleeping men who at night had come to them from the sea. Nothing moved. The fronds of palms stood still against the sky. Not a branch stirred along the shore, and the brown roofs of hidden houses peeped through the green foliage, through the big leaves that hung shining and still like leaves forged of heavy metal. This was the East of the ancient navigators, so old, so mysterious, resplendent and somber, living and unchanged, full of danger and promise. And these were the men. I sat up suddenly. A wave of movement passed through the crowd from end to end, passed along the heads, swayed the bodies, ran along the jetty like a ripple on the water, like a breath of wind on a field—and all was still again. I see it now—the wide sweep of the bay, the glittering sands, the wealth of green infinite and varied, the sea blue like the sea of a dream, the crowd of attentive faces, the blaze of vivid color—the water reflecting it all, the curve of the shore, the jetty, the high-sterned outlandish craft floating still, and the three boats with the tired men from the West sleeping, unconscious of the land and the people and of the violence of sunshine. They slept thrown across the thwarts, curled on bottomboards, in the careless attitudes of death. The head of the old skipper, leaning back in the stern of the longboat, had fallen on his breast, and he looked as though he would never wake. Farther out old Mahon's face was upturned to the sky, with the long white beard spread out on his breast, as though he had been shot where he sat at the tiller; and a man, all in a heap in the bows of the boat, slept with both arms embracing the stemhead and with his cheek laid on the gunwale. The East looked at them without a sound.

"I have known its fascination since; I have seen the mysterious shores, the still water, the lands of brown nations, where a stealthy Nemesis lies in wait, pursues, overtakes so many of the conquering race, who are proud of their wisdom, of their knowledge, of their strength. But for me all the East is contained in that vision of my youth. It is all in that moment when I opened my young eyes on it. I came upon it from a tussle with the sea—and I was young—and I saw it looking at me. And this is all that is left of it! Only a moment; a moment of strength, of romance, of glamor—of youth! . . . A flick of sunshine upon a strange shore, the time to remember, the time for a sigh, and—good-by!—Night—Good-by . . . !"

He drank.

"Ah! The good old time—the good old time. Youth and the sea. Glamor and the sea! The good, strong sea, the salt, bitter sea, that could whisper to you and roar at you and knock your breath out of you."

He drank again.

"By all that's wonderful it is the sea, I believe, the sea itself—or is it youth alone? Who can tell? But you here—you all had something out of life: money, love—whatever one gets on shore—and, tell me, wasn't that the best time, that time when we were young at sea; young and had nothing, on the sea that gives nothing, except hard knocks—and sometimes a chance to feel your strength—that only—that you all regret?"

And we all nodded at him: the man of finance, the man of accounts, the man of law, we all nodded at him over the polished table that like a still sheet of brown water reflected our faces, lined, wrinkled; our faces marked by toil, by deceptions, by success, by love; our weary eyes looking still, looking always, looking anxiously for something out of life, that while it is expected is already gone—has passed unseen, in a sigh, in a flash—together with the youth, with the strength, with the romance of illusions.

Rudyard Kipling
(1865–1936)

Like Conrad and Maugham, Rudyard Kipling used foreign settings for his novels to great advantage. Born in Bombay, India, Kipling was educated in England, but returned to India at nineteen, where he worked as a journalist and an editor. The country profoundly affected nearly everything that he wrote, whether children's stories, novels for adult reading, or poems that both supported and warned against English imperialism. A list of Kipling's major works shows his indebtedness to his Indian background and to his sympathy for England's imperialistic venture there. In 1907, he received the Nobel Prize for literature; he was England's first laureate. Kipling was quite prolific, as we can see from the dates of his books: early poems, Departmental Ditties *(1886) and* Barrack-Room Ballads *(1892); short stories,* Plain Tales from the Hills *(1888) and* Soldiers Three *(1888); novels for adults and children,* The Light That Failed *(1890),* Captains Courageous *(1897), and* Kim *(1901); and the famous jungle stories,* The Jungle Book *and the* Second Jungle Book, *in 1894 and 1895. Kipling's poems were also wildly popular:* "Gunga Din," "Recessional," "Mandalay." *After his marriage in 1892, he lived in Vermont for four years and then moved back to England, where he remained until his death.*

The Mark of the Beast

> *Your Gods and my Gods*
> —*do you or I know which are the stronger?*
>
> *Native Proverb*

East of Suez, some hold, the direct control of Providence ceases; Man being there handed over to the power of the

Gods and Devils of Asia, and the Church of England Providence only exercising an occasional and modified supervision in the case of Englishmen.

This theory accounts for some of the more unnecessary horrors of life in India: it may be stretched to explain my story.

My friend Strickland of the Police, who knows as much of natives of India as is good for any man, can bear witness to the facts of the case. Dumoise, our doctor, also saw what Strickland and I saw. The inference which he drew from the evidence was entirely incorrect. He is dead now; he died in a rather curious manner, which has been elsewhere described.

When Fleete came to India he owned a little money and some land in the Himalayas, near a place called Dharmsala. Both properties had been left him by an uncle, and he came out to finance them. He was a big, heavy, genial, and inoffensive man. His knowledge of natives was, of course, limited, and he complained of the difficulties of the language.

He rode in from his place in the hills to spend New Year in the station, and he stayed with Strickland. On New Year's Eve there was a big dinner at the club, and the night was excusably wet. When men foregather from the uttermost ends of the Empire, they have a right to be riotous. The Frontier had sent down a contingent o' Catch-'em-Alive-O's who had not seen twenty white faces for a year, and were used to ride fifteen miles to dinner at the next Fort at the risk of a Khyberee bullet where their drinks should lie. They profited by their new security, for they tried to play pool with a curled-up hedgehog found in the garden, and one of them carried the marker round the room in his teeth. Half a dozen planters had come in from the south and were talking "horse" to the Biggest Liar in Asia, who was trying to cap all their stories at once. Everybody was there, and there was a general closing up of ranks and taking stock of our losses in dead or disabled that had fallen during the past year. It was a very wet night, and I remember that we sang "Auld Lang Syne" with our feet in the Polo Championship Cup, and our heads among the stars, and swore that we were all dear friends. Then some of us went away and annexed Burma, and some tried to open up the Soudan and were opened up by Fuzzies in that cruel scrub outside Suakim, and some found stars and medals, and some were married, which was bad, and some did other things which were worse, and the others of us stayed in our chains and strove to make money on insufficient experiences.

Fleete began the night with sherry and bitters, drank champagne steadily up to dessert, then raw, rasping Capri with all the strength of whiskey, took Benedictine with his coffee, four or five whiskies and sodas to improve his pool strokes, beer and bones at half-past two, winding up with old brandy. Consequently, when he came out, at half-past three in the morning, into fourteen degrees of frost, he was very angry with his horse for coughing, and tried to leapfrog into the saddle. The horse broke away and went to the stables; so Strickland I formed a Guard of Dishonour to take Fleete home.

Our road lay through the bazar, close to a little temple of Hanuman, the Monkey-god, who is a leading divinity worthy of respect. All gods have good points, just as have all priests. Personally, I attach much importance to Hanuman, and am kind to his people—the great gray apes of the hills. One never knows when one may want a friend.

There was a light in the temple, and as we passed we could hear voices of men chanting hymns. In a native temple the priests rise at all hours of the night to do honour to their god. Before we could stop him, Fleete dashed up the steps, patted two priests on the back, and was gravely grinding the ashes of his cigar-butt into the forehead of the red stone image of Hanuman. Strickland tried to drag him out, but he sat down and said solemnly:

"Shee that? Mark of the B-beasht! *I* made it. Ishn't it fine?"

In half a minute the temple was alive and noisy, and Strickland, who knew what came of polluting gods, said that things might occur. He, by virtue of his official position, long residence in the country, and weakness for going among the natives, was known to the priests, and he felt unhappy. Fleete sat on the ground and refused to move. He said that "good old Hanuman" made a very soft pillow.

Then, without any warning, a Silver Man came out of a recess behind the image of the god. He was perfectly naked in that bitter, bitter cold, and his body shone like frosted silver, for he was what the Bible calls "a leper as white as snow." Also he had no face, because he was a leper of some years' standing, and his disease was heavy upon him. We two stooped to haul Fleete up, and the temple was filling and filling with folk who seemed to spring from the earth, when the Silver Man ran in under our arms, making a noise exactly like the mewing of an otter, caught Fleete around the body and dropped his head on Fleete's breast before we could wrench him away. Then he retired to a corner and sat mewing while the crowd blocked all the doors.

The priests were very angry until the Silver Man touched Fleete. That nuzzling seemed to sober them.

At the end of a few minutes' silence one of the priests came to Strickland and said, in perfect English, "Take your friend away. He has done with Hanuman, but Hanuman has not done with him." The crowd gave room and we carried Fleete into the road.

Strickland was very angry. He said that we might all three have been knifed, and that Fleete should thank his stars that he had escaped without injury.

Fleete thanked no one. He said that he wanted to go to bed. He was gorgeously drunk.

We moved on, Strickland silent and wrathful, until Fleete was taken with violent shivering fits and sweating. He said that the smells of the bazar were overpowering, and he wondered why slaughterhouses were permitted so near English residences. "Can't you smell the blood?" said Fleete.

We put him to bed at last, just as the dawn was breaking, and Strickland invited me to have another whiskey and soda. While we were drinking he talked of the trouble in the temple, and admitted that it baffled him completely. Strickland hates being mystified by natives, because his business in life is to overmatch them with their own weapons. He has not yet succeeded in doing this, but in fifteen or twenty years he will have made some small progress.

"They should have mauled us," he said, "instead of mewing at us. I wonder what they meant. I don't like it one little bit."

I said that the Managing Committee of the temple would in all probability bring a criminal action against us for insulting their religion. There was a section of the Indian Penal Code which exactly met Fleete's offence. Strickland said he only hoped and prayed that they would do this. Before I left I looked into Fleete's room, and saw him lying on his right side, scratching his left breast. Then I went to bed, cold, depressed, and unhappy at seven o'clock in the morning.

At one o'clock I rode over to Strickland's house to inquire after Fleete's head. I imagined that it would be a sore one. Fleete was breakfasting and seemed unwell. His temper was gone, for he was abusing the cook for not supplying him with an underdone chop. A man who can eat raw meat after a wet night is a curiosity. I told Fleete this, and he laughed.

"You breed queer mosquitos in these parts," he said. "I've been bitten to pieces, but only in one place."

"Let's have a look at the bite," said Strickland. "It may have gone down since this morning."

While the chops were being cooked, Fleete opened his shirt and showed us, just over his left breast, a mark, the perfect double of the black rosettes—the five or six irregular blotches arranged in a circle—on a leopard's hide. Strickland looked and said, "It was only pink this morning. It's grown black now."

Fleete ran to a glass.

"By Jove!" he said, "this is nasty. What is it?"

We could not answer. Here the chops came in, all red and juicy, and Fleete bolted three in a most offensive manner. He ate on his right grinders only, and threw his head over his right shoulder as he snapped the meat. When he had finished, it struck him that he had been behaving strangely, for he said apologetically, "I don't think I ever felt so hungry in my life. I've bolted like an ostrich."

After breakfast Strickland said to me, "Don't go. Stay here, and stay for the night."

Seeing that my house was not three miles from Strickland's, this request was absurd. But Strickland insisted, and was going to say something when Fleete interrupted by declaring in a shame-faced way that he felt hungry again. Strickland sent a man to my house to fetch over my bedding and a horse, and we three went down to Strickland's stables to pass the hours until it was time to go out for a ride. The man who has a weakness for horses never wearies of inspecting them; and when two men are killing time in this way they gather knowledge and lies the one from the other.

There were five horses in the stables, and I shall never forget the scene as we tried to look them over. They seemed to have gone mad. They reared and screamed and nearly tore up their pickets; they sweated and shivered and lathered and were distraught with fear. Strickland's horses used to know him as well as his dogs; which made the matter more curious. We left the stable for fear of the brutes throwing themselves in their panic. Then Strickland turned back and called me. The horses were still frightened, but they let us "gentle" and make much of them, and put their heads in our bosoms.

"They aren't afraid of *us*," said Strickland. "D'you know, I'd give three months' pay if Outrage here could talk."

But Outrage was dumb, and could only cuddle up to his

master and blow out his nostrils, as is the custom of horses when they wish to explain things but can't. Fleete came up when we were in the stalls, and as soon as the horses saw him their fright broke out afresh. It was all that we could do to escape from the place unkicked. Strickland said, "They don't seem to love you, Fleete."

"Nonsense," said Fleete; "my mare will follow me like a dog." He went to her; she was in a loose-box; but as he slipped the bars she plunged, knocked him down, and broke away into the garden. I laughed, but Strickland was not amused. He took his moustache in both fists and pulled at it till it nearly came out. Fleete, instead of going off to chase his property, yawned, saying that he felt sleepy. He went to the house to lie down, which was a foolish way of spending New Year's Day.

Strickland sat with me in the stables and asked if I had noticed anything peculiar in Fleete's manner. I said that he ate his food like a beast; but that this might have been the result of living alone in the hills out of the reach of society as refined and elevating as ours, for instance. Strickland was not amused. I do not think that he listened to me, for his next sentence referred to the mark on Fleete's breast, and I said that it might have been caused by blister-flies, or that it was possibly a birth-mark newly born and now visible for the first time. We both agreed that it was unpleasant to look at, and Strickland found occasion to say that I was a fool.

"I can't tell you what I think now," said he, "because you would call me a madman; but you must stay with me for the next few days if you can. I want you to watch Fleete, but don't tell me what you think till I have made up my mind."

"But I am dining out to-night," I said.

"So am I," said Strickland, "and so is Fleete. At least if he doesn't change his mind."

We walked about the garden smoking, but saying nothing—because we were friends, and talking spoils good tobacco—till our pipes were out. Then we went to wake up Fleete. He was wide awake and fidgeting about his room.

"I say, I want some more chops," he said. "Can I get them?"

We laughed and said, "Go and change. The ponies will be round in a minute."

"All right," said Fleete. "I'll go when I get the chops—underdone ones, mind."

He seemed to be quite in earnest. It was four o'clock, and

we had had breakfast at one; still, for a long time, he demanded those underdone chops. Then he changed into riding clothes and went out into the verandah. His pony—the mare had not been caught—would not let him come near. All three horses were unmanageable—mad with fear—and finally Fleete said that he would stay at home and get something to eat. Strickland and I rode out wondering. As we passed the temple of Hanuman, the Silver Man came out and mewed at us.

"He is not one of the regular priests of the temple," said Strickland. "I think I should peculiarly like to lay my hands on him."

There was no spring in our gallop on the racecourse that evening. The horses were stale, and moved as though they had been ridden out.

"The fright after breakfast has been too much for them," said Strickland.

That was the only remark he made through the remainder of the ride. Once or twice I think he swore to himself; but that did not count.

We came back in the dark at seven o'clock, and saw that there were no lights in the bungalow. "Careless ruffians my servants are!" said Strickland.

My horse reared at something on the carriage-drive, and Fleete stood up under its nose.

"What are you doing, grovelling about the garden?" said Strickland.

But both horses bolted and nearly threw us. We dismounted by the stables and returned to Fleete, who was on his hands and knees under the orange-bushes.

"What the devil's wrong with you?" said Strickland.

"Nothing, nothing in the world," said Fleete, speaking very quickly and thickly. "I've been gardening—botanising, you know. The smell of the earth is delightful. I think I'm going for a walk—a long walk—all night."

Then I saw that there was something excessively out of order somewhere, and I said to Strickland, "I am not dining out."

"Bless you!" said Strickland. "Here, Fleete, get up. You'll catch fever there. Come in to dinner and let's have the lamps lit. We'll all dine at home."

Fleete stood up unwillingly, and said, "No lamps—no lamps. It's much nicer here. Let's dine outside and have some more chops—lots of 'em and underdone—bloody ones with gristle."

Now a December evening in Northern India is bitterly cold, and Fleete's suggestion was that of a maniac.

"Come in," said Strickland sternly. "Come in at once."

Fleete came, and when the lamps were brought, we saw that he was literally plastered with dirt from head to foot. He must have been rolling in the garden. He shrank from the light and went to his room. His eyes were horrible to look at. There was a green light behind them, not in them, if you understand, and the man's lower lip hung down.

Strickland said, "There is going to be trouble—big trouble—to-night. Don't you change your riding-things."

We waited and waited for Fleete's reappearance, and ordered dinner in the meantime. We could hear him moving about his own room, but there was no light there. Presently from the room came the long-drawn howl of a wolf.

People write and talk lightly of blood running cold and hair standing up and things of that kind. Both sensations are too horrible to be trifled with. My heart stopped as though a knife had been driven through it, and Strickland turned as white as the tablecloth.

The howl was repeated, and was answered by another howl far across the fields.

That set the gilded roof on the horror. Strickland dashed into Fleete's room. I followed, and we saw Fleete getting out of the window. He made beast-noises in the back of his throat. He could not answer us when we shouted at him. He spat.

I don't quite remember what followed, but I think that Strickland must have stunned him with the long boot-jack or else I should never have been able to sit on his chest. Fleete could not speak, he could only snarl, and his snarls were those of a wolf, not of a man. The human spirit must have been giving way all day and have died out with the twilight. We were dealing with a beast that had once been Fleete.

The affair was beyond any human and rational experience. I tried to say "Hydrophobia," but the word wouldn't come, because I knew that I was lying.

We bound this beast with leather thongs of the punkah-rope, and tied its thumbs and big toes together, and gagged it with a shoe-horn, which makes a very efficient gag if you know how to arrange it. Then we carried it into the dining-room, and sent a man to Dumoise, the doctor, telling him to come over at once. After we had despatched the messenger and were drawing breath, Strickland said, "It's no good. This isn't any doctor's work." I, also, knew that he spoke the truth.

The beast's head was free, and it threw it about from side to side. Any one entering the room would have believed that we were curing a wolf's pelt. That was the most loathsome accessory of all.

Strickland sat with his chin in the heel of his fist, watching the beast as it wriggled on the ground, but saying nothing. The shirt had been torn open in the scuffle and showed the black rosette mark on the left breast. It stood out like a blister.

In the silence of the watching we heard something without mewing like a she-otter. We both rose to our feet, and, I answer for myself, not Strickland, felt sick—actually and physically sick. We told each other, as did the men in "Pinafore," that it was the cat.

Dumoise arrived, and I never saw a little man so unprofessionally shocked. He said that it was a heart-rending case of hydrophobia, and that nothing could be done. At least any palliative measures would only prolong the agony. The beast was foaming at the mouth. Fleete, as we told Dumoise, had been bitten by dogs once or twice. Any man who keeps half a dozen terriers must expect a nip now and again. Dumoise could offer no help. He could only certify that Fleete was dying of hydrophobia. The beast was then howling, for it had managed to spit out the shoe-horn. Dumoise said that he would be ready to certify to the cause of death, and that the end was certain. He was a good little man, and he offered to remain with us; but Strickland refused the kindness. He did not wish to poison Dumoise's New Year. He would only ask him not to give the real cause of Fleete's death to the public.

So Dumoise left, deeply agitated; and as soon as the noise of the cart-wheels had died away, Strickland told me, in a whisper, his suspicions. They were so wildly improbable that he dared not say them out aloud; and I, who entertained all Strickland's beliefs, was so ashamed of owning to them that I pretended to disbelieve.

"Even if the Silver Man had bewitched Fleete for polluting the image of Hanuman, the punishment could not have fallen so quickly."

As I was whispering this the cry outside the house rose again, and the beast fell into a fresh paroxysm of struggling till we were afraid that the thongs that held it would give way.

"Watch!" said Strickland. "If this happens six times I shall take the law into my own hands. I order you to help me."

He went into his room and came out in a few minutes with

the barrels of an old shot-gun, a piece of fishing-line, some thick cord, and his heavy wooden bedstead. I reported that the convulsions had followed the cry by two seconds in each case, and the beast seemed perceptibly weaker.

Strickland muttered, "But he can't take away the life! He can't take away the life!"

I said, though I knew that I was arguing against myself, "It may be a cat. It must be a cat. If the Silver Man is responsible, why does he dare to come here?"

Strickland arranged the wood on the hearth, put the gun-barrels into the glow of the fire, spread the twine on the table, and broke a walking-stick in two. There was one yard of fishing-line, gut, lapped with wire, such as is used for *mahseer*-fishing, and he tied the two ends together in a loop.

Then he said, "How can we catch him? He must be taken alive and unhurt."

I said that we must trust in Providence, and go out softly with polo-sticks into the shrubbery at the front of the house. The man or animal that made the cry was evidently moving round the house as regularly as a nightwatchman. We could wait in the bushes till he came by, and knock him over.

Strickland accepted this suggestion, and we slipped out from a bath-room window into the front verandah and then across the carriage-drive into the bushes.

In the moonlight we could see the leper coming round the corner of the house. He was perfectly naked, and from time to time he mewed and stopped to dance with his shadow. It was an unattractive sight, and thinking of poor Fleete, brought to such degradation by so foul a creature, I put away all my doubts and resolved to help Strickland from the heated gun-barrels to the loop of twine—from the loins to the head and back again—with all tortures that might be needful.

The leper halted in the front porch for a moment and we jumped out on him with the sticks. He was wonderfully strong, and we were afraid that he might escape or be fatally injured before we caught him. We had an idea that lepers were frail creatures, but this proved to be incorrect. Strickland knocked his legs from under him, and I put my foot on his neck. He mewed hideously, and even through my riding-boots I could feel that his flesh was not the flesh of a clean man.

He struck at us with his hand and feet-stumps. We looped the lash of a dog-whip round him, under the arm-pits, and dragged him backwards into the hall and so into the dining-room where the beast lay. There we tied him with trunk-straps. He made no attempt to escape, but mewed.

When we confronted him with the beast the scene was beyond description. The beast doubled backwards into a bow, as though he had been poisoned with strychnine, and moaned in the most pitiable fashion. Several other things happened also, but they cannot be put down here.

"I think I was right," said Strickland. "Now we will ask him to cure this case."

But the leper only mewed. Strickland wrapped a towel round his hand and took the gun-barrels out of the fire. I put the half of the broken walking-stick through a loop of fishing-line and buckled the leper comfortably to Strickland's bed-stead. I understood then how men and women and little children can endure to see a witch burnt alive; for the beast was moaning on the floor, and though the Silver Man had no face, you could see horrible feelings passing through the slab that took its place, exactly as waves of heat play across red-hot iron—gun-barrels for instance.

Strickland shaded his eyes with his hands for a moment, and we got to work. This part is not to be printed.

The dawn was beginning to break when the leper spoke. His mewings had not been satisfactory up to that point. The beast had fainted from exhaustion, and the house was very still. We unstrapped the leper and told him to take away the evil spirit. He crawled to the beast and laid his hand upon the left breast. That was all. Then he fell face down and whined, drawing in his breath as he did so.

We watched the face of the beast, and saw the soul of Fleete coming back into the eyes. Then a sweat broke out on the forehead, and the eyes—they were human eyes—closed. We waited for an hour, but Fleete still slept. We carried him to his room and bade the leper go, giving him the bedstead, and the sheet on the bedstead to cover his nakedness, the gloves and the towels with which we had touched him, and the whip that had been hooked round his body. He put the sheet about him and went out into the early morning without speaking or mewing.

Strickland wiped his face and sat down. A night-gong, far away in the city, made seven o'clock.

"Exactly four-and-twenty hours!" said Strickland. "And I've done enough to ensure my dismissal from the service, besides permanent quarters in a lunatic asylum. Do you believe that we are awake?"

The red-hot gun-barrel had fallen on the floor and was singeing the carpet. The smell was entirely real.

That morning at eleven we two together went to wake up Fleete. We looked and saw that the black leopard-rosette on his chest had disappeared. He was very drowsy and tired, but as soon as he saw us, he said, "Oh! Confound you fellows. Happy New Year to you. Never mix your liquors. I'm nearly dead."

"Thanks for your kindness, but you're over time," said Strickland. "To-day is the morning of the second. You've slept the clock round with a vengeance."

The door opened, and little Dumoise put his head in. He had come on foot, and fancied that we were laying out Fleete.

"I've brought a nurse," said Dumoise. "I suppose that she can come in for . . . what is necessary."

"By all means," said Fleete cheerily, sitting up in bed. "Bring on your nurses."

Dumoise was dumb. Strickland led him out and explained that there must have been a mistake in the diagnosis. Dumoise remained dumb and left the house hastily. He considered that his professional reputation had been injured, and was inclined to make a personal matter of the recovery. Strickland went out too. When he came back, he said that he had been to call on the temple of Hanuman to offer redress for the pollution of the god, and had been solemnly assured that no white man had ever touched the idol, and that he was an incarnation of all the virtues laboring under a delusion. "What do you think?" said Strickland.

I said, "There are more things . . ."

Not respecting what we know

H. G. Wells
(1866–1946)

Herbert George Wells was the first great writer of science fiction. Notable were The Time Machine *(1896),* The Invisible Man *(1897), and* The War of the Worlds *(1901). Influenced by Thomas Henry Huxley, who was himself a disciple of Darwin, Wells trained himself in biology and taught the subject until he began his writing career. He wrote in many other areas besides science fiction and established himself as an important novelist in his day, with* Tono-Bungay *and* Ann Veronica *in 1909,* The History of Mr. Polly *(1910), and* Mr. Britling Sees It Through *(1916), as well as numerous others. Prolific as a short story writer, historian (the hugely successful* Outline of History, *1920), autobiographer, and political scientist, Wells considered himself a prophet about man's history and a wise counsel on social questions. By the year of his death, he had seen World War II destroy all his ideas about man's ability to cooperate and to found a Socialist state.*

The Magic Shop

I had seen the magic shop from afar several times; I had passed it once or twice, a shop window of alluring little objects, magic balls, magic hens, wonderful cones, ventriloquist dolls, the material of the basket trick, packs of cards that *looked* all right, and all that sort of thing, but never had I thought of going in until one day, almost without warning, Gip hauled me by my finger right up to the window, and so conducted himself that there was nothing for it but to take him in. I had not thought the place was there, to tell the truth—a modest-size frontage in Regent Street, between the picture shop and the place where the chicks run about just out of patent incubators,—but there it was sure enough. I had fancied it was down nearer the Circus, or round the corner in Oxford Street, or even in Holborn; always over the way and a little inaccessible it had been, with something of the mirage in its position; but here it was now quite indisputably, and the fat end of Gip's pointing finger made a noise upon the glass.

"If I was rich," said Gip, dabbing a finger at the Disappearing Egg, "I'd buy myself that. And that"—which was The Crying Baby, Very Human—"and that," which was a mystery, and called, so a neat card asserted, "Buy One and Astonish Your Friends."

"Anything," said Gip, "will disappear under one of those cones. I have read about it in a book.

"And there, dadda, is the Vanishing Halfpenny—only they've put it this way up so's we can't see how it's done."

Gip, dear boy, inherits his mother's breeding, and he did not propose to enter the shop or worry in any way; only, you know, quite unconsciously he lugged my finger doorward, and he made his interest clear.

"That," he said, and pointed to the Magic Bottle.

"If you had that?" I said; at which promising inquiry he looked up with a sudden radiance.

"I could show it to Jessie," he said, thoughtful as ever of others.

"It's less than a hundred days to your birthday, Gibbles," I said, and laid my hand on the door-handle.

Gip made no answer, but his grip tightened on my finger, and so we came into the shop.

It was no common shop this; it was a magic shop, and all the prancing precedence Gip would have taken in the matter of mere toys was wanting. He left the burthen of the conversation to me.

It was a little, narrow shop, not very well lit, and the door-bell pinged again with a plaintive note as we closed it behind us. For a moment or so we were alone and could glance about us. There was a tiger in *papier-mâché* on the glass case that covered the low counter—a grave, kind-eyed tiger that waggled his head in a methodical manner; there were several crystal spheres, a china hand holding magic cards, a stock of magic fish-bowls in various sizes, and an immodest magic hat that shamelessly displayed its springs. On the floor were magic mirrors; one to draw you out long and thin, one to swell your head and vanish your legs, and one to make you short and fat like a draught; and while we were laughing at these the shopman, as I suppose, came in.

At any rate, there he was behind the counter—a curious, sallow, dark man, with one ear larger than the other and a chin like the toe-cap of a boot.

"What can we have the pleasure?" he said, spreading his long, magic fingers on the glass case; and so with a start we were aware of him.

"I want," I said, "to buy my little boy a few simple tricks."

"Legerdemain?" he asked. "Mechanical? Domestic?"

"Anything amusing," said I.

"Um!" said the shopman, and scratched his head for a moment as if thinking. Then, quite distinctly, he drew from his head a glass ball. "Something in this way?" he said, and held it out.

The action was unexpected. I had seen the trick done at entertainments endless times before—it's part of the common stock of conjurers—but I had not expected it here. "That's good," I said, with a laugh.

"Isn't it?" said the shopman.

Gip stretched out his disengaged hand to take this object and found merely a blank palm.

"It's in your pocket," said the shopman, and there it was!

"How much will that be?" I asked.

"We make no charge for glass balls," said the shopman politely. "We get them"—he picked one out of his elbow as he spoke—"free." He produced another from the back of his neck, and laid it beside its predecessor on the counter. Gip regarded his glass ball sagely, then directed a look of inquiry at the two on the counter, and finally brought his round-eyed scrutiny to the shopman, who smiled. "You may have those too," said the shopman, "and, if you *don't* mind, one from my mouth. *So!*"

Gip counselled me mutely for a moment, and then in a profound silence put away the four balls, resumed my reassuring finger, and nerved himself for the next event.

"We get all our smaller tricks in that way," the shopman remarked.

I laughed in the manner of one who subscribes to a jest. "Instead of going to the wholesale shop," I said. "Of course, it's cheaper."

"In a way," the shopman said. "Though we pay in the end. But not so heavily—as people suppose. . . . Our larger tricks, and our daily provisions and all the other things we want, we get out of that hat. . . . And you know, sir, if you'll excuse my saying it, there *isn't* a wholesale shop not for Genuine Magic goods, sir. I don't know if you noticed our inscription—the Genuine Magic shop." He drew a business-card from his cheek and handed it to me. "Genuine," he said, with his finger on the word, and added, "There is absolutely no deception, sir."

He seemed to be carrying out the joke pretty thoroughly, I thought.

He turned to Gip with a smile of remarkable affability. "You, you know, are the Right Sort of Boy."

I was surprised at his knowing that, because, in the interests of discipline, we keep it rather a secret even at home; but Gip received it in unflinching silence, keeping a steadfast eye on him.

"It's only the Right Sort of Boy gets through that doorway."

And, as if by way of illustration, there came a rattling at the door, and a squeaking little voice could be faintly heard. "Nyar! I *warn* 'a go in there, dadda, I WARN 'a go in there. Ny-a-a-ah!" and then the accents of a down-trodden parent, urging consolations and propitiations. "It's locked, Edward," he said.

"But it isn't," said I.

"It is, sir," said the shopman, "always—for that sort of child," and as he spoke we had a glimpse of the other youngster, a little, white face, pallid from sweet-eating and over-sapid food, and distorted by evil passions, a ruthless little egotist, pawing at the enchanted pane. "It's no good, sir," said the shopman, as I moved, with my natural helpfulness, doorward, and presently the spoilt child was carried off howling.

"How do you manage that?" I said, breathing a little more freely.

"Magic!" said the shopman, with a careless wave of the hand, and behold! sparks of coloured fire flew out of his fingers and vanished into the shadows of the shop.

"You were saying," he said, addressing himself to Gip, "before you came in, that you would like one of our 'Buy One and Astonish your Friends' boxes?"

Gip, after a gallant effort, said "Yes."

"It's in your pocket."

And leaning over the counter—he really had an extraordinarily long body—this amazing person produced the article in the customary conjurer's manner. "Paper," he said, and took a sheet out of the empty hat with the springs; "string," and behold his mouth was a string-box, from which he drew an unending thread, which when he had tied his parcel he bit off—and, it seemed to me, swallowed the ball of string. And then he lit a candle at the nose of one of the ventriloquist's dummies, stuck one of his fingers (which had become sealing-wax red), into the flame, and so sealed the parcel. "Then there was the Disappearing Egg," he remarked, and produced one from within my coat-breast and packed it, and also The Crying Baby, Very Human. I handed each parcel to Gip as it was ready, and he clasped them to his chest.

He said very little, but his eyes were eloquent; the clutch of his arms was eloquent. He was the playground of unspeakable emotions. These, you know, were *real* Magics.

Then, with a start, I discovered something moving about in my hat—something soft and jumpy. I whipped it off, and a ruffled pigeon—no doubt a confederate—dropped out and ran on the counter, and went, I fancy, into a cardboard box behind the *papier-mâché* tiger.

"Tut, tut!" said the shopman, dexterously relieving me of my headdress; "careless bird, and—as I live—nesting!"

He shook my hat, and shook out into his extended hand two or three eggs, a large marble, a watch, about half-a-dozen of the inevitable glass balls, and then crumpled, crinkled paper, more and more and more, talking all the time of the way in which people neglect to brush their hats *inside* as well as out, politely, of course, but with a certain personal application. "All sorts of things accumulate, sir. . . . Not *you*, of course, in particular. . . . Nearly every customer. . . . Astonishing what they carry about with them. . . ." The crumpled paper rose and billowed on the counter more and more and more, until he was nearly hidden from us, until he was altogether hidden, and still his voice went on and on. "We none of us know what the fair semblance of a human being may conceal, sir. Are we all then no better than brushed exteriors, whited sepulchres—"

His voice stopped—exactly like when you hit a neighbour's gramophone with a well-aimed brick, the same instant silence, and the rustle of the paper stopped, and everything was still. . . .

"Have you done with my hat?" I said, after an interval.

There was no answer.

I stared at Gip, and Gip stared at me, and there were our

distortions in the magic mirrors, looking very rum, and grave, and quiet. . . .

"I think we'll go now," I said. "Will you tell me how much all this comes to? . . .

"I say," I said, on a rather louder note, "I want the bill; and my hat, please."

It might have been a sniff from behind the paper pile. . . .

"Let's look behind the counter, Gip," I said. "He's making fun of us."

I led Gip round the head-wagging tiger, and what do you think there was behind the counter? No one at all! Only my hat on the floor, and a common conjurer's lop-eared white rabbit lost in meditation, and looking as stupid and crumpled as only a conjurer's rabbit can do. I resumed my hat, and the rabbit lolloped a lollop or so out of my way.

"Dadda!" said Gip, in a guilty whisper.

"What is it, Gip?" said I.

"I *do* like this shop, dadda."

"So should I," I said to myself, "if the counter wouldn't suddenly extend itself to shut one off from the door." But I didn't call Gip's attention to that. "Pussy!" he said, with a hand out to the rabbit as it came lolloping past us; "Pussy, do Gip a magic!" and his eyes followed it as it squeezed through a door I had certainly not remarked a moment before. Then this door opened wider, and the man with one ear larger than the other appeared again. He was smiling still, but his eye met mine with something between amusement and defiance. "You'd like to see our showroom, sir," he said, with an innocent sauvity. Gip tugged my finger forward. I glanced at the counter and met the shopman's eye again. I was beginning to think the magic just a little too genuine. "We haven't *very* much time," I said. But somehow we were inside the show-room before I could finish that.

"All goods of the same quality," said the shopman, rubbing his flexible hands together, "and that is the Best. Nothing in the place that isn't genuine Magic, and warranted thoroughly rum. Excuse me, sir!"

I felt him pull at something that clung to my coat-sleeve, and then I saw he held a little, wriggling red demon by the tail—the little creature bit and fought and tried to get at his hand—and in a moment he tossed it carelessly behind a counter. No doubt the thing was only an image of twisted indiarubber, but for the moment—! And his gesture was exactly that of a man who handles some petty biting bit of vermin. I glanced at Gip, but Gip was looking at a magic rocking-horse. I was glad he hadn't seen the thing. "I say," I said, in an undertone, and indicating Gip and the red demon with my eyes, "you haven't many things like *that* about, have you?"

"None of ours! Probably brought it with you," said the shopman—also in an undertone, and with a more dazzling smile than ever. "Astonishing what people *will* carry about with them unawares!" And then to Gip, "Do you see anything you fancy here?"

There were many things that Gip fancied there.

He turned to this astonishing tradesman with mingled confidence and respect. "Is that a Magic Sword?" he said.

"A Magic Toy Sword. It neither bends, breaks, nor cuts the fingers. It renders the bearer invincible in battle against any one under eighteen. Half-a-crown to seven and sixpence, according to size. These panoplies on cards are for juvenile knights-errant and very useful—shield of safety, sandals of swiftness, helmet of invisibility."

"Oh, daddy!" gasped Gip.

I tried to find out what they cost, but the shopman did not heed me. He had got Gip now; he had got him away from my finger; he had embarked upon the exposition of all his confounded stock, and nothing was going to stop him. Presently I saw with a qualm of distrust and something very like jealousy that Gip had hold of this person's finger as usually he has hold of mine. No doubt the fellow was interesting, I thought, and had an interestingly faked lot of stuff, really *good* faked stuff, still—

I wandered after them, saying very little, but keeping an eye on this prestidigital fellow. After all, Gip was enjoying it. And no doubt when the time came to go we should be able to go quite easily.

It was a long, rambling place, that show-room, a gallery broken up by stands and stalls and pillars, with archways leading off to other departments, in which the queerest-looking assistants loafed and stared at one, and with perplexing mirrors and curtains. So perplexing, indeed, were these that I was presently unable to make out the door by which we had come.

The shopman showed Gip magic trains that ran without steam or clockwork, just as you set the signals, and then some very, very valuable boxes of soldiers that all came alive directly you took off the lid and said—. I myself haven't a very quick ear and it was a tongue-twisting sound, but Gip—he has his mother's ear—got it in no time. "Bravo!" said the shopman, putting the men back into the box unceremoniously and handing it to Gip. "Now," said the shopman, and in a moment Gip had made them all alive again.

"You'll take that box?" asked the shopman.

"We'll take that box," said I, "unless you charge its full value. In which case it would need a Trust Magnate—"

"Dear heart! *No!*" and the shopman swept the little men back again, shut the lid, waved the box in the air, and there it was, in brown paper, tied up and—*with Gip's full name and address on the paper!*

The shopman laughed at my amazement.

"This is the genuine magic," he said. "The real thing."

"It's a little too genuine for my taste," I said again.

After that he fell to showing Gip tricks, odd tricks, and still odder the way they were done. He explained them, he turned them inside out, and there was the dear little chap nodding his busy bit of a head in the sagest manner.

I did not attend as well as I might. "Hey, presto!" said the Magic Shopman, and then would come the clear, small "Hey, presto!" of the boy. But I was distracted by other things. It was being borne in upon me just how tremendously rum this place was; it was, so to speak, inundated by a sense of rumness. There was something a little rum about the fixtures even, about the ceiling, about the floor, about the casually distributed chairs. I had a queer feeling that whenever I wasn't looking at them straight they went askew, and moved about, and played a noiseless puss-in-the-corner behind my back. And the cornice had a serpentine design with masks—masks altogether too expressive for proper plaster.

Then abruptly my attention was caught by one of the odd-looking assistants. He was some way off and evidently unaware of my presence—I saw a sort of three-quarter length of him over a pile of toys and through an arch—and, you know, he was leaning against a pillar in an idle sort of way doing the most horrid things with his features! The particular horrid thing he did was with his nose. He did it just as though he was idle and wanted to amuse himself. First of all it was a short, blobby nose, and then suddenly he shot it out like a telescope, and then out it flew and became thinner and thinner until it was like a long, red, flexible whip. Like a thing in a nightmare it was! He flourished it about and flung it forth as a fly-fisher flings his line.

My instant thought was that Gip mustn't see him. I turned about, and there was Gip quite preoccupied with the shopman, and thinking no evil. They were whispering together and looking at me. Gip was standing on a little stool, and the shopman was holding a sort of big drum in his hand.

"Hide and seek, dadda!" cried Gip. "You're He!"

And before I could do anything to prevent it, the shopman had clapped the big drum over him.

I saw what was up directly. "Take that off," I cried, "this instant! You'll frighten the boy. Take it off!"

The shopman with the unequal ears did so without a word, and held the big cylinder towards me to show its emptiness. And the little stool was vacant! In that instant my boy had utterly disappeared? . . .

You know, perhaps, that sinister something that comes like a hand out of the unseen and grips your heart about. You know it takes your common self away and leaves you tense and deliberate, neither slow nor hasty, neither angry nor afraid. So it was with me.

I came up to this grinning shopman and kicked his stool aside.

"Stop this folly!" I said. "Where is my boy?"

"You see," he said, still displaying the drum's interior, "there is no deception—"

I put out my hand to grip him, and he eluded me by a dexterous movement. I snatched again, and he turned from me and pushed open a door to escape. "Stop!" I said, and he laughed, receding. I leapt after him—into utter darkness.

Thud!

"Lor' bless my 'eart! I didn't see you coming, sir!"

I was in Regent Street, and I had collided with a decent-looking working man; and a yard away, perhaps, and looking a little perplexed with himself, was Gip. There was some sort of apology, and then Gip had turned and come to me with a bright little smile, as though for a moment he had missed me.

And he was carrying four parcels in his arm!

He secured immediate possession of my finger.

For the second I was rather at a loss. I stared round to see the door of the magic shop, and, behold, it was not there! There was no door, no shop, nothing, only the common pilaster between the shop where they sell pictures and the window with the chicks! . . .

I did the only thing possible in that mental tumult; I walked to the kerbstone and held up my umbrella for a cab.

" 'Ansoms," said Gip, in a note of culminating exultation.

I helped him in, recalled my address with an effort, and got in also. Something unusual proclaimed itself in my tail-coat pocket, and I felt and discovered a glass ball. With a petulant expression I flung it into the street.

Gip said nothing.

For a space neither of us spoke.

"Dadda!" said Gip, at last, "that *was* a proper shop!"

I came round with that to the problem of just how the whole thing had seemed to him. He looked completely undamaged—so far, good; he was neither scared nor unhinged, he was simply tremendously satisfied with the afternoon's entertainment, and there in his arms were the four parcels.

Confound it! what could be in them?

"Um!" I said. "Little boys can't go to shops like that every day."

He received this with his usual stoicism, and for a moment I was sorry I was his father and not his mother, and so couldn't suddenly there, *coram publico*, in our hansom, kiss him. After all, I thought, the thing wasn't so very bad.

But it was only when we opened the parcels that I really began to be reassured. Three of them contained boxes of soldiers, quite ordinary lead soldiers, but of so good a quality as to make Gip altogether forget that originally these parcels had been Magic Tricks of the only genuine sort, and the fourth contained a kitten, a little living white kitten, in excellent health and appetite and temper.

I saw this unpacking with a sort of provisional relief. I hung about in the nursery for quite an unconscionable time. . . .

That happened six months ago. And now I am beginning to believe it is all right. The kitten had only the magic natural to all kittens, and the soldiers seem as steady a company as any colonel could desire. And Gip—?

The intelligent parent will understand that I have to go cautiously with Gip. But I went so far as this one day. I said, "How would you like your soldiers to come alive, Gip, and march about by themselves?"

"Mine do," said Gip. "I just have to say a word I know before I open the lid."

"Then they march about alone?"

"Oh, *quite*, dadda. I shouldn't like them if they didn't do that."

I displayed no unbecoming surprise, and since then I have taken occasion to drop in upon him once or twice, unannounced, when the soldiers were about, but so far I have never discovered them performing in anything like a magical manner. . . .

It's so difficult to tell.

There's also a question of finance. I have an incurable habit of paying bills. I have been up and down Regent Street several times, looking for that shop. I am inclined to think, indeed, that in that matter honour is satisfied, and that, since Gip's name and address are known to them, I may very well leave it to these people, whoever they may be, to send in their bill in their own time.

The
Twentieth
Century

Saki
(1870–1916)

Saki—H. H. Munro—was born in Burma. In his brief life, he had several careers, as a military policeman in Burma (like George Orwell, later), as a newspaper correspondent in the Balkans, and as a short story writer. His first volume of satires, Reginald, *appeared in 1904; his* Complete Short Stories of Saki *was published posthumously, in 1930. He was killed on the Western front while serving in the British army.*

The Open Window

"My aunt will be down presently, Mr. Nuttel," said a very self-possessed young lady of fifteen; "in the meantime you must try to put up with me."

Framton Nuttel endeavoured to say the correct something which should duly flatter the niece of the moment without unduly discounting the aunt that was to come. Privately he doubted more than ever whether these formal visits on a succession of total strangers would do much toward helping the nerve cure which he was supposed to be undergoing.

"I know how it will be," his sister had said when he was preparing to migrate to this rural retreat; "you will bury yourself down there and not speak to a living soul, and your nerves will be worse than ever from moping. I shall just give you letters of introduction to all the people I know there. Some of them, as far as I can remember, were quite nice."

Framton wondered whether Mrs. Sappleton, the lady to whom he was presenting one of the letters of introduction, came into the nice division.

"Do you know many of the people round here?" asked the

niece, when she judged that they had had sufficient silent communion.

"Hardly a soul," said Framton. "My sister was staying here, at the rectory, you know, some four years ago, and she gave me letters of introduction to some of the people here."

He made the last statement in a tone of distinct regret.

"Then you know practically nothing about my aunt?" pursued the self-possessed young lady.

"Only her name and address," admitted the caller. He was wondering whether Mrs. Sappleton was in the married or widowed state. An indefinable something about the room seemed to suggest masculine habitation.

"Her great tragedy happened just three years ago," said the child; "that would be since your sister's time."

"Her tragedy?" asked Framton; somehow, in this restful country spot, tragedies seemed out of place.

"You may wonder why we keep that window wide open on an October afternoon," said the niece, indicating a large French window that opened on to a lawn.

"It is quite warm for the time of the year," said Framton; "but has that window got anything to do with the tragedy?"

"Out through that window, three years ago to a day, her husband and her two young brothers went off for their day's shooting. They never came back. In crossing the moor to their favourite snipe-shooting ground they were all three engulfed in a treacherous piece of bog. It had been that dreadful wet summer, you know, and places that were safe in other years gave way suddenly without warning. Their bodies were never recovered. That was the dreadful part of it." Here the child's voice lost its self-possessed note and became falteringly human. "Poor aunt always thinks that they will come back some day, they and the little brown spaniel that was lost with them, and walk in at that window just as they used to do. That is why the window is kept open every evening till it is quite dusk. Poor dear aunt, she has often told me how they went out, her husband with his white waterproof coat over his arm, and Ronnie, her youngest brother, singing 'Bertie, why do you bound?' as he always did to tease her, because she said it got on her nerves. Do you know, sometimes on still, quiet evenings like this, I almost get a creepy feeling that they will all walk in through that window—"

She broke off with a little shudder. It was a relief to Framton when the aunt bustled into the room with a whirl of apologies for being late in making her appearance.

"I hope Vera has been amusing you?" she said.

"She has been very interesting," said Framton.

"I hope you don't mind the open window," said Mrs. Sappleton briskly; "my husband and brothers will be home directly from shooting, and they always come in this way. They've been out for snipe in the marshes to-day, so they'll make a fine mess over my poor carpets. So like you menfolks, isn't it?"

She rattled on cheerfully about the shooting and the scarcity of birds and the prospects for duck in the winter. To Framton it was all purely horrible. He made a desperate but only partially successful effort to turn the talk on to a less ghastly topic; he was conscious that his hostess was giving him only a fragment of her attention, and her eyes were constantly straying past him to the open window and the lawn beyond. It was certainly an unfortunate coincidence that he should have paid his visit on this tragic anniversary.

"The doctors agree in ordering me complete rest, an absence of mental excitement, and avoidance of anything in the nature of violent physical exercise," announced Framton, who laboured under the tolerably wide-spread delusion that total strangers and chance acquaintances are hungry for the least detail of one's ailments and infirmities, their cause and cure. "On the matter of diet they are not so much in agreement," he continued.

"No?" said Mrs. Sappleton, in a voice which replaced a yawn only at the last moment. Then she suddenly brightened into alert attention—but not to what Framton was saying.

"Here they are at last!" she cried. "Just in time for tea, and don't they look as if they were muddy up to the eyes!"

Framton shivered slightly and turned toward the niece with a look intended to convey sympathetic comprehension. The child was staring out through the open window with dazed horror in her eyes. In a chill shock of nameless fear Framton swung round in his seat and looked in the same direction.

In the deepening twilight three figures were walking across the lawn toward the window; they all carried guns under their arms, and one of them was additionally burdened with a white coat hung over his shoulders. A tired brown spaniel kept close at their heels. Noiselessly they neared the house, and then a hoarse young voice chanted out of the dusk: "I said, Bertie, why do you bound?"

Framton grabbed wildly at his stick and hat; the hall-door, the gravel-drive, and the front gate were dimly-noted stages in his headlong retreat. A cyclist coming along the road had to run into the hedge to avoid imminent collision.

"Here we are, my dear," said the bearer of the white mackintosh, coming in through the window; "fairly muddy, but most of it's dry. Who was that who bolted out as we came up?"

"A most extraordinary man, a Mr. Nuttel," said Mrs. Sappleton; "could only talk about his illness, and dashed off without a word of good-bye or apology when you arrived. One would think he had seen a ghost."

"I expect it was the spaniel," said the niece calmly; "he told me he had a horror of dogs. He was once hunted into a cemetery somewhere on the banks of the Ganges by a pack of pariah dogs and had to spend the night in a newly dug grave with the creatures snarling and grinning and foaming just above him. Enough to make anyone lose their nerve."

Romance at short notice was her specialty.

W. Somerset Maugham
(1874–1965)

One of the most popular English authors of the twentieth century, W. Somerset Maugham was born in Paris. In his long life of ninety-one years, he turned out hundreds of short stories and dozens of novels, as well as several commercially successful plays and numerous essays. All of his fictional work is characterized by his stress on storytelling, on the well-made story, often with a surprise ending. He resisted the influence of Modernism, with its disregard for narrative and plot; Maugham relished the very act of narrative. After studying medicine as a young man, he turned to plays and wrote Lady Frederick *in 1907, preceded by the naturalistic novel* Liza of Lambeth *in 1897. His plays included* The Circle *(1921),* Our Betters *(1923), and his most popular,* The Constant Wife *(1927). His best-known novel and his masterpiece was* Of Human Bondage *(1915), whose content draws on Maugham's own background as a physician and a severe stammerer (an affliction which, for the novel, was transformed into a clubfoot). Other Maugham books that solidified his popular reputation are* The Moon and Sixpence *(1919),* Cakes and Ale *(1930), and* The Razor's Edge *(1944); his most famous stories include "The Letter" and "Miss Thompson." Several of his fictions were turned into successful motion pictures.*

Mr. Know-All

I was prepared to dislike Max Kelada even before I knew him. The war had just finished and the passenger traffic in the ocean-going liners was heavy. Accommodation was very hard to get and you had to put up with whatever the agents chose to offer you. You could not hope for a cabin to yourself and I was thankful to be given one in which there were only two berths. But when I was told the name of my companion my heart sank. It suggested closed port-holes and the night air rigidly excluded. It was bad enough to share a cabin for fourteen days with anyone (I was going from San Francisco to Yokohama), but I should have looked upon it with less dismay if my fellow-passenger's name had been Smith or Brown.

When I went on board I found Mr. Kelada's luggage already below. I did not like the look of it; there were too many labels on the suitcases, and the wardrobe trunk was too big. He had unpacked his toilet things, and I observed that he was a patron of the excellent Monsiéur Coty; for I saw on the washing-stand his scent, his hair-wash and his brilliantine. Mr. Kelada's brushes, ebony with his monogram in gold, would have been all the better for a scrub. I did not at all like Mr. Kelada. I made my way into the smoking-room. I called for a pack of cards and began to play patience. I had scarcely started before a man came up to me and asked me if he was right in thinking my name was so-and-so.

"I am Mr. Kelada," he added, with a smile that showed a row of flashing teeth, and sat down.

"Oh, yes, we're sharing a cabin, I think."

"Bit of luck, I call it. You never know who you're going to be put in with. I was jolly glad when I heard you were English. I'm all for us English sticking together when we're abroad, if you understand what I mean."

I blinked.

"Are you English?" I asked, perhaps tactlessly.

"Rather. You don't think I look like an American, do you? British to the backbone, that's what I am."

To prove it, Mr. Kelada took out of his pocket a passport and airily waved it under my nose.

King George has many strange subjects. Mr. Kelada was short and of a sturdy build, clean-shaven and dark-skinned, with a fleshy, hooked nose and very large, lustrous and liquid eyes. His long black hair was sleek and curly. He spoke with a fluency in which there was nothing English and his gestures were exuberant. I felt pretty sure that a closer inspection of that British passport would have betrayed the fact that Mr. Kelada was born under a bluer sky than is generally seen in England.

"What will you have?" he asked me.

I looked at him doubtfully. Prohibition was in force and to all appearances the ship was bone-dry. When I am not thirsty

I do not know which I dislike more, ginger-ale or lemon-squash. But Mr. Kelada flashed an oriental smile at me.

"Whisky and soda or a dry Martini, you have only to say the word."

From each of his hip-pockets he fished a flask and laid them on the table before me. I chose the Martini, and calling the steward he ordered a tumbler of ice and a couple of glasses.

"A very good cocktail," I said.

"Well, there are plenty more where that came from, and if you've got any friends on board, you tell them you've got a pal who's got all the liquor in the world."

Mr. Kelada was chatty. He talked of New York and of San Francisco. He discussed plays, pictures, and politics. He was patriotic. The Union Jack is an impressive piece of drapery, but when it is flourished by a gentleman from Alexandria or Beirut, I cannot but feel that it loses somewhat in dignity. Mr. Kelada was familiar. I do not wish to put on airs, but I cannot help feeling that it is seemly in a total stranger to put mister before my name when he addresses me. Mr. Kelada, doubtless to set me at my ease, used no such formality. I did not like Mr. Kelada. I had put aside the cards when he sat down, but now, thinking that for this first occasion our conversation had lasted long enough, I went on with my game.

"The three on the four," said Mr. Kelada.

There is nothing more exasperating when you are playing patience than to be told where to put the card you have turned up before you have had a chance to look for yourself.

"It's coming out, it's coming out," he cried. "Then ten on the knave."

With rage and hatred in my heart I finished. Then he seized the pack.

"Do you like card tricks?"

"No, I hate card tricks," I answered.

"Well, I'll just show you this one."

He showed me three. Then I said I would go down to the dining-room and get my seat at table.

"Oh, that's all right," he said. "I've already taken a seat for you. I thought that as we were in the same state-room we might just as well sit at the same table."

I did not like Mr. Kelada.

I not only shared a cabin with him and ate three meals a day at the same table, but I could not walk round the deck without his joining me. It was impossible to snub him. It never occurred to him that he was not wanted. He was certain that

you were as glad to see him as he was to see you. In your
own house you might have kicked him downstairs and slammed
the door in his face without the suspicion dawning on him
that he was not a welcome visitor. He was a good mixer, and
in three days knew everyone on board. He ran everything.
He managed the sweeps, conducted the auctions, collected
money for prizes at the sports, got up quoit and golf matches,
organised the concert and arranged the fancy dress ball. He
was everywhere and always. He was certainly the best-hated
man in the ship. We called him Mr. Know-All, even to his
face. He took it as a compliment. But it was at meal times
that he was most intolerable. For the better part of an hour
then he had us at his mercy. He was hearty, jovial, loquacious
and argumentative. He knew everything better than anybody
else, and it was an affront to his overweening vanity that you
should disagree with him. He would not drop a subject, however unimportant, till he had brought you round to his way
of thinking. The possibility that he could be mistaken never
occurred to him. He was the chap who knew. We sat at the
doctor's table. Mr. Kelada would certainly have had it all his
own way, for the doctor was lazy and I was frigidly indifferent,
except for a man called Ramsay who sat there also. He was
as dogmatic as Mr. Kelada and resented bitterly the Levantine's cocksureness. The discussions they had were acrimon-
ious and interminable.

Ramsay was in the American Consular Service, and was
stationed at Kobe. He was a great heavy fellow from the
Middle West, with loose fat under a tight skin, and he bulged
out of his ready-made clothes. He was on his way back to
resume his post, having been on a flying visit to New York
to fetch his wife, who had been spending a year at home.
Mrs. Ramsay was a very pretty little thing, with pleasant
manners and a sense of humour. The Consular Service is ill
paid, and she was dressed always very simply; but she knew
how to wear her clothes. She achieved an effect of quiet
distinction. I should not have paid any particular attention to
her but that she possessed a quality that may be common
enough in women, but nowadays is not obvious in their demeanour. You could not look at her without being struck by
her modesty. It shone in her like a flower on a coat.

One evening at dinner the conversation by chance drifted
to the subject of pearls. There had been in the papers a good
deal of talk about the culture pearls which the cunning Japanese were making, and the doctor remarked that they must

inevitably diminish the value of real ones. They were very good already; they would soon be perfect. Mr. Kelada, as was his habit, rushed the new topic. He told us all that was to be known about pearls. I do not believe Ramsay knew anything about them at all, but he could not resist the opportunity to have a fling at the Levantine, and in five minutes we were in the middle of a heated argument. I had seen Mr. Kelada vehement and voluble before, but never so voluble and vehement as now. At last something that Ramsay said stung him, for he thumped the table and shouted:

"Well, I ought to know what I am talking about. I'm going to Japan just to look into this Japanese pearl business. I'm in the trade and there's not a man in it who won't tell you that what I say about pearls goes. I know all the best pearls in the world and what I don't know about pearls isn't worth knowing."

Here was news for us, for Mr. Kelada, with all his loquacity, had never told anyone what his business was. We only knew vaguely that he was going to Japan on some commercial errand. He looked round the table triumphantly.

"They'll never be able to get a culture pearl that an expert like me can't tell with half an eye." He pointed to a chain that Mrs. Ramsay wore. "You take my word for it, Mrs. Ramsay, that chain you're wearing will never be worth a cent less than it is now."

Mrs. Ramsay in her modest way flushed a little and slipped the chain inside her dress. Ramsay leaned forward. He gave us all a look and a smile flickered in his eyes.

"That's a pretty chain of Mrs. Ramsay's, isn't it?"

"I noticed it at once," answered Mr. Kelada. "Gee, I said to myself, those are pearls all right."

"I didn't buy it myself, of course. I'd be interested to know how much you think it cost."

"Oh, in the trade somewhere round fifteen thousand dollars. But if it was bought on Fifth Avenue I shouldn't be surprised to hear that anything up to thirty thousand was paid for it."

Ramsay smiled grimly.

"You'll be surprised to hear that Mrs. Ramsay bought that string at a department store the day before we left New York, for eighteen dollars."

Mr. Kelada flushed.

"Rot. It's not only real, but it's as fine a string for its size as I've ever seen."

"Will you bet on it? I'll bet you a hundred dollars it's imitation."

"Done."

"Oh, Elmer, you can't bet on a certainty," said Mrs. Ramsay.

She had a little smile on her lips and her tone was gently deprecating.

"Can't I? If I get a chance of easy money like that I should be all sorts of a fool not to take it."

"But how can it be proved?" she continued. "It's only my word against Mr. Kelada's."

"Let me look at the chain, and if it's imitation, I'll tell you quickly enough. I can afford to lose a hundred dollars," said Mr. Kelada.

"Take it off, dear. Let the gentleman look at it as much as he wants."

Mrs. Ramsay hesitated a moment. She put her hands to the clasp.

"I can't undo it," she said. "Mr. Kelada will just have to take my word for it."

I had a sudden suspicion that something unfortunate was about to occur, but I could think of nothing to say.

Ramsay jumped up.

"I'll undo it."

He handed the chain to Mr. Kelada. The Levantine took a magnifying glass from his pocket and closely examined it. A smile of triumph spread over his smooth and swarthy face. He handed back the chain. He was about to speak. Suddenly he caught sight of Mrs. Ramsay's face. It was so white that she looked as though she were about to faint. She was staring at him with wide and terrified eyes. They held a desperate appeal; it was so clear that I wondered why her husband did not see it.

Mr. Kelada stopped with his mouth open. He flushed deeply. You could almost *see* the effort he was making over himself.

"I was mistaken," he said. "It's a very good imitation, but of course as soon as I looked through my glass I saw that it wasn't real. I think eighteen dollars is just about as much as the damned thing's worth."

He took out his pocket-book and from it a hundred-dollar note. He handed it to Ramsay without a word.

"Perhaps that'll teach you not to be so cocksure another time, my young friend," said Ramsay as he took the note.

I noticed that Mr. Kelada's hands were trembling.

The story spread over the ship as stories do, and he had to put up with a good deal of chaff that evening. It was a fine joke that Mr. Know-All had been caught out. But Mrs. Ramsay retired to her state-room with a headache.

Next morning I got up and began to shave. Mr. Kelada lay on his bed smoking a cigarette. Suddenly there was a small scraping sound and I saw a letter pushed under the door. I opened the door and looked out. There was nobody there. I picked up the letter and saw that it was addressed to Max Kelada. The name was written in block letters. I handed it to him.

"Who's this from?" He opened it. "Oh!"

He took out of the envelope, not a letter, but a hundred-dollar note. He looked at me and again he reddened. He tore the envelope into little bits and gave them to me.

"Do you mind just throwing them out of the port-hole?"

I did as he asked, and then I looked at him with a smile.

"No one likes being made to look a perfect damned fool," he said.

"Were the pearls real?"

"If I had a pretty little wife I shouldn't let her spend a year in New York while I stayed at Kobe," said he.

At that moment I did not entirely dislike Mr. Kelada. He reached out for his pocket-book and carefully put in it the hundred-dollar note.

E.M. Forster
(1879–1970)

Edward Morgan Forster was born at the height of the Victorian era, and lived to an age when most of his important writing was forty years behind him. A graduate of Cambridge University, Forster wrote four novels in quick succession: Where Angels Fear to Tread *(1905),* The Longest Journey *(1907),* A Room with a View *(1908), and* Howards End *(1910). What is generally considered to be his finest novel—although some readers prefer* Howards End—*came fourteen years later,* A Passage to India, *in 1924. Forster also wrote short stories, collecting them in* The Celestial Omnibus *(1911) and* The Eternal Moment *(1928). His occasional essays established him as a critic of importance, especially in books such as* Aspects of the Novel *(1927),* Abinger Harvest *(1936), and* Two Cheers for Democracy *(1951).* Maurice, *a novel about a young man's awakening to his homosexuality, was published posthumously, in 1971. Always a gentle and civilized voice, Forster showed a toughness in defending what he considered to be esssential human values: the need to connect with other human beings; the difficulty people have in understanding each other, especially when they derive from different cultural backgrounds; and the comic sense that is an indispensable civilizing factor in human relationships. As a marginal member of the Bloomsbury Group, Forster has been identified with Virginia and Leonard Woolf, John Maynard Keynes, Lytton Strachey, and others; but he remained his own man to the end, a twentieth-century writer who insisted on certain nineteenth-century amenities.*

The Story of a Panic

Eustace's career—if career it can be called—certainly dates from that afternoon in the chestnut woods above Ravello. I confess at once that I am a plain, simple man, with no pretensions to literary style. Still, I do flatter myself that I can tell a story without exaggerating, and I have therefore decided to give an unbiassed account of the extraordinary events of eight years ago.

Ravello is a delightful place with a delightful little hotel in which we met some charming people. There were the two Miss Robinsons, who had been there for six weeks with Eustace, their nephew, then a boy of about fourteen. Mr. Sandbach had also been there some time. He had held a curacy in the north of England, which he had been compelled to resign on account of ill-health, and while he was recuperating at Ravello he had taken in hand Eustace's education—which was then sadly deficient—and was endeavouring to fit him for one of our great public schools. Then there was Mr. Leyland, a would-be artist, and, finally, there was the nice landlady, Signora Scafetti, and the nice English-speaking waiter, Emmanuele—though at the time of which I am speaking Emmanuele was away, visiting a sick father.

To this little circle, I, my wife, and my two daughters made, I venture to think, a not unwelcome addition. But though I liked most of the company well enough, there were two of them to whom I did not take at all. They were the artist, Leyland, and the Miss Robinsons' nephew, Eustace.

Leyland was simply conceited and odious, and, as those qualities will be amply illustrated in my narrative, I need not enlarge upon them here. But Eustace was something besides: he was indescribably repellent.

I am fond of boys as a rule, and was quite disposed to be friendly. I and my daughters offered to take him out—"No, walking was such a fag." Then I asked him to come and bathe—"No, he could not swim."

"Every English boy should be able to swim," I said, "I will teach you myself."

"There, Eustace dear," said Miss Robinson; "here is a chance for you."

But he said he was afraid of the water!—a boy afraid!—and of course I said no more.

I would not have minded so much if he had been a really studious boy, but he neither played hard nor worked hard. His favourite occupations were lounging on the terrace in an easy chair and loafing along the high road, with his feet shuffling up the dust and his shoulders stooping forward. Naturally enough, his features were pale, his chest contracted, and his muscles undeveloped. His aunts thought him delicate; what he really needed was discipline.

That memorable day we all arranged to go for a picnic up in the chestnut woods—all, that is, except Janet, who stopped behind to finish her water-colour of the Cathedral—not a very successful attempt, I am afraid.

I wander off into these irrelevant details, because in my mind I cannot separate them from an account of the day; and it is the same with the conversation during the picnic: all is imprinted on my brain together. After a couple of hours' ascent, we left the donkeys that had carried the Miss Robinsons and my wife, and all proceeded on foot to the head of the valley—Vallone Fontana Caroso is its proper name, I find.

I have visited a good deal of fine scenery before and since, but have found little that has pleased me more. The valley ended in a vast hollow, shaped like a cup, into which radiated ravines from the precipitous hills around. Both the valley and the ravines and the ribs of hill that divided the ravines were covered with leafy chestnut, so that the general appearance was that of a many-fingered green hand, palm upwards, which was clutching convulsively to keep us in its grasp. Far down the valley we could see Ravello and the sea, but that was the only sign of another world.

"Oh, what a perfectly lovely place," said my daughter Rose. "What a picture it would make!"

"Yes," said Mr. Sandbach. "Many a famous European gallery would be proud to have a landscape a tithe as beautiful as this upon its walls."

"On the contrary," said Leyland, "it would make a very poor picture. Indeed, it is not paintable at all."

"And why is that?" said Rose, with far more deference than he deserved.

"Look, in the first place," he replied, "how intolerably straight against the sky is the line of the hill. It would need breaking up and diversifying. And where we are standing the whole thing is out of perspective. Besides, all the colouring is monotonous and crude."

"I do not know anything about pictures," I put in, "and I do not pretend to know: but I know what is beautiful when I see it, and I am thoroughly content with this."

"Indeed, who could help being contented!" said the elder Miss Robinson; and Mr. Sandbach said the same.

"Ah!" said Leyland, "you all confuse the artistic view of Nature with the photographic."

Poor Rose had brought her camera with her, so I thought this positively rude. I did not wish any unpleasantness; so I merely turned away and assisted my wife and Miss Mary Robinson to put out the lunch—not a very nice lunch.

"Eustace, dear," said his aunt, "come and help us here."

He was in a particularly bad temper that morning. He had, as usual, not wanted to come, and his aunts had nearly allowed him to stop at the hotel to vex Janet. But I, with their permission, spoke to him rather sharply on the subject of exercise; and the result was that he had come, but was even more taciturn and moody than usual.

Obedience was not his strong point. He invariably questioned every command, and only executed it grumbling. I should always insist on prompt and cheerful obedience, if I had a son.

"I'm—coming—Aunt—Mary," he at last replied, and dawdled to cut a piece of wood to make a whistle, taking care not to arrive till we had finished.

"Well, well, sir!" said I, "you stroll in at the end and profit by our labours." He sighed, for he could not endure being chaffed. Miss Mary, very unwisely, insisted on giving him the wing of the chicken, in spite of all my attempts to prevent her. I remember that I had a moment's vexation when I thought that, instead of enjoying the sun, and the air, and the woods, we were all engaged in wrangling over the diet of a spoilt boy.

But, after lunch, he was a little less in evidence. He withdrew to a tree trunk, and began to loosen the bark from his whistle. I was thankful to see him employed, for once in a way. We reclined, and took a *dolce far niente*.

Those sweet chestnuts of the South are puny striplings compared with our robust Northerners. But they clothed the contours of the hills and valleys in a most pleasing way, their veil being only broken by two clearings, in one of which we were sitting.

And because these few trees were cut down, Leyland burst into a petty indictment of the proprietor.

"All the poetry is going from Nature," he cried, "her lakes and marshes are drained, her seas banked up, her forests cut down. Everywhere we see the vulgarity of desolation spreading."

I have had some experience of estates, and answered that

cutting was very necessary for the health of the larger trees. Besides, it was unreasonable to expect the proprietor to derive no income from his lands.

"If you take the commercial side of landscape, you may feel pleasure in the owner's activity. But to me the mere thought that a tree is convertible into cash is disgusting."

"I see no reason," I observed politely, "to despise the gifts of Nature because they are of value."

It did not stop him. "It is no matter," he went on, "we are all hopelessly steeped in vulgarity. I do not except myself. It is through us, and to our shame, that the Nereids have left the waters and the Oreads the mountains, that the woods no longer give shelter to Pan."

"Pan!" cried Mr. Sandbach, his mellow voice filling the valley as if it had been a great green church, "Pan is dead. That is why the woods do not shelter him." And he began to tell the striking story of the mariners who were sailing near the coast at the time of the birth of Christ, and three times heard a loud voice saying: "The great God Pan is dead."

"Yes. The great God Pan is dead," said Leyland. And he abandoned himself to that mock misery in which artistic people are so fond of indulging. His cigar went out, and he had to ask me for a match.

"How very interesting," said Rose. "I do wish I knew some ancient history."

"It is not worth your notice," said Mr. Sandbach. "Eh, Eustace?"

Eustace was finishing his whistle. He looked up, with the irritable frown in which his aunts allowed him to indulge, and made no reply.

The conversation turned to various topics and then died out. It was a cloudless afternoon in May, and the pale green of the young chestnut leaves made a pretty contrast with the dark blue of the sky. We were all sitting at the edge of the small clearing for the sake of the view, and the shade of the chestnut saplings behind us was manifestly insufficient. All sounds died away—at least that is my account: Miss Robinson says that the clamour of the birds was the first sign of uneasiness that she discerned. All sounds died away, except that, far in the distance, I could hear two boughs of a great chestnut grinding together as the tree swayed. The grinds grew shorter and shorter, and finally that sound stopped also. As I looked over the green fingers of the valley, everything was absolutely motionless and still; and that feeling of suspense which one so often experiences when Nature is in repose, began to steal over me.

Suddenly, we were all electrified by the excruciating noise of Eustace's whistle. I never heard any instrument give forth so ear-splitting and discordant a sound.

"Eustace, dear," said Miss Mary Robinson, "you might have thought of poor Aunt Julia's head."

Leyland who had apparently been asleep, sat up.

"It is astonishing how blind a boy is to anything that is elevating or beautiful," he observed. "I should not have thought he could have found the wherewithal out here to spoil our pleasure like this."

Then the terrible silence fell upon us again. I was now standing up and watching a catspaw of wind that was running down one of the ridges opposite, turning the light green to dark as it travelled. A fanciful feeling of foreboding came over me; so I turned away, to find to my amazement, that all the others were also on their feet, watching it too.

It is not possible to describe coherently what happened next: but I, for one, am not ashamed to confess that, though the fair blue sky was above me and the green spring woods beneath me, and the kindest of friends around me, yet I became terribly frightened, more frightened than I ever wish to become again, frightened in a way I never have known either before or after. And in the eyes of the others, too, I saw blank, expressionless fear, while their mouths strove in vain to speak and their hands to gesticulate. Yet, all around us were prosperity, beauty, and peace, and all was motionless, save the catspaw of wind, now travelling up the ridge on which we stood.

Who moved first has never been settled. It is enough to say that in one second we were tearing away along the hillside. Leyland was in front, then Mr. Sandbach, then my wife. But I only saw for a brief moment; for I ran across the little clearing and through the woods and over the undergrowth and the rocks and down the dry torrent beds into the valley below. The sky might have been black as I ran, and the trees short grass, and the hillside a level road; for I saw nothing and heard nothing and felt nothing, since all the channels of sense and reason were blocked. It was not the spiritual fear that one has known at other times, but brutal overmastering physical fear, stopping up the ears, and dropping clouds before the eyes, and filling the mouth with foul tastes. And it was no ordinary humiliation that survived; for I had been afraid, not as a man, but as a beast.

II

I cannot describe our finish any better than our start; for our fear passed away as it had come, without cause. Suddenly I was able to see, and hear, and cough, and clear my mouth. Looking back, I saw that the others were stopping too; and, in a short time, we were all together, though it was long before we could speak, and longer before we dared to.

No one was seriously injured. My poor wife had sprained her ankle, Leyland had torn one of his nails on a tree trunk, and I myself had scraped and damaged my ear. I never noticed it till I had stopped.

We were all silent, searching one another's faces. Suddenly Miss Mary Robinson gave a terrible shriek. "Oh, merciful heavens! where is Eustace?" And then she would have fallen, if Mr. Sandbach had not caught her.

"We must go back, we must go back at once," said my Rose, who was quite the most collected of the party. "But I hope—I feel he is safe."

Such was the cowardice of Leyland, that he objected. But, finding himself in a minority, and being afraid of being left alone, he gave in. Rose and I supported my poor wife, Mr. Sandbach and Miss Robinson helped Miss Mary, and we returned slowly and silently, taking forty minutes to ascend the path that we had descended in ten.

Our conversation was naturally disjointed, as no one wished to offer an opinion on what had happened. Rose was the most talkative: she startled us all by saying that she had very nearly stopped where she was.

"Do you mean to say that you weren't—that you didn't feel compelled to go?" said Mr. Sandbach.

"Oh, of course, I did feel frightened"—she was the first to use the word—"but I somehow felt that if I could stop on it would be quite different, that I shouldn't be frightened at all, so to speak." Rose never did express herself clearly: still, it is greatly to her credit that she, the youngest of us, should have held on so long at that terrible time.

"I should have stopped, I do believe," she continued, "if I had not seen mamma go."

Rose's experience comforted us a little about Eustace. But a feeling of terrible foreboding was on us all, as we painfully climbed the chestnut-covered slopes and neared the little clearing. When we reached it our tongues broke loose. There, at the further side, were the remains of our lunch, and close to them, lying motionless on his back, was Eustace.

With some presence of mind I at once cried out: "Hey, you young monkey! jump up!" But he made no reply, nor did he answer when his poor aunts spoke to him. And, to my unspeakable horror, I saw one of those green lizards dart out from under his shirt-cuff as we approached.

We stood watching him as he lay there so silently, and my ears began to tingle in expectation of the outbursts of lamentations and tears.

Miss Mary fell on her knees beside him and touched his hand, which was convulsively entwined in the long grass.

As she did so, he opened his eyes and smiled.

I have often seen that peculiar smile since, both on the possessor's face and on the photographs of him that are beginning to get into the illustrated papers. But, till then, Eustace had always worn a peevish, discontented frown; and we were all unused to this disquieting smile, which always seemed to be without adequate reason.

His aunts showered kisses on him, which he did not reciprocate, and then there was an awkward pause. Eustace seemed so natural and undisturbed; yet, if he had not had astonishing experiences himself, he ought to have been all the more astonished at our extraordinary behaviour. My wife, with ready tact, endeavoured to behave as if nothing had happened.

"Well, Mr. Eustace," she said, sitting down as she spoke, to ease her foot, "how have you been amusing yourself since we have been away?"

"Thank you, Mrs. Tytler, I have been very happy."

"And where have you been?"

"Here."

"And lying down all the time, you idle boy?"

"No, not all the time."

"What were you doing before?"

"Oh; standing or sitting."

"Stood and sat doing nothing! Don't you know the poem 'Satan finds some mischief still for—'"

"Oh, my dear madam, hush! hush!" Mr. Sandbach's voice broke in; and my wife, naturally mortified by the interruption, said no more and moved away. I was surprised to see Rose immediately take her place, and, with more freedom than she generally displayed, run her fingers through the boy's tousled hair.

"Eustace! Eustace!" she said, hurriedly, "tell me everything—every single thing."

Slowly he sat up—till then he had lain on his back.

"Oh Rose—," he whispered, and, my curiosity being aroused, I moved nearer to hear what he was going to say. As I did so, I caught sight of some goats' footmarks in the moist earth beneath the trees.

"Apparently you have had a visit from some goats," I observed. "I had no idea they fed up here."

Eustace laboriously got on to his feet and came to see; and when he saw the footmarks he lay down and rolled on them, as a dog rolls in dirt.

After that there was a grave silence, broken at length by the solemn speech of Mr. Sandbach.

"My dear friends," he said, "it is best to confess the truth bravely. I know that what I am going to say now is what you are all now feeling. The Evil One has been very near us in bodily form. Time may yet discover some injury that he has wrought among us. But, at present, for myself at all events, I wish to offer up thanks for a merciful deliverance."

With that he knelt down, and, as the others knelt, I knelt too, though I do not believe in the Devil being allowed to assail us in visible form, as I told Mr. Sandbach afterwards. Eustace came too, and knelt quietly enough between his aunts after they had beckoned to him. But when it was over he at once got up, and began hunting for something.

"Why! Someone has cut my whistle in two," he said. (I had seen Leyland with an open knife in his hand—a superstitious act which I could hardly approve.)

"Well, it doesn't matter," he continued.

"And why doesn't it matter?" said Mr. Sandbach, who has ever since tried to entrap Eustace into an account of that mysterious hour.

"Because I don't want it any more."

"Why?"

At that he smiled; and, as no one seemed to have anything more to say, I set off as fast as I could through the wood, and hauled up a donkey to carry my poor wife home. Nothing occurred in my absence, except that Rose had again asked Eustace to tell her what had happened; and he, this time, had turned away his head, and had not answered her a single word.

As soon as I returned, we all set off. Eustace walked with difficulty, almost with pain, so that, when we reached the other donkeys, his aunts wished him to mount one of them and ride all the way home. I make it a rule never to interfere between relatives, but I put my foot down at this. As it turned out, I was perfectly right, for the healthy exercise, I suppose, began to thaw Eustace's sluggish blood and loosen his stiffened muscles. He stepped out manfully, for the first time in his life, holding his head up and taking deep draughts of air into his chest. I observed with satisfaction to Miss Mary Robinson, that Eustace was at last taking some pride in his personal appearance.

Mr. Sandbach sighed, and said that Eustace must be carefully watched, for we none of us understood him yet. Miss Mary Robinson being very much—over much, I think—guided by him, sighed too.

"Come, come, Miss Robinson," I said, "there's nothing wrong with Eustace. Our experiences are mysterious, not his. He was astonished at our sudden departure, that's why he was so strange when we returned. He's right enough—improved, if anything."

"And is the worship of athletics, the cult of insensate activity, to be counted as an improvement?" put in Leyland, fixing a large, sorrowful eye on Eustace, who had stopped to scramble on to a rock to pick some cyclamen. "The passionate desire to rend from Nature the few beauties that have been still left her—that is to be counted as an improvement too?"

It is mere waste of time to reply to such remarks, especially when they come from any unsuccessful artist, suffering from a damaged finger. I changed the conversation by asking what we should say at the hotel. After some discussion, it was agreed that we should say nothing, either there or in our letters home. Importunate truth-telling, which brings only bewilderment and discomfort to the hearers, is, in my opinion, a mistake; and, after a long discussion, I managed to make Mr. Sandbach acquiesce in my view.

Eustace did not share in our conversation. He was racing about, like a real boy, in the wood to the right. A strange feeling of shame prevented us from openly mentioning our fright to him. Indeed, it seemed almost reasonable to conclude that it had made but little impression on him. So it disconcerted us when he bounded back with an armful of flowering acanthus, calling out:

"Do you suppose Gennaro'll be there when we get back?"

Gennaro was the stop-gap waiter, a clumsy, impertinent fisher-lad, who had been had up from Minori in the absence of the nice English-speaking Emmanuele. It was to him that we owed our scrappy lunch; and I could not conceive why Eustace desired to see him, unless it was to make mock with him of our behaviour.

"Yes, of course he will be there," said Miss Robinson. "Why do you ask, dear?"

"Oh, I thought I'd like to see him."

"And why?" snapped Mr. Sandbach.

"Because, because I do, I do; because, because I do." He danced away into the darkening wood to the rhythm of his words.

"This is very extraordinary," said Mr. Sandbach. "Did he like Gennaro before?"

"Gennaro has only been here two days," said Rose, "and I know that they haven't spoken to each other a dozen times."

Each time Eustace returned from the wood his spirits were higher. Once he came whooping down on us as a wild Indian, and another time he made believe to be a dog. The last time he came back with a poor dazed hare, too frightened to move, sitting on his arm. He was getting too uproarious, I thought; and we were all glad to leave the wood, and start upon the steep staircase path that leads down into Ravello. It was late and turning dark; and we made all the speed we could, Eustace scurrying in front of us like a goat.

Just where the staircase path debouches on the white high road, the next extraordinary incident of this extraordinary day occurred. Three old women were standing by the wayside. They, like ourselves, had come down from the woods, and they were resting their heavy bundles of fuel on the low parapet of the road. Eustace stopped in front of them, and, after a moment's deliberation, stepped forward and—kissed the left-hand one on the cheek!

"My good fellow!" exclaimed Mr. Sandbach, "are you quite crazy?"

Eustace said nothing, but offered the old woman some of his flowers, and then hurried on. I looked back; and the old woman's companions seemed as much astonished at the proceeding as we were. But she herself had put the flowers in her bosom, and was murmuring blessings.

This salutation of the old lady was the first example of Eustace's strange behaviour, and we were both surprised and alarmed. It was useless talking to him, for he either made silly replies, or else bounded away without replying at all.

He made no reference on the way home to Gennaro, and I hoped that that was forgotten. But, when we came to the Piazza, in front of the Cathedral, he screamed out: "Gennaro! Gennaro!" at the top of his voice, and began running up the little alley that led to the hotel. Sure enough, there was Gennaro at the end of it, with his arms and legs sticking out of the nice little English-speaking waiter's dress suit, and a dirty fisherman's cap on his head—for, as the poor landlady truly said, however much she superintended his toilette, he always managed to introduce something incongruous into it before he had done.

Eustace sprang to meet him, and leapt right up into his arms, and put his own arms round his neck. And this in the presence, not only of us, but also of the landlady, the chambermaid, the facchino, and of two American ladies who were coming for a few days' visit to the little hotel.

I always make a point of behaving pleasantly to Italians, however little they may deserve it; but this habit of promiscuous intimacy was perfectly intolerable, and could only lead to familiarity and mortification for all. Taking Miss Robinson aside, I asked her permission to speak seriously to Eustace on the subject of intercourse with social inferiors. She granted it; but I determined to wait till the absurd boy had calmed down a little from the excitement of the day. Meanwhile, Gennaro, instead of attending to the wants of the two new ladies, carried Eustace into the house, as if it was the most natural thing in the world.

"Ho capito," I heard him say as he passed me. "Ho capito" is the Italian for "I have understood"; but, as Eustace had not spoken to him, I could not see the force of the remark. It served to increase our bewilderment, and, by the time we sat down at the dinner-table, our imaginations and our tongues were alike exhausted.

I omit from this account the various comments that were made, as few of them seem worthy of being recorded. But, for three or four hours, seven of us were pouring forth our bewilderment in a stream of appropriate and inappropriate exclamations. Some traced a connection between our behaviour in the afternoon and the behaviour of Eustace now. Others saw no connection at all. Mr. Sandbach still held to the possibility of infernal influences, and also said that he ought to have a doctor. Leyland only saw the development of "that unspeakable Philistine, the boy." Rose maintained, to my surprise, that everything was excusable; while I began to see that the young gentleman wanted a sound thrashing. The poor Miss Robinsons swayed helplessly about between these diverse opinions; inclining now to careful supervision, now to acquiescence, now to corporal chastisement, now to Eno's Fruit Salt.

Dinner passed off fairly well, though Eustace was terribly fidgety, Gennaro as usual dropping the knives and spoons, and hawking and clearing his throat. He only knew a few words of English, and we were all reduced to Italian for making known our wants. Eustace, who had picked up a little somehow, asked for some oranges. To my annoyance, Gennaro, in his answer made use of the second person singular—a form only used when addressing those who are both intimates and equals. Eustace had brought it on himself; but an impertinence of this kind was an affront to us all, and I was determined to speak, and to speak at once.

When I heard him clearing the table I went in, and, summoning up my Italian, or rather Neapolitan—the Southern dialects are execrable—I said, "Gennaro! I heard you address Signor Eustace with 'Tu.' "

"It is true."

"You are not right. You must use 'Lei' or 'Voi'—more polite forms. And remember that, though Signor Eustace is sometimes silly and foolish—this afternoon for example—yet you must always behave respectfully to him; for he is a young English gentleman, and you are a poor Italian fisher-boy."

I know that speech sounds terribly snobbish, but in Italian one can say things that one would never dream of saying in English. Besides, it is no good speaking delicately to persons of that class. Unless you put things plainly, they take a vicious pleasure in misunderstanding you.

An honest English fisherman would have landed me one in the eye in a minute for such a remark, but the wretched down-trodden Italians have no pride. Gennaro only sighed, and said: "It is true."

"Quite so," I said, and turned to go. To my indignation I heard him add: "But sometimes it is not important."

"What do you mean?" I shouted.

He came close up to me with horrid gesticulating fingers.

"Signor Tytler, I wish to say this. If Eustazio asks me to call him 'Voi,' I will call him 'Voi.' Otherwise, no."

With that he seized up a tray of dinner things, and fled

from the room with them; and I heard two more wine-glasses go on the courtyard floor.

I was now fairly angry, and strode out to interview Eustace. But he had gone to bed, and the landlady, to whom I also wished to speak, was engaged. After more vague wonderings, obscurely expressed owing to the presence of Janet and the two American ladies, we all went to bed, too, after a harassing and most extraordinary day.

III

But the day was nothing to the night.

I suppose I had slept for about four hours, when I woke suddenly thinking I heard a noise in the garden. And, immediately, before my eyes were open, cold terrible fear seized me—not fear of something that was happening, like the fear in the wood, but fear of something that might happen.

Our room was on the first floor, looking out on to the garden—or terrace, it was rather: a wedge-shaped block of ground covered with roses and vines, and intersected with little asphalt paths. It was bounded on the small side by the house; round the two long sides ran a wall, only three feet above the terrace level, but with a good twenty feet drop over it into the olive yards, for the ground fell very precipitously away.

Trembling all over I stole to the window. There, pattering up and down the asphalt paths, was something white. I was too much alarmed to see clearly; and in the uncertain light of the stars the thing took all manner of curious shapes. Now it was a great dog, now an enormous white bat, now a mass of quickly travelling cloud. It would bounce like a ball, or take short flights like a bird, or glide slowly like a wraith. It gave no sound—save the pattering sound of what, after all, must be human feet. And at last the obvious explanation forced itself upon my disordered mind; and I realized that Eustace had got out of bed, and that we were in for something more.

I hastily dressed myself, and went down into the dining-room which opened upon the terrace. The door was already unfastened. My terror had almost entirely passed away, but for quite five minutes I struggled with a curious cowardly feeling, which bade me not interfere with the poor strange boy, but leave him to his ghostly patterings, and merely watch him from the window, to see he took no harm.

But better impulses prevailed and, opening the door, I called out:

"Eustace! what on earth are you doing? Come in at once."

He stopped his antics, and said: "I hate my bedroom. I could not stop in it, it is too small."

"Come! come! I'm tired of affectation. You've never complained of it before."

"Besides I can't see anything—no flowers, no leaves, no sky: only a stone wall." The outlook of Eustace's room certainly was limited; but, as I told him, he had never complained of it before.

"Eustace, you talk like a child. Come in! Prompt obedience, if you please."

He did not move.

"Very well: I shall carry you in by force," I added, and made a few steps towards him. But I was soon convinced of the futility of pursuing a boy through a tangle of asphalt paths, and went in instead, to call Mr. Sandbach and Leyland to my aid.

When I returned with them he was worse than ever. He would not even answer us when we spoke, but began singing and chattering to himself in a most alarming way.

"It's a case for the doctor now," said Mr. Sandbach, gravely tapping his forehead.

He had stopped his running and was singing, first low, then loud—singing five-finger exercises, scales, hymn tunes, scraps of Wagner—anything that came into his head. His voice—a very untuneful voice—grew stronger and stronger, and he ended with a tremendous shout which boomed like a gun among the mountains, and awoke everyone who was still sleeping in the hotel. My poor wife and the two girls appeared at their respective windows, and the American ladies were heard violently ringing their bell.

"Eustace," we all cried, "stop! stop, dear boy, and come into the house."

He shook his head, and started off again—talking this time. Never have I listened to such an extraordinary speech. At any other time it would have been ludicrous, for here was a boy, with no sense of beauty and puerile command of words, attempting to tackle themes which the greatest poets have found almost beyond their power. Eustace Robinson, aged fourteen, was standing in his nightshirt saluting, praising, and blessing, the great forces and manifestations of Nature.

He spoke first of night and the stars and planets above his

head, of the swarms of fire-flies below him, of the invisible sea below the fire-flies, of the great rocks covered with anemones and shells that were slumbering in the invisible sea. He spoke of the rivers and waterfalls, of the ripening bunches of grapes, of the smoking cone of Vesuvius and the hidden fire-channels that made the smoke, of the myriads of lizards who were lying curled up in the crannies of the sultry earth, of the showers of white rose-leaves that were tangled in his hair. And then he spoke of the rain and the wind by which all things are changed, of the air through which all things live, and of the woods in which all things can be hidden.

Of course, it was all absurdly high faluting: yet I could have kicked Leyland for audibly observing that it was "a diabolical caricature of all that was most holy and beautiful in life."

"And then,"—Eustace was going on in the pitiable conversational doggerel which was his only mode of expression—"and then there are men, but I can't make them out so well." He knelt down by the parapet, and rested his head on his arms.

"Now's the time," whispered Leyland. I hate stealth, but we darted forward and endeavoured to catch hold of him from behind. He was away in a twinkling, but turned round at once to look at us. As far as I could see in the starlight, he was crying. Leyland rushed at him again, and we tried to corner him among the asphalt paths, but without the slightest approach to success.

We returned, breathless and discomfited, leaving him at his madness in the further corner of the terrace. But my Rose had an inspiration.

"Papa," she called from the window, "if you get Gennaro, he might be able to catch him for you."

I had no wish to ask a favour of Gennaro, but, as the landlady had by now appeared on the scene, I begged her to summon him from the charcoal-bin in which he slept, and make him try what he could do.

She soon returned, and was shortly followed by Gennaro, attired in a dress coat, without either waistcoat, shirt, or vest, and a ragged pair of what had been trousers, cut short above the knees for purposes of wading. The landlady, who had quite picked up English ways, rebuked him for the incongruous and even indecent appearance which he presented.

"I have a coat and I have trousers. What more do you desire?"

"Never mind, Signora Scafetti," I put in. "As there are no

ladies here, it is not of the slightest consequence." Then,
turning to Gennaro, I said: "The aunts of Signor Eustace
wish you to fetch him into the house."

He did not answer.

"Do you hear me? He is not well. I order you to fetch him
into the house."

"Fetch! fetch!" said Signora Scafetti, and shook him roughly
by the arm.

"Eustazio is well where he is."

"Fetch! fetch!" Signora Scafetti screamed, and let loose a
flood of Italian, most of which, I am glad to say, I could not
follow. I glanced up nervously at the girls' window, but they
hardly know as much as I do, and I am thankful to say that
none of us caught one word of Gennaro's answer.

The two yelled and shouted at each other for quite ten
minutes, at the end of which Gennaro rushed back to his
charcoal-bin and Signora Scafetti burst into tears, as well she
might, for she greatly valued her English guests.

"He says," she sobbed, "that Signor Eustace is well where
he is, and that he will not fetch him. I can do no more."

But I could, for, in my stupid British way, I have got some
insight into the Italian character. I followed Mr. Gennaro to
his place of repose, and found him wriggling down on to a
dirty sack.

"I wish you to fetch Signor Eustace to me," I began.

He hurled at me an unintelligible reply.

"If you fetch him, I will give you this." And out of my
pocket I took a new ten lira note.

This time he did not answer.

"This note is equal to ten lire in silver," I continued, for
I knew that the poor-class Italian is unable to conceive of a
single large sum.

"I know it."

"That is, two hundred soldi."

"I do not desire them. Eustazio is my friend."

I put the note into my pocket

"Besides, you would not give it me."

"I am an Englishman. The English always do what they
promise."

"That is true." It is astonishing how the most dishonest of
nations trust us. Indeed they often trust us more than we trust
one another. Gennaro knelt up on his sack. It was too dark
to see his face, but I could feel his warm garlicky breath

coming out in gasps, and I knew that the eternal avarice of the South had laid hold upon him.

"I could not fetch Eustazio to the house. He might die there."

"You need not do that," I replied patiently. "You need only bring him to me; and I will stand outside in the garden." And to this, as if it were something quite different, the pitiable youth consented.

"But give me first the ten lire."

"No"—for I knew the kind of person with whom I had to deal. Once faithless, always faithless.

We returned to the terrace, and Gennaro, without a single word, pattered off towards the pattering that could be heard at the remoter end. Mr. Sandback, Leyland, and myself moved away a little from the house, and stood in the shadow of the white climbing roses, practically invisible.

We heard "Eustazio" called, followed by absurd cries of pleasure from the poor boy. The pattering ceased, and we heard them talking. Their voices got nearer, and presently I could discern them through the creepers, the grotesque figure of the young man, and the slim little white-robed boy. Gennaro had his arm round Eustace's neck, and Eustace was talking away in his fluent, slip-shod Italian.

"I understand almost everything," I heard him say. "The trees, hills, stars, water, I can see all. But isn't it odd! I can't make out men a bit. Do you know what I mean?"

"Ho capito," said Gennaro gravely, and took his arm off Eustace's shoulder. But I made the new note crackle in my pocket; and he heard it. He stuck his hand out with a jerk; and the unsuspecting Eustace gripped it in his own.

"It is odd!" Eustace went on—they were quite close now—"It almost seems as if—as if—"

I darted out and caught hold of his arm, and Leyland got hold of the other arm, and Mr. Sandbach hung on to his feet. He gave shrill heart-piercing screams; and the white roses, which were falling early that year, descended in showers on him as we dragged him into the house.

As soon as we entered the house he stopped shrieking; but floods of tears silently burst forth, and spread over his upturned face.

"Not to my room," he pleaded. "It is so small."

His infinitely dolorous look filled me with strange pity, but what could I do? Besides, his window was the only one that had bars to it.

"Never mind, dear boy," said kind Mr. Sandbach. "I will bear you company till the morning."

At this his convulsive struggles began again. "Oh, please, not that. Anything but that. I will promise to lie still and not to cry more than I can help, if I am left alone."

So we laid him on the bed, and drew the sheets over him, and left him sobbing bitterly, and saying: "I nearly saw everything, and now I can see nothing at all."

We informed the Miss Robinsons of all that had happened, and returned to the dining-room, where we found Signora Scafetti and Gennaro whispering together. Mr. Sandbach got pen and paper, and began writing to the English doctor at Naples. I at once drew out the note, and flung it down on the table to Gennaro.

"Here is your pay," I said sternly, for I was thinking of the Thirty Pieces of Silver.

"Thank you very much, sir," said Gennaro, and grabbed it.

He was going off, when Leyland, whose interest and indifference were always equally misplaced, asked him what Eustace had meant by saying 'he could not make out men a bit.'

"I cannot say. Signor Eustazio" (I was glad to observe a little deference at last) "has a subtle brain. He understands many things."

"But I heard you say you understood," Leyland persisted.

"I understand, but I cannot explain. I am a poor Italian fisher-lad. Yet, listen: I will try." I saw to my alarm that his manner was changing, and tried to stop him. But he sat down on the edge of the table and started off, with some absolutely incoherent remarks.

"It is sad," he observed at last. "What has happened is very sad. But what can I do? I am poor. It is not I."

I turned away in contempt. Leyland went on asking questions. He wanted to know who it was that Eustace had in his mind when he spoke.

"That is easy to say," Gennaro gravely answered. "It is you, it is I. It is all in this house, and many outside it. If he wishes for mirth, we discomfort him. If he asks to be alone, we disturb him. He longed for a friend, and found none for fifteen years. Then he found me, and the first night I—I who have been in the woods and understood things too—betray him to you, and send him in to die. But what could I do?"

"Gently, gently," said I.

"Oh, assuredly he will die. He will lie in the small room all night, and in the morning he will be dead. That I know for certain."

"There, that will do," said Mr. Sandbach. "I shall be sitting with him."

"Filomena Giusti sat all night with Caterina, but Caterina was dead in the morning. They would not let her out, though I begged, and prayed, and cursed, and beat the door, and climbed the wall. They were ignorant fools, and thought I wished to carry her away. And in the morning she was dead."

"What is all this?" I asked Signora Scafetti.

"All kinds of stories will get about," she replied, "and he, least of anyone, has reason to repeat them."

"And I am alive now," he went on, "because I had neither parents nor relatives nor friends, so that, when the first night came, I could run through the woods, and climb the rocks, and plunge into the water, until I had accomplished my desire!"

We heard a cry from Eustace's room—a faint but steady sound, like the sound of wind in a distant wood heard by one standing in tranquillity.

"That," said Gennaro, "was the last noise of Caterina. I was hanging on to her window then, and it blew out past me."

And, lifting up his hand, in which my ten lira note was safely packed, he solemnly cursed Mr. Sandbach, and Leyland, and myself, and Fate, becauase Eustace was dying in the upstairs room. Such is the working of the Southern mind; and I verily believe that he would not have moved even then, had not Leyland, that unspeakable idiot, upset the lamp with his elbow. It was a patent self-extinguishing lamp, bought by Signora Scafetti, at my special request, to replace the dangerous thing that she was using. The result was, that it went out; and the mere physical change from light to darkness had more power over the ignorant animal nature of Gennaro than the most obvious dictates of logic and reason.

I felt, rather than saw, that he had left the room and shouted out to Mr. Sandbach: "Have you got the key to Eustace's room in your pocket?" But Mr. Sandbach and Leyland were both on the floor, having mistaken each other for Gennaro, and some more precious time was wasted in finding a match. Mr. Sandbach had only just time to say that he had left the key in the door, in case the Miss Robinsons wished to pay

Eustace a visit, when we heard a noise on the stairs, and there
was Gennaro, carrying Eustace down.

We rushed out and blocked up the passage, and they lost
heart and retreated to the upper landing.

"Now they are caught," cried Signora Scafetti. "There is
no other way out."

We were cautiously ascending the staircase, when there
was a terrific scream from my wife's room, followed by a
heavy thud on the asphalt path. They had leapt out of her
window.

I reached the terrace just in time to see Eustace jumping
over the parapet of the garden wall. This time I knew for
certain he would be killed. But he alighted in an olive tree,
looking like a great white moth, and from the tree he slid on
to the earth. And as soon as his bare feet touched the clods
of earth he uttered a strange loud cry, such as I should not
have thought the human voice could have produced, and
disappeared among the trees below.

"He has understood and he is saved," cried Gennaro, who
was still sitting on the asphalt path. "Now, instead of dying
he will live!"

"And you, instead of keeping the ten lire, will give them
up," I retorted, for at this theatrical remark I could contain
myself no longer.

"The ten lire are mine," he hissed back, in a scarcely audible voice. He clasped his hand over his breast to protect
his ill-gotten gains, and, as he did so, he swayed forward and
fell upon his face on the path. He had not broken any limbs,
and a leap like that would never have killed an Englishman,
for the drop was not great. But those miserable Italians have
no stamina. Something had gone wrong inside him, and he
was dead.

The morning was still far off, but the morning breeze had
begun, and more rose leaves fell on us as we carried him in.
Signora Scafetti burst into screams at the sight of the dead
body, and, far down the valley towards the sea, there still
resounded the shouts and the laughter of the escaping boy.

Virginia Woolf
(1882–1941)

Virginia Woolf was the daughter of the celebrated man of letters Leslie Stephen. Privately educated at home, she grew up among books, intellectual conversation, and socially well-placed visitors. Although the atmosphere seemed perfect for a budding novelist, it was filled with tensions that created in Woolf lifelong migraines and a mental instability that often brought her close to death. In 1912, she married Leonard Woolf, a writer on economics and an essayist of note, and in 1917 they started the Hogarth Press, which published, among other books, the works of Sigmund Freud in translation. At this time, their home near the British Museum became the center for a group of writers, intellectuals, and artists who came to be known as the Bloomsbury Group. Woolf began as a traditionalist, in The Voyage Out *(1915) and* Night and Day *(1919), but in the 1920s she wrote the novels that brought her an international reputation. Influenced by Freud, Bergson, and Joyce and drawing on her own resources as a woman ahead of her times, she created a sensitive, uniquely modulated prose style in such works as* Jacob's Room *(1922),* Mrs. Dalloway *(1925),* To the Lighthouse *(1927), and* The Waves *(1931). She was a true woman of letters, producing numerous reviews, writing essays on diverse literary subjects, and continuing as a novelist and short story writer until, in despair at the war, she drowned herself in 1941. Some of her other volumes include novels such as* Orlando *(1928),* The Years *(1937), and* Between the Acts *(1941); essays in* The Common Reader *(1925),* The Second Common Reader *(1933), and* The Death of the Moth and Other Essays *(1942). Of particular interest to later feminists were her tracts,* A Room of One's Own *(1929) and* Three Guineas *(1938).*

The Mark on the Wall

Perhaps it was the middle of January in the present year that I first looked up and saw the mark on the wall. In order to fix a date it is necessary to remember what one saw. So now I think of the fire; the steady film of yellow light upon the page of my book; the three chrysanthemums in the round glass bowl on the mantelpiece. Yes, it must have been the winter time, and we had just finished our tea, for I remember that I was smoking a cigarette when I looked up and saw the mark on the wall for the first time. I looked up through the smoke of my cigarette and my eye lodged for a moment upon the burning coals, and that old fancy of the crimson flag flapping from the castle tower came into my mind, and I thought of the cavalcade of red knights riding up the side of the black rock. Rather to my relief the sight of the mark interrupted the fancy, for it is an old fancy, an automatic fancy, made as a child perhaps. The mark was a small round mark, black upon the white wall, about six or seven inches above the mantelpiece.

How readily our thoughts swarm upon a new object, lifting it a little way, as ants carry a blade of straw so feverishly, and then leave it. . . . If that mark was made by a nail, it can't have been for a picture, it must have been for a miniature—the miniature of a lady with white powdered curls, powder-dusted cheeks, and lips like red carnations. A fraud of course, for the people who had this house before us would have chosen pictures in that way—an old picture for an old room. That is the sort of people they were—very interesting people, and I think of them so often, in such queer places, because one will never see them again, never know what happened next. They wanted to leave this house because they wanted to change their style of furniture, so he said, and he was in process of saying that in his opinion art should have ideas behind it when we were torn asunder, as one is torn from the old lady about to pour out tea and the young man about to hit the tennis ball in the back garden of the suburban villa as one rushes past in the train.

But for that mark, I'm not sure about it; I don't believe it was made by a nail after all; it's too big, too round, for that.

I might get up, but if I got up and looked at it, ten to one I shouldn't be able to say for certain; because once a thing's done, no one ever knows how it happened. Oh! dear me, the mystery of life; the inaccuracy of thought! The ignorance of humanity! To show how very little control of our possessions we have—what an accidental affair this living is after all our civilization—let me just count over a few of the things lost in one lifetime, beginning, for that seems always the most mysterious of losses—what cat would gnaw, what rat would nibble—three pale blue canisters of book-binding tools? Then there were the bird cages, the iron hoops, the steel skates, the Queen Anne coal-scuttle, the bagatelle board, the hand organ—all gone, and jewels, too. Opals and emeralds, they lie about the roots of turnips. What a scraping paring affair it is to be sure! The wonder is that I've any clothes on my back, that I sit surrounded by solid furniture at this moment. Why, if one wants to compare life to anything, one must liken it to being blown through the Tube at fifty miles an hour—landing at the other end without a single hairpin in one's hair! Shot out at the feet of God entirely naked! Tumbling head over heels in the asphodel meadows like brown paper parcels pitched down a shoot in the post office! With one's hair flying back like the tail of a race-horse. Yes, that seems to express the rapidity of life, the perpetual waste and repair; all so casual, all so haphazard. . . .

But after life. The slow pulling down of thick green stalks so that the cup of the flower, as it turns over, deluges one with purple and red light. Why, after all, should one not be born there as one is born here, helpless, speechless, unable to focus one's eyesight, groping at the roots of the grass, at the toes of the Giants? As for saying which are trees, and which are men and women, or whether there are such things, that one won't be in a condition to do for fifty years or so. There will be nothing but spaces of light and dark, intersected by thick stalks, and rather higher up perhaps, rose-shaped blots of an indistinct colour—dim pinks and blues—which will, as time goes on, become more definite, become—I don't know what. . . .

And yet that mark on the wall is not a hole at all. It may even be caused by some round black substance, such as a small rose leaf, left over from the summer, and I, not being a very vigilant housekeeper—look at the dust on the mantelpiece, for example, the dust which, so they say, buried

Troy three times over, only fragments of pots utterly refusing annihilation, as one can believe.

The tree outside the window taps very gently on the pane. . . . I want to think quietly, calmly, spaciously, never to be interrupted, never to have to rise from my chair, to slip easily from one thing to another, without any sense of hostility, or obstacle. I want to sink deeper and deeper, away from the surface, with its hard separate facts. To steady myself, let me catch hold of the first idea that passes . . . Shakespeare. . . . Well, he will do as well as another. A man who sat himself solidly in an arm-chair, and looked into the fire, so—A shower of ideas fell perpetually from some very high Heaven down through his mind. He leant his forehead on his hand, and people, looking in through the open door—for this scene is supposed to take place on a summer's evening—But how dull this is, this historical fiction! It doesn't interest me at all. I wish I could hit upon a pleasant track of thought, a track indirectly reflecting credit upon myself, for those are the pleasantest thoughts, and very frequent even in the minds of modest mouse-coloured people, who believe genuinely that they dislike to hear their own praises. They are not thoughts directly praising oneself; that is the beauty of them; they are thoughts like this:

"And then I came into the room. They were discussing botany. I said how I'd seen a flower growing on a dust heap on the site of an old house in Kingsway. The seed, I said, must have been sown in the reign of Charles the First. What flowers grew in the reign of Charles the First?" I asked— (But I don't remember the answer.) Tall flowers with purple tassels to them perhaps. And so it goes on. All the time I'm dressing up the figure of myself in my own mind, lovingly, stealthily, not openly adoring it, for if I did that, I should catch myself out, and stretch my hand at once for a book in self-protection. Indeed, it is curious how instinctively one protects the image of oneself from idolatry or any other handling that could make it ridiculous, or too unlike the original to be believed in any longer. Or is it not so very curious after all? It is a matter of great importance. Suppose the looking-glass smashes, the image disappears, and the romantic figure with the green of forest depths all about it is there no longer, but only that shell of a person which is seen by other people— what an airless, shallow, bald, prominent world it becomes! A world not to be lived in. As we face each other in omnibuses and underground railways we are looking into the mirror;

that accounts for the vagueness, the gleam of glassiness, in our eyes. And the novelists in future will realize more and more the importance of these reflections, for of course there is not one reflection but an almost infinite number; those are the depths they will explore, those the phantoms they will pursue, leaving the description of reality more and more out of their stories, taking a knowledge of it for granted, as the Greeks did and Shakespeare perhaps—but these generalizations are very worthless. The military sound of the word is enough. It recalls leading articles, cabinet ministers—a whole class of things indeed which, as a child, one thought the thing itself, the standard thing, the real thing, from which one could not depart save at the risk of nameless damnation. Generalizations bring back somehow Sunday in London, Sunday afternoon walks, Sunday luncheons, and also ways of speaking of the dead, clothes, and habits—like the habit of sitting all together in one room until a certain hour, although nobody liked it. There was a rule for everything. The rule for tablecloths at that particular period was that they should be made of tapestry with little yellow compartments marked upon them, such as you may see in photographs of the carpets in the corridors of the royal palaces. Tablecloths of a different kind were not real tablecloths. How shocking, and yet how wonderful it was to discover that these real things, Sunday luncheons, Sunday walks, country houses, and tableclothes were not entirely real, were indeed half phantoms, and the damnation which visited the disbeliever in them was only a sense of illegitimate freedom. What now takes the place of those things I wonder, those real standard things? Men perhaps, should you be a woman; the masculine point of view which governs our lives, which sets the standard, which establishes Whitaker's Table of Precedency,[1] which has become, I suppose, since the war, half a phantom to many men and women, which soon, one may hope, will be laughed into the dustbin where the phantoms go, the mahogany sideboards and the Landseer prints, Gods and Devils, Hell and so forth, leaving us all with an intoxicating sense of illegitimate freedom—if freedom exists. . . .

In certain lights that mark on the wall seems actually to project from the wall. Nor is it entirely circular. I cannot be

---

[1] A table listing the rank order of the British aristocracy and notables in *Whitaker's Almanack*, (est. 1868), an annual publication like the *World Almanac* in the United States.

sure, but it seems to cast a perceptible shadow, suggesting that if I ran my finger down that strip of the wall it would, at a certain point, mount and descend a small tumulus, a smooth tumulus like those barrows on the South Downs which are, they say, either tombs or camps. Of the two I should prefer them to be tombs, desiring melancholy like most English people, and finding it natural at the end of a walk to think of the bones stretched beneath the turf. . . . There must be some book about it. Some antiquary must have dug up those bones and given them a name. . . . What sort of a man is an antiquary, I wonder? Retired Colonels for the most part, I daresay, leading parties of aged labourers to the top here, examining clods of earth and stone, and getting into correspondence with the neighboring clergy, which, being opened at breakfast time, gives them a feeling of importance, and the comparison of arrow-heads necessitates cross-country journeys to the county towns, an agreeable necessity both to them and to their elderly wives, who wish to make plum jam or to clean out the study, and have every reason for keeping that great question of the camp or the tomb in perpetual suspension, while the Colonel himself feels agreeably philosophic in accumulating evidence on both sides of the question. It is true that he does finally incline to believe in the camp; and, being opposed, indites a pamphlet which he is about to read at the quarterly meeting of the local society when a stroke lays him low, and his last conscious thoughts are not of wife or child, but of the camp and that arrow-head there, which is now in the case at the local museum, together with the foot of a Chinese murderess, a handful of Elizabethan nails, a great many Tudor clay pipes, a piece of Roman pottery, and the wineglass that Nelson drank out of—proving I really don't know what.

No, no, nothing is proved, nothing is known. And if I were to get up at this very moment and ascertain that the mark on the wall is really—what shall we say?—the head of a gigantic old nail, driven in two hundred years ago, which has now, owing to the patient attrition of many generations of housemaids, revealed its head above the coat of paint, and is taking its first view of modern life in the sight of a white-walled fire-lit room, what should I gain?—Knowledge? Matter for further speculation? I can think sitting still as well as standing up. And what is knowledge? What are our learned men save the descendants of witches and hermits who crouched in caves and in woods brewing herbs, interrogating shrew-mice and writing down the language of the stars? And the less we honour them as our superstitions dwindle and our respect for beauty and health of mind increases. . . . Yes, one could imagine a very pleasant world. A quiet, spacious world, with the flowers so red and blue in the open fields. A world without professors or specialists or house-keepers with the profiles of policemen, a world which one could slice with one's thought as a fish slices the water with his fin, grazing the stems of the water-lilies, hanging suspended over nests of white sea eggs. . . . How peaceful it is down here, rooted in the centre of the world and gazing up through the grey waters, with their sudden gleams of light, and their reflections—if it were not for Whitaker's Almanack—if it were not for the Table of Precedency!

I must jump up and see for myself what that mark on the wall really is—a nail, a rose-leaf, a crack in the wood?

Here is nature once more at her old game of self-preservation. This train of thought, she perceives, is threatening mere waste of energy, even some collision with reality, for who will ever be able to lift a finger against Whitaker's Table of Precedency? The Archbishop of Canterbury is followed by the Lord High Chancellor; the Lord High Chancellor is followed by the Archbishop of York. Everybody follows somebody, such is the philosophy of Whitaker; and the great thing is to know who follows whom. Whitaker knows, and let that, so Nature counsels, comfort you, instead of enraging you; and if you can't be comforted, if you must shatter this hour of peace, think of the mark on the wall.

I understand Nature's game—her prompting to take action as a way of ending any thought that threatens to excite or to pain. Hence, I suppose, comes our slight contempt for men of action—men, we assume, who don't think. Still, there's no harm in putting a full stop to one's disagreeable thoughts by looking at a mark on the wall.

Indeed, now that I have fixed my eyes upon it, I feel that I have grasped a plank in the sea; I feel a satisfying sense of reality which at once turns the two Archbishops and the Lord High Chancellor to the shadows of shades. Here is something definite, something real. Thus, waking from a midnight dream of horror, one hastily turns on the light and lies quiescent, worshipping the chest of drawers, worshipping solidity, worshipping reality, worshipping the impersonal world which is a proof of some existence other than ours. That is what one wants to be sure of. . . . Wood is a pleasant thing to think

about. It comes from a tree; and trees grow, and we don't
know how they grow. For years and years they grow, without
paying any attention to us, in meadows, in forests, and by
the side of rivers—all things one likes to think about. The
cows swish their tails beneath them on hot afternoons; they
paint rivers so green that when a moorhen dives one expects
to see its feathers all green when it comes up again. I like to
think of the fish balanced against the stream like flags blown
out; and of water-beetles slowly raising domes of mud upon
the bed of the river. I like to think of the tree itself: first of
the close dry sensation of being wood; then the grinding of
the storm; then the slow, delicious ooze of sap; I like to think
of it, too, on winter's nights standing in the empty field with
all leaves close-furled, nothing tender exposed to the iron
bullets of the moon, a naked mast upon an earth that goes
tumbling, tumbling, all night long. The song of birds must
sound very loud and strange in June; and how cold the feet
of insects must feel upon it, as they make laborious progresses
up the creases of the bark, or sun themselves upon the thin
green awning of the leaves, and look straight in front of them
with diamond-cut red eyes. . . . One by one the fibres snap
beneath the immense cold pressure of the earth, then the last
storm comes and, falling, the highest branches drive deep
into the ground again. Even so, life isn't done with; there are
a million patient, watchful lives still for a tree, all over the
world, in bedrooms, in ships, on the pavement, lining rooms,
where men and women sit after tea, smoking cigarettes. It is
full of peaceful thoughts, happy thoughts, this tree. I should
like to take each one separately—but something is getting in
the way. . . . Where was I? What has it all been about? A
tree? A river? The Downs? Whitaker's Almanack? The fields
of asphodel? I can't remember a thing. Everything's moving,
falling, slipping, vanishing. . . . There is a vast upheaval of
matter. Someone is standing over me and saying:

"I'm going out to buy a newspaper."

"Yes?"

"Though it's no good buying newspapers. . . . Nothing ever
happens. Curse this war; God damn this war! . . . All the
same, I don't see why we should have a snail on our wall."

Ah, the mark on the wall! It was a snail.

James Joyce
(1882–1941)

James Joyce, Franz Kafka, and Marcel Proust are generally considered the most influential writers of the twentieth century; to these, one might add Thomas Mann and Virginia Woolf and the poets T. S. Eliot and William Butler Yeats. In terms of technique and verbal facility, Joyce stands alone. James Joyce was born in Dublin, a city that was to occupy him and his work for the rest of his life, although he was an exile from his native city during his adult years. After an elitist education that could have been preparation for the priesthood, he turned his back on church, country, and family and began to produce the stories and novels that established his reputation. He saw himself as an exile, isolated, an alien figure; but his persona, Stephen Dedalus, is representative of all artists, not only of Joyce. The stories that make up Dubliners, from which "Araby" derives, were written during the period when he was also working on the final version of A Portrait of the Artist As a Young Man (published in 1916, but written much earlier). Joyce followed this with his masterpiece, Ulysses, in 1922, which is the most influential novel of the twentieth century. In order to represent the interworkings of Dublin, Joyce moved to interiors, and his development of interior monologue and stream of consciousness in Stephen Dedalus, Leopold Bloom, and his wife, Molly, carried the novel to its furthest reaches. Joyce spent the next seventeen years working on what became the most avant-garde of fictions, the dreamlike, ever-shifting Finnegans Wake (1939). He died in Zurich, Switzerland, where he is buried. Like Kafka, Proust, Conrad, Lawrence, Woolf, and Rilke, Joyce failed to win the Nobel Prize for literature.

Araby

North Richmond Street, being blind, was a quiet street except at the hour when the Christian Brothers' School set the boys free. An uninhabited house of two stories stood at the blind end, detached from its neighbours in a square ground. The other houses of the street, conscious of decent lives within them, gazed at one another with brown imperturbable faces.

The former tenant of our house, a priest, had died in the back drawing-room. Air, musty from having been long enclosed, hung in all the rooms, and the waste room behind the kitchen was littered with old useless papers. Among these I found a few paper-covered books, the pages of which were curled and damp: *The Abbot*, by Walter Scott, *The Devout Communicant* and *The Memoirs of Vidocq*. I liked the last best because its leaves were yellow. The wild garden behind the house contained a central apple-tree and a few straggling bushes under one of which I found the late tenant's rusty bicycle-pump. He had been a very charitable priest; in his will he had left all his money to institutions and the furniture of his house to his sister.

When the short days of winter came, dusk fell before we had well eaten our dinner. When we met in the streets the houses had grown somber. The space of sky above us was the color of ever-changing violet and towards it the lamps of the street lifted their feeble lanterns. The cold air stung us and we played till our bodies glowed. Our shouts echoed in the silent street. The career of our play brought us through the dark muddy lanes behind the houses where we ran the gauntlet of the rough tribes from the cottages, to the back doors of the dark dripping gardens where odours arose from the ashpits, to the dark odourous stables where a coachman smoothed and combed the horse or shook music from the buckled harness. When we returned to the street, light from the kitchen windows had filled the areas. If my uncle was seen turning the corner we hid in the shadow until we had seen him safely housed. Or if Mangan's sister came out on the doorstep to call her brother in to his tea we watched her from our shadow peer up and down the street. We waited to see whether she would remain or go in and, if she remained,

we left our shadow and walked up to Mangan's steps re-
signedly. She was waiting for us, her figure defined by the
light from the half-opened door. Her brother always teased
her before he obeyed and I stood by the railings looking up
at her. Her dress swung as she moved her body and the soft
rope of her hair tossed from side to side.

Every morning I lay on the floor in the front parlour watching her door. The blind was pulled down to within an inch
of the sash so that I could not be seen. When she came out
on the doorstep my heart leaped. I ran to the hall, seized my
books and followed her. I kept her brown figure always in
my eye and, when we came near the point at which our ways
diverged, I quickened my pace and passed her. This happened
morning after morning. I had never spoken to her, except for
a few casual words, and yet her name was like a summons to
all my foolish blood.

Her image accompanied me even in places the most hostile
to romance. On Saturday evenings when my aunt went mar-
keting I had to go to carry some of the parcels. We walked
through the flaring streets, jostled by drunken men and bargaining women, amid the curses of labourers, the shrill litanies
of shop-boys who stood on guard by the barrels of pigs' cheeks,
the nasal chanting of street-singers, who sang a *come-all-you*
about O'Donovan Rossa, or a ballad about the troubles in
our native land. These noises converged in a single sensation
of life for me: I imagined that I bore my chalice safely through
a throng of foes. Her name sprang to my lips at moments in
strange prayers and praises which I myself did not understand.
My eyes were often full of tears (I could not tell why) and at
times a flood from my heart seemed to pour itself out into
my bosom. I thought little of the future. I did not know
whether I would ever speak to her or not or, if I spoke to
her, how I could tell her of my confused adoration. But my
body was like a harp and her words and gestures were like
fingers running upon the wires.

One evening I went into the back drawing-room in which
the priest had died. It was a dark rainy evening and there
was no sound in the house. Through one of the broken panes
I heard the rain impinge upon the earth, the fine incessant
needles of water playing in the sodden beds. Some distant
lamp or lighted window gleamed below me. I was thankful
that I could see so little. All my senses seemed to desire to
veil themselves and, feeling that I was about to slip from

them, I pressed the palms of my hands together until they trembled, murmuring: *"O love! O love!"* many times.

At last she spoke to me. When she addressed the first words to me I was so confused that I did not know what to answer. She asked me was I going to *Araby*. I forgot whether I answered yes or no. It would be a splendid bazaar, she said; she would love to go.

"And why can't you?" I asked.

While she spoke she turned a silver bracelet round and round her wrist. She could not go, she said, because there would be a retreat that week in her convent. Her brother and two other boys were fighting for their caps and I was alone at the railings. She held one of the spikes, bowing her head towards me. The light from the lamp opposite our door caught the white curve of her neck, lit up her hair that rested there and, falling, lit up the hand upon the railing. It fell over one side of her dresss and caught the white border of a petticoat, just visible as she stood at ease.

"It's well for you," she said.

"If I go," I said, "I will bring you something."

What innumerable follies laid waste my waking and sleeping thoughts after that evening! I wish to annihilate the tedious intervening days. I chafed against the work of school. At night in my bedroom and by day in the classroom her image came between me and the page I strove to read. The syllables of the word *Araby* were called to me through the silence in which my soul luxuriated and cast an Eastern enchantment over me. I asked for leave to go to the bazaar on Saturday night. My aunt was surprised and hoped it was not some Freemason affair. I answered few questions in class. I watched my master's face pass from amiability to sternness; he hoped I was not beginning to idle. I could not call my wandering thoughts together. I had hardly any patience with the serious work of life which, now that it stood between me and my desire, seemed to me child's play, ugly monotonous child's play.

On Saturday morning I reminded my uncle that I wished to go to the bazaar in the evening. He was fussing at the hallstand, looking for the hat-brush, and answered me curtly:

"Yes, boy, I know."

As he was in the hall I could not go into the front parlour and lie at the window. I left the house in bad humor and walked slowly towards the school. The air was pitilessly raw and already my heart misgave me.

When I came home to dinner my uncle had not yet been home. Still it was early. I sat staring at the clock for some time and, when its ticking began to irritate me, I left the room. I mounted the staircase and gained the upper part of the house. The high cold empty gloomy rooms liberated me and I went from room to room singing. From the front window I saw my companions playing below in the street. Their cries reached me weakened and indistinct and, leaning my forehead against the cool glass, I looked over at the dark house where she lived. I may have stood there for an hour, seeing nothing but the brown-clad figure cast by my imagination, touched discreetly by the lamplight at the curved neck, at the hand upon the railings and at the border below the dress.

When I came downstairs again I found Mrs. Mercer sitting at the fire. She was an old garrulous woman, a pawnbroker's widow, who collected used stamps for some pious purpose. I had to endure the gossip of the tea-table. The meal was prolonged beyond an hour and still my uncle did not come. Mrs. Mercer stood up to go: she was sorry she couldn't wait any longer, but it was after eight o'clock and she did not like to be out late, as the night air was bad for her. When she had gone I began to walk up and down the room, clenching my fists. My aunt said:

"I'm afraid you may put off your bazaar for this night of Our Lord."

At nine o'clock I heard my uncle's latchkey in the hall door. I heard him talking to himself and heard the hallstand rocking when it had received the weight of his overcoat. I could interpret these signs. When he was midway through his dinner I asked him to give me the money to go to the bazaar. He had forgotten.

"The people are in bed and after their first sleep now," he said.

I did not smile. My aunt said to him energetically:

"Can't you give him the money and let him go? You've kept him late enough as it is."

My uncle said he was very sorry he had forgotten. He said he believed in the old saying, "All work and no play makes Jack a dull boy." He asked me where I was going and, when I had told him a second time, he asked me did I know *The Arab's Farewell to his Steed*. When I left the kitchen he was about to recite the opening lines of the piece to my aunt.

I held a florin tightly in my hand as I strode down Buckingham Street towards the station. The sight of the streets thronged with buyers and glaring with gas recalled to me the purpose of my journey. I took my seat in a third-class carriage of a deserted train. After an intolerable delay the train moved out of the station slowly. It crept onward among ruinous houses and over the twinkling river. At Westland Row Station a crowd of people pressed to the carriage doors; but the porters moved them back, saying that it was a special train for the bazaar. I remained alone in the bare carriage. In a few minutes the train drew up beside an improvised wooden platform. I passed out on to the road and saw by the lighted dial of a clock that it was ten minutes to ten. In front of me was a large building which displayed the magical name.

I could not find any sixpenny entrance and, fearing that the bazaar would be closed, I passed in quickly through a turnstile, handing a shilling to a weary-looking man. I found myself in a big hall girdled at half its height by a gallery. Nearly all the stalls were closed and the greater part of the hall was in darkness. I recognized a silence like that which pervades a church after a service. I walked into the center of the bazaar timidly. A few people were gathered about the stalls which were still open. Before a curtain, over which the words *Café Chantant* were written in coloured lamps, two men were counting money on a salver. I listened to the fall of the coins.

Remembering with difficulty why I had come I went over to one of the stalls and examined porcelain vases and flowered tea-sets. At the door of the stall a young lady was talking and laughing with two young gentlemen. I remarked their English accents and listened vaguely to their conversation.

"O, I never said such a thing!"

"O, but you did!"

"O, but I didn't!"

"Didn't she say that?"

"Yes. I heard her."

"O, there's a . . . fib!"

Observing me the young lady came over and asked me did I wish to buy anything. The tone of her voice was not encouraging; she seemed to have spoken to me out of a sense of duty. I looked humbly at the great jars that stood like eastern guards at either side of the dark entrance to the stall and murmured:

"No, thank you."

The young lady changed the position of one of the vases and went back to the two young men. They began to talk of the same subject. Once or twice the young lady glanced at me over her shoulder.

I lingered before her stall, though I knew my stay was useless, to make my interest in her wares seem the more real. Then I turned away slowly and walked down the middle of the bazaar. I allowed the two pennies to fall against the sixpence in my pocket. I heard a voice call from one end of the gallery that the light was out. The upper part of the hall was now completely dark.

Gazing up into the darkness I saw myself as a creature driven and derided by vanity; and my eyes burned with anguish and anger.

D. H. Lawrence
(1885–1930)

David Herbert Lawrence began his career as a schoolmaster, was early recognized by Ford Madox Ford as a talented poet, and then moved rapidly into the writing of novels. The fiction on which his reputation rests is Sons and Lovers *(1913),* The Rainbow *(1915), and* Women in Love *(1920); of almost equal importance are* The Plumed Serpent *(1926) and* Lady Chatterley's Lover *(1928), and several shorter works, such as "St. Mawr," "The Woman Who Rode Away," and "The Prussian Officer." The openly sexual content of many of these books, as well as the explicitness of his paintings, kept him in difficulty with the English censors for most of his adult life. After his marriage to Frieda von Richthofen of the famous "Red Baron" German family, he traveled extensively until his death from tuberculosis. It was these travels, to Mexico, Australia, the United States, Italy, and elsewhere, which provided settings for many of his works. In his forty-four years, he poured out, in addition to novels and short fiction, travel books, hundreds of poems, and essays that attacked virtually every aspect of modern life.*

Things

They were true idealists, from New England. But that is some time ago: before the war. Several years before the war, they met and married; he a tall, keen-eyed young man from Connecticut, she a smallish, demure, Puritan-looking young woman from Massachusetts. They both had a little money. Not much, however. Even added together, it didn't make three thousand dollars a year. Still—they were free. Free!

Ah! Freedom! To be free to live one's own life! To be twenty-five and twenty-seven, a pair of true idealists with a mutual love of beauty, and an inclination towards "Indian thought"—meaning alas, Mrs. Besant—and an income a little under three thousand dollars a year! But what is money? All one wishes to do is to live a full and beautiful life. In Europe, of course, right at the fountainhead of tradition. It might possibly be done in America: in New England, for example. But at a forfeiture of a certain amount of "beauty." True beauty takes a long time to mature. The baroque is only half-beautiful, half-matured. No, the real silver bloom, the real golden-sweet bouquet of beauty had its roots in the Renaissance, not in any later or shallower period.

Therefore the two idealists, who were married in New Haven, sailed at once to Paris: Paris of the old days. They had a studio apartment on the Boulevard Montparnasse, and they became real Parisians, in the old, delightful sense, not in the modern, vulgar. It was the shimmer of the pure impressionists, Monet and his followers, the world seen in terms of pure light, light broken and unbroken. How lovely! How lovely the nights, the river, the mornings in the old streets and by the flower-stalls and the book-stalls, the afternoons up on Montmartre or in the Tuileries, the evenings on the boulevards!

They both painted, but not desperately. Art had not taken them by the throat, and they did not take Art by the throat. They painted: that's all. They knew people—nice people, if possible, though one had to take them mixed. And they were happy.

Yet it seems as if human beings must set their claws in *something*. To be "free," to be "living a full and beautiful life," you must, alas, be attached to something. A "full and beautiful life" means a tight attachment to *something*—at least, it is so for all idealists—or else a certain boredom supervenes; there is a certain waving of loose ends upon the air, like the waving, yearning tendrils of the vine that spread and rotate, seeking something to clutch, something up which to climb towards the necessary sun. Finding nothing, the vine can only trail, half-fulfilled, upon the ground. Such is freedom!—a clutching of the right pole. And human beings are all vines. But especially the idealist. He is a vine, and he needs to clutch and climb. And he despises the man who is a mere *potato*, or turnip, or lump of wood.

Our idealists were frightfully happy, but they were all the time reaching out for something to cotton on to. At first, Paris was enough. They explored Paris *thoroughly*. And they learned French till they almost felt like French people, they could speak it so glibly.

Still, you know, you never talk French with your *soul*. It can't be done. And though it's very thrilling, at first, talking in French to clever Frenchmen—they seem so much cleverer than oneself—still, in the long run, it is not satisfying. The endlessly clever *materialism* of the French leaves you cold, in the end, gives a sense of barrenness and incompatibility with true New England depth. So our two idealists felt.

They turned away from France—but ever so gently. France had disappointed them. "We've loved it, and we've got a great deal out of it. But after a while, after a considerable while, several years, in fact, Paris leaves one feeling disappointed. It hasn't quite got what one wants."

"But Paris isn't France."

"No, perhaps not. France is quite different from Paris. And France is lovely—quite lovely. But to *us*, though we love it, it doesn't say a great deal."

So, when the war came, the idealists moved to Italy. And they loved Italy. They found it beautiful, and more poignant than France. It seemed much nearer to the New England conception of beauty: something pure, and full of sympathy, without the *materialism* and *cynicism* of the French. The two idealists seemed to breathe their own true air in Italy.

And in Italy, much more than in Paris, they felt they could thrill to the teachings of the Buddha. They entered the swelling stream of modern Buddhistic emotion, and they read the books, and they practised meditation, and they deliberately set themselves to eliminate from their own souls greed, pain, and sorrow. They did not realize—yet—that Buddha's very eagerness to free himself from pain and sorrow is in itself a sort of greed. No, they dreamed of a perfect world, from which all greed, and nearly all pain, and a great deal of sorrow, were eliminated.

But America entered the war, so the two idealists had to help. They did hospital work. And though their experience made them realize more than ever that greed, pain, and sorrow *should* be eliminated from the world, nevertheless the Buddhism, or the theosophy, didn't emerge very triumphant from the long crisis. Somehow, somewhere, in some part of themselves, they felt that greed, pain, and sorrow would never be eliminated, because most people don't care about eliminating them, and never will care. Our idealists were far too western to think of abandoning all the world to damnation, while they saved their two selves. They were far too unselfish to sit tight under a bho-tree and reach Nirvana in a mere couple.

It was more than that, though. They simply hadn't enough *Sitzfleisch* to squat under a bho-tree and get to Nirvana by contemplating anything, least of all their own navel. If the whole wide world was not going to be saved, they, personally, were not so very keen on being saved just by themselves. No, it would be so lonesome. They were New Englanders, so it must be all or nothing. Greed, pain, and sorrow must either be eliminated from *all the world*, or else, what was the use of eliminating them from oneself? No use at all! One was just a victim.

And so, although they still loved "Indian thought," and felt very tender about it: well, to go back to our metaphor, the pole up which the green and anxious vines had clambered so far now proved dry-rotten. It snapped, and the vines came slowly subsiding to earth again. There was no crack and crash. The vines held themselves up by their own foliage, for a while. But they subsided. The beanstalk of "Indian thought" had given way before Jack and Jill had climbed off the tip of it to a further world.

They subsided with a slow rustle back to earth again. But they made no outcry. They were again "disappointed." But they never admitted it. "Indian thought" had let them down. But they never complained. Even to one another, they never said a word. They were disappointed, faintly but deeply disillusioned, and they both knew it. But the knowledge was tacit.

And they still had so much in their lives. They still had Italy—dear Italy. And they still had freedom, the priceless treasure. And they still had so much "beauty." About the fulness of their lives they were not quite so sure. They had one little boy, whom they loved as parents should love their children, but whom they wisely refrained from fastening upon, to build their lives on him. No, no, they must live their own lives! They still had strength of mind to know that.

But they were now no longer so very young. Twenty-five and twenty-seven had become thirty-five and thirty-seven. And though they had had a very wonderful time in Europe, and though they still loved Italy—dear Italy!—yet: they were disappointed. They had got a lot out of it: oh, a very great deal indeed! Still, it hadn't given them quite, not *quite*, what they had expected. Europe was lovely, but it was dead. Living in Europe, you were living on the past. And Europeans, with all their superficial charm, were not *really* charming. They were materialistic, they had no *real* soul. They just did not understand the inner urge of the spirit, because the inner urge was dead in them, they were all survivals. There, that was the truth about Europeans: they were survivals, with no more getting ahead in them.

It was another bean-pole, another vine-support crumbled under the green life of the vine. And very bitter it was, this time. For up the old tree-trunk of Europe the green vine had been clambering silently for more than ten years, ten hugely important years, the years of real living. The two idealists had *lived* in Europe, lived on Europe and on European life and European things as vines in an everlasting vineyard.

They had made their home here: a home such as you could never make in America. Their watchword had been "beauty." They had rented, the last four years, the second floor of an old palazzo on the Arno, and here they had all their "things." And they derived a profound, profound satisfaction from their apartment: the lofty, silent, ancient rooms with windows on the river, with glistening dark-red floors, and the beautiful furniture that the idealists had "picked up."

Yes, unknown to themselves, the lives of the idealists had been running with a fierce swiftness horizontally, all the time. They had become tense, fierce hunters of "things" for their home. While their souls were climbing up to the sun of old European culture or old Indian thought, their passions were running horizontally, clutching at "things." Of course they did not buy the things for the things' sakes, but for the sake of "beauty." They looked upon their home as a place entirely furnished by loveliness, not by "things" at all. Valerie had some very lovely curtains at the windows of the long *salotto*, looking on the river: curtains of queer ancient material that looked like finely knitted silk, most beautifully faded down from vermilion and orange, and gold, and black, down to a sheer soft glow. Valerie hardly ever came into the *salotto* without mentally falling on her knees before the curtains. "Chartres!" she said. "To me they are Chartres!" And Melville never turned and looked at his sixteenth-century Venetian bookcase, with its two or three dozen of choice books, without feeling his marrow stir in his bones. The holy of holies!

The child silently, almost sinisterly, avoided any rude contact with these ancient monuments of furniture, as if they had been nests of sleeping cobras, or that "thing" most perilous to the touch, the Ark of the Covenant. His childish awe was silent and cold, but final.

Still, a couple of New England idealists cannot live merely on the bygone glory of their furniture. At least, one couple could not. They got used to the marvellous Bologna cupboard, they got used to the wonderful Venetian bookcase, and the books, and the Siena curtains and bronzes, and the lovely sofas and side-tables and chairs they had "picked up" in Paris. Oh, they had been picking things up since the first day they landed in Europe. And they were still at it. It is the last interest Europe can offer to an outsider: or to an insider either.

When people came, and were thrilled by the Melville interior, then Valerie and Erasmus felt they had not lived in vain: that they still were living. But in the long mornings, when Erasmus was desultorily working at Renaissance Florentine literature, and Valerie was attending to the apartment: and in the long hours after lunch; and in the long, usually very cold and oppressive evenings in the ancient palazzo: then the halo died from around the furniture, and the things became things, lumps of matter that just stood there or hung there *ad infinitum*, and said nothing; and Valerie and Erasmus almost hated them. The glow of beauty, like every other glow, dies down unless it is fed. The idealists still dearly loved their things. But they had got them. And the sad fact is, things that glow vividly while you're getting them, go almost quite cold after a year or two. Unless, of course, people envy them very much, and the museums are pining for them. And the Melvilles' "things," though very good, were not quite so good as that.

So, the glow gradually went out of everything, out of Europe, out of Italy—"the Italians are dears"—even out of that marvellous apartment on the Arno. "Why, if I had this apartment, I'd never, never even want to go out of doors! It's too lovely and perfect." That was something, of course—to hear that.

And yet Valerie and Erasmus went out of doors: they even went out to get away from its ancient, cold-floored, stone-heavy silence and dead dignity. "We're living on the past, you know, Dick," said Valerie to her husband. She called him Dick.

They were grimly hanging on. They did not like to give in. They did not like to own up that they were through. For twelve years now, they had been "free" people living a "full and beautiful life." And America for twelve years had been their anathema, the Sodom and Gomorrah of industrial materialism.

It wasn't easy to own that you were "through." They hated to admit that they wanted to go back. But at last, reluctantly, they decided to go, "for the boy's sake."—"We can't *bear* to leave Europe. But Peter is an American, so he had better look at America while he's young." The Melvilles had an entirely English accent and manner; almost; a little Italian and French here and there.

They left Europe behind, but they took as much of it along with them as possible. Several van-loads, as a matter of fact. All those adorable and irreplaceable "things." And all arrived in New York, idealists, child, and the huge bulk of Europe they had lugged along.

Valerie had dreamed of a pleasant apartment, perhaps on Riverside Drive, where it was not so expensive as east of Fifth Avenue, and where all their wonderful things would look marvellous. She and Erasmus house-hunted. But alas! their income was quite under three thousand dollars a year. They found—well, everybody knows what they found. Two small rooms and a kitchenette, and don't let us unpack a *thing!*

The chunk of Europe which they had bitten off went into a warehouse, at fifty dollars a month. And they sat in two small rooms and a kitchenette, and wondered why they'd done it.

Erasmus, of course, ought to get a job. This was what was written on the wall, and what they both pretended not to see. But it had been the strange, vague threat that the Statue of Liberty had always held over them: "Thou shalt get a job!" Erasmus had the tickets, as they say. A scholastic career was still possible for him. He had taken his exams brilliantly at Yale, and had kept up his "researches," all the time he had been in Europe.

But both he and Valerie shuddered. A scholastic career! The scholastic world! The *American* scholastic world! Shudder upon shudder! Give up their freedom, their full and beautiful life? Never! Never! Erasmus would be forty next birthday.

The "things" remained in warehouse. Valerie went to look at them. It cost her a dollar an hour, and horrid pangs. The "things," poor things, looked a bit shabby and wretched, in that warehouse.

However, New York was not all America. There was the great clean West. So the Melvilles went West, with Peter, but without the things. They tried living the simple life, in the mountains. But doing their own chores became almost a nightmare. "Things" are all very well to look at, but it's awful handling them, even when they're beautiful. To be the slave of hideous things, to keep a stove going, cook meals, wash dishes, carry water and clean floors: pure horror of sordid anti-life!

In the cabin on the mountains, Valerie dreamed of Florence, the lost apartment; and her Bologna cupboard and Louis-Quinze chairs, above all, her "Chartres" curtains, stood in New York and costing fifty dollars a month.

A millionaire friend came to the rescue, offering them a cottage on the California coast—California! Where the new soul is to be born in man. With joy the idealists moved a little farther west, catching at new vine-props of hope.

And finding them straws! The millionaire cottage was perfectly equipped. It was perhaps as labour-savingly perfect as is possible: electric heating and cooking, a white-and-pearl enameled kitchen, nothing to make dirt except the human being himself. In an hour or so the idealists had got through their chores. They were "free"—free to hear the great Pacific pounding the coast, and to feel a new soul filling their bodies.

Alas! The Pacific pounded the coast with hideous brutality, brute force itself! And the new soul, instead of sweetly stealing into their bodies, seemed only meanly to gnaw the old soul out of their bodies. To feel you are under the fist of the most blind and crunching brute force: to feel that your cherished idealist's soul is being gnawed out of you, and only irritation left in place of it: well, it isn't good enough.

After about nine months, the idealists departed from the California west. It had been a great experience, they were glad to have had it. But, in the long run, the West was not the place for them, and they knew it. No, the people who wanted new souls had better get them. They, Valerie and Erasmus Melville, would like to develop the old soul a little further. Anyway, they had not felt any influx of new soul, on the California coast. On the contrary.

So, with a slight hole in their material capital, they returned to Massachusetts and paid a visit to Valerie's parents, taking the boy along. The grandparents welcomed the child—poor expatriated boy—and were rather cold to Valerie, but really cold to Erasmus. Valerie's mother definitely said to Valerie, one day, that Erasmus ought to take a job, so that Valerie could live decently. Valerie haughtily reminded her mother of the beautiful apartment on the Arno, and the "wonderful" things in store in New York, and of the "marvellous and satisfying life" she and Erasmus had led. Valerie's mother said that she didn't think her daughter's life looked so very marvellous at present: homeless, with a husband idle at the age of forty, a child to educate, and a dwindling capital: looked the reverse of marvellous to *her*. Let Erasmus take some post in one of the universities.

"What post? What university?" interrupted Valerie.

"That could be found, considering your father's connections and Erasmus's qualifications," replied Valerie's mother. "And you could get all your valuable things out of store, and have a really lovely home, which everybody in America would be proud to visit. As it is, your furniture is eating up your income, and you are living like rats in a hole, with nowhere to go to."

This was very true. Valerie was beginning to pine for a home, with her "things." Of course she could have sold her furniture for a substantial sum. But nothing would have induced her to. Whatever else passed away, religions, cultures, continents, and hopes, Valerie would *never* part from the "things" which she and Erasmus had collected with such passion. To these she was nailed.

But she and Erasmus still would not give up that freedom, that full and beautiful life they had so believed in. Erasmus cursed America. He did not want to earn a living. He panted for Europe.

Leaving the boy in charge of Valerie's parents, the two idealists once more set off for Europe. In New York they paid two dollars and looked for a brief, bitter hour at their "things." They sailed "student class"—that is, third. Their income now was less than two thousand dollars, instead of three. And they made straight for Paris—cheap Paris.

They found Europe, this time, a complete failure. "We have returned like dogs to our vomit," said Erasmus; "but the vomit has staled in the meantime." He found he couldn't stand Europe. It irritated every nerve in his body. He hated America too. But America at least was a darn sight better than this miserable, dirt-eating continent; which was by no means cheap any more, either.

Valerie, with her heart on her things—she had really burned to get them out of that warehouse, where they had stood now for three years, eating up two thousand dollars—wrote to her mother she thought Erasmus would come back if he could get some suitable work in America. Erasmus, in a state of frustration bordering on rage and insanity, just went round Italy in a poverty-stricken fashion, his coat-cuffs frayed, hating everything with intensity. And when a post was found for him in Cleveland University, to teach French, Italian, and Spanish literature, his eyes grew more beady, and his long, queer face grew sharper and more ratlike, with utter baffled fury. He was forty, and the job was upon him.

"I think you'd better accept, dear. You don't care for Europe any longer. As you say, it's dead and finished. They offer us a house on the college lot, and mother says there's room in it for all our things. I think we'd better cable 'Accept.' "

He glowered at her like a cornered rat. One almost expected to see rat's whiskers twitching at the sides of the sharp nose.

"Shall I send the cablegram?" she asked.

"Send it!" he blurted.

And she went out and sent it.

He was a changed man, quieter, much less irritable. A load was off him. He was inside the cage.

But when he looked at the furnaces of Cleveland, vast and like the greatest of black forests, with red and white hot cascades of gushing metal, and tiny gnomes of men, and terrific noises, gigantic, he said to Valerie:

"Say what you like, Valerie, this is the biggest thing the modern world has to show."

And when they were in their up-to-date little house on the college lot of Cleveland University and that woebegone débris of Europe, Bologna cupboard, Venice book-shelves, Ravenna bishop's chair, Louis-Quinze side-tables, "Chartres" curtains, Siena bronze lamps, all were arrayed, and all looked perfectly out of keeping, and therefore very impressive; and when the idealists had had a bunch of gaping people in, and Erasmus had showed off in his best European manner, but still quite cordial and American; and Valerie had been most ladylike, but for all that, "we prefer America"; then Erasmus said, looking at her with the queer sharp eyes of a rat:

"Europe's the mayonnaise all right, but America supplies the good old lobster—what?"

"Every time!" she said, with satisfaction.

And he peered at her. He was in the cage: but it was safe inside. And she, evidently, was her real self at last. She had got the goods. Yet round his nose was a queer, evil, scholastic look, of pure scepticism. But he liked lobster.

Katherine Mansfield
(1888–1923)

Katherine Mansfield (Kathleen Beauchamp) was born in New Zealand, but hers was a wandering life, somewhat reminiscent of the lives of her friends D. H. and Frieda Lawrence. At fifteen Mansfield left New Zealand for London, to study music at Queen's College; then she returned to New Zealand upon graduation, married, unhappily, and went back to London. Her first volume of stories, In a German Pension *(1911), began her career as a short story writer; she gained considerable fame with the subsequent publication of* Bliss *(1920),* The Garden Party *(1922), and* The Dove's Nest *(1923). After her death, (of tuberculosis, in Fontainebleau, France), her second husband, the critic John Middleton Murry, edited her* Journal Letters *(1928) and* Novels and Novelists *(1930), her critical essays. Mansfield's representative stories recall Chekhov's short fictions, especially in their attention to craft, the cleanness of their line, and their delicate stress upon a moment or nuance that opens up or destroys a life.*

Marriage À La Mode

On his way to the station William remembered with a fresh pang of disappointment that he was taking nothing down to the kiddies. Poor little chaps! It was hard lines on them. Their first words always were as they ran to greet him, "What have you got for me, daddy?" and he had nothing. He would have to buy them some sweets at the station. But that was what he had done for the past four Saturdays; their faces had fallen last time when they saw the same old boxes produced again.

And Paddy had said, "I had red ribbing on mine *bee*-fore!"

And Johnny had said, "It's always pink on mine. I hate pink."

But what was William to do? The affair wasn't so easily settled. In the old days, of course, he would have taken a taxi off to a decent toyshop and chosen them something in five minutes. But nowadays they had Russian toys, French toys, Serbian toys—toys from God knows where. It was over a year since Isabel had scrapped the old donkeys and engines and so on because they were so "dreadfully sentimental" and "so appallingly bad for the babies' sense of form."

"It's so important," the new Isabel had explained, "that they should like the right things from the very beginning. It saves so much time later on. Really, if the poor pets have to spend their infant years staring at these horrors, one can imagine them growing up and asking to be taken to the Royal Academy."

And she spoke as though a visit to the Royal Academy was certain immediate death to any one. . . .

"Well, I don't know," said William slowly. "When I was their age I used to go to bed hugging an old towel with a knot in it."

The new Isabel looked at him, her eyes narrowed, her lips apart.

"*Dear* William! I'm sure you did!" She laughed in the new way.

Sweets it would have to be, however, thought William gloomily, fishing in his pocket for change for the taxi-man. And he saw the kiddies handing the boxes round—they were awfully generous little chaps—while Isabel's precious friends didn't hesitate to help themselves. . . .

What about fruit? William hovered before a stall just inside the station. What about a melon each? Would they have to share that, too? Or a pineapple for Pad, and a melon for Johnny? Isabel's friends could hardly go sneaking up to the nursery at the children's meal-times. All the same, as he bought the melon William had a horrible vision of one of Isabel's young poets lapping up a slice, for some reason, behind the nursery door.

With his two very awkward parcels he strode off to his train. The platform was crowded, the train was in. Doors banged open and shut. There came such a loud hissing from the engine that people looked dazed as they scurried to and fro. William made straight for a first-class smoker, stowed away his suit-case and parcels, and taking a huge wad of papers out of his inner pocket, he flung down in the corner and began to read.

"Our client moreover is positive. . . . We are inclined to reconsider . . . in the event of—" Ah, that was better. William pressed back his flattened hair and stretched his legs across the carriage floor. The familiar dull gnawing in his breast quietened down. "With regard to our decision—" He took out a blue pencil and scored a paragraph slowly.

Two men came in, stepped across him, and made for the farther corner. A young fellow swung his golf clubs into the rack and sat down opposite. The train gave a gentle lurch, they were off. William glanced up and saw the hot, bright station slipping away. A red-faced girl raced along the carriages, there was something strained and almost desperate in the way she waved and called. "Hysterical!" thought William dully. Then a greasy, black-faced workman at the end of the platform grinned at the passing train. And William thought, "A filthy life!" and went back to his papers.

When he looked up again there were fields, and beasts standing for shelter under the dark trees. A wide river, with naked children splashing in the shallows, glided into sight and was gone again. The sky shone pale, and one bird drifted high like a dark fleck in a jewel.

"We have examined our client's correspondence files. . . ." The last sentence he had read echoed in his mind. "We have examined . . ." William hung on to that sentence, but it was no good; it snapped in the middle, and the fields, the sky, the sailing bird, the water, all said, "Isabel." The same thing happened every Saturday afternoon. When he was on his way to meet Isabel there began those countless imaginary meetings. She was at the station, standing just a little apart from everybody else; she was sitting in the open taxi outside; she was at the garden gate; walking across the parched grass; at the door, or just inside the hall.

And her clear, light voice said, "It's William," or "Hillo, William!" or "So William has come!" He touched her cool hand, her cool cheek.

The exquisite freshness of Isabel! When he had been a little boy, it was his delight to run into the garden after a shower of rain and shake the rose-bush over him. Isabel was that rose-bush, petal-soft, sparkling and cool. And he was still that little boy. But there was no running into the garden now, no laughing and shaking. The dull, persistent gnawing in his breast started again. He drew up his legs, tossed the papers aside, and shut his eyes.

"What is it, Isabel? What is it?" he said tenderly. They

were in their bedroom in the new house. Isabel sat on a painted stool before the dressing table that was strewn with little black and green boxes.

"What is what, William?" And she bent forward, and her fine light hair fell over her cheeks.

"Ah, you know!" He stood in the middle of the strange room and he felt a stranger. At that Isabel wheeled round quickly and faced him.

"Oh, William!" she cried imploringly, and she held up the hair-brush: "Please! Please don't be so dreadfully stuffy and—tragic. You're always saying or looking or hinting that I've changed. Just because I've got to know really congenial people, and go about more, and am frightfully keen on—on everything, you behave as though I'd—" Isabel tossed back her hair and laughed—"killed our love or something. It's so awfully absurd"—she bit her lip—"and it's so maddening, William. Even this new house and the servants you grudge me."

"Isabel!"

"Yes, yes, it's true in a way," said Isabel quickly. "You think they are another bad sign. Oh, I know you do. I feel it," she said softly, "every time you come up the stairs. But we couldn't have gone on living in that other poky little hole, William. Be practical, at least! Why, there wasn't enough room for the babies even."

No, it was true. Every morning when he came back from chambers it was to find the babies with Isabel in the back drawing-room. They were having rides on the leopard skin thrown over the sofa back, or they were playing shops with Isabel's desk for a counter, or Pad was sitting on the hearthrug rowing away for dear life with a little brass fire shovel, while Johnny shot at pirates with the tongs. Every evening they each had a pick-a-back up the narrow stairs to their fat old Nanny.

Yes, he supposed it was a poky little house. A little white house with blue curtains and a window-box of petunias. William met their friends at the door with "Seen our petunias? Pretty terrific for London, don't you think?"

But the imbecile thing, the absolutely extraordinary thing was that he hadn't the slightest idea that Isabel wasn't as happy as he. God, what blindness! He hadn't the remotest notion in those days that she really hated that inconvenient little house, that she thought the fat Nanny was ruining the babies, that she was desperately lonely, pining for new people and new music and pictures and so on. If they hadn't gone to that studio party at Moira Morrison's—if Moira Morrison hadn't said as they were leaving, "I'm going to rescue your wife, selfish man. She's like an exquisite little Titania"—if Isabel hadn't gone with Moira to Paris—if—if . . .

The train stopped at another station. Bettingford. Good heavens! They'd be there in ten minutes. William stuffed the papers back into his pockets; the young man opposite had long since disappeared. Now the other two got out. The late afternoon sun shone on women in cotton frocks and little sunburnt, barefoot children. It blazed on a silky yellow flower with coarse leaves which sprawled over a bank of rock. The air ruffling through the window smelled of the sea. Had Isabel the same crowd with her this week-end, wondered William?

And he remembered the holidays they used to have, the four of them, with a little farm girl, Rose, to look after the babies. Isabel wore a jersey and her hair in a plait; she looked about fourteen. Lord! how his nose used to peel! And the amount they ate, and the amount they slept in that immense feather bed with their feet locked together. . . . William couldn't help a grim smile as he thought of Isabel's horror if she knew the full extent of his sentimentality.

"Hillo, William!" She was at the station after all, standing just as he had imagined, apart from the others, and—William's heart leapt—she was alone.

"Hallo, Isabel!" William stared. He thought she looked so beautiful that he had to say something, "You look very cool."

"Do I?" said Isabel. "I don't feel very cool. Come along, your horrid old train is late. The taxi's outside." She put her hand lightly on his arm as they passed the ticket collector. "We've all come to meet you," she said. "But we've left Bobby Kane at the sweet shop, to be called for."

"Oh!" said William. It was all he could say for the moment.

There in the glare waited the taxi, with Bill Hunt and Dennis Green sprawling on one side, their hats tilted over their faces, while on the other, Moira Morrison, in a bonnet like a huge strawberry, jumped up and down.

"No ice! No ice! No ice!" she shouted gaily.

And Dennis chimed in from under his hat. "*Only* to be had from the fishmonger's."

And Bill Hunt, emerging, added, "With *whole* fish in it."

"Oh, what a bore!" wailed Isabel. And she explained to William how they had been chasing round the town for ice while she waited for him. "Simply everything is running down the steep cliffs into the sea, beginning with the butter."

"We shall have to anoint ourselves with the butter," said Dennis. "May thy head, William, lack not ointment."

"Look here," said William, "how are we going to sit? I'd better get up by the driver."

"No, Bobby Kane's by the driver," said Isabel. "You're to sit between Moira and me." The taxi started. "What have you got in those mysterious parcels?"

"De-cap-it-ated heads!" said Bill Hunt, shuddering beneath his hat.

"Oh, fruit!" Isabel sounded very pleased. "Wise William! A melon and a pineapple. How too nice!"

"No, wait a bit," said William, smiling. But he really was anxious. "I brought them down for the kiddies."

"Oh, my dear!" Isabel laughed, and slipped her hand through his arm. "They'd be rolling in agonies if they were to eat them. No"—she patted his hand—"you must bring them something next time. I refuse to part with my pineapple."

"Cruel Isabel! Do let me smell it!" said Moira. She flung her arms across William appealingly. "Oh!" The strawberry bonnet fell forward: she sounded quite faint.

"A Lady in Love with a Pineapple," said Dennis, as the taxi drew up before a little shop with a striped blind. Out came Bobby Kane, his arms full of little packets.

"I do hope they'll be good. I've chosen them because of the colours. There are some round things which really look too divine. And just look at this nougat," he cried ecstatically, "just look at it! It's a perfect little ballet."

But at that moment the shopman appeared. "Oh, I forgot. They're none of them paid for," said Bobby, looking frightened. Isabel gave the shopman a note, and Bobby was radiant again. "Hallo, William! I'm sitting by the driver." And bareheaded, all in white, with his sleeves rolled up to the shoulders, he leapt into his place. "Avanti!" he cried. . . .

After tea the others went off to bathe, while William stayed and made his peace with the kiddies. But Johnny and Paddy were asleep, the rose-red glow had paled, bats were flying, and still the bathers had not returned. As William wandered downstairs, the maid crossed the hall carrying a lamp. He followed her into the sitting-room. It was a long room, coloured yellow. On the wall opposite William some one had painted a young man, over life-size, with very wobbly legs, offering a wide-eyed daisy to a young woman who had one

very short arm and one very long, thin one. Over the chairs
and sofa there hung strips of black material, covered with big
splashes like broken eggs, and everywhere one looked there
seemed to be an ash-tray full of cigarette ends. Williams sat
down in one of the arm-chairs. Nowadays, when one felt with
one hand down the sides, it wasn't to come upon a sheep with
three legs or a cow that had lost one horn, or a very fat dove
out of the Noah's Ark. One fished up yet another little paper-
covered book of smudged-looking poems. . . . He thought of
the wad of papers in his pocket, but he was too hungry and
tired to read. The door was open; sounds came from the
kitchen. The servants were talking as if they were alone in
the house. Suddenly there came a loud screech of laughter
and an equally loud "Sh!" They had remembered him. William got up and went through the French windows into the
garden, and as he stood there in the shadow he heard the
bathers coming up the sandy road; their voices rang through
the quiet.

"I think it's up to Moira to use her little arts and wiles."

A tragic moan from Moira.

"We ought to have a gramophone for the week-ends that
played 'The Maid of the Mountains.' "

"Oh no! Oh no!" cried Isabel's voice. "That's not fair to
William. Be nice to him, my children! He's only staying until
to-morrow evening."

"Leave him to me," cried Bobby Kane. "I'm awfully good
at looking after people."

The gate swung open and shut. William moved on the
terrace; they had seen him. "Hallo, William!" And Bobby
Kane, flapping his towel, began to leap and pirouette on the
parched lawn. "Pity you didn't come, William. The water was
divine. And we all went to a little pub afterwards and had
sloe gin."

The others had reached the house. "I say, Isabel," called
Bobby, "would you like me to wear my Nijinsky dress to-
night?"

"No," said Isabel, "nobody's going to dress. We're all
starving. William's starving, too. Come along, *mes amis*, let's
begin with sardines."

"I've found the sardines," said Moira, and she ran into the
hall, holding a box high in the air.

"A Lady with a Box of Sardines," said Dennis gravely.

"Well, William, and how's London?" asked Bill Hunt,
drawing the cork out of a bottle of whisky.

"Oh, London's not much changed," answered William.

"Good old London," said Bobby, very hearty, spearing a sardine.

But a moment later William was forgotten. Moira Morrison began wondering what colour one's legs really were under water.

"Mine are the palest, palest mushroom colour."

Bill and Dennis ate enormously. And Isabel filled glasses, and changed plates, and found matches, smiling blissfully. At one moment she said, "I do wish, Bill, you'd paint it."

"Paint what?" said Bill loudly, stuffing his mouth with bread.

"Us," said Isabel, "round the table. It would be so fascinating in twenty years' time."

Bill screwed up his eyes and chewed. "Light's wrong," he said rudely, "far too much yellow"; and went on eating. And that seemed to charm Isabel, too.

But after supper they were all so tired they could do nothing but yawn until it was late enough to go to bed. . . .

It was not until William was waiting for his taxi the next afternoon that he found himself alone with Isabel. When he brought his suit-case down into the hall, Isabel left the others and went over to him. She stooped down and picked up the suit-case. "What a weight!" she said, and she gave a little awkward laugh. "Let me carry it! To the gate."

"No, why should you," said William. "Of course not. Give it to me."

"Oh, please do let me," said Isabel. "I want to, really." They walked together silently. William felt there was nothing to say now.

"There," said Isabel triumphantly, setting the suit-case down, and she looked anxiously along the sandy road. "I hardly seem to have seen you this time," she said breathlessly. "It's so short, isn't it? I feel you've only just come. Next time—" The taxi came into sight. "I hope they look after you properly in London. I'm so sorry the babies have been out all day, but Miss Neil had arranged it. They'll hate missing you. Poor William, going back to London." The taxi turned. "Goodbye!" She gave him a little hurried kiss; she was gone.

Fields, trees, hedges streamed by. They shook through the empty, blind-looking little town, ground up the steep pull to the station.

The train was in. William made straight for a first-class smoker, flung back into the corner, but this time he let the papers alone. He folded his arms against the dull, persistent gnawing, and began in his mind to write a letter to Isabel.

The post was late as usual. They sat outside the house in long chairs under coloured parasols. Only Bobby Kane lay on the turf at Isabel's feet. It was dull, stifling; the day drooped like a flag.

"Do you think there will be Mondays in Heaven?" asked Bobby childishly.

And Dennis murmured, "Heaven will be one long Monday."

But Isabel couldn't help wondering what had happened to the salmon they had for supper last night. She had meant to have fish mayonnaise for lunch and now . . .

Moira was asleep. Sleeping was her latest discovery. "It's *so* wonderful. One simply shuts one's eyes, that's all. It's *so* delicious."

When the old ruddy postman came beating along the sandy road on his tricycle one felt the handlebars ought to have been oars.

Bill Hunt put down his book. "Letters," he said complacently, and they all waited. But, heartless postman—O malignant world! There was only one, a fat one for Isabel. Not even a paper.

"And mine's only from William," said Isabel mournfully.

"From William—already?"

"He's sending you back your marriage lines as a gentle reminder."

"Does everybody have marriage lines? I thought they were only for servants."

"Pages and pages! Look at her! A Lady reading a Letter," said Dennis.

My darling, precious Isabel. Pages and pages there were. As Isabel read on her feeling of astonishment changed to a stifled feeling. What on earth had induced William . . . ? How extraordinary it was. . . What could have made him . . . ? She felt confused, more and more excited, even frightened. It was just like William. Was it? It was absurd, of course, it must be absurd, ridiculous. "Ha, ha, ha! Oh dear!" What was she to do? Isabel flung back in her chair and laughed till she couldn't stop laughing.

"Do, do tell us," said the others. "You must tell us."

"I'm longing to," gurgled Isabel. She sat up, gathered the

letter, and waved it at them. "Gather round," she said. "Listen, it's too marvellous. A love-letter!"

"A love-letter! But how divine!" *Darling, precious Isabel.* But she had hardly begun before their laughter interrupted her.

"Go on, Isabel, it's perfect."

"It's the most marvellous find."

"Oh, do go on, Isabel!"

God forbid, my darling, that I should be a drag on your happiness.

"Oh! oh! oh!"

"Sh! sh! sh!"

And Isabel went on. When she reached the end they were hysterical: Bobby rolled on the turf and almost sobbed.

"You must let me have it just as it is, entire, for my new book," said Dennis firmly. "I shall give it a whole chapter."

"Oh, Isabel," moaned Moira, "that wonderful bit about holding you in his arms!"

"I always thought those letters in divorce cases were made up. But they pale before this."

"Let me hold it. Let me read it, mine own self," said Bobby Kane.

But to their surprise, Isabel crushed the letter in her hand. She was laughing no longer. She glanced quickly at them all; she looked exhausted. "No, not just now. Not just now," she stammered.

And before they could recover she had run into the house, through the hall, up the stairs into her bedroom. Down she sat on the side of the bed. "How vile, odious, abominable, vulgar," muttered Isabel. She pressed her eyes with her knuckles and rocked to and fro. And again she saw them, but not four, more like forty, laughing, sneering, jeering, stretching out their hands while she read them William's letter. Oh, what a loathsome thing to have done. How could she have done it! *God forbid, my darling, that I should be a drag on your happiness.* William! Isabel pressed her face into the pillow. But she felt that even the grave bedroom knew her for what she was, shallow, tinkling, vain. . . .

Presently from the garden below there came voices.

"Isabel, we're all going for a bathe. Do come!"

"Come, thou wife of William!"

"Call her once before you go, call once yet!"

Isabel sat up. Now was the moment, now she must decide. Would she go with them, or stay here and write to William.

Which, which should it be? "I must make up my mind." Oh, but how could there be any question? Or course she would stay here and write.

"Titania!" piped Moira.

"Isa-bel?"

No, it was too difficult. "I'll—I'll go with them, and write to William later. Some other time. Later. Not now. But I shall *certainly* write," thought Isabel hurriedly.

And, laughing in the new way, she ran down the stairs.

Stella Benson
(1892–1933)

Stella Benson was born in England, traveled extensively on the continent and in America, and lived for a lengthy period of time in China. Although she was an essayist, novelist, and poet, her best work was done in shorter fictional forms. Her Collected Short Stories *was published posthumously, in 1936.*

The Man Who Missed the Bus

Mr. Robinson's temper was quite sore by the time he reached St. Pierre. The two irritations that most surely found the weak places in his nervous defenses were noise and light in his eyes. And, as he told Monsieur Dupont, the proprietor of Les Trois Moineaux at St. Pierre, "If there is one thing, monsieur, that is offensive—essentially offensive—that is to say, a danger in itself—I mean to say noise doesn't have to have a meaning. . . . What I mean is, monsieur, that noise—"

"*Numéro trente,*" said Monsieur Dupont to the chasseur.

Mr. Robinson always had to explain things very thoroughly in order to make people really appreciate the force of what he had to say; and even then it was a hard task to get them to acknowledge receipt, so to speak, of his message. But he was a humble man, and he accounted for the atmosphere of unanswered and unfinished remarks in which he lived by admitting that his words were unfortunately always inadequate to convey to a fellow-mortal the intense interest to be found in the curiosities of behavior and sensation. His mind was overstocked with by-products of the business of life. He felt that every moment disclosed a new thing worth thinking of among the phenomena that his senses presented to him. Other people, he saw, let these phenomenal moments slip by unanalyzed; but if he had had the words and the courage, he felt, he could have awakened those of his fellow-creatures whom he met from their trance of shallow living. As it was, the relation of his explorations and wonderings sounded, even to his own ears, flat as the telling at breakfast of an ecstatic dream.

What he had meant to say about noise, for instance, had been that noise was *in itself* terrifying and horrible—not as a warning of danger but as a physical assault. Vulgar people treat noise only as a language that *means* something, he would have said, but really noise could not be translated, any more than rape could be translated. There was no such thing as an ugly harmless noise. The noise of an express train approaching and shrieking through a quiet station; the noise of heavy rain sweeping towards one through a forest; the noise of loud concerted laughter at an unheard joke—all benevolent noises if translated into concrete terms, were *in themselves* calamities. All this Mr. Robinson would have thought worth saying to Monsieur Dupont—worth continuing to say until Monsieur Dupont should have confessed to an understanding of his meaning; but as usual the words collapsed as soon as they left Mr. Robinson's lips.

Monsieur Dupont stood in the doorway of Les Trois Moineaux with his back to the light. Mr. Robinson could see the shape of his head set on stooping shoulders, with a little frail fluff of hair beaming round a baldness. He could see the rather crumpled ears with outleaning lobes bulging sharply against the light. But between ear and ear, between bald brow and breast he could see nothing but a black blank against the glare. Mr. Robinson had extremely acute sight—perhaps too acute, as he often wanted to tell people, since this was perhaps why the light in his eyes affected him so painfully.

"If my sight were less acute," he would have said, "I should not mind a glare so much—I mean to say, my eyes are so extremely receptive that they receive too much, or in other words the same cause that makes my eyes so very sensitive is . . ."

But nobody ever leaned forward eagerly and said, "I understand you perfectly, Mr. Robinson, and what you say is most interesting. Your sight includes so much that it cannot exclude excessive light, and this very naturally irritates your nerves, though the same peculiarity accounts for your intense powers of observation." Nobody ever said anything like that, but then, people are so self-engrossed.

Mr. Robinson was not self-engrossed—he was simply extravagantly interested in *things*, not people. For instance, he looked round now, as the chasseur sought in the shadows for his suitcase, and saw the terrace striped by long beams of light—broad flat beams that were strung like yellow sheets from every window and door in the hotel to the trees, tall urns, and tables of the terrace. A murmur of voices enlivened the air, but there were no human creatures in any beam— only blocked dark figures in the shadows—and, in every patch of light, a sleeping dog or cat or two. Dogs and cats lay extended or curled comfortably on the warm uneven paving stones, and Mr. Robinson's perfect sight absorbed the shape of every brown, tortoise-shell, or black marking on their bodies, as a geographer might accept the continents on a new unheard-of globe.

"It's just like geography—the markings on animals," Mr. Robinson had once said to an American who couldn't get away. "What I mean to say is that the markings on a dog or a rabbit have just as much sense as the markings on this world of ours—or in other words the archipelagoes of spots on this pointer puppy are just as importantly isolated from one another as they could be in any Adriatic sea."

But the American had only replied, "Why, no, Mr. Robinson, not half so important; I am taking my wife, with the aid of the American Express Company, to visit the Greek islands this summer; and we shall be sick on the sea and robbed on the land—whereas nobody but a flea ever visits the spots on that puppy, and the flea don't know and don't care a damn what color he bites into." Showing that nobody except Mr. Robinson ever really studied things impersonally.

Mr. Robinson, a very ingenious-minded and sensitive man with plenty of money, was always seeking new places to go to, where he might be a success—or rather, where his unaccountable failures elsewhere might not be known. St. Pierre, he thought, was an excellent venture, although the approach to it had been so trying. As soon as he had heard of it— through reading a short thoughtless sketch by a popular novelist in the *Daily Call*—he had felt hopeful about it. A little Provençal walled town on a hill, looking out over vineyards to the blue Mediterranean; a perfect little hotel—clean and with a wonderful cook—frequented by an interesting few. . . .

"By the time I get downstairs," thought Mr. Robinson as he carefully laid his trousers under the mattress in his room and donned another pair, "the lights will be lighted on the terrace, and I shall be able to see my future friends. I must tell some one about that curious broken reflection in the river Rhone."

He went downstairs and out onto the terrace, where the tinkle of glasses and plates made him feel hungry. He could hear, as he stood in the doorway looking out, one man's voice making a series of jokes in quick succession, each excited pause in his voice being filled by a gust and scrape of general laughter—like waves breaking on a beach with a clatter and then recoiling with a thin, hopeful, lonely sound. "Probably all his jokes are personalities," thought Mr. Robinson, "and, therefore, not essentially funny. No doubt they are slightly pornographic, at that. When will people learn how interesting and exciting *things* are? . . ."

A waiter behind him drew out a chair from a table in one of the squares of light thrown from a window. Mr. Robinson, after sitting down abstractedly, was just going to call the waiter back to tell him that his eyes were ultra-sensitive to light and that he could see nothing in that glare, when a large dog, with the bleached, patched, innocent face of a circus clown, came and laid its head on his knee. Mr. Robinson could never bear to disappoint an animal. He attributed to animals all the hot and cold variations of feeling that he himself habitually experienced, identifying the complacent fur of the brute with his own thin human skin. So that when the waiter, coming quietly behind him, put the wine list into his hand, Mr. Robinson merely said, "Thank you, garçon, but I never touch alcohol in any form—or, for the matter of that, tobacco either. In my opinion—" and did not call the rapidly escaping waiter back to ask him to move his table. The dog's chin was now comfortably pressed against his knee, and the dog's paw hooked in a pathetically prehensile way about his ankle.

Mr. Robinson made the best of his position in the dazzle and tried to look about him. The Trois Moineaux was built just outside the encircling wall of the tightly corseted little town of St. Pierre and, since St. Pierre clung to the apex of a conical hill, it followed that the inn terrace jutted boldly out over a steep, stepped fall of vineyards overhanging the plain. The plain was very dim now, overlaid by starlit darkness, yet at the edge of the terrace there was a sense of *view*, and all the occupied tables stood in a row against the low wall, diluting the food and drink they bore with starlight and space. The men and women sitting at these tables all had their faces to the world and their backs to Mr. Robinson. He could not see a single human face. He had come down too late to secure one of the outlooking tables, and his place was imprisoned in a web of light under an olive tree. In the middle of the table, peaches and green grapes were heaped on a one-legged dish. And on the edge of the dish a caterpillar waved five-sixths of its length drearily in the air, unable to believe that its world could really end at this abrupt slippery rim. Mr. Robinson, shading his eyes from the light, could see every detail of the caterpillar's figure, and it seemed to him worth many minutes of absorbed attention. Its color was a pale greenish-fawn, and it had two dark bumps on its brow by way of eyes.

"How unbearably difficult and lonely its life would seem to us," thought Mr. Robinson, leaning intensely over it. "How frightful if by mistake the merest spark of self-consciousness should get into an insect's body (an accidental short-circuit in the life current, perhaps), and it should know itself absolutely alone—appallingly free." He put his finger in the range of its persistent wavings and watched it crawl with a looping haste down his fingernail, accepting without question a quite fortuitous salvation from its dilemma. He laid his finger against a leaf, and the caterpillar disembarked briskly after its journey across alien elements. When it was gone, Mr. Robinson looked about him, dazed. "My goodness," he thought, "that caterpillar's face is the only one I have seen tonight!"

The noise of chatter and laughter went up like a kind of smoke from the flickering creatures at the tables near the edge of the terrace. At each table the heads and shoulders of men and women leaned together—were sucked together like flames in a common upward draft. "My dear, she looked like a . . . Oh, well, if you want to. . . . He's the kind of man who . . . *No*, my dear, not in my *bedroom*. . . . A rattling good yarn. . . . Stop me if I've told you this one before. . . ." One man, standing up a little unsteadily facing the table nearest to Mr. Robinson, made a speech: ". . . the last time . . . delightful company . . . fair sex . . . happiest hours of my life . . . mustn't waste your time . . . us mere men . . .

as the Irishman said to the Scotchman when . . . happiest
moments of all my life . . . one minute and I shall be done
. . . always remember the happiest days of all my . . . well,
I mustn't keep you . . . I heard a little story the other day.
. . ." And all the time his audence leaned together round
their table, embarrassed, looking away over the dark plain
or murmuring together with bent heads.

The only woman whose face Mr. Robinson might have seen
was shielding her face with her hands and shaking with silent
laughter. The speaker was wavering on his feet very much as
the caterpillar had wavered on its tail, and his wide gestures,
clawing the air in search of the attention of his friends, suggested to Mr. Robinson the caterpillar's wild gropings for
foothold where no foothold was. "Yes," thought Mr. Robinson, "the caterpillar was *my* host. No other face is turned to
me."

However, as he thought this, a man came from a farther
table and stood quite close, under the olive tree, between
Mr. Robinson and the lighted doorway, looking down on him.
The man stretched out his hand to the tree and leaned upon
it. A freak of light caught the broad short hand, walnut-
knuckled and brown, crooked over the bough. Mr. Robinson
could not see the man's face at all, but he felt that the visit
was friendly. To conciliate this sympathetic stranger, he would
even have talked about the weather, or made a joke about
pretty girls or beer; but he could not think of anything of that
kind to say to a man whose hand, grasping an olive bough,
was all that could be known of him. All that Mr. Robinson
could do for the moment was to wonder what could have sent
the man here. "It could not have been," thought Mr. Robinson humbly, "that he was attracted by my face, because
nobody ever is." And then he began thinking how one man's
loss is nearly always another man's gain, if considered broadly
enough. For one to be forsaken, really, means that another
has a new friend.

"This young man," thought Mr. Robinson, gazing at the
black outline of the stranger's head, "has probably come here
blindly, because of some sudden hurt, some stab, some insult,
inflicted by his friends at that table over there—probably by
a woman. Perhaps he thinks he has a broken heart (for he
has young shoulders). Nothing short of a wound that temporarily robbed him of his social balance could make him do
so strange a thing as suddenly to leave his friends and come
here to stand silent by me in the shade. Yet if he only could—

as some day, I am convinced, we all shall—know that the
sum remains the same—that some other lover is the happier
for this loss of his—and that if he had gained a smile from
her, the pain he now feels would simply have been shifted to
another heart—not dispelled . . . We only have to think
impersonally enough, and even death—well, we are all either
nearly dead or just born, more or less, and the balance of
birth and death never appreciably alters. Personal thinking is the cure of existence. Why are we all crushed under
the weight of this strangling *me*—this snake in our
garden . . . ?"

So he said to the young man, "Isn't it a curious thing,
looking round at young people and old people, that it doesn't
really matter if they are born or dead—I mean to say, it's all
the same whatever happens, if you follow me, and so many
people mind when they needn't, if people would only realize—" At this moment there was a burst of clapping from
the far table and the young man bounded from Mr. Robinson's side back to his friends, shouting, "Good egg—have
you thought of a word already? Animal, vegetable, or min-
eral—and remember to speak up because I'm rather hard of
hearing."

Mr. Robinson suddenly felt like Herbert Robinson, personally affronted. The sum of happiness (which of course
remained unaltered by his setback) for a moment did not
matter in the least. He pushed back his chair and walked
away, leaving his cheese uneaten and the clown-faced dog
without support. He went to his bedroom and sat down opposite his mirror, smooth, plump, pale, with small pouched
eyes and thick, straight, wet-looking hair.

"What is this?" asked Mr. Robinson, studying the reflection of his disappointed face—the only human face he had
seen that evening. "Look at me—I *am* alive—I am indeed
very acutely alive—more alive, perhaps, than all these men
and women half-blind—half-dead in their limitations of greed
and sex. . . . It is true I have no personal claim on life; I am
a virgin and I have no friends—yet I live intensely—and there
are—there *are*—there *are* other forms of life than personal
life. The eagle and the artichoke are equally alive; and perhaps my way of life is nearer to the eagle's than the artichoke's. And must I be alone—must I live behind cold shoulders because I see *out* instead of *in*—the most vivid form of
life conceivable, if only it could be lived perfectly?"

He tried to see himself in the mirror, as was his habit, as

a mere pliable pillar of life, a turret of flesh with a prisoner called *life* inside it. He stared himself out of countenance, trying, as it were, to dissolve his poor body by understanding it—poor white, sweating, rubbery thing that was called Herbert Robinson and had no friends. But tonight the prisoner called *life* clung to his prison—tonight his body tingled with egotism—tonight the oblivion that he called wisdom would not come, and he could not become conscious, as he longed to, of the live sky above the roof, the long winds streaming about the valleys, the billions of contented, wary, or terrifed creatures moving about the living dust, weeds, and waters of the world. He remained just Herbert Robinson who had not seen any human face while in the midst of his fellow men.

He began to feel an immediate craving—an almost revengeful lust—to be alone, far from men, books, mirrors, and lights, watching, all his life long, the bodiless, mindless movements of animals—ecstatic living things possessing no *me*. "I should scarcely know I was alive, then, and perhaps never even notice when I died. . . ." He decided he would go away next day, and give no group again the chance to excommunicate him.

He remembered that he had seen a notice at the door of the hotel giving the rare times at which an auto-bus left and arrived at St. Pierre. "I will leave by the early bus, before any one is awake to turn his back on me."

He could not sleep, but lay uneasily on his bed reading the advertisements in a magazine he had brought with him. Advertisements always comforted him a good deal, because advertisers really, he thought, took a broad view; they wrote of—and to—their fellow men cynically and subtly, taking advantage of the vulgar passion for personal address, and yet treating humanity as one intricate mass—an instrument to be played upon. This seemed the ideal standpoint to Mr. Robinson, and yet he was insulted by the isolation such an ideal involved.

He dressed himself early, replaced in his suitcase the few clothes he had taken out, put some notes in an envelope addressed to Monsieur Dupont, and leaned out of the window to watch for the bus. St. Pierre, a sheaf of white-and-pink plaster houses, was woven together on a hill, like a haycock. The town, though compact and crowned by a sharp white bell-tower, seemed to have melted a little, like a thick candle; the centuries and the sun had softened its fortress outlines. The other hills, untopped by towns, seemed much more definitely constructed; they were austerely built of yellow and green blocks of vineyard, cemented by the dusty green of olive trees. Gleaming, white fluffy clouds peeped over the hills—"like kittens," thought Mr. Robinson, who had a fancy for trying to make cosmic comparisons between the small and the big. On the terrace of the inn half a dozen dogs sprawled in the early sun. Over the valley a hawk balanced and swung in the air, so hungry after its night's fast that it swooped rashly and at random several times, and was caught up irritably into the air again after each dash, as though dangling on a plucked thread. Mr. Robinson leaned long on his sill looking at it, until his elbows felt sore from his weight, and he began to wonder where the bus was that was going to take him away to loneliness. He went down to the terrace, carrying his suitcase, and stood in the archway. There was no sound of a coming bus—no sound at all, in fact, except a splashing and a flapping and a murmuring to the left and right of him. A forward step or two showed him that there were two long washing troughs, one on each side of the archway, each trough shaded by a stone gallery and further enclosed in a sort of trellis of leaning kneading women.

Mr. Robinson noticed uneasily that he could not see one woman's face; all were so deeply bent and absorbed. After a moment, however, a woman's voice from the row behind him asked him if he was waiting for the bus. He turned to reply, hoping to break the spell by finding an ingenuous rustic face lifted to look at him. But all the faces were bent once more, and it was another woman behind him again who told him that the bus had left ten minutes before. Once more the speaker bent over her work before Mr. Robinson had time to turn and see her face. "What a curious protracted accident," he thought, and had time to curse his strange isolation before he realized the irritation of being unable to leave St. Pierre for another half dozen hours. He flung his suitcase into the hall of the inn and walked off up a path that led through the vineyards. As if the whole affair had been prearranged, all the dogs on the terrace rose up and followed him, yawning and stretching surreptitiously, like workers reluctantly leaving their homes at the sound of a factory whistle.

Mr. Robinson, true to his habit, concentrated his attention on—or rather diffused it to embrace—the colors about him. The leaves of the vines especially held his eye; they were the same frosty bloom that grapes themselves often wear—a sky-blue dew on the green leaf. Two magpies, with a bottle-green sheen on their wings, gave their police-rattle cry as he came near and then flew off, flaunting their long tails clumsily. A hundred feet higher, where the ground became too steep even for vines, Mr. Robinson found a grove of gnarled old olive trees, edging a thick wood of Spanish chestnuts. Here he sat down and looked between the tree-trunks and over the distorted shadows at the uneven yellow land and the thin blade of mat-blue sea stabbing the farthest hills. The dogs stood round him, expecting him to rise in a minute and lead them on again. Seeing that he still sat where he was, they wagged their tails tolerantly but invitingly. Finally they resigned themselves to the inevitable and began philosophically walking about the grove, sniffing gently at various points in search of a makeshift stationary amusement.

Mr. Robinson watched them with a growing sense of comfort. "Here," he thought, "are the good undeliberate beasts again; I knew they would save me. They don't shut themselves away from life in their little individualites, or account uniquely for their lusts on the silly ground of personality. Their bodies aren't prisons—they're just dormitories. . . ." He delighted in watching the dogs busily engrossed in being alive without self-consciousness. After all, he thought, he did not really depend on men. (For he had been doubting his prized detachment most painfully.)

One of the dogs discovered a mouse-hole and, after thrusting his nose violently into it to verify the immediacy of the smell, began digging, but not very cleverly because he was too large a dog for such petty sports. The other dogs hurried to the spot and, having verified the smell for themselves, stood restively round the first discoverer, wearing the irritable look we all wear when watching some one else bungle over something we feel (erroneously) that we could do very much better ourselves. Finally they pushed the original dog aside and began trying to dig, all in the same spot, but, finding this impossible, they tapped different veins of the same lode-smell. Soon a space of some ten feet square was filled with a perfect tornado of flying dust, clods, grass, and piston-like forepaws. Hind legs remained rooted while forelegs did all the work, but whenever the accumulation of earth to the rear of each dog became inconveniently deep, hindlegs, with a few impatient strong strokes, would dash the heap away to some distance—even as far as Mr. Robinson's boots. Quite suddenly all the dogs, with one impulse, admitted themselves beaten; they concluded without rancor that the area was unmistakably mouseless. They signified their contempt for the place in the usual canine manner, and walked away, sniffing, panting, sniffing again for some new excitement.

Mr. Robinson, who had been, for the duration of the affair, a dog in spirit, expecting at every second that a horrified mouse would emerge from this cyclone of attack, imitated his leaders and quieted down with an insouciance equal to theirs. But he had escaped from the menace of humanity; he was eased—he was sleepy. . . .

He slept for a great many hours, and when he awoke the sunlight was slanting down at the same angle as the hill, throwing immense shadows across the vineyards. The dogs had gone home. And there, on a space of flattened earth between two spreading tree-roots, was a mouse and its family. Mr. Robinson, all mouse now, with no memory of his canine past, lay quite still on his side. The mother mouse moved in spasms, stopping to quiver her nose over invisible interests in the dust. Her brood were like little curled feathers, specks of down blown about by a fitful wind. There seemed to be only one license to move shared by this whole mouse family; when mother stopped, one infant mouse would puff forward, and as soon as its impulse expired, another thistledown brother would glide erratically an inch or two. In this leisurely way the family moved across the space of earth and into the grass, appearing again and again between the green blades. Mr. Robinson lay still, sycophantically reverent.

Between two blades of grass the senior mouse came out onto a little plateau, about eighteen inches away from Mr. Robinson's unwinking eye. At that range Mr. Robinson could see its face as clearly as one sees the face of a wife over a breakfast table. It was a dignified but greedy face; its eyes, in so far as they had any expression at all, expressed a cold heart; its attraction lay in its texture, a delicious velvet—and that the mouse would never allow a human finger, however friendly, to enjoy. It would have guarded its person as a classical virgin guarded her honor. As soon as Mr. Robinson saw the mouse's remote expression he felt as a lost sailor on a sinking ship might feel, who throws his last rope—and no saving hands grasp it.

He heard the sound of human footsteps behind him. There was a tiny explosion of flight beside him—and the mouse family was not there. Through the little grove marched a line of men in single file, going home from their work in the vineyards over the hill. Mr. Robinson sat up and noticed, with a cold heart, that all the men wore the rush hats of the country pulled down against the low last light of the sun, and that not one face was visible.

Mr. Robinson sat for some time with his face in his hands. He felt his eyes with his finger, and the shape of his nose and cheekbone; he bit his finger with his strong teeth. Here was a face—the only human face in the world. Suddenly craving for the sight of that friend behind the mirror, he got up and walked back to the Trois Moineaux. He found himself very hungry, having starved all day; but his isolation gave him a so much deeper sense of lack than did his empty stomach that, although dinner was in progress among the bands of light and shade on the terrace, his first act was to run to his room and stand before the mirror. There was a mistiness in the mirror. He rubbed it with his hand. The mistiness persisted—a compact haze of blankness that exactly covered the reflection of his face. He moved to a different angle—he moved the mirror—he saw clearly the reflection of the room, of his tweed-clad figure, of his tie, of his suitcase in the middle of the floor; but his face remained erased, like an unsatisfactory charcoal sketch. Filled with an extraordinary fear, he stood facing the mirror for some minutes, feeling with tremulous fingers for his eyes, his lips, his forehead. There seemed to him to be the same sensation of haze in his sense of touch as in his eyesight—a nervelessness—a feeling of nauseating contact with a dead thing. It was like touching with an unsuspecting hand one's own limb numbed by cold or by an accident of position.

Mr. Robinson walked downstairs, dazed, and out onto the terrace. As before, the shadowed tables looking out over the edge of the terrace were already surrounded by laughing, chattering parties. Mr. Robinson took his seat, as before, under the olive tree. "Bring me a bottle of . . . Sauterne," he said to the waiter (for he remembered that his late unmarried sister used to sustain upon this wine a reputation for wit in the boarding house in which she had lived). "And, waiter, isn't there a table free looking out at the view? I can't see anything here." It was not the view he craved, of course, but only a point of vantage from which to see the faces of his mysterious noisy neighbors. His need for seeing faces was more immediate than ever, now that his one friend had failed him.

"There will be tables free there in a moment," said the waiter. "They are all going to dance soon. They're only wait-

ing for the moon." And the waiter nodded his shadowed face
towards a distant hill, behind which—looking at this moment
like a great far red fire—the moon was coming up. "Look,
the moon, the moon, the moon, look . . ." every one on the
terrace was saying. And a few moments later, the moon—
now completely round but cut in half by a neat bar of cloud,
took flight lightly from the top of the hill.

There was a scraping of chairs, the scraping of a gramophone, and half a dozen couples of young men and women
began dancing between the tall Italian urns and the olive trees
on the terrace. Mr. Robinson poured himself out a large
tumbler of Sauterne. "Waiter, I don't want a table at the edge
now—I want one near the dancers—I want to see their faces."

"There are no tables free in the center of the terrace now.
Several are vacant at the edge."

"I can see a table there, near the dancers, with only two
chairs occupied. Surely I could sit with them."

"That table is taken by a large party, but most of them are
dancing. They will come back there in a moment."

Mr. Robinson, disregarding the waiter and clutching his
tumbler in one hand and his bottle in the other, strode to the
table he had chosen. "I'm *too* lonely—I must sit here."

"So lonely, poo-oo-oor man," said the woman at the table,
a stout middle-aged woman with high shoulders and a high
bosom clad in saxe-blue sequins. She turned her face towards
him in the pink light of the moon. Mr. Robinson, though
desperate, was not surprised. Her face was the same blank—
the same terrible disc of nothingness that he had seen in his
mirror. Mr. Robinson looked at her companion in dreadful
certainty. A twin blank faced him.

"Sh-lonely, eh?" came a thick young voice out of nothingness. "Well, m'lad, you'll be damn sight lonelier yet in minute
'f y' come buttin' in on—"

"Ow, Ronnie," expostulated his frightful friend—but at
that moment the gramophone fell silent and the dancers came
back to their table. Mr. Robinson scanned the spaces that
should have been their faces one by one; they were like discs
of dazzle seen after unwisely meeting the eye of the sun.

"This old feller sayzzz—lonely—pinched your chair,
Belle—"

"Never mind, duckie," said Belle—and threw herself across
Mr. Robinson's knee. "Plenty of room for little me."

The white emptiness of her face that was no face blocked
out Mr. Robinson's view of the world.

"Oh, my God!" she cried, jumping up suddenly. "I know why he's lonely—why—the man's not alive. Look at his face!"

"I am—I am—I am—" shouted Mr. Robinson in terror. "I'll show you I am . . ." He lurched after her and dragged her among the dancers as the music began again. He shut his eyes. He could hear her wild animal shrieks of laughter and feel her thin struggling body under his hands.

Mr. Robinson sat, quite still but racked by confusion, excitement, and disgust, beside the road on the wall of a vineyard, watching the last star slip down into the haze that enhaloed the hills. The moon had gone long ago. All Mr. Robinson's heart was set on catching the bus this morning; to him the dawn that was even now imperceptibly replacing the starlight was only a herald of the bus and of escape. He had no thoughts and no plans beyond catching the bus. He knew that he was cold, but flight would warm him; that he was hungry and thirsty, but flight would nourish him; that he was exhausted and broken-hearted, but flight would ease and comfort him.

A white glow crowned a hill, behind which the sky had long been pearly, and in a minute an unbearably bright ray shot from the hill into Mr. Robinson's eyes. The dazzling domed brow of the sun rose between a tree and a crag, and a lily-white light rushed into the valley.

The bus, crackling and crunching, waddled round the bend. Mr. Robinson hailed it with a distraught cry and gesture.

"*Enfin . . . très peu de places, m'sieu—n'y a qu'un tout p'tit coin par ici . . .*"

Mr. Robinson had no need now to look at the face of the driver, or at the rows of senseless sunlit ghosts that filled the bus. He knew his curse by now. He climbed into the narrow place indicated beside the driver. The bus lurched on down the narrow winding road that overhung the steep vineyards of the valley. Far below—so far below that one could not see the movement of the water—a yellow stream enmeshed its rocks in a net of plaited strands.

Mr. Robinson sat beside the driver, not looking at that phantom faceless face—so insulting to the comfortable sun—but looking only at the road that was leading him to escape. How far to flee he did not know, but all the hope there was, he felt, lay beyond the farthest turn of the road. After one spellbound look at the sun-blinded face of St. Pierre, clinging to its hivelike hill, he looked forward only, at the winding perilous road.

And his acute eyes saw, in the middle of the way, half a dozen specks of live fur, blowing about a shallow rut. . . . The bus's heavy approach had already caused a certain panic in the mouse family. One atom blew one way, one another; there was a sort of little muddled maze of running mice in the road.

Mr. Robinson's heart seemed to burst. Before he was aware, he had sprung to his feet and seized the wheel of the bus from the driver. He had about twenty seconds in which to watch the mice scuttling into the grass—to watch the low loose wall of the outer edge of the road crumble beneath the plunging weight of the bus. He saw, leaning crazily towards him, the face—the *face*—rolling eyes, tight grinning lips—of the driver, looking down at death. There, far down, was the yellow net of the river, spread to catch them all.

Sylvia Townsend Warner
(1893–1978)

Sylvia Townsend Warner, novelist, short story writer, and poet, first published poetry before turning to fiction. In 1948, her Corner That Held Them *helped establish her reputation as a serious and careful stylist. Throughout her career, the short story dominated, with* The Cat's Cradle Book *in 1940, followed by several other volumes,* Swans on an Autumn River *(1966) and* The Innocent and the Guilty *(1971).*

The Phoenix

Lord Strawberry, a nobleman, collected birds. He had the finest aviary in Europe, so large that eagles did not find it uncomfortable, so well laid out that both humming-birds and snow-buntings had a climate that suited them perfectly. But for many years the finest set of apartments remained empty, with just a label saying: "PHŒNIX. *Habitat: Arabia.*"

Many authorities on bird life had assured Lord Strawberry that the phœnix is a fabulous bird, or that the breed was long extinct. Lord Strawberry was unconvinced: his family had always believed in phœnixes. At intervals he received from his agents (together with statements of their expenses) birds which they declared were the phœnix but which turned out to be orioles, macaws, turkey buzzards dyed orange, etc., or stuffed cross-breeds, ingeniously assembled from various plumages. Finally Lord Strawberry went himself to Arabia, where, after some months, he found a phœnix, won its confidence, caught it, and brought it home in perfect condition.

It was a remarkably fine phœnix, with a charming character—affable to the other birds in the aviary and much attached to Lord Strawberry. On its arrival in England it made a great stir among ornithologists, journalists, poets, and milliners, and was constantly visited. But it was not puffed by these attentions, and when it was no longer in the news, and the visits fell off, it showed no pique or rancour. It ate well, and seemed perfectly contented.

It costs a great deal of money to keep up an aviary. When Lord Strawberry died he died penniless. The aviary came on the market. In normal times the rarer birds, and certainly the phœnix, would have been bid for by the trustees of Europe's great zoological societies, or by private persons in the U.S.A.; but as it happened Lord Strawberry died just after a world war, when both money and bird-seed were hard to come by (indeed the cost of bird-seed was one of the things which had ruined Lord Strawberry). The London *Times* urged in a leader that the phœnix be bought for the London Zoo, saying that a nation of bird-lovers had a moral right to own such a rarity; and a fund, called the Strawberry Phœnix Fund, was opened. Students, naturalists, and schoolchildren contributed according to their means; but their means were small, and there were no large donations. So Lord Strawberry's executors (who had the death duties to consider) closed with the higher offer of Mr. Tancred Poldero, owner and proprietor of Poldero's Wizard Wonderworld.

For quite a while Mr. Poldero considered his phœnix a bargain. It was a civil and obliging bird, and adapted itself readily to its new surroundings. It did not cost much to feed, it did not mind children; and though it had no tricks, Mr. Poldero supposed it would soon pick up some. The publicity of the Strawberry Phœnix Fund was now most helpful. Almost every contributor now saved up another half-crown in order to see the phœnix. Others, who had not contributed to the fund, even paid double to look at it on the five-shilling days.

But then business slackened. The phœnix was as handsome as ever, and as amiable; but, as Mr. Poldero said, it hadn't got Udge. Even at popular prices the phœnix was not really popular. It was too quiet, too classical. So people went instead to watch the antics of the baboons, or to admire the crocodile who had eaten the woman.

One day Mr. Poldero said to his manager, Mr. Ramkin:

"How long since any fool paid to look at the phœnix?"

"Matter of three weeks," replied Mr. Ramkin.

"Eating his head off," said Mr. Poldero. "Let alone the insurance. Seven shillings a week it costs me to insure that bird, and I might as well insure the Archbishop of Canterbury."

"The public don't like him. He's too quiet for them, that's the trouble. Won't mate nor nothing. And I've tried him with no end of pretty pollies, ospreys, and Cochin-Chinas, and the Lord knows what. But he won't look at them."

"Wonder if we could swap him for a livelier one," said Mr. Poldero.

"Impossible. There's only one at a time."

"Go on!"

"I mean it. Haven't you ever read what it says on the label?"

They went to the phœnix's cage. It flapped its wings politely, but they paid no attention. They read:

"PANSY. *Phœnix phœnixissima formosissima arabiana.* This rare and fabulous bird is UNIQUE. The World's Old Bachelor. Has no mate and doesn't want one. When old, sets fire to itself and emerges miraculously reborn. Specially imported from the East."

"I've got an idea," said Mr. Poldero. "How old do you suppose that bird is?"

"Looks in its prime to me," said Mr. Ramkin.

"Suppose," continued Mr. Poldero, "we could somehow get him alight? We'd advertise it beforehand, of course, work up interest. Then we'd have a new bird, and a bird with some romance about it, a bird with a life-story. We could sell a bird like that."

Mr. Ramkin nodded.

"I've read about it in a book," he said. "You've got to give them scented woods and what not, and they build a nest and sit down on it and catch fire spontaneous. But they won't do it till they're old. That's the snag."

"Leave that to me," said Mr. Poldero. "You get those scented woods, and I'll do the ageing."

It was not easy to age the phœnix. Its allowance of food was halved, and halved again, but though it grew thinner its eyes were undimmed and its plumage glossy as ever. The heating was turned off; but it puffed out its feathers against the cold, and seemed none the worse. Other birds were put into its cage, birds of a peevish and quarrelsome nature. They pecked and chivied it; but the phœnix was so civil and amiable that after a day or two they lost their animosity. Then Mr. Poldero tried alley cats. These could not be won by manners, but the phœnix darted above their heads and flapped its golden wings in their faces, and daunted them.

Mr. Poldero turned to a book on Arabia, and read that the climate was dry. "Aha!" said he. The phœnix was moved to a small cage that had a sprinkler in the ceiling. Every night the sprinkler was turned on. The phœnix began to cough. Mr. Poldero had another good idea. Daily he stationed himself in front of the cage to jeer at the bird and abuse it.

When spring was come, Mr. Poldero felt justified in beginning a publicity campaign about the ageing phœnix. The old public favourite, he said, was nearing its end. Meanwhile he tested the bird's reactions every few days by putting a few tufts of foul-smelling straw and some strands of rusty barbed wire into the cage, to see if it were interested in nesting yet. One day the phœnix began turning over the straw. Mr. Poldero signed a contract for the film rights. At last the hour seemed ripe. It was a fine Saturday evening in May. For some weeks the public interest in the ageing phœnix had been working up, and the admission charge had risen to five shillings. The enclosure was thronged. The lights and the cameras were trained on the cage, and a loud-speaker proclaimed to the audience the rarity of what was about to take place.

"The phœnix," said the loud-speaker, "is the aristocrat of bird-life. Only the rarest and most expensive specimens of oriental wood, drenched in exotic perfumes, will tempt him to construct his strange love-nest."

Now a neat assortment of twigs and shavings, strongly scented, was shoved into the cage.

"The phœnix," the loud-speaker continued, "is as capricious as Cleopatra, as luxurious as la du Barry, as heady as a strain of wild gypsy music. All the fantastic pomp and passion of the ancient East, its languorous magic, its subtle cruelties . . ."

"Lawks!" cried a woman in the crowd. "He's at it!"

A quiver stirred the dulled plumage. The phœnix turned its head from side to side. It descended, staggering from its perch. Then wearily it began to pull about the twigs and shavings.

The cameras clicked, the lights blazed full on the cage. Rushing to the loud-speaker Mr. Poldero exclaimed:

"Ladies and gentlemen, this is the thrilling moment the world has breathlessly awaited. The legend of centuries is materializing before our modern eyes. The phœnix . . ."

The phœnix settled on its pyre and appeared to fall asleep.

The film director said:

"Well, if it doesn't evaluate more than this, mark it instructional."

At that moment the phœnix and the pyre burst into flames. The flames streamed upwards, leaped out on every side. In a minute or two everything was burned to ashes, and some thousand people, including Mr. Poldero, perished in the blaze.

Aldous Huxley
(1894–1963)

Aldous Huxley was a product of a distinguished lineage that included Thomas Henry Huxley (his grandfather) and Matthew Arnold; his brothers were Julian and Andrew Fielding Huxley, two eminent scientists. Although he had a conventional gentleman's education, at Eton and Oxford, Aldous Huxley was anything but conventional. His novels and stories, which appeared with great regularity, were cynical and caustic treatments of England and of modern life as a whole. His satiric bent appeared first in Crome Yellow *(1921) and* Antic Hay *(1923) and continued in novels that helped define the very world Huxley was attacking:* Point Counter Point *(1928),* Brave New World *(1932),* Eyeless in Gaza *(1936),* After Many a Summer Dies the Swan *(1939),* Ape and Essence *(1948), and* The Devils of Loudun *(1952). Huxley came to California in the late 1930s and there coupled his disgust with modern life with a sympathetic view of mysticism and the occult. Essays that resulted from this new interest include* Ends and Means *(1937) and* Brave New World Revisited *(1958). A volume of representative, corrosive short stories,* Mortal Coils, *appeared early in his career, in 1922.*

Sir Hercules

The infant who was destined to become the fourth baronet of the name of Lapith was born in the year 1740. He was a very small baby, weighing not more than three pounds at birth, but from the first he was sturdy and healthy. In honour of his maternal grandfather, Sir Hercules Occam of Bishop's Occam, he was christened Hercules. His mother, like many other mothers, kept a notebook, in which his progress from month to month was recorded. He walked at ten months, and before his second year was out he had learnt to speak a number of words. At three years he weighed but twenty-four pounds, and at six, though he could read and write perfectly and showed a remarkable aptitude for music, he was no larger and heavier than a well-grown child of two. Meanwhile, his mother had borne two other children, a boy and a girl, one of whom died of croup during infancy, while the other was carried off by smallpox before it reached the age of five. Hercules remained the only surviving child.

On his twelfth birthday Hercules was still only three feet and two inches in height. His head, which was very handsome and nobly shaped, was too big for his body, but otherwise he was exquisitely proportioned and, for his size, of great strength and agility. His parents, in the hope of making him grow, consulted all the most eminent physicians of the time. Their various prescriptions were followed to the letter, but in vain. One ordered a very plentiful meat diet; another exercise; a third constructed a little rack, modelled on those employed by the Holy Inquisition, on which young Hercules was stretched, with excruciating torments, for half an hour every morning and evening. In the course of the next three years Hercules gained perhaps two inches. After that his growth stopped completely, and he remained for the rest of his life a pigmy of three feet and four inches. His father, who had built the most extravagant hopes upon his son, planning for him in his imagination a military career equal to that of Marlborough, found himself a disappointed man. "I have brought an abortion into the world," he would say, and he took so violent a dislike to his son that the boy dared scarcely come into his presence. His temper, which had been serene, was turned by disappointment to moroseness and savagery. He avoided all company (being, as he said, ashamed to show himself, the father of a *lusus naturæ*, among normal, healthy human beings), and took to solitary drinking, which carried him very rapidly to his grave; for the year before Hercules came of age his father was taken off by an apoplexy. His mother, whose love for him had increased with the growth of his father's unkindness, did not long survive, but little more than a year after her husband's death succumbed, after eating two dozen oysters, to an attack of typhoid fever.

Hercules thus found himself at the age of twenty-one alone in the world, and master of a considerable fortune, including the estate and mansion of Crome. The beauty and intelligence of his childhood had survived into his manly age, and, but for his dwarfish stature, he would have taken his place among the handsomest and most accomplished young men of his time. He was well read in Greek and Latin authors, as well as in all the moderns of any merit who had written in English, French, or Italian. He had a good ear for music, and was no indifferent performer on the violin, which he used to play like a bass viol, seated on a chair with the instrument between his legs. To the music of the harpsichord and clavichord he was extremely partial, but the smallness of his hands made it impossible for him ever to perform upon these instruments. He had a small ivory flute made for him, on which, whenever he was melancholy, he used to play a simple country air or jig, affirming that this rustic music had more power to clear and raise the spirits than the most artificial productions of the masters. From an early age he practised the composition of poetry, but, though conscious of his great powers in this art, he would never publish any specimen of his writing. "My stature," he would say, "is reflected in my verses; if the public were to read them it would not be because I am a poet, but because I am a dwarf." Several MS. books of Sir Hercules's poems survive. A single specimen will suffice to illustrate his qualities as a poet.

> *In ancient days, while yet the world was young,*
> *Ere Abram fed his flocks or Homer sung;*
> *When blacksmith Tubal tamed creative fire,*
> *And Jabal dwelt in tents and Jubal struck the lyre;*
> *Flesh grown corrupt brought forth a monstrous birth*
> *And obscene giants trod the shrinking earth,*
> *Till God, impatient of their sinful brood,*
> *Gave rein to wrath and drown'd them in the Flood.*
> *Teeming again, repeopled Tellus bore*
> *The lubber Hero and the Man of War;*
> *Huge towers of Brawn, topp'd with an empty Skull,*
> *Witlessly bold, heroically dull.*
> *Long ages pass'd and Man grown more refin'd,*
> *Slighter in music but of vaster Mind,*
> *Smiled at his grandsire's broadsword, bow and bill,*
> *And learn'd to wield the Pencil and the Quill.*
> *The glowing canvas and the written page*
> *Immortaliz'd his name from age to age,*
> *His name emblazon'd on Fame's temple wall;*
> *For Art grew great as Humankind grew small.*
> *Thus man's long progress step by step we trace;*

The Giant dies, the hero takes his place; David & Goliath?
The Giant vile, the dull heroic Block:
At one we shudder and at one we mock.
Man last appears. In him the Soul's pure flame
Burns brightlier in a not inord'nate frame.
Of old when Heroes fought and Giants swarmed,
Men were huge mounds of matter scarce inform'd;
Wearied by leavening so vast a mass,
The spirit slept and all the mind was crass.
The smaller carcase of these later days
Is soon inform'd; the Soul unwearied plays
And like a Pharos darts abroad her mental rays.
But can we think that Providence will stay
Man's footsteps here upon the upward way?
Mankind in understanding and in grace
Advanc'd so far beyond the Giants' race?
Hence impious thought! Still led by GOD'S own Hand,
Mankind proceeds towards the Promised Land.
A time will come (prophetic, I descry
Remoter dawns along the gloomy sky),
When happy mortals of a Golden Age
Will backward turn the dark historic page,
And in our vaunted race of Men behold
A form as gross, a Mind as dead and cold,
As we in Giants see, in warriors of old.
A time will come, wherein the soul shall be
From all superfluous matter wholly free:
When the light body, agile as a fawn's,
Shall sport with grace along the velvet lawns.
Nature's most delicate and final birth,
Mankind perfected shall possess the earth.
But ah, not yet! For still the Giants' race,
Huge, though diminish'd, tramps the Earth's fair face;
Gross and repulsive, yet perversely proud,
Men of their imperfections boast aloud.
Vain of their bulk, of all they still retain
Of giant ugliness absurdly vain;
At all that's small they point their stupid scorn
And, monsters, think themselves divinely born.
Sad is the Fate of those, ah, sad indeed,
The rare precursors of the nobler breed!
Who come man's golden glory to foretell,
But pointing Heav'nwards live themselves in Hell.

* . *

As soon as he came into the estate, Sir Hercules set about remodelling his household. For though by no means ashamed of his deformity—indeed, if we may judge from the poem quoted above, he regarded himself as being in many ways superior to the ordinary race of man—he found the presence of full-grown men and women embarrassing. Realizing, too, that he must abandon all ambitions in the great world, he determined to retire absolutely from it and to create, as it were, at Crome a private world of his own, in which all should be proportionable to himself. Accordingly, he discharged all the old servants of the house and replaced them gradually, as he was able to find suitable successors, by others of dwarfish stature. In the course of a few years he had assembled about himself a numerous household, no member of which was above four feet high and the smallest among them scarcely two feet and six inches. His father's dogs, such as setters, mastiffs, greyhounds, and a pack of beagles, he sold or gave away as too large and too boisterous for his house, replacing them by pugs and King Charles spaniels and whatever other breeds of dog were the smallest. His father's stable was also sold. For his own use, whether riding or driving, he had six black Shetland ponies, with four very choice piebald animals of New Forest breed.

Having thus settled his household entirely to his own satisfaction, it only remained for him to find some suitable companion with whom to share this paradise. Sir Hercules had a susceptible heart, and had more than once, between the ages of sixteen and twenty, felt what it was to love. But here his deformity had been a source of the most bitter humiliation, for, having once dared to declare himself to a young lady of his choice, he had been received with laughter. On his persisting, she had picked him up and shaken him like an importunate child, telling him to run away and plague her no more. The story soon got about—indeed, the young lady herself used to tell it as a particularly pleasant anecdote—and the taunts and mockery it occasioned were a source of the most acute distress to Hercules. From the poems written at this period we gather that he meditated taking his own life. In course of time, however, he lived down this humiliation; but never again, though he often fell in love, and that very passionately, did he dare to make any advances to those in whom he was interested. After coming to the estate and finding that he was in a position to create his own world as he desired it, he saw that, if he was to have a wife—which he very much desired, being of an affectionate and, indeed, amorous temper—he must choose her as he had chosen his servants—from among the race of dwarfs. But to find a suitable wife was, he found, a matter of some difficulty; for he would marry none who was not distinguished by beauty and gentle birth. The dwarfish daughter of Lord Bemboro he refused on the ground that besides being a pigmy she was hunchbacked; while another young lady, an orphan belonging to a very good family in Hampshire, was rejected by him because her face, like that of so many dwarfs, was wizened and repulsive. Finally, when he was almost despairing of success, he heard from a reliable source that Count Titimalo, Venetian nobleman, possessed a daughter of exquisite beauty and great accomplishments, who was but three feet in height. Setting out at once for Venice, he went immediately on his arrival to pay his respects to the count, whom he found living with his wife and five children in a very mean apartment in one of the poorer quarters of the town. Indeed, the count was so far reduced in his circumstances that he was even then negotiating (so it was rumoured) with a travelling company of clowns and acrobats, who had had the misfortune to lose their performing dwarf, for the sale of his diminutive daughter Filomena. Sir Hercules arrived in time to save her from this untoward fate, for he was so much charmed by Filomena's grace and beauty, that at the end of three days' courtship he made her a formal offer of marriage, which was accepted by her no less joyfully than by her father, who perceived in an English son-in-law a rich and unfailing source of revenue. After an unostentatious marriage, at which the English ambassador acted as one of the witnesses, Sir Hercules and his bride returned by sea to England, where they settled down, as it proved, to a life of uneventful happiness.

Crome and its household of dwarfs delighted Filomena, who felt herself now for the first time to be a free woman living among her equals in a friendly world. She had many tastes in common with her husband, especially that of music. She had a beautiful voice, of a power surprising in one so small, and could touch A in alt without effort. Accompanied by her husband on his fine Cremona fiddle, which he played, as we have noted before, as one plays a bass viol, she would sing all the liveliest and tenderest airs from the operas and cantatas of her native country. Seated together at the harpsichord, they found that they could with their four hands play all the music written for two hands of ordinary size, a circumstance which gave Sir Hercules unfailing pleasure.

When they were not making music or reading together, which they often did, both in English and Italian, they spent their time in healthful outdoor exercises, sometimes rowing in a little boat on the lake, but more often riding or driving, occupations in which, because they were entirely new to her, Filomena especially delighted. When she had become a perfectly proficient rider, Filomena and her husband used often to go hunting in the park, at that time very much more extensive than it is now. They hunted not foxes nor hares, but rabbits, using a pack of about thirty black and fawn-colored pugs, a kind of dog which, when not overfed, can course a rabbit as well as any of the smaller breeds. Four dwarf grooms, dressed in scarlet liveries and mounted on white Exmoor ponies, hunted the pack, while their master and mistress, in green habits, followed either on the black Shetlands or on the piebald New Forest ponies. A picture of the whole hunt—dogs, horses, grooms, and masters—was painted by William Stubbs, whose work Sir Hercules admired so much that he invited him, though a man of ordinary stature, to come and stay at the mansion for the purpose of executing this picture. Stubbs likewise painted a portrait of Sir Hercules and his lady driving in their green enamelled calash drawn by four black Shetlands. Sir Hercules wears a plum-coloured velvet coat and white breeches; Filomena is dressed in flowered muslin and a very large hat with pink feathers. The two figures in their gay carriage stand out sharply against a dark background of trees; but to the left of the picture the trees fall away and disappear, so that the four black ponies are seen against a pale and strangely lurid sky that has the golden-brown colour of thunderclouds lighted up by the sun.

In this way four years passed happily by. At the end of that time Filomena found herself great with child. Sir Hercules was overjoyed. "If God is good," he wrote in his daybook, "the name of Lapith will be preserved and our rarer and more delicate race transmitted through the generations until in the fullness of time the world shall recognize the superiority of those beings whom now it uses to make mock of." On his wife's being brought to bed of a son he wrote a poem to the same effect. The child was christened Ferdinando in memory of the builder of the house.

With the passage of the months a certain sense of disquiet began to invade the minds of Sir Hercules and his lady. For the child was growing with an extraordinary rapidity. At a year he weighed as much as Hercules had weighed when he was three. "Ferdinando goes *crescendo*," wrote Filomena in her diary. "It seems not natural." At eighteen months the baby was almost as tall as their smallest jockey, who was a man of thirty-six. Could it be that Ferdinando was destined to become a man of the normal, gigantic dimensions? It was a thought to which neither of his parents dared yet give open utterance, but in the secrecy of their respective diaries they brooded over it in terror and dismay.

On his third birthday Ferdinando was taller than his mother and not more than a couple of inches short of his father's height. "To-day for the first time," wrote Sir Hercules, "we discussed the situation. The hideous truth can be concealed no longer: Ferdinando is not one of us. On this, his third birthday, a day when we should have been rejoicing at the health, the strength, and beauty of our child, we wept together over the ruin of our happiness. God give us strength to bear this cross."

At the age of eight Ferdinando was so large and so exuberantly healthy that his parents decided, though reluctantly, to send him to school. He was packed off to Eton at the beginning of the next half. A profound peace settled upon the house. Ferdinando returned for the summer holidays larger and stronger than ever. One day he knocked down the butler and broke his arm. "He is rough, inconsiderate, unamenable to persuasion," wrote his father. "The only thing that will teach him manners is corporal chastisement." Ferdinando, who at this age was already seventeen inches taller than his father, received no corporal chastisement.

One summer holidays about three years later Ferdinando returned to Crome accompanied by a very large mastiff dog. He had bought it from an old man at Windsor who found the beast too expensive to feed. It was a savage, unreliable animal; hardly had it entered the house when it attacked one of Sir Hercules's favourite pugs, seizing the creature in its jaws and shaking it till it was nearly dead. Extremely put out by this occurrence, Sir Hercules ordered that the beast should be chained up in the stable-yard. Ferdinando sullenly answered that the dog was his, and he would keep it where he pleased. His father, growing angry, bade him take the animal out of the house at once, on pain of his utmost displeasure. Ferdinando refused to move. His mother at this moment coming into the room, the dog flew at her, knocked her down, and in a twinkling had very severely mauled her arm and shoulder; in another instant it must infallibly have had her by the throat, had not Sir Hercules drawn his sword and stabbed the animal to the heart. Turning on his son, he ordered him to leave the room immediately, as being unfit to remain in the same place with the mother whom he had nearly murdered. So awe-inspiring was the spectacle of Sir Hercules standing with one foot on the carcase of the gigantic dog, his sword drawn and still bloody, so commanding were his voice, his gestures, and the expression of his face, that Ferdinando slunk out of the room in terror and behaved himself for all the rest of the vacation in an entirely exemplary fashion. His mother soon recovered from the bites of the mastiff, but the effect on her mind of this adventure was ineradicable; from that time forth she lived always among imaginary terrors.

The two years which Ferdinando spent on the Continent, making the Grand Tour, were a period of happy repose for his parents. But even now the thought of the future haunted them; nor were they able to solace themselves with all the diversions of their younger days. The Lady Filomena had lost her voice and Sir Hercules was grown too rheumatical to play the violin. He, it is true, still rode after his pugs, but his wife felt herself too old and, since the episode of the mastiff, too nervous for such sports. At most, to please her husband, she would follow the hunt at a distance in a little gig drawn by the safest and oldest of the Shetlands.

The day fixed for Ferdinando's return came round. Filomena, sick with vague dreads and presentiments, retired to her chamber and her bed. Sir Hercules received his son alone. A giant in a brown travelling-suit entered the room. "Welcome home, my son," said Sir Hercules in a voice that trembled a little.

"I hope I see you well, sir." Ferdinando bent down to shake hands, then straightened himself up again. The top of his father's head reached to the level of his hip.

Ferdinando had not come alone. Two friends of his own age accompanied him, and each of the young men had brought a servant. Not for thirty years had Crome been desecrated by the presence of so many members of the common race of men. Sir Hercules was appalled and indignant, but the laws of hospitality had to be obeyed. He received the young gentlemen with grave politeness and sent the servants to the kitchen, with orders that they should be well cared for.

The old family dining-table was dragged out into the light

and dusted (Sir Hercules and his lady were accustomed to dine at a small table twenty inches high). Simon, the aged butler, who could only just look over the edge of the big table, was helped at supper by the three servants brought by Ferdinando and his guests.

Sir Hercules presided, and with his usual grace supported a conversation on the pleasures of foreign travel, the beauties of art and nature to be met with abroad, the opera at Venice, the singing of the orphans in the churches of the same city, and on other topics of a similar nature. The young men were not particularly attentive to his discourses; they were occupied in watching the efforts of the butler to change the plates and replenish the glasses. They covered their laughter by violent and repeated fits of coughing or choking. Sir Hercules affected not to notice, but changed the subject of the conversation to sport. Upon this one of the young men asked whether it was true, as he had heard, that he used to hunt the rabbit with a pack of pug dogs. Sir Hercules replied that it was, and proceeded to describe the chase in some detail. The young men roared with laughter.

When supper was over, Sir Hercules climbed down from his chair and, giving as his excuse that he must see how his lady did, bade them good-night. The sound of laughter followed him up the stairs. Filomena was not asleep; she had been lying on her bed listening to the sound of enormous laughter and the tread of strangely heavy feet on the stairs and along the corridors. Sir Hercules drew a chair to her bedside and sat there for a long time in silence, holding his wife's hand and sometimes gently squeezing it. At about ten o'clock they were startled by a violent noise. There was a breaking of glass, a stamping of feet, with an outburst of shouts and laughter. The uproar continuing for several minutes, Sir Hercules rose to his feet and, in spite of his wife's entreaties, prepared to go and see what was happening. There was no light on the staircase, and Sir Hercules groped his way down cautiously, lowering himself from stair to stair and standing for a moment on each tread before adventuring on a new step. The noise was louder here; the shouting articulated itself into recognizable words and phrases. A line of light was visible under the dining-room door. Sir Hercules tiptoed across the hall towards it. Just as he approached the door there was another terrific crash of breaking glass and jangled metal. What could they be doing? Standing on tiptoe he managed to look through the keyhole. In the middle of

the ravaged table old Simon, the butler, so primed with drink
that he could scarcely keep his balance, was dancing a jig.
His feet crunched and tinkled among the broken glass, and
his shoes were wet with spilt wine. The three young men sat
round, thumping the table with their hands or with the empty
wine bottles, shouting and laughing encouragement. The three
servants leaning against the wall laughed too. Ferdinando
suddenly threw a handful of walnuts at the dancer's head,
which so dazed and surprised the little man that he staggered
and fell down on his back, upsetting a decanter and several
glasses. They raised him up, gave him some brandy to drink,
thumped him on the back. The old man smiled and hic-
coughed. "To-morrow," said Ferdinando, "we'll have a concerted ballet of the whole household." "With father Hercules
wearing his club and lion-skin," added one of his companions,
and all three roared with laughter.

Sir Hercules would look and listen no further. He crossed
the hall once more and began to climb the stairs, lifting his
knees painfully high at each degree. This was the end; there
was no place for him now in the world, no place for him and
Ferdinando together.

His wife was still awake; to her questioning glance he answered, "They are making mock of old Simon. To-morrow
it will be our turn." They were silent for a time.

At last Filomena said, "I do not want to see to-morrow."

"It is better not," said Sir Hercules. Going into his closet
he wrote in his day-book a full and particular account of all
the events of the evening. While he was still engaged in this
task he rang for a servant and ordered hot water and a bath
to be made ready for him at eleven o'clock. When he had
finished writing he went into his wife's room, and preparing
a dose of opium twenty times as strong as that which she was
accustomed to take when she could not sleep, he brought it
to her, saying, "Here is your sleeping-draught."

Filomena took the glass and lay for a little time, but did
not drink immediately. The tears came into her eyes. "Do
you remember the songs we used to sing, sitting out there
sulla terrazza in summer-time?" She began singing softly in
her ghost of a cracked voice a few bars from Stradella's *"Amor,
amor, non dormir più."* "And you playing on the violin. It
seems such a short time ago, and yet so long, long, long.
Addio, amore. A rivederti." She drank off the draught and,
laying back on the pillow, closed her eyes. Sir Hercules kissed
her hand and tiptoed away, as though he were afraid of wak-

ing her. He returned to his closet, and having recorded his wife's last words to him, he poured into his bath the water that had been brought up in accordance with his orders. The water being too hot for him to get into the bath at once, he took down from the shelf his copy of Suetonius. He wished to read how Seneca had died. He opened the book at random. "But dwarfs," he read, "he held in abhorrence as beng *lusus naturæ* and of evil omen." He winced as though he had been struck. This same Augustus, he remembered, had exhibited in the amphitheatre a young man called Lucius, of good family, who was not quite two feet in height and weighed seventeen pounds, but had a stentorian voice. He turned over the pages. Tiberius, Caligula, Claudius, Nero: it was a tale of growing horror. "Seneca his preceptor, he forced to kill himself." And there was Petronius, who had called his friends about him at the last, bidding them to talk to him, not of the consolations of philosophy, but of love and gallantry, while the life was ebbing away through his opened veins. Dipping his pen once more in the ink he wrote on the last page of his diary: "He died a Roman death." Then, putting the toes of one foot into the water and finding that it was not too hot, he threw off his dressing-gown and, taking a razor in his hand, sat down in the bath. With one deep cut he severed the artery in his left wrist, then lay back and composed his mind to meditation. The blood oozed out, floating through the water in dissolving wreaths and spirals. In a little while the whole bath was tinged with pink. The colour deepened; Sir Hercules felt himself mastered by an invincible drowsiness; he was sinking from vague dream to dream. Soon he was sound asleep. There was not much blood in his small body.

Jean Rhys
(1894–1979)

Jean Rhys was born in Domenica, in the West Indies, the daughter of a Welsh doctor and a Creole mother. She attended school in England and married the Dutch poet Max Hamer, experiencing the bohemian continental life that became the basis for her novels The Left Bank *and* Good Morning, Midnight. Quartet *appeared in 1928,* After Leaving Mr. Mackenzie *in 1930, and then she more or less fell into obscurity until the late 1950s. A BBC dramatization of* Good Morning, Midnight *in 1958 revived interest in her work, and in the 1960s her work was of special concern to feminists. Her later writings include* Tigers Are Better Looking, *a collection of stories, and* Wide Sargasso Sea, *an ingenious novel based on the Charlotte Brontë character in* Jane Eyre, *Bertha Rochester (who was from the West Indies).* Sleep It Off, Lady *appeared in 1976, and an unfinished autobiography,* Smile Please, *was left behind at her death.*

Mannequin

Twelve o'clock. Déjeuner chez Jeanne Veron,[1] Place Vendome.

Anna, dressed in the black cotton, chemise-like garment of the mannequin off duty was trying to find her way along dark passages and down complicated flights of stairs to the underground room where lunch was served.

She was shivering, for she had forgotten her coat, and the garment that she wore was very short, sleeveless, displaying her rose-coloured stocking to the knee. Her hair was flamingly and honestly red; her eyes, which were very gentle in expres-

---

[1] Lunch at Jeanne Veron's.

sion, brown and heavily shadowed with kohl; her face small and pale under its professional rouge. She was fragile, like a delicate child, her arms pathetically thin. It was to her legs that she owed this dazzling, this incredible opportunity.

Madame Veron, white-haired with black eyes incredibly distinguished, who had given them one sweeping glance, the glance of the connoisseur, smiled imperiously and engaged her at an exceedingly small salary. As a beginner, Madame explained, Anna could not expect more. She was to wear the jeune fille[2] dresses. Another smile, another sharp glance.

Anna was conducted from the Presence by an underling who helped her to take off the frock she had worn temporarily for the interview. Aspirants for an engagement are always dressed in a model of the house.

She had spent yesterday afternoon in a delirium tempered by a feeling of exaggerated reality, and in buying the necessary make-up. It had been such a forlorn hope, answering the advertisement.

The morning had been dreamlike. At the back of the wonderfully decorated salons she had found an unexpected sombreness; the place, empty, would have been dingy and melancholy, countless puzzling corridors and staircases, a rabbit warren and a labyrinth. She despaired of ever finding her way.

In the mannequins' dressing-room she spent a shy hour making up her face—in an extraordinary and distinctive atmosphere of slimness and beauty; white arms and faces vivid with rouge; raucous voices and the smell of cosmetics; silken lingerie. Coldly critical glances were bestowed upon Anna's reflection in the glass. None of them looked at her directly. . . . A depressing room, taken by itself, bare and cold, a very inadequate conservatory for these human flowers. Saleswomen in black rushed in and out, talking in sharp voices; a very old woman hovered, helpful and shapeless, showing Anna where to hang her clothes, presenting to her the black garment that Anna was wearing, going to lunch. She smiled with professional motherliness, her little, sharp, black eyes travelling rapidly from la nouvelle's[3] hair to her ankles and back again.

She was Madame Pecard, the dresser.

Before Anna had spoken a word she was called away by a small boy in buttons to her destination in one of the salons:

[2] Young girl.
[3] The newcomer's.

there, under the eye of a vendeuse,[4] she had to learn the way to wear the innocent and springlike air and garb of the jeune fille. Behind a yellow, silken screen she was hustled into a leather coat and paraded under the cold eyes of an American buyer. This was the week when the spring models are shown to important people from big shops all over Europe and America: the most critical week of the season. . . . The American buyer said that he would have that, but with an inch on to the collar and larger cuffs. In vain the saleswoman, in her best English with its odd Chicago accent, protested that that would completely ruin the chic of the model. The American buyer knew what he wanted and saw that he got it.

The vendeuse sighed, but there was a note of admiration in her voice. She respected Americans: they were not like the English, who, under a surface of annoying moroseness of manner, were notoriously timid and easy to turn round your finger.

"Was that all right?" Behind the screen one of the saleswomen smiled encouragingly and nodded. The other shrugged her shoulders. She had small, close-set eyes, a long thin nose and tight lips of the regulation puce colour. Behind her silken screen Anna sat on a high white stool. She felt that she appeared charming and troubled. The white and gold of the salon suited her red hair.

A short morning. For the mannequin's day begins at ten and the process of making up lasts an hour. The friendly saleswoman volunteered the information that her name was Jeannine, that she was in the lingerie, that she considered Anna rudement jolie,[5] that noon was Anna's lunch hour. She must go down the corridor and up those stairs, through the big salon then. . . . Anyone would tell her. But Anna, lost in the labyrinth, was too shy to ask her way. Besides, she was not sorry to have time to brace herself for the ordeal. She had reached the regions of utility and oilcloth: the decorative salons were far overhead. Then the smell of food—almost visible, it was so cloudlike and heavy—came to her nostrils, and high-noted, and sibilant, a buzz of conversation made her draw a deep breath. She pushed a door open.

She was in a big, very low-ceilinged room, all the floor space occupied by long wooden tables with no cloths. . . . She was sitting at the mannequins' table, gazing at a thick and hideous

---

[4] Saleslady.
[5] Very pretty.

white china plate, a twisted tin fork, a wooden-handled stained knife, a tumbler so thick it seemed unbreakable.

There were twelve mannequins at Jeanne Veron's: six of them were lunching, the others still paraded, goddesslike, till their turn came for rest and refreshment. Each of the twelve was of a distinct and separate type: each of the twelve knew her type and kept to it, practising rigidly in clothing, manner, voice and conversation.

Round the austere table were now seated: Babette, the gamine, the traditional blonde enfant: Mona, tall and darkly beautiful, the femme fatale, the wearer of sumptuous evening gowns. Georgette was the garçonne:[6] Simone with green eyes Anna knew instantly for a cat whom men would and did adore, a sleek, white, purring, long-lashed creature. . . . Eliane was the star of the collection.

Eliane was frankly ugly and it did not matter: no doubt Lilith, from whom she was obviously descended, had been ugly too. Her hair was henna-tinted, her eyes small and black, her complexion bad under her thick make-up. Her hips were extraordinarily slim, her hands and feet exquisite, every movement she made was as graceful as a flower's in the wind. Her walk . . . But it was her walk which made her the star there and earned her a salary quite fabulous for Madame Veron's, where large salaries were not the rule. . . . Her walk and her "chic of the devil" which lit an expression of admiration in even the cold eyes of American buyers.

Eliane was a quiet girl, pleasant-mannered. She wore a ring with a beautiful emerald on one long, slim finger, and in her small eyes were both intelligence and mystery.

Madame Pecard, the dresser, was seated at the head of the mannequin's table, talking loudly, unlistened to, and gazing benevolently at her flock.

At other tables sat the sewing girls, pale-faced, black-frocked—the workers, heroically gay, but with the stamp of labour on them: and the saleswomen. The mannequins, with their sensual, blatant charms and their painted faces were watched covertly, envied and apart.

Babette the blonde enfant was next to Anna, and having started the conversation with a few good, round oaths at the quality of the sardines, announced proudly that she could speak English and knew London very well. She began to tell Anna the history of her adventures in the city of coldness,

[6] Perennially single woman.

dark and fogs. . . . She had gone to a job as a mannequin in Bond Street and the villainous proprietor of the shop having tried to make love to her and she being rigidly virtuous, she had left. And another job, Anna must figure to herself, had been impossible to get, for she, Babette, was too small and slim for the Anglo-Saxon idea of a mannequin.

She stopped to shout in a loud voice to the woman who was serving: "Hé, my old one, don't forget your little Babette. . . ."

Opposite, Simone the cat and the sportive Georgette were having a low-voice conversation about the tristeness of a monsieur of their acquaintance. "I said to him," Georgette finished decisively, "Nothing to be done, my rabbit. You have not looked at me well, little one. In my place would you not have done the same?"

She broke off when she realized that the others were listening, and smiled in a friendly way at Anna.

She too, it appeared, had ambitions to go to London because the salaries were so much better there. Was it difficult? Did they really like French girls? Parisiennes?

The conversation became general.

"The English boys are nice," said Babette, winking one divinely candid eye. "I had a chic type who used to take me to dinner at the Empire Palace. Oh, a pretty boy. . . ."

"It is the most chic restaurant in London," she added importantly.

The meal reached the stage of dessert. The other tables were gradually emptying; the mannequins all ordered very strong coffee, several a liqueur. Only Mona and Eliane remained silent; Eliane, because she was thinking of something else; Mona, because it was her type, her genre to be haughty.

Her hair swept away from her white, narrow forehead and her small ears: her long earrings nearly touching her shoulders, she sipped her coffee with a disdainful air. Only once, when the blonde enfant, having engaged in a passage of arms with the waitress and got the worst of it was momentarily discomfited and silent, Mona narrowed her eyes and smiled an astonishingly cruel smile.

As soon as her coffee was drunk she got up and went out.

Anna produced a cigarette, and Georgette, perceiving instantly that here was the sportive touch, her genre, asked for one and lit it with a devil-may-care air. Anna eagerly passed her cigarettes round, but the Mère Pecard interfered weightily. It was against the rules of the house for the mannequins to smoke, she wheezed. The girls all lit their cigarettes and smoked. The Mère Pecard rumbled on: "A caprice, my children. All the world knows that mannequins are capricious. Is it not so?" She appealed to the rest of the room.

As they went out Babette put her arm round Anna's waist and whispered: "Don't answer Madame Pecard. We don't like her. We never talk to her. She spies on us. She is a camel."

That afternoon Anna stood for an hour to have a dress draped on her. She showed this dress to a stout Dutch lady buying for The Hague, to a beautiful South American with pearls, to a silver-haired American gentleman who wanted an evening cape for his daughter of seventeen, and to a hook-nosed odd English lady of title who had a loud voice and dressed, under her furs, in a grey jersey and stout boots.

The American gentleman approved of Anna, and said so, and Anna gave him a passionately grateful glance. For, if the vendeuse Jeannine had been uniformly kind and encouraging, the other, Madame Tienne, had been as uniformly disapproving and had once even pinched her arm hard.

About five o'clock Anna became exhausted. The four white and gold walls seemed to close in on her. She sat on her high white stool staring at a marvellous nightgown and fighting an intense desire to rush away. Anywhere! Just to dress and rush away anywhere, from the raking eyes of the customers and the pinching fingers of Irene.

"I will one day. I can't stick it," she said to herself. "I won't be able to stick it." She had an absurd wish to gasp for air.

Jeannine came and found her like that.

"It is hard at first hein? . . . One asks oneself: Why? For what good? It is all idiot. We are all so. But we go on. Do not worry about Irene." She whispered: "Madame Veron likes you very much. I heard her say so."

At six o'clock Anna was out in the rue de la Paix; her fatigue forgotten, the feeling that now she really belonged to the great, maddening city possessed her and she was happy in her beautifully cut tailor-made and a beret.

Georgette passed her and smiled; Babette was in a fur coat.

All up the street the mannequins were coming out of the shops, pausing on the pavements a moment, making them as gay and as beautiful as beds of flowers before they walked swiftly away and the Paris night swallowed them up.

Liam O'Flaherty
(1896–1984)

Liam O'Flaherty was born in the Aran Islands, off the western coast of Ireland. His background first with the Irish Guards in the British army and then with the Irish Republican Army during the civil war with England prepared him for his best-known novel, The Informer (1925). He followed with several volumes of short and long fictions, Spring Sowing (1926), Famine (1937), and Two Lovely Beasts and Other Stories (1948). His autobiographical works include Two Years (1930) and Shame the Devil (1934). From 1924 to 1950, his output was prodigious, comprising more than forty volumes of novels, short story collections, and autobiographies. His themes were almost always the desperation of the Irish struggle for independence, the violence attendant upon that struggle, and the division within men who, while yearning for independence, also desire something else in their lives.

The Touch

A white mare galloped west along the strand against the fierce Spring wind. Her tail was stretched out stiff and motionless. Flecks of foam dropped from her jaws with each outrush of her breath. Her wide-open nostrils were blood red. Hailstones, carried slantwise at a great speed by the wind's power, struck with a loud noise against the canvas of her straddle. Two horsehair ropes trailed low from the holed bottoms of her wicker panniers which flapped with her heaving gait, their halters whining as they shifted round the pegs of the straddle's wooden yoke. The wind tore loose wisps from the layer of straw that cushioned her back against the rough canvas. The wisps were maintained afloat upon the air by the sweeping blast. They sailed away to the east, in a straggling line, frolicking like butterflies at dance.

Cáit Paudeen Pheadair, a girl of eighteen, sat sideways on the mare's haunches, crouching forward over the straddle yoke. She gripped one of the upright pegs with her mittened left hand. A can of hot tea bundled up in a woolen cloth, was held aloft in her right hand. She wore a heavy dress of purple frieze, a sheepskin jacket, rawhide shoes and a head shawl that was knotted under her chin. Her blue eyes were half-closed for protection against the stinging hail. She rode with skill, in complete union with the movement of the mare.

Over at the western end of the strand, the people of the district had been gathering drift weed from the surf since a long time before dawn. Now there were many cocks of the red weed scattered over the gray sand, up from the curving limit of the breaking waves.

Nearly all the men stopped working when they saw the girl come riding towards them on the white mare at a fierce gallop.

"There is a virgin that is fit partner for a king," one man said.

"By the blade of the lance!" said a second man. "If I were single today, it would be on her finger I'd want to put my ring."

"Aye," said the third, "and in her womb my son."

A young man named Bartla Choilm Brighde was working for Cáit's father as a day laborer that spring. He flushed with anger on hearing these remarks. He was in love with the girl.

"Loose-mouthed devils!" he muttered under his breath, as he came out of the tide with a load of seaweed on his pitchfork. "May the swine be maimed and gouged! I'd like to choke them all."

He glanced towards the girl furtively as he threw the weed from his pitchfork onto the cock. Then he hurried back into the sea for another load. He was anxious to conceal his emotion from the other men. He was chilled to the marrow of his bones after wading back and forth through the icy water for many hours. His hands and feet were numbed. His thighs were scalded. Yet the intensity of his love for the girl made him feel there was a warm fire burning within him. His blood was coursing madly through his veins.

The girl deftly brought the mare to an abrupt halt near her father's gathered weed. Then she leaped to the sand, still holding aloft her can of hot tea.

"God bless the work," she called out gaily to the people.

"You, too," they answered her.

Her father, Paudeen Pheadair Reamoinn, came over in a state of great anger. He was a stooped little man. His crabbed features were distorted by the cold. He was about sixty. His wife had given him no sons. His daughters, with the exception of Cáit, had all emigrated in search of a livelihood. That was why he was obliged to take a laboring man to help him with the sowing that Spring.

"Are you crazy?" he said, catching the mare by the head.

"Why so?" said Cáit.

"For racing this one west along the strand," he said. "That's the reason."

Cáit laughed. She was much taller than her father, a splendid supple girl with the exuberance of health in her wild countenance.

"I couldn't hold her," she said. "It must have been the Spring she felt in her blood. She wanted no part of quick-walking or trotting. She only wanted to gallop. There is no end to her courage, even though she is only a little one."

"You are sillier than your mother," Paudeen said. "God help me, having to deal with the two of ye."

He loosened the bellyband and put his hand in between the straw and the mare's back.

"Aie!" he said. "She's half drowned in her own sweat."

The mare shuddered when she felt the coldness of his hand touching her heated skin.

"Aie!" Paudeen said again. "A silly girl racing this poor creature that's as fat as a pig after her winter's idleness."

Cáit laughed again as she walked over to a big granite rock.

"Ara! That's fool's talk," she said. "That race will only do her good."

Paudeen put the padded tailpiece outside the mare's tail. Then he moved the straddle from side to side, in order to air her heated back. When she began to shiver violently he returned the tailpiece and half-tightened the bellyband.

"Aie!" he said mournfully. "Woe to him who is without a son to tend horses."

He put a small basketful of hay to the mare's head. He took a handful of straw from the straddle and began to rub her legs.

"Aie!" he repeated. "A man is cursed truly, when he has only a female to guide his horses."

Cáit took shelter under the rock and loosened her sheepskin jacket. Her apron was wound around her waist beneath

it. She loosened the apron also and spread the bundle it
contained upon the sand. There were large slices of buttered
griddle cake, boiled eggs, salt, two spoons and two mugs.
When she had everything arranged she unwound a cloth from
the can of tea. She opened the can and poured hot tea into
the mugs.

"Come on over now," she shouted at the two men. "Drink
this warm sup. Don't let it get cold."

Bartla hurried over to the rock. He sat down on his heels,
took off his cap and made the sign of the cross on his forehead.
Cáit handed him a mug.

"God increase you," he said as he accepted it.

"Same to you," she said.

They looked one another in the eyes. They blushed. Even
though the few words they had spoken were those of common
courtesy, they got as shy as if they had disclosed the secret
of their love. Cáit looked away suddenly. Bartla bent over
his food.

Paudeen came over to the rock blowing on his cupped
hands.

"Go on over and catch hold of her head," he said to Cáit,
"for fear she might take fright. She's as wild as the devil on
account of the cold."

He sat down on the sand and put his legs crosswise under
him. He blessed himself hurriedly and began to eat. He bolted
his food like a person half-dead from hunger.

"Lord God!" Cáit said as she handed him a mug of tea.
"Why don't you have patience with your bite?"

"Bad cess to you!" Paudeen said. "Clear off over there."

Cáit went to the mare and began to rub her forehead.
Another shower of hailstones was now falling. The mare was
trying to pull her halter. She was very excited.

"Easy now, treasure," Cáit whispered to her. "Take it easy,
darling. Preoil! My little hag!"

The mare soon lowered her snout to the hay once more,
as she grew quiet under the touch of the girl's gentle hand.

"Hurry up there," Paudeen said to Bartla. "Poor people
can't take the whole day with their meal. Hurry, I say. We
have a lot to do and the day is nearly spent already."

The young man did not speak. Although he had felt faint
from hunger for two hours previously, he was unable to eat
more than a few morsels. He found difficulty in swallowing
even that little. Hunger left him when he saw the holy light
of love in Cáit's eyes as they looked at one another.

Every other time she looked at him he had only seen the gay light of mockery in her eyes. Every other time, her lips smiled when she looked at him. This time her lips did not smile. They had frowned in wonder and awe.

That was why his hunger left him. That was why his throat contracted, making it difficult to swallow. So that, instead of eating, he kept looking back furtively over his shoulder in her direction.

The father soon noticed these furtive glances that the young laborer cast in the direction of his daughter. His anger blazed.

"They say a cat is entitled to look at a princess," he said. "That may be, but it is certain that a boorish land-slave has no such right. The worthless land-slave has no right in the world to look at the daughter of an honorable freeman. Do you understand what I'm saying, son of Choilm Brighde?"

The young man's anger blazed. He looked sharply at Paudeen. There was no outward sign of his anger in any part of his countenance except in his eyes, which shone fiercely. He did not speak.

"Watch out for yourself, I say," the old man continued. "You have only a small garden by the door of your cottage, two goats and an ass. You have neither father, nor brother, nor sister. You have only your mother, and she is sick for the past ten years and she is depending on you like a newborn infant for every little service. Nobody belonging to you ever had land or foreshore in this district. They were only rogues and vagrants, stray people that were driven to our place by the famine long ago."

Bartla jumped to his feet. His hands were trembling with rage.

"You have said enough, son of Pheardair Reomoinn," he cried. "There was never a rogue of my kindred. Only honest, God-fearing people belong to my kindred."

"Devil a bit I care," said Paudeen. "Stay clear of my daughter. It's not on a girl that was born in a house of two cows that a man of two goats should cast eyes."

"You have said enough, old man," Bartla repeated.

"Clear off, then," Paudeen said. "If you have eaten, go on over and be loading weed."

Bartla rushed over to the mare. He pushed aside one of the baskets with his shoulder and tightened the bellyband fiercely. Then he began to load seaweed into the two baskets. When they were full to overflowing, he picked up his fork and continued to load the weed onto the top of the straddle.

Cáit's heart now beat wildly as she watched the young man. The fierce movement of his laboring strength made her intoxicated. She had to lean against the mare's shoulder, with dazed eyes and open lips. Even though hailstones were still falling and striking sharply against the side of her face, she was unaware of their bitter touch. She was only aware of the desire that possessed her heart and soul.

Paudeen noticed her prepossession as he came over from the rock. He understood at once. He halted with his back to the shower. He rubbed his chin with his thumb and forefinger.

"There now!" said he to himself. "That young scoundrel has got hold of her. There now!"

He looked at Bartla. Now he hated the young man bitterly. He hated the young back that was as straight as an oar. He hated the fair hair and the shining blue eyes that were able to drive women to folly with desire.

"Damn him," he said with venom. "The beggar! The devil of a beggar! Without a penny-piece in his pocket! The beggar! I'll soon put an end to his shaping. The stinking fellow!"

He went to the mare and caught up his pitchfork. He began to load seaweed. The two men worked fiercely, one on each side of the mare. The weed was soon heaped high above the straddle in a tower. It was time to throw the first rope.

"Look out for the rope," Paudeen said.

"Let me have it," said Bartla.

Paudeen threw the rope across the top of the load.

"Got it?" he said to Bartla.

The wind blew the rope-end out ahead. It fell across Cáit's bosom. She caught it and handed it to Bartla.

"Did you get it?" Paudeen called again.

Bartla made no answer. When he was taking the rope-end from Cáit, his fingers touched the back of her hand. The two of them started as a result of the touch. They became dizzy.

They let go their hold of the rope-end. They seized one another by the hands. They stood breast to breast. They trembled from head to foot. Their faces were ablaze.

They remained standing breast to breast like that, touching, for several moments. Then Paudeen screamed.

"What the devil ails you, scoundrel?" he yelled. "Why don't you speak?"

Bartla started. He dropped Cáit's hands, picked up the rope-end and tied it around a tooth that projected from the bottom of the basket. Then he threw across the second rope.

"Here it comes," he cried.

Paudeen caught the second rope and tied it around the tooth. When he had his knee against the side of the basket, tightening the rope, the mare let one of her hind legs go dead. The load became unbalanced. It almost fell on top of the old man.

"Stand!" Bartla yelled, as he kicked the mare in the shin.

She returned her weight to the defaulting leg and the load righted itself at once.

"You're all right now," Bartla said to Paudeen. "You can fasten."

Paudeen secured the rope and then he ran over to Bartla's side, his teeth chattering with rage.

"You devil!" he cried. "Were you trying to kill me?"

"It wasn't my fault," Bartla said. "It was how she let her foot go dead."

"You're a dirty scoundrel. There was a day when I'd. . . ."

"You've said enough," Bartla said.

"Scoundrel!" Paudeen said. "Rogue!"

"Shut up," Bartla said. "Don't say anything you might regret, if I were to lose patience with you."

Paudeen went over to his own side of the mare, boasting as he went.

"There was a day," he cried, "when I'd chastise the best men in the place, if they dared insult me."

"I don't hear you," Bartla said.

The young man and Cáit looked at one another. Now there was terror in their eyes and despair. They both understood there was a chasm which could not be bridged standing between them and their love. Bartla stretched out his hand and touched her lightly on the shoulder. Overcome with emotion, she turned away from him and sobbed. She hid her face in the mare's white mane and her whole body shook as she wept. Bartla took his pitchfork and began to work fiercely once more.

The two men loaded seaweed and threw ropes and tightened until there was as much seaweed above the straddle as the mare could carry. The load was like a wet red tower.

"Be off now," Paudeen said sharply to the young man. "Hurry. We have at least ten loads to bring to the potato garden."

Bartla took the halter from Cáit. Now they did not look at one another. He twisted the halter around his left hand, with which he then took hold of the load. He picked up a sea-rod from the cock.

"Go on!" he cried to the mare, flashing the sea-rod by her head. "Twous!"

The mare went forward slowly, up the strand through the cocks of gathered weed, her feet sinking deep into the soft sand, under the heavy load.

"Go on!" Bartla kept shouting angrily, as he shook the sea-rod at her head.

They mounted the slope onto the sand bank that bound the road, a red tower walking on long white feet and a young man guiding it.

Cáit went over to the rock and knelt beside the remains of the meal. Then she watched Bartla with longing until he went from sight. Darkness fell upon her soul when he disappeared beyond the sand bank, just as if she would never see him again. Indeed, she knew that she had just suffered an eternal loss. When she tried to pick up the gear she discovered that she was unable to lift the lightest object. She had to lower her head on her bosom and give way once more to her tears.

Paudeen also stood looking after the young man until he was out of sight. The old man was talking to himself and there was an evil expression on his countenance.

"There, now!" he was saying. "Nice kettle of fish. A dirty beggar planning to come into my house as son-in-law. I'll soon put an end to his foolish ideas. The beggar!"

He went east along the strand to the place where Marcus Joyce was working.

"Listen," he said to Marcus.

Marcus was a big strong man with a head of red hair. He and Paudeen took shelter under a cock of weed, both of them sitting on their heels. They lighted a pipe.

"You were talking of a match a short while ago," Paudeen said.

"I was," said Marcus. "I was thinking of that second son I have, Red Mike."

"A good man, God bless him," Paudeen said. "I've no fault with him at all, but with the amount of money you intended to give him and he getting a lovely girl as well as two-fourths of land."

" 'Faith two hundred and fifty is no trifle," Marcus said.

"Put another hundred with it," Paudeen said, "and that makings of a bull you have. The yearling."

"Oh! You devil!" Marcus said. "Where would I get that riches?"

"Listen, Marcus," Paudeen said. "Whisper. You have half a score of Roscommon sheep and . . ."

When Cáit had wept a little she was able to gather up her belongings. She tied the bundle under her jacket and then looked round for her father. When she saw him in earnest conversation with Marcus Joyce under the cock of seaweed she took great fright. She made the sign of the cross on her lips.

"God between me and misfortune!" she said earnestly.

She knew well that they spoke of a match between her and Red Mike. She also knew that the match was practically settled, judging by their gestures. The two men were striking one another's palms forcefully and shouldering one another and passing the pipe after every few words. These were indications that the bargain was already concluded, except for the minor details.

"Oh! Lord God!" Cáit said to herself, as she hurried east along the strand towards her home. "The damage is done. He has sold me to Red Mike Joyce, just as if I were a cow or a sheep."

She mounted the sand bank and then went south along the narrow road that led to her village. Another great shower of hailstones came. She took shelter under the fence that bound the road. She sat on the ground with her back to the fence, a finger between her teeth, staring at the ground, with her mind a blank. Then she suddenly thought of Bartla. She started just as if she had been struck. Her eyes opened wide and she stared at the opposite fence.

At first she thought of his hands touching her hands and of his bosom touching her bosom. She thought of the intoxication produced in her being by that touch.

Then the suffering of eternal hell came upon her with the memory of that touch; for it was manifest to her that this first touch of love would be her last.

A wail of despair came to her throat but it went no farther up into her mouth. She only stared in silence at the far fence and at the cold hailstones that lashed against the cold gray stones.

Aie! Aie! Hailstones! Cold hailstones and a young girl staring without tears at her stillborn love.

Elizabeth Bowen
(1899–1973)

Born in Dublin, Elizabeth Bowen is a novelist and short story writer whose work straddles England and Ireland. She is known primarily for a group of novels that appeared within a fifteen-year period: The House in Paris *(1936),* The Death of the Heart *(1938), and* The Heat of the Day *(1949). To these should be added* To the North *(1932) and several volumes of short stories:* Look at All Those Roses *(1941),* Ivy Gripped the Steps *(1946), and* A Day in the Dark and Other Stories *(1965). She also wrote several nonfiction works, which are semiautobiographical in content:* Bowen's Court *(1942),* The Shelbourne Hotel *(1951),* Seven Winters, *and* Afterthoughts *(1962). In both her novels and stories, Bowen's characteristic subject matter was in the tradition of Virginia Woolf and Katherine Mansfield—psychological rather than realistic, stressing moments or "epiphanies" rather than social activity. In* Notes on Writing a Novel, *Bowen defined the object of a novel as the "non-poetic statement of a poetic truth," further qualifying that the "essence of a poetic truth is that no statement of it can be final." These ideas are perhaps best exemplified in what is her masterpiece,* The Death of the Heart.

The Demon Lover

Toward the end of her day in London Mrs. Drover went round to her shut-up house to look for several things she wanted to take away. Some belonged to herself, some to her family, who were by now used to their country life. It was late August; it had been a steamy, showery day: at the moment the trees down the pavement glittered in an escape of humid yellow afternoon sun. Against the next batch of clouds, already piling up ink-dark, broken chimneys and parapets

stood out. In her once familiar street, as in any unused channel, an unfamiliar queerness had silted up; a cat wove itself
in and out of railings, but no human eye watched Mrs. Drover's return. Shifting some parcels under her arm, she slowly
forced round her latchkey in an unwilling lock, then gave the
door, which had warped, a push with her knee. Dead air
came out to meet her as she went in.

The staircase window having been boarded up, no light
came down into the hall. But one door, she could just see,
stood ajar, so she went quickly through into the room and
unshuttered the big window in there. Now the prosaic woman,
looking about her, was more perplexed than she knew by
everything that she saw, by traces of her long former habit
of life—the yellow smoke-stain up the white marble mantelpiece, the ring left by a vase on the top of the escritoire; the
bruise in the wallpaper where, on the door being thrown open
widely, the china handle had always hit the wall. The piano,
having gone away to be stored, had left what looked like
claw-marks on its part of the parquet. Though not much dust
had seeped in, each object wore a film of another kind; and,
the only ventilation being the chimney, the whole drawing
room smelled of the cold hearth. Mrs. Drover put down her
parcels on the escritoire and left the room to proceed upstairs;
the things she wanted were in the bedroom chest.

She had been anxious to see how the house was—the part-
time caretaker she shared with some neighbors was away this
week on his holiday, known to be not yet back. At the best
of times he did not look in often, and she was never sure that
she trusted him. There were some cracks in the structure, left
by the last bombing, on which she was anxious to keep an
eye. Not that one could do anything—

A shaft of refracted daylight now lay across the hall. She
stopped dead and stared at the hall table—on this lay a letter
addressed to her.

She thought first—then the caretaker *must* be back. All the
same, who, seeing the house shuttered, would have dropped
a letter in at the box? It was not a circular, it was not a bill.
And the post office redirected, to the address in the country,
everything for her that came through the post. The caretaker
(even if he *were* back) did not know she was due in London
today—her call here had been planned to be a surprise—so
his negligence in the matter of this letter, leaving it to wait
in the dusk and dust, annoyed her. Annoyed, she picked up
the letter, which bore no stamp. But it cannot be important,

or they would know. . . . She took the letter rapidly upstairs
with her, without a stop to look at the writing till she reached
what had been her bedroom, where she let in light. The room
looked over the garden and other gardens: the sun had gone
in; as the clouds sharpened and lowered, the trees and rank
lawns seemed already to smoke with dark. Her reluctance to
look again at the letter came from the fact that she felt in-
truded upon—and by someone contemptuous of her ways.
However, in the tenseness preceding the fall of rain she read
it: it was a few lines.

> *Dear Kathleen,*
> *You will not have forgotten that today is our anniversary,*
> *and the day we said. The years have gone by at once*
> *slowly and fast. In view of the fact that nothing has changed,*
> *I shall rely upon you to keep your promise. I was sorry*
> *to see you leave London, but was satisfied that you would*
> *be back in time. You may expect me, therefore, at the*
> *hour arranged.*
>
> > *Until then . . .*
> >
> > > *K.*

Mrs. Drover looked for the date: it was today's. She dropped
the letter on to the bedsprings, then picked it up to see the
writing again—her lips, beneath the remains of lipstick, beginning to go white. She felt so much the change in her own
face that she went to the mirror, polished a clear patch in it
and looked at once urgently and stealthily in. She was confronted by a woman of forty-four, with eyes staring out under
a hat brim that had been rather carelessly pulled down. She
had not put on any more powder since she left the shop where
she ate her solitary tea. The pearls her husband had given
her on their marriage hung loose round her now rather thinner
throat, slipping into the V of the pink wool jumper her sister
knitted last autumn as they sat round the fire. Mrs. Drover's
most normal expression was one of controlled worry, but of
assent. Since the birth of the third of her little boys, attended
by a quite serious illness, she had had an intermittent muscular flicker to the left of her mouth, but in spite of this she
could always sustain a manner that was at once energetic and
calm.

Turning from her own face as precipitately as she had gone
to meet it, she went to the chest where the things were,
unlocked it, threw up the lid and knelt to search. But as the
rain began to come crashing down she could not keep from

looking over her shoulder at the stripped bed on which the letter lay. Behind the blanket of rain the clock of the church that still stood struck six—with rapidly heightening apprehension she counted each of the slow strokes. "The hour arranged. . . . My God," she said, "*what* hour? How should I . . . ? After twenty-five years . . ."

The young girl talking to the soldier in the garden had not ever completely seen his face. It was dark; they were saying goodbye under a tree. Now and then—for it felt, from not seeing him at this intense moment, as though she had never seen him at all—she verified his presence for these few moments longer by putting out a hand, which he each time pressed, without very much kindness, and painfully, on to one of the breast buttons of his uniform. That cut of the button on the palm of her hand was, principally, what she was to carry away. This was so near the end of a leave from France that she could only wish him already gone. It was August 1916. Being not kissed, being drawn away from and looked at intimidated Kathleen till she imagined spectral glitters in the place of his eyes. Turning away and looking back up the lawn she saw, through branches of trees, the drawing room window alight: she caught a breath for the moment when she could go running back there into the safe arms of her mother and sister, and cry: "What shall I do, what shall I do? He has gone."

Hearing her catch her breath, her fiancé said, without feeling: "Cold?"

"You're going away such a long way."

"Not so far as you think."

"I don't understand?"

"You don't have to," he said. "You will. You know what we said."

"But that was—suppose you—I mean, suppose."

"I shall be with you," he said, "sooner or later. You won't forget that. You need do nothing but wait."

Only a little more than a minute later she was free to run up the silent lawn. Looking in through the window at her mother and sister, who did not for the moment perceive her, she already felt that unnatural promise drive down between her and the rest of all human kind. No other way of having given herself could have made her feel so apart, lost and forsworn. She could not have plighted a more sinister troth.

Kathleen behaved well when, some months later, her fiancé

was reported missing, presumed killed. Her family not only supported her but were able to praise her courage without stint because they could not regret, as a husband for her, the man they knew almost nothing about. They hoped she would, in a year or two, console herself—and had it been only a question of consolation things might have gone much straighter ahead. But her trouble, behind just a little grief, was a complete dislocation from everything. She did not reject other lovers, for these failed to appear: for years she failed to attract men—and with the approach of her thirties she became natural enough to share her family's anxiousness on this score. She began to put herself out, to wonder; and at thirty-two she was very greatly relieved to find herself being courted by William Drover. She married him, and the two of them settled down in this quiet, arboreal part of Kensington: in this house the years piled up, her children were born and they all lived till they were driven out by the bombs of the next war. Her movements as Mrs. Drover were circumscribed, and she dismissed any idea that they were still watched.

As things were—dead or living the letter-writer sent her only a threat. Unable, for some minutes, to go on kneeling with her back exposed to the empty room, Mrs. Drover rose from the chest to sit on an upright chair whose back was firmly against the wall. The desuetude of her former bedroom, her married London home's whole air of being a cracked cup from which memory, with its reassuring power, had either evaporated or leaked away, made a crisis—and at just this crisis the letter-writer had, knowledgeably, struck. The hollowness of the house this evening cancelled years on years of voices, habits and steps. Through the shut windows she only heard rain fall on the roofs around. To rally herself, she said she was in a mood—and, for two or three seconds shutting her eyes, told herself that she had imagined the letter. But she opened them—there it lay on the bed.

On the supernatural side of the letter's entrance she was not permitting her mind to dwell. Who, in London, knew she meant to call at the house today? Evidently, however, this had been known. The caretaker, *had* he come back, had had no cause to expect her: he would have taken the letter in his pocket, to forward it, at his own time, through the post. There was no other sign that the caretaker had been in—but, if not? Letters dropped in at doors of deserted houses do not fly or walk to tables in halls. They do not sit on the dust of empty tables with the air of certainty that they will be found. There is needed some human hand—but nobody but the caretaker had a key. Under circumstances she did not care to consider, a house can be entered without a key. It was possible that she was not alone now. She might be being waited for, downstairs. Waited for—until when? Until "the hour arranged." At least that was not six o'clock: six had struck.

She rose from the chair and went over and locked the door.

The thing was, to get out. To fly? No, not that: she had to catch her train. As a woman whose utter dependability was the keystone of her family life she was not willing to return to the country, to her husband, her little boys and her sister, without the objects she had come up to fetch. Resuming work at the chest she set about making up a number of parcels in a rapid, fumbling decisive way. These, with her shopping parcels, would be too much to carry; these meant a taxi—at the thought of the taxi her heart went up and her normal breathing resumed. I will ring up the taxi now; the taxi cannot come too soon: I shall hear the taxi out there running its engine, till I walk calmly down to it through the hall. I'll ring up—But no: the telephone is cut off. . . . She tugged at a knot she had tied wrong.

The idea of flight . . . He was never kind to me, not really. I don't remember him kind at all. Mother said he never considered me. He was set on me, that was what it was—not love. Not love, not meaning a person well. What did he do, to make me promise like that? I can't remember.—But she found that she could.

She remembered with such dreadful acuteness that the twenty-five years since then dissolved like smoke and she instinctively looked for the weal left by the button on the palm of her hand. She remembered not only all that he said and did but the complete suspension of *her* existence during that August week. I was not myself—they all told me so at the time. She remembered—but with one white burning blank as where acid has dropped on a photograph: *under no conditions* could she remember his face.

So, wherever he may be waiting, I shall not know him. You have no time to run from a face you do not expect.

The thing was to get to the taxi before any clock struck what could be the hour. She would slip down the street and round the side of the square to where the square gave on the main road. She would return in the taxi, safe, to her own door, and bring the solid driver into the house with her to

pick up the parcels from room to room. The idea of the taxi
driver made her decisive, bold: she unlocked her door, went
to the top of the staircase and listened down.

She heard nothing—but while she was hearing nothing the
passé air of the staircase was disturbed by a draught that
travelled up to her face. It emanated from the basement:
down there a door or window was being opened by someone
who chose this moment to leave the house.

The rain had stopped; the pavements steamily shone as
Mrs. Drover let herself out by inches from her own front door
into the empty street. The unoccupied houses opposite continued to meet her look with their damaged stare. Making
towards the thoroughfare and the taxi, she tried not to keep
looking behind. Indeed, the silence was so intense—one of
those creeks of London silence exaggerated this summer by
the damage of war—that no tread could have gained on hers
unheard. Where her street debouched on the square where
people went on living she grew conscious of and checked her
unnatural pace. Across the open end of the square two buses
impassively passed each other; women, a perambulator, cy-
clists, a man wheeling a barrow signalized, once again, the
ordinary flow of life. At the square's most populous corner
should be—and was—the short taxi rank. This evening, only
one taxi—but this, although it presented its blank rump, appeared already to be alertly waiting for her. Indeed, without
looking around the driver started his engine as she panted up
from behind and put her hand on the door. As she did so,
the clock struck seven. The taxi faced the main road: to make
the trip back to her house it would have to turn—she had
settled back on the seat and the taxi *had* turned before she,
surprised by its knowing movement, recollected that she had
not "said where." She leaned forward to scratch at the glass
panel that divided the driver's head from her own.

The driver braked to what was almost a stop, turned round
and slid the glass panel back: the jolt of this flung Mrs. Drover
forward till her face was almost into the glass. Through the
aperture driver and passenger, not six inches between them,
remained for an eternity eye to eye. Mrs. Drover's mouth
hung open for some seconds before she could issue her first
scream. After that she continued to scream freely and to beat
with her gloved hands on the glass all round as the taxi,
accelerating without mercy, made off with her into the hin-
terland of deserted streets.

Sean O'Faolain
(1900–)

Sean O'Faolain was born in Ireland, and nearly all of his work is marked by his relationship to the country and its anguished history. Although a novelist as well as a short story writer, he is best known for his work in the latter genre, with volumes of shorter fiction such as Midsummer Night Madness *(1932),* The Man Who Invented Sin *(1948),* The Heat of the Sun *(1966), and* The Talking Trees *(1971). They have been brought together in* Collected Stories. *O'Faolain's persistent theme is the relationship between individuals and society, a motif which also runs through his novels,* A Nest of Simple Folk *(1933), with its allusion to Turgenev, and* Come Back to Erin *(1940). Works of a purely Irish nature include biographies of Eamon De Valera (1933) and Daniel O'-Connor (1938), as well as* Song of Ireland *(1943) and* The Irish *(1948), both of them historical-cultural studies of his native country.*

The Human Thing

It is not always cold in the Basses-Alpes—but on that late September evening (was it as long as ten years ago?) when I rang his presbytery bell it was very cold. The only answer to my call was the wind funnelling down that tiny, flagged street of his, narrow as a bedspread and smelly as a bedpan. It was like aerial gunnery aimed over thirty miles of forest and ravines to strike the sea five miles out beyond the warm beaches of Nice where I had toasted myself that morning in the Riviera sun. Was I to have to spend the night alone up here in Argons? And, if so, was there even a half-decent hotel in Argons? It would be dusk within an hour. I rang again and pressed for shelter against his studded door. Suddenly it opened and a woman passed hastily out into the narrow street. All I saw was a snapshot glimpse of a brightly made-up mouth in a dark face, a stocky figure, well dressed, a bit over-blown in the Italian way that you so often see along this border. Afterwards I wondered if she had been wearing a long black veil like a war-widow. The old housekeeper all but closed the door after her, glared at me with two sooty eyes from under a top-knot like the ace of spades, accepted my card and my tiny letter of introduction, closed the door within an inch of its jamb and backed into the house. This meant at least that he was at home, and I straightway forgot everything except what the Abbé de Saint Laurent had told me about him a few days before in his sunbathed little study in Nice.

"Argons?" he had said. "In that case I know the very man for you. You must call on my good confrère the Abbé Morfé. He will tell you everything you want to know about the traditional life of the Basses-Alpes."

And straightway sat to his desk and began to write on a small sheet of paper, murmuring over one sunlit shoulder as he wrote:

"He is not French, of course. Although you would never suspect it he has been with us so long—for at least twenty years. He is an Irishman. One of several who volunteered for the French mission after the War, when we were badly in need of priests. As we still are! You may talk to him freely. "Not," he smiled back at me around the corner of his glasses, "that you will need to. He will do the talking. How do you spell your name? Thank you. A very outspoken man. Sometimes, I think, a little too outspoken. But," and here he turned right around to me, "zealous! Beyond my vocabulary. A downright man. And absolutely fearless." He turned back to his desk to inscribe the tiny envelope. "The perfect priest for the mountains. Ireland, as you must know, was never Romanized. So you, as an Englishman . . ." (He did not observe my sigh; I am always being mistaken for an Englishman.) ". . . will understand readily what I mean when I say that he represents the best, the very best of *l'eglise des barbares*."

He folded his small letter into its small envelope, handed it to me courteously, and wafted me upwards and onwards towards nether Gaul.

As if under another wild blast of wind the door was flung open. I saw a powerful-looking countryman. His face was the colour of raw bacon cured by the sun and the wind. In his

left hand he held my card, in his right a fat claw-hammer
which he flung behind the door with such a clatter that for a
second I was taken aback by the violence of the gesture; all
the more so because he was shouting back into the house,
"Mais, je vous ai dis que je ne la connais pas!" He turned
back to me, warmly welcoming, cried, "Come in, Sean! Come
in!" and I was straightway back in the County Mayo; though
in Ireland only a Protestant clergyman would have looked so
indigent. His soutane was old and dusty, his boots were un-
laced, he wore an old, fraying straw hat on the back of his
balding poll, he was smoking a pipe mended with twine.

"I was making a coop for the hens!" he said.

"I'm interrupting you?"

"The most pleasant interruption in the world!" he laughed,
and with one big hand on my shoulder he drew me in and
invited me to stay not only for the night but for as long as I
pleased: to which I cautiously replied that it could, alas, only
be for one night. When we were in his living-room—oh! the
joy of that sizzling log fire!—he at once produced a full bottle
of Tullamore Dew, which, I noticed, was not only dusty but
had never been opened. He sank as slowly as an elephant
into his leather-covered armchair and began to talk non-stop
about Ireland.

Everything in the room was of the region, and it was all as
darkly impersonal as a convent: the hand-wrought firedogs,
the heavy furniture that had obviously been made on the spot
a long time ago, the greying, pious prints, the brown tiles,
the adze-marked beams under a ceiling that had once been
white plaster and was now tea-coloured from years of wood
smoke and nicotine. As my feet thawed my heart rose—all
this was exactly the sort of thing I needed for my article. But
for well over an hour he did not give me a chance to ask him
any of the questions that had brought me to his door—he
asked all the questions, and rarely waited for my answers. I
could see only three tokens of our common country: the until-
now unopened bottle of whiskey; the corner of *The Sunday
Independent*, still in its folder, still bearing its green Irish
stamp, edging out from under the papers of the *midi*; and a
small cushion embroidered with green and red leprechauns
bulging from under his fat elbow. I could imagine it coming
to him, with "Merry Christmas," from some distant Deirdre
or Mary.

At long last he let Ireland drop. Touching the Abbé's note
(a little frigidly?) he said:

"Well, so you are going to write about us? And what have you discovered so far, pray?"

"More or less what you'd expect."

"And," a little guardedly, "what would I expect?"

"What every traveller in a strange place expects, that the truth about every place is the sum of everybody's contradictions."

"Such as?"

"Well, for example, everybody I meet east of the Var tells me that the old, traditional life now exists nowhere except west of the Var, and everybody west of the Var tells me that if I want to see the old ways I must come up here into the mountains. What would you say to that?"

He sniffed, and at once struck the chord that dominated everything else that was to follow.

"Do you know phwat it is?" he said in a buttermilk brogue, with a buttermilk smile, "I'm not sure that I'm fit to tawlk about this ould counthry at all, at all. 'Tis a quare counthry. To tell you the honest truth, Sean, I'm gettin' a bit fed up with the Frinch. I have to live with them you know."

Meaning that I was just a tourist? The jab and the brogue delighted and alerted me. A false brogue, as every Irishman knows, is a sure sign that the speaker is about to say something so true that he wants to blunt the edge of it by presenting it as a kind of family joke. I said, adopting the same sword-in-the-scabbard technique:

"Shure and all, isn't it a bit late in the day for you to be feeling that way now, Father? After all your thirty-odd years shepherding thim?"

He looked at me unamiably. A point apiece. We were playing that ancient Irish game known as conversational poker, a game which nobody can win and nobody can lose because nobody may utter the open truth but everybody must give and take a few sharp little smacks of it or the game is no good at all.

"Better late than never," he said sourly. "As is the way with most of us?"

He began to talk slowly. Was he feeling his way into my mind? Or into his own? He casually refreshed my glass. But as we progressed I thought I noticed a difference in his way of playing the Game: if we were playing the Game. After all he was a priest, and a French priest, and a French priest of the mountains—a man, that is, for whom the stakes in every game are infinite.

"The Basses-Alpes? Mind you, Sean, the Basses-Alpes aren't such a bad country. Not rich, of course. Anyway not rich the way the coast is rich. But it has things the coast never had and never will have. There are people who like to bask on the Riviera, who like to have Nice sunny apartments and Nice sunny congregations. But, sure, the Riviera isn't country at all! What is the Riviera but one blooming esplanade forty miles long? A string of international resorts without a stem of local character? Without any character! Without any values except cold, commercial cash values. But we aren't poor either. The land down there, you've seen it, is all ravined and gorged. Hard, stony uplands. With their olive groves abandoned, and their villages crumbling, or turned into tourist traps, and their farmhouses for sale to foreigners. And all the young people going. Gone! Lured away down to the bright lights along the coast. All of them wanting to be croupiers, or traffic cops in white helmets, or factory workers in white overalls. When I think of places like St. Paul! A sink of iniquity I call it. For all I know it may be a place that you like to visit. And for good reasons, comfortable hotels, good food. But fifty years ago that was a decent, little country hill village. What is it today? Packed to the last corner with what, with who! The *haut monde*! Paahrisians! In bikinis and beach pyjamas! Do you know who the organist in that little church is today! A Protestant! And glad to have him. And now don't start talking to me about arty-arty chapels like that one by Matisse up in Vence. A chapel? It's a bathroom designed by a freethinker."

"Was Matisse a freethinker?"

"You can have him! Listen! There's one thing on earth that I can't stand and that's milk and water Catholics."

His eyes glinted. If this was, by any chance, a jab at me, maybe we were still playing the Game. He went on:

"Up here it is different. Up here the forests mean—well, you might call it comparative wealth for some and a good living for all. So our people have stayed on. The bright lights are farther away." His voice slowed. "Yes, our people have stayed on."

"And," I leaned forward eagerly, "kept the old life ways?"

He knocked his pipe out with slow, careful taps on the head of a firedog. I had the feeling that the Game was over.

"I'll explain to you what I mean by milk and water religion. I know of instances of women in these parts deliberately going off and having affairs—and I mean respectable, married women with families—for no reason but because it is the modern fashion. Women born and reared in these parts, copying, that's all it is, the ways of places they think better than their own. To be as smart as the best. To be in the fashion. I find that utterly contemptible."

He was so passionate about it that I demurred, though cautiously since he felt so strongly about it.

"Surely," I proposed gently, "one must go by cases? I mean a woman might be terribly unhappy. Her husband might be a boor, or a bore, or even a drunk. She might have met with some man whom she wished she had married, some man she loved or thought she loved . . ."

"That has nothing whatever to do with it! I could understand it if there was a bit of real passion in it. I could make allowances. I could even forgive it. It is my job to forgive. But they do it for the most vulgar of all reasons, just to be up to the minute. To be *à la page*. They do it simply to have something to boast about at the tea-table."

"And the men?"

"The same! People like that have no religion, no character. They have nothing. That's what I mean by milk and water religion."

"And for this you blame the gentry?"

"I never mentioned the gentry."

"You said they want to be as smart as the best. To be in the fashion. Which best? Whose fashion? The nobs'?"

"You never get this sort of thing among the gentry, certainly not among the real noblesse. Oh, of course, you will find sinners among them, as you will everywhere. The flesh is the flesh, high or low. We are all creatures of the flesh. But this thing doesn't come from the flesh. It isn't even honest sensuality. It comes from the corruption of the mind. It comes from meanness of the mind. It's plain, vulgar, bloody tom-foolery. It is indifference. It is spiritual death. It is apostasy."

He slapped the side of his armchair. An uncomfortable silence fell on us. Was he always as irascible as this?

"Maybe I'm in a pessimistic mood," he grumbled. "Gimme your glass. I'm a bad host. Maybe what I need is a week after the grouse in County Mayo."

"Aye," I said, more than willing to return to the Game. "They say there's nothing like a good grouse for a bad theologian."

"Why is it bad theology, pray?"

"Well, after all, 'the greatest of these is charity.' "

"Oho! There is always charity."

(He sounded as if he was a bit sick of charity.)

"This couldn't be a long backwash from the French Revolution? I notice your little street here is called the Rue Carnot."

"There is also," he parried back, "A Rue Saint Roch. That's San Rocco. The good Italian influence. The bond with Rome."

"Yes!" I said dryly. "I noticed that Italian influence. In the Place Garibaldi."

He snarled it:

"That crew!"

We both laughed. (There really is a lot to be said for the urbanity of the Game.) Just then old Ace of Spades came in to say in her sullen voice:

"Dinner is served, Father. And that lady telephoned to say the funeral will be tomorrow at nine o'clock."

He looked hard at her.

"Anastasia, do you know this Madame Bailly?"

"She has been living in Alberon this five years."

"Funny that I can't remember her. I'll just ring Father Benoit." He turned to me. "He is one of my curates. We have a big parish. We divide it among the three of us."

I had driven up through Alberon: one of those small places with a couple of sawmills, and with more garages than hotels, which means that everything goes stone-dead after October when the big passes get clogged with snow.

"Let's eat!"

We went into his dining-room. As he flung out his serviette, tucked it under his jaw and began to pour the wine, he said:

"The poor woman's husband was killed this afternoon in an accident. A tree fell right across his back. He owned a hotel, a garage and a sawmill in Alberon. She came about the funeral." He paused in the act of filling his own glass. "Bailly?" I know a couple of Baillys around Grasse. And," he growled, "nothing much good about any of them."

"Liberals?" I teased.

"Puh! You mentioned Garibaldi. And Carnot. It would be very interesting study for you to find out at what date these names came in . . . and at what date a lot of other things began to come in."

We talked at random. Presently he said:

"I don't want you to misunderstand me about the gentry. When all is said and done they are still the best people in France. They're on the way out, of course. They have no

political gumption. And no money. And no influence. Your
Liberals, as you choose to call them, are pushing them over
the last edge of the ravines. What's left of them." He sipped
his wine and frowned. "Bailly? Somehow or other that name
keeps ringing a bell somewhere in what's left of my poor old
head."

"Haven't you the Liber Animarum?" I asked, meaning the
thick, black notebook I had been shown once in an Irish
presbytery by an old priest who had once been a dear friend
of mine. These stubby books have a page to every parishioner:
name, business, address, married or single, whether he prac-
tises his religion or not, and sometimes, though rarely, a more
intimate comment if the priest considers it necessary to probe
more deeply. He snorted.

"Ha! Liber Animarum, how are you? 'Tis easy seen that
you come from Holy Ireland. Themselves and their card-
indexes. What I call IBM Catholicism. It's as much as my
two curates and myself can do to get around to visiting our
parishioners once every two years. If that! And sometimes
none too welcome at that! Have you any idea at all of the
size of our parishes? If it wasn't for our housekeepers . . ."
He stopped dead. He sighed. "I must be getting old. I'm
losing my grip."

He rang the little brass bell on the table and waited for her
to appear at the door.

"Tell me," he said. "Do you really know this Madame
Bailly?"

"Everybody in Alberon knows her."

"Yes, yes, you told me she is from Alberon."

"I said she lives in Alberon."

He pushed his chair back and faced her.

"Anastasia! What are you trying to say exactly? Where did
she come from?"

"Cannes."

"And Bailly married her and brought her to Alberon five
years ago?"

"M. Bailly's wife and four children are living in Grasse with
his mother."

There was a long silence. He said, "Bailly sent them away?"

Her sooty eyes stared at him. Her shoulders barely moved.
He thanked her and nodded her out. He pushed his dinner
away and his face was pale about his tightly clenched lips—
the only part of that ruddy face that could grow pale.

"Five years! What sort of a priest am I? What sort of a

parish do I run? Under my very nose! And now this person
has the insolence to come here and ask me to give him a
Christian burial! I'll soon put a stop to that!"

"My God! You can't refuse to bury the man? You can't
let him be put into a hole in the ground like an animal?"

"And do you think that after leading this kind of life, giving
public scandal for five years, openly and brazenly, that I am
going to give him public burial now as a good Catholic? What
would my parisioners say? What would they think? Do you
think that it's for this I came here thirty-three years ago, to
bless scandalmongers like those two apostates?"

"Isn't that a bit extreme? Sinners, yes. Call them that if
you like. That, of course. But in mere charity . . ."

"Charity! Everybody always talks to me about charity! What
is charity?"

"Love, I suppose. I suppose those two unfortunate people
loved one another."

"And his wife? And his four children? Did he love *them*?"

"But he may, even at the last minute, have hoped for
forgiveness. If you had been there when that tree fell on him
would you not have given him Extreme Unction? Anointed
his eyes, and hands, and mouth, and prayed for his forgiveness?"

Outside, a wild rush of wind rattled leaves against the pane
like a million clamouring fingers.

"Well, I was *not* there," he said heavily. "He died as he
lived, struck down by the hand of God. I'm going to phone
Father Benoit."

Alone in the room I tired to visualize that stocky Italianate
woman I had seen hurrying away from his door. I tried to
see her and her dead lover in their hotel in Alberon, and I
realized that this was one life story that I would never know.
All I could imagine was a hundred spade-heads like old Anastasia in that little hill town besieging her with their cruel
silence and their bitter eyes. He came back and slumped into
his chair.

"He is out."

I sat opposite him and I thought: "And here is another life-
story that I will never know!" After a few moments he said,
quietly:

"Charity, Sean, is a virtue. It is, as you say, love—the love
of all things through God, the love of God in all things. As
for your love, human love? It is that, too. As Saint Bona-

venture said, it is the life that couples the lover to the beloved. *Vita copulans amantem cum amato.* But it is that in the name of God, for God and by God. One act of love in a lifetime is an immensity. But one mortal sin can of itself destroy all love, and all life, as that man destroyed two lives over and over again before the eyes of the world." He stopped and got up again. "This thing must be ended publicly! As it was begun publicly. I must go down there at once."

"Tonight?"

We both looked at the window. The mistral was at its full force. A wild sheaf of leaves whirled horizontally past the window.

"Let me drive you," I offered, miserably.

"I'd be glad if you did. I'm in no fit state to drive."

We buttoned ourselves up in our overcoats, pulled on our berets, and crushed into my little Dauphine. He directed me on the long, winding road where the woods on each side waved in one solid mass like a turbulent sea. I was too busy watching the road to talk. All the way he never spoke except to say "Fork left," or "Right here." I felt like a man driving an executioner to the place of execution and I did not know which of the two of us I disliked the more at that moment. When we entered Alberon the streets were empty and dark. Two cafés were lighted, their windows opaque with condensed moisture. He suddenly said, revealing that he had been thinking in that language:

"C'est dans la Place. Il s'appelle Le Chamois."

It was a three-storey house with the usual Alpine roof pitched to a peak and smoothing out at the base to let the great weight of snow slide down and melt on the gutters. On the ground floor there was a café, all dark and buttoned-up. Two windows on the storey above it were lighted. When he got out and was ringing at the door I withdrew to the centre of the little Place to park and wait. It took a couple of rings to produce an answer. When the door opened I saw, against the light inside, the dark outline of the woman who called herself Madame Bailly. He stepped inside at once, the door closed. I was alone with the mistral, the darkness and the empty Place.

The perfect priest for the mountains. Getting a bit fed-up with the Frinch. Nice people and Nice apartments. Absolutely fearless. Downright. A finger on a switch lit up two more windows upstairs. *Vita copulans amantem cum amato.* Would he be laid out in there on his bed of love? Zealous beyond my vocabulary. The mistral blew around and around me in

Sean O'Faolain

moaning circles. Two men, an older and a younger, came, heads down, into the square from the left. I saw them pause at the closed up Café le Chamois, look at its dark window, making some gestures that could only mean, "Ah yes! I heard that . . ." Then one of them stretched his arm forward and they went on again, heads down, to, I presumed, one of the other cafés, where no doubt as in every house in the town . . . I started the engine and turned on the heat.

After another long wait those two extra windows went dark. Still he did not come out. One mortal act of love in a lifetime is an immensity. One mortal sin can destroy the whole of that love and of that life for ever. Damn it, why doesn't he finish her off quickly? That, at least, would be a small act of Charity! A big truck and trailer laden with long baulks of timber trundled into the square and out at the other end. Then only the wind and the darkness again.

At last a flood of light beamed out on the pavement as the door opened and I saw his great bulky outline. He was shaking hands with the woman in black. As I peered forward I saw that it was not the same woman. He bowed to her and looked around for me. I drove over to meet him. She slowly closed the door, he clambered in, and silently waved me onward.

I could not see his face in the darkness but by the dashboard light I saw his hand, lying loosely on his thigh, shaking like a man with the palsy.

"Well?" I asked.

He spoke so softly I could barely hear him.

"I could not believe such love existed on this earth."

"Madame Bailly?"

"She came down from Grasse. With her four children. For the funeral."

"There will be a funeral?"

"Could I refuse his wife?"

"And the other?"

"The two of them are there together. Comforting one another."

No more was said until we were back in his living-room, in his dark presbytery, in his tiny, smelly street. There, standing by the grey ash of his dying fire, still in his beret and his long overcoat, he turned on me a face twisted by agony and cried:

"Did I do right?"

"You did the human thing, Father."

"Ah! The human thing?" He shook his head, uncomforted.

He laid his hand in a kindly way on my shoulder. "Sleep well, you!"—as one who would not. "And I never told you anything at all, at all, about the ould Basses-Alpes!"

I hardly slept at all. All night the wind moaned through his narrow street, down over every forest, village and black ravine. Were those two women awake? I wished I was down where the bright lights of the esplanades glinted in the whispering sea.

Frank O'Connor
(1903–1966)

Born in Cork, Ireland, Frank O'Connor (Michael O'Donovan) after a stint as a librarian turned to short fiction. His first volume, Guests of the Nation, *appeared in 1931, in Gaelic. He then turned to English and published over the next twenty years a number of volumes that established his reputation as the "Irish Chekhov." These include* Dutch Interior *(1940),* More Stories *(1954), and* Domestic Relations *(1957). O'Connor immersed himself thoroughly in Irish life, literature, and language, serving as director of the Abbey Theatre for a period and translating Gaelic poetry into English. His reputation, however, is based on his short stories.*

The Face of Evil

I could never understand all the old talk about how hard it is to be a saint. I was a saint for quite a bit of my life and I never saw anything hard in it. And when I stopped being a saint, it wasn't because the life was too hard.

I fancy it is the sissies who make it seem like that. We had quite a few of them in our school, fellows whose mothers intended them to be saints and who hadn't the nerve to be anything else. I never enjoyed the society of chaps who wouldn't commit sin for the same reason that they wouldn't dirty their new suits. That was never what sanctity meant to me, and I doubt if it is what it means to other saints. The companions I enjoyed were the tough gang down the road, and I liked going down of an evening and talking with them under the gas lamp about football matches and school, even if they did sometimes say things I wouldn't say myself. I was never one for criticizing; I had enough to do criticizing myself, and I knew they were decent chaps and didn't really mean much harm by the things they said about girls.

No, for me the main attraction of being a saint was the way it always gave you something to do. You could never say you felt time hanging on your hands. It was like having a room of your own to keep tidy; you'd scour it and put everything neatly back in its place, and within an hour or two it was beginning to look as untidy as ever. It was a full-time job that began when you woke and stopped only when you fell asleep.

I would wake in the morning, for instance, and think how nice it was to lie in bed and congratulate myself on not having to get up for another half hour. That was enough. Instantly a sort of alarm-clock would go off in my mind; the mere thought that I could enjoy half an hour's comfort would make me aware of an alternative, and I'd begin an argument with myself. I had a voice in me that was almost the voice of a stranger, the way it nagged and jeered. Sometimes I could almost visualize it, and then it took on the appearance of a fat and sneering teacher I had some years before at school— a man I really hated. I hated that voice. It always began in the same way, smooth and calm and dangerous. I could see the teacher rubbing his fat hands and smirking.

"Don't get alarmed, boy. You're in no hurry. You have another half hour."

"I know well I have another half hour," I would reply, trying to keep my temper. "What harm am I doing? I'm only imagining I'm down in a submarine. Is there anything wrong in that?"

"Oho, not the least in the world. I'd say there's been a heavy frost. Just the sort of morning when there's ice in the bucket."

"And what has that to do with it?"

"Nothing, I tell you. Of course, for people like you it's easy enough in the summer months, but the least touch of frost in the air soon makes you feel different. I wouldn't worry trying to keep it up. You haven't the stuff for this sort of life at all."

And gradually my own voice grew weaker as that of my tormentor grew stronger, till all at once, I would strip the clothes from off myself and lie in my nightshirt, shivering and muttering: "So I haven't the stuff in me, haven't I?" Then I would go downstairs before my parents were awake, strip, and wash in the bucket, ice or no ice, and when Mother came down she would cry in alarm: "Child of grace, what has you up at this hour? Sure, 'tis only half past seven." She almost took it as a reproach to herself, poor woman, and I couldn't tell her the reason, and even if I could have done so, I wouldn't. It was a thing you couldn't talk about to anybody.

Then I went to Mass and enjoyed again the mystery of the streets and lanes in the early morning; the frost which made your feet clatter off the walls at either side of you like falling masonry, and the different look that everything wore, as though, like yourself, it was all cold and scrubbed and new. In the winter the lights would still be burning red in the little white-washed cottages, and in summer their walls were ablaze with sunshine so that their interiors were dimmed to shadows. Then there were the different people, all of whom recognized one another, like Mrs. MacEntee, who used to be a stew-ardess on the boats, and Macken, the tall postman; people who seemed ordinary enough when you met them during the day but carried something of their mystery with them at Mass, as though they, too, were reborn.

I can't pretend I was ever very good at school, but even there it was a help. I might not be clever, but I had always a secret reserve of strength to call on in the fact that I had what I wanted, and that besides it I wanted nothing. People frequently gave me things, like fountain pens or pencil-shar-peners, and I would suddenly find myself becoming attached to them and immediately know I must give them away, and then feel the richer for it. Even without throwing my weight around, I could help and protect kids younger than myself and yet not become involved in their quarrels. Not to become involved, to remain detached—that was the great thing; to care for things and for people, yet not to care for them so much that your happiness became dependent on them.

It was like no other hobby, because you never really got the better of yourself, and all at once you would suddenly find yourself reverting to childish attitudes; flaring up in a wax with some fellow, or sulking when Mother asked you to go for a message, and then it all came back; the nagging of the infernal alarm-clock, which grew louder with every mo-ment until it incarnated as a smooth, fat, jeering face.

"Now, that's the first time you've behaved sensibly for months, boy. That was the right way to behave to your mother."

"Well, it *was* the right way. Why can't she let me alone once in a while? I only want to read. I suppose I'm entitled to a bit of peace some time?"

"Ah, of course you are, my dear fellow. Isn't that what I'm saying? Go on with your book! Imagine you're a cowboy, riding to the rescue of a beautiful girl in a cabin in the woods, and let that silly woman go for the messages herself. She probably hasn't long to live anyway, and when she dies you'll be able to do all the weeping you like."

And suddenly tears of exasperation would come to my eyes and I'd heave the story-book to the other side of the room and shout back at the voice that gave me no rest: "Cripes, I might as well be dead and buried. I have no blooming life." After that I would apologize to Mother (who, poor woman, was more embarrassed than anything else and assured me that it was all her fault), go on the message, and write another tick in my notebook against the heading of "Bad Temper" so as to be able to confess it to Father O'Regan when I went to Confession on Saturday. Not that he was ever severe with me, no matter what I did; he thought I was the last word in holiness, and was always asking me to pray for some special intention of his own. And though I was depressed, I never lost interest, for no matter what I did, I could scarcely ever reduce the total of times I had to tick off that item in my notebook.

Oh, I don't pretend it was any joke, but it did give me the feeling that my life had some meaning; that inside me I had a real source of strength; that there was nothing I could not do without and yet remain sweet, self-sufficient, and content. Sometimes, too, there was the feeling of something more than mere content, as though my body were transparent, like a window, and light shone through it as well as on it, onto the road, the houses, and the playing children, as though it were I who was shining on them, and tears of happiness would come into my eyes, and I hurled myself among the playing children just to forget it.

But, as I say, I had no inclination to mix with other kids who might be saints as well. The fellow who really fascinated me was a policeman's son named Dalton, who was easily the most vicious kid in the locality. The Daltons lived on the terrace above ours. Mrs. Dalton was dead; there was a younger brother called Stevie who was next door to an imbecile, and there was something about that kid's cheerful grin that was even more frightening than the malice on Charlie's broad face. Their father was a tall melancholy man with a big black moustache, and the nearest thing imaginable to one of the Keystone cops. Everyone was sorry for his loss in his wife, but you knew that if it hadn't been that, it would have been something else—maybe the fact that he hadn't lost her. Charlie was only an additional grief. He was always getting into trouble, stealing and running away from home; and only his father's being a policeman prevented his being sent to an industrial school. One of my most vivid recollections is that of Charlie's education. I'd hear a shriek, and there would be Mr. Dalton dragging Charlie along the pavement to school and, whenever the names his son called him grew a little more obscene than usual, pausing to give Charlie a good going-over with the belt which he carried loose in his hand. It is an exceptional father who can do this without getting some pleasure out of it, but Mr. Dalton looked as though even it were an additional burden. Charlie's screams could always fetch me out.

"What is it?" Mother would cry after me.

"Ah, nothing. Only Charlie Dalton again."

"Come in! Come in!"

"I won't be seen."

"Come in, I say. 'Tis never right."

And even when Charlie uttered the most atrocious indecencies, she only joined her hands as if in prayer and muttered, "The poor child! The poor unfortunate child!" I never could understand the way she felt about Charlie. He wouldn't have been Charlie if it hadn't been for the leatherings and the threats of the industrial school.

Looking back on it, the funniest thing is that I seemed to be the only fellow on the road he didn't hate. They were all terrified of him, and some of the kids would go a mile to avoid him. He was completely unclassed: being a policeman's son, he should have been way up the social scale, but he hated the respectable kids worse than the others. When we stood under the gas lamp at night and saw him coming up the road, everybody fell silent. He looked suspiciously at the group, ready to spring up anyone's throat if he saw the shadow of offence; ready even when there wasn't a shadow. He fought like an animal, by instinct, without judgment, and without ever reckoning the odds, and he was terribly strong. He wasn't clever; several of the older chaps could beat him to a frazzle when it was merely a question of boxing or wrestling, but it never was that with Dalton. He was out for blood and usually got it. Yet he was never that way with me. We weren't friends. All that ever happened when we passed each other was that I smiled at him and got a cold, cagey nod in return. Sometimes we stopped and exchanged a few words, but it was an ordeal because we never had anything to say to each other.

It was like the signalling of ships, or, more accurately, the courtesies of great powers. I tried, like Mother, to be sorry for him in having no proper home, and getting all those leatherings, but the feeling that came uppermost in me was never pity but respect—respect for a fellow who had done all the things I would never do: stolen money, stolen bicycles, run away from home, slept with tramps and criminals in barns and doss-houses, and ridden without a ticket on trains and on buses. It filled my imagination. I have a vivid recollection of one summer morning when I was going up the hill to Mass. Just as I reached the top and saw the low, sandstone church perched high up ahead of me, he poked his bare head round the corner of a lane to see who was coming. It startled me. He was standing with his back to the gable of a house; his face was dirty and strained; it was broad and lined, and the eyes were very small, furtive and flickering, and sometimes a sort of spasm would come over them and they flickered madly for half a minute on end.

"Hullo, Charlie," I said. "Where were you?"

"Out," he replied shortly.

"All night?" I asked in astonishment.

"Yeah," he replied with a nod.

"What are you doing now?"

He gave a short, bitter laugh.

"Waiting till my old bastard of a father goes out to work and I can go home."

His eyes flickered again, and self-consciously he drew his hand across them as though pretending they were tired.

"I'll be late for Mass," I said uneasily. "So long."

"So long."

That was all, but all the time at Mass, among the flowers and the candles, watching the beautiful, sad old face of Mrs. MacEntee and the plump, smooth, handsome face of Macken, the postman, I was haunted by the image of that other face, wild and furtive and dirty, peering round a corner like an animal looking from its burrow. When I came out, the morning was brilliant over the valley below me; the air was punctuated with bugle calls from the cliff where the barrack stood, and Charlie Dalton was gone. No, it wasn't pity I felt for him. It wasn't even respect. It was almost like envy.

Then, one Saturday evening, an incident occurred which changed my attitude to him; indeed, changed my attitude to myself, though it wasn't until long after that I realized it. I was on my way to Confession, preparatory to Communion next morning. I always went to Confession at the parish church in town where Father O'Regan was. As I passed the tramway terminus at the Cross, I saw Charlie sitting on the low wall above the Protestant church, furtively smoking the butt-end of a cigarette which somebody had dropped, getting on the tram. Another tram arrived as I reached the Cross, and a number of people alighted and went off in different directions. I crossed the road to Charlie and he gave me his most distant nod.

"Hullo."

"Hullo, Cha. Waiting for somebody?"

"No. Where are you off to?"

"Confession."

"Huh." He inhaled the cigarette butt deeply and then tossed it over his shoulder into the sunken road beneath without looking where it alighted. "You go a lot."

"Every week," I said modestly.

"Jesus!" he said with a short laugh. "I wasn't there for twelve months."

I shrugged my shoulders. As I say, I never went in much for criticizing others, and anyway Charlie wouldn't have been Charlie if he had gone to Confession every week.

"Why do you go so often?" he asked challengingly.

"Oh, I don't know," I said doubtfully. "I suppose it keeps you out of harm's way."

"But you don't do any harm," he growled, just as though he were defending me against someone who had been attacking me.

"Ah, we all do harm."

"But, Jesus Christ, you don't do anything," he said almost angrily, and his eyes flickered again in that curious nervous spasm, and almost as if they put him into a rage, he drove his knuckles into them.

"We all do things," I said. "Different things."

"Well, what do you do?"

"I lose my temper a lot," I admitted.

"Jesus!" he said again, and rolled his eyes.

"It's a sin just the same," I said obstinately.

"A sin? Losing your temper? Jesus, I want to kill people. I want to kill my bloody old father, for one. I will too, one of those days. Take a knife to him."

"I know, I know," I said, at a loss to explain what I meant. "But that's just the same thing as me."

I wished to God I could talk better. It wasn't any missionary zeal. I was excited because for the first time I knew that Charlie felt about me exactly as I felt about him, with a sort of envy, and I wanted to explain to him that he didn't have to envy me, and that he could be as much a saint as I was just as I could be as much a sinner as he was. I wanted to explain that it wasn't a matter of tuppence ha'penny worth of sanctity as opposed to tuppence worth that made the difference, that it wasn't what you did but what you lost by doing it that mattered. The whole Cross had become a place of mystery—the grey light, drained of warmth; the trees hanging over the old crumbling walls; the tram, shaking like a boat when someone mounted it. It was the way I sometimes felt afterwards with a girl, as though everything about you melted and fused and became one with a central mystery.

"But when what you do isn't any harm?" he repeated angrily with that flickering of the eyes I had almost come to dread.

"Look, Cha," I said, "you can't say a thing isn't any harm. Everything is harm. It might be losing my temper with me and murder with you, like you say, but it would only come to the same thing. If I show you something, will you promise not to tell?"

"Why would I tell?"

"But promise."

"Oh, all right."

Then I took out my little notebook and showed it to him. It was extraordinary, and I knew it was extraordinary. I found myself, sitting on that wall, showing a notebook I wouldn't have shown to anyone else in the world to Charlie Dalton, a fellow any kid on the road would go a long way to avoid, and yet I had the feeling that he would understand it as no one else would do. My whole life was there, under different headings—Disobedience, Bad Temper, Bad Thoughts, Selfishness, and Laziness—and he looked through it quietly, studying the ticks I had placed against each count.

"You see," I said, "you talk about your father, but look at all the things I do against my mother. I know she's a good mother, but if she's sick or if she can't walk fast when I'm in town with her, I get mad just as you do. It doesn't matter what sort of mother or father you have. It's what you do to yourself when you do things like that."

"What do you do to yourself?" he asked quietly.

"It's hard to explain. It's only a sort of peace you have inside yourself. And you can't be just good, no matter how hard you try. You can only do your best, and if you do your best you feel peaceful inside. It's like when I miss Mass of a morning. Things mightn't be any harder on me that day than any other day, but I'm not as well able to stand up to them. It makes things a bit different for the rest of the day. You don't mind it so much if you get a hammering. You know there's something else in the world besides the hammering."

I knew it was a feeble description of what morning Mass really meant to me, the feeling of strangeness which lasted throughout the whole day and reduced reality to its real proportions, but it was the best I could do. I hated leaving him.

"I'll be late for Confession," I said regretfully, getting off the wall.

"I'll go down a bit of the way with you," he said, giving a last glance at my notebook and handing it back to me. I knew he was being tempted to come to Confession along with me, but my pleasure had nothing to do with that. As I say, I never had any missionary zeal. It was the pleasure of understanding rather than that of conversion.

He came down the steps to the church with me and we went in together.

"I'll wait here for you," he whispered, and sat in one of the back pews.

It was dark there; there were just a couple of small, unshaded lights in the aisles above the confessionals. There was a crowd of old women outside Father O'Regan's box, so I knew I had a long time to wait. Old women never got done with their confessions. For the first time I felt it long, but when my turn came it was all over in a couple of minutes: the usual "Bless you, my child. Say a prayer for me, won't you?" When I came out, I saw Charlie Dalton sitting among the old women outside the confessional, waiting to go in. He looked very awkward and angry, his legs wide and his hands hanging between them. I felt very happy about it in a quiet way, and when I said my penance I said a special prayer for him.

It struck me that he was a long time inside, and I began to grow worried. Then he came out, and I saw by his face that it was no good. It was the expression of someone who is saying to himself with a sort of evil triumph: "There, I told you what it was like."

"It's all right," he whispered, giving his belt a hitch. "You go home."

"I'll wait for you," I said.

"I'll be a good while."

I knew then Father O'Regan had given him a heavy penance, and my heart sank.

"It doesn't matter," I said. "I'll wait."

And it was only long afterwards that it occurred to me that I might have taken one of the major decisions of my life without being aware of it. I sat at the back of the church in the dusk and waited for him. He was kneeling up in front, before the altar, and I knew it was no good. At first I was too stunned to feel. All I knew was that my happiness had all gone. I admired Father O'Regan; I knew that Charlie must have done things that I couldn't even imagine—terrible things—but the resentment grew in me. What right had Father O'-Regan or anyone to treat him like that? Because he was down, people couldn't help wanting to crush him further. For the first time in my life I knew real temptation. I wanted to go with Charlie and share his fate. For the first time I realized that the life before me would have complexities of emotion which I couldn't even imagine.

The following week he ran away from home again, took a bicycle, broke into a shop to steal cigarettes, and, after being arrested seventy-five miles from Cork in a little village on the coast, was sent to an industrial school.

1ˢᵗ person you get a character development faster.
The purpose of s.s. is technique and credibility

Graham Greene
(1904–   )

Born in Hertfordshire, England, Graham Greene began his career as a journalist and as a writer of what he called "entertainments" to separate them from his weightier fictions. Some of these are The Man Within *(1929),* Stamboul Train *(1932), and* This Gun for Hire *(1936). As a Roman Catholic convert, Greene often establishes value systems in his serious work that run up against received religious tenets: the ensuing tensions sustain these "novels of ideas." His most important work began, in 1938, with* Brighton Rock, *which was followed by* The Power and the Glory *(1940),* The Heart of the Matter *(1948), and* The End of the Affair *(1951), the four novels that established him as an important and compelling writer. Prolific and successful, Greene has had several of his novels made into films—*The Third Man, The Quiet American, Our Man in Havana, A Burnt-Out Case—*as well as several of the early entertainments and shorter pieces. Although he is renowned as a novelist, his work as a memoirist, travel writer, film critic, playwright, and short story writer should not be neglected.*

Brother

The Communists were the first to appear. They walked quickly, a group of about a dozen, up the boulevard which runs from Combat to Ménilmontant; a young man and a girl lagged a little way behind because the man's leg was hurt and the girl was helping him along. They looked impatient, harassed, hopeless, as if they were trying to catch a train which they knew already in their hearts they were too late to catch.

The proprietor of the café saw them coming when they were still a long way off; the lamps at that time were still alight (it was later that the bullets broke the bulbs and dropped darkness all over that quarter of Paris), and the group showed up plainly in the wide barren boulevard. Since sunset only one customer had entered the café, and very soon after sunset firing could be heard from the direction of Combat; the Métro station had closed hours ago. And yet something obstinate and undefeatable in the proprietor's character prevented him from putting up the shutters; it might have been avarice; he could not himself have told what it was as he pressed his broad yellow forehead against the glass and stared this way and that, up the boulevard and down the boulevard.

But when he saw the group and their air of hurry he began immediately to close his café. First he went and warned his only customer, who was practising billiard shots, walking round and round the table, frowning and stroking a thin moustache between shots, a little green in the face under the low diffused lights.

"The Reds are coming," the proprietor said, "you'd better be off. I'm putting up the shutters."

"Don't interrupt. They won't harm me," the customer said. "This is a tricky shot. Red's in baulk. Off the cushion. Screw on spot." He shot his ball straight into a pocket.

"I knew you couldn't do anything with that," the proprietor said, nodding his bald head. "You might just as well go home. Give me a hand with the shutter first. I've sent my wife away." The customer turned on him maliciously, rattling the cue between his fingers. "It was your talking that spoilt the shot. You've cause to be frightened, I dare say. But I'm a poor man. I'm safe. I'm not going to stir." He went across to his coat and took out a dry cigar. "Bring me a bock." He walked round the table on his toes and the balls clicked and the proprietor padded back into the bar, elderly and irritated. He did not fetch the beer but began to close the shutters; every move he made was slow and clumsy. Long before he had finished the group of Communists was outside.

He stopped what he was doing and watched them with furtive dislike. He was afraid that the rattle of the shutters would attract their attention. If I am very quiet and still, he thought, they may go on, and he remembered with malicious pleasure the police barricade across the Place de la République. That will finish them. In the meanwhile I must be very quiet, very still, and he felt a kind of warm satisfaction at the idea that worldly wisdom dictated the very attitude most suited to his nature. So he stared through the edge of a shutter, yellow, plump, cautious, hearing the billiard balls crackle in the other room, seeing the young man come limping up the pavement on the girl's arm, watching them stand and stare with dubious faces up the boulevard towards Combat.

But when they came into the café he was already behind the bar, smiling and bowing and missing nothing, noticing how they had divided forces, how six of them had begun to run back the way they had come.

The young man sat down in a dark corner above the cellar stairs and the others stood round the door waiting for something to happen. It gave the proprietor an odd feeling that they should stand there in his café not asking for a drink, knowing what to expect, when he, the owner, knew nothing, understood nothing. At last the girl said "Cognac," leaving the others and coming to the bar, but when he had poured it out for her, very careful to give a fair and not a generous measure, she simply took it to the man sitting in the dark and held it to his mouth.

"Three francs," the proprietor said. She took the glass and sipped a little and turned it so that the man's lips might touch the same spot. Then she knelt down and rested her forehead against the man's forehead and so they stayed.

"Three francs," the proprietor said, but he could not make his voice bold. The man was no longer visible in his corner, only the girl's back, thin and shabby in a black cotton frock, as she knelt, leaning forward to find the man's face. The proprietor was daunted by the four men at the door, by the knowledge that they were Reds who had no respect for private property, who would drink his wine and go away without paying, who would rape his women (but there was only his wife, and she was not there), who would rob his bank, who would murder him as soon as look at him. So with fear in his heart he gave up the three francs as lost rather than attract any more attention.

Then the worst that he contemplated happened.

One of the men at the door came up to the bar and told him to pour out four glasses of cognac. "Yes, yes," the proprietor said, fumbling with the cork, praying secretly to the Virgin to send an angel, to send the police, to send the Gardes Mobiles, now, immediately, before the cork came out, "that will be twelve francs."

"Oh, no," the man said, "we are all comrades here. Share and share alike. Listen," he said, with earnest mockery, leaning across the bar, "all we have is yours just as much as it's ours, comrade," and stepping back a pace he presented himself to the proprietor, so that he might take his choice of stringy tie, of threadbare trousers, of starved features. "And it follows from that, comrade, that all you have is ours. So four cognacs. Share and share alike."

"Of course," the proprietor said, "I was only joking." Then he stood with bottle poised, and the four glasses tingled upon the counter. "A machine-gun," he said, "up by Combat," and smiled to see how for the moment the men forgot their brandy as they fidgeted near the door. Very soon now, he thought, and I shall be quit of them.

"A machine-gun," the Red said incredulously, "they're using machine-guns?"

"Well," the proprietor said, encouraged by this sign that the Gardes Mobiles were not very far away, "you can't pretend that you aren't armed yourselves." He leant across the bar in a way that was almost paternal. "After all, you know, your ideas—they wouldn't do in France. Free love."

"Who's talking of free love?" the Red said.

The proprietor shrugged and smiled and nodded at the corner. The girl knelt with her head on the man's shoulder, her back to the room. They were quite silent and the glass of brandy stood on the floor beside them. The girl's beret was pushed back on her head and one stocking was laddered and darned from knee to ankle.

"What, those two? They aren't lovers."

"I," the proprietor said, "with my bourgeois notions would have thought . . ."

"He's her brother," the Red said.

The men came clustering round the bar and laughed at him, but softly as if a sleeper or a sick person were in the house. All the time they were listening for something. Between their shoulders the proprietor could look out across the boulevard; he could see the corner of the Faubourg du Temple.

"What are you waiting for?"

"For friends," the Red said. He made a gesture with open palm as if to say, You see, we share and share alike. We have no secrets.

Something moved at the corner of the Faubourg du Temple.

"Four more cognacs," the Red said.

"What about those two?" the proprietor asked.

"Leave them alone. They'll look after themselves. They're tired."

How tired they were. No walk up the boulevard from Ménilmontant could explain the tiredness. They seemed to have come farther and fared a great deal worse than their companions. They were more starved; they were infinitely more hopeless, sitting in their dark corner away from the friendly gossip, the amicable desperate voices which now confused the proprietor's brain, until for a moment he believed himself to be a host entertaining friends.

He laughed and made a broad joke directed at the two of them; but they made no sign of understanding. Perhaps they were to be pitied, cut off from the camaraderie round the counter; perhaps they were to be envied for their deeper comradeship. The proprietor thought for no reason at all of the bare grey trees of the Tuileries like a series of exclamation marks drawn against the winter sky. Puzzled, disintegrated, with all his bearings lost, he stared out through the door towards the Faubourg.

It was as if they had not seen each other for a long while and would soon again be saying good-bye. Hardly aware of what he was doing he filled the four glasses with brandy. They stretched out worn blunted fingers for them.

"Wait," he said. "I've got something better than this"; then paused, conscious of what was happening across the boulevard. The lamplight splashed down on blue steel helmets; the Gardes Mobiles were lining out across the entrance to the Faubourg, and a machine-gun pointed directly at the café windows.

So, the proprietor thought, my prayers are answered. Now I must do my part, not look, not warn them, save myself. Have they covered the side door? I will get the other bottle. Real Napoleon brandy. Share and share alike.

He felt a curious lack of triumph as he opened the trap of the bar and came out. He tried not to walk quickly back towards the billiard room. Nothing that he did must warn these men; he tried to spur himself with the thought that every slow casual step he took was a blow for France, for his café, for his savings. He had to step over the girl's feet to pass her; she was asleep. He noted the sharp shoulder blades thrusting through the cotton, and raised his eyes and met her brother's, filled with pain and despair.

He stopped. He found he could not pass without a word. It was as if he needed to explain something, as if he belonged to the wrong party. With false bonhomie he waved the cork-screw he carried in the other's face. "Another cognac, eh?"

"It's no good talking to them," the Red said. "They're German. They don't understand a word."

"German?"

"That's what's wrong with his leg. A concentration camp."

The proprietor told himself that he must be quick, that he must put a door between him and them, that the end was very close, but he was bewildered by the hopelessness in the man's gaze. "What's he doing here?" Nobody answered him. It was as if his question were too foolish to need a reply. With his head sunk upon his breast the proprietor went past, and the girl slept on. He was like a stranger leaving a room where all the rest are friends. A German. They don't understand a word; and up, up through the heavy darkness of his mind, through the avarice and the dubious triumph, a few German words remembered from very old days climbed like spies into the light: a line from the *Lorelei* learnt at school, *Kamerad* with its war-time suggestion of fear and surrender, and oddly from nowhere the phrase *mein Bruder*. He opened the door of the billiard room and closed it behind him and softly turned the key.

"Spot in baulk," the customer explained and leant across the great green table, but while he took aim, wrinkling his narrow peevish eyes, the firing started. It came in two bursts with a rip of glass between. The girl cried out something, but it was not one of the words he knew. Then feet ran across the floor, the trap of the bar slammed. The proprietor sat back against the table and listened and listened for any further sound; but silence came in under the door and silence through the keyhole.

"The cloth. My God, the cloth," the customer said, and the proprietor looked down at his own hand which was work-ing the corkscrew into the table.

"Will this absurdity never end?" the customer said. "I shall go home."

"Wait," the proprietor said. "Wait." He was listening to voices and footsteps in the other room. These were voices he did not recognize. Then a car drove up and presently drove away again. Somebody rattled the handle of the door.

"Who is it?" the proprietor called.

"Who are you? Open that door."

"Ah," the customer said with relief, "the police. Where was I now? Spot in baulk." He began to chalk his cue. The

proprietor opened the door. Yes, the Gardes Mobiles had
arrived; he was safe again, though his windows were smashed.
The Reds had vanished as if they had never been. He looked
at the raised trap, at the smashed electric bulbs, at the broken
bottle which dripped behind the bar. The café was full of
men, and he remembered with odd relief that he had not had
time to lock the side door.

"Are you the owner?" the officer asked. "A bock for each
of these men and a cognac for myself. Be quick about it."

The proprietor calculated: "Nine francs fifty," and watched
closely with bent head the coins rattle down upon the counter.

"You see," the officer said with significance, "we pay." He
nodded towards the side door. "Those others: did they pay?"

No, the proprietor admitted, they had not paid, but as he
counted the coins and slipped them into the till, he caught
himself silently repeating the officer's order—"A bock for
each of these men." Those others, he thought, one's got to
say that for them, they weren't mean about the drink. It was
four cognacs with them. But, of course, they did not pay.
"And my windows," he complained aloud with sudden as-
perity, "what about my windows?"

"Never you mind," the officer said, "the government will
pay. You have only to send in your bill. Hurry up now with
my cognac. I have no time for gossip."

"You can see for yourself," the proprietor said, "how the
bottles have been broken. Who will pay for that?"

"Everything will be paid for," the officer said.

"And now I must go to the cellar to fetch more."

He was angry at the reiteration of the word pay. They enter
my café, he thought, they smash my windows, they order me
about and think that all is well if they pay, pay, pay. It occurred to him that these men were intruders.

"Step to it," the officer said and turned and rebuked one
of the men who had leant his rifle against the bar.

At the top of the cellar stairs the proprietor stopped. They
were in darkness, but by the light from the bar he could just
make out a body half-way down. He began to tremble violently, and it was some seconds before he could strike a match.
The young German lay head downwards, and the blood from
his head had dropped on to the step below. His eyes were
open and stared back at the proprietor with the old despairing
expression of life. The proprietor would not believe that he
was dead. "Kamerad," he said bending down, while the match
singed his fingers and went out, trying to recall some phrase

in German, but he could only remember, as he bent lower still, "mein Bruder." Then suddenly he turned and ran up the steps, waved the match-box in the officer's face, and called out in a low hysterical voice to him and his men and to the customer stooping under the low green shade, "Cochons. Cochons."

"What was that? What was that?" the officer exclaimed. "Did you say that he was your brother? It's impossible," and he frowned incredulously at the proprietor and rattled the coins in his pocket.

Samuel Beckett
(1906–   )

The leading playwright of his generation, Samuel Beckett was born in Dublin. Educated in both French and English, he made his permanent home in Paris in 1936. Much of his earlier career followed the lines of his friend James Joyce, as did his concern with the sounds and rhythms of language. Like Joyce, Beckett has created a world of words, writing in both English and French, and then translating back and forth from each language, as the need arose. Two novels, Murphy (1938) and Watt (published 1953), and then the trilogy of fictions called Molloy (1951), Malone Dies (1952), and The Unnamable (1953) helped to readdress the whole idea of prose fiction for the twentieth century. Obviously indebted to Joyce, Beckett's fictions break free of the master and explore more deeply underground situations and underworld philosophers, tramps, bums, and madmen. Notwithstanding his achievement in the novel, Beckett became best known for his plays, beginning with the ground-breaking Waiting for Godot in 1952. This was followed by Endgame (1957), Krapp's Last Tape (1959), Happy Days (1961), and several one-acters or brief, single-sequence plays, some without words. Also a poet, Beckett published Poems in 1963, and a number of volumes of short poetic-prose pieces: Stories and Texts for Nothing (1967), No's Knife (1970), and More Pricks Than Kicks (written earlier, published in 1970). In 1969, Beckett was awarded the Nobel Prize for literature. In the story "Yellow," Belacqua is a typical Beckett hero from More Pricks Than Kicks, from which the story is taken, reminiscent of the two derelicts in Waiting for Godot and the wanderers in his five early novels.

Yellow

The night-nurse bounced in on the tick of five and turned on the light. Belacqua waked feeling greatly refreshed and eager to wrestle with this new day. He had underlined, as quite a callow boy, a phrase in Hardy's *Tess*, won by dint of cogging in the Synod: "When grief ceases to be speculative, sleep sees her opportunity." He had manipulated that sentence for many years now, amending its terms, as "joy" for "grief," to answer his occasions, even calling upon it to bear the strain of certain applications for which he feared it had not been intended, and still it held good through it all. He waked with it now in his mind, as though it had been there all the time he slept, holding that fragile place against dreams.

The nurse brought a pot of tea and a glass of strong salts on a tray.

"Pfui!" exclaimed Belacqua.

But the callous girl preferred to disregard this.

"When are they doing me?" he asked.

"You are down for twelve," she said.

Down . . . !

She took herself off.

He drank the salts and two cups of tea, and be damned to the whole of them. Then of course he was wide awake, poor fellow. But what cared he, what cared saucy Belacqua? He switched off the lamp and lay on his back in this the darkest hour, smoking.

Carry it off as he might, he was in a dreadful situation. At twelve sharp he would be sliced open—zeep!—with a bistoury. This was the idea that his mind, for the moment, was in no fit state to entertain. If this Hunnish idea once got a foothold in his little psyche in its present unready condition, topsy-turvy after yesterday's debauch of anxiety and then the good night's sleep coming on top of that, it would be annihilated. The psyche, not the idea—which was precisely the reverse of what he wished. For himself, to do him justice, he did not care. His mind might cave in for all he cared, he was tired of the old bastardo. But the unfortunate part of it was that this would appear in his behavior, he would scream and kick and bite and scratch when they came for him, beg for execution to be stayed and perhaps even wet the bed, and what a reflection on his late family that would be! The grand old Huguenot family guts, he could not do the dirty on them like that (to say nothing of his natural anxiety to be put to rights with as little fuss as possible.)

"My sufferings under the anesthetic," he reflected, "will be exquisite, but I shall not remember them."

He dashed out his cigarette and put on the lamp, this not so much for the company of the light as in order to postpone daybreak until he should feel a little more sure of himself. Daybreak, with its suggestion of a nasty birth, he could not bear. Downright and all as he was, he could not bear the sight of this punctilious and almost, he sometimes felt, superfluous delivery. This was mere folly and well he knew it. He tried hard to cure himself, to frighten or laugh himself out of this weakness, but to no avail. He would grow tired and say to himself: "I am what I am." That was the end of all his meditations and endeavours: "I am what I am." He had read the phrase somewhere and liked it and made it his own.

But God at least was good—as He usually is if we only know how to take Him—in this way: that six hours separated him, Belacqua, from the ordeal, six hours were allotted to him in which to make up his mind, as a pretty drab her face for an enemy. His getting the fleam in the neck, his suffering the tortures of the damned while seeming to slumber as peacefully as a little child, were of no consequence, as hope-saved they were not, so long as his mind was master of the thought of them. What he had to do, and had with typical slackness put off doing till the last moment, was to arrange a hot reception in his mind for the thought of all the little acts of kindness that he was to endure before the day was out. Then he would be able to put a good face on it. Otherwise not. Otherwise he would bite, scratch, etc., when they came for him. Now the good face was all that concerned him, the bold devil-may-care expression (except of course that he was also anxious to be made well with the least possible ado). He did not pause to consider himself in this matter, nor the light that the coming ordeal would shed on his irrevocable self, because he really was tired of that old bastardo. No, his whole concern was with other people, the lift-boy, nurses and sisters, the local doc coming to put him off, the eminent surgeon, the handy man at hand to clean up and put the bits into the incinerator, and all the friends of his late family, who would ferret out the whole truth. It did not matter about him, he was what he was. But these outsiders, the family guts, and so on and so forth, all these things had to be considered.

An asthmatic in the room overhead was coughing his heart up. "God bless you," thought Belacqua, "you make things easier for me." But when did the unfortunate sleep? During the day, the livelong day, through the stress of the day. At twelve sharp he would be sound, or, better again, just dozing off. Meantime he coughed, as Crusoe labored to bring his gear ashore, the snugger to be.

Belacqua made a long arm and switched off the lamp. It threw shadows. He would close his eyes, he would bilk the dawn in that way. What were the eyes anyway? The posterns of the mind. They were safer closed.

If only he were well-bred or, failing that, plucky. Blue blood or gamecock! Even if he lived in his mind as much as was his boast. Then he need not be at all this pains to make himself ready. Then it would only be a question of finding a comfortable position in the strange bed, trying to sleep or reading a book, waiting calmly for the Angelus. But he was an indolent bourgeois poltroon, very talented up to a point, but not fitted for private life in the best and brightest sense, in the sense to which he referred when he bragged of how he furnished his mind and lived there, because it was the last ditch when all was said and done. But he preferred not to wait till then, he fancied it might be wiser to settle down there straight away and not wait till he was kicked into it by the world, just at the moment maybe when he was beginning to feel at home in the world. He could no more go back into his heart in that way than he could keep out of it altogether. So now there was nothing for it but to lie on his back in the dark, and exercise his talent. Unless of course he chose to distress the friends of his late family (to say nothing of perhaps jeopardizing the cure for which the friends of his late family were paying). But he had too much of the grocer's sense of honor for that. Rather than have that happen he would persist with his psyche, he would ginger up his little psyche for the occasion.

Poor Belacqua, he seems to be having a very dull, irksome morning, preparing for the fray in this manner. But he will make up for it later on, there is a good time coming for him later on, when the doctors have given him a new lease of apathy.

What were his tactics in this crisis?

In a less tight corner he might have been content to bar-ricade his mind against the idea. But this was at the best a slipshod method, since the idea, howsoever blatant an enemy and despite the strictest guard, was almost certain to sidle in sooner or later under the skirts of a friend, and then the game was up. Still, in the ordinary run of adversity, he would doubt-less have bowed to his natural indolence and adopted such a course, he would have been content merely to think of other things and hope for the best. But this was no common or garden fix, he was properly up against it this time, there could be no question of half-measures on this melancholy occasion.

His plan therefore was not to refuse admission to the idea, but to keep it at bay until his mind was ready to receive it. Then let it in and pulverize it. Obliterate the bastard. He ground his teeth in the bed. Flitter the——, tear it into pieces like a priest. So far so good. But by what means? Belacqua ransacked his mind for a suitable engine of destruction.

At this crucial point the good God came to his assistance with a phrase from a paradox of Donne: "Now among our wise men, I doubt not but many would be found, who would laugh at Heraclitus weeping, none which would weep at De-mocritus laughing." This was a godsend and no error. Not the phrase as a judgment, but its terms, the extremes of wisdom that it tendered to Belacqua. It is true that he did not care for these black and white alternatives as a rule. Indeed he even went so far as to hazard a little paradox on his own account, to the effect that between contraries no alternation was possible. But was it the moment for a man to be nice? Belacqua snatched eagerly at the issue. Was it to be laughter or tears? It came to the same thing in the end, but which was it to be *now*? It was too late to arrange for the luxury of both. Now in a moment he would fill his mind with one or other of these two orders of rays, shall we say ultrared and ultraviolet, and prepare to perforate his adversary.

"Really," thought Belacqua, "I cannot remember having ever spent a more dreary morning; but needs must, that was a true saying, when the devil drives."

At this all-important juncture of his delirium Belacqua found himself blinking his eyes rapidly, a regular nictation, so that little flaws of dawn gushed into his mind. This had not been done with intent, but when he found that it seemed to be benefiting him in some curious way he kept it up, until gradually the inside of his skull began to feel sore. Then he desisted and went back to the dilemma.

Here, as indeed at every crux of the enterprise, he sacrificed his sense of what was personal and proper to himself to the desirability of making a certain impression on other people, an impression almost of gallantry. He must efface himself altogether and do the little soldier. It was this paramount consideration that made him decide in favor of Bim and Bom, Grock, Democritus, whatever you are pleased to call it, and postpone its dark converse to a less public occasion. This was an abnegation if you like, for Belacqua could not resist a lachrymose philosopher, and still less when, as was the case with Heraclitus, he was obscure at the same time. He was in his element in dingy tears, and luxuriously so when these were furnished by a pre-Socratic man of acknowledged distinction. How often had he not exclaimed, skies being grey: "Another minute of this and I consecrate the remnant of my life to Heraclitus of Ephesus, I shall be that Delian diver who, after the third or fourth submersion, returns no more to the surface!"

But weeping in this charnel house would be misconstrued. All the staff, from matron to lift-boy, would make the mistake of ascribing his tears, or, perhaps better, his tragic demeanor, not to the follies of humanity at large—which of course covered themselves—but rather to the tumor the size of a brick that he had on the back of his neck. This would be a very natural mistake and Belacqua was not blaming them. No blame attached to any living person in this matter. But the news would get round that Belacqua, so far from grinning and bearing, had piped his eye, or had been on the point of doing so. Then he would be disgraced and, by extension, his late family also.

So now his course was clear. He would arm his mind with laughter—laughter is not quite the word but it will have to serve—at every point, then he would admit the idea and blow it to pieces. Smears, as after a gorge of blackberries, of hilarity—which is not quite the word either—would be adhering to his lips as he stepped smartly, *ohne Hast aber ohne Rast,* into the torture-chamber. His fortitude would be generally commended.

How did he proceed to put this plan into execution?

He has forgotten, he has no use for it any more.

The night-nurse broke in upon him at seven with another pot of tea and two cuts of toast.

"That's all you'll get now," she said.

The impertinent slut! Belacqua very nearly told her to work it up. "Did the salts talk to you?" she said.

The sick man appraised her as she took his temperature and pulse. She was a tight, trim little bit.

"They whispered to me," he said.

When she was gone, he thought, What an all-but-flawless brunette, so spick and span too after having been on the go all night, at the beck and call of the first lousy old squaw who let fall her book or could not sleep for the roar of the traffic in Merrion Row. What the hell did anything matter anyway!

Pale wales in the east beyond the Land Commission. The day was going along nicely.

The night-nurse came back for the tray. That made her third appearance, if he was not mistaken. She would very shortly be relieved, she would eat her supper and go to bed. But not to sleep. The place was too full of noise and light at that hour, her bed a refrigerator. She could not get used to this night duty, she really could not. She lost weight and her little face became cavernous. Also it was very difficult to arrange anything with her fiancé. What a life!

"See you later," she said.

There was no controverting this. Belacqua cast about wildly for a reply that would please her and do him justice at the same time. *"Au plaisir"* was of course the very thing, but the wrong language. Finally he settled on "I suppose so" and discharged it at her in a very halfhearted manner, when she was more than half out of the door. He would have been very much better advised to let it alone and say nothing.

While he was still wasting his valuable time cursing himself for a fool, the door burst open and the day-nurse came in with a mighty rushing sound of starched apron. She was to have charge of him by day. She just missed being beautiful, this Presbyterian from Aberdeen. Aberdeen!

After a little conversation *obiter*, Belacqua let fall casually, as though the idea had only just occurred to him, whereas in fact it had been tormenting him insidiously for some time:

"Oh nurse the W.C. perhaps it might be as well to know." Like that, all in a rush, without any punctuation.

When she had finished telling him, he knew roughly where the place was. But he stupidly elected to linger on in the bed with his uneasy load, codding himself that it would be more decent not to act incontinent on intelligence of so intimate a kind. In his anxiety to give color to this pause he asked Miranda when he was being done.

"Didn't the night-nurse tell you?" she said sharply. "At twelve."

So the night-nurse had split. The treacherous darling!

He got up and set out, leaving Miranda at work on the bed. When he got back she was gone. He got back into the made bed.

Now the sun, that creature of habit, shone in through the window.

A little Aschenputtel, gummy and pert, skipped in with sticks and coal for the fire.

"Morning," she said.

"Yes," said Belacqua. But he retrieved himself at once. "What a lovely room," he exclaimed. "All the morning sun."

No more was needed to give Aschenputtel his measure.

"Very lovely," she said bitterly, "right on me fire." She tore down the blind. "Putting out me good fire," she said.

That was certainly one way of looking at it.

"I had one old one in here," she said, "and he might be snoring but he wouldn't let the blind down."

Some old put had crossed her, that was patent.

"Not for God," she said, "so what did I do?" She screwed round on her knees from building the fire. Belacqua obliged her.

"What was that?" he said.

She turned back with a chuckle to her task. "I block it with a chair," she said, "and his shirt over the back."

"Ha," exclaimed Belacqua.

"Again he'd be up," she exulted, "don't you know." She laughed happily at the memory of this little deception. "I kep' it off all right," she said.

She talked and talked, and poor Belacqua, with his mind unfinished, had to keep his end up. Somehow he managed to create a very favorable impression.

"Well," she said at last, in an indescribable singsong, "g'bye now. See you later."

"That's right," said Belacqua.

Aschenputtel was engaged to be married to handy Andy; she had been for years. Meantime she gave him a dog's life.

Soon the fire was roaring up the chimney and Belacqua could not resist the temptation to get up and sit before it, clad only in his thin blue 100,000 Chemises pajamas. The coughing aloft had greatly abated since he first heard it. The man was gradually settling down, it did not require a Sherlock Holmes to realize that. But on the grand old yaller wall, crowding in upon his left hand, a pillar of higher tone, representing the sun, was spinning out its placid deiseal. This dribble of time, thought Belacqua, like sanies into a bucket, the world wants a new washer. He would draw the blind, both blinds.

But he was foiled by the entry of the matron with the morning paper—this, save the mark, by way of taking his mind off it. It is impossible to describe the matron. She was all right. She made him nervous the way she flung herself about.

Belacqua turned on the flow:

"What a lovely morning," he gushed, "a lovely room, all the morning sun."

The matron simply disappeared, there is no other word for it. The woman was there one moment and gone the next. It was extraordinary.

The theater sister came in. What a number of women there seemed to be in this place! She was a great raw châteaubriant of a woman, like the one on the Wincarnis bottle. She took a quick look at his neck.

"Pah," she scoffed, "that's nothing."

"Not at all," said Belacqua.

"Is that the lot?"

Belacqua did not altogether care for her tone.

"And a toe," he said, "to come off, or rather, portion of a toe."

"Top," she guffawed, "and bottom."

There was no controverting this. But he had learned his lesson. He let it pass.

This woman was found to improve on acquaintance. She had a coarse manner, but she was exceedingly gentle. She taught all her more likely patients to wind bandages. To do this well with the crazy little hand-windlass that she provided was no easy matter. The roll would become fusiform. But when one got to know the humors of the apparatus, then it could be coaxed into yielding the hard slender spools, perfect cylinders, that delighted her. All these willing slaves that passed through her hands, she blandished each one in turn. "I never had such tight, straight bandages," she would say. Then, just as the friendship established on this basis seemed about to develop into something more—how shall I say?— substantial, the patient would all of a sudden be well enough to go home. Some malignant destiny pursued this splendid woman. Years later, when the rest of the staff was forgotten, she would drift into the mind. She marked down Belacqua for the bandages.

Miranda came back, this time with the dressing tray. That voluptuous undershot cast of mouth, the clenched lips, almost *bocca romanã*, how had he failed to notice it before? Was it the same woman?

"Now," she said.

She lashed into the part with picric and ether. It beat him to understand why she should be so severe on his little bump of amativeness. It was not septic to the best of his knowledge. Then why this severity? Merely on the off-chance of its coming in for the fag end of a dig? It was very strange. It had not even been shaved. It jutted out under the short hairs like a cuckoo's bill. He trusted it would come to no harm. Really he could not afford to have it curtailed. His little bump of amativeness.

When his entire nape was as a bride's adorned (bating the obscene stain of the picric) and so tightly bandaged that he felt his eyes bulging, she transferred her compassion to the toes. She scoured the whole phalanx, top and bottom. Suddenly she began to titter. Belacqua nearly kicked her in the eye, he got such a shock. How dared she trespass on his program! He refusing to be tickled in this petty local way, trying with his teeth to reach his under lip and gouging his palms, and she forgetting herself, there was no other word for it. There were limits, he felt, to Democritus.

"Such a lang tootsy," she giggled.

Heavenly Father, the creature was bilingual. A lang tootsy! Belacqua swallowed his choler.

"Soon to be syne," he said in a loud voice. What his repartee lacked in wit it made up for in style. But it was lost on this granite Medusa.

"A long foot," he said agreeably, "I know, or a long nose. But a long toe, what does that denote?"

No answer. Was the woman then altogether cretinous? Or did she not hear him? Belting away there with her urinous picric and cooling her porridge in advance. He would try her again.

"I say," he roared, "that that toe you like so much will soon be only a memory." He could not put it plainer than that.

"Yes,"—the word died away and was repeated—"yes, his troubles are nearly over."

Belacqua broke down completely, he could not help it. This distant voice, like a *cor anglais* coming through the eve-

ning, and then the "his," the "his" was the last straw. He
buried his face in his hands, he did not care who saw him.

"I would like," he sobbed, "the cat to have it, if I might."

She would never have done with her bandage, it cannot
have measured less than a furlong. But of course it would
never do to leave anything to chance, Belacqua could appreciate that. Still, it seemed somehow disproportioned to the
length of even his toe. At last she made all fast round his
shin. Then she packed her tray and left. Some people go,
others leave. Belacqua felt like the rejected of these two that
night in a bed. He felt he had set Miranda somehow against
him. Was this then the haporth of paint? Miranda on whom
so much depended. *Merde!*

It was all Lister's fault. These damned happy Victorians.

His heart gave a great leap in its box with a fulminating
sense that he was all wrong, that anger would stand by him
better than the other thing, the laugh seemed so feeble, so
like a whinge in the end. But on second thoughts, no; anger
would turn aside when it came to the point, leaving him like
a sheep. Anyhow it was too late to turn back. He tried cautiously what it felt like to have the idea in his mind. . . .
Nothing happened, he felt no shock. So at least he had spiked
the brute, that was something.

At this point he went downstairs and had a truly military
evacuation, Army Service Corps. Coming back he did not
doubt that all would yet be well. He whistled a snatch outside
the duty-room. There was nothing left of his room when he
got back but Miranda, Miranda more prognathous than ever,
loading a syringe. Belacqua tried to make light of this.

"What now?" he said.

But she had the weapon into his bottom and discharged before he realized what was happening. Not a cry escaped him.

"Did you hear what I said?" he said. "I insist, it is my
right, on knowing the meaning of this, the purpose of this
injection, do you hear me?"

"It is what every patient gets," she said, "before going
down to the theater."

Down to the theater! Was there a conspiracy in this place to
destroy him, body and soul? His tongue clave to his palate.
They had desiccated his secretions. First blood to the profession!

The theater-socks were the next little bit of excitement.
Really, the theater seemed to take itself very seriously. To
hell with your socks, he thought, it's your mind I want.

Now events began to move more rapidly. First of all an angel of the Lord came to his assistance with a funny story, really very funny indeed—it always made Belacqua laugh till he cried—about the parson who was invited to take a small part in an amateur production. All he had to do was to snatch at his heart when the revolver went off, cry "By God! I'm shot!" and drop dead. The parson said certainly, he would be most happy, if they would have no objection to his drawing the line at "By God!" on such a secular occasion. He would replace it, if they had no objection, by "Mercy!" or "Upon my word!" or something of that kind. "Oh my! I'm shot!," how would that be?

But the production was so amateur that the revolver went off indeed and the man of God was transfixed.

"Oh!" he cried, "Oh! . . . BY CHRIST! I *AM* SHOT!"

It was a mercy that Belacqua was a dirty, low-down Low Church Protestant highbrow and able to laugh at this sottish jest. Laugh! How he did laugh, to be sure. Till he cried.

He got up and began to titivate himself. Now he could hear the asthmatic breathing if he listened hard. The day was out of danger, any fool could see that. A little sealed cardboard box lying on the mantelpiece caught his eye. He read the inscription: Fraisse's Ferruginous Ampoules for the Intensive Treatment of Anaemia by Intramuscular Squirtation. Registered Trademark—Mozart. The little Hexenmeister of Don Giovanni, now in his narrow cell forever mislaid, dragged into bloodlessness! How very amusing. Really, the world was in great form this morning.

Now two further women—there was no end to them—the one of a certain age, the other not, entered, ripping off their regulation cuffs as they advanced. They pounced on the bed. The precautionary oil sheet, the cradle . . . Belacqua padded up and down before the fire, the ends of his pajamas tucked like a cyclist's into the sinister socks. He would smoke one more cigarette, nor count the cost. It was astonishing, when he came to think of it, how the entire routine of this place, down to the meanest detail, was calculated to a cow's toe to promote a single end, the relief of suffering in the long run. Observe how he dots his i's now and crucifies his t's to the top of his bent. He was being put to his trumps.

Surreptitiously they searched his yellow face for signs of discomposure. In vain. It was a mask. But perhaps his voice would tremble. One, she whose life had changed, took it upon herself to say in a peevish tone:

"Sister Beamish won't bless you for soiling her good socks."

Sister Beamish would not bless him.

The voice of this person was in ruins, but she abused it further.

"Would you not stand on the mat?"

His mind was made up in a flash: he would stand on the mat. He would meet them in this matter. If he refused to stand on the mat he was lost in the eyes of these two women.

"Anything," he said, "to oblige Sister Beamish."

Miranda was having a busy morning. Now she appeared for the fourth or fifth time, he had lost count, complete with shadowy assistants. The room seemed full of grey women. It was like a dream.

"If you have any false teeth," she said, "you may remove them."

His hour was at hand, there was no blinking at the fact.

Going down in the lift with Miranda he felt his glasses under his hand. This was a blessed accident if you like, just when the silence was becoming awkward.

"Can I trust you with these?" he said.

She put them into her bosom. The divine creature! He would assault her in another minute.

"No smoking," she said, "in the operating theater."

The surgeon was washing his invaluable hands as Belacqua swaggered through the antechamber. He that hath clean hands shall be stronger. Belacqua cut the surgeon. But he flashed a dazzling smile at the Wincarnis. She would not forget that in a hurry.

He bounced up on to the table like a bridegroom. The local doc was in great form, he had just come from standing best man, he was all togged up under his vestments. He recited his exhortation and clapped on the nozzle.

"Are you right?" said Belacqua.

The mixture was too rich, there could be no question about that. His heart was running away, terrible yellow yerks in his skull. "One of the best," he heard those words that did not refer to him. The expression reassured him. The best man clawed at his tap.

By Christ! He did die!

They had clean forgotten to auscultate him!

William Sansom
(1912–   )

Wiliam Sansom was born in England and educated there and on the continent. Although he has written novels (for example, The Body, 1945), he is best known for his short stories. Since 1944, with Fireman Flower, he has published several collections: The Face of Innocence (1951), Something Terrible Something Lovely (1954), A Bed of Roses (1954), and The Ulcerated Milkman (1966). From these, he picked those stories that he wished to have appear in his Collected Stories. His short pieces are written in a sharp, edgy prose that helps to catch people at key moments in their lives, when they are to be either illuminated or annihilated.

How Claeys Died

In Germany, two months after the capitulation, tall green grass and corn had grown up round every remnant of battle, so that the war seemed to have happened many years ago. A tank, nosing up from the corn like a pale grey toad, would already be rusted, ancient: the underside of an overturned carrier exposed intricacies red-brown and clogged like an agricultural machine abandoned for years. Such objects were no longer the contemporary traffic, they were exceptional carcasses; one expected their armour to melt like the armour of crushed beetles, to enter the earth and help fertilize further the green growth in which they were already drowned.

Claeys and his party—two officers and a driver—drove past many of these histories, through miles of such fertile green growth stretching flatly to either side of the straight and endless grey avenues. Presently they entered the outskirts of a town. This was a cathedral town, not large, not known much—

until by virtue of a battle its name now resounded in black letters the size of the capital letters on the maps of whole countries. This name would now ring huge for generations, it would take its part in the hymn of a national glory, such a name had already become sacred, stony, a symbol of valour. Claeys looked about him with interest—he had never seen the town before, only heard of the battle and suffered with the soldiers who had taken it and held it for four hopeful days with the hope dying each hour until nearly all were dead, hope and soldiers. Now as they entered the main street, where already the white tram-trains were hooting, where the pale walls were chipped and bullet-chopped, where nevertheless there had never been the broad damage of heavy bombs and where therefore the pavements and shop-fronts were already washed and civil—as they entered these streets decked with summer dresses and flecked with leaf patterns, Claeys looked in vain for the town of big letters, and smelled only perfume; a wall of perfume; they seemed to have entered a scent-burg, a sissy-burg, a town of female essences, Grasse—but it was only that this town happened to be planted with lime-trees, lime-trees everywhere, and these limes were all in flower, their shaded greenery alive with the golden powdery flower whose essence drifted down to the streets and filled them. The blood was gone, the effort of blood had evaporated. Only scent, flowers, sunlight, trams, white dresses.

"A nice memorial," Claeys thought. "Keep it in the geography book." Then the car stopped outside a barracks. The officers got out. Claeys said he would wait in the car. He was not in uniform, he was on a civil mission, attached temporarily to the army. It does not matter what mission. It was never fulfilled. All that need be said is that Claeys was a teacher, engaged then on relief measures, a volunteer for this work of rehabilitation of the enemy, perhaps a sort of half-brother-of-mercy as during the occupation he had been a sort of half-killer. Now he wanted to construct quickly the world of which he had dreamed during the shadow years; now he was often as impatient of inaction as he had learned to be patient before. Patience bends before promise: perhaps this curiosity for spheres of action quickened his interest as now a lorry-load of soldiers drew up and jumped down at the barrack-gate. One of the soldiers said: "They're using mortars." Another was saying: "And do you blame 'em?"

There had been trouble, they told Claeys, up at the camp for expatriates—the camp where forced labourers imported from all over Europe waited for shipment home. A group of these had heard that a released German prisoner-of-war was returning to work his farm in the vicinity of the camp. They had decided to raid the farm at nightfall, grab as much food as possible, teach the German a trick or two. But the German had somehow got hold of a grenade—from the fields, or perhaps hidden in the farmhouse. At any rate, he had thrown it and killed two of the expatriates. The others had retreated, the story had spat round, before long the expatriates were coming back on the farm in full strength. They had rifles and even mortars. The news got back to the occupational military and a picket had been sent over. The mortars were opening fire as it arrived: but they were stopped, the expatriates respected the British. Yet to maintain this respect they had to keep a picket out there for the night. Not all the polskis or czechskis or whoever they were had gone home. A few had hung about, grumbling. The air was by no means clear.

When the officers returned, Claeys told them that he had altered his plans, he wanted to go up and take a look at this expatriates' camp. He gave no reason, and it is doubtful whether he had then a special reason; he felt only that he ought to see these expatriates and talk to them. He had no idea of what to say, but something of the circumstances might suggest a line later.

So they drove out into the country again, into the green. Rich lucent corn stretched endlessly to either side of the straight and endless road. Regularly, in perfect order, precisely intervalled beeches flashed by: a rich, easy, discreet roof of leaves shaded their passage as the foliage met high above. Occasionally a notice at the roadside reminded them of mines uncleared beyond the verges, occasionally a tree bore an orderly white notice addressed to civil traffic. And occasionally a unit of civil traffic passed—a family wheeling a handcart, a cyclist and his passenger, and once a slow-trudging German soldier making his grey way back along the long road to his farm. But there was nothing about this figure in gray-green to suggest more than a farmer dressed as a soldier; he walked slowly, he seemed to be thinking slowly, secure in his destination and free of time as any countryman walking slowly home on an empty road.

All was order. Birds, of course, sang. A green land, unbelievably quiet and rich, sunned its moisture. Each square yard lay unconcerned with the next, just as each measure of the road lay back as they passed, unconcerned with their passing, contented, remaining where it had always been under its own beech, a piece of land. And when at last the beech-rows stopped, the whole of that flat country seemed to spread itself suddenly open. The sky appeared, blue and sailing small white clouds to give it air. Those who deny the flatlands forget the sky—over flat country the sky approaches closer than anywhere else, it takes a shape, it becomes the blue-domed lid on a flat plate of earth. Here is a greater intimacy between the elements; and for once, for a little, the world appears finite.

The carload of four travelled like a speck over this flat space. And Claeys was thinking: "Such a summer, such still air—something like a mother presiding heavily and quietly, while down in her young the little vigours boil and breed . . . air almost solid, a sort of unseen fruit fibre . . . a husk guarding the orderly chaos of the breeding ground. . . ."

Such a strict order seemed indeed to preside within the intricate anarchy—success and failure, vigorous saplings from the seeds of good fortune, a pennyworth of gas from the seeds that fall on stony ground: yet a sum total of what might appear to be complete achievement, and what on the human level appears to be peace. And on that level, the only real level, there appeared—over by the poplar plumes? Or by the wind-mill? Or at some flat point among the converged hedges?—there appeared one scar, a scar of purely human disorder: over somewhere lay this camp of ten thousand displaced souls, newly freed but imprisoned still by their strange environment and by their great expectations born and then as instantly barred. On the face of it, these seemed to represent disorder, or at most a residue of disorder. But was this really so? Would such disorder not have appeared elsewhere, in similar quantity and under conditions of apparent order? Were they, perhaps, not anything more than stony-grounders—the disfavoured residue of an anarchic nature never governed directly, only impalpably guided by more general and less concerned governments? Was it right to rationalize, to impose order upon such seed, was it right—or at least, was it sensible? It was right, obviously—for a brain to reason is itself a part of nature and it would be wrong to divert it from its necessitous reasoning. But right though reason may be, there was no more reason to put one's faith in the impeccable work of the reasoning brain than to imagine that any other impressive yet deluded machine—like, for instance, the parachute seed—should by its apparent ingenuity succeed. Look at the parachute seed—this amazing seed actually flies off the insensate plant-mother! It sails on to the wind! The seed itself hangs beneath such an intricate parasol, it is carried from the roots of its mother to land on fertile ground far away and set up there an emissary generation! And more—when it lands, this engine is so constructed that draughts inch-close to the soil drag, drag at the little parachute, so that the seed beneath actually erodes the earth, digs for itself a little trench of shelter, buries itself! Amazing! And what if the clever little seed is borne on the wrong wind to a basin of basalt?

Claeys was thinking: "The rule of natural anarchy—a few succeed, many waste and die. No material waste: only a huge waste of effort. The only sure survival is the survival of the greater framework that includes the seed and all other things on the earth—the furious landcrab, the bright young Eskimo, the Antiguan cornbroker—every thing and body . . . and these thrive and decay and compensate . . . just as we, on the threshold of some golden age of reason, just as we are the ones to harness some little nuclear genius, pack it into neat canisters, store it ready to blow up all those sunny new clinics when the time comes, the time for compensation. . . ."

Just then the car drove into a small town on the bank of a broad river. Instantly, in a matter of yards, the green withered and the party found themselves abruptly in what seemed to be some sort of a quarry, dry, dug-about, dust-pale, slagged up on either side with excavated stones.

It was indeed an excavation; it was of course the street of a town. This town was dead. It had been bombed by a thousand aircraft, shelled by an entire corps of artillery and then fought through by land soldiers. No houses were left, no streets. The whole had been churned up, smashed and jigsawed down again, with some of the jig-saw pieces left upended—those gaunt walls remaining—and the rest of the pieces desiccated into mounds and hollows and flats. No grass grew. The air hung sharp with vaporized dust. A few new alleys had been bulldozed through; these seemed pointless, for now there was no traffic, the armies had passed through, the town was deserted. Somewhere in the centre Claeys stopped the car. He held up his hand for silence. The four men listened. Throughout that wasted city there was no sound. No distant muttering, no murmur. No lost hammering, no drowned cry. No word, no footstep. No wheels. No wind shifting a branch—for there were no trees. No flapping of torn cloth, this avalanche had covered all the cloth. No birds—but one, a small bird that flew straight over, without singing; above such a desert it moved like a small vulture, a shadow, a bird without destination. Brick, concrete, gravel-dust—with only two shaped objects as far all round as they could see: one, an intestinal engine of fat iron pipes, black and big as an up-ended lorry, something thrown out of a factory; and leaning on its side a pale copper-green byzantine cupola like a gigantic sweet-kiosk blown over by the wind, the tower fallen from what had been the town church. This—in a town that had been the size of Reading.

Almost reverently, as on sacred ground, they started the car and drove off again. Through the pinkish-white mounds the sound of the motor seemed now to intrude garishly. Claeys wanted only to be out of the place. Again, this destruction seemed to have occurred years before; but now because of the very absence of green, of any life at all, of any reason to believe that people had ever lived there. Not even a torn curtain. They wormed through and soon, as abruptly as before, the country began and as from a seasonless pause the summer embraced them once more.

Claeys stood up off his seat to look over the passing hedges. The camp was somewhere near now. The driver said, two kilometres. Surely, Claeys thought, surely with that dead town so near the men in this camp could realize the extent of the upheaval, the need for a pause before their journey could be organized? Surely they must see the disruption, this town, the one-way bridges over every stream far around, the roads pitted and impassable? Yet . . . what real meaning had these evidences? Really, they were too negative to be understood, too much again of something long finished. It was not as if something positive, like an army passing, held up one's own purpose; not even a stream of aircraft, showing that at least somewhere there was an effort and direction. No, over these fields there was nothing, not even the sense of a pause, when something might be restarted; instead a vacuity stretched abroad, a vacuum of human endeavour, with the appalling contrast of this vegetable growth continuing evenly and unconcerned. That was really the comprehensible evidence, this sense of the land and of the essence of life continuing, so that one must wish to be up and walking away, to be off to take part not in a regrowth but in a simple continuation of what had always been. For every immediate moment there was food to be sought, the pleasures of taste to be enjoyed: what was more simple than to walk out and put one's hands on a cap-full of eggs, a pig, a few fat hens? And if a grey uniform intervened, then it was above all a grey uniform, something instinctively obstructive, in no real sense connected with the dead town. The only real sympathy that ever came sometimes to soften the greyness of this grey was a discovery, felt occasionally with senses of wonder and unease, that this uniform went walking and working through its own mined cornfields and sometimes blew itself up—that therefore there must be a man inside it, a farmer more than a soldier. But the grey was mostly an obstruction to the ordinary daily desire for food, for fun, for something to be tasted. The day for these men was definitely a day. It was no twenty-four hours building up to a day in the future when something would happen. No future day had been promised. There was, therefore, no succession of days, no days for ticking off, for passing through and storing in preparation. There were in fact the days themselves, each one a matter for living, each a separate dawning and tasting and setting.

Suddenly Claeys heard singing, a chorus of men's voices. A second later the driver down behind the windshield heard it. He nodded, as though they had arrived. The singing grew louder, intimate—as though it came from round a corner that twisted the road immediately ahead. But it came from a lane just before, it flourished suddenly into a full-throated slavic anthem—and there was the lane crowded with men, some sitting, others marching four abreast out into the road. The car whirred down to a dead halt. The singing wavered and stopped. Claeys saw that the driver had only his left hand on the wheel—his other hand was down gripping the black butt of a revolver at his knee. (He had never done this driving through German crowds earlier.)

"It's not the camp," the driver said. "These are some of them, though. The camp's a kilometre up the road." He kept his eyes scanning slowly up and down the line of men crowding in the lane's entry, he never looked up at Claeys. Then the men came a few paces forward, though they looked scarcely interested. Probably they were pushed forward by the crowd behind, many of whom could not have seen the car, many of whom were still singing.

Claeys stood upright and said: "I'd like to talk to these . . . you drive on, get round the corner and wait. I don't want that military feeling."

The men looked on with mild interest, as though they might

have had many better things to do. They looked scarcely
"displaced"; they had a self-contained air, an independence.
There was no censure in their stare; equally no greeting; nor
any love. Their clothes were simple, shirts and greyish trousers and boots: though these were weather-stained, they were
not ragged.

Claeys jumped down. An interest seemed to quicken in
some of the watching men as they saw how Claeys was dressed—
béret, plus-fours, leather jacket. It was because of these clothes
that the military in the car gave Claeys no salute as they drove
off; also because they disapproved of this kind of nonsense,
and this may have been why they neither smiled nor waved,
but rather nodded impersonally and whirred off round the
corner. They might, for instance, have been dropping Claeys
after giving him some sort of a lift.

So that Claeys was left quite alone on the road, standing
and smiling at the crowd of expatriates grouped at the entrance to the lane. The car had disappeared. It had driven
off the road and round the corner. There, as often happens
when a vehicle disappears from view, its noise had seemed
to vanish too. Presumably it had stopped. But equally it might
have been presumed far away on its journey to the next town.

The men took a pace or two forward, now beginning to
form a crescent-shape round Claeys, while Claeys began to
speak in English: "Good afternoon, mates. Excuse me, I'm
Pieter Claeys—native of Belgique." None of the men smiled.
They only stared hard. They were too absorbed now even to
mutter a word between themselves. They were searching for
an explanation, a sign that would clarify this stranger. They
were unsure, and certainly it seemed unimpressed. "Good
afternoon, comrades," Claeys shouted. "Gentlemen, hello!"

Without waiting, for the silence was beginning to weigh,
he turned into French. "Suis Claeys de Belgique. Je veux
vous aider. Vous permettez—on peut causer un peu?"

He repeated: "Peut-être?" And in the pause while no one
answered he looked up and above the heads of these men,
feeling that his smile might be losing its first flavour, that
somehow an embarrassment might be dissolved if he looked
away.

The country again stretched wide and green. Claeys was
startled then to see sudden huge shapes of paint-box colour
erecting themselves in the distance. But then immediately he
saw what they were—the wings and fuselages of broken gliders. They rose like the fins of huge fish, tilted at queer angles,

grounded and breathlessly still. Difficult at first to understand, for their shapes were strange and sudden, and of an artifice dangerously like something natural: brightly coloured, they might have been shapes torn from an abstract canvas and stuck wilfully on this green background: or the bright broken toys left by some giant child.

Claeys tried again: "Gijmijneheeren zijt blijkbaar in moeilijkheden. Ik zou die gaarne vernemen. . . ."

The Dutch words came ruggedly out with a revival of his first vigour, for Claeys was more used to Dutch and its familiarity brought some ease again to his smile. It brought also a first muttering from the men.

They began to mutter to each other in a Slav-sounding dialect—Polish, Ukrainian, Czech, Russian?—and as this muttering grew it seemed to become an argument. Claeys wanted instantly to make himself clearer, he seemed to have made some headway at last and so now again he repeated the Dutch. This time he nodded, raised his arm in a gesture, even took a pace forward in his enthusiasm. But now one of the men behind began to shout angrily, and would have pushed himself forward shaking his fist—had the others not held him.

It was not clear to Claeys—he felt that the Dutch had been understood, and yet what he had said was friendly . . . he began to repeat the words again. Then, half-way through, he thought of a clearer way. He broke into German. There was every chance that someone might understand German; they might have been working here for three years or more; or anyway it was the obvious second language. ". . . So bin ich hier um Ihnen zu hilfen gekommen. Bitte Kameraden, hören Sie mal. . . ."

The muttering rose, they were plainly talking—and now not to each other but to him. The crescent had converged into a half-circle, these many men with livening faces were half round him. Claeys stood still. Overhead the summer sky made its huge dome, under which this small group seemed to make the pin-point centre. The green quiet stretched endlessly away to either side, the painted gliders stuck up brightly. No traffic.

". . . Bitte ein Moment . . . ich bin Freund, Freund, FREUND. . . ." And as he repeated this word "friend" he realized what his tongue had been quicker to understand—that none of his listeners knew the meaning of these German words. They knew only that he was speaking German, they knew the intonation well.

He stopped. For a moment, as the men nudged each other nearer, as the Slav words grew into accusation and imprecation, Claeys's mind fogged up appalled by this muddle, helplessly overwhelmed by such absurdity, such disorder and misunderstanding.

Then, making an effort to clear himself, he shook his head and looked closely from one man to the other. But the composure had gone: they were all mouth, eyes, anger and desire—they were no longer independent. And this was accumulating, breeding itself beyond the men as men. They had become a crowd.

Knowing that words were of no further use, Claeys did the natural thing—wearily, slowly he raised his arm in a last despairing bid for silence.

An unfortunate gesture. The shouting compounded into one confused roar. One of the men on the edge of the crowd jumped out and swung something in the air—a scythe. It cut Claeys down, and then all the pack of them were on him, kicking, striking, grunting and shouting less.

Claeys must have screamed as the scythe hit him—two shots thundered like two full stops into that muddle, there was an abrupt silence and two men fell forward; and then another shot and the men scattered crying into the lane.

Those three soldiers came running up to Claeys's body. They shot again into the men crowding the lane; but then the men, bottled up in the narrow lane, suddenly turned and raised their arms above their heads. The soldiers held their fire, their particular discipline actuated more strongly than their emotions. Two of them kept their guns alert, gestured the men forward. They came, hands raised, shambling awkwardly. The other officer bent down to Claeys.

He was almost finished, messed with blood and blue-white where the flesh showed. He was breathing, trying to speak; and the officer knelt down on both his knees and raised Claeys's head up. But Claeys never opened his eyes—they were bruised shut, anyway. And no words came from his lips, though the officer lowered his head and listened very carefully.

Through the pain, through his battered head, one thought muddled out enormously. "Mistake . . . mistake. . . ." And this split into two other confused, unanswered questions, weakening dulling questions. Broadly, if they could have been straightened out, these questions would have been: "Order or Disorder? Those fellows were the victims of an attempt to rule men into an impeccable order, my killing was the result of the worst, that is, the most stupid disorder. . . ."

But he couldn't get the words out, or any like them. Only—weakly, slowly he raised his right hand. He groped for the officer's hand, and the officer knew what he wanted and met the hand with his own in a handshake. Claeys just managed to point at the place where the men had been, where they still were. Then his head sank deep on to his neck. Again the officer knew what he wanted. He rose, his hand still outstretched from Claeys's grasp, like a hand held out by a splint. Then he started over towards the men.

Instinctively, for this hand of his was wet with blood, he wiped it on his tunic as he walked forward. Without knowing this, he raised his hand again into its gesture of greeting. There was a distasteful expression on his face, for he hardly liked such a duty.

So that when he shook hands with the first of the men, proffering to them, in fact, Claeys's handshake, none of these expatriates knew whether the officer was giving them Claeys's hand or whether he had wiped Claeys's gesture away in distaste and was now offering them his congratulation for killing such a common enemy as Claeys.

Dylan Thomas
(1914–1953)

Dylan Thomas, who became one of the three or four most significant English poets of his generation, was born in Swansea, Wales. He left school at seventeen to become a journalist. He entered the literary world with his Eighteen Poems *in 1934, and followed this with* Twenty-Five Poems *(1936),* The Map of Love *(1939),* The World I Breathe *(1939),* Deaths and Entrances *(1946), and* In Country Sleep and Other Poems *(1952). Thomas's poetry was conceived in striking, discordant images, its themes of birth, love, and death juxtaposed to mythic patterns derived from Christian legend, Welsh sources, and Thomas's individualistic reading of Freud. He became known as a brilliant reader of his often difficult work, also as a writer of evocative plays (especially* Under Milk Wood*), and the author of prose works such as* Adventures in the Skin Trade *(published posthumously in 1955) and* Portrait of the Artist As a Young Dog *(1940). Always one to burn the candle at both ends, Thomas died before his fortieth birthday.*

One Warm Saturday

The young man in a sailor's jersey, sitting near the summer huts to see the brown and white women coming out and the groups of pretty-faced girls with pale vees and scorched backs who picked their way delicately on ugly, red-toed feet over the sharp stones to the sea, drew on the sand a large, indented woman's figure; and a naked child, just out of the sea, ran over it and shook water, marking on the figure two wide wet eyes and a hole in the footprinted middle. He rubbed the woman away and drew a paunched man: the child ran over it, tossing her hair, and shook a row of buttons down its belly

476

and a line of drops, like piddle in a child's drawing, between the long legs stuck with shells.

In a huddle of picnicking women and their children, stretched out limp and damp in the sweltering sun or fussing over paper carriers or building castles that were at once destroyed by the tattered march of other picnickers to different pieces of the beach, among the ice-cream cries, the angrily happy shouts of boys playing ball, and the screams of girls as the sea rose to their waists, the young man sat alone with the shadows of his failure at his side. Some silent husbands, with rolled up trousers and suspenders dangling, paddled slowly on the border of the sea, paddling women, in thick, black picnic dresses, laughed at their own legs, dogs chased stones, and one proud boy rode the water on a rubber seal. The young man, in his wilderness, saw the holiday Saturday set down before him, false and pretty, as a flat picture under the vulgar sun; the disporting families with paper bags, buckets and spades, parasols and bottles, the happy, hot, and aching girls with sunburn liniments in their bags, the bronzed young men with chests, and the envious, white young men in waistcoats, the thin, pale, hairy, pathetic legs of the husbands silently walking through the water, the plump and curly, shaven-headed and bowed-backed children up to no sense with unrepeatable delight in the dirty sand, moved him, he thought dramatically in his isolation, to an old shame and pity; outside all holiday, like a young man doomed for ever to the company of his maggots, beyond the high and ordinary, sweating, sun-awakened power and stupidity of the summer flesh on a day and a world out, he caught the ball that a small boy had whacked into the air with a tiny tray, and rose to throw it back.

The boy invited him to play. A friendly family stood waiting some way off, the tousled women with their dresses tucked in their knickers, the bare-footed men in shirtsleeves, a number of children in slips and cut-down underwear. He bowled bitterly to a father standing with a tray before a wicket of hats. "The lone wolf playing ball," he said to himself as the tray whirled. Chasing the ball towards the sea, passing undressing women with a rush and a wink, tripping over a castle into a coil of wet girls lying like snakes, soaking his shoes as he grabbed the ball off a wave, he felt his happiness return in a boast of the body, and, "Look out, Duckworth, here's a fast one coming," he cried to the mother behind the hats. The ball bounced on a boy's head. In and out of the scattered families, among the sandwiches and clothes, uncles and mothers fielded the bouncing ball. A bald man, with his shirt hanging out, returned it in the wrong direction, and a collie carried it into the sea. Now it was mother's turn with the tray. Tray and ball together flew over her head. An uncle in a panama smacked the ball to the dog, who swam with it out of reach. They offered the young man egg-and-cress sandwiches and warm stout, and he and an uncle and a father sat down on the *Evening Post* until the sea touched their feet.

Alone again, hot and unhappy, for the boasting minute when he ran among the unknown people lying and running loudly at peace was struck away, like a ball, he said, into the sea, he walked to a space on the beach where a hell-fire preacher on a box marked "Mr. Matthews" was talking to a congregation of expressionless women. Boys with peashooters sat quietly near him. A ragged man collected nothing in a cap. Mr. Matthews shook his cold hands, stormed at the holiday, and cursed the summer from his shivering box. He cried for a new warmth. The strong sun shone into his bones, and he buttoned his coat collar. Valley children, with sunken, impudent eyes, quick tongues and singing voices, chest thin as shells, gathered round the Punch and Judy and the Stop Me tricycles, and he denied them all. He contradicted the girls in their underclothes combing and powdering, and the modest girls cleverly dressing under tents of towels.

As Mr. Matthews cast down the scarlet town, drove out the bare-bellied boys who danced around the ice-cream man, and wound the girls' sunburnt thighs about with his black overcoat—"Down! down!" he cried, "the night is upon us"—the young man in dejection stood, with a shadow at his shoulder, and thought of Porthcawl's Coney Beach, where his friends were rocking with girls on the Giant Racer or tearing in the Ghost Train down the skeletons' tunnel. Leslie Bird would have his arms full of coconuts. Brenda was with Herbert at the rifle-range. Gil Morris was buying Molly a cocktail with a cherry at the "Esplanade." Here he stood, listening to Mr. Matthews, the retired drinker, crying darkness on the evening sands, with money hot in his pocket and Saturday burning away.

In his loneliness he had refused their invitations. Herbert, in his low, red sports car, G. B. at the back, a sea-blown nymph on the radiator, called at his father's house, but he said: "I'm not in the mood, old man. I'm going to spend a quiet day. Enjoy yourselves. Don't take too much pop." Only waiting for the sun to set, he stood in the sad circle with the pleasureless women who were staring at a point in the sky behind their prophet, and wished the morning back. Oh, boy! to be wasting his money now on the rings and ranges of the fair, to be sitting in the chromium lounge with a short worth one and six and a Turkish cigarette, telling the latest one to the girls, seeing the sun, through the palms in the lounge window, sink over the promenade, over the Bath chairs, the cripples and widows, the beach-trousered, kerchiefed, week-end wives, the smart, kiss-curled girls with plain and spectacled girl friends, the innocent, swaggering, loud bad boys, and the poms at the ankles, and the cycling sweetmen. Ronald had sailed to Ilfracombe on the *Lady Moira*, and, in the thick saloon, with a party from Brynhyfryd, he'd be knocking back nips without a thought that on the sands at home his friend was alone and pussyfoot at six o'clock, and the evening dull as a chapel. All his friends had vanished into their pleasures.

He tought: Poets live and walk with their poems; a man with visions needs no other company; Saturday is a crude day; I must go home and sit in my bedroom by the boiler. But he was not a poet living and walking, he was a young man in a sea town on a warm bank holiday, with two pounds to spend; he had no visions, only two pounds and a small body with its feet on the littered sand; serenity was for old men; and he moved away, over the railway points, on to the tramlined road.

He snarled at the flower clock in Victoria Gardens.

"And what shall a prig do now?" he said aloud, causing a young woman on a bench opposite the white-tiled urinal to smile and put her novel down.

She had chestnut hair arranged high on her head in an old-fashioned way, in loose coils and a bun, and a Woolworth's white rose grew out of it and drooped to touch her ear. She wore a white frock with a red paper flower pinned on the breast, and rings and bracelets that came from a fun-fair stall. Her eyes were small and quite green.

He marked, carefully and coldly in one glance, all the unusual details of her appearance; it was the calm, unstartled certainty of her bearing before his glance from head to foot, the innocent knowledge, in her smile and the set of her head, that she was defended by her gentleness and accessible strangeness against all rude encounters and picking looks, that made his fingers tremble. Though her frock was long and the collar high, she could as well be naked there on the blis-

tered bench. Her smile confessed her body bare and spotless
and willing and warm under the cotton, and she waited without guilt.

How beautiful she is, he thought, with his mind on words
and his eyes on her hair and red and white skin, how beautifully she waits for me, though she does not know she is
waiting and I can never tell her.

He had stopped and was staring. Like a confident girl before a camera, she sat smiling, her hands folded, her head
slightly to one side so that the rose brushed her neck. She
accepted his admiration. The girl in a million took his long
look to herself, and cherished his stupid love.

Midges flew into his mouth. He hurried on shamefully. At
the gates of the Gardens he turned to see her for the last
time on earth. She had lost her calm with his abrupt and
awkward going, and stared in confusion after him. One hand
was raised as though to beckon him back. If he waited, she
would call him. He walked round the corner and heard her
voice, a hundred voices, and all hers, calling his name, and
a hundred names that were all his, over the bushy walls.

And what shall the terrified prig of a love-mad young man
do next? he asked his reflection silently in the distorting mirror of the empty "Victoria" saloon. His ape-like, hanging
face, with "Bass" across the forehead, gave back a cracked
sneer.

If Venus came in on a plate, said the two red, melon-slice
lips, I would ask for vinegar to put on her.

She could drive my guilt out; she could smooth away my
shame; why didn't I stop to talk to her? he asked.

You saw a queer tart in a park, his reflection answered,
she was a child of nature, oh my! oh my! Did you see the
dewdrops in her hair? Stop talking to the mirror like a man
in a magazine, I know you too well.

A new head, swollen and lop-jawed, wagged behind his
shoulder. He spun round, to hear the barman say:

"Has the one and only let you down? You look like death
warmed up. Have this one on the house. Free beer to-day.
Free X's." He pulled the beer handle. "Only the best served
here. Straight from the rust. You do look queer," he said,
"the only one saved from the wreck and the only wreck saved.
Here's looking at you!" He drank the beer he had drawn.

"May I have a glass of beer, please?"

"What do you think this is, a public house?"

On the polished table in the middle of the saloon the young

man drew, with a finger dipped in strong, the round head of a girl and piled a yellow froth of hair upon it.

"Ah! dirty, dirty!" said the barman, running round from behind the counter and rubbing the head away with a dry cloth.

Shielding the dirtiness with his hat, the young man wrote his name on the edge of the table and watched the letters dry and fade.

Through the open bay-window, across the useless railway covered with sand, he saw the black dots of bathers, the stunted huts, the jumping dwarfs round the Punch and Judy, and the tiny religious circle. Since he had walked and played down there in the crowded wilderness, excusing his despair, searching for company though he refused it, he had found his own true happiness and lost her all in one bewildering and clumsy half a minute by the "Gentlemen" and the flower clock. Older and wiser and no better, he would have looked in the mirror to see if his discovery and loss had marked themselves upon his face in shadows under the eyes or lines about the mouth, were it not for the answer he knew he would receive from the distorted reflection.

The barman came to sit near him, and said in a false voice: "Now you tell me all about it, I'm a regular storehouse of secrets."

"There isn't anything to tell. I saw a girl in Victoria Gardens and I was too shy to speak to her. She was a piece of God help us all right."

Ashamed of his wish to be companionable, even in the depth of love and distress, with her calm face before his eyes and her smile reproving and forgiving him as he spoke, the young man defiled his girl on the bench, dragged her down into the spit and sawdust and dolled her up to make the barman say:

"I like them big myself. Once round Bessy, once round the gasworks. I missed the chance of a lifetime, too. Fifty lovelies in the rude and I'd left my Bunsen burner home."

"Give me the same, please."

"You mean similar."

The barman drew a glass of beer, drank it, and drew another.

"I always have one with the customers," he said, "It puts us on even terms. Now we're just two heart-broken bachelors together." He sat down again.

"You can't tell me anything I don't know," he said. "I've

seen over twenty chorines from the Empire in this bar, drunk as printers. Oh, les girls! les limbs!"

"Will they be in to-night?"

"There's only a fellow sawing a woman in half this week."

"Keep a half for me."

A drunk man walked in on an invisible white line, and the barman, reeling in sympathy across the room, served him with a pint. "Free beer to-day," he said. "Free X's. You've been out in the sun."

"I've been out in the sun all day," said the man.

"I thought you looked sunburnt."

"That's drink," said the man. "I've been drinking."

"The holiday is drawing to an end," the young man whispered into his glass. Bye-bye blackbird, the moment is lost, he thought, examining, with an interest he could not forgive, the comic coloured postcards of mountain-buttocked women on the beach and hen-pecked, pin-legged men with telescopes, pasted on the wall beneath the picture of a terrier drinking stout; and now, with a jolly barman and a drunk in a crushed cap, he was mopping the failing day down. He tipped his hat over his forehead, and a lock of hair that fell below the hat tickled his eyelid. He saw, with a stranger's darting eye that missed no single subtlety of the wry grin or the faintest gesture drawing the shape of his death on the air, an unruly-haired young man who coughed into his hand in the corner of a rotting room and puffed the smoke of his doped Weight.

But as the drunk man weaved towards him on wilful feet, carrying his dignity as a man might carry a full glass around a quaking ship, as the barman behind the counter clattered and whistled and dipped to drink, he shook off the truthless, secret tragedy with a sneer and a blush, straightened his melancholy hat into a hard-brimmed trilby, dismissed the affected stranger. In the safe centre of his own identity, the familiar world about him like another flesh, he sat sad and content in the plain room of the undistinguished hotel at the sea-end of the shabby, spreading town where everything was happening. He had no need of the dark interior world when Tawe pressed in upon him and the eccentric ordinary people came bursting and crawling, with noise and colours, out of their houses, out of the graceless buildings, the factories and avenues, the shining shops and blaspheming chapels, the terminuses and the meeting-halls, the falling alleys and brick lanes, from the arches and shelters and holes behind the hoardings, out of the common, wild intelligence of the town.

At last the drunk man had reached him. "Put your hand here," he said, and turned about and tapped himself on the bottom.

The barman whistled and rose from his drink to see the young man touch the drunk man on the seat of the trousers.

"What can you feel there?"

"Nothing."

"That's right. Nothing. Nothing. There's nothing there to feel."

"How can you sit down then?" asked the barman.

"I just sit down on what the doctor left," the man said angrily. "I had as good a bottom as you've got once. I was working underground in Dowlais, and the end of the world came down on me. Do you know what I got for losing my bottom? Four and three! Two and three ha'pence a cheek. That's cheaper than a pig."

The girl from Victoria Gardens came into the bar with two friends: a blonde young girl almost as beautiful as she was, and a middle-aged woman dressed and made up to look young. The three of them sat at the table. The girl he loved ordered three ports and gins.

"Isn't it delicious weather?" said the middle-aged woman.

The barman said: "Plenty of sky about." With many bows and smiles he placed their drinks in front of them. "I thought the princesses had gone to a better pub," he said.

"What's a better pub without you, handsome?" said the blonde girl.

"This is the 'Ritz' and the 'Savoy,' isn't it, *garçon* darling?" the girl from the Gardens said, and kissed her hand to him.

The young man in the window seat, still bewildered by the first sudden sight of her entering the darkening room, caught the kiss to himself and blushed. He thought to run out of the room and through the miracle-making Gardens, to rush into his house and hide his head in the bed-clothes and lie all night there, dressed and trembling, her voice in his ears, her green eyes wide awake under his closed eyelids. But only a sick boy with tossed blood would run from his proper love into a dream, lie down in a bedroom that was full of his shames, and sob against the feathery, fat breast and face on the damp pillow. He remembered his age and poems, and would not move.

"Tanks a million, Lou," said the barman.

Her name was Lou, Louise, Louisa. She must be Spanish or French or a gipsy, but he could tell the street that her voice came from; he knew where her friends lived by the rise and fall of their sharp voices, and the name of the middle-aged woman was Mrs. Emerald Franklin. She was to be seen every night in the "Jew's Harp," sipping and spying and watching the clock.

"We've been listening to Matthews Hellfire on the sands. Down with this and down with that, and he used to drink a pint of biddy before his breakfast," Mrs. Franklin said. "Oh, there's a nerve!"

"And his eye on the fluff all the time," said the blonde girl. "I wouldn't trust him any further than Ramon Navarro behind the counter."

"Whoops! I've gone up in the world. Last week I was Charley Chase," said the barman.

Mrs. Franklin raised her empty glass in a gloved hand and shook it like a bell. "Men are deceivers ever," she said. "And a drop of mother's ruin right around."

"Especially Mr. Franklin," said the barman.

"But there's a lot in what the preacher says, mind," Mrs. Franklin said, "about the carrying on. If you go for a constitutional after stop-tap along the sands you might as well be in Sodom and Gomorrah."

The blonde girl laughed. "Hark to Mrs. Grundy! I see her with a black man last Wednesday, round by the museum."

"He was an Indian," said Mrs. Franklin, "from the university college, and I'd thank you to remember it. Every one's brothers under the skin, but there's no tarbrush in my family."

"Oh, dear! oh, dear!" said Lou. "Lay off it, there's loves. This is my birthday. It's a holiday. Put a bit of fun in it. Miaow! miaow! Marjorie, kiss Emerald and be friends." She smiled and laughed at them both. She winked at the barman, who was filling their glasses to the top. "Here's to your blue eyes, *garçon!*" She had not noticed the young man in the corner. "And one for granddad there," she said, smiling at the swaying, drunk man. "He's twenty-one to-day. There! I've made him smile."

The drunk man made a deep, dangerous bow, lifted his hat, stumbled against the mantelpiece, and his full pint in his free hand was steady as a rock. "The prettiest girl in Carmarthenshire," he said.

"This is Glamorganshire, dad," she said, "where's your geography? Look at him waltzing! mind your glasses! He's got that Kruschen feeling. Come on, faster! give us the Charleston."

The drunk man, with his pint held high, danced until he fell, and all the time he never spilt a drop. He lay at Lou's feet on the dusty floor and grinned up at her in confidence and affection. "I fell," he said. "I could dance like a trooper when I had a beatyem."

"He lost his bottom at the last trump," the barman explained.

"When did he lose his bottom?" said Mrs. Franklin.

"When Gabriel blew his whistle down in Dowlais."

"You're pulling my leg."

"It's a pleasure, Mrs. Em. Hoi, you! get up from the vomitorium."

The man wagged his end like a tail, and growled at Lou's feet.

"Put your head on my foot. Be comfy. Let him lie there," she said.

He went to sleep at once.

"I can't have drunks on the premises."

"You know where to go then."

"Cru-el Mrs. Franklin!"

"Go on, attend to your business. Serve the young man in the corner, his tongue's hanging out."

"Cru-el lady!"

As Mrs. Franklin called attention to the young man, Lou peered shortsightedly across the saloon and saw him sitting with his back to the window.

"I'll have to get glasses," she said.

"You'll have plenty of glasses before the night's out."

"No, honest, Marjorie, I didn't know any one was there. I do beg your pardon, you in the corner," she said.

The barman switched on the light. "A bit of *lux in tenebris*."

"Oh!" said Lou.

The young man dared not move for fear that he might break the long light of her scrutiny, the enchantment shining like a single line of light between them, or startle her into speaking; and he did not conceal the love in his eyes, for she could pierce through to it as easily as she could turn his heart in his chest and make it beat above the noises of the two friends' hurried conversation, the rattle of glasses behind the counter where the barman spat and polished and missed nothing, and the snores of the comfortable sleeper. Nothing can hurt me. Let the barman jeer. Giggle in your glass, our Em.

I'm telling the world, I'm walking in clover, I'm staring at
Lou like a fool, she's my girl, she's my lily. O love! O love!
She's no lady, with her sing-song Tontine voice, she drinks
like a deep-sea diver; but Lou, I'm yours, and Lou, you're
mine. He refused to meditate on her calmness now and twist
her beauty into words. She was nothing under the sun or
moon but his. Unashamed and certain, he smiled at her: and,
though he was prepared for all, her answering smile made
his fingers tremble again, as they had trembled in the Gardens, and reddened his cheeks and drove his heart to a gallop.

"Harold, fill the young man's glass up," Mrs. Franklin said.

The barman stood still, a duster in one hand and a dripping
glass in the other.

"Have you got water in your ears? Fill the young man's
glass!"

The barman put the duster to his eyes. He sobbed. He
wiped away the mock tears.

"I thought I was attending a *première* and this was the royal
box," he said.

"He's got water on the brain, not in his earhole," said
Marjorie.

"I dreamt it was a beautiful tragi-comedy entitled 'Love at
First Sight, or, Another Good Man gone wrong.' Act one in
a boozer by the sea."

The two women tapped their foreheads.

Lou said, still smiling: "Where was the second act?"

Her voice was as gentle as he had imagined it to be before
her gay and nervous playing with the over-familiar barman
and the inferior women. He saw her as a wise, soft girl whom
no hard company could spoil, for her soft self, bare to the
heart, broke through every defence of her sensual falsifiers.
As he thought this, phrasing her gentleness, faithlessly running to words away from the real room and his love in the
middle, he woke with a start and saw her lively body six steps
from him, no calm heart dressed in a sentence, but a pretty
girl, to be got and kept. He must catch hold of her fast. He
got up to cross to her.

"I woke before the second act came on," said the barman.
"I'd sell my dear old mother to see that. Dim light. Purple
couches. Ecstatic bliss. Là, là chérie!"

The young man sat down at the table, next to her.

Harold, the barman, leaned over the counter and cupped
his hand to his ear.

The man on the floor rolled in his sleep, and his head lay in the spittoon.

"You should have come and sat here a long time ago," Lou whispered. "You should have stopped to talk to me in the Gardens. Were you shy?"

"I was too shy," the young man whispered.

"Whispering isn't manners. I can't hear a word," said the barman.

At a sign from the young man, a flick of the fingers that sent the waiters in evening dress bustling with oysters about the immense room, the barman filled the glasses with port, gin, and Nutbrown.

"We never drink with strangers," Mrs. Franklin said, laughing.

"He isn't a stranger," said Lou, "are you, Jack?"

He threw a pound note on the table: "Take the damage."

The evening that had been over before it began raced along among the laughter of the charming women sharp as knives, and the stories of the barman, who should be on the stage, and Lou's delighted smiles and silences at his side. Now she is safe and sure, he thought, after her walking like my doubtful walking, around the lonely distances of the holiday. In the warm, spinning middle they were close and alike. The town and the sea and the last pleasure-makers drifted into the dark that had nothing to do with them, and left this one room burning.

One by one, some lost men from the dark shuffled into the bar, drank sadly, and went out. Mrs. Franklin, flushed and dribbling, waved her glass at their departures. Harold winked behind their backs. Majorie showed them her long, white legs.

"Nobody loves us except ourselves," said Harold. "Shall I shut the bar and keep the riff-raff out?"

"Lou is expecting Mr. O'Brien, but don't let that stop you," Marjorie said. "He's her sugar daddy from old Ireland."

"Do you love Mr. O'Brien?" the young man whispered.

"How could I, Jack?"

He could see Mr. O'Brien as a witty, tall fellow of middle age, with waved greying hair and a clipped bit of dirt on his upper lip, a flash ring on his marriage finger, a pouched, knowing eye, dummy dressed with a whaleboned waist, a broth of a man about Cardiff, Lou's horrible lover tearing towards her now down the airless streets in the firm's car. The young man clenched his hand on the table covered with dead, and sheltered her in the warm strength of his fist. "My round, my round," he said, "up again, plenty! Doubles, trebles, Mrs. Franklin is a jibber."

"My mother never had a jibber."

"Oh, Lou!" he said, "I am more than happy with you."

"Coo! coo! hear the turtle doves."

"Let them coo," said Marjorie. "I could coo, too."

The barman looked around him in surprise. He raised his hands, palms up, and cocked his head.

"The bar is full of birds," he said.

"Emerald's laying an egg," he said, as Mrs. Franklin rocked in her chair.

Soon the bar was full of customers. The drunk man woke up and ran out, leaving his cap in a brown pool. Sawdust dropped from his hair. A small, old, round, red-faced, cheery man sat facing the young man and Lou, who held hands under the table and rubbed their legs against each other.

"What a night for love!" said the old man. "On such a night as this did Jessica steal from the wealthy Jew. Do you know where that comes from?"

"*The Merchant of Venice*," Lou said. "But you're an Irishman, Mr. O'Brien."

"I could have sworn you were a tall man with a little tish," said the young man gravely.

"What's the weapons, Mr. O'Brien?"

"Brandies at dawn, I should think, Mrs. Franklin."

"I never described Mr. O'Brien to you at all. You're dreaming!" Lou whispered. "I wish this night could go on for ever."

"But not here. Not in the bar. In a room with a big bed."

"A bed in a bar," said the old man, "if you'll pardon me hearing you, that's what I've always wanted. Think of it, Mrs. Franklin."

The barman bobbed up from behind the counter.

"Time, gentlemen and others!"

The sober strangers departed to Mrs. Franklin's laughter. The lights went out.

"Lou, don't you lose me."

"I've got your hand."

"Press it hard, hurt it."

"Break his bloody neck," Mrs. Franklin said in the dark. "No offence meant."

"Marjorie smack hand," said Marjorie. "Let's get out of the dark. Harold's a rover in the dark."

"And the girl guides."

"Let's take a bottle each and go down to Lou's," she said.

"I'll buy the bottles," said Mr. O'Brien.

"It's you don't lose me now," Lou whispered. "Hold on to me, Jack. The others won't stay long. Oh, Mr. Christ, I wish it was just you and me!"

"Will it be just you and me?"

"You and me and Mr. Moon."

Mr. O'Brien opened the saloon door. "Pile into the Rolls, you ladies. The gentlemen are going to see to the medicine."

The young man felt Lou's quick kiss on his mouth before she followed Marjorie and Mrs. Franklin out.

"What do you say we split the drinks?" said Mr. O'Brien.

"Look what I found in the lavatory," said the barman, "he was singing on the seat." He appeared behind the counter with the drunk man leaning on his arm.

They all climbed into the car.

"First stop, Lou's."

The young man, on Lou's knee, saw the town in a daze spin by them, the funnelled and masted smoke-blue outline of the still, droning docks, the lightning lines of the poor streets growing longer, and the winking shops that were snapped out one by one. The car smelt of scent and powder and flesh. He struck with his elbow, by accident, Mrs. Franklin's upholstered breast. Her thighs, like cushions, bore the drunk man's rolling weight. He was bumped and tossed on a lump of women. Breasts, legs, bellies, hands, touched, warmed, and smothered him. On through the night, towards Lou's bed, towards the unbelievable end of the dying holiday, they tore past black houses and bridges, a station in a smoke cloud, and drove up a steep side street with one weak lamp in a circle of railings at the top, and swerved into a space where a tall tenement house stood surrounded by cranes, standing ladders, poles and girders, barrows, brick-heaps.

They climbed to Lou's room up many flights of dark, perilous stairs. Washing hung on the rails outside closed doors. Mrs. Franklin, fumbling alone with the drunk man, behind the others, trod in a bucket, and a lucky black cat ran over her foot. Lou led the young man by the hand through a passage marked with names and doors, lit a match, and whispered: "It won't be very long. Be good and patient with Mr. O'Brien. Here it is. Come in first. Welcome to you, Jack!" She kissed him again at the door of her room.

She turned on the light, and he walked with her proudly

into her own room, into the room that he could come to know, and saw a wide bed, a gramophone on a chair, a washbasin half-hidden in a corner, a gas fire and a cooking ring, a closed cupboard, and her photograph in a cardboard frame on the chest of drawers with no handles. Here she slept and ate. In the double bed she lay all night, pale and curled, sleeping on her left side. When he lived with her always, he would not allow her to dream. No other men must lie and love in her head. He spread his fingers on her pillow.

"Why do you live at the top of the Eiffel Tower?" said the barman, coming in.

"What a climb!" said Mr. O'Brien. "But it's very nice and private when you get here."

"If you get here!" said Mrs. Franklin. "I'm dead beat. This old nuisance weighs a ton. Lie down, lie down on the floor and go to sleep. The old nuisance!" she said fondly. "What's your name?"

"Ernie," the drunk man said, raising his arm to shield his face.

"Nobody's going to bite you, Ernie. Here, give him a nip of whisky. Careful! Don't pour it on your waistcoat; you'll be squeezing your waistcoat in the morning. Pull the curtains, Lou, I can see the wicked old moon," she said.

"Does it put ideas in your head?"

"I love the moon," said Lou.

"There never was a young lover who didn't love the moon." Mr. O'Brien gave the young man a cheery smile, and patted his hand. His own hand was red and hairy. "I could see at the flash of a glance that Lou and this nice young fellow were made for each other. I could see it in their eyes. Dear me, no! I'm not so old and blind I can't see love in front of my nose. Couldn't you see it, Mrs. Franklin? Couldn't you see it, Marjorie?"

In the long silence, Lou collected glasses from the cupboard as though she had not heard Mr. O'Brien speak. She drew the curtains, shut out the moon, sat on the edge of her bed with her feet tucked under her, looked at her photograph as at a stranger, folded her hands as she had folded them, on the first meeting, before the young man's worship in the Gardens.

"A host of angels must be passing by," said Mr. O'Brien. "What a silence there is! Have I said anything out of place? Drink and be merry, to-morrow we die. What do you think I bought these lovely shining bottles for?"

The bottles were opened. The dead were lined on the mantelpiece. The whisky went down. Harold the barman and Marjorie, her dress lifted, sat in the one arm-chair together. Mrs. Franklin, with Ernie's head on her lap, sang in a sweet, trained contralto voice *The Shepherd's Lass*. Mr. O'Brien kept rhythm with his foot.

I want Lou in my arms, the young man said to himself, watching Mr. O'Brien tap and smile and the barman drew Marjorie down deep. Mrs. Franklin's voice sang sweetly in the small bedroom where he and Lou should be lying in the white bed without any smiling company to see them drown. He and Lou could go down together, one cool body weighted with a boiling stone, on to the falling, blank white, entirely empty sea, and never rise. Sitting on their bridal bed, near enough to hear his breath, she was farther from him than before they met. Then he had everything but her body; now she had given him two kisses, and everything had vanished but that beginning. He must be good and patient with Mr. O'Brien. He could wipe away the embracing, old smile with the iron back of his hand. Sink lower, lower, Harold and Marjorie, tumble like whales at Mr. O'Brien's feet.

He wished that the light would fail. In the darkness he and Lou could creep beneath the clothes and imitate the dead. Who would look for them there, if they were dead still and soundless? The others would shout to them down the dizzy stairs or rummage in the silence about the narrow, obstacled corridors or stumble out into the night to search for them among the cranes and ladders in the desolation of the destroyed houses. He could hear, in the made-up dark, Mr. O'Brien's voice cry, "Lou, where are you? Answer! answer!" the hollow answer of the echo, "answer!" and hear her lips in the cool pit of the bed secretly move around another name, and feel them move.

"A fine piece of singing, Emerald, and very naughty words. That was a shepherd, that was," Mr. O'Brien said.

Ernie, on the floor, began to sing in a thick, sulking voice but Mrs. Franklin placed her hand over his mouth and he sucked and nuzzled it.

"What about this young shepherd?" said Mr. O'Brien, pointing his glass at the young man. "Can he sing as well as make love? You ask him kindly, girlie," he said to Lou, "and he'll give us a song like a nightingale."

"Can you sing, Jack?"

"Like a crow, Lou."

"Can't he even talk poetry? What a young man to have who can't spout the poets to his lady!" Mr. O'Brien said.

From the cupboard Lou brought out a red-bound book and gave it to the young man, saying: "Can you read us a piece out of here? The second volume's in the hatbox. Read us a dreamy piece, Jack. It's nearly midnight."

"Only a love poem, no other kind," said Mr. O'Brien. "I won't hear anything but a love poem."

"Soft and sweet," Mrs. Franklin said. She took her hand away from Ernie's mouth and looked at the ceiling.

The young man read, but not aloud, lingering on her name, the inscription on the fly-leaf of the first volume of the collected poems of Tennyson: "To Louisa, from her Sunday School teacher, Miss Gwyneth Forbes. God's in His Heaven, all's right with the world."

"Make it a love poem, don't forget."

The young man read aloud, closing one eye to steady the dancing print, *Come into the Garden, Maud*. And when he reached the beginning of the fourth verse his voice grew louder:

> "I said to the lily, 'There is but one
> With whom she has heart to be gay.
> When will the dancers leave her alone?
> She is weary of dance and play.'
> Now half to the setting moon are gone,
> And half to the rising day;
> Low on the sand and loud on the stone
> The last wheel echoes away.
> "I said to the rose, 'The brief night goes
> In babble and revel and wine.
> O young lord-lover, what sighs are those,
> For one that will never be thine?
> But mine, but mine,' so I sware to the rose,
> 'For ever and ever, mine.'"

At the end of the poem, Harold said, suddenly, his head hanging over the arm of the chair, his hair made wild, and his mouth red with lipstick: "My grandfather remembers seeing Lord Tennyson, he was a little man with a hump."

"No," said the young man, "he was tall and he had long hair and a beard."

"Did you ever see him?"

"I wasn't born then."

"My grandfather saw him. He had a hump."

"Not Alfred Tennyson."

"Lord Alfred Tennyson was a little man with a hump."

"It couldn't have been the same Tennyson."

"You've got the wrong Tennyson, this was the famous poet with a hump."

Lou, on the wonderful bed, waiting for him alone of all the men, ugly or handsome, old or young, in the wide town and the small world that would be bound to fall, lowered her head and kissed her hand to him and held her hand in the river of light on the counterpane. The hand, to him, became transparent, and the light on the counterpane glowed up steadily through it in the thin shape of her palm and fingers.

"Ask Mr. O'Brien what Lord Tennyson was like," said Mrs. Franklin. "We appeal to you, Mr. O'Brien, did he have a hump or not?"

Nobody but the young man, for whom she lived and waited now, noticed Lou's little loving movements. She put her glowing hand to her left breast. She made a sign of secrecy on her lips.

"It depends," Mr. O'Brien said.

The young man closed one eye again, for the bed was pitching like a ship: a sickening, hot storm out of a cigarette cloud unsettled cupboard and chest. The motions of the seagoing bedroom were calmed with the cunning closing of his eye, but he longed for night air. On sailor's legs he walked to the door.

"You'll find the House of Commons on the second floor at the end of the passage," said Mr. O'Brien.

At the door, he turned to Lou and smiled with all his love, declaring it to the faces of the company and making her, before Mr. O'Brien's envious regard, smile back and say: "Don't be long, Jack. Please! You mustn't be long."

Now every one knew. Love had grown up in an evening.

"One minute, my darling," he said. "I'll be here."

The door closed behind him. He walked into the wall of the passage. He lit a match. He had three left. Down the stairs, clinging to the sticky, shaking rails, rocking on seesaw floorboards, bruising his shin on a bucket, past the noises of secret lives behind doors he slid and stumbled and swore and heard Lou's voice in a fresh fever drive him on, call him to return, speak to him with such passion and abandonment that even in the darkness and the pain of his haste he was dazzled and struck still. She spoke, there on the rotting stairs in the middle of the poor house, a frightening rush of love words;

from her mouth, at his ear, endearments were burned out. Hurry! hurry! Every moment is being killed. Love, adored, dear, run back and whistle to me, open the door, shout my name, lay me down. Mr. O'Brien has his hands on my side.

He ran into a cavern. A draught blew out his matches. He lurched into a room where two figures on a black heap on the floor lay whispering, and ran from there in a panic. He made water at the dead end of the passage and hurried back towards Lou's room, finding himself at last on a silent patch of stairway at the top of the house: he put out his hand, but the rail was broken and nothing there prevented a long drop to the ground down a twisted shaft that would echo and double his cry, bring out from their holes in the wall the sleeping or stirring families, the whispering figures, the blind startled turners of night into day. Lost in a tunnel near the roof, he fingered the damp walls for a door; he found a handle and gripped it hard, but it came off in his hand. Lou had led him down a longer passage than this. He remembered the number of doors: there were three on each side. He ran down the broken-railed flight into another passage and dragged his hand along the wall. Three doors, he counted. He opened the third door, walked into darkness, and groped for the switch on the left. He saw, in the sudden light, a bed and a cupboard and a chest of drawers with no handles, a gas fire, a wash-basin in the corner. No bottles. No glasses. No photograph of Lou. The red counterpane on the bed was smooth. He could not remember the colour of Lou's counterpane.

He left the light burning and opened the second door, but a strange woman's voice cried, half-asleep: "Who is there? Is it you, Tom? Tom, put the light on." He looked for a line of light at the foot of the next door, and stopped to listen for voices. The woman was still calling in the second room.

"Lou, where are you?" he cried. "Answer! answer!"

"Lou, what Lou? There's no Lou here," said a man's voice through the open door of the first dark room at the entrance to the passage.

He scampered down another flight and counted few doors with his scratched hand. One door opened and a woman in a nightdress put out her head. A child's head appeared below her.

"Where does Lou live? Do you know where Lou lives?"

The woman and child stared without speaking.

"Lou! Lou! her name is Lou!" he heard himself shout. "She lives here, in this house! Do you know where she lives?"

The woman caught the child by the hair and pulled her into the room. He clung to the edge of her door. The woman thrust her arm round the edge and brought down a bunch of keys sharply on his hands. The door slammed.

A young woman with a baby in a shawl stood at an open door on the opposite side of the passage, and caught his sleeve as he ran by. "Lou who? You woke my baby."

"I don't know her other name. She's with Mrs. Franklin and Mr. O'Brien."

"You woke my baby."

"Come in and find her in the bed," a voice said from the darkness behind the young woman.

"He's woken up the baby."

He ran down the passage, holding his wet hand to his mouth. He fell against the rails of the last flight of stairs. He heard Lou's voice in his head once more whisper to him to return as the ground floor rose, like a lift full of dead towards the rails. Hurry! hurry! I can't, I won't wait, the bridal night is being killed.

Up the rotten, bruising, mountainous stairs he climbed, in his sickness, to the passage where he had left the one light burning in an end room. The light was out. He tapped all the doors and whispered her name. He beat on the doors and shouted, and a woman, dressed in a vest and a hat, drove him out of the passage with a walking-stick.

For a long time he waited on the stairs, though there was no love now to wait for and no bed but his own too many miles away to lie in, and only the approaching day to remember his discovery. All around him the disturbed inhabitants of the house were falling back into sleep. Then he walked out of the house on to the waste space and under the leaning cranes and ladders. The light of the one weak lamp in a rusty circle fell across the brick-heaps and the broken wood and the dust that had been houses once, where the small and hardly known and never-to-be-forgotten people of the dirty town had lived and loved and died and, always, lost.

Arthur C. Clarke
(1917–   )

Arthur C. Clarke was born in England and educated at King's College, London. After serving for five years in the RAF during World War II, he engaged in scientific research and did original work on communications satellites. But his real reputation has been made in his science fiction books, both fiction and non-fiction. Beginning in 1951 with The Sands of Mars, *he has been enormously prolific, with books, articles, stories, and essays pouring out each year. Some of his best-known works are:* Islands in the Sky *(1952);* Across the Sea of Stars *(1959);* 2001: A Space Odyssey *(1968), which was made into a highly successful film by Stanley Kubrick;* The Lost Worlds of 2001 *(1972); and several sequels to the above books. Clarke now lives in Colombo, Sri Lanka.*

Jesuit have strict academic rules, very intelligent.

The Star

It is three thousand light-years to the Vatican. Once, I believed that space could have no power over faith, just as I believed that the heavens declared the glory of God's handiwork. Now I have seen that handiwork, and my faith is sorely troubled. I stare at the crucifix that hangs on the cabin wall above the Mark VI Computer, and for the first time in my life I wonder if it is no more than an empty symbol.

I have told no one yet, but the truth cannot be concealed. The facts are there for all to read, recorded on the countless miles of magnetic tape and the thousands of photographs we are carrying back to Earth. Other scientists can interpret them as easily as I can, and I am not one who would condone that tampering with the truth which often gave my order a bad name in the olden days.

The crew are already sufficiently depressed: I wonder how they will take this ultimate irony. Few of them have any religious faith, yet they will not relish using this final weapon in their campaign against me—that private, good-natured, but fundamentally serious, war which lasted all the way from Earth. It amused them to have a Jesuit as chief astrophysicist: Dr. Chandler, for instance, could never get over it (why are medical men such notorious atheists?). Sometimes he would meet me on the observation deck, where the lights are always low so that the stars shine with undiminished glory. He would come up to me in the gloom and stand staring out of the great oval port, while the heavens crawled slowly around us as the ship turned end over end with the residual spin we had never bothered to correct.

"Well, Father," he would say at last, "it goes on forever and forever, and perhaps *Something* made it. But how can you believe that *Something* has a special interest in us and our miserable little world—that just beats me." Then the argument would start, while the stars and nebulae would swing around us in silent, endless arcs beyond the flawlessly clear plastic of the observation port.

It was, I think, the apparent incongruity of my position that caused most amusement to the crew. In vain I would point to my three papers in the *Astrophysical Journal*, my five in the *Monthly Notices of the Royal Astronomical Society*. I would remind him that my order has long been famous for its scientific works. We may be few now, but ever since the eighteenth century we have made contributions to astronomy and geophysics out of all proportion to our numbers. Will my report on the Phoenix Nebula end our thousand years of history? It will end, I fear, much more than that.

I do not know who gave the nebula its name, which seems to me a very bad one. If it contains a prophecy, it is one that cannot be verified for several billion years. Even the word nebula is misleading: this is a far smaller object than those stupendous clouds of mist—the stuff of unborn stars—that are scattered throughout the length of the Milky Way. On the cosmic scale, indeed, the Phoenix Nebula is a tiny thing— a tenuous shell of gas surrounding a single star.

Or what is left of a star . . .

The Rubens engraving of Loyola seems to mock me as it hangs there above the spectrophotometer tracings. What would *you*, Father, have made of this knowledge that has come into my keeping, so far from the little world that was all the universe you knew? Would your faith have risen to the challenge, as mine has failed to do?

You gaze into the distance, Father, but I have traveled a distance beyond any that you could have imagined when you founded our order a thousand years ago. No other survey ship has been so far from Earth: we are at the very frontiers of the explored universe. We set out to reach the Phoenix Nebula, we succeeded, and we are homeward bound with our burden of knowledge. I wish I could lift that burden from my shoulders, but I call to you in vain across the centuries and the light-years that lie between us.

On the book you are holding the words are plain to read. AD MAIOREM DEI GLORIAM, the message runs, but it is a message I can no longer believe. Would you still believe it, if you could see what we have found?

We knew, of course, what the Phoenix Nebula was. Every year, in our galaxy alone, more than a hundred stars explode, blazing for a few hours or days with thousands of times their normal brilliance before they sink back into death and obscurity. Such are the ordinary novae—the commonplace disasters of the universe. I have recorded the spectrograms and light curves of dozens since I started working at the Lunar Observatory.

But three or four times in every thousand years occurs something beside which even a nova pales into total insignificance.

When a star becomes a supernova, it may for a little while outshine all the massed suns of the galaxy. The Chinese astronomers watched this happen in A.D. 1054, not knowing what it was they saw. Five centuries later, in 1572, a supernova blazed in Cassiopeia so brilliantly that it was visible in the daylight sky. There have been three more in the thousand years that have passed since then.

Our mission was to visit the remnants of such a catastrophe, to reconstruct the events that led up to it, and, if possible, to learn its cause. We came slowly in through the concentric shells of gas that had been blasted out six thousand years before, yet were expanding still. They were immensely hot, radiating even now with a fierce violet light, but were far too tenuous to do us any damage. When the star had exploded, its outer layers had been driven upward with such speed that they had escaped completely from its gravitational field. Now they formed a hollow shell large enough to engulf a thousand solar systems, and at its center burned the tiny, fantastic object which the star had now become—a White Dwarf, smaller than the Earth, yet weighing a million times as much.

The glowing gas shells were all around us, banishing the normal night of interstellar space. We were flying into the center of a cosmic bomb that had detonated millennia ago and whose incandescent fragments were still hurtling apart. The immense scale of the explosion, and the fact that the debris already covered a volume of space many billions of miles across, robbed the scene of any visible movement. It would take decades before the unaided eye could detect any motion in those tortured wisps and eddies of gas, yet the sense of turbulent expansion was overwhelming.

We had checked our primary drive hours before, and were drifting slowly toward the fierce little star ahead. Once it had been a sun like our own, but it had squandered in a few hours the energy that should have kept it shining for a million years. Now it was a shrunken miser, hoarding its resources as if trying to make amends for its prodigal youth.

No one seriously expected to find planets. If there had been any before the explosion, they would have been boiled into puffs of vapor, and their substance lost in the greater wreckage of the star itself. But we made the automatic search, as we always do when approaching an unknown sun, and presently we found a single small world circling the star at an immense distance. It must have been the Pluto of this vanished solar system, orbiting on the frontiers of the night. Too far from the central sun ever to have known life, its remoteness had saved it from the fate of all its lost companions.

The passing fires had seared its rocks and burned away the mantle of frozen gas that must have covered it in the days before the disaster. We landed, and we found the Vault.

Its builders had made sure that we would. The monolithic marker that stood above the entrance was now a fused stump, but even the first long-range photographs told us that here was the work of intelligence. A little later we detected the continent-wide pattern of radioactivity that had been buried in the rock. Even if the pylon above the Vault had been destroyed, this would have remained, an immovable and all but eternal beacon calling to the stars. Our ship fell toward this gigantic bull's-eye like an arrow into its target.

The pylon must have been a mile high when it was built, but now it looked like a candle that had melted down into a puddle of wax. It took us a week to drill through the fused rock, since we did not have the proper tools for a task like this. We were astronomers, not archaeologists, but we could improvise. Our original purpose was forgotten: this lonely monument, reared with such labor at the greatest possible distance from the doomed sun, could have only one meaning. A civilization that knew it was about to die had made its last bid for immortality.

It will take us generations to examine all the treasures that were placed in the Vault. They had plenty of time to prepare, for their sun must have given its first warnings many years before the final detonation. Everything that they wished to preserve, all the fruit of their genius, they brought here to this distant world in the days before the end, hoping that some other race would find it and that they would not be utterly forgotten. Would we have done as well, or would we have been too lost in our own misery to give thought to a future we could never see or share?

If only they had had a little more time! They could travel freely enough between the planets of their own sun, but they had not yet learned to cross the interstellar gulfs, and the nearest solar system was a hundred light-years away. Yet even had they possessed the secret of the Transfinite Drive, no more than a few millions could have been saved. Perhaps it was better thus.

Even if they had not been so disturbingly human as their sculpture shows, we could not have helped admiring them and grieving for their fate. They left thousands of visual records and the machines for projecting them, together with elaborate pictorial instructions from which it will not be difficult to learn their written language. We have examined many of these records, and brought to life for the first time in six thousand years the warmth and beauty of a civilization that in many ways must have been superior to our own. Perhaps they only showed us the best, and one can hardly blame them. But their worlds were very lovely, and their cities were built with a grace that matches anything of man's. We have watched them at work and play, and listened to their musical speech sounding across the centuries. One scene is still before my eyes—a group of children on a beach of strange blue sand, playing in the waves as children play on Earth. Curious whip-like trees line the shore, and some very large animal is wading in the shadows yet attracting no attention at all.

And sinking into the sea, still warm and friendly and life-giving, is the sun that will soon turn traitor and obliterate all this innocent happiness.

Perhaps if we had not been so far from home and so vulnerable to loneliness, we would not have been so deeply moved. Many of us had seen the ruins of ancient civilizations on other worlds, but they had never affected us so profoundly. This tragedy was unique. It is one thing for a race to fail and die, as nations and cultures have done on Earth. But to be destroyed so completely in the full flower of its achievement, leaving no survivors—how could that be reconciled with the mercy of God?

My colleagues have asked me that, and I have given what answers I can. Perhaps you could have done better, Father Loyola, but I have found nothing in the *Exercitia Spiritualia* that helps me here. They were not an evil people: I do not know what gods they worshiped, if indeed they worshiped any. But I have looked back at them across the centuries, and have watched while the loveliness they used their last strength to preserve was brought forth again into the light of their shrunken sun. They could have taught us much: why were they destroyed?

I know the answers that my colleagues will give when they get back to Earth. They will say that the universe has no purpose and no plan, that since a hundred suns explode every year in our galaxy, at this very moment some race is dying in the depths of space. Whether that race has done good or evil during its lifetime will make no difference in the end: there is no divine justice, for there is no God.

Yet, of course, what we have seen proves nothing of the sort. Anyone who argues thus is being swayed by emotion, not logic. God has no need to justify His actions to man. He who built the universe can destroy it when He chooses. It is arrogance—it is perilously near blasphemy—for us to say what He may or may not do.

This I could have accepted, hard though it is to look upon whole worlds and peoples thrown into the furnace. But there comes a point when even the deepest faith must falter, and now, as I look at the calculations lying before me, I know I have reached that point at last.

We could not tell, before we reached the nebula, how long ago the explosion took place. Now, from the astronomical evidence and the record in the rocks of that one surviving planet, I have been able to date it very exactly. I know in what year the light of this colossal conflagration reached our

Earth. I know how brilliantly the supernova whose corpse now dwindles behind our speeding ship once shone in terrestrial skies. I know how it must have blazed low in the east before sunrise, like a beacon in that oriental dawn.

There can be no reasonable doubt: the ancient mystery is solved at last. Yet, oh God, there were so many stars you could have used. What was the need to give these people to the fire, that the symbol of their passing might shine above Bethlehem?

The mystery was what was the thing that the 3 wise men saw.
The Jesuit can't understand that when the bright star appeared it destroyed the civilization when it should give life
Why do things happen?

Doris Lessing
(1919–   )

Novelist, playwright, and short story writer, Doris Lessing was born in Kermanshah (then Persia), where her father was director of a bank, and then moved to a farm in southern Rhodesia (present-day Zimbabwe). She grew up on the family farm, then moved to the city, married, had two children, and separated from her husband in 1943. After that, she began to establish herself as a writer. Her major work is considered to be the Martha Quest series: Martha Quest *(1952),* A Proper Marriage *(1954),* The Ripple from the Storm *(1958),* Landlocked *(1965), and* The Four-Gated City *(1969), along with* The Golden Notebook *(1962), a novel whose contents foreshadowed many aspects of the feminist movement. Lessing's other work includes* The Grass is Singing *(1950), her first novel, about growing up in Africa; and several volumes of shorter fiction:* Five *(1953),* The Habit of Loving *(1957), and* A Man and Two Women *(1963). By 1949, Lessing had established herself in London as a writer interested in political and feminist issues. Her recent work has turned toward a kind of apocalyptic science fiction, the group of novels called* Canopus in Argus: Archives. *These include* Shikasta; The Marriages Between Zones Three, Four, and Five; The Sirian Experiments; and* The Sentimental Agents.

An Old Woman
and Her Cat

Her name was Hetty, and she was born with the twentieth century. She was seventy when she died of cold and malnutrition. She had been alone for a long time, since her husband had died of pneumonia in a bad winter soon after the Second

World War. He had not been more than middleaged. Her
four children were now middleaged, with grown children. Of
these descendants one daughter sent her Christmas cards, but
otherwise she did not exist for them. For they were all respectable people, with homes and good jobs and cars. And
Hetty was not respectable. She had always been a bit strange,
these people said, when mentioning her at all.

When Fred Pennefather, her husband, was alive and the
children just growing up, they all lived much too close and
uncomfortable in a council flat in that part of London which
is like an estuary, with tides of people flooding in and out:
they were not half a mile from the great stations of Euston,
St. Pancras, and King's Cross. The blocks of flats were pi-
oneers in that area, standing up grim, grey, hideous, among
many acres of little houses and gardens, all soon to be demol-
ished so that they could be replaced by more tall grey blocks.
The Pennefathers were good tenants, paying their rent, keeping out of debt; he was a building worker, "steady," and
proud of it. There was no evidence then of Hetty's future
dislocation from the normal, unless it was that she very often
slipped down for an hour or so to the platforms where the
locomotives drew in and ground out again. She liked the smell
of it all, she said. She liked to see people moving about,
"coming and going from all those foreign places." She meant
Scotland, Ireland, the North of England. These visits into the
din, the smoke, the massed swirling people were for her a
drug, like other people's drinking or gambling. her husband
teased her, called her a gypsy. She was in fact part-gypsy, for
her mother had been one, but had chosen to leave her people
and marry a man who lived in a house. Fred Pennefather
liked his wife for being different from the run of the women
he knew, and had married her because of it, but her children
were fearful that her gypsy blood might show itself in worse
ways than haunting railway stations. She was a tall woman
with a lot of glossy black hair, a skin that tanned easily, and
dark strong eyes. She wore bright colours, and enjoyed quick
tempers and sudden reconciliations. In her prime she attracted attention, was proud and handsome. All this made it
inevitable that the people in those streets should refer to her
as "that gypsy woman." When she heard them, she shouted
back that she was none the worse for that.

After her husband died and the children married and left,
the Council moved her to a small flat in the same building.
She got a job selling food in a local store, but found it boring.

There seem to be traditional occupations for middleaged women living alone, the busy and responsible part of their lives being over. Drink. Gambling. Looking for another husband. A wistful affair or two. That's about it. Hetty went through a period of, as it were, testing out all these, like hobbies, but tired of them. While still earning her small wage as a saleswoman, she began a trade in buying and selling secondhand clothes. She did not have a shop of her own, but bought or begged clothes from householders, and sold these to stalls and the secondhand shops. She adored doing this. It was a passion. She gave up her respectable job and forgot all about her love of trains and travellers. Her room was always full of bright bits of cloth, a dress that had a pattern she fancied and did not want to sell, strips of beading, old furs, embroidery, lace. There were street traders among the people in the flats, but there was something in that way Hetty went about it that lost her friends. Neighbours of twenty or thirty years' standing said she had gone queer, and wished to know her no longer. But she did not mind. She was enjoying herself too much, particularly the moving about the streets with her old perambulator, in which she crammed what she was buying or selling. She liked the gossiping, the bargaining, the wheedling from householders. It was this last which—and she knew this quite well of course—the neighbours objected to. It was the thin edge of the wedge. It was begging. Decent people did not beg. She was no longer decent.

Lonely in her tiny flat, she was there as little as possible, always preferring the lively streets. But she had after all to spend some time in her room, and one day she saw a kitten lost and trembling in a dirty corner, and brought it home to the block of flats. She was on a fifth floor. While the kitten was growing into a large strong tom, he ranged about that conglomeration of staircases and lifts and many dozens of flats, as if the building were a town. Pets were not actively persecuted by the authorities, only forbidden and then tolerated. Hetty's life from the coming of the cat became more sociable, for the beast was always making friends with somebody in the cliff that was the block of flats across the court, or not coming home for nights at a time so that she had to go and look for him and knock on doors and ask, or returning home kicked and limping, or bleeding after a fight with his kind. She made scenes with the kickers, or the owners of the enemy cats, exchanged cat lore with cat lovers, was always having to bandage and nurse her poor Tibby. The cat was soon a scarred warrior with fleas, a torn ear, and a ragged look to him. He was a multicoloured cat and his eyes were small and yellow. He was a long way down the scale from the delicately coloured, elegantly shaped pedigree cats. But he was independent, and often caught himself pigeons when he could no longer stand the tinned cat food, or the bread and packet gravy Hetty fed him, and he purred and nestled when she grabbed him to her bosom at those times she suffered loneliness. This happened less and less. Once she had realised that her children were hoping that she would leave them alone because the old rag trader was an embarrassment to them, she accepted it, and a bitterness that always had wild humour in it, only welled up at times like Christmas. She sang or chanted to the cat: "You nasty old beast, filthy old cat, nobody wants you, do they Tibby, no, you're just an alley tom, just an old stealing cat, hey Tibs, Tibs, Tibs."

The building teemed with cats. There were even a couple of dogs. They all fought up and down the grey cement corridors. There were sometimes dog and cat messes which someone had to clear up, but which might be left for days and weeks as part of neighbourly wars and feuds. There were many complaints. Finally an official came from the Council to say that the ruling about keeping animals was going to be enforced. Hetty, like others, would have to have her cat destroyed. This crisis coincided with a time of bad luck for her. She had 'flu; had not been able to earn money, had found it hard to get out for her pension, had run into debt. She owed a lot of back rent, too. A television set she had hired and was not paying for attracted the visits of a television representative. The neighbours were gossiping that Hetty had "gone savage." This was because the cat had brought up the stairs and along the passageways a pigeon he had caught, shedding feathers and blood all the way; a woman coming in to complain found Hetty plucking the pigeon to stew it, as she had done with others, sharing the meal with Tibby.

"You're filthy," she would say to him, setting the stew down to cool in his dish. "Filthy old thing. Eating that dirty old pigeon. What do you think you are, a wild cat? Decent cats don't eat dirty birds. Only those old gypsies eat wild birds."

One night she begged help from a neighbour who had a car, and put into the car herself, the television set, the cat, bundles of clothes, and the pram. She was driven across London to a room in a street that was a slum because it was waiting to be done up. The neighbour made a second trip to bring her bed and her mattress, which were tied to the roof of the car, a chest of drawers, an old trunk, saucepans. It was in this way that she left the street in which she had lived for thirty years, nearly half her life.

She set up house again in one room. She was frightened to go near "them" to re-establish pension rights and her identity, because of the arrears of rent she had left behind, and because of the stolen television set. She started trading again, and the little room was soon spread, like her last, with a rainbow of colours and textures and lace and sequins. She cooked on a single gas ring and washed in the sink. There was no hot water unless it was boiled in saucepans. There were several old ladies and a family of five children in the house, which was condemned.

She was in the ground floor back, with a window which opened onto a derelict garden, and her cat was happy in a hunting ground that was a mile around this house where his mistress was so splendidly living. A canal ran close by, and in the dirty city-water were islands which a cat could reach by leaping from moored boat to boat. On the islands were rats and birds. There were pavements full of fat London pigeons. The cat was a fine hunter. He soon had his place in the hierarchies of the local cat population and did not have to fight much to keep it. He was a strong male cat, and fathered many litters of kittens.

In that place Hetty and he lived five happy years. She was trading well, for there were rich people close by to shed what the poor needed to buy cheaply. She was not lonely, for she made a quarrelling but satisfying friendship with a woman on the top floor, a widow like herself who did not see her children either. Hetty was sharp with the five children, complaining about their noise and mess, but she slipped them bits of money and sweets after telling their mother that "she was a fool to put herself out for them, because they wouldn't appreciate it." She was living well, even without her pension. She sold the television set and gave herself and her friend upstairs some day-trips to the coast, and bought a small radio. She never read books or magazines. The truth was that she could not write or read, or only so badly it was no pleasure to her. Her cat was all reward and no cost, for he fed himself, and continued to bring in pigeons for her to cook and eat, for which in return he claimed milk.

"Greedy Tibby, you greedy *thing*, don't think I don't know, oh yes I do, you'll get sick eating those old pigeons, I do keep telling you that, don't I?''

At last the street was being done up. No longer a uniform, long, disgraceful slum, houses were being brought by the middle-class people. While this meant more good warm clothes for trading—or begging, for she still could not resist the attraction of getting something for nothing by the use of her plaintive inventive tongue, her still flashing handsome eyes—Hetty knew, like her neighbours, that soon this house with its cargo of poor people would be bought for improvement.

In the week Hetty was seventy years old, came the notice that was the end of this little community. They had four weeks to find somewhere else to live.

Usually, the shortage of housing being what it is in London—and everywhere else in the world, of course—these people would have had to scatter, fending for themselves. But the fate of this particular street was attracting attention, because a municipal election was pending. Homelessness among the poor was finding a focus in this street which was a perfect symbol of the whole area, and indeed the whole city, half of it being fine converted tasteful houses, full of people who spent a lot of money, and half being dying houses tenanted by people like Hetty.

As a result of speeches by councillors and churchmen, local authorities found themselves unable to ignore the victims of this redevelopment. The people in the house Hetty was in were visited by a team consisting of an unemployment officer, a social worker, and a rehousing officer. Hetty, a strong gaunt old woman wearing a scarlet wool suit she had found among her castoffs that week, a black knitted teacosy on her head, and black buttoned Edwardian boots too big for her, so that she had to shuffle, invited them into her room. But although all were well used to the extremes of poverty, none wished to enter the place, but stood in the doorway and made her this offer: that she should be aided to get her pension—why had she not claimed it long ago? and that she, together with the four other old ladies in the house should move to a Home run by the Council out in the northern suburbs. All these women were used to, and enjoyed, lively London, and while they had no alternative but to agree, they fell into a saddened and sullen state. Hetty agreed too. The last two winters had set her bones aching badly, and a cough was never far away. And while perhaps she was more of an urban soul even than the others, since she had walked up and down so many streets with her old perambulator loaded with rags and laces, and since she knew so intimately London's texture and taste, she minded least of all the idea of a new home "among green fields." There were, in fact, no fields near the promised Home, but for some reason all the old ladies had chosen to bring out this old song of a phrase, as if it belonged to their situation, that of old women not far off death. "It will be nice to be near green fields again," they said to each other over cups of tea.

The housing officer came to make final arrangements. Hetty Pennefather was to move with the others in two weeks' time. The young man, sitting on the very edge of the only chair in the crammed room, because it was greasy and he suspected it had fleas or worse in it, breathed as lightly as he could because of the appalling stink: there was a lavatory in the house, but it had been out of order for three days, and it was just the other side of a thin wall. The whole house smelled.

The young man, who knew only too well the extent of the misery due to lack of housing, who knew how many old people abandoned by their children did not get the offer to spend their days being looked after by the authorities, could not help feeling that this wreck of a human being could count herself lucky to get a place in this "Home," even if it was—and he knew and deplored the fact—an institution in which the old were treated like naughty and dimwitted children until they had the good fortune to die.

But just as he was telling Hetty that a van would be coming to take her effects and those of the other four old ladies, and that she need not take anything more with her than her clothes "and perhaps a few photographs," he saw what he had thought was a heap of multicoloured rags get up and put its ragged gingery-black paws on the old woman's skirt. Which today was a cretonne curtain covered with pink and red roses that Hetty had pinned around her because she liked the pattern.

"You can't take that cat with you," he said automatically. It was something he had to say often, and knowing what misery the statement caused, he usually softened it down. But he had been taken by surprise.

Tibby now looked like a mass of old wool that has been matting together in dust and rain. One eye was permanently half-closed, because a muscle had been ripped in a fight. One ear was vestigial. And down a flank was a hairless slope with a thick scar on it. A cat-hating man had treated Tibby as he

treated all cats, to a pellet from his air-gun. The resulting
wound had taken two years to heal. And Tibby smelled.

No worse, however, than his mistress, who sat stiffly still,
bright-eyed with suspicion, hostile, watching the wellbrushed
tidy young man from the Council.

"How old is that beast?"

"Ten years, no, only eight years, he's a young cat about
five years old," said Hetty, desperate.

"It looks as if you'd do him a favour to put him out of his
misery," said the young man.

When the official left, Hetty had agreed to everything. She
was the only one of the old women with a cat. The others
had budgerigars[1] or nothing. Budgies were allowed in the
Home.

She made her plans, confided in the others, and when the
van came for them and their clothes and photographs and
budgies, she was not there, and they told lies for her. "Oh,
we don't know where she can have gone, dear," the old
women repeated again and again to the indifferent van driver.
"She was here last night, but she did say something about
going to her daughter in Manchester." And off they went to
die in the Home.

Hetty knew that when houses have been emptied for redevelopment they may stay empty for months, even years.
She intended to go on living in this one until the builders
moved in.

It was a warm autumn. For the first time in her life she
lived like her gypsy forbears, and did not go to bed in a room
in a house like respectable people. She spent several nights,
with Tibby, sitting crouched in a doorway of an empty house
two doors from her own. She knew exactly when the police
would come around, and where to hide herself in the bushes
of the overgrown shrubby garden.

As she had expected, nothing happened in the house, and
she moved back in. She smashed a back windowpane so that
Tibby could move in and out without her having to unlock
the front door for him, and without leaving a window suspiciously open. She moved to the top back room and left it
every morning early, to spend the day in the streets with her
pram and her rags. At night she kept a candle glimmering
low down on the floor. The lavatory was still out of order,
so she used a pail on the first floor, instead, and secretly

---

[1] Small Australian parrots. "Budgies" is an abbreviated form.

emptied it at night into the canal which in the day was full of pleasure boats and people fishing.

Tibby brought her several pigeons during that time.

"Oh you are a clever puss, Tibby, Tibby! Oh you're clever, you are. You know how things are, don't you, you know how to get around and about."

The weather turned very cold; Christmas came and went. Hetty's cough came back, and she spent most of her time under piles of blankets and old clothes, dozing. At night she watched the shadows of the candle flame on floor and ceiling—the windowframes fitted badly, and there was a draught. Twice tramps spent the night in the bottom of the house and she heard them being moved on by the police. She had to go down to make sure the police had not blocked up the broken window the cat used, but they had not. A blackbird had flown in and had battered itself to death trying to get out. She plucked it, and roasted it over a fire made with bits of floorboard in a baking pan: the gas of course had been cut off. She had never eaten very much, and was not frightened that some dry bread and a bit of cheese was all that she had eaten during her sojourn under the heap of clothes. She was cold, but did not think about that much. Outside there was slushy brown snow everywhere. She went back to her nest thinking that soon the cold spell would be over and she could get back to her trading. Tibby sometimes got into the pile with her, and she clutched the warmth of him to her. "Oh you clever cat, you clever old thing, looking after yourself, aren't you? That's right my ducky, that's right my lovely."

And then, just as she was moving about again, with snow gone off the ground for a time but winter only just begun, in January, she saw a builder's van draw up outside, a couple of men unloading their gear. They did not come into the house: they were to start work next day. By then Hetty, her cat, her pram piled with clothes and her two blankets, were gone. She also took a box of matches, a candle, an old saucepan and a fork and spoon, a tinopener, a candle and a rattrap. She had a horror of rats.

About two miles away, among the homes and gardens of amiable Hampstead, where live so many of the rich, the intelligent and the famous, stood three empty, very large houses. She had seen them on an occasion, a couple of years before, when she had taken a bus. This was a rare thing for her, because of the remarks and curious looks provoked by her mad clothes, and by her being able to appear at the same

time such a tough battling old thing, and a naughty child. For
the older she got, this disreputable tramp, the more there
strengthened in her a quality of fierce, demanding childish-
ness. It was all too much of a mixture; she was uncomfortable
to have near.

She was afraid that "they" might have rebuilt the houses,
but there they still stood, too tumbledown and dangerous to
be of much use to tramps, let alone the armies of London's
homeless. There was no glass left anywhere. The flooring at
ground level was mostly gone, leaving small platforms and
juts of planking over basements full of water. The ceilings
were crumbling. The roofs were going. The houses were like
bombed buildings.

But on the cold dark of a late afternoon she pulled the
pram up the broken stairs and moved cautiously around the
frail boards of a second floor room that had a great hole in
it right down to the bottom of the house. Looking into it was
like looking into a well. She held a candle to examine the
state of the walls, here more or less whole, and saw that rain
and wind blowing in from the window would leave one corner
dry. Here she made her home. A sycamore tree screened the
gaping window from the main road twenty yards away. Tibby,
who was cramped after making the journey under the clothes
piled in the pram, bounded down and out and vanished into
neglected undergrowth to catch his supper. He returned fed
and pleased, and seemed happy to stay clutched in her hard
thin old arms. She had come to watch for his return after
hunting trips, because the warm purring bundle of bones and
fur did seem to allay, for a while, the permanent ache of cold
in her bones.

Next day she sold her Edwardian boots for a few shillings—
they were fashionable again—and bought a loaf and some
bacon scraps. In a corner of the ruins well away from the one
she had made her own, she pulled up some floor boards, built
a fire, and toasted bread and the bacon scraps. Tibby had
brought in a pigeon, and she roasted that, but not very effi-
ciently. She was afraid of the fire catching and the whole mass
going up in flames; she was afraid too of the smoke showing
and attracting the police. She had to keep damping down the
fire, and so the bird was bloody and unappetising, and in the
end Tibby got most of it. She felt confused, and discouraged,
but thought it was because of the long stretch of winter still
ahead of her before spring could come. In fact, she was ill.
She made a couple of attempts to trade and earn money to

feed herself before she acknowledged she was ill. She knew she was not yet dangerously ill, for she had been that in her life, and would have been able to recognise the cold listless indifference of a real last-ditch illness. But all her bones ached, and her head ached, and she coughed more than she ever had. Yet she did not think of herself as suffering particularly from the cold, even in that sleety January weather. She had never, in all her life, lived in a properly heated place, had never known a really warm home, not even when she lived in the Council flats. Those flats had electric fires, and the family had never used them, for the sake of economy, except in very bad spells of cold. They piled clothes onto themselves, or went to bed early. But she did know that to keep herself from dying now she could not treat the cold with her usual indifference. She knew she must eat. In the comparatively dry corner of the windy room, away from the gaping window through which snow and sleet were drifting, she made another nest—her last. She had found a piece of plastic sheeting in the rubble, and she laid that down first, so that the damp would not strike up. Then she spread her two blankets over that. Over them were heaped the mass of old clothes. She wished she had another piece of plastic to put on top, but she used sheets of newspaper instead. She heaved herself into the middle of this, with a loaf of bread near to her hand. She dozed, and waited, and nibbled bits of bread, and watched the snow drifting softly in. Tibby sat close to the old blue face that poked out of the pile and put up a paw to touch it. He miaowed and was restless, and then went out into the frosty morning and brought in a pigeon. This the cat put, still struggling and fluttering a little, close to the old woman. But she was afraid to get out of the pile in which the heat was being made and kept with such difficulty. She really could not climb out long enough to pull up more splinters of plank from the floors, to make a fire, to pluck the pigeon, to roast it. She put out a cold hand to stroke the cat.

"Tibby you old thing, you brought it for me then did you? You did, did you? Come here, come in here . . ." But he did not want to get in with her. He miaowed again, pushed the bird closer to her. It was now limp and dead.

"You have it then. You eat it. I'm not hungry, thank you Tibby."

But the carcase did not interest him. He had eaten a pigeon before bringing this one up to Hetty. He fed himself well. In spite of his matted fur, and his scars and his half-closed yellow eye, he was a strong healthy cat.

At about four the next morning there were steps and voices downstairs. Hetty shot out of the pile and crouched behind a fallen heap of plaster and beams, now covered with snow, at the end of the room near the window. She could see through the hole in the floorboards down to the first floor, which had collapsed entirely, and through it to the ground floor. She saw a man in a thick overcoat and muffler and leather gloves holding a strong torch to illuminate a thin bundle of clothes lying on the floor. She saw this bundle was a sleeping man or woman. She was indignant—*her* home was being trespassed upon. And she was afraid because she had not been aware of this other tenant of the ruin. Had he, or she, heard her talking to the cat? And where was the cat? If he wasn't careful he would be caught, and that would be the end of him. The man with a torch went off and came back with a second man. In the thick dark far below Hetty, was a small cave of strong light, which was the torchlight. In this space of light two men bent to lift the bundle, which was the corpse of a man or a woman like Hetty. They carried it out across the dangertraps of fallen and rotting boards that made gangplanks over the waterfilled basements. One man was holding the torch in the hand that supported the dead person's feet, and the light jogged and lurched over trees and grasses: the corpse was being taken through the shrubberies to a car.

There are men in London who, between the hours of two and five in the morning, when the real citizens are asleep, who should not be disturbed by such unpleasantness as the corpses of the poor, make the rounds of all the empty, rotting houses they know about, to collect the dead, and to warn the living that they ought not to be there at all, inviting them to one of the official Homes or lodgings for the homeless.

Hetty was too frightened to get back into her warm heap. She sat with the blankets pulled around her, and looked through gaps in the fabric of the house, making out shapes and boundaries and holes and puddles and mounds of rubble, as her eyes, like her cat's, became accustomed to the dark.

She heard scuffling sounds and knew they were rats. She had meant to set the trap, but the thought of her friend Tibby, who might catch his paw, had stopped her. She sat up until the morning light came in grey and cold, after nine. Now she did know herself to be very ill and in danger, for she had lost all the warmth she had huddled into her bones under the rags.

She shivered violently. She was shaking herself apart with shivering. In between spasms she drooped limp and exhausted. Through the ceiling above her—but it was not a ceiling, only a cobweb of slats and planks, she could see into a dark cave which had been a garret, and through the roof above that, the grey sky, teeming with incipient rain. The cat came back from where he had been hiding, and sat crouched on her knees, keeping her stomach warm, while she thought out her position. These were her last clear thoughts. She told herself that she would not last out until spring unless she allowed "them" to find her, and take her to hospital. After that, she would be taken to a "Home."

But what would happen to Tibby, her poor cat? She rubbed the old beast's scruffy head with the ball of her thumb and muttered: "Tibby, Tibby, they won't get you, no, you'll be all right, yes, I'll look after you."

Towards midday, the sun oozed yellow through miles of greasy grey cloud, and she staggered down the rotting stairs, to the shops. Even in those London streets, where the extraordinary has become usual, people turned to stare at a tall gaunt woman, with a white face that had flaming red patches on it, and blue compressed lips, and restless black eyes. She wore a tightly buttoned man's overcoat, torn brown woollen mittens, and an old fur hood. She pushed a pram loaded with old dresses and scraps of embroidery and torn jerseys and shoes, all stirred into a tight tangle, and she kept pushing this pram up against people as they stood in queues, or gossiped, or stared into windows, and she muttered: "Give me your old clothes darling, give me your old pretties, give Hetty something, poor Hetty's hungry." A woman gave her a handful of small change, and Hetty bought a roll filled with tomato and lettuce. She did not dare go into a cafe, for even in her confused state she knew she would offend, and would probably be asked to leave. But she begged a cup of tea at a street stall, and when the hot liquid flooded through her she felt she might survive the winter. She bought a carton of milk and pushed the pram back through the slushy snowy street to the ruins.

Tibby was not there. She urinated down through the gap in the boards, muttering "A nuisance, that old tea," and wrapped herself in a blanket and waited for the dark to come.

Tibby came in later. He had blood on his foreleg. She had heard scuffling and she knew that he had fought a rat, or several, and had been bitten. She poured the milk into the tilted saucepan and Tibby drank it all.

She spent the night with the animal held against her chilly bosom. They did not sleep, but dozed off and on. Tibby would normally be hunting, the night was his time, but he had stayed with the old woman now for three nights.

Early next morning they again heard the corpse removers among the rubble on the ground floor, and saw the beams of the torch moving on wet walls and collapsed beams. For a moment the torch light was almost straight on Hetty, but no one came up: who could believe that a person could be desperate enough to climb those dangerous stairs, to trust those crumbling splintery floors, and in the middle of winter?

Hetty had now stopped thinking of herself as ill, of the degrees of her illness, of her danger—of the impossibility of her surviving. She had cancelled out in her mind the presence of winter and its lethal weather, and it was as if spring was nearly here. She knew that if it had been spring when she had had to leave the other house, she and the cat could have lived here for months and months, quite safely and comfortably. Because it seemed to her an impossible and even a silly thing that her life, or rather, her death, could depend on something so arbitrary as builders starting work on a house in January rather than in April, she could not believe it: the fact would not stay in her mind. The day before she had been quite clearheaded. But today her thoughts were cloudy, and she talked and laughed aloud. Once she scrambled up and rummaged in her rags for an old Christmas card she had got four years before from her good daughter.

In a hard harsh angry grumbling voice she said to her four children that she needed a room of her own now that she was getting on. "I've been a good mother to you," she shouted to them before invisible witnesses—former neighbours, welfare workers, a doctor. "I never let you want for anything, never! When you were little you always had the best of everything! You can ask anybody, go on, ask them then!"

She was restless and made such a noise that Tibby left her and bounded onto the pram and crouched watching her. He was limping, and his foreleg was rusty with blood. The rat had bitten deep. When the daylight came, he left Hetty in a kind of a sleep, and went down into the garden where he saw a pigeon feeding on the edge of the pavement. The cat pounced on the bird, dragged it into the bushes, and ate it all, without taking it up to his mistress. After he had finished eating, he stayed hidden, watching the passing people. He stared at them intently with his blazing yellow eye, as if he were thinking, or planning. He did not go into the old ruin and up the crumbling wet stairs until late—it was as if he knew it was not worth going at all.

He found Hetty, apparently asleep, wrapped loosely in a blanket, propped sitting in a corner. Her head had fallen on her chest, and her quantities of white hair had escaped from a scarlet woollen cap, and concealed a face that was flushed a deceptive pink—the flush of coma from cold. She was not yet dead, but she died that night. The rats came up the walls and along the planks and the cat fled down and away from them, limping still, into the bushes.

Hetty was not found for a couple of weeks. The weather changed to warm, and the man whose job it was to look for corpses was led up the dangerous stairs by the smell. There was something left of her, but not much.

As for the cat, he lingered for two or three days in the thick shrubberies, watching the passing people and beyond them, the thundering traffic of the main road. Once a couple stopped to talk on the pavement, and the cat, seeing two pairs of legs, moved out and rubbed himself against one of the legs. A hand came down and he was stroked and patted for a little. Then the people went away.

The cat saw he would not find another home, and he moved off, nosing and feeling his way from one garden to another, through empty houses, finally into an old churchyard. This graveyard already had a couple of stray cats in it, and he joined them. It was the beginning of a community of stray cats going wild. They killed birds, and the field mice that lived among the grasses, and they drank from puddles. Before winter had ended the cats had had a hard time of it from thirst, during the two long spells when the ground froze and there was snow and no puddles and the birds were hard to catch because the cats were so easy to see against the clean white. But on the whole they managed quite well. One of the cats was female, and soon there were a swarm of wild cats, as wild as if they did not live in the middle of a city surrounded by streets and houses. This was just one of half a dozen communities of wild cats living in that square mile of London.

Then an official came to trap the cats and take them away. Some of them escaped, hiding till it was safe to come back again. But Tibby was caught. He was not only getting old and stiff—he still limped from the rat's bite—but he was friendly, and did not run away from the man, who had only to pick him up in his arms.

"You're an old soldier, aren't you?" said the man. "A real tough one, a real old tramp."

It is possible that the cat even thought that he might be finding another human friend and a home.

But it was not so. The haul of wild cats that week numbered hundreds, and while if Tibby had been younger a home might have been found for him, since he was amiable, and wished to be liked by the human race, he was really too old, and smelly and battered. So they gave him an injection and, as we say, "put him to sleep."

Brian Moore
(1921–)

Born in Belfast, Northern Ireland, Brian Moore has spent more than half of his life in Canada and the United States. After service in the World War II, he turned to writing, and his novel The Luck of Ginger Coffey, in 1960, gained him several awards. Before that, he had distinguished himself with The Lonely Passion of Judith Hearne (1956) and The Feast of Lupercal (1957). By this time, he had established what would be one of his major themes, the quality of suffering and anguish as it is experienced by isolated, lonely people; a type of guilt that they have taken on as part of their existence. After 1960, Moore wrote several more novels, among them The Emperor of Ice Cream (1965, after Wallace Stevens's title), I Am Mary Dunne (1968), and Catholics (1973). He has also written numerous film scripts.

Uncle T

Vincent Bishop, standing at his hotel room window saw in momentary reflection from the windowpane a nervous young man with dark eyes and undisciplined black hair. Above Times Square the sky hemorrhaged in an advertising glare. His reflection dissolved. He turned away.

"Are you nearly ready, Barbara?" he called.

She was in the bathroom putting polish on her nails. His uncle was due any minute. Maybe he should have bought a bottle to offer his uncle a drink before they started off? The half-dozen roses he had chosen for his aunt—maybe he should have taken them out of the box and let them stand in water for a while? Were half a dozen roses enough?

"Barbara, do you think I should run down to the lobby and get a box of chocolates?"

She did not hear him. Her and her nails. If this was the way she kept him waiting on the second day of their honeymoon, what faced him in the years to come? What would his uncle think of her? Or of him? How could he tell? He had never met his uncle. This morning, as soon as he and his bride checked into the hotel after the flight from Toronto, his uncle had been on the phone to invite them to dinner at his apartment. He was coming now to pick them up. He sounded very kind, but what could you tell from a voice on the phone?

Of course there was his letter. That was the important thing.

> Grenville Press
> 182 West 15th St.
> New York, N.Y. 10011

Dear Vincent,

I am delighted to hear that you are planning to get married and that you are contemplating a honeymoon trip to New York. Both Bernadette and I offer our heartiest congratulations to you and our best wishes to your fiancée. Needless to say, we are looking forward to meeting you at last, but unfortunately, I cannot offer to put you up, as ours is a very small apartment. However, don't worry, I will find you a hotel room.

I was most interested to read that you do not want to return to Ireland when your exchange teaching year in Canada is completed. I can well see the problems of going home with a new bride who is neither Irish nor Catholic and not likely to enjoy the atmosphere there at all. Now, as you also mention that you are fed up with teaching and would like to find something else, let me make you a proposal. How would you consider joining me here at Grenville Press? I'm sure that a young man with your background would be ideal for the editorial side of the business. As you know, Bernadette and I have no children and we consider you very much a member of our family. I might add that since I bought out old Grenville's widow last year, I am now the proprietor of this firm.

Anyway, since you are coming to visit us in New York, we can talk about this in more detail. In the meantime, let me say that although we know each other only from letters, I have long thought that you—a rebel, a wanderer and a lover of literature—must be very much like me when I was your age. I look forward to our meeting. Till then,

Affectionately,
Uncle T

Uncle T. Three years ago, in Ireland, Vincent sat in his bedroom sending letters over all the world's oceans, messages in bottles, appeals for rescue. *I am twenty-two years old and have just completed an Honors English Language and Literature degree at the Queen's University of Belfast. I am anxious to live abroad.* Resident clerk in the Shan States, shipping aide in Takoradi, plantation overseer in British Guiana—any job, anywhere, which would exorcise the future then facing him: a secondary school in an Ulster town, forty lumps of boys waiting at forty desks, rain on the windowpanes, two local cinemas, a dance on Saturday nights.

Back with the foreign postmarks, the form replies, the we-regret-to-inform-you's came a letter signed "Uncle T." A letter in answer to Vincent's veiled appeal to a never-seen uncle who was now, Vincent's mother said, a partner in a New York publishing firm. The letter contained a fifty-dollar money order. The writer regretted that he could not suggest any job at that time, but hoped that, relations established, he and Vincent would keep in touch.

They kept in touch. Even for a young iconoclast there was comfort in a precedent. And what better precedent than Uncle Turlough Carnahan, who, like himself, had published poems in undergraduate magazines, who had once formed a university socialist club, and who (again, like Vincent) had left his parents' house forever after a bitter anticlerical dispute? Vincent wanted to escape from Ireland. Uncle Turlough lived in America. Vincent dreamed of some sort of literary career. Uncle Turlough, by all accounts, had achieved it. Was it any wonder then that this relative was the one Vincent boasted of to his bride?

"Well, will I pass muster for the great man?" Barbara asked, coming from the bathroom, her nail polish still wet, her hands extended before her like a temple dancer's. She was small and fair and neat; her girlish dresses drew attention to her breasts and legs. They had met three months ago when she began to teach modern dance at the Toronto high school where Vincent was spending his exchange year. Since then, she and he had rarely been separated; yet they were strangers still, unsure of each other, too anxious to please.

"Pass muster?" he said. "You'll do more than that." He bent to kiss her ear as the room telephone growled twice.

"That must be him, Vincent."

"Hello," said the telephone voice. "Are you decent? Can I come up for a moment?"

"Of course."

The phone went dead. "He's on his way up," Vincent told her.

"Oh Vincent, I'm so nervous."

How could she be? What was Uncle Turlough to her, who three months ago had never even heard is name? Whereas he, for how many years had he dreamed that one day his uncle might beckon him into his literary world he dreamed of? How would she understand his panic now as he waited at the door of their room, remembering the slight, dark youth he had seen so often in his mother's photograph album, wondering how the person who knocked lightly on the door would differ from that youth. Of course, those photographs would be thirty-five years old. Uncle Turlough must be almost sixty.

He opened the door.

"Vincent, how are you? Welcome to New York." The stranger shook hands, then moved past Vincent. "And this must be Barbara. How are you, my dear? Why, you're even more lovely than he said you were. Welcome, welcome."

On the telephone Vincent had noticed it but had not been sure. Now, he was. The stranger's voice had no trace of his own harsh Ulster burr, but was soft, broguey, nasal, like the voice of an American imitating an Irish accent. Confidential and cozy, it told Barbara, "Do you know, it's an extraordinary thing, my dear, but this husband of yours is the spitting image of me when I was his age. Look at us together. Don't you still see a resemblance?

What resemblance? Vincent thought, but hoped Barbara would have the sense to pretend.

"Oh, yes," she said, "of course, I see it."

The stranger bobbed his head in acknowledgment, and as he did Vincent noticed his hair, black and shiny as a crow's wing, unexpected as the chocolate-brown overcoat and blood-colored shoes. Resemblance?

"Do you have a couple of glasses, by any chance?" the stranger said, unbuttoning his overcoat to reveal a rumpled gray suit, too tight at the middle button. From his jacket pocket he took a pint bottle of whiskey and broke the seal. "Bernadette won't be expecting us for a while," he said. "I left the office early. I thought we might have one for the road here, before we start."

Obediently, Barbara went into the bathroom, returning with two water glasses. "I'd better phone for ice," she said.

"Don't bother," the stranger said. "Just run the cold tap awhile. There's no sense letting them rob you blind with their room service."

He poured two large whiskies and presented them to his guests. "I don't need a glass," he said, raising the pint to his lips. "It's bottles up for me." Silent, they watched, their own drinks untasted. Then Barbara took the two glasses of neat whiskey and went to run the cold tap, as ordered. If it were one of her relatives, Vincent thought, there'd be no surprise, the uncle would be just as advertised, solid, Canadian, safe; he would be the man he said he was and not—what? Oh, Uncle, what uneasy eyes you have! What ruddy cheeks you have, Uncle dear!

"And how's your mother keeping?" the stranger asked.

"She's well."

"Dear little Eileen. Many is the time I've wanted to go home and see her and my other brothers and sisters and all the rest of the Carnahan clan. Maybe I will, some day. Maybe I will."

He recorked the pint and put it on their dressing table. "I'll just leave this here in case you youngsters need a little refreshment when you get home tonight. After all, it's your honeymoon." He winked at Barbara, who was coming out of the bathroom, a wink at once collusive and apologetic. "Although you know, Barbara, my old mother used to say you should never give an Irishman the choice between a girl and the bottle. Because it's a proven fact that most of them will prefer the bottle. Am I right, Vince?" He punched Vincent's shoulder in uncertain good-fellowship. "Now, finish up that sup of drink and we'll be on our way."

Obediently, they drank their whiskies. Obediently they got their coats and followed him to the elevator. At the lobby entrance the hotel doorman approached, asking if they wanted a cab. The stranger shook his head. "You two wait here," he said, and ran a block down the street to find a cab himself.

"Well," Barbara said.

"Well, what?"

She made a face. "I do not like thee, Uncle T, the reason why is plain to see."

"What are you talking about?"

"Just look at him, Vincent. His hair, for one thing."

"What about it?"

"Lovely head of hair," she said. "It's dyed."

"Oh, come off it."

"It's d-y-e-d," she said. "And I'll bet that's not the only phony thing about him."

"Now wait a minute. What do you mean?"

"Darling," she said, "if he's a publisher, I'm Mrs. Roosevelt."

"Now give the man a chance, will you? Why jump to conclusions?"

She did not answer, for at that moment, a cab drew up in full view of the doorman and the stranger leaned out, beckoning them to come. In shame, they passed the doorman's contempt. *Give the man a chance. . . .* But as the taxi rushed them onto the bright carnival rink of Times Square, Vincent heard his father's dry, diagnostic voice: "If your mother's family have a weakness, it's that never in my life have I known any of them to spoil a good story for the sake of the truth." Upgrading their relations, exaggerating their triumphs, hiding their shortcomings under a bluster of palaver—wasn't that what his father thought of the Carnahan clan? Even his mother, hadn't she a touch of it? When twenty-five exchange teachers had been picked to go out to Canada, hadn't she told all her friends the story as though her son were the only one chosen? And this stranger was his mother's brother. Could those letters about Grenville Press be Carnahan exaggeration? No, of course no. *Give the man a chance.*

"Your wife's an American, isn't she, Mr. Carnahan?" Barbara asked.

"Yes, Bernadette was born right here in New York City, although she's of good Irish stock. Where do you people come from, my dear?"

"My grandparents came from England," Barbara said.

"Both sides?"

"Both sides."

And wasn't there a certain Anglo-Saxon attitude in the way she said that? But the stranger did not seem to notice. On and on he went, telling about the Tenderloin district, pointing out the Flatiron building, keeping the small talk afloat as though to distract his listeners from the true facts of the journey. For their taxi was moving from bad to worse, entering streets that Vincent would not have dreamed of in his afternoon of sightseeing along the elegance of Fifth Avenue, streets of houses whose front entrances looked like rear exits, of stale little basement shops left over from an older New York, of signs which proposed *Keys Made, Rooms to Let, Shoes Repaired*. A group of sallow-skinned men played pitchpenny on the pavement. The taxi stopped.

"Here we are," the broguey voice said. "It's very convenient, you know, because it's right downtown."

They skirted the pitchpenny players, entered the apartment building, and climbed two narrow flights of stairs, their guide hurrying ahead of them to press a buzzer outside one of the corridor doors. He rang twice, and as on a signal, a woman opened the door, drawing a mauve woolen stole tight about her bosom as she met the corridor draft. To Vincent's surprise, she was in her late thirties, a brassy blonde, blown stout, wearing a gray sateen dress one size too small for her, moving her weight uncomfortably on tiny ankles and feet. "Bernadette," the stranger said. And kissed her cheek.

Those heads together, kissing, made Vincent think of their mutual hair-dressing problems. Did they dye each other's? Awkwardly, he offered his gift of flowers.

"Oh, roses! Aren't they lovely! Thank you, Vincent. Aren't you the perfect gentleman! Barbara, dear, do you want to come with me and freshen up a little? Turlough, take their coats, will you?"

The sight of their overcoats disappearing into a closet reminded Vincent that the evening was a sentence still to be served. If only he had come alone to New York, if only he hadn't told Barbara that this job would be the end of their worries about what to do when his exchange year was over. If only—he thought of his father's remark—yes, if only he hadn't behaved like a Carnahan. And now, in confirmation of his mother's blood, the first thing he noticed in the living room was a familiar face in a familiar oval frame. Dyed hair or not, publisher or not, this stranger was his kinsman. The photograph was of Vincent's maternal grandmother.

The living room was strangely bare, its furniture worn and discolored, as though his uncle and aunt had several small children and had long ago given up the struggle with appearances. Yet the letter said there were no children. He looked at the bookcase near what must be his uncle's easy chair. Shakespeare, and some poetry, secondhand copies of

Goethe, Swift, Dante, Dickens, Flaubert. All were dusty as though they had not been disturbed since the flat was first moved into. By a small table near the reading lamp were several well-used copies of *The Saturday Evening Post*.

"Glass of sherry?" his uncle said, coming in with a tray on which were four glasses, none of them used. But the newly broken tinfoil seal of the sherry bottle lay beside them and the sherry bottle had already been depleted. Dark, uneasy eyes saw Vincent notice the diminished bottle level, skittered nervously toward the door as Aunt Bernadette reappeared with Barbara. Everyone sat down. Sherry was poured. The verbal gropings began. Aunt Bernadette brought out her wedding present (an ugly salad bowl) and was duly thanked for it. She asked about the wedding. Had they had a big reception? Had they sent photographs to Vincent's mother? How was his mother keeping, by the way?

"She's in great form, from the letters she sends," Vincent said.

"And your Dad, how is he? Turlough tells me you and your Dad didn't always hit it off too well. I hope you made it up with him before you came out here?"

Made it up? He had gone back to Drumconer Avenue the week before he sailed as an exchange teacher. His mother received him, talked to him for a long while, then asked him to wait. He sat alone in the drawing room, listening for his father's step. He heard his father leave the surgery and go along the hall. His father did not come up. He went out of the drawing room and looked over the banister. His father was at the front door, putting on his hat and coat. "Father?" he said. "Father? . . ."

His father did not look up. "I have to go out on a sick call," his father said.

"But couldn't you spare a minute? Or could I come with you?"

His father did not answer. His father reached down into the monk's bench for his consulting bag. His father's attitude had not changed since that day two years before when he looked up from the breakfast table, the newspaper shaking in his fingers. "So this is your damn socialism, is it? Have you seen the paper? My son up on a platform at the university, helping a couple of Protestants to run down his religion and his country. My son! Oh, haven't I reared a right pup. You're going to apologize, do you hear? You're going to sit down this minute and write a public apology and send it out to this newspaper. Do you hear me? This minute!"

Vincent refused. His sister wept: she said his conduct had broken their mother's heart. His mother packed a suitcase and went on a pilgrimage to Lough Derg, walking in her bare feet over the stones of that penitential island, praying God to give her son back the gift of faith. But despite his father's rage, his sister's tears, his mother's penance, he could not recant. Oh, yes, he loved them, he loved them all. But fourteen and eight made twenty-two, eight years of hypocrisy, of going to Mass and the sacraments for their sake. He tried to tell the truth in that university debate. The truth troubled him. But his father belonged to a generation who had had their troubles; they had no time for any others. And so after a month of his father's silent anger, Vincent left home to become a schoolmaster in a provincial town. And two years later when he returned, hoping to see his father, his father reached down into the monk's bench in the hall, picked up his consulting bag and opened the front door, leaving his plea unanswered. What answer had he wanted, he wondered? Forgiveness? Or merely some sign that they still were kin? They knew, both he and his father, that if he crossed the Atlantic he might never return. But his father had to go out on a sick call. His father walked down the path, opened the garden gate, did not look back. Went down the avenue, turned the corner, no look back.

And now, remembering this, what should he say to his uncle's wife? What should he answer this strange woman who asked if he had "made it up"?

"Ah, your father always was stubborn," Uncle Turlough said, seeing his hesitation. "I remember well. He and I were schoolmates. . . ."

"Stubborn?" Aunt Bernadette said. "But isn't it children that are stubborn when they go against their own parents? Don't be putting excuses into the boy's head, Turlough. You've no right. Look what happened with your own father. When you heard he was dead you sat in this room and wept." She turned to Vincent. "Too late to make it up then," she said. "Too late."

Her face was very close. Her flabby, powdered cheeks were pitted and spongy as angel food cake. Yet a few years ago she must have been pretty enough to make an old fool dye his hair. A few years ago, before the fat, before the coarseness, before the skin began to sag as though the body had sprung a slow leak. An old man marries a pretty face and ends up in a room with a monster. Strange monster, what right have you to reproach me with my father? He turned from her, determined to ignore her.

She would not be ignored. "Oh, I know you think it's none of my business," she said. "But Turlough tells me you're just like he was when he first came out here. So, I'm warning you, Vincent. Don't make his mistake."

"Now Bernadette, now dear," Uncle Turlough said. "You're confusing two different cases entirely."

"Am I? You never went home because you were too stubborn to go back on all your boasting. You were even ashamed of me."

"Now, that's not true, sweetheart. . . ."

"It is true." She turned to Barbara. "He's always complaining that I don't have his education. Well, I don't, but is that my fault? Oh, let me tell you dear, your troubles are only starting when you marry into this Carnahan clan."

"I can't believe I'll have any trouble," Barbara said, smiling.

"Do you mean because you're better educated than me?"

"I didn't mean that at all, Mrs. Carnahan."

"Oh yes, you did. But don't forget you're a Protestant. Show me the mixed marriage that doesn't have its troubles. You'll have your share of tears."

"Drinks? Drinks, anyone?" Uncle Turlough said in a hoarse voice. "Barbara, a little more? Vincent, can I top that up for you? Bernadette? Anyone? . . ."

No one answered him. Barbara sat stiff in her chair, her eyes fixed on the lamp across the room. Aunt Bernadette, her neck red beneath the powder line, looked at Barbara in open dislike.

"Charity," Uncle Turlough said, pouring himself the drink that no one else wanted. "Charity for the other person's point of view, that's what counts. Don't try to make everyone else the same as you, that's the thing I've learned as I get older. . . . Vincent, maybe you'd like to switch to a shot of whiskey?"

Maybe he would. Getting drunk might be the only way to survive this evening. So Vincent said yes, aware of Barbara's sudden disapproval, watching her gather up her handbag as though she were preparing to walk out on him. In that moment he felt her Protestant prejudice against all the things which the words "Irish Catholic" must bring into her mind: vulgarity, backwardness, bigotry, drunkenness. But the litanies of love he had recited to her these past three months, didn't they count for anything? Didn't she know very well that he was no longer Catholic, that it was not his fault that he had been born Irish, that he could hardly be held responsible for relatives he had never laid eyes on? If her lovemaking last night meant anything more than animal desire, wouldn't she be suffering with him now, not sitting in judgment on him as though he had tricked her?

Still, he had tricked her, hadn't he? Tricked her by boasting of his publisher uncle, tricked her by holding out New York as bait, knowing how bored she was with Toronto. Yes, he had. She knew it and she would make him pay for it. She stirred in her chair, turned toward his uncle, and in a disarmingly innocent voice, asked the question Vincent had feared all evening. "By the way, Mr. Carnahan, we've been wondering what sort of books you publish. Is it mostly fiction, or nonfiction?"

Aunt Bernadette looked at her husband. "Fiction?"

"What about the dinner, dear?" Uncle Turlough asked. "Isn't it nearly ready?"

"I'll go and see."

In the silence which followed Aunt Bernadette's departure, Uncle Turlough poured himself another sherry. "Well . . ." he said. "Well, I thought Vincent and I would talk business tomorrow at the office. Tonight, let's just enjoy ourselves, eh?"

"Oh, I wasn't thinking of it in that sense," Barbara said. "I was just wondering if perhaps I've read some of your authors?"

"Authors?" Dark, uneasy eyes appealed to Vincent, found no support, fixed their gaze on a neutral corner. "We—ah—we don't do any fiction, my dear. Not that I wouldn't be happy to, mind you. But you see—perhaps I've never explained this properly in my letters—we're in a more specialized field."

"Oh, really?"

Vincent stared at her, willing her to look at him. Drop it, can't you? But she had no mercy. "Well," she said, "what sort of books do you do, then?"

"Books? Not too many books, I'm afraid. You see we're not what you might call book publishers. We do a few directories. And we do brochures and booklets and pamphlets—that sort of work."

"Directories?"

"Well, for instance, we do a dental directory that's a very profitable line. We try to get out a new edition every five years. You'd be surprised how many dentists can afford to shell out five dollars for a nicely got-up book that has their name in it."

"Dinner's ready," said Aunt Bernadette.

Dinner. The fusty dining room was crowded with heavy walnut furniture which, by the awkwardness of its presence, announced that their hosts did not often eat there. There was, however, a bottle of wine, and the main dish of roast beef and baked potatoes was good and plentiful. A plated silver candlestick with three candles lit. An Irish linen tablecloth still glistening new, its folds heavily creased from the years of lying in a gift box, proclaimed that in honor of Vincent and his bride Aunt Bernadette had set out her best. But Barbara did not relent; the questions continued. Behind his uncle's apologetic smiles, behind the evasions, the unwillingness to be specific, Barbara laid the imposture bare; Grenville Press, those boastful letters nowithstanding, was in reality a hole-and-corner print shop whose main activity consisted in cooking up lists of names in the manner of a spurious *Who's Who*. There was, Uncle Turlough admitted, a great deal of work in canvassing people to get them to buy the books and brochures in which their names would be included, a great deal of "sounding out groups in specialized fields to see if the response merits publication."

"And what exactly did you have in mind for Vincent in all this?" Barbara asked.

"Well. . . ." His uncle's dark eyes sought out Aunt Bernadette, who sat silent, eating with a concentration which showed plainly how she had come to lose her looks. "Well, I thought he might take Miss Henshaw's place. Eh, Bernadette?"

Aunt Bernadette nodded, still chewing.

"As a matter of fact, Vincent, the week you wrote to me saying you wanted to stay, that was the week we found out Miss Henshaw had cancer of the bowel. She was our editor, my right arm, and old Grenville's before me. Wonderful woman, she could turn out anything you wanted, from a seed catalogue to a school prospectus. She was a great loss, but"—he smiled painfully at Vincent—"if it had to happen, then what better time than now, which it gives me a chance to offer you a good job with the firm. Which you'll accept, I hope."

Barbara was waiting. He must speak. "Well," he said, "of course my teaching year isn't over yet. I haven't really made up my mind."

"But you're fed up with teaching, your letter said."

"Yes."

"And you have to find some sort of job here, don't you?"

"Yes."

"And you wrote that you'd like to live in New York, didn't you?"

"Yes."

"Well, then?"

Vincent did not answer. "I think Vincent was under the impression that you were a book publisher," Barbara said.

"Book publisher? Book publisher. I see. So you thought we were something on the order of Scribner's, did you? Something in that class. Ah, I'm afraid that's not the case, although who knows, great trees from little acorns, as the saying goes. Well, maybe it's my fault. Maybe I made the firm sound a little more important than it really is. But that's only human, isn't it? Isn't it, Vincent?"

Vincent nodded, his eyes on the tablecloth. Aunt Bernadette, speaking for the first time since she had started eating, announced that she would serve coffee in the front room.

"Coffee, yes," Uncle Turlough said, lurching to his feet, tossing his napkin on the table. "Coffee it is. And we'll have a spot of brandy in your honor, children. Come along, Barbara, let me take you in."

Coffee was poured. Aunt Bernadette took her cup and retired to the kitchen, refusing Barbara's halfhearted offer to help with the dishes. Uncle Turlough handed brandies around, then moved uncertaintly into the center of the room, his own glass held aloft.

"A toast," he said. "I mean, I want to tell you both how happy I am that you're here at last. I want to tell you how much tonight means to me. You see, Vincent, you're the first relative I've laid eyes on since the day I left Ireland. Yes, this is a great occasion. As you know, I've no children of my own and reading Vincent's letters was like living my own life over again. Funny, isn't it, how you and I have done so many of the same things? Yes. . . . So, *Cead Mile Failte* to you and to this lovely bride of yours, and may this might be the beginning of your long and happy memories of New York."

Vincent raised his glass but Barbara put hers down. "I'm superstitious," she said, smiling. "I never like to drink to something before we've really made our minds up."

"Well then, let's say, here's hoping," his uncle said. "Here's hoping you'll like it enough to stay. Eh, Vincent?"

"Here's hoping," Vincent said, smiling in embarrassment. He and his uncle drank, Barbara did not pick up her glass. His uncle noticed that.

"As for the money," his uncle said. "I think I'll be able to start you on more than you're earning as a schoolmaster." He turned to Barbara, empty glass in his hand, in an attitude which reminded Vincent of a beggar asking alms. "And you know, Barbara," he said, "if it's moving to a new place that worries you, Bernadette and I will do all we can to help you get settled."

"It's not the moving that worries me," she said.

"Then what is it, my dear?"

"Well, if you must know," she said, "I'm worried about the job and whether it's what Vincent wants."

Said, her sentence hung in the air like smoke after a bullet. His uncle turned toward Vincent, waiting, his puffy face curiously immobile, his dark eyes stilled at last. In the kitchen Aunt Bernadette could be heard turning on taps, stacking dinner dishes. No one spoke, and after a few moments his uncle pulled out his handkerchief and coughed into it. Coughed and coughed, bending almost double while Vincent watched, heartsick, waiting for the paroxysm to wear itself out, watching as his uncle straightened up again, handkerchief still shielding his mouth, eyes staring at them in bloodshot, watery contrition. "Yes . . . well, of course, that's for you and Vincent to decide," his uncle said. "Excuse me—this cough. Sorry. Anyway, it's my fault, talking business to a young couple on their honeymoon. *Mea culpa.* Now, let's talk about something else. How was your trip?"

"Very tiring," Barbara said. "I don't know about Vincent, but I feel quite exhausted."

"Sorry to hear that," his uncle said. "If you're tired we mustn't keep you too late. But it's still the shank of the evening, after all. Would you like another cup of coffee?"

"No, thank you."

Again there was silence. "Vincent tells me you teach modern dance," his uncle began. "I'm a great admirer of Katherine Dunham. Have you ever seen her troupe?"

"Yes."

"And Martha Graham's 'Letter to the World,' " his uncle continued. "Yes, I used to go to a lot of ballet once upon a time." He smiled at her as he spoke, smiled as though pleading for her friendship. But Barbara did not return his smile and so, rejected, he reached unsteadily for the bottle and poured himself another brandy. Vincent tried to speak; in that moment he felt embarrassed for this man who had written a letter, booked a hotel room, bought a festive meal, made a speech of welcome, and who, his illusion of family feeling destroyed, sat silent, half drunk, his smile rejected. Vincent talked. He talked of the Abbey Theatre, of the plays he had seen in Toronto. For a few minutes, he and his uncle stumbled over broken rocks of conversation, recalling the sights and spectacles of former days. But a conversation with no dark corners could no longer be sustained. The talk died. Aunt Bernadette came back into the room to collect the coffee cups. Barbara gathered up her handbag.

"It's been a lovely evening, Mrs. Carnahan," she said, "and a wonderful dinner. But I'm afraid you must excuse me. I'm awfully tired from the plane trip. We had to be up so early this morning."

Aunt Bernadette bent down, put the coffee pot on her tray, stacked the saucers, heaped the cups on top.

"Leave those dishes, won't you dear?" Uncle Turlough said. "What's it matter?"

"I just want to put them in the sink."

"But Barbara's leaving, dear."

"I won't be a minute." She picked up the tray, went out of the room, and again they heard the rush of water taps in the kitchen.

"Bernadette won't be a minute," Uncle Turlough said. "She . . . she likes to get the dishes done in one washing. I'll just go and hurry her up. Sit down for a second, Barbara, I'll be back in a moment."

He went out.

"My God, Barbara, it's not ten o'clock yet. You could have been a bit more polite to them."

"I didn't feel like it," she said. "I'm sick. Why didn't you have the guts to tell him? You'd be insane to take that job. *Insane.* Why didn't you speak up?"

"Shh! They'll hear you."

"Well, what do I care? Do you think I want to spend our honeymoon being shown around by him and that floozy of his? My God, Vincent—"

But at that moment the sound of unmistakably quarrelsome voices reached them from the kitchen. "I don't care," Aunt Bernadette's voice said. "Let them go."

"Ah now, wait a minute, sweetheart—"

"Oh, shut up! I know you. It's your own fault. It's an old

story, making yourself out to be something you never were."

"Shh!" his uncle's voice pleaded. Mumbling, indistinct, the argument died to whispers. A door shut. Uncle Turlough came from the kitchen, his face again fixed in its apologetic smile.

"We really must go," Barbara said, standing up.

"Oh? Well then, I'll just run down and find a taxi for you. Just a minute, I won't be long. Bernadette? . . . Bernadette, will you get the children's coats?"

In answer the water taps roared again in the kitchen.

"Won't be long," Uncle Turlough said, opening the apartment door. "Vincent, get yourself a drink."

The front door shut. Vincent stood up and walked toward the brandy bottle. He had drunk too much. He felt slow, uncoordinated, dull.

"Vincent, you're not going to have another drink!"

"I am."

"I'm getting my coat then. Where is it?"

"In the closet in the hall."

He heard her leave the room. He picked up the bottle. Perhaps in twenty years his face would bloat and blotch as his uncle's had. Drink, that was an Irish weakness. Self-deceit, that was an Irish weakness. He drank the brandy. He stared at the bookshelves with their dusty, unused books. Drunkenly, he turned to face his Carnahan grandmother on the mantelpiece. Never give an Irishman the choice between a girl and the bottle, she had said. Most of them will prefer the bottle.

The front door opened and he heard his uncle call, "Barbara, let me help you with that coat. And is this Vincent's coat? I have a cab waiting downstairs. Where's Vincent?"

His uncle came in, his step unsteady, his face still fixed in that apologetic smile which was, wasn't it, the very mirror of the man? "Here's your coat, Vincent lad. And wait till I get your aunt. Bernadette? Bernadette?"

He went out again and Vincent heard him go into the kitchen. A moment later, the front door shut. Vincent ran out to the hall. She was gone. Furious at her, he opened the front door to call her back, but as he did, his uncle returned from the kitchen. "Oh, there you are," his uncle said. "Bernadette asked me to say goodnight for her, she has a touch of migraine." He held out a clumsy parcel. "Your wedding present," he said. "I wrapped it up for you. Now, what about a nightcap? One for the road. Where's Barbara?"

"I asked her to go down and hold the cab."

His lie, complementing his uncle's, their mutual shame as they stood face to face, each seeking to atone for his wife's rudeness, each hoping to preserve the fiction of family unity . . . Oh God, Vincent thought, we are alike. Quickly, he opened the front door. "No thanks," he said. "Good night, and thank you for a very nice evening. Don't bother to come down, please."

"No bother at all. But are you sure now, you wouldn't stay a wee while? You could send Barbara home if she's tired and then we could sit down over a glass, just the two of us."

"I'm afraid I'd better go. Barbara is waiting, you see."

"I see," his uncle said. "Yes, of course. All right, I'll come down and say goodnight to her."

"Please, it's not necessary."

"No bother," his uncle said, following him out, pursuing him down two flights of stairs, coming with him into the street. The taxi waited, its bright ceiling light showing Barbara huddled in the far corner of the back seat. She did not appear to see them, and Vincent, afraid that she would refuse to say good-bye, hurried ahead of his uncle and pulled open the taxi door. "Say good-bye to him, will you?" he whispered.

"Where is he?" She looked past him, peering into the darkness of the shabby street. But his uncle had stopped about twelve feet from the taxi. She waved to him and he raised his hand and waved back. "Goodnight, my dear," he called. "Have a good rest."

"Goodnight, Mr. Carnahan. And thank you." She smiled at him and leaned back in her seat. For her it was over; she wanted to go back to the hotel, to escape forever from these people she despised. "Come on," she said. "Get in."

But as she spoke, Vincent heard a low voice behind him. "Vincent? Vincent?"

Father? he had called. Father? But his father had not looked back. His father had walked down the path, opened the gate, no look back. Went down the avenue, turned the corner, no look back.

He turned back. There, half drunk on the pavement stood a fat old man with dyed hair. Where was the boy who once wrote poems, the young iconoclast who once spoke out against the priests? What had done this to him? Was it drink, or exile, or this marriage to a woman twenty years his junior? Or had that boy never been? What did this old man want of him now, Vincent wondered? Forgiveness? Or merely some sign that they still were kin?

"Vincent," his uncle said. "I'll see you tomorrow, won't I?"

"Yes."

"And Vincent? It's a good job, on my word of honor it is I hope you'll take it, Vincent."

"Well, I must think about it, Uncle Turlough."

"Of course, of course. And Vincent? Bernadette, ah, you shouldn't mind her. Some days she's not herself. I'm sorry you didn't enjoy yourself this evening."

"But we did. We had a very good time."

"Thanks, Vince, thanks for saying that. Now, I don't want to keep you but I wish we'd had more time to talk. I know you don't like the looks of the job. I think you don't like the looks of me, either. Well, I can't say I blame you, no, I can't say I blame you one bit. But, Vincent?"

"Yes, Uncle Turlough?"

"I was counting on your coming in with me. I had great hopes of passing on the business—but, never mind, if you don't want the job you don't want it and there's no use talking. Go on back now. You're on your honeymoon, you have better things to do than sit around at night with the likes of me. So off with you, lad, and good luck to you."

"Goodnight, Uncle Turlough."

As he shook hands with his uncle, Vincent looked at the taxi. There she sat, her pretty face averted in contempt. Was that all last night's lovemaking had meant to her? Didn't she know it was for both their sakes that he had come here this evening, that unless he could find something to do on this side of the water, she would be condemned to a life of drizzling boredom as a schoolteacher's wife in an Irish country town?

He leaned into the taxi. "Barbara, let's not go just yet."

"I'm tired," she said. "I'm leaving."

He fumbled in his trouser pocket. "Here's your fare then." He pushed the money at her and shut the taxi door. The taxi moved away from the curb. He watched; she did not look back.

"What's the matter, Vincent?"

He turned, his face forming an apologetic smile, his dark, uneasy eyes searching his kinsman's face. "I've changed my mind," he said. "Maybe I'll have one for the road, after all."

"I knew it, I knew it," said his spitting image.

Nadine Gordimer
(1924–   )

Nadine Gordimer was born in the Transvaal, South Africa. A prolific novelist and short story writer, she is best known for her subtle but defiant opposition to the apartheid laws in her native country and for the embodiment of this opposition in her fiction. Along with fellow novelist Alan Paton and playwright Athol Fugard, she is the most renowned of the South African writers who have taken a position against Pretoria's restrictive racial policies. Among her novels are A Guest of Honor *(1970) and* The Conservationist *(1975). While "The Defeated" (from* The Soft Voice of the Serpent, *1952) is not precisely about apartheid and its dehumanization, it does represent various types of racial and religious exclusion in her native country.*

The Defeated

My mother did not want me to go near the Concession stores because they smelled, and were dirty, and the natives spat tuberculosis germs into the dust. She said it was no place for little girls.

But I used to go down there sometimes, in the afternoon, when static four o'clock held the houses of our Mine, and the sun washed over them like the waves of the sea over sand castles. I felt that life was going on down there at the Concession stores: noise, and movement and—yes, bad smells, even—and so I would wander down the naked road, with the hot sun uncomfortably drying the membrane inside my nose, seeing the irregular line of narrow white shops lying away ahead like a jumble of shoe boxes.

The signs of life that I craved were very soon evident: rich and careless of its vitality, it overflowed from the crowded pavement of the stores, and the surrounding veld was littered with sucked-out oranges and tatters of dirty paper, and worn into the shabby barrenness peculiar to earth much trampled upon by the feet of men. A fat, one-legged native, with the patient detachment of the businessman who knows himself indispensable, sat on the bald veld beside the path that led from the Compound, his stock of walking sticks, standing up, handles tied together, points splayed out fanwise, his pyramids of bright, thin-skinned oranges waiting. Sometimes he had mealies as well—those big, hard, full-grown ears with rows of yellowish tombstones instead of little pearly teeth— and a brazier made from a paraffin tin to roast them by. Propped against the chipped pillars of the pavement, there were always other vendors, making their small way in lucky beans, herbs, bracelets beaten from copper wire, knitted caps in wonderful colors—blooming like great hairy petunias, or bursting suns, from the needles of old, old native women— and, of course, oranges. Everywhere there were oranges; the pushing, ambling crowds filling the pavement ate them as they stared at the windows, the gossips, sitting with their blankets drawn close and their feet in the gutter, sucked at them, the Concession store cats sniffed at the skins where they lay, hollow-cheeked, discarded in every doorway.

Quite often I had to flick the white pith from where it had landed, on my shoe or even my dress, spat negligently by some absorbed orange-eater contemplating a shirt through breath-smudged plate glass. The wild, wondering dirty men came up from the darkness of the mine and they lay themselves out to the sun on the veld, and to their mouths they put the round fruit of the sun; and it was the expression of their need.

I would saunter along the shopwindows amongst them, and for me there was a quickening of glamour about the place: the air was thicker with their incense-like body smell, and the sudden rank shock of their strongest sweat, as a bare armpit lifted over my head. The clamor of their voices— always shouting, but so merry, so angry!—and the size of their laughter, and the open-mouthed startle with which they greeted every fresh sight: I felt vaguely the spell of the books I had read, returning; markets in Persia, bazaars in Cairo. . . . Nevertheless, I was careful not to let them brush too closely past me, lest some unnamable *something* crawl from their dusty blankets or torn cotton trousers onto my clean self, and I did not like the way they spat, with that terrible gurgle in the throat, into the gutter, or, worse still, blew their noses loudly between finger and thumb, and flung the excrement horribly to the air.

And neither did I like the heavy, sickening, greasy carrion-breath that poured from the mouth of the Hotela la Bantu, where the natives hunched intent at zinc-topped forms, eating steaming no-color chunks of horror that bore no relation to meat as I knew it. The down on my arms prickled in revulsion from the pulpy entrails hanging in dreadful enticement at the window, and the blood-embroidered sawdust spilling out of the doorway.

I know that I wondered how the storekeepers' wives, who sat on soap boxes outside the doorways of the shops on either side of the eating house, could stand the breath of that maw. How they could sit, like lizards in the sun; and all the time they breathed in the breath of the eating house: took it deep into the recesses of their being, whilst my throat closed against it in disgust.

It was down there one burning afternoon that I met Mrs. Saiyetovitz. She was one of the storekeepers' wives, and I had seen her many times before, sitting before the deep, blanket-hung cave of her husband's store, where a pile of tinsel-covered wooden trunks shimmered and flashed a pink or green eye out of the gloom into the outside—wearing her creased alpaca apron, her fat insteps leaning over her down-at-heel shoes. Sometimes she knitted, and sometimes she just sat. On this day there was a small girl hanging about her, drawing on the shopwindow with a sticky forefinger. When the child turned to look at me, I recognized her as one of the girls from "our school"; a girl from my class, as a matter of fact, called Miriam Saiyetovitz. Yes, that was her name: I remembered it because it was ugly—I was always sorry for girls with ugly names.

Miriam was a tousled, black-haired little girl, who wore a red bow in her hair. Now she recognized me, and we stood looking at one another; all at once the spare line of the name "Miriam Saiyetovitz," that was like the scrolled pattern of an iron gate with only the sky behind it, shifted its perspective in my mind, so that now between the cold curly M's and the implacable A's of that gate's framework, I saw a house, a complication of buildings and flowers and figures walking, where before there was nothing but the sky. Miriam Saiye-tovitz—and this: behind her name and her school self, the hot and buzzing world of the stores. And I smiled at her, very friendly.

So she knew we had decided to recognize one another and she sauntered over to talk to me. I stood with her in the doorway of her father's store, and I, too, wrote my name and drew cats composed of two capital O's and a sausage tail, with the point of my hot and sticky finger on the window. Of course, she did not exactly introduce me to her mother—children never do introduce their mothers; they merely let it be known, by referring to the woman in question offhand, in the course of play, or going up to speak to her in such a way that the relationship becomes obvious. Miriam went up to her mother and said diffidently: "Ma, I know this girl from school—she's in class with me, can we have some red lemonade?"

And the woman lifted her head from where she sat, wide-legged, so that you couldn't help seeing the knee-elastic of her striped pink silk bloomers holding over the cotton tops of her stockings and said, peering, "Take it! Take it! Go, have it!"

Because I did not then know her, I thought that she was angry, she spoke with such impatience; but soon I knew that it was only her eager generosity that made her fling permission almost fiercely at Miriam whenever the child made some request. Mrs. Saiyetovitz's glance wavered over to me, but she did not seem to be seeing me very clearly: indeed, she could not, for her small, pale, pale eyes narrowed into her big, simple, heavy face were half-blind, and she had always to peer at everything, and never quite see.

I saw that she was very ugly.

Ugly, with the blunt ugliness of a toad; the ugliness of seeming not entirely at home in any element—as if the earth were the wrong place, too heavy and magnetic for a creature already so blunt; and the water would be no better: too subtle and contour-swayed for a creature so graceless. And yet her ugliness was without repellence. When I grew older I often wondered why; she should have been repellent, one should have turned from her, but one did not. She was only ugly. She had the short, stunted yet heavy bones of generations of oppression in the Ghettos of Europe; breasts, stomach, hips crowded sadly, no height, wide strong shoulders and a round back. Her head settled right down between her shoulders without even the grace of a neck, and her dun flat hair was cut at the level of her ears. Her features were not essentially

Semitic; there was nothing so *definite* as that about her: she had no distinction whatever.

Miriam reappeared from the shades of the store, carrying two bottles of red lemonade. A Shangaan emerged at the same time, clutching a newspaper parcel and puzzling over his handful of change, not looking where he was going. Miriam swept past him, the dusty African with his odd, troglodyte unsureness, and his hair plastered into savage whorls with red clay. With one swift movement she knocked the tin caps off the bottles against the scratched frame of the shopwindow, and handed my lemonade to me. "Where did you get it so quickly?" I asked, surprised. She jerked her head back towards the store: "In the kitchen," she said—and applied herself to the bottle.

And so I knew that the Saiyetovitzes lived there, behind the Concession store.

Saturday afternoons were the busiest. Mrs. Saiyetovitz's box stood vacant outside and she helped her husband in the shop. Saturday afternoon was usually my afternoon for going down there, too; my mother and father went out to golf, and I was left with the tick of the clock, the purring monologue of our cat, and the doves gurgling in the empty garden.

On Saturdays every doorway was crowded; a continual shifting stream snaked up and down the pavements; flies tangled overhead, the air smelled hotter, and from the doorway of every store the high, wailing blare and repetition of native songs, played on the gramophone, swung out upon the air and met in discord with the tune of the record being played next door.

Miriam's mother's brother was the proprietor of the Hotela la Bantu, and another uncle had the bicycle shop two doors down. Sometimes she had a message to deliver at the bicycle shop, and I would go in with her. Spare wheels hung across the ceiling, there was a battered wooden counter with a pile of puncture repair outfits, a sewing machine or two for sale, and, in the window, bells and pumps and mascots cut out of tin, painted yellow and red for the adornment of handle bars. We were invariably offered a lemonade by the uncle, and we invariably accepted. At home I was not allowed to drink lemonades unlimited; they might "spoil my dinner"; but Miriam drank them whenever she pleased.

Wriggling in and out amongst the gray-dusty bodies of the natives—their silky brown skin dies in the damp fug underground: after a few months down the mine, it reflects only weariness—Miriam looked with her own calm, quick self-possession upon the setting in which she found herself. Like someone sitting in a swarm of ants; and letting them swarm, letting them crawl all over and about her. Not lifting a hand to flick them off. Not crying out against them in disgust; nor explaining, saying, well, I *like* ants. Just sitting there and letting them swarm, and looking out of herself as if to say: What ants? What ants are you talking about? I giggled and shuddered in excitement at the sight of the dried bats and cobwebby snakeskins rotting in the bleary little window of the medicine shop, but Miriam tugged at my dress and said, "Oh, come on—" I exclaimed at the purple and red shirts lying amongst the dead flies in the wonderful confusion of Saiyetovitz's store window, but Miriam was telling me about her music exam in September, and only frowned at the interruption. I was approaching the confusion of adolescence, and sometimes an uncomfortable, terrible, fascinating curiosity—like a headless worm which lay shamefully hidden in the earth of my soul—crawled out into my consciousness at the sight of the animal obviousness of the natives' male bodies in their scanty covering; but the flash of my guilt at these moments met no answer in Miriam, although she was the same age as I.

If the sight of a boy interrupting his conversation to step out a yard or two onto the veld to relieve himself filled me with embarrassment and real disgust, so that I wanted to go and look at flowers—it seemed that Miriam did not see.

It was quite a long time before she took me into her father's store.

For months it remained a vague, dark, dust-moted world beyond the blanket-hung doorway, into which she was swallowed up and appeared again, whilst I waited outside, with the boys who looked and looked and looked at the windows. Then one day, as she was entering, she paused, and said suddenly and calmly: "Aren't you coming . . . ?" Without a word, I followed her in.

It was cool in the store, and the coolness was a surprise. Out of the sun-baked pavement—and into the store that was cool, like a cellar! Light danced only furtively along the folds of the blankets that hung from the ceiling: crackling silent and secret little fires in the curly woolen furze. The blankets were dark somber hangings, in proud colors, bold and primal. They hung like dark stalactites in the cave, still and heavy, communing only their own colors back to themselves. They brooded over the shop; and over Mr. Saiyetovitz there beneath, treading the worn cement with his disgruntled, dispossessed air of doing his best, but . . . I had glimpsed him before. He lurked within the depths of his store like a beast in its lair, and now and then I had seen the glimmer of his pale, pasty face with the wide upper lip under which the lower closed glumly and puffily.

John Saiyetovitz (his name wasn't John at all, really—it was Yanka, but when he arrived at Cape Town, long ago, the Immigration authorities were tired of attempting to understand and spell the unfamiliar names of the immigrants pouring off the boat, and by the time they'd got the "Saiyetovitz" spelt right, they couldn't be bothered puzzling over the "Yanka," so they scrawled "John" on his papers, and John he was)—John Saiyetovitz was a gentle man, with an almost hangdog gentleness, but when he was trading with the natives, strange blasts of power seemed to blow up in his soul. Africans are the slowest buyers in the world; to them, buying is a ritual, a slow and solemn undertaking. They must go carefully; they nervously scent pitfalls on every side. And confronted with a selection of different kinds of the one thing they want, they are as confused as a child before a plate of pastries; fingering, hesitating, this or that . . . ? On a busy Saturday they must be allowed to stand about the shop endlessly, looking up and about, pausing to shake their heads and give a profound "OW!"; sauntering off; going to press their noses against the window again; coming back. And Mr. Saiyetovitz—always the same, unshaven and collarless—lugging a blanket down from the shelves, flinging it upon the counter—and another, and then another, and standing, arms hanging, sullen and smoldering before the blank-faced purchaser. The boy with his helpless stance, and his eyes rolling up in the agony of decision, filling the shop with the sickly odor of his anxious sweat, and clutching his precious guitar.

Waiting, waiting.

And then Mr. Saiyetovitz swooping away in a gesture of rage and denial; don't care, sick-to-death. And the boy anxious, edging forward to feel the cloth again, and the whole business starting up all over again; more blankets, different colors, down from the shelf and hooked from the ceiling— stalactites crumpled to woolen heaps to wonder over. Mr. Saiyetovitz throwing them down, moving in jerks of rage now, and then roughly bullying the boy into a decision. Shouting

at him, bundling his purchase into his arms, snatching the
money, gesturing him cowed out of the store.

Mr. Saiyetovitz treated the natives honestly, but with bad
grace. He forced them to feel their ignorance, their inade-
quacy, and their submission to the white man's world of money.
He spiritually maltreated them, and bitterly drove his nail
into the coffin of their confidence.

With me, he was shy, he smiled widely and his hand went
to the stud swinging loose at the neck of his half-buttoned
shirt, and drew as if in apology over the stubbled landscape
of his jaw. He always called me "little girl" and he liked to
talk to me in the way that he thought children like to be
talked to, but I found it very difficult to make a show of reply,
because his English was so broken and fragmentary. So I used
to stand there, and say yes, Mr. Saiyetovitz, and smile back
and say thank you! to anything that sounded like a question,
because the question usually was did I want a lemonade?,
and of course, I usually did.

The first time Miriam ever came to my home was the day
of my birthday party.

Our relationship at school had continued unchanged, just
as before; she had her friends and I had mine, but outside
of school there was the curious plane of intimacy on which
we had, as it were, surprised one another wandering, and so
which was shared peculiarly by us.

I had put Miriam's name down on my guest list; she was
invited; and she came. She wore a blue taffeta dress which
Mrs. Saiyetovitz had made for her (on the old Singer on the
counter in the shop, I guessed) and it was quite nice if a bit
too frilly. My home was pretty and well-furnished and full of
flowers and personal touches of my mother's hands; there
was space, and everything shone. Miriam did not open her
eyes at it; I saw her finger a bowl of baby-skinned pink roses
in the passing, but all afternoon she looked out indifferently
as she did at home.

The following Saturday at the store we were discussing the
party. Miriam was telling Mrs. Saiyetovitz about my presents,
and I was standing by in a pleasurable embarrassment at my
own importance.

"Well, please God, Miri," said Mrs. Saiyetovitz at the finish, "you'll also have a party for your birday in April. . . . .
Ve'll be in d'house, and everyting'll be nice, just like you
want."—They were leaving the rooms behind the shop—the

mournful green plush curtains glooming the archway between the bedroom and the living room; the tarnished samovar; the black beetles in the little kitchen; Miriam's old black piano with the candlesticks, wheezing in the drafty passage; the damp puddly yard piled with empty packing cases and egg-shells and banana skins; the hovering smell of fish frying. They were going to live in a little house in the township nearby.

But when April came, Miriam took ten of her friends to the Saturday afternoon bioscope in celebration of her birth-day. "And to Costas Café afterwards for ice cream," she stated to her mother, looking out over her head. I think Mrs. Saiyetovitz was disappointed about the party, but she rea-soned then, as always, that as her daughter went to school and was educated and could speak English, whilst she herself knew nothing, wasn't clever at all, the little daughter must know best what was right and what was *nice*.

I know now what of course I did not know then: that Miriam Saiyetovitz and I were intelligent little girls into whose brains there never had, and never would, come the freak and won-derful flash that is brilliance. Ours were alabaster intellects: clear, perfect, light; no streaks of dark, unknown granite splitting to reveal secret veins of brightness, like thin gold, between stratum and stratum. We were fitted to be good schoolteachers, secretaries, organizers; we did everything well, nothing badly, and nothing remarkably. But to the Saiyeto-vitzes, Miriam's brain blazed like the sun, warming their hum-bleness.

In the year-by-year passage through school, our classmates thinned out one by one; the way seedlings come up in a bunch to a certain stage in their development, and then by some inexplicable process of natural selection, one or two continue to grow and branch up into the air, whilst the others wither or remain small and weedy. The other girls left to go and learn shorthand-and-typewriting: weeded out by the necessity of earning a living. Or moved, and went to other schools: transplanted to some ground of their own. Miriam and I re-mained, growing straight and steadily. . . .

During our matriculation year a sense of wonder and im-pending change came upon us both; the excitement of coming to an end that is also a beginning. We felt this in one another, and so were drawn together in new earnestness. Miriam came to study with me in the garden at my house, and oftener than ever, I slipped down to the Concession stores to exhange a book or discuss work with her. For although they now had a house, the Saiyetovitzes crept about, very quiet, talking to one another only in hoarse, respectful whispers.

It was during this year, when the wonder of our own capacity to learn was reaching out and catching into light like a veld fire within us, that we began to talk of the University. And, all at once, we talked of nothing else. I spoke to my father of it, and he was agreeable, although my mother thought a girl could do better with her time. But so long as my father was willing to send me, I knew I should go. Ah yes, said Miriam. She liked my father very much; I knew that. In fact she said to me once—it was a strange thing to say, and almost emotionally, she said it, and at a strange time, because we were on the bus going into the town to buy a new winter coat which she had wanted very badly and talked about longingly for days, and her father had just given her the money to get it—she said to me: You know, I think your father's just right.— I mean, if you had to choose somebody, a certain kind of person for a father, well, your father'd be just the kind you'd want.

When she broached the subject of University to her parents, they were agreeable for her to go, too. Indeed, they wanted her to go almost more than she herself did. But they worried a great deal about the money side of it; every time I went down to the store there'd be a discussion of ways and means, Saiyetovitz slowly munching his bread and garlic polony lunch, and worrying. Miriam didn't worry about it; they'll find the money, she said. She was a tall girl, now, with beautiful breasts, and a large, dark-featured face that had a certain capable elegance, although her father's glum mouth was unmistakable and on her upper lip faint dark down foreshadowed a heavy middle-age. Her parents were peasants; but she was the powerful young Jewess. Beside her, I felt pale in my Scotch gingery-fairness: lightly drawn upon the mind's eye, whilst she was painted in oils.

We both matriculated; not so well as we thought we should, but well enough; and we went to the University. And there too, we did well enough. We had both decided upon the same course: teaching. In the end, it had seemed the only thing to do. Neither of us had any particular bent.

It must have been a hard struggle for the Saiyetovitzes to keep Miriam at the University, buy her clothes, and pay for her board and lodging in Johannesburg. There is a great deal of money to be made out of native trade concessions purchased from the government; and it doesn't require education or trained commercial astuteness to make it—in fact, trading of this sort seems to flourish in response to something very different: what is needed is instinctive peasant craftiness such as can only be found in the uneducated, in those who have scratched up their own resources. Storekeepers with this quality of peasant craft made money all about Mr. Saiyetovitz, bought houses and motorcars and banded their wives' retired hands with diamonds in mark of their new idleness. But Mr. Saiyetovitz was a peasant without the peasant's craft; without that flaw in his simplicity that might have given him checks and deeds of transfer to sign, even if he were unable to read the print on the documents. . . . Without this craft, the peasant has only one thing left to him: hard work, dirty work, with the sweet, sickly body-smell of the black men about him all day. Saiyetovitz made no money: only worked hard and long, standing in his damp shirt amidst the clamor of the stores and the death-smell from the eating house always in his nose.

Meanwhile, Miriam fined down into a lady. She developed a half-bored, half-intolerant shrug of the shoulders in place of the childish sharpness that had been filed jagged by the rub-rub of rough life and harsh contrasts. She became soft-voiced, where she had been loud and gay. She watched and conformed; and soon took on the attitude of liberal-mindedness that sets the doors of the mind slackly open, so that any idea may walk in and out again, leaving very little impression: she could appreciate Bach and Stravinsky, and spend a long evening listening to swing music in the dark of somebody's flat.

Race and creed had never meant very much to Miriam and me, but at the University she sifted naturally towards the young Jews who were passing easily and enthusiastically, with their people's extraordinary aptitude for creative and scientific work, through Medical School. They liked her; she was invited to their homes for tennis parties, swimming on Sundays, and dances, and she seemed as unimpressed by the luxury of their ten-thousand-pound houses as she had been by the contrast of our clean, pleasant little home, long ago, when she herself was living behind the Concession store.

She usually spent part of the vacations with friends in Johannesburg; I missed her—wandering about the Mine on my own, out of touch, now, with the girls I had left behind in the backwater of the small town. During the second half of one July vacation—she had spent the first two weeks in Johannesburg—she asked me if she could come and spend Sunday at my home, and in the afternoon, one of the Medical students arrived at our house in his small car. He had come from Johannesburg; Miriam had evidently told him she would be with us. I gathered her parents did not know of the young man's visit, and I did not speak of it before them.

So the four years of our training passed. Miriam Saiyetovitz and I had dropped like two leaves, side by side into the same current, and been carried downstream together: now the current met a swirl of dead logs, reeds, and the force of other waters, and broke up, divided its drive and its one direction. The leaves floated clear; divergent from one another. Miriam got a teaching post in Johannesburg, but I was sent to a small school in the Northern Transvaal. We met seldom during the first six months of our adult life: Miriam went to Capetown during the vacation, and I flew to Rhodesia with the first profits of my independence. Then came the war, and I, glad to escape so soon the profession I had once anticipated with such enthusiasm, joined the nursing service and went away for the long, strange interlude of four years. Whilst I was with a field hospital in Italy, I heard that Miriam had married—a Doctor Somebody-or-other: my informant wasn't sure of the name. I guessed it must be one of the boys whom she had known as students, I sent a cable of congratulation, to the Saiyetovitzes' address.

And then, one day, I came back to the small mining town and found it there, the same; like a face that has been waiting a long time. My Mother, and my Dad, the big wheels of the shaft turning, the trees folding their wings about the Mine houses; and our house, with the green, square lawn and the cat watching the doves. For the first few weeks I faltered about the old life, feeling my way in dream so like the old reality that it hurt.

There was a feel about an afternoon that made my limbs tingle with familiarity. . . . What . . . ? And then, lying on our lawn under the hot sky, I knew: just the sort of glaring summer afternoon that used to send me down to the Concession stores, feeling isolated in the heat. Instantly, I thought of the Saiyetovitzes, and I wanted to go and see them, see if they were still there; what Miriam was doing; where she was, now.

Down at the stores it was the same as ever, only dirtier, smaller, more chipped and smeared—the way reality often is in contrast with the image carried long in the mind. As I stepped so strangely on that old pocked pavement, with the skeleton cats and the orange peel and the gobs of spit, my heart tightened with the thought of the Saiyetovitzes. I was in a kind of excitement to see the store again. And there it was; and excitement sank out at the evidence of the monotony of "things." Blankets swung a little in the doorway. Flies crawled amongst the shirts and shoes posed in the window, the hot, wet, sickening fatty smell came over from the eating house. I met it with the old revulsion: it was like breathing inside someone's stomach. And in the store, amongst the wicked glitter of the tin trunks, beneath the secret whispering of the blankets, the old Saiyetovitzes sat glumly, with patience, waiting. . . . As animals wait in a cage; for nothing.

In their delight at seeing me again, I saw that they were older, sadder; that they had somehow given themselves into the weight of their own humbleness, they were without a pinnacle on which to fix their eyes. Whatever place it was that they looked upon now, it was flat.

Mr. Saiyetovitz's mouth had creased in further to the dead folds of his chin; his hair straggled to the rims of his ears. As he spoke to me, I noticed that his hands lay, with a curious helpless indifference, curled on the counter. Mrs. Saiyetovitz shuffled off at once to the back of the shop to make a cup of tea for me, and carried it in, slopping over into the saucer. She was uglier than ever, now, her back hunched up to meet her head, her old thick legs spiraled in crêpe bandages because of varicose veins. And blinder too, I could see: that enquiring look of the blind or deaf smiling unsure at you from her face.

The talk turned almost at once to Miriam, and as they answered my questions about her, I saw them go inert. Yes, she was married; had married a doctor—a flicker of pride in the old man at this. She lived in Johannesburg. Her husband was doing very well. There was a photograph of her home, in one of the more expensive suburbs; a large, white modern house, with flower borders and a fishpond. And there was Miri's little boy, sitting on his swing; and a studio portrait of him, taken with his mother.

There was the face of Miriam Saiyetovitz, confident, carefully made-up and framed in a good hairdresser's version of her dark hair, smiling queenly over the face of her child. One hand lay on the child's shoulder, a smooth hand, wearing large, plain, expensive diamond rings. Her bosom was proud and rounded now—a little too heavy, a little overripe in the climate of ease.

I could see in her face that she had forgotten a lot of things.

When his wife had gone into the back of the shop to refill my teacup, old Saiyetovitz went silent, looking at the hand that lay before him on the counter, the fingers twitching a little under the gaze.

It doesn't come out like you think, he said, it doesn't come out like you think.

He looked up at me with a comforting smile.

And then he told me that they had seen Miriam's little boy only three times since he was born. Miriam they saw hardly at all; her husband never. Once or twice a year she came out from Johannesburg to visit them, staying an hour on a Sunday afternoon, and then driving herself back to Town again. She had not invited her parents to her home at any time; they had been there only once, on the occasion of the birth of their grandson.

Mrs. Saiyetovitz came back into the store: she seemed to know of what we had been speaking. She sat down on a shot-purple tin trunk, and folded her arms over her breast. Ah yes, she breathed, ah yes. . . .

I stood there in Miriam's guilt before the Saiyetovitzes, and they were silent, in the accusation of the humble.

But a little while a Swazi in a tobacco-colored blanket sauntered dreamily into the shop, and Mr. Saiyetovitz rose heavy with defeat.

Through the eddy of dust in the lonely interior and the wavering fear round the head of the native and the bright hot dance of the jazz blankets and the dreadful submission of Mrs. Saiyetovitz's conquered voice in my ear, I heard his voice strike like a snake at my faith: angry and browbeating, sullen and final, lashing weakness at the weak.

Mr. Saiyetovitz and the native.

Defeated, and without understanding in their defeat.

Edna O'Brien
(1930–   )

Edna O'Brien was born in County Clare, Ireland and left home at sixteen to study pharmacy. After marrying and bearing two children, she moved to London in 1959 and began to publish novels and stories. Her best-known books are The Love Object *(stories),* Girl with Green Eyes, Married Bliss, August Is a Wicked Month, *and* A Scandalous Woman. *Her work is noted for its candor in sexual matters and for her defiance of restrictions placed upon women, especially in her native Ireland.*

How to Grow a Wisteria

When they were first married they saw no one. That was his wish. They spent their days in their wooden house, high up, on a mountain. There was snow for four or five months of each year, and in the early morning when the sun shone they sat on the veranda admiring the expanse of white fields and the pines that were weighed down with snow. Beyond the fields reigned mountains, great mountains. She did not feel lonely in the morning. But at night she sometimes sighed. Stabbed she would be by some small memory—a voice, a song, once it was by the taste of warm beetroot. These stray memories she had no control over, no idea when they might occur. They came like spirits to disconcert her. Even when making love they were capable of intruding. She sometimes asked herself why she had chosen a man who insisted on exile. The answer was easy: his disposition and his face fitted in with some brainless dream of hers. He was someone she would never really know.

The only outsider that came was the village idiot, who

cycled up to do the garden. He grinned his way through hoeing and digging, never knowing how to answer her questions. Little questions about his mother, his father, his rusted lady's bicycle, and how he came to possess it. Once he rooted up a creeper, and she laughed and talked to her husband about it incessantly as if it were something of major importance. They planted another.

The seasons brought variety—first a false spring, a premature thaw, then a real one, then the flowers, small and soft like the pupils of eyes, and sheep lambing, and the things that they had sowed appearing above the ground. When the rains came the wood swelled, and then when the rains went the wood had a terrible time shrinking and settling down. The creak in the house was unnerving. She was not with child. They no longer got up in the middle of lunch or breakfast or supper and walked to their vast bed in a quiver of passion. They chopped wood, they lit the stove, they kept busy; there is always something to do in a house.

When summer came he took a sleeping bag out of doors, saying nothing. He chose the forest. At first she cried, then she became reconciled to it, but she was always hungry and always cold.

At length, feeling the bleakness himself, he agreed to move into a city but on the understanding that they would live perfectly privately. He went first to find an apartment because it had to be suitable, it had to look out on a stretch of green and in a city that is a difficult thing to find.

She missed him. It was the first time in years that they had been parted, and when he came back and walked along the dark lane carrying a torch she ran and embraced him. In their embrace there was tenderness and a reconciliation.

The apartment had a high ceiling, double doors, and a radiator concealed behind wooden bars. They missed the stove. He fitted up his machines—his tape recorder, his record player, his infrared lamp. Since they had only one room she made a point of being out a lot to leave him to his solitude. In her walks she came to know the streets, intimately. She knew where ill-fitting slabs of stone caused a ridge in the pavement, the rust stains on the red paper kiosks, nannies, prams; she never looked at those inside the prams. She knew the dogs that were at war with their owners and those that followed meekly on their leashes. One or two people smiled at her. There was one square of houses she found particularly enchanting. They were four-story houses set well back from the road with flight of steps leading to the tiled porchways. In this square she studied curtains, gateways and the paintwork, thinking she could tell the life of the house by these external signs. She loved that hour of evening when things perked up as people hurried home with provisions for their dinner. Their urgency excited her. She often hurried with them and then found she was going in the wrong direction. In the daytime she made bus journeys, going from terminus to terminus simply to overhear. When she came home she told her husband all that she had seen and all that she heard and he sometimes laughed because she heard some amusing things.

At Christmas she plucked up courage to invite people to dinner. They owned a gallery where she had passed many pleasant hours. It entailed maneuvering beforehand and a war afterward. They did not meet with his approval. The woman confessed to a weakness for leather suitcases and that he found distasteful. They had three sets of guests throughout a winter and only one of these evenings went well.

Christmas again, the anniversary of their betrothal and she left him. She walked out of the house and down the street. There were stars, a moon, and a succession of street lights to show the way. The frost which was severe seemed to fix and make permanent her action as the frost had fastened the hoof marks of animals on their mountain walks long before. Her friends drove to his apartment and handed him her note saying that she had gone. "Peace, peace at last," was what he had said.

He went back to the mountain and wrote her a chain of letters. They were all abusive, and she could not read them through without succumbing to tears.

She moved to a larger city and got a job in a gallery. The intention was to meet people. She lived modestly well. Her old life and her new life, they could not be more opposing. Things went from one extreme to another. It was all parties and friendship and telephone calls now. Not a week, not a day, not an hour went by but she saw someone or was telephoned by someone and made plans. She had plans it seemed for the rest of her life. Life stories were dropped in her ear and though she felt flattered she was also unable to sleep at night, for all the incidents that crowded in on her.

There were lovers, too, drunken lovers in drunken beds after parties, and the more expedient ones were those who called just before dinner and seduced her in the kitchen or the hallway or wherever they happened to be. There were some well-conducted affairs and presents and bunches of flowers and eating in restaurants. There were all these exciting things but the proper feelings of enjoyment refused to come. In fact something else happened. She was filling up with secret revulsion. "I need a rest, a rest from people," she would say, but it was impossible to escape.

At one of her parties a tap flew off a cider barrel and though the cider gushed ponderously over the floor no one made any attempt to control it. Someone had made bows out of mauve lavatory paper and was passing them round and everyone was laughing about this. She wished that they would all leave together, at once, and like a swarm of flies.

Then she made a resolution. She tried being with people and not seeing and not hearing. But they got through. They always found some chink. It was not difficult—an insult, a well-placed line of flattery, some new gossip, and she was theirs. Theirs to make promises to, theirs to be obligated to, theirs to hide her distaste from. She thought there are not left in the world two people who really like one another. Two parts of her were in deadly enmity, the her that welcomed them in and the her that shrank away from them. It was all terrible and tiring and meaningless.

One evening in a friend's house she overturned a glass of red wine. It pooled into a wide stain and went through the holes of the crocheted cloth. Under the cloth there was red crepe paper so that the stain—a savage red—was out of all proportion to the amount of wine spilt. She apologized of course and her hostess was more than forgiving. In fact they all moved to another room to rid themselves of its unsightliness.

Next time she disgraced herself in a hotel. A tumbler—there had been whiskey in it—simply shot out of her hand and missed the very polished boot of a gentleman passing by. Her friend (a new man) found it very funny.

In a drawing room just before lunch she kicked some bottles which were put to warm by a hearth. She tried mopping it up with a handkerchief before anyone could see. She even used the corner of her flimsy dress. Just like a child.

After that it became inevitable. No matter where she went, no matter who she was, it simply had to happen. It began to control her life, her outings. Her friends laughed indulgently. They made jokes as she entered rooms and yet it was always mortifying and always shocking when it occurred. Lying down at night it assailed her. She saw herself spilling her way across rooms, dance floors, countries, continents. In her sleep she spilled and when she wakened she dreaded the encounters of the day, knowing what must happen.

The decision took months to arrive at, but one day it was easy to execute. As easy as the night she left her husband, knowing it was for ever. She had to give up seeing people. She was quite methodical about it. She had blinds put on the windows, asked for the telephone to be removed. That was a wrench. To make matters worse the workmen left her the extension saying she might like it for her kiddies. Though unconnected she feared it was in danger of ringing because it had developed the habit. People wrote. Some assumed that she was having a wicked affair with somebody so notorious that he had to be hidden. They were maddeningly coy about it. When they came she hid, telling herself that the ringing would die down once they had run out of patience. An order was delivered once a week and left on the doorstep. On the doorstep, too, she left the empties, letters for posting and the list of necessities for the following week. To her friends she wrote, "Thank you for asking me, I wish I could, but at the moment I dare not come out of doors. Perhaps another time, perhaps next year?" Each letter always the same. She could have had them printed but she didn't. Each one she wrote carefully in heavy black ink. She did not wish to offend. They had been friends once and she might meet them again before she died. She knew that it needed only a toothache, a burst pipe, or an excess of high spirits to lure her back into the world. "Not yet, not yet," she would say resolutely to herself.

The day passed agreeably. There were things to be done. Dust assembles of its own accord. She kept everything spotless. She had a small massage machine which she used on herself twice a day. Its effect was both bracing and relaxing and she used it all over. She dressed for dinner, and each evening had two martinis. During dinner she put on some records and allowed herself to be animated. Otherwise it was quiet, quiet. The quiet, ordered days lay ahead like a foreseeable stretch of path. She had no wish to go out. She had nothing to say, nothing to hear. She had only one quibble: the timing of her affliction. Had it happened sooner the marriage need not have ended and they might have stayed together, two withdrawn people in a house, on a mountain.

Ted Hughes
(1930–   )

Ted Hughes was born in Mytholmyroyd, in the western part of Yorkshire, England. Although best known as a poet, he has also worked intensely in the shorter fictional form, as well as on radio and television scripts. His characteristic style is one of great intensity and controlled passion, and his images are frequently feral and primitive. His books include The Hawk in the Rain (1957), Lupercal (1960), Wodwo (1967), and Crow: From the Life and Songs of the Crow (1971). His Selected Poems was published in 1973. Hughes was married to the American poet Sylvia Plath, with whom he had two children. He is now poet-laureate of England.

Snow

And let me repeat this over and over again: beneath my feet is the earth, some part of the surface of the earth. Beneath the snow beneath my feet, that is. What else could it be? It is firm, I presume, and level. If it is not actually soil and rock, it must be ice. It is very probably ice. Whichever it may be, it is proof—the most substantial proof possible—that I am somewhere on the earth, the known earth. It would be absurd to dig down through the snow, just to determine exactly what is underneath, earth or ice. This bedded snow may well be dozens of feet deep. Besides, the snow filling all the air and rivering along the ground would pour into the hole as fast as I could dig, and cover me too—very quickly.

This could be no other planet: the air is perfectly natural, perfectly good.

Our aircraft was forced down by this unusual storm. The

pilot tried to make a landing, but misjudged the extraordinary power of the wind and the whereabouts of the ground. The crash was violent. The fuselage buckled and gaped, and I was flung clear. Unconscious of everything save the need to get away from the disaster, I walked farther off into the blizzard and collapsed, which explains why when I came to full consciousness and stood up out of the snow that was burying me I could see nothing of either the aircraft or my fellow passengers. All around me was what I have been looking at ever since. The bottomless dense motion of snow. I started to walk.

Of course, everything previous to that first waking may have been entirely different since I don't remember a thing about it. Whatever chance dropped me here in the snow evidently destroyed my memory. That's one thing of which there is no doubt whatsoever. It is, so to speak, one of my facts. The aircraft crash is a working hypothesis, that merely.

There's no reason why I should not last quite a long time yet. I seem to have an uncommon reserve of energy. To keep my mind firm, that is the essential thing, to fix it firmly in my reasonable hopes, and lull it there, encourage it. Mesmerize it slightly with a sort of continuous prayer. Because when my mind is firm, my energy is firm. And that's the main thing here—energy. No matter how circumspect I may be, or how lucid, without energy I am lost on the spot. Useless to think about it. Where my energy ends I end, and all circumspection and all lucidity end with me. As long as I have energy I can correct my mistakes, outlast them, outwalk them—for instance the unimaginable error that as far as I know I am making at this very moment. This step, this, the next five hundred, or five thousand—all mistaken, all absolute waste, back to where I was ten hours ago. But we recognize that thought. My mind is not my friend. My support, my defense, but my enemy too—not perfectly intent on getting me out of this. If I were mindless perhaps there would be no difficulty whatsoever. I would simply go on aware of nothing but my step by step success in getting over the ground. The thing to do is to keep alert, keep my mind fixed in alertness, recognize these treacherous paralyzing, yes, lethal thoughts the second they enter, catch them before they can make that burrowing plunge down the spinal cord.

Then gently and without any other acknowledgment push them back—out into the snow where they belong. And that is where they belong. They are the infiltrations of the snow, encroachments of this immensity of lifelessness. But they en-

ter so slyly! We are true, they say, or at least very probably
true, and on that account you must entertain us and even
give us the run of your life, since above all things you are
dedicated to the truth. That is the air they have, that's how
they come in. What do I know about the truth? As if simple-
minded dedication to truth were the final law of existence! I
only know more and more clearly what is good for me. It's
my mind that has this contemptible awe for the probably true,
and my mind, I know, I prove it every minute, is not me and
is by no means sworn to help me. Am I a lie? I must survive—
that's a truth sacred as any, and as the hungry truths devour
the sleepy truths I shall digest every other possible truth to
the substance and health and energy of my own, and the ones
I can't digest I shall spit out, since in this situation my intention to survive is the one mouth, the one digestive tract, so
to speak, by which I live. But those others! I relax for a
moment, I leave my mind to itself for a moment—and they
are in complete possession. They plunge into me, exultantly,
mercilessly. There is no question of their intention of their
power. Five seconds of carelessness, and they have struck.
The strength melts from me, my bowels turn to water, my
consciousness darkens and shrinks, I have to stop.

What are my facts? I do have some definite facts.

Taking six steps every five seconds, I calculate—allowing
for my brief regular sleeps—that I have been walking through
this blizzard for five months and during that time have covered
something equal to the breadth of the Atlantic between
Southampton and New York. Two facts, and a third: throughout those five months this twilight of snow has not grown
either darker or brighter.

So.

There seems no reason to doubt that I am somewhere within
either the Arctic or the Antarctic Circle. That's a comfort.
It means my chances of survival are not uniquely bad. Men
have walked the length of Asia simply to amuse themselves.

Obviously I am not traveling in a straight line. But that
needn't give me any anxiety. Perhaps I made a mistake when
I first started walking, setting my face against the wind instead
of downwind. Coming against the wind I waste precious energy and there is always this wearisome snow blocking my
eyes and mouth. But I had to trust the wind. This resignation
to the wind's guidance is the very foundation of my firmness
of mind. The wind is not simply my compass. In fact, I must
not think of it as a compass at all. The wind is my law. As a

compass nothing could be more useless. No need to dwell on that. It's extremely probable indeed and something I need not hide from myself that this wind is leading me to and fro in quite a tight little maze—always shifting too stealthily for me to notice the change. Or if the sun is circling the horizon, it seems likely that the wind is swinging with it through the three hundred and sixty degrees once in every twenty-four hours, turning me as I keep my face against it in a perfect circle not more than seven miles across. This would explain the otherwise strange fact that in spite of the vast distance I have covered the terrain is still dead level, exactly as when I started. A frozen lake, no doubt. This is a strong possibility and I must get used to it without letting it overwhelm me, and without losing sight of its real advantages.

The temptation to trust to luck and instinct and cut out across wind is to be restricted. The effect on my system of confidence would be disastrous. My own judgment would naturally lead me in a circle. I would have to make deliberate changes of direction to break out of that circle—only to go in a larger circle or a circle in the opposite direction. So more changes. Wilder and more sudden changes, changes of my changes—all to evade an enemy that showed so little sign of itself it might as well not have existed. It's clear where all that would end. Shouting and running and so on. Staggering round like a man beset by a mob. Falling, groveling. So on. The snow.

No. All I have to do is endure: that is, keep my face to the wind. My face to the wind, a firm grip on my mind, and everything else follows naturally. There is not the slightest need to be anxious. Any time now the Polar night will arrive, bringing a drastic change of climate—inevitable. Clearing the sky and revealing the faultless compass of the stars.

The facts are overwhelmingly on my side. I could almost believe in Providence. After all, if one single circumstance were slightly—only slightly—other than it is! If, for instance, instead of waking in a blizzard on a firm level place I had come to consciousness falling endlessly through snow cloud. Then I might have wondered very seriously whether I were in the gulf or not. Or if the atmosphere happened to consist of, say, ammonia. I could not have existed. And in the moment before death by asphyxiation I would certainly have been convinced I was out on some lifeless planet. Or if I had no body but simply arms and legs growing out of a head, my whole system of confidence would have been disoriented from the start. My dreams, for instance, would have been meaningless to me, or rather an argument of my own meaninglessness. I would have died almost immediately, out of sheer bewilderment. I wouldn't need nearly such extreme differences either. If I had been without these excellent pigskin boots, trousers, jacket, gloves and hood, the cold would have extinguished me at once.

And even if I had double the clothing that I have, where would I be without my chair? My chair is quite as important as one of my lungs. As both my lungs, indeed, for without it I should be dead. Where would I have slept? Lying in the snow. But lying flat, as I have discovered, I am buried by the snow in just under a minute, and the cold begins to take over my hands and my feet and my face. Sleep would be impossible. In other words, I would very soon collapse of exhaustion and be buried. As it is, I unsnap my chair harness, plant the chair in the snow, sit on it, set my feet on the rung between the front legs, my arms folded over my knees and my head resting on my arms, and am able in this way to take a sleep of fully ten minutes before the snow piles over me.

The chain of providential coincidences is endless. Or rather, like a chain mail, it is complete without one missing link to betray and annul the rest. Even my dreams are part of it. They are as tough and essential a link as any, since there can no longer be any doubt that they are an accurate reproduction of my whole previous life, of the world as it is and as I knew it—all without one contradictory detail. Yet if my amnesia had been only a little bit stronger!—it needed only that. Because without this evidence of the world and my identity I could have known no purpose in continuing the ordeal. I could only have looked, breathed, and died, like a nestling fallen from the nest.

Everything fits together. And the result—my survival, and my determination to survive. I should rejoice.

The chair is of conventional type: nothing in the least mystifying about it. A farmhouse sort of chair: perfectly of a piece with my dreams, as indeed are my clothes, my body, and all the inclinations of my mind. It is of wood, painted black, though in places showing a coat of brown beneath the black. One of the nine struts in the back is missing and some child—I suppose it was a child—has stuck a dab of chewing gum into the empty socket. Obviously the chair has been well used, and not too carefully. The right foreleg has been badly chewed, evidently by a puppy, and on the seat both black and brown paints are wearing through, showing the dark grain of the pale wood. If all this is not final evidence of a reality beyond my own, of the reality of the world it comes from, the world I redream in my sleeps—I might as well lie down in the snow and be done with.

The curious harness needn't worry me. The world, so far as I've dreamed it at this point, contains no such harness, true. But since I've not yet dreamed anything from after my twenty-sixth birthday, the harness might well have been invented between that time and the time of my disaster. Probably it's now in general use. Or it may be the paraphernalia of some fashionable game that came in during my twenty-seventh or later year, and to which I got addicted. Sitting on snow peaks in nineteenth-century chairs. Or perhaps I developed a passion for painting polar scenery and along with that a passion for this particular chair as my painting seat, and had the harness designed specially. A lucky eccentricity! It is perfectly adapted to my present need. But all that's in the dark still. There's a lot I haven't dreamed yet. From my twenty-third and twenty-fourth years I have almost nothing— a few insignificant episodes. Nothing at all after my twenty-sixth birthday. The rest, though, is about complete, which suggests that any time now I ought to be getting my twenty-third and twenty-fourth years in full and, more important, my twenty-seventh year, or as much of it as there is, along with the accurate account of my disaster and the origin of my chair.

There seems little doubt of my age. Had I been dreaming my life chronologically there would have been real cause for worry. I could have had no idea how much was still to come. Of course, if I were suddenly to dream something from the middle of my sixtieth year I would have to reorganize all my ideas. What really convinces me of my youth is my energy. The appearance of my body tells me nothing. Indeed, from my hands and feet—which are all I have dared to uncover— one could believe I was several hundred years old, or even dead, they are so black and shrunken on the bone. But the emaciation is understandable, considering that for five months I have been living exclusively on willpower, without the slightest desire for food.

I have my job to get back to, and my mother and father will be in despair. And God knows what will have happened to Helen. Did I marry her? I have no wedding ring. But we were engaged. And it is another confirmation of my youth that my feelings for her are as they were then—stronger, in fact, yes a good deal stronger, though speaking impartially these feelings that seem to be for her might easily be nothing but my desperate longing to get back to the world in general— a longing that is using my one-time affection for Helen as a sort of form or model. It's possible, very possible, that I have in reality forgotten her, even that I am sixty years old, that she has been dead for thirty-four years. Certain things may be very different from what I imagine. If I were to take this drift of thoughts to the logical extreme there is no absolute proof that my job, my parents, Helen, and the whole world are not simply my own invention, fantasies my imagination has improvised on the simple themes of my own form, my clothes, my chair, and the properties of my present environment. I am in no position to be sure about anything.

But there is more to existence, fortunately, than consideration of possibilities. There is conviction, faith. If there were not, where would I be? The moment I allow one of these "possibilities" the slightest intimacy—a huge futility grips me, as it were physically, by the heart, as if the organ itself were despairing of this life and ready to give up.

Courageous and calm. That should be my prayer. I should repeat that, repeat it like the Buddhists with their "O jewel of the lotus." Repeat it till it repeats itself in my very heart, till every heartbeat drives it through my whole body. Courageous and calm. This is the world, think no more about it.

My chair will keep me sane. My chair, my chair, my chair, my chair—I might almost repeat that. I know every mark on it, every grain. So near and true! It alone predicates a Universe, the entire Universe, with its tough carpentering, its sprightly, shapely design—so delicate, so strong. And while I have the game I need be afraid of nothing. Though it is dangerous. Tempting, dangerous, but—it is enough to know that the joy is mine. I set the chair down in the snow, letting myself think I am going to sleep, but instead of sitting I step back a few paces into the snow. How did I think of that? The first time, I did not dare look away from it. I had never before let it out of my hand, never let it go for a fraction between unbuckling it and sitting down on it. But then I let it go and stepped back into the snow. I had never heard my voice before. I was astonished at the sound that struggled up out of me. Well, I need the compensations. And this game does rouse my energies, so it is, in a sense, quite practical. After the game, I could run. That's the moment of danger, though, the moment of overpowering impatience when I could easily lose control and break out, follow my instinct, throw myself on luck, run out across the wind.

But there is a worse danger. If I ran out across the wind I would pretty soon come to my senses, turn my face back into the wind. It is the game itself, the stage of development it has reached, that is dangerous now. I no longer simply step back. I set the chair down, turn my face away, and walk off into the blizzard, counting my steps carefully. At fourteen paces I stop. Fifteen is the limit of vision in this dense flow of snow, so at fourteen I stop, and turn. Let those be the rules. Let me fix the game at that. Because at first I see nothing. That should be enough for me. Everywhere, pouring silent gray, a silence like a pressure, like the slow coming to bear of some incalculable pressure, too gradual to detect. If I were simply to stand there my mind would crack in a few moments. But I concentrate, I withdraw my awe from the emptiness and look pointedly into it. At first, everything is as usual—as I have seen it for five months. Then my heart begins to thump unnaturally, because I seem to make out a dimness, a shadow that wavers deep in the gray turmoil, vanishes and darkens, rises and falls. I step one pace forward and using all my willpower stop again. The shadow is as it was. Another step. The shadow seems to be a little darker. Then it vanishes and I lunge two steps forward but immediately stop because there it is, quite definite, no longer moving. Slowly I walk towards it. The rules are that I keep myself under control, that I restrain all sobs or shouts though of course it is impossible to keep the breathing regular—at this stage at least, and right up to the point where the shadow resolves into a chair. In that vast gray dissolution—my chair! The snowflakes are drifting against the legs and gliding between the struts, bumping against them, clinging and crawling over the seat. To control myself then is not within human power. Indeed I seem to more or less lose consciousness at that point. I'm certainly not responsible for the weeping, shouting thing that falls on my chair, embracing it, kissing it, brushing his cheeks against it. As the snowflakes tap and run over my gloves and over the chair I begin to call them names. I peer into each one as if it were a living face, full of speechless recognition, and I call to them—Willy, Joanna, Peter, Jesus, Ferdinand, anything that comes into my head, and shout to them and nod and laugh. Well, it's harmless enough madness.

The temptation to go beyond the fourteen paces is now

becoming painful. To go deep into the blizzard. Forty paces. Then come back, peering. Fifteen paces, twenty paces. Stop. A shadow.

That would not be harmless madness. If I were to leave my chair like that the chances are I would never find it again. My footprints do not exist in this undertow of snow. Weeks later, I would still be searching, casting in great circles, straining at every moment to pry a shadow out of the gray sameness. My chair meanwhile a hundred miles away in the blizzard, motionless—neat legs and elegant back, sometimes buried, sometimes uncovering again. And for centuries, long after I'm finished, still sitting there, intact with its tooth-marks and missing strut, waiting for a darkening shape to come up out of the nothingness and shout to it and fall on it and possess it.

But my chair is here, on my back, here. There's no danger of my ever losing it. Never so long as I keep control, keep my mind firm. All the facts are on my side. I have nothing to do but endure.

Enduring British Classics

☐ **BEST SHORT STORIES OF RUDYARD KIPLING.** The fascination of India, adventure in exotic places, the British at home and at war, love complicated by entanglements, and unexpected endings. Kiplings versatility of style truly makes him, as W. Somerset Maughan declared, "the best short story writer that our country can boast." (521404—$4.50)

☐ **THE SECRET AGENT by Joseph Conrad.** In this world of plot and counterplot, where identities are deceptions and glowing slogans mask savage realities, each character becomes an ever more helpless puppet of forces beyond control—until one woman's love, grief, and anger rips through the entire fabric of the conspiracy with a passionate, profoundly human act. (518047—$2.50)*

☐ **THE PICTURE OF DORIAN GRAY by Oscar Wilde,** with **Lord Arthur Savile's Crime, The Happy Prince,** and **The Birthday of the Infanta.** The controversial novel of a youth whose features, year after year, retain the same youthful appearance of innocent beauty, while the shame of his hideous vices become mirrored on the face of his portrait.
(519671—$2.95)*

☐ **PRIDE AND PREJUDICE by Jane Austen.** The romantic clash of two opinionated young people provides the sustaining theme of Jane Austen's famous novel, which captures the affections of class-conscious 18th-century English families with matrimonial aims and rivalries.
(520750—$1.95)*

☐ **TRISTRAM SHANDY by Laurence Sterne.** Perhaps the most capriciously written classic of all time, this delightfully delirious novel masks a carefully constructed design beneath a facade of aimless frivolity. Dialogues between the student of philosophy and the simple-minded sentimentalist evoke the sum of human nature. (518683—$4.95)

☐ **THE SHERLOCK HOLMES MYSTERIES by Sir Arthur Conan Doyle.** Indisputably the greatest fiction detective of all time, Sherlock Holmes lives—in film, on television, and of course through Sir Arthur Conan Doyle's inimitable craft. These twenty-two stories—including all the Holmes mysteries shown on PBS-TV—is Holmes at his brilliant and ever-delightful best. (521064—$3.50)

*Prices slightly higher in Canada

There's an epidemic with 27 million victims. And no visible symptoms.

It's an epidemic of people who can't read.

Believe it or not, 27 million Americans are functionally illiterate, about one adult in five.

The solution to this problem is you... when you join the fight against illiteracy. So call the Coalition for Literacy at toll-free **1-800-228-8813** and volunteer.

Volunteer Against Illiteracy. The only degree you need is a degree of caring.